A precious little boy...

A beloved little girl...

But family life isn't always so easy.

They fell madly in love, but circumstances pulled them apart. Can their child finally reunite them?

Emotional, exciting and always unexpected!

Next month, don't miss

featuring

THE WILD CHILD

by Judith Bowen

&

SPENCER'S CHILD

by Joan Kilby

More Little Secrets

Volume 1

Michael's Father

Melinda Curtis

Keeping Faith

Janice Macdonald

First published in Great Britain 2007 by Harlequin Mills & Boon Limited, Eton House, 18-24 Paradise Road, Richmond, Surrey TW9 1SR

ISBN 978 0 263 85846 4

10-0807

Printed and bound in Spain by Litografia Rosés S.A., Barcelona

Michael's Father

Melinda Curtis

Dear Reader,

Have you ever experienced the Sonoma County wine country? If you have, you may have stumbled across one of the smaller, family-run wineries, met the owner (grower/winemaker), his wife (tasting-room hostess) and his teenage son (souvenir-stand clerk). It takes a dedicated family to make a privately owned winery prosper. Cori Sinclair belongs to one such family, the Messinas, whose winery has found some measure of success and expanded beyond a tasting room in their driveway.

Cori dreams of escaping the all-consuming commitment her family's winery requires and wants to prove herself on her own terms. She doesn't plan to fall in love with Blake Austin, a man in search of family and stability, whose career hinges on the support of Cori's grandfather, Salvatore Messina, and staying in Sonoma. When Cori finally achieves her independence, it's not as satisfying as she'd hoped. Coming home, Cori must face Blake, the man she left behind, the man she still loves, the man whose career she could destroy – if she tells her family the truth about Michael's fathering.

I hope you enjoy Cori and Blake's story. I love to hear from readers. You can contact me at PO Box 2596, Turlock, CA 95381, USA or through my website at www.melindacurtis.net.

Enjoy!

Melinda Curtis

With much love and thanks to…

My patient and supportive family (Curt, Mason, Colby, Chelsea, Mom, Dad, Paul and John), who don't mind waiting for calls to be returned or suffering through pizza and bagged salad instead of home cooking.

Brian and Andrea Skonovd, who shared their vineyard growing stories and advice. Any mistakes are mine alone,

Lori Green, Karen Johnson and Sigal Kremer, for encouragement, reading time and promotion ideas.

Valleyrose, the Sacramento chapter of RWA, who helped me put all the pieces together.

Susan Floyd, Anna Adams and Jennifer LaBrecque, fellow authors who shared laughter, tears and dreams. DoBelieve, ladies!

PROLOGUE

"YOU ARE *not* pregnant!" Salvatore Messina railed at his granddaughter's announcement.

Cori Sinclair had never seen him so angry. And growing up in a household with three generations of Italians, she'd seen plenty of her grandfather's anger. Suddenly, she regretted blurting out her plight just before her college graduation.

Out in the hallway, the voices of eager Stanford graduates rang through the air. Inside Cori's room, Salvatore Messina's Italian loafers marched a stormy cadence across the beige industrial carpet. Her grandfather's stride was still as strong and obstinate as the eighty-year-old man himself. Standing over six feet, olive-skinned, with lightning silver hair and black eyes and dressed in unwrinkled charcoal slacks and matching jacket, Salvatore overwhelmed the small room.

"This kind of thing isn't supposed to happen to us," he proclaimed, adding something under his breath she didn't quite catch.

Shrinking into a corner of a worn red couch, Cori tugged at the hem of her short, blue dress, forcing a weak laugh past her parched throat. Clearly, her grandfather assumed she was as invincible as he saw himself.

"It could happen to anyone." Even to those who used condoms. Cori represented that rare statistic where the latex had failed.

When her grandfather didn't immediately answer, Cori gathered her tattered courage and looked at him. His jaw was clenched as tightly as his fists. With relief, Cori realized his cast-iron gaze and frown were directed at the black graduation robe hanging above the couch she sat on.

She breathed deeply before swallowing what was left of her pride and apologizing, but just then a wave of nausea hit, sending Cori stumbling for the little private bathroom. This was a humbling experience she was starting to get used to.

As she pulled her head out of the toilet minutes later, a large, gnarled hand dropped to her shoulder, then tentatively stroked Cori's spine. She took a deep breath, moved by the uncharacteristic display of affection. He removed his hand and she shivered, trying to find the strength to stand and face her problems.

The hand returned, lifting her and cleansing her face and neck with a wet cloth, demonstrating a gentleness Cori would never have expected from her grandfather. Eyes closed, she sighed and rested her head on her forearm.

This is how families are supposed to act.

For the first time in weeks, Cori's spirits rose. Everything was going to be okay.

"You should have told me sooner," her grandfather said quietly.

He couldn't know how she'd agonized over how to tell her conservative, Italian family, and the baby's father, about her predicament. Or how she'd watched her dreams of independence, which had seemed so close, slip away.

"It's not too late to correct this."

Cori gasped and lifted her head gingerly, not sure what she'd heard. Her gaze collided with her grandfather's cold, black eyes and she realized he was proposing the unthinkable.

He wants me to have an abortion.

Footsteps and joyful conversation moved past Cori's dorm room, heading toward the commencement ceremony. This wasn't one of the lighthearted practical jokes her grandfather was known to pull on her. If there'd been anything left in Cori's stomach, she would have given it up.

Unexpectedly, his dark eyes fell to the floor. "You'll marry the boy."

Cori's heart sank, pulled by the combined weight of relief and dread. Relief because she'd misunderstood him, and dread because her grandfather's statement made it sound as if a resolution were simple. But Cori knew better. Her grandfather was the founder of Messina Vineyards, one of the most prestigious wineries in Northern California. He'd built the winery all by himself, without the backing of venture capitalists, lawyers or movie producers. He'd succeeded by snaring those around him within his intricate plans for success, disregarding their personal goals or dreams while pursuing his own. If she allowed her grandfather to force her into marriage with her baby's father, his life—all of their lives—would never be their own again. Proud and independent, her former lover would never forgive her. It would be a shell of a marriage, despite the love for him that she still guarded.

Rising unsteadily to her feet, Cori shook her head, unable to speak past the tangle of hurt and disappointment. She avoided looking at herself in the mirror, knowing what she'd see—a pale, straggly haired blonde with hollow cheeks and dull brown eyes that should be radiating happiness and hope for the future on this, her graduation day. Instead, everything about her was thin and sunken after two weeks of morning sickness.

On shaky legs, Cori almost made it back to the small red couch before Salvatore Messina spoke.

"I want you to consider this carefully, because I will not support a *bastard.*"

His words dropped heavily between them. A line was being drawn.

Slowly, Cori turned to face her grandfather, trapped by the determined look in his eyes, emphasized by silver brows drawn low.

"He doesn't want me." The words, no less than the truth, still had the ability to wound her. After the awful things she'd said to her lover, the hurtful way they'd parted, she was sure he never wanted to see her again. He certainly hadn't called since the night their baby had been conceived. Cori was convinced that their love had blossomed at the wrong time. They were young; they each had goals. Goals that were too divergent for even love to overcome.

Cori hadn't thought her grandfather's expression could get any darker.

"Then, we'll buy this baby a name. Everyone has his price." Salvatore Messina pushed past Cori and began to pace the small room once more. "We'll find his, just like we did with John Sinclair."

"No." Dismay guided Cori's hands over the slight swelling of her belly as if she could cover the ears of the little one growing inside her. She'd picked up hints over the years that her grandfather and her long-estranged father, John Sinclair, hadn't gotten along, but to have her grandfather confirm that Sophia and John Sinclair's marriage had been forced shook Cori's composure. Was that why John Sinclair left them without a backward glance, abandoning his young family and a promising career in the wine industry? Cori couldn't let this happen to her—or to her baby's father.

"History repeats itself," Salvatore said, as if reading her thoughts. His pace quickened and his eyes speared madly about the room as if looking for a target. He pulled a slim, chrome cell phone out of his pocket. "You can't represent Messina Vineyards on the wine tour this summer unmarried *and* pregnant. Tell me his name and I won't totally ruin him."

Cori drew an unsteady breath, knowing she couldn't divulge his name now. Her grandfather didn't make idle threats. Destroying someone's career in the wine industry would be easy for him. He'd hound Cori until she slipped and told him what he wanted to know. How was she going to protect her former lover? Mama had intervened between Cori and her grandfather in the past. Cori grimaced, imagining the disappointed expression on her mother's face when she realized Cori was repeating her mistakes. A forced marriage? No way. Yet what could she do?

And then Cori knew. There was only one way to protect everyone. But it would only work if Cori was brave enough to stand alone. It was what she wanted, wasn't it? To finally be independent, not an appendage of Messina Vineyards? To make something of herself without standing in her grandfather's shadow?

"There won't be any unmarried pregnant women on the wine tour," she said, hoping she could support her convictions, and follow her dreams.

"Good. It's not the way of you young people, but it used to happen a lot. And in this case, it's for the best." Her grandfather took a deep breath and smiled at her. As smiles went, it wasn't one of his warmer ones. "We'll call the priest this afternoon, after the ceremony."

He'd misunderstood her rebellious statement. "No, Grandfather. I'm having this baby *alone*." Ignoring her roiling stomach, Cori drew herself up. "And I'm not going on the wine tour."

His smile faded.

"I've taken a job in L.A. I start in two weeks." Until that moment, Cori hadn't found the courage to tell him she was accepting a job at a public relations firm. In fact, since she'd discovered her pregnancy, she'd all but given up on the job and her own goals. She just hadn't had the heart to officially turn down the offer.

"Like hell you are!" His eyes found their mark. Her. "If you're having that baby, you'll be married and home where you belong."

For the first time since Cori had admitted her condition, she felt the full force of her grandfather's anger directed upon her. His scorching ire had her nearly breaking out in a sweat. Never having stood up to her grandfather before, Cori's determination slipped. It would be so much easier to let him have his way. Her baby would never want for anything.

"Without me, you won't be able to support that child *alone* in Los Angeles. You won't see a penny from me." He glared down at her, a triumphant smile on his face—as if he'd discovered her weakness. "His name, Corinne."

Cori's resolve wavered. What was she thinking? Single parenthood was going to be hard enough. How could she hope to launch a career at the same time? She did still love him. Maybe they could work out their differences. Maybe…

When she didn't answer, her grandfather's voice crackled with fire. "Didn't you learn about birth control at any of those expensive schools I sent you to?" He waved a hand in the direction of her stomach. "Damn it, Corinne, I won't stand by and see you ruin what I've built with *this*—this mistake of yours."

"Ruin what you've built?" Cori's words were a weak echo of Salvatore's venomous declaration. "How could I possibly ruin what you've built?" In Cori's estimation, nothing could shatter the success her grandfather had created. Certainly not an illegitimate great-grandchild.

Her grandfather leaned over Cori, his face coming within inches of hers. "Illegitimate babies tear families apart. This is a family venture, and you won't destroy it because you let some boy have his fun. At least your mother recognized what she had to do." Her grandfather pulled back and glanced at his Rolex. "Everyone's waiting to see you graduate. Pull yourself together and meet me downstairs in five minutes. We'll take care of this later."

It took Cori a few minutes to collect herself after he left—a few minutes to try to erase the image of her grandfather walking out of her life.

CHAPTER ONE

"YOU'RE NOT HAPPY to see me." Cori Sinclair could have sworn the house she'd grown up in stared down on her, dark and forbidding. "Maybe I'm not so happy to see you, either."

It was a long time to be cast out of a family. Nearly five years had passed since that fateful day in June when her grandfather had issued his ultimatum. Since then, she hadn't spoken to her grandfather, and had kept only limited, infrequent contact with her mother and brother, who were still as committed to the family business as she had once been. Her family's dedication kept them immersed in the Messina Winery in Sonoma, California. For most of her life, Cori had thrived on that feeling of purpose and belonging. Until she realized she needed to prove herself on her own terms, without her grandfather's guidance.

She wasn't ready to face her past, wasn't ready to step through the black, double doors into the depths of the three-story mansion with its multi-angled roof, dark-gray brick facings and coal shutters, wasn't ready to step away from the small freedom her dented yellow Mustang represented. Cori hadn't even been able to bring herself to park her car in the garage. She'd pulled up on the far side of the front entry as if she were a guest, then stood in the warm spring sun, waiting, fighting her dread, and wondering.

Cori's gaze trailed away from the house, toward the main highway. The drive to the Messina compound was beautiful and winding, lined with ancient oak trees and rows of neatly tended grapevines just getting ready to burst forth with spring life.

Home. After so long, Cori still thought of this as home.

Cori bit her lip and, not for the first time that day, pondered her choice of attire. She'd wanted to wear something stylish and feminine for her mother, something to show her grandfather he didn't control her anymore.

What had she been thinking to have donned the deep red, form-fitting sheath with its teasing neckline and short hem? Add the high-heeled, scallop-edged scarlet pumps she'd slipped into upon her arrival and there was no way Cori looked as if she'd come home to fit in with her conservative wine-making family.

But Cori wasn't here to fit in. She had to remember that. She was here to help Mama, but was not home to stay.

Her boss Sidney, had approved her request to telecommute and reduce her public relations workload so that she could return home indefinitely. Cori had a successful career guiding public relations for several imported beer brands distributed by Bell-Diva, including Nightshade, the hottest beer in the clubs this year. It just about killed her to work outside the wine industry, but she couldn't bring herself to work for another winery.

The sound of a door being opened drew Cori's attention back to the house. She stiffened as she recognized the man closing the imposing front door.

He looked up toward the driveway, freezing for a moment when Cori came into his line of vision. Then his chin dropped slightly and he stared at her in a way that made her feel she had his complete attention. The gesture was so familiar that Cori's heart immediately scaled up her throat. With effort, she forced herself to be calm, to look as if he were just another one of Messina's field managers.

Despite his bulky work boots, fluid strides carried him closer. Her eyes drank in the changes to his body, easily discernible through his faded blue jeans and T-shirt. He'd filled out since she'd seen him last, but he was still lean and muscular. His red-brown hair, cut short on the sides, longer on top, glinted in the California afternoon sunlight.

"Miss Sinclair." He stopped five feet away from her, hands on his hips as if he owned the place.

He was far enough away that she could tell things hadn't changed between them, but close enough for her to note how his ice-gray eyes stroked impassively over her red dress, down her legs to her pumps and back over her dress…pausing in the area of her cleavage.

Maybe not so impassively.

For once, those ten extra pregnancy pounds she hadn't shed didn't seem so bad. With more courage than she had felt moments before, Cori met his gaze.

"Blake Austin, isn't it?"

Blake's jaw clenched. Cori allowed herself a small smile, then tossed a hand through her hair for good measure. She was, after all, the woman in red.

"Back for a visit after all this time?"

The bravado drained out of her. "You know why I'm back," she replied flatly.

Blake glanced toward the house, then pinned Cori with his chilling eyes.

"She needs people around her to be strong."

"And you think I'm not." Smoothing her dress with her hands, Cori tried to hide the tremor of apprehension that made her knees weak. She questioned her own resolve. *Am I strong enough to handle Mama's cancer one more time?*

Blake shrugged unapologetically. "If the shoe fits." He glanced significantly at her red heels, then moved closer to the Mustang.

"You're still driving this? What is it? Four years old?"

"Five." It was the last car her grandfather had bought for her, a graduation gift. Living in Los Angeles, she'd been unable to afford anything else while paying exorbitant rent and day-care costs.

"Kind of passé, isn't it?"

At least she knew now what he thought of her. Cori squared her shoulders. Blake didn't know what she'd been through these past few years. "It runs great and it's paid for."

He snorted, irritating her.

"I bet you still drive that beat-up, old truck," she snapped, regretting the words as soon as they spilled from her lips. The memory of Blake's taut body, of tangled limbs and an ill-placed steering wheel suddenly made it hard to breathe.

His eyes held her gaze, and Cori's entire body stilled. Silently, they acknowledged their shared past.

Blake broke the moment first, looking toward the car.

"I've never known a Messina to drive a car longer than two years. I know you can afford ten of these. Why are you really driving it? What, has it got crushed, red velvet interior or something?" Blake leaned into the open window for a closer look, his dark blue T-shirt caressing the lean muscles of his back as she once had done.

Belatedly realizing what Blake was about to find, Cori tried to stop him. "Don't—" But she was too late.

A thin scream cut through the air.

Cori hadn't planned to tell him like this. She wasn't ready.

"Mommy, get me out! Mommy!"

The high-pitched plea startled Blake so much that he hit his head as he pulled out of the car. "What the hell?" He rubbed the back of his scalp with one hand.

"Mommy!"

"Coming, Michael." She opened the door, then with practiced ease moved the passenger seat forward, reached in and released the belt on her son's car seat. His little face was scrunched up, his eyes tightly shut. But Cori knew Michael considered himself awake. The sooner she freed him, the less likely Blake was to experience one of Michael's tantrums.

"It's okay, baby." He'd only fallen asleep about thirty minutes before they arrived, which was one reason why she'd postponed braving the mansion. Cranky didn't begin to describe Michael when he hadn't slept a full hour.

Cori pulled him out and into her arms, guiding his head to her shoulder, away from Blake's view. Michael settled easily against her, relaxed and content to be free. She rubbed his little back and kissed the crown of his head, familiar gestures meant to reassure her son.

"He's yours?" Blake frowned at her, his eyes dipping to her legs.

"All thirty-five pounds of him." Realizing her dress was riding up, she held Michael's bottom away from her with one hand and smoothed her skirt with the other.

Cori blushed. Actually blushed. She couldn't remember the last time that had happened. Of all the ways she'd imagined seeing Blake Austin again, flashing her panties hadn't made the list.

"I heard about someone named Michael. I just..." His frown deepened.

"I'm not married. Never was, if that's what you're asking." Where had that come from? Blake certainly wasn't asking, much to her heart's dismay.

She wasn't ready for this. Granted, Michael was small for his age, so Cori didn't think Blake would suspect the boy was his son. Heaven knows, he would be furious if he guessed the truth before Cori had a chance to tell him. She just wanted to tell Blake when things were right. Looking at his disapproving frown, she didn't think this was the time.

Blake's expression became closed and unreadable as the moment turned excruciatingly awkward. "And the kid..." Blake stepped to his left, craning his neck to see Michael's face.

"Michael." Cori stepped slightly back and away, her hand on Michael's head as she shielded him from view. She didn't like Blake referring to Michael as *the kid.*

Blake paused. Scratched his head.

Cori hadn't been prepared for this kind of reception. So much for her fantasy of Blake seeing Michael and claiming them. Hugging Michael tighter, Cori fought back the tears. Only Michael mattered. And Mama. "Your point?"

Blake looked as if someone had sucker punched him, as if he didn't know what to say. Then he blurted, "I wasn't expecting a kid, that's all."

"His name is Michael," Cori said through a throat so tight

she struggled for air. "Now, if you'll excuse me, I need to see my mother and get settled."

Cori stepped past Blake and marched with as much dignity as she could muster on high heels while holding thirty-five pounds of angel. She was practically bent over backward to keep her balance.

"Who is that man, Mommy? I don't like him."

"No one we need to worry about, Peanut." Half of her wished Blake had heard her words.

How could Blake not recognize his own son?

BLAKE REACTED to Cori's walking away instinctively. He hurried around her and opened the front door, ignoring the blank, unwelcome look from the kid and getting a hesitant "thank you" without a smile from Cori. She'd always been unfailingly polite, inspiring the best behavior in him.

Cori Sinclair had come home. With a kid in tow. Blake's heart stumbled every time he looked at Cori, dropped to his gut every time he laid eyes on her kid.

He should have called her. They'd shared one unbelievable night together, argued and never spoken again. Stubborn, wounded pride had kept him from contacting her. And she hadn't come back. Until now.

Despite years of service to Messina Vineyards, it was clear Blake was still an outsider. The Messinas were such a private family, they made the Kennedys look like chatterboxes. Blake respected their silence and hadn't asked about Cori when she hadn't returned from school. About a year or more after Cori's graduation, when it seemed the Messinas had accepted Blake, he'd started accompanying Mr. Messina to award dinners, charity events and the like. Only then did he hear snippets of conversation about Cori and Michael. Sophia, especially, was quick to point out to Mr. Messina and Luke, Cori's brother, how good Michael was for Cori.

All this time, Blake had assumed Michael was Cori's lover, not her child. He felt so stupid. At least now, he could lay to rest that nagging suspicion that he'd been the reason Cori had never returned to her family.

As Blake watched, Cori made a beeline for the steep, sweeping staircase without slowing to take in the bronze and burgundy opulence that still impressed Blake. Of course, she'd grown up in this house and probably took the mix of antique furnishings, original artwork and oriental carpets for granted.

Blake realized she meant to climb the steps in those neck-breaking high heels while holding the kid. So he followed her up the stairs to make sure she wouldn't fall. Then he had to knock on Sophia's door for Cori and open it, as well. His mother was undoubtedly praising his manners in heaven.

Blake felt more like the butler—one more reason why he hadn't called her.

"Mama," Cori said in a heart-wrenching whisper as she swept past him.

Sophia smiled brilliantly, her expression lighting up the room, and making Blake believe for just a moment that she wasn't terminally ill, losing a second battle with breast cancer.

Not stopping to put down her son, Cori rushed to her mother's side despite her heels sinking into the thick taupe carpet. She hung on to the boy as if he were her lifeline.

Blake had once thought he could fill that role. Resolutely, he tugged the door closed, shutting away the scene, and his memories.

"I'M SO GLAD YOU'RE HERE." Mama's voice came out in a breathy whisper as she patted the edge of the bed in invitation.

Trying her best to bury her unsettled emotions toward Blake, Cori sat on the rose-patterned brocade bedspread, carefully watching her mother for any sign of pain the jostling might cause. When she didn't see any, Cori lifted Michael onto her lap so that he could see his grandmother. She took her mother's thin hand and gave it a tender squeeze. Mama looked terrible, with no luster to her once dark hair, and eyes that were sluggish. Her pale pink satin nightgown was the brightest thing about her appearance.

"You remember Grandma, don't you, Michael?"

Michael nodded and tucked his head under Cori's chin.

"Well..." Cori floundered for something to say. She'd stayed in touch with her mother, but only by telephone and over the occasional dinner when Mama came to Los Angeles. They usually filled the time exchanging news and avoiding the issue of Michael's parentage. Idle chitchat seemed inappropriate now. She glanced around the room, noting the same rose curtains, pine paneling and Queen Anne furniture. Other than a plastic water pitcher, cup and straw on the bedside table, nothing seemed to have changed in the room except her mother's health.

To keep the conversation from lagging, Cori fell back on good manners. "Can I get you anything?"

"No." Her mother seemed content just to look at the two of them.

Cori bobbed her head nervously. "You look good. You've got color in your cheeks," she lied. Her mother's complexion was as white as a lily.

"Maria did my makeup this morning, since you were coming, but she's no good with hair." Mama raised a weak hand and touched the thin, gray hair on her head. Cori remembered when it had gleamed as black as night. Now everything about her mother seemed dull.

"I can pull it up, if you like," Cori offered thickly, uncomfortable when faced with the reality of her mother's illness. Blake's doubts about her returned and echoed in her head.

Am I strong enough to help her? The tasks ahead of her were overwhelming. Could she help her mother die and still be a good mom? Cover myriad duties her job required? Be near Blake without letting him know she still loved him?

"Not now. I just want to look at you." Mama's dark eyes were large in her pinched face. "Stand up so I can see your dress."

Cori tried to set Michael down on the floor, but he clung to her leg. She bent to tuck his Digimon T-shirt over the ketchup stain on his denim shorts, wishing she'd remembered to change his shirt as she'd planned before coming upstairs. Her mother hadn't seen Michael that often, and Cori wanted him to make a good impression.

"Wonderful cut," Mama murmured, looking first at Cori's shoes, then at Michael clutching her leg. "What an unusual accessory that little angel is."

"He's beautiful." Cori tousled Michael's straight brown hair. "A little shy, maybe."

"Uh-huh," her mother agreed. "How long are you here?"

"Awhile." Cori sank back onto the bed and took her mother's hand.

Mama smiled weakly. "Me, too."

BLAKE SHUT HIMSELF OUT of the Messina mansion, letting his feet put physical distance between himself and Cori. But thoughts of his old love lingered.

He'd met Salvatore Messina's granddaughter that first summer he'd worked at Messina Vineyards. Blake and his half sister, Jennifer, had just moved into the house at the back of the property and Blake was struggling to meet the needs of a new, demanding employer. Two years after his mother and stepfather died in a car accident, Blake had worked his way through a few corporate farming jobs. With half a degree and no chip on his shoulder—he couldn't afford one with a younger sister to care for—Blake had done well. Still, he hadn't felt good enough for Mr. Messina's granddaughter. She was the Sonoma County equivalent of royalty.

Blake rounded a bend in the drive and paused, looking out across the successive rows of vines. He imagined that instead of bare wood, the canes were thick with leaves shading clusters of purple grapes, as they had been when he'd first met Cori. The scene painted a rich backdrop to a younger Cori Sinclair, home from college and a nuisance, following him around the vineyard, telling him what he did wrong, showing up in the darndest places—like down by the Russian River in the barest of bikinis.

He'd told Cori to get lost. He'd warned her to stay away

from him. After all, she was his employer's granddaughter. But Cori just laughed and flashed him that dazzling smile of hers, as if he could never hurt her feelings, as if she knew they were destined to be together. Maybe it wouldn't have been so bad if she hadn't been so vibrant. Cori's dark, Italian complexion combined with soft brown eyes and long, wavy blond hair often drew glances. At only five foot four, she'd had the sleek proportions of a model several inches taller. But it was Cori's bubbly personality that kept Blake's attention, because Blake had given up on enjoying life after his mother and stepfather died.

Blake sighed, opening the floodgates to more memories.

The summer progressed and things intensified as he and Cori became friends teetering on the edge of something more. Blake lived with the unexpected daily pain of seeing Cori go out with those spoiled rich kids in their foreign sports cars to all those soirees, wine tastings and balls. All dressed up in her fancy clothes, ears and slender neck decked out in expensive jewelry even though she was only a kid—barely nineteen—looking like a delicious piece of eye candy. It hurt to see her go, especially when Cori admitted that she'd rather stay home with him.

As those summer days passed, Blake grew more frustrated because he knew what those rich boys had in mind when they took Cori out. Despite Blake's best intentions, he'd struggled with the same forbidden desire for Cori Sinclair that he knew the rich kids did. But Blake had two things stopping him from doing anything about his feelings—Salvatore Messina and the need to provide for Jennifer. He couldn't afford to lose his job. Blake was sure it would take wild horses to get him to touch Cori Sinclair.

In the end, it had taken much less than that.

Blake shook his head, stopping himself from reliving that memory. It was bad enough that Cori still invaded his dreams. He couldn't have her hovering in his thoughts during the day.

Rather than veer deeper into the vineyards on his rounds, Blake walked farther down the driveway in the dappled shade provided by the oak trees lining the drive. Out of habit, he scanned the neat rows of grapevines as he passed, looking for the impending bud break that signaled spring had arrived in the vineyard, when a new set of duties would face Blake. At this time of year, the grapevines stood bare, unadorned by the heavy foliage that sheltered grape clusters from the sun in early summer.

Not ten steps later, Blake's thoughts returned to Cori.

The optimistic, naive Cori wasn't in evidence today. Neither was her heart-stopping smile. This Cori Sinclair was tougher, undoubtedly hardened because the son of a bitch who got her pregnant hadn't been honorable enough to marry her. He knew Cori. She wouldn't choose to be an unwed mother.

The image of Cori leaning against her car in the driveway returned. She'd cut her hair so that it fell in tousled, golden waves around her face and shoulders. Having a baby had transformed her sleek frame into a curvy figure. Cori was a knockout in that red dress. It was short enough to make her legs look long, particularly when she'd leaned into the car to pick up the kid. And when the hem had hiked up in front, well…

Blake frowned. Not only was Cori off-limits, then and now, but she'd made it abundantly clear one night, years ago, that Blake wasn't good enough for her.

The school bus rumbled into the drive of Messina Vineyards, and a moment later, Jennifer stepped off. Fleetingly, Blake wondered if he'd been thinking about Cori to avoid thinking about the problems he was having raising his sister, or the helplessness he suffered when he thought about Sophia dying.

Jennifer looked like any normal almost thirteen-year-old in blue jeans, an Old Navy T-shirt and bulky leather shoes, her long brown hair lifting gently on the breeze. Blake was glad to see her. Glad they had each other. Glad of the choices he'd made to keep them together.

Then Jen opened her mouth.

"I've told you before, I don't need to be picked up at the bus." Her steps changed to the swagger of a soon-to-be woman and her expression turned sullen.

Blake sighed. "I wanted some company," he said, realizing

it was true. Sophia was having one of her better days, which made the thought of losing her that much harder to bear.

"Huh."

Jen's code for "leave me alone." They headed back to the main house, carefully walking on opposite sides of the road, careful to keep their thoughts to themselves. Blake longed for the days when Jen had slipped her hand into his, chattering freely about her day.

"How's Sophia?"

Blake read the anxiety Jennifer tried to hide in her voice and felt sorry for her. Sophia Sinclair was like a grandmother to Jennifer, inviting her to fancy dinners, opening the big house to her when Blake traveled for the winery. It was hard enough for a girl to lose her parents when she was four. Why did the only other woman Jen had bonded with have to die early, as well?

"It's a good day." Blake wished he could tell her Sophia was getting better. "You're doing your homework with her, right?"

"Don't I always?"

Too late, Blake realized that Cori was here to keep Sophia company and might consider Jen an intruder. Well, too bad. Jennifer was just as much a part of Sophia's family as Cori was. Sophia and Jennifer shared a special relationship.

"Don't put me down!"

The shrill plea cut through the air, shuddering along Blake's nerves like fingernails on a chalkboard. It was the kid. Whining again. Brush concealed the part of the driveway where Cori's car was parked, but the boy's voice definitely came from there.

"I need to get our suitcases out, Peanut. I can't do that with one hand."

"Houseguests," Blake warned Jennifer as they rounded the curve of the driveway, hoping his expression communicated that she should behave.

Jennifer frowned.

"Can we help you with those?" Blake offered, watching the

kid squirm in Cori's arms. Her dress hiked up again, and he forced his eyes to stay on her face.

"Mommy, I want to go home," wailed the kid.

Cori looked as if she'd rather accept help from her worst enemy than from Blake, but after a moment's consideration, she nodded.

"You remember Cori, don't you, Jen?" Blake asked as he approached, trying to lay the foundation of peace.

"No. Who are you?" Jen asked sweetly, when Blake knew full well that his sister remembered who Cori was.

Blake gave his sister a stern glance before looking into Cori's trunk. He was surprised at what he found. Only two medium, black wheelie-bags—not even an expensive brand but the cheap kind that you got at a discount store—a computer satchel, a sleeping bag and one well-worn, stained backpack.

Cori introduced herself and the kid to Jennifer. The back of the boy's head nestled against Cori's neck, his chin rested on her shoulder. Short, spindly legs dangled on either side of Cori's hips. From his size, Blake guessed him to be around three. The kid eyed Jennifer suspiciously, earning a bit of reluctant respect from Blake. Lately, his sister rode an emotional pendulum from heated disdain to cool affection. An unsuspecting little boy would be an easy mark for her derision.

Blake handed the laptop to Cori and passed the backpack to Jen, who held it out as if it had germs. He carried the sleeping bag and two wheelies into the house.

"Where to?" Blake asked as he headed upstairs.

"My old room."

Blake heard Jen huff in outrage behind him. She'd been sleeping in Cori's bedroom when she stayed with Sophia and had become rather proprietary about it, even going so far as to refer to it as "my room." Blake hoped Jennifer decided to use good manners today so that she wouldn't embarrass him.

"It's only got one single bed. Maybe you should stay in the guest room," Blake said as they climbed the stairs, trying to avoid a blowup.

"I'm not a guest," Cori answered firmly, then nudged the

child and added, ''Besides, you like camping out on the floor, don't you, Peanut?''

Shouldering open the door to Cori's room, Blake entered, glad he was accustomed to the color.

''It's pretty pink, isn't it,'' Cori said, with a forced laugh. ''I'd forgotten *how* pink.''

Everything was pink. Pink carpet, pink frilly drapes, pink satin bedspread, pink striped wallpaper and pink champagne furniture. Blake couldn't relate to it at all. Jennifer loved it. The black suitcases seemed somber and out of place.

''It's a girl's room, Mommy.''

''I'm a girl.''

''You're a mommy.''

''Give your mommy a kiss and thank Jennifer for carrying your backpack.'' Cori finally managed to disengage herself from the little cling-on.

''You're staying in *this* room?'' Jennifer handed over the backpack without acknowledging the kid's thanks.

''I'll survive, I think. I can always wear my sunglasses.'' Cori flashed a little smile in Jennifer's direction.

Whether Cori was deliberately misreading Jennifer's meaning or just being polite, Blake couldn't tell. She seemed tense. Her eyes ping-ponged from Michael to Blake. What was making her so uncomfortable?

Jennifer crossed her arms over her chest and raised her eyebrows, giving Cori her version of the evil eye, but Cori didn't notice as she kicked off those killer pumps, bent and pulled a suitcase across the floor.

''Jen, why don't you go check on Sophia and get started on your homework?'' Blake suggested, trying to breathe normally as Cori showed several inches of bare thigh while leaning over. Just a little bit farther and she'd expose everything. Blake made himself look away.

''Mama's resting right now,'' Cori said, as if she was now in charge of her mother's well-being.

''That's okay,'' Jennifer said with saccharine sweetness. ''She's used to me being there *every day.*''

And with that direct hit, Jen flounced out of the room.

Straightening, Cori gnawed on her lower lip, then gave Blake a worried look, brown eyes as big and soulful as a puppy's.

''Mama said she was going to rest while I unpacked.''

Blake shrugged, unwilling to let her distress bother him. ''Jen does her homework in there most afternoons. I think Sophia likes the company.''

Cori turned away, but not before he noted the tears filling her eyes. Blake pulled the door closed between them before he did something stupid like pull her into his arms.

SALVATORE MESSINA SAT in the limousine staring at the yellow Mustang in the driveway. His granddaughter had come home. For years, he'd lived without her sunny smiles, her shining diplomacy and her fierce love of the land. Messina Vineyards wasn't as strong a presence in the wine industry without her, especially these days. And the family? Well, the family had become less talkative, less humorous and—he'd admit this only to himself—less loving. Here in the shadowy twilight of his dark car, Salvatore could admit that he had missed Corinne.

A silly, sentimental feeling swept through him, filling Salvatore's eyes with tears, making him uncomfortably aware of the driver sitting patiently in the front seat. He hardened his jaw, then blinked back the tears with a measured breath.

Show no weakness.

His car door swung open, startling Salvatore and sending a shaft of pain through his hips and a fresh wave of tears to his eyes.

Blake Austin peered in. ''Everything okay?''

''Fine,'' Salvatore replied gruffly as the pain eased, despite the fact that nothing was right. His daughter was dying, his granddaughter had never forgiven him his unfortunate ultimatum, and both his hips were giving out on him. He carried on through each day on painkillers that did nothing to numb the torment that was his life.

The Mustang's splashy yellow color caught Salvatore's eye

once more, causing a different pang, albeit one just as painful, not in his hips but in his heart.

"Manny just dropped me off from the north property. Can I help you out?"

Salvatore wouldn't accept pity, even from an employee as loyal as Blake Austin. "Do I look helpless?" he snapped, carefully stepping out, using the car's frame for support as unobtrusively as possible. Standing upright was excruciating, but Salvatore Messina grappled with life as staunchly as life wrestled with him.

He bared his teeth in a smile as he straightened, swallowing a groan of agony.

Blake observed the process, most likely not fooled but too considerate to say anything. He nodded, as if acknowledging his employer's strength of will.

Shame weakened Salvatore's anger, but anger was the only thing aside from medicine that made the pain manageable, so he gave it free rein.

"Everything's right in the vineyards? With the crew?"

"Everything's great, sir."

As well as being a tireless worker, Blake Austin always treated Salvatore with respect. Over the past few years, Blake had become almost one of the family, yet he still called Salvatore "sir" or "Mr. Messina." Blake was respectful, faithful, and knew when to mind his own business. The perfect employee. Salvatore didn't receive that kind of treatment from his own grandchildren. He glanced over his shoulder at the yellow Mustang.

Would Corinne offer an apology as due to the head of the family? It didn't matter who was right or wrong, the younger deferred to the elder if she wanted to make peace. He didn't know what he'd do if she didn't ask his forgiveness.

Salvatore Messina bid Blake good-night and moved stiffly up the steps as the spring shadows deepened the sky.

BLAKE STEPPED into the mudroom in his house at the back of the Messina property. Lately, it seemed that every day sapped his energy, but seeing Cori had unexpectedly drained him. Blake removed his muddy boots, grateful that the day was nearly over, grateful to be on his own turf. The small, two-story house belonged to Messina Vineyards, but Blake and Jennifer called it home.

The steamy smells of dinner drifted out to him, taunting him with the promise of welcome. He hesitated before entering the kitchen. Out in the mudroom, it was easier for Blake to believe that he and Jennifer were still close. Prepared to tackle the final duty of the day, he took a deep breath and entered the brightly lit kitchen, stocking feet treading softly on the hardwood floor.

Jennifer bustled about the kitchen counter while MTV blared from the small television on top of the refrigerator. Blake noticed immediately that, as dinners went, it wasn't much—hamburger with noodles, a green salad, canned pears and wheat toast. Jen wasn't much of a cook, but at least she made a lot of food. He washed his hands with dish soap in the sink, and then he switched the television to a channel with news and lowered the volume in the hopes that they might actually have a conversation.

''What? No vegetables?'' Blake teased as he surveyed the food Jennifer dished onto foam plates.

''Sliced bell pepper on the salad. The sauce on the noodles is red, so it must have tomato in it.'' Jen rolled her gray eyes, but didn't smile or look at him as she carried the plates to the table. She never made eye contact with Blake anymore, unless she was angry. He wished he knew what to say or do to make her smile at him again, to share that special camaraderie he'd once taken for granted.

''Tomato is a fruit.'' Blake eyed the three slices of bell pepper she'd referred to that miraculously garnished the top of his salad, not hers, before he delivered the milk to the table.

''So you say.'' She took her place on one of the old wooden kitchen chairs. The one by the telephone. Undoubtedly, she hoped it would ring during dinner.

That's when Blake noticed that four pear halves graced his plate. She had one. Not only that, but barely any salad or hamburger with noodles sat on her plate. He clenched his jaw. It didn't matter that Jen thought she knew how to take care of herself. She didn't. At this rate, the school would be calling him to say she had an eating disorder. Maybe they weren't as close as they'd once been, but that didn't mean Blake wasn't still responsible for her.

Snatching a small bag of carrots from the refrigerator, Blake poked his finger through the plastic and tossed some onto Jen's plate. Then he ladled another helping of hamburger mixture on top of what she'd originally taken. He couldn't stop himself from tossing a slice of bell pepper from his own salad onto her greens, as well.

"That ought to help balance the food groups for you."

Jen uttered a teenage sound of disgust.

"And make you regular," Blake added for good measure.

"Gross." She prodded her food for a moment, then sighed and started to eat.

Disaster averted, Blake slid into his seat and picked up a fork even though he was no longer hungry. Sophia's illness was hitting him harder than he'd expected. It was as if he were losing his parents all over again—only this time he was losing Jen, too. How many more years would it be before he came home to an empty house?

They ate in quiet efficiency, with newscasters filling the silence between them and, for once, no telephone calls. Blake wasn't sure anymore if Jennifer's silence was due to teenage angst or sorrow for Sophia. He just knew he couldn't fill it.

As they were cleaning up, Blake asked, "Want to watch some TV?" He needed a distraction; otherwise he'd worry about things he didn't want to, like Jen, Sophia and Cori.

Jennifer grunted.

"I guess that means no." Blake tried to hide his disappointment as he took a chocolate candy bar—his cure for the blues—out of the refrigerator and trudged into the living room. Maybe when Jen went up to her room, he'd flip through one of his parenting books.

Other than the school pictures of Jennifer on the fireplace

mantel, the living room hadn't changed since they'd moved in. There was a small television on a stand, a large green sectional sofa and two glass-topped coffee tables planted on a blue carpet—all castoffs from the last time Sophia remodeled the main house.

Blake slouched into the couch with his remote, expecting to be alone the rest of the evening. Miraculously, Jen hung out in the doorway.

"*Star Trek?* ESPN?" he offered, afraid that the tiny ray of hope welling inside him would be extinguished if he put too much faith in it.

Jen shrugged, poised awkwardly in the hall.

With a click of a button, ESPN's upbeat theme song filled the room. Then an announcer launched into the day's sports scores. Sports were easy. You played within the rules and won or lost. Not like parenting. The rules of parenting changed as the child aged.

"We had a substitute teacher in English today. Man, was she messed up." Jen warmed to her story and relaxed her shoulders against the wall, her face lighting up. "Some of the kids switched seats and pretended to be someone else."

Blake noticed all of this out of the corner of his eye. Caution kept him from looking directly at her until he deciphered her mood.

"By the end of the period, she didn't know who was who."

Blake's eyes landed on Jen's face in a blink. She was smiling. Her demeanor fairly shouted for approval. Blake passed the remote control from one hand to the other.

Let it go. Jennifer was reaching out to him. He should just smile, pat the couch next to him and share in her harmless little prank. But Blake remembered what it was like to be twelve, had once been on the path to becoming a destructive, unchecked teen himself. That had been in junior high school, while his mom struggled to keep them off welfare. Too tired each night to do much more than ask her wayward son about his day, Blake had become something of a campus hellion. When she finally found out the truth about what a bully Blake had become, through a visit to the principal's office the day he was suspended, the sorrow and disappointment in her tears combined with a transfer to a new school helped straighten him out.

''Did you go along with it?'' His words came out in a low growl and his chin dropped until it almost touched his chest, his eyes on his sister.

Jen's expression crumbled. She sniffed, then drew belligerence around her like a cloak. ''So what if I did? There's no harm done.''

''That's not an answer. I think you know how I expect you to behave.''

Hostile eyes stared right back at him. That was new. She hadn't been able to hold his stern gaze before. The realization that he was losing control of her ignited his temper.

''Jennifer Louise,'' he warned, sitting up straighter.

''You expect better from me, don't you.'' Her eyes flashed.

Blake's eyes widened. A frontal attack. This, too, was new.

''You know I do.'' Blake realized he should leave her alone, but he couldn't. ''Like today. You were rude to Cori Sinclair and that *boy*.'' Blake uttered the last word distastefully.

''As if they care about me.'' Arms crossed guardedly over her chest.

Why did she have to take everything so personally? As if the world were out to get her?

''That doesn't matter. What matters is that you treat people with respect.'' He stood, trying to regain some control over the situation. Over her. ''Especially to those in the Messina household.''

''You act like we're second-class citizens. Everything is about the Messinas. Like they're royalty or something.''

''Look at all they've done for us.'' He spread his arms and gestured around the room. ''How they opened up their home to us.''

''We'll never be allowed in the house again after Sophia dies.'' Jen's brows pulled disdainfully low.

Blake eyed her in disbelief. ''Is that what this is about? *Your* room? She's dying, Jen. How much more selfish can you be?''

''I must be such a disappointment to you.'' Her face reddened while her arms clutched herself tighter. ''If it wasn't for me, you would've finished college. And you'd be somewhere...else.''

For a moment, two pairs of gray eyes clashed. It was true. Blake resented the fact that responsibility for his sister had been thrust upon him, and still felt inferior working in a world where everyone had a degree except him.

But none of it was her fault.

In a blink, Jen spun, escaping to the stairs, her footfalls beating sharply on each step, trampling his heart.

''Jen, wait.'' Moving just as quickly, Blake reached the foot of the stairs.

Jen stopped but didn't turn, her thin shoulders hunched. One hand clutched the railing, the other covered her face. She was crying.

Blake's heart cracked. He couldn't find his voice, trapped as it was behind his fear. Fear of losing Jen. Fear for Sophia and the pain they were all going through. And he'd accused Cori of not being strong enough today.

''You're the most important person in the world to me.'' He managed to push the words past the lump in his throat. ''I've got your picture in my wallet. Yours, Mom's and Dad's. Do you want to see?'' It was the olive branch he used with Jen. He'd been using it a lot more frequently lately. Sometimes Blake wondered if he'd ever reach a point where it wouldn't work anymore.

Slowly, Jen turned, showing him her pale, tear-streaked face. Yet she remained on the steps. The tears just about killed him. Gone were the thoughts that Jen was becoming a pain in the ass. How could he be so insensitive as to make his little sister cry?

''I'm worried about Sophia, too.'' Blake took a guess that this latest mood swing hung on Sophia's failing health. ''I could use a hug about now, Jenny Lou.'' It was his final bit of ammo. *Jenny Lou.* Their mother's version of Jennifer's given name, Jennifer Louise. Blake had begun calling her that eight years ago after Kevin and Mary Austin were killed in a car crash on Interstate 80. Blake had been twenty-two, just starting his junior year at the university in Davis. Jennifer had been only four years old.

After hearing the devastating news of their deaths, Blake rushed home to find a neighbor cooking a truckload of vegetable casseroles in his parents' kitchen and Jen hiding in her bedroom.

Blake pushed past the woman, then barreled into Jen's bedroom, scooping up his sprite of a half sister and taking her outside. The Indian-summer sun had already warmed the late-morning air. Blake sought the old oak tree behind the farmhouse, and settled down on the sparse, brown, wild grass beneath the oak's thick, spreading branches, with Jen in his lap.

Looking down, he saw Jen's eyes tightly shut and her thumb planted firmly in her mouth. Rather than pull it out as he'd done on numerous other occasions, Blake allowed the little girl the luxury of whatever comfort she could claim. They sat together under that tree until the sun had set. Neither spoke for a long while. The only sound was the gentle smack of her lips against her thumb and the brush of cornstalks stroked by the wind.

"I'm never leaving you, Jenny Lou." Blake never knew if it was the endearment that his mother used or if any words would have reached her, but Jennifer turned her small body into his and started to cry.

He'd been calling her Jenny Lou in times of upheaval ever since.

Now Jennifer flew down the stairs into Blake's arms, practically knocking him over, chasing away the cobwebs of the past, making Blake wish this truce between them would last.

CHAPTER TWO

IGNORING THE NERVOUS flutter in her stomach, Cori entered the empty Messina dining room with Michael in tow. Would her grandfather welcome her back? Or order her to go? She squared her shoulders. There was no way she'd leave when Mama had asked her to come home.

Cori pulled Michael back as he extended a small hand toward an antique Japanese tea set on the sideboard. The last thing she needed on her first day home was one of Michael's *accidents.*

The opulent room, with its dark, heavy wood furniture, deep burgundy and bronze decor and crystal chandelier felt familiar. Her mind panned through dinners with congressmen, wine makers and her family. Back then, her mother and grandfather were nearly always laughing at some story her brother had retold or some joke her grandfather had pulled on Cori.

Cori sighed. She'd lived here in another lifetime, one she couldn't relate to now. The long, formal dining table sparkled with expensive china—a sharp contrast to the serviceable Chinette set they used in their little apartment in Los Angeles. A portrait of Cori's grandmother gazed down upon them, the only warmth in an otherwise impersonal room.

The ornate grandfather clock in the hallway chimed the hour—seven o'clock. Late for dinner by Michael's standards but early for the Messinas, who usually ate after a full day of work.

''There's my favorite rug rat,'' came a voice behind her.

Cori turned to greet Luke with a warm smile. Cori suspected her brother was wearing the same faded jeans, scuffed work boots and dark flannel shirt he'd worn the last time she'd been home. Five years her senior, Luke Sinclair was becoming a seasoned winemaker. Like Cori, he had the dark complexion and eyes of their Italian ancestors. But there the similarities between the siblings ended. Luke stood over six feet tall, with jet-black hair and a smile that dazzled women from birth to sixty.

"You didn't dress for dinner?" Cori asked. Not that dinner in the household was a formal affair, but the only time jeans were ever allowed was during the fall harvest season. Cori still had her red dress on and had finally changed Michael's shirt.

"I don't do that anymore," Luke responded cryptically.

Michael squealed with delight as Luke picked him up, then spun him around in a dizzying circle, sending grubby shoelaces flying like streamers around the room.

"Watch out," Cori warned.

"We're fine." Smiling, Luke lowered Michael carefully to the thick oriental carpet, keeping a steadying hand on the boy until he stood without swaying.

"Have you seen Blake and Jen?" he asked.

Cori met her brother's inquisitive gaze with a quick nod. All afternoon, she'd battled her emotions for Blake. She always knew she'd have to tell Blake he was a father. Except, if Blake couldn't recognize his own son, did he deserve to know? Or was that just a coward's excuse to not tell him?

Blake wasn't making things easier for her. He'd been so sarcastic toward Cori when he'd first seen her, then he'd turned coolly distant, throwing her off balance. Just before she'd come downstairs, she'd watched Blake help her grandfather out of a car, noting his patience despite her grandfather's gruffness. The gesture had melted her heart.

No matter what she decided, the attraction was still there. She'd lived with the memory of the man she'd fallen in love with for almost five years. That image was hard to tear down in just one afternoon.

Michael giggled and staggered dramatically, bringing Cori

back to the present. Obviously, Luke's charm didn't end with women.

"Thanks for coming, Sis. Things have been incredibly difficult without you here."

She blinked back tears at his admission, for her family rarely expressed feelings aloud. "I wish someone had told me earlier."

"There was hope earlier." Luke's expression turned grim and he looked down at Michael, who tugged on his long leg as if looking for a wrestling match.

The sliver of hope Cori had been carrying for her mother was rapidly disintigrating. Even though a part of her knew this was the end, Cori refused to believe her mother couldn't beat the cancer again.

"Michael, behave like a gentleman," Cori admonished, making sure she caught her son's attention before turning back to Luke. "How've you managed to spend time with Mama and keep up with your work?"

Luke scratched the back of his neck, not looking directly at Cori. "You know how it is around here. We're going from first thing in the morning until dinner, sometimes later. But I stop by to visit her every night." He shot a look toward the hallway, then back at Cori, a smile on his face. "We've got some catching up to do. I want to tell you about—"

Luke clamped his mouth shut as Salvatore Messina strode rigidly into the room wearing his usual dark wool suit, silencing further conversation. Hard, black eyes took in Cori's short red dress with a frown. Cori wasn't sure what would have been worse—dressing down like her brother or keeping the dress, her symbol of independence. With effort, Cori kept her hands from knotting nervously in front of her. This was the moment she'd been waiting for.

Salvatore's frown deepened, showing lines etched more severely than she remembered. He finally broke the silence.

"So, Corinne. It takes death to bring you home. I wondered when you'd remember your obligations."

Luke shook his head, shooting a look of disapproval at their grandfather.

Along with disappointment, guilt washed over Cori at her grandfather's words. She'd been raised to believe the family came before any personal obligations or dreams she might have. It took her a moment to remind herself that she would've come home if she'd been allowed to do so on her terms.

Cori lifted her chin. She'd done nothing wrong. Her grandfather was the one who'd shut her out. But there were fences that needed to be mended, even if he wasn't letting her come home to stay.

''Michael, this is your great-grandfather.'' Cori bent to gently urge her son forward. ''Shake his hand.''

Her pride and joy cast a glance at Luke, who smiled and nodded reassuringly. Raising his small hand solemnly, Michael hesitated, then stepped forward to meet Salvatore Messina.

Time hung on Michael's extended arm. No one moved. No one spoke.

''Playing at royalty, are we?'' Salvatore finally said brusquely, glaring at Cori. ''It won't work. He gets nothing from either me or your mother.''

Michael smashed into Cori's leg at record speed, then pivoted behind her, little arms wrapping around her bare leg. Luke looked uncomfortable but said nothing.

''Don't.'' Cori had known seeing her grandfather would be awkward, but was shocked at his icy reception toward her, and especially toward Michael.

''Maria, what's for dinner?'' Salvatore bellowed, dismissing them as he moved to the head of the elegant table.

Luke sat to his right, leaving Cori and Michael to sit to his left. After standing indecisively for a few moments, Cori dragged out two heavy straight-back chairs and tried to settle Michael into the place farthest from her grandfather—but Michael was having none of it.

''Michael, I need you to sit in your chair.'' Cori kept her voice low while trying to guide Michael's little body into his seat, hating that her grandfather observed their struggle.

''No.'' The high pitch of his young voice was adamant. He stared up at his great-grandfather with untrusting eyes, chin tucked into his chest.

Ignoring the clash over seating, Maria served lamb chops, asparagus, sweet potatoes and sourdough rolls. This seemed to be the last straw for Michael, who had wriggled halfway into Cori's lap.

''Not that,'' he wailed, his little finger pointing to the asparagus and sweet potatoes. ''I want McDonald's.''

''He's a mama's boy,'' her grandfather noted, not bothering to look up from his meal.

Years of training at the Messina dinner table, where opinions were expressed hotly but rebuttals against her grandfather were not allowed, kept Cori silent, even as her body heated with the need to defend herself and her son. Michael's warm presence in Cori's lap didn't help. Any minute now, she feared she'd break out in a sweat.

''We took you everywhere when you were a child,'' Salvatore Messina continued. ''You ate everything. You never hung on your mother's skirts.''

They'd joked so much back then, she and her grandfather, each trying to put one over on the other. It was hard to believe this man, or the man in her dorm room that fateful day, was the grandfather who had doted on her during her childhood.

''He's only four,'' Luke said, receiving a cool stare from Salvatore Messina for his defense.

''I didn't have any freedom,'' Cori declared, thinking of the one thing she'd been lacking in her highly structured childhood, the one thing she'd longed for.

Her grandfather scoffed. ''You had family. And you were confident of yourself.''

Had she been confident? Cori didn't think so. She'd traveled so much until she was eighteen, she'd perfected the veneer of sophistication. Her insecurities were kept hidden behind an arsenal of good manners and a smile that eased her out of most difficulties. She'd reveled in her independence in college and started making close friends, finally telling her grandfather she couldn't travel or help him entertain during the school year because it interfered with her studies. She'd dutifully returned for spring break, summer vacation and the holidays, finding comfort in the familiar bustle of activity, and the sense of belonging home and family offered.

And then she'd met Blake, so proudly self-sufficient, so staunchly convinced that he could make it on his own. Little had she known that Blake would be her role model in the years to come.

"But I guess we didn't teach you any morals, since you decided to be just another unwed mother, bringing another unwanted child into the world."

"He isn't unwanted." Cori strove to keep her voice calm, uncomfortably conscious of Michael on her lap.

Salvatore raised one bushy, silver brow and leaned toward Cori and her son. "You said his father didn't want you. Maybe because he had a *wife?*"

Cori almost refuted his spiteful words, but caught herself. What her grandfather believed didn't matter.

"Or maybe it was because you didn't know who the father was." Her grandfather flung the words at her.

Cori's stomach sank to her toes.

"Grandpa! That's enough." Luke growled at Salvatore Messina.

"How dare you?" Cori managed to push the heavy chair back from the table and lift Michael from her lap and into her arms, attempting escape before her grandfather said anything worse.

"I'll tell you how I dare." Unrelenting, Salvatore shouted at her back. "It says *unknown* on that boy's birth certificate. That means he's a bastard. When I find out who fathered him, I'll make sure he knows what a coward he's been and make him pay."

She spun on her grandfather with an outraged gasp, Michael clinging silently to her chest. "It doesn't matter what his birth certificate says in this day and age. If you ever call him that again, you'll be sorry."

''Idle threat.'' Everything about her grandfather was as tight as steel, from the set of his shoulders to the taut lines framing his eyes.

Cori struggled to keep her body from shaking. How could he be so horrible? How would they manage to stay in the same house together? There was only one person who could make him behave. And then, only when he wanted to behave. So Cori drew on the only defense she had left.

''I'll tell Mama. About the choice you gave me.'' Cori caught Luke's frown and ignored him. She'd never told Mama or Luke why she hadn't come home. Mama had attempted to talk about Michael's father once, but Cori deftly changed the subject and Mama had never tried again. Cori hadn't wanted to tell her mother and brother, risking them taking sides and dividing the family just as her grandfather had predicted.

Cori waited for her words to sink in before she turned away from her grandfather. She noticed his expression sag into something resembling regret. If her grandfather felt any remorse, he had a strange way of showing it.

Cori stumbled up the stairs and into her room. Completely drained, she sank onto the bed with Michael still clinging to her, his head tucked into her neck. Somewhere, in the farthest corner of Cori's mind, she'd hoped that things had changed, that her grandfather would accept Michael without knowing who his father was. But Salvatore Messina's feelings on the matter were clear.

She fought her tears, not even slightly appeased to know she had a bargaining chip with her grandfather—her silence.

Cori could never let her grandfather know the truth about Michael. She didn't understand why he'd kept alive his desire to punish both Cori and Michael's father for their unplanned pregnancy. His animosity was overwhelming. Worse, Salvatore Messina still had the power to destroy Blake, to fire him, kick him out of his home and attempt to make sure he wouldn't find work in the wine industry again.

''He's mean, Mommy.''

Reflexively, Cori's hands stroked a soothing pattern on his back.

''Yes, he can be, Peanut.''

''He's loud. He yelled about daddies.'' Michael snuffled and wiped his nose on her dress. ''And I don't have one.''

This was a phrase Michael used often. Cori's heart ached over her son's desire for a father.

''No. Your father doesn't live with us.'' Recalling Blake's disapproving scowl, Cori didn't expect that to change.

''I want him to.'' Michael pulled back so that she could see his little brow furrowed in a serious expression. ''Everybody has dads but me.''

''Lots of kids only have mommies.'' Cori smoothed his soft brown hair away from his forehead. ''We've talked about this before.''

''It's not fair. I want a daddy.'' Michael threw himself dramatically at Cori, nearly knocking her backward onto the bed. ''I want to go home.''

Cori didn't blame him. Leaving would be the least painful way out of this. She'd been happy in this house once. Her family would never understand the choices she'd made—the choices she'd been forced to make.

''We can't go home until...'' She almost said *until Grandma goes to heaven,* but she stopped herself. She still had hope. ''We have to take care of Grandma.''

''I want to go home now.'' Michael flopped onto the bed, sending pink ruffles rippling. ''Nobody's nice. And this room is pink.'' He kicked at the bed.

Cori looked around the room with all her dolls and feminine memorabilia still displayed as if she'd just left for college, as if she'd never grown up and made her own decisions. The pink room held no appeal for her anymore. Why should it offer any comfort to a little boy?

''How about if you and I decorate this room while we help Grandma get well?'' She could pack away the dolls and other childhood treasures she'd never missed in more than four years.

''Orange?''

Cori suffered an eye-blinding vision of orange against pink walls.

"Purple?" she proposed hopefully. Purple could be mixed with pink without too much trouble.

"Blue," he announced with finality. "Can I look at my book, Mommy?"

"I'm sorry, honey. We left your baby book at home." Michael used his baby book to comfort himself. Having memorized much of it, Michael could tell Cori when he'd cut his first tooth and how tall he was.

"No, Mommy. You forgot but I packed it," Michael said, hopping off the bed and running to his backpack.

She hadn't wanted to bring the book here. Michael's baby book was the one place she'd been honest about Michael's parentage. She'd written Blake's name on the inside cover where it said "Father." She'd planned to tell Michael about his father someday, sometime after he started to read and before he graduated from college. Or maybe when Blake was no longer working for her grandfather.

Cori's pulse quickened as she realized how dangerous the book could be. If Michael left his baby book anywhere he shouldn't, if someone picked it up and flipped to the first page, they'd know the truth.

Oblivious to her turmoil, Michael retrieved the book from his backpack, then climbed back up on the bed. He wriggled into her lap, turning to the first page.

"This is all about me," he said proudly, the night's drama temporarily forgotten.

BLAKE SAT ON THE BANK of the Russian River in the darkness, letting the fog envelop him in its chilly embrace. Behind him, hidden by the thick mist, acres of grapevines separated the Messina mansion from the river. Before him, the river flowed silently by, accented by the night symphony of crickets and an occasional plaintive cry from a frog or owl. Obscured by the fog, Blake's old truck was parked a few feet away, next to a tangle of blackberry bushes.

He'd said good-night to Jen and checked on Sophia long ago, but he'd avoided going to bed. Blake knew he'd be plagued with thoughts of Cori Sinclair that would keep him from sleep. Instead, like a sentimental fool, he'd ended up here, where he and Cori used to meet, reliving thoughts he had no right to think in the first place.

It wasn't as if he was staying and waiting for her to show up. He knew that wasn't going to happen. For so many years, this had been his spot.

I loved her. The thought rippled through Blake, eliciting more anguish than he'd felt in years. But Blake's love hadn't been good enough for Salvatore Messina's granddaughter.

Something stumbled in the night. In one smooth motion, Blake shot up and swung the beam of his flashlight in the direction of the noise. It wasn't uncommon for a puma or a vagabond to wander through the area, and Blake wanted to recapture the element of surprise.

An arm came up against the light. A female voice cursed.

She looked like a vision stepped out of the past. Worn blue denim clung to her legs. A faded red Stanford sweatshirt covered her other curves. Drops of water from the fog were sprinkled on the hair around her forehead, glowing like a halo in the beam of his flashlight.

"Damn it, Cori. What are you doing here?" He'd said something similar years ago, the first time he'd found her down by the river after dark. Blake's heart beat just as rapidly now as it had then.

"Could you shine the light on my feet instead of in my eyes?"

He readjusted the beam toward her sneakers, incredibly white despite the soft, muddy ground she'd hiked through to get this far.

"Thanks."

She was always so polite. Too damn polite. Even that one precious night they were together and they'd argued, she'd said thank you as she'd left him alone in bed. "You don't always have to thank me."

"I needed some air," she said, as if explaining why she was here in this place. Their place.

"Where's the kid?"

"Michael," she reiterated gently. "Asleep. He's a good sleeper. Always has been. Even when he was a baby."

She was babbling, but Blake didn't care. Part of him was fascinated by the idea that she'd tackled motherhood on her own. Another part of him—the stupid part—was jealous that she'd let some other man touch her as intimately as he had.

"And the boy's father?" he found himself asking, even as he kicked himself for letting his curiosity fall between them. "Forget it. I don't need to know." Wishing she'd go, Blake turned back toward the river, flicking off the flashlight and plunging the area into a darkness that was only dimly lit by the distant lights from the mansion.

Her footsteps carried her closer. Blake's pulse picked up a notch when he imagined he could smell her flowery perfume.

"We were a burden he didn't need." Her voice carried a note of sadness.

Fool. Blake wished he could wrap his hands around the bastard's neck and make him regret causing Cori pain. Had they argued? Or had Cori just accepted the jerk's excuses when he left her?

Blake swore under his breath and wiped a hand over his face. "Looks like you've done well with Jen."

"She's a handful for only being twelve," Blake admitted. No sense telling Cori Sinclair about his problems.

"No boy trouble yet?"

"No, thank God." Her question sent his mind back to the first time he'd kissed Cori.

"She's going to be a knockout. You'll be fighting them off."

Her words brought back the memory of what had crumbled Blake's guard against his feelings for Cori. By the end of that first summer, Blake had fallen into the habit of tucking Jennifer into bed, then waiting up for Cori, reluctant to slip into his empty bed until she made it safely back within the Messina compound. His instincts told him Cori would find herself in trouble eventually. She was beautiful, and the Messinas didn't seem to mind that she dressed like a woman of the world.

He knew that they couldn't be anything more than friends. But he enjoyed their late-night private conversations, her brilliant smiles and the knowledge that she was home safe.

Blake had been waiting for Cori to come home from some function the Messinas had required her to attend. She'd gone to the event in a sleek little sports car with a young, blond, next-in-line-to-be-a-millionaire college boy.

The new British convertible had pulled up, and with a heavy heart, Blake realized the driver was going to kiss Cori. He couldn't tear his eyes away. Then, just as the boy's lips neared Cori's, Blake heard her say "No."

Blake snapped. He sprang into action. Ran to the car. Yanked the guy out and threw him to the driveway.

"Don't touch her!" He went cold just remembering that primitive territorial note of warning in his voice.

Cori was at Blake's side in an instant. Holding her trembling body against his, Blake never wanted to let go. Moments later, when her soft lips touched his, he knew he was lost.

He loved her.

She was everything he wasn't—well educated, wealthy, someone important. None of that mattered when they were together. Or so he'd thought.

Blake fought the memory of the feel of Cori's body against his. Luckily, the physical memory was overshadowed by the burning need to know what had been happening to Cori all these years.

"What kind of man were you involved with, that wouldn't want to marry the mother of his child?"

Cori sat down on the far end of the steep riverbank, several feet away from Blake, choosing her words as carefully as she had chosen her seat.

"We wanted different things."

"Obviously you wanted the same thing at least once. You created a child together." *She created a child with someone else.* The thought burned in his belly, worse than the jealousy he'd carried all these years imagining her in a happy relationship with someone else—someone who was good for her, as Sophia put it.

Cori didn't answer. Blake peered through the fog but couldn't make out her features without turning on the flashlight. "Were you the one who decided you wanted different things?"

"Why do you ask?"

"Déjà vu. That's what you said to me the last time I saw you." He'd confessed his love and plans for the future. Hell, he'd done everything but propose marriage. She'd practically tripped over herself in her haste to flee.

"I needed to make it on my own first, remember?" The words spilled out bitterly from the shadows.

Blake didn't remember it that way. He only remembered the rejection. For a moment, he wondered if he'd mistaken her meaning years ago. But he'd never had the chance to find out. She'd eventually fallen into the arms of another man.

"You never came back."

"No." The word signaled the end of the conversation. "I had Michael and that's all that mattered."

That's all that mattered to *her*. She didn't seem to care about how her actions affected others, saddened them or ripped them apart inside.

"You don't come home for the holidays." Having his family torn from him left Blake with this need to set down and foster roots, kept him here with the Messinas, who'd become a second family to him and Jennifer. Blake would do anything for them.

"I let them down."

How could she have disappointed the Messinas? She'd been the dutiful granddaughter—once—until she met somebody who changed her mind. Someone other than Blake.

"And you've been raising him alone?" He'd have bet money Cori would have come right back to the family's money and security. He knew firsthand that raising a child was too difficult to do alone if you didn't have to.

"Yes. Is that so hard to believe? That I could make it on

my own without my family?'' She laughed but the sound lacked humor. ''You must really think I'm something special.'' She stood up, her face still unreadable in the gray shadows. ''Sleep well, Blake.''

But Blake knew sleep would elude him.

CORI SLIPPED INTO HER mother's room and lowered herself carefully onto the bed. Soft light from the hallway crept across the thick carpet, casting her mother's gaunt face in shadow. Luke dozed on the sofa on the far side of the room, his stocking feet dangling over the edge of the sofa's arm. Gently, Cori drew the covers on the bed up around Mama's thin shoulders, tucking her in, in much the same way she did Michael every night. Seeing her mother asleep and unmoving, Cori was sure she was losing her battle with cancer.

Cori smoothed the blankets along the edge of the bed, unwilling to leave her mother's side. She could still hear Blake's tone, full of condemnation, his words ripe with disbelief. After her confrontation with her grandfather, Cori had needed some reassurance that she'd done the right thing by keeping Blake's fatherhood from him. For years, the secret had chipped away at her conscience. Irrationally, she'd wanted some sign from Blake that her decision had been for the best, that she should continue to guard her secret. So, she'd walked down to the Russian River in the foggy darkness.

Her conversation with Blake had been much like their talks that first summer. The intimacy of the night. Questions asked that one wouldn't dare ask in the daylight. She'd wanted to tell him about Michael, had even started to gather her courage. Then, sensing Blake's disappointment in her, the fragile mood between them collapsed. Just as her world seemed to be.

''You're worried about something.'' Sophia spoke softly, her eyes still closed as if she lacked the strength to open them. ''I could always tell when you were worried, by how carefully you paid attention to what you were doing.''

''I'm a mother. I worry about everything.'' Cori hoped her voice sounded lighter than she felt.

"I'm here if you want to talk."

How long will you be here? The question paralyzed Cori's thoughts, and she fell silent. She wouldn't accept her mother was dying, despite the evidence in front of her.

Sophia sighed, then opened her eyes. "You're wondering why I'm not in a hospital."

Cori's hand slipped under the blanket and found her mother's. It was such a small, fragile hand. "Ye-es." Cori's thin acknowledgment cracked, the word as brittle as her fears.

"There comes a time when you have to decide, Cori. And I realized it was my time to stop fighting."

Closing her eyes, Cori turned her head toward the hallway, away from this reality. "The doctors can't do anything for you?"

"The doctors can ease my pain or they can continue to attack the cancer. Either way is a losing battle."

Cori bit her lip, trying to hold herself together. "Why don't you have a nurse?" They could afford an army of nurses.

"No nurses. No doctors. No tubes or shots. Just my family and my home." Mama squeezed Cori's hand.

"How long?" Cori closed her eyes against her tears. "How long have you known?"

"I found out the cancer metastasized right after Christmas."

It was now late February. Her mother had kept the illness hidden from her for nearly two months. The guilt was almost as debilitating as the truth she wouldn't accept. Cori's hand crept to her throat. She had to know more.

"When did you decide to…?" *Die.* Cori couldn't say the word aloud. To do so was to admit defeat. "To stop fighting?"

"When I asked you to come home and you said yes. They took all the tubes out of me after I hung up. Blake brought me home from the hospital that same day."

How was Cori supposed to deal with that? Her mother had given up because Cori had agreed to come home. In need of a distraction, she opened her eyes and focused on her mother's last words.

"Blake took you home?"

"Blake and Jennifer are so supportive. They spent quite a bit of time with me at the hospital. Blake has some spare time until bud break."

Spare time? Every month was busy in the vineyard. January and February were filled with pruning and replanting damaged stock. February sometimes offered a few weeks of respite until the warmer weather coaxed buds to open on the vine. Maybe Blake relied on the other staff to cover for him while he helped Sophia.

No. Cori doubted Blake had much, if any, spare time.

"What about Luke and Grandpa?" Cori cast a glance back at her sleeping brother, snoring softly on the couch.

"Lucas and Father have been focusing on the business. We're introducing internationally, you know." Sophia's voice sounded drowsy.

"I didn't know," Cori murmured. She couldn't do anything about her grandfather's absence from Sophia's life, but she was going to take Luke to task for having his priorities screwed up. His saving grace was the fact that he guarded Mama through the night.

"Do you have regular checkups, Corinne?" Sophia's eyes opened and fixed wearily on Cori. "That's very important."

Momentarily consumed with fear when she couldn't remember the last time she'd visited the doctor, Cori could only stare blankly at her mother. When she blinked, her memory returned.

Last summer. She'd been to the doctor last summer and everything was okay. And then came the awful thought: *Who would take care of Michael if something happened to me?*

"Honesty is important, too. I wish I had been honest with your father. Maybe then he'd have stayed with me. You don't ever see your father, do you?"

"No." Cori drew back. John Sinclair wasn't discussed in the Messina household. He didn't call or send birthday cards. He'd walked out of their lives about twenty years ago and never looked back. Did her mother know that Salvatore had paid John Sinclair to marry her? And most likely paid him to leave?

"It's too bad that you don't see your father. I've always regretted losing touch. A child needs a father. You should tell him, for Michael's sake."

Struggling to follow her mother's logic, Cori asked, "Tell John Sinclair?"

"No. Tell Blake he has a son."

Cori forced herself to breathe normally. She couldn't read her mother's expression; her eyes were closed again. Cori peeked at Luke to make sure he still slept. Finally, she asked, "How long have you known?"

"I suspected all along, but couldn't really see it until today. Michael looks less like a baby and more like a little Austin." Sophia moved her head listlessly as if trying to get comfortable. "Blake's a good man. He deserves to know the truth no matter what your reasons for keeping it from him."

Cori wanted—at times needed—to tell Blake, but she doubted Blake would want to keep his fatherhood a secret. He was a proud, honorable man who'd want Michael to call him Dad. In which case, Cori didn't think she could protect Blake from her grandfather.

"WELL, IF IT ISN'T Sleeping Beauty," Blake greeted Cori with sarcasm at the door to Sophia's bedroom the next morning. He checked his watch. "Nine o'clock. Kind of early for you, isn't it?" He slouched farther in the flowery chair, stretching his jean-clad legs toward Sophia's bed frame. He should be out in the vineyards. But not wanting Sophia to be alone, he'd waited for Cori to appear.

Sophia either didn't catch or ignored the dig in Blake's greeting. "She certainly looks lovely today." From Sophia's smile, it seemed the sight of Cori made her happy—while it confused, irritated and hurt Blake.

"I've been working since five. Got to pay the bills," Cori replied mildly, with a quick glance at Blake's bootless feet, enveloped in dingy socks.

What had she expected from a workingman? Socks in pristine condition? Self-consciously, Blake pulled his feet back to the edge of the chair. He often left his boots at the back door when he'd been traversing a particularly muddy patch of vineyard.

Tugging her short, clingy blue sweater over her khaki walking shorts, Cori moved to her mother's side. The kid dragged his feet behind her, one hand clutching the bottom of the long-sleeved denim shirt she wore over the sweater.

Ignoring her excuse, flimsy as it was, Blake's eyes surveyed Cori's legs and bare feet. It was less dangerous than looking at her curves in that skimpy sweater. ''It's a bit chilly out for shorts,'' he found himself saying.

''If the sun's out, Southern Californians wear shorts,'' Cori replied, her words as brisk as the weather. Cori stepped between Blake and Sophia, presenting him with her backside.

Blake swallowed and wet his lips, finding it hard to have Cori so near and untouchable. The kid popped free to lurk on the far side of the bed, a welcome distraction to Blake at this point.

''There's nothing like a little sun to give a woman that glow,'' Sophia conceded, obviously missing the subtext of the conversation.

''A little sunshine would do you good,'' Blake said to Sophia, leaning to one side so he could see her face, trying not to look at Cori's slender figure. She'd left him. He shouldn't be reacting to her this way now, with interest as inappropriate now as it had been years ago.

''Not today.'' Sophia rolled her head. She smiled wanly at Michael, who ducked behind the bed out of sight. ''I must look frightening.''

''Nonsense.'' Cori's hand gently encompassed her mother's. ''If that's a hint, I'll style your hair.''

''That would be heaven.''

The kid chose that moment to jump onto Sophia's bed.

''Grandma, we're going to change the pink room to blue.'' The kid's thin voice rang out as he hopped, jolting Sophia's limp body with each bounce.

''Michael, don't—'' Cori reached for her son, but Blake reacted faster.

''Can't you control him?'' Blake snatched the boy off the bed with two hands on his little waist, holding him none too gently in the air, inches from his face. ''Don't ever do that again.''

The brat's dark eyes rounded as they stared at Blake. His mouth puckered tremulously.

Immediately, Blake knew he'd overreacted from stress and lack of sleep, and some other dark reason he was reluctant to acknowledge. Resentment.

I should have been this boy's father.

Air escaped Blake's lungs, taking his strength with him. Suddenly, the kid felt as if he weighed a hundred pounds.

''Put him down.'' Cori spoke with the unchecked fury of a mother protecting her young. She held out her arms for her son.

Blake met her gaze squarely before setting the kid down. Holding the boy's sticklike arms, Blake knelt to his level. ''I want you to promise me you won't do that again. You could have hurt your grandmother.'' Blake may not have been his father, but he could still be a positive influence on the child. ''Are you all right, Sophia?''

''Yes. More startled than anything,'' she answered breathlessly.

Cori stood between her mother and her son, seemingly torn as to which needed her the most.

''Promise?'' Blake prompted, returning his full attention to the boy. Blake had forgotten how frail a little kid's emotions were. The boy was small, yet not as fragile as Sophia was.

When the kid nodded, his face full of fear, Blake released him. In the blink of an eye, Cori's son fled the room. Blake stood, his stomach clenching from what he'd done, not blaming the kid one bit for his hasty retreat.

''That was uncalled for.'' Cori's voice shook, her eyes still focused on the floor where the boy had stood.

Blake shrugged, not backing down, even when he knew only

a parent had the right to punish, even when he loathed his own actions. "You want the kid to behave, start setting some rules."

"Rules—" Cori sputtered, eyes narrowing.

Blake cut her off before she could gather steam. "I have to go. Maria's downstairs, but I told her you'd stay close to Sophia today. Do you think you can handle that?"

CHAPTER THREE

HOW COULD HE NOT SEE *that Michael was his son?*

Looking down upon the heads of her son and his father, she'd noted the same swirling pattern of brown hair on each crown. She'd vacillated between anger at Blake for tossing Michael around like a sack of potatoes and disappointment that he couldn't see the similarities between himself and his son. Yet, should she expect Blake to recognize what she'd tried so hard to hide?

Crash! Tinkle, tinkle.

Cori froze as she slid the last hairpin into her mother's lifeless hair.

''Michael?'' she asked, just as her cell phone rang in her shorts pocket.

''It wasn't me!'' Michael called from the hallway.

''It's probably that crystal vase,'' Sophia observed calmly.

''The one that good-looking actor gave you?'' Cori asked, trying to keep her tone light as she reached for her phone.

''Ronald Reagan was our president,'' Sophia replied with mock dignity.

Ever since Ronald Reagan had given the vase to Sophia, Luke and Cori had teased her about her crush on him. Cori hoped she wouldn't find that vase in pieces in the hall.

As Cori answered the telephone, she went in search of her son. His fast-retreating footsteps on the hardwood floor, punctuated with a door slam, signaled his escape to the pink room.

''Cori, I need some PR angles for Nightshade, pronto,'' Sidney Collins, Cori's boss, trilled in her ear. ''They liked what you proposed last week, but they want to hear some other ideas from you, just to be sure the first one is the best.''

Cori sighed heavily, as much in response to Sidney's request as at the sight of Ronald Reagan's vase in pieces scattered across the floor.

''Not again.'' Cori peered into the bedroom at Michael, shaking a finger at him when he looked up from his cartoons.

''I didn't do it,'' he whispered.

''Yes, again.'' Sidney didn't sound happy, either. ''Just because they're so forward thinking they can't recognize brilliance when it's right in front of them doesn't mean we don't jump through the hoop when they snap their fingers.''

''Tell them we're out of recommendations. Tell them that was our best idea and the others were so bad we won't even show them.'' Cori stomped down the back stairs in search of a broom.

''No way. Bell-Diva's new vice president of marketing was talking to the Parker Agency, just testing the waters, he said, but we'll lose the account if we don't shine, and shine brightly, in the next few months.''

''I did shine. That last press release was picked up for a segment on the *Today Show*. Let Adam Parker deliver that.'' Collins & Co. was taking off, creating great buzz for their clients, who told others of their success. They were so busy that Cori was starting to wonder if she had any fresh ideas left. The pace had become grueling. If Sidney hadn't taken a chance on Cori right out of college and stuck with her through the pregnancy, Cori would have moved on by now to someplace where she could be in the spotlight less and with her son more.

''I'm sure Adam Parker will promise them everything. You know him. He'd sell his mother the Brooklyn Bridge if he thought he could make a buck. Seriously, Cori, Bell-Diva is half our billings right now.''

Cori lowered her voice to a whisper. ''And more than half of my headaches. I really don't have time for this.'' She knew that the deal she'd struck with Sidney to work from Sonoma was going to cause a snag or two along the way, but she hadn't expected a problem to arise so soon. At least she could do her public relations/spokesperson job with a telephone, e-mail and fax—as long as her clients didn't require a meeting or hold an event where her presence was mandatory.

"Nobody has time for this, but nobody knows their business better than you do."

"And they pay their retainer on time." Wearily, Cori beat Sidney to the punch, resigned to the fact that she was going to have to work some more today, realizing that keeping her job while helping her mother wasn't going to be easy. Even as she thought this, several rough ideas started teasing their way through her brain. She would need to go to the store to check on some things first. She ended her call with a promise to get back to her as soon as possible.

Luke strode into the hallway, cell phone glued to his ear while he listened intently, muttering an occasional "Uh-huh."

"Thank God, Luke. Can you stay with Mama for an hour, maybe two? I've got to run to the store."

"Uh-huh," Luke mumbled, stepping past Cori into Mama's bedroom.

BLAKE STUCK HIS HEAD in Sophia's open bedroom door, expecting to see Cori sitting with her. But Cori's mother was alone.

"Where's your posse, Sophia?" Blake tried to make light of his concern as he held back a frown.

"I'm not sure." Sophia blinked rapidly. Midday sunlight streamed through the windows directly into her eyes. "I called..."

"She left you alone?" Arthritis kept Maria downstairs most of the time now. A second maid cleaned the upstairs twice a week. Blake wouldn't have left Sophia for so long if he'd known Cori wasn't going to be with her. And here he'd hoped Cori's presence would make it possible for him to handle his full workload again.

Blake crossed the room and yanked the drapes closed.

"Cori has a little boy to take care of." Sophia defended her daughter. Her frail hand moved slowly back and forth over the bedspread and her small feet fidgeted under the covers.

''Do you need anything? Water? Something to eat?''

''Maybe some help to the ladies' room.''

Blake's jaw clenched as he wondered how long Sophia had been waiting. She was too weak to stand by herself without help.

Footsteps coming upstairs, along with the excited voice of a child and the crackle of bags, indicated Cori and the kid were back.

Blake's face settled into a disapproving frown. Why would Cori leave her mother alone on her first morning back?

''I told you before, Michael, you cannot drink anything we bought today except the soda.'' Cori peeked in the room and waved, her smile strained.

''I like beer. I do,'' the kid whined.

Blake's mouth fell open. The kid liked beer?

''No, Michael, you don't.''

Although Cori lowered her voice, Blake still caught her words and her blush before she ducked out of the room.

What the hell was that all about?

Blake helped Sophia to the bathroom, then stood outside the door while she did her business. He helped her back to bed, his body rigid with tension. With her mother dying, Cori was off shopping for beer? The more he thought about it, the angrier he got. But when Blake excused himself, intending to seek out Cori to force-feed her a much-needed dose of reality, Sophia stopped him on his way to the door.

''Don't.''

Blake tried to relax his taut features as he gazed down at the woman who'd taken him and Jennifer into her heart. Sophia Sinclair had to be one of the kindest, most generous women on earth. She deserved better treatment from her daughter.

''You need her,'' he said, not even pretending to misunderstand.

''This is harder on Corinne than you think. I've been in her shoes, watching helplessly as my mother died. She was in school and traveling with my father when I had cancer the last time. I thought it would be easier on her.'' She drew a shaky breath. ''Let me decide how she helps me.''

Okay, so maybe Sophia had spotted Blake's irritation and suspected his reaction. She always had been one sharp lady. But this was hard on everyone, and Blake wasn't about to shelter Cori. Sophia wanted her here, so Cori needed to stay by her side and make sure Sophia was comfortable. Blake took one purposeful stride toward the hall.

''Promise you'll let me handle Corinne.'' Sophia's soft words stopped Blake again.

He looked back at the frail, dying woman. Blake wanted to make Sophia's last days as peaceful as possible. Allowing Cori to behave irresponsibly would make things that much more difficult for everyone, especially Sophia. She was getting weaker every day—she was nearly bed-ridden—yet all Cori seemed to see was a sick woman resting in bed.

Blake struggled with his anger for a moment before asking ''Why?''

''I have my reasons.'' Sophia's eyes closed tightly as if she were fighting an unpleasant thought. ''I need you to honor my request.''

''Of course,'' Blake replied, yet he headed for Cori's room, anyway. If he couldn't explain to Cori how much help Sophia really needed, he could at least make her feel guilty for her behavior.

The door to the pink room stood open and several shopping bags littered the floor. What was all this stuff? Then Blake noticed the two six-packs of expensive, imported beer on the desk.

The kid was staring at the television while Cori opened her laptop.

''Busy morning?'' Blake asked, allowing sarcasm to weigh down his words when what he really wanted to do was raise his voice and ask her what the hell she'd been doing. But a promise to Sophia was to be honored.

''We needed to buy something blue,'' the kid said solemnly.

He pulled a large blue pillow out of a bag, then wrestled it to the floor and flopped on top of it. "And buy some beer. Mommy buys a lot of beer."

Blake took a deep, controlling breath and searched Cori's features carefully. Did Cori have a drinking problem? Was that why Sophia didn't want him to interfere?

Cori's computer booted up with a series of beeps. Ignoring his tone, she stared at the small black machine intently, as if it might disappear if her gaze strayed. "Thank you for watching Mama. She was asleep when we left and Luke was around. Is he still here?" she asked with a nervous laugh and a quick glance up at Blake.

"He's not here, is he. I thought for sure he'd stay." Cori frowned. "Okay. I'll sit with her once I send this e-mail."

"If you're up to it." If she was sober. How did he know Cori hadn't stopped off at some bar somewhere or had lunch and drinks while they were out? Blake considered asking her outright if she had a problem. He'd be right there to help her if she did. But being a Messina, she'd probably just hide the problem and refuse his help.

Cori tilted her head and regarded him carefully. "Why wouldn't I be up to it?"

"I don't know. It's just that you've always put yourself first and I can see that hasn't changed." Blake kept his voice low. That first summer Cori followed him everywhere during the day although she claimed to have come home from school to work. As if going out at night with her family was work. Blake gave a snort of disgust. He'd had plenty of time over the years to analyze Cori's behavior and pinpoint her deficiencies. In spite of her warmth and vibrancy, Cori did what she wanted *when* she wanted.

Cori's eyes dropped to the floor as though his words had the power to wound her. For a moment, his resolve wavered. After all, it was her mother dying down the hall.

"Go ahead and send that e-mail. I'm sure it's real important," he added, just to see if she really was the ice princess he'd made her out to be. If she crumpled, he'd be sorry. But not sorry enough to offer her a comforting shoulder to lean on. That route led to certain disaster, no matter how strongly it beckoned.

Cori's eyes swept the floor, and then she gathered a shuddering breath and transformed into Mr. Messina's granddaughter. The line of her mouth became uncharacteristically firm. Hands drew to rest on softly curved hips. Her brown eyes met his with the veneer of indifference she'd worn yesterday in the driveway.

"Yes, I *was* shopping. Thank you for noticing. I do all the public relations for Nightshade. Occasionally, when I'm stuck, I like to look at their packaging. Now, if you don't mind, I have other things to do to make sure I can pay the rent this month."

Because he was out of line, way off base and embarrassed beyond belief, Blake performed an abrupt about-face and exited the pink room. He slid the pocket door to the back stairs open on its silent coasters and retreated to the vineyards.

JENNIFER SAT IN THE public library with her best friend, Shelly Broder. They were supposed to be working on their social studies project—a report on the life of Chinese teenagers—but Jen's stomach hurt and she found it hard to concentrate. Doodles covered her lined notebook page. She pretty much lived with a knotted stomach every day. As unobtrusively as possible, she placed a hand over the button of her jeans. The pain got worse whenever she thought about Sophia.

Shelly nudged Jen under the table and then looked pointedly toward the door of the library.

Devon Hamlisch came in with his social studies partner and closest friend, Skyler Wight. Devon was the cutest boy in junior high school, with his short dark hair, deep blue eyes and cool swagger. His smile made Jen go all fluttery inside. Not that he smiled at Jen very often.

Devon and Skyler were jocks, so they were part of the popular crowd. Playing on a school sports team practically guaranteed you were "in." Even Flavio Martinez, who'd been the fat kid everybody picked on just last year, made the seventh-grade flag football team and was suddenly cool.

Kids like Jen and Shelly, who were too uncoordinated to be a cheerleader or play girls basketball, were stuck in the ditch of unpopularity. It didn't help that Jen and Shelly were about as developed as a fence post. Jen was still in a training bra and she was almost thirteen years old. There was no hope of Devon Hamlisch smiling at Jen anytime soon. The social lines were clearly drawn.

Devon and Skyler walked past table after table, ever closer to Jen and Shelly. Jen couldn't believe it. Devon Hamlisch and Skyler Wight were going to sit with them. She tried to look calm, as if popular boys walked up to her every day, but her hands began to shake and her eyes widened.

What do I say when they sit down?

Then, at the last moment, the two boys turned away and sat at the table next to them, where Veronica Anderson and Kitten Alley had been giggling for an hour. Jen should have known. Ronnie and Kitten were both cheerleaders. They wore stylish low-waisted jeans and tight sweaters that hugged their small breasts. Jen hoped they'd get an *F* on their social studies assignment.

"We're such dorks," Shelly whispered, obviously having been caught in the same fantasy as Jen.

Jen nodded her head in miserable agreement and pretended to return her attention to the book in front of her. No matter how hard she tried, the words weren't sinking in. She didn't want to let Shelly down, but Jen just couldn't seem to focus lately.

A few minutes later, Shelly nudged Jen and motioned almost frantically for her to look toward Devon's table.

Devon leaned back into his chair, a thin strand of pink gum linking his mouth to Ronnie's. The gum stretched too far and broke apart, hanging like two lizards' tongues from each of their mouths. Devon, Ronnie and Kittie dissolved into near-silent laughter.

The librarian stared menacingly from her post behind the

desk. Skyler glanced at Jen and shrugged almost apologetically, his fingers fanning the pages of his book.

"Oh. My. God. That's disgusting," Shelly whispered, pulling Jen's attention back to her own table.

It was the grossest thing Jen had ever seen in her life. And yet she yearned with all of her adolescent being to trade places with Ronnie.

"Let's go. Blake should be outside." Jen closed her notebook. She didn't think she'd ever felt like such an outsider. She wanted to go home and play her music really loud. At least while she sang alone in her room, she felt like she belonged somewhere.

The two girls walked out of the library, hugging their notebooks to their slim chests as if the bound paper could hide the fact that they lacked cleavage. Sometimes Jen thought her plain brown hair, gray eyes and pale skin made her invisible, like a ghost to boys like Devon.

Jen stepped out of the library first and skipped down the steps with Shelly right behind her, anticipating Blake pulling up in his new, shiny black pickup truck. At least her brother had the decency to own such a smooth vehicle. He wasn't so bad. Some of her friends even thought he was cute. Maybe Devon would come outside and see Jen get into the truck. Jen smiled, imagining Devon salivating over her cool ride.

A faded, dented truck that looked a lot like their old one pulled up to the curb. It even sported a big gray spot of primer in the back. Thank heavens Jennifer knew Blake never drove the old wreck anymore outside of the vineyard. That was the last thing she needed tonight.

The driver honked just as Jennifer was halfway down the steps. Jen's feet planted themselves so quickly that Shelly bumped into her from behind, sending Jen's notebook flying from suddenly limp arms. Papers scattered everywhere.

It *was* their old truck. What was her brother doing driving that piece of junk?

Shelly and Jen scrambled to pick up the papers. Jen needed

to leave quickly before anybody spotted her in that pickup. Blake was such a geek. Why was he doing this to her?

Jen chased her math homework as it danced up the steps on a breeze. She had almost reached it when Devon Hamlisch bent in front of her and picked it up. He handed it to Jen with a casual toss of his beautiful head and a smooth "Hey."

"Thanks," Jennifer managed to choke out. Devon Hamlisch had picked up her math homework. She'd tuck it under her pillow and never turn it in.

Blake revved the truck. Jen knew he had to keep the idle running fast or the engine would die.

"Is that your ride?" Ronnie asked, her voice rich with derision.

Jen cringed in horror. She hadn't noticed the others come outside. She'd only had eyes for Devon. Jen's face flamed with heat and she was grateful for the darkness. With her light coloring, she couldn't hide even the barest blush.

Jen managed a weak excuse. "It's our work truck."

"Farm workers." Kitty sniffed scornfully, looking away.

"I don't think I've ever heard one that loud." Ronnie wrinkled her nose.

"It sounds cool," Skyler offered, as Blake gunned the engine again.

Jen thought she'd pass out. Skyler Wight was sticking up for her against the most popular girl in school?

"Definitely not. God, can you smell the fumes from that thing?" Ronnie cocked her hip and rested her fist on it. The pose threw out her A-cup cleavage, making Jen feel even more like a loser. Jen wanted to melt into a puddle so that Ronnie could more easily stomp all over her.

"I gotta go," Jen said, escaping down the steps. She tried to walk normally, but too much adrenaline coursed through her legs, making her hips sway almost uncontrollably.

Shelly waited for her at the bottom of the steps. "Skyler Wight talked to you."

Jen dragged her friend toward the truck, opened the door and pushed Shelly in next to Blake.

Jen hopped in and slammed the old metal door.

Blake shifted the truck into gear. Predictably, it died.

"Satisfied?" Jen sniped at her lame brother, willing her eyes away from the snickering group in front of the library. If there was such a thing as dorkdom, Jen was in it.

BLAKE TOOK A SWIG OF BEER and put the cold bottle to his forehead. He'd needed something stronger than chocolate tonight. Things weren't getting any better. Jennifer had cried silently in the truck after they'd dropped Shelly off. He realized now that driving the old truck into town was a mistake. Given that he and Cori used to sit in it and talk for hours when it got too cold to sit outside by the river, and had almost made love on the bench seat of that old pickup, he'd wanted to flaunt it in Cori's face. Kind of like saying "I don't think of you every time I slide behind the wheel." What a lie that was. Look where that smart move got him. Cori had never even seen him driving the truck. Instead of making sure Cori realized he was over her, he'd crushed his teenage sister's fragile ego.

Muted sports scores buzzed irritatingly on the television. Blake switched to the weather channel and turned down the sound. Upstairs, one of Jen's favorite songs about being misunderstood ended. There was a brief respite before, predictably, the same song started again.

Blake stared down at the book filled with parental advice on his lap, unable to concentrate on the words. His own teenage years had been relatively happy ones. Blake was sure he hadn't given Kevin Austin, his adopted father, as many headaches or near-ulcer episodes as Jennifer was giving him. What was he doing wrong?

The music started again. The haunting melody tugged at Blake's floundering spirits and jolted him out of his seat.

SALVATORE STARED BLINDLY at the figures in front of him, while he tried to gather the strength to go upstairs. The trip was a double agony at the end of the day now. His hips ached all the time. It hurt to walk, much less climb, the tall, sweeping staircase he'd been so proud of when he'd approved the architectural plans years ago. Once on the second floor, Salvatore could barely bring himself to look at the wan face of his dying daughter. How could God be so cruel as to take his two most precious gems early—his beloved Anna and now their precious Sophia? Both victims of breast cancer.

With hands on each chair arm, Salvatore pushed himself painfully to his feet. It was becoming harder to keep his torment hidden. Yet, how could he complain when his daughter suffered with such grace? If only the doctors had been able to save her. Salvatore's own doctor wanted him to undergo double hip replacement surgery. Salvatore couldn't afford the two-month recovery period. He was risking quite a bit on the international introduction of his wines and needed to stay sharply focused.

He moved with deliberate steps toward the office door and the dreaded staircase, toward the light of his life, Sophia. And his pills. He'd spend fifteen minutes with Sophia. Then, he'd swallow one of those chalky pills and fifteen minutes later he'd feel relief. He told himself he only needed to endure the pain for another half hour. He could take it. He was a Messina.

It had cost him all his energy to hold things together when Anna died nearly twenty years ago. Salvatore would have lost his sanity and his business many times over if not for Sophia. With her brilliant smile, endless energy and quiet dignity, Sophia stepped into the social role created by her mother. A man couldn't ask for a better daughter. What was he to do now? Lucas held other priorities and Corinne was not an option. It was unfortunate that she'd been unable to break the chain of illegitimacy that seemed to plague the Messinas. At least she was making a name for herself in the public relations world. Salvatore tried to discreetly keep track of her career, in case she needed his help.

He reached the staircase and had started grimly up when he recalled Corinne's lack of respect at dinner last night. Clearly, she was raising that boy all wrong. Salvatore should have stepped in before this and provided the firm guidance the child so obviously needed. Refusing to eat dinner and asking, right there in the dining room, for fast food! It was inconceivable that the boy shared the same blood as Salvatore.

Halfway to the top. Sixteen more steps to go. The pain in his hips radiated up his backbone. Salvatore clenched his teeth and concentrated on his frustrating thoughts.

It wasn't like the old days when children didn't dare talk back to their elders. No. The old days were different. Children and grandchildren obeyed their patriarch, were silent when receiving their comeuppance and then did what the patriarch thought was best for the family. And heaven help the person that wronged the family.

The caustic words of Francesca Camilletti, his wife's sister, echoed as sharply as if she were beside him today rather than fifty-some-odd years ago. *"The Messinas are cursed with wine-making talent in America, a land that doesn't appreciate wine. They'll work their fingers to the bone and still be poor and unhappy. Don't go, Anna. He's a failure. He'll ruin your life."* She'd spit out those words of bitter advice to Anna on the New Jersey train platform, as she, Salvatore and Sophia, just a baby with wisps of silky black hair and sparkling brown eyes, were about to board the train to California. Francesca already believed Salvatore Messina had ruined her sister's life by getting her pregnant before they were married. Taking her away from the family was almost a worse sin.

Salvatore had known that if he and Anna stayed in New Jersey, Francesca would have made Salvatore's life a living hell. As luck would have it, Anna wanted to break free of her family's influence and her sister's suffocating love.

Anna had kissed her sister's cheek, told her she'd write, and then slipped her delicate hand into Salvatore's, her dark eyes radiating trust and love. Salvatore knew then that he'd have to make something of himself to validate the love Anna blessed him with. Come hell or high water, Messina Vineyards would grow and succeed, outliving them all and proving Francesca Camilletti wrong.

He paused to catch his breath, wondering for the first time if his desire to punish the man responsible for Cori's pregnancy was in any way similar to Francesca's irrational vendetta against him, which had lasted until the day she died. He frowned, unhappy with the notion, and shoved the thought aside. More pressing matters required his attention.

Salvatore stepped heavily onto the second-floor landing. Thankfully, Sophia's room was just at the top of the stairs. After a few shuffling steps, he swung Sophia's door open, leaning some of his weight on the door handle.

"Do you need anything, Mama?" Cori asked.

"No, thank you."

Corinne. Salvatore wanted to spin around and come back later. But any quick move would send him tumbling to the floor.

Sophia's gaze settled upon him. Even in the dim light, he could tell Sophia wasn't comfortable. He moved resolutely forward, intent on easing things for his daughter in any way possible.

From her perch on the bed, Corinne turned and stiffened when she saw him. She wore faded jeans and a sweatshirt. Without makeup, she looked barely seventeen. To her credit, Corinne didn't shrink away when her eyes met his, but there was no mistaking the unwelcoming expression on her face. A part of Salvatore preened with pride at her strength. Simultaneously, the voices of his Italian ancestors railed against her open disrespect. Not that any of that mattered at the moment. Sophia needed him.

Salvatore made every effort to move his legs smoothly under two pairs of dark, watchful eyes. With luck, Sophia's pain medication and Corinne's contempt would cloud their perceptive powers.

"It's time you retired, Corinne." He stopped in front of the two women. This close, he could see Sophia's pinched features. Yes, something was definitely wrong.

Eyes flashing, Corinne straightened her spine and opened her mouth, only to be cut off by her mother.

"Yes, dear. It's getting late. Why don't you go to bed? I'm sure my grandson is an early riser."

Corinne wasn't quick enough to hide the hurt in her eyes at her dismissal, but she didn't fight. She gave Sophia a small smile and a quick kiss on the cheek, then bid her mother good-night.

Salvatore didn't receive as much as a glance from his granddaughter.

When he heard the door close behind him, Salvatore reached for his daughter's delicate hand. He longed to sit next to her on the bed, but doubted he could stand back up without giving away his weakness.

"Tell me what you need, *cara.*"

IT WASN'T UNTIL BLAKE stood outside the kitchen door of the main house that he realized where he'd been heading. A soft glow through the kitchen windows lit the night. A shadow too large to be Cori moved past one window toward the refrigerator.

Suppressing his disappointment, Blake climbed the two steps to the door and entered without knocking. He didn't want to see Cori, anyway, not after the way he'd humiliated himself that morning.

"Beer or wine?" Luke asked, not at all surprised to see Blake at this hour. Both were night owls. Many a late night they'd shared a drink in this kitchen, illuminated, as they were now, by the light above the stove.

"Beer." Blake didn't equate drowning his sorrows with wine. He was one beer down already and could use at least one more to numb the feelings of helplessness he confronted in almost every aspect of his life. Blake slouched into a wooden kitchen chair and stretched out his legs. "Any reason the lights aren't on?"

Without getting up, Luke reached into the refrigerator to get a bottle, then slid the beer across the table to him. Blake opened the bottle before he realized it was the same brand Cori had purchased earlier. After a moment's hesitation, he took a swig. It wasn't anything special.

"Seemed the right thing to do at the time," Luke said, shrugging.

"You okay?" Blake uncapped his beer and took a sip. They drank for a few minutes in silence. Luke was a true Messina. Catch him in any social situation with any mix of people and he would fit right in, setting others at ease and never missing a conversational beat. As with the other Messinas, when you got too personal or they didn't want to tell you something, he shut down. It was one of the reasons Blake would never be one of them. After nearly six years of evolving friendship, they had never let him get that close.

"Have you seen Sophia tonight?" Blake asked.

"Briefly. Cori's been up there."

"And you can't be up there with her?" That seemed odd.

Luke shrugged again. "My grandfather heads up about now and he wants time alone with her, too."

"So you file in one by one? Is there a time limit?"

Luke rubbed the skin below his eyes, shadowed from the dim lighting, lack of sleep, or both. "It's...odd." He shook his head. "It was easier when we were younger. Before..." The Messina response kicked in and Luke went mute.

Blake waited a full five seconds before filling in Luke's thought. "Before Cori left?"

Luke didn't answer verbally, just gave his beer a rueful half smile.

AFTER CHECKING TO MAKE sure that Michael still snoozed peacefully in his sleeping bag on the floor of the pink room, Cori took the back stairs to the kitchen in search of a drink.

Maybe she should have been trying to make up with her grandfather instead of avoiding him these past few days. She'd been dismissed, as if she were a child of twelve, not twenty-five, a mother with a career and responsibilities. Everyone in the Messina household treated her as if she needed to be protected and couldn't make contributions of her own.

Some things never changed.

It was as if her own family was fooled into believing she was nothing more than the polished facade they'd created. As if they'd forgotten she'd been charming businessmen and politicians at the finest of restaurants in San Francisco while other girls were playing with Barbies. As if they assumed she didn't know the difference between a Chardonnay and a Zinfandel vine. As if grape growing, wine-making and business acumen didn't flow in her veins.

Now, if she'd been a man…

She trotted down the steps in the dim stairway, unhappy with the familiar train of thought. Cori hated those mental "what if" games, but couldn't always stop playing. She stepped into the large kitchen before her mind registered that she wasn't alone.

Luke and Blake sat at the kitchen table in the semidarkness, each nursing a beer. Nightshades.

"Hey, Sis." Luke greeted her. "Everything okay upstairs?"

Blake took a drink from his beer, gray eyes regarding her sharply. Cori felt his disapproval target her as clearly as if he'd spoken. She should be the one sending him dark glances. He'd accused her of being selfish today, hinted that she might have a drinking problem.

As if she had time to drink in her hectic everyday life.

"Grandfather is with her now." Cori looked away and crossed the black marble to the refrigerator. They both wanted news about Mama. Cori didn't want to talk. She'd get a beer and take it out by the pool so she could wallow in self-pity in private.

Chrome-plated, the refrigerator was twice as large as hers at home. Cori practically stepped into it to escape from view. Somewhere in this cavernous thing there had to be a beer. She'd put in four earlier, saving the rest for PR inspiration. She poked around until she found one long-necked brown bottle that had somehow managed to get shoved behind everything else.

Luke stood as Cori clutched her prize. "I'll go up and say good night."

Cori nodded, practically charging for the back door before Blake had time to say anything to her.

The fifty-degree air welcomed her back to Northern California, just as Cori's bare feet reminded her it was only February. Still, she wore blue jeans and a sweatshirt. Compared to the alternative of going back into the kitchen with Blake, she had no choice but to stay outside. On the bright side, her beer wouldn't become warm before she finished it.

Wisps of fog rose sparsely from the ground and crept toward the treetops, lit only by the light spilling out of the windows upstairs.

The pool sat behind a tall hedge to the right of the kitchen, and Cori quickly settled herself into a cushioned glider near the deep end, tucking her bare feet beneath her for warmth. The glider moved almost as soundlessly as the mist. Cori loved quiet nights like this, when the air smelled fresh with the new growth of spring. In Los Angeles, there were constant reminders that people were all around—smog, cars, sirens and loud music. Out here, a sense of peace and privacy prevailed.

Cori twisted off the top of her beer and took a sip. With a sigh, she eased her head back against the cushions, cradling the beer in her lap. She traitorously preferred beer over wine. It didn't even have to be good beer. She just liked the taste of malt over grapes. Her grandfather had been horrified to learn that. He took it as some kind of personal failure on her part. For Cori, it was just one more reason she didn't fit in, which was why she'd asked Maria to feed her and Michael dinner early from now on. It would be easier to avoid her grandfather.

The kitchen door latch clicked open, then shut. Cori strained to catch Blake's footfalls, but despite the fact that she knew he always wore boots, he walked as silently as a cat. No matter. He wasn't going to seek her out. Cori closed her eyes and pretended she didn't care. She'd known coming home would be painful. She just had never imagined the slights would be nonstop and come from every quarter. Even Mama was reluctant to talk about her condition.

And Cori couldn't have imagined that the weight of her secret would fluctuate from confinable to bursting. The pressure of Blake's disapproval was enough to keep her secret locked away. Most times, Blake seemed barely able to look at Michael, much less study his features and mannerisms and recognize himself there. His scorn scorched her in every word and look he directed her way. Those few times she'd glimpsed the Blake she'd fallen in love with—him helping her grandfather out of his car; those first few words they'd shared last night at the river; the stained, worn socks of a man not afraid to get his hands dirty with honest work—that's when Cori longed to tell him the truth—

''Are you asleep?''

CHAPTER FOUR

CORI NEARLY JUMPED OFF the glider at Blake's words. He stood not two feet in front of her, seeming to rise out of the shadows. Her eyes traveled over his jean-clad legs, past his lined denim jacket covering a red-and-black checked flannel shirt, up to his mouth parted in a tentative half smile, then away to the calm water in the swimming pool.

"I guess you weren't."

"No." She swung her bare feet down to the cold flagstones, prepared to go.

"Wait."

Cori glanced up at his face, anxious as to why he would want her to stay. Her heart pounded with apprehension. Could he have guessed about Michael? Should she tell him now? His gray eyes held hers steadily, with no anger or persecution, making her hesitate.

"They need time alone with her," he said unapologetically, as if she were some visitor rather than family. "They don't spend near enough time with her. And they'll probably leave her if you go up, too, seeing as how you've been gone so much."

Cori blinked but held Blake's gaze, refusing to acknowledge the pain his statement inflicted. He seemed more a Messina than she did. For years, she'd comforted herself with the thought that her mother and brother were still on her side. The visits and telephone calls had been sparse, but warm. Here on Messina turf, the separation burned more acutely than before and was all the more painful since she'd discovered this little piece of herself that wanted to belong.

The long hours away from Michael, the hard work for people who were never satisfied, the anonymity of living in L.A. without anyone to rely on. It wasn't how she'd grown up and it wasn't what she wanted for Michael. Not that she wanted to give up her career or her independence. She certainly didn't want to play the role her grandfather preferred for her. She just wanted her family back.

But her grandfather wouldn't allow it.

The only way she could be assured that her grandfather would treat Michael fairly was if she divulged her secret. Yet, if she told everyone the truth, her grandfather would either fire Blake or try to control him. She couldn't do that to Blake five years ago and she wouldn't do that to him now.

Having nothing to say without giving away things she shouldn't, Cori took a sip of beer. Now that she was being warned away from the house, she really wanted to go back inside. The air seemed sharper than before. Her toes were beginning to sting and her hands were cold and wet from the condensation on the beer bottle. When Blake didn't say anything or leave, Cori wiped her wet hands on her jeans, one at a time, careful to keep her eyes off him.

After what seemed an unusually long silence, Cori laughed dryly and tucked her feet back under her.

''I guess I should thank you. For standing guard,'' she said, for that was certainly what it seemed like. ''You can go on home. I won't go inside yet.''

''No.''

She glanced at him then. Blake stood awkwardly, hands at his sides, brows drawn down and a slight frown on his face. He looked irritated.

''You don't have to thank me. I'm doing this for Sophia.''

''Of course.'' She choked out the words. She meant nothing to him now, had probably meant nothing to him all those years ago. ''She's lucky to have you...and Jennifer...around. Thank you.'' If Cori hadn't been so set on making her own way all those years ago, if the condom hadn't failed, she would have been the one her mother relied on now. Still, she had to be grateful that Blake watched over Mama so carefully.

Cori sighed. She couldn't live in the world of "what ifs" with Blake standing close enough for her to touch. If she lifted her arm, she could easily slip her fingers into the curve of his palm. She looked at his strong hand and then away. Mistake. She knew what those fingers felt like coasting over her skin. The thought sent a tingling response down her spine.

Cori took another sip of beer. She'd been home two days and the wanting was killing her. She wanted to be part of her family again, to be accepted for who she was, not judged by mistakes she'd made. She wanted to buy back these past few years with her mother.

And she still wanted Blake. She wanted to coax that begrudging smile out of him. She missed talking with him before going to bed each night. She craved his touch.

There. She'd admitted it to herself. She longed to be with the man whose heart she'd scrambled over in her bid for independence. He was a good man. Responsible, loyal, honorable. And sexy. She could still feel the whisper of his lips beneath her ear.

She brought her cool palm up to her neck in an attempt to erase the memory.

When he still didn't move or speak, Cori tilted the beer to her lips and used the opportunity to look him in the eye, daring him to speak, because there were so many things she couldn't say to him, that she had to keep locked tightly inside. At any minute she expected to blurt out that Michael was his son or that if he was going to stand there forever looking at her, she could use a lot more than just his looking. It'd been a long time since she'd experienced the touch of a man.

Who was she kidding? Blake had been the last man to touch her. Cori took another pull on the beer bottle just to keep herself contained.

"Chocolate?" He thrust his hand in her direction, palm up, offering her a choice of several colorful M&M's.

Cori shook her head. It wasn't that she didn't like chocolate.

Chocolate just didn't seem the right treat to mix with beer. She'd noticed when they first met that chocolate was one of Blake's few weaknesses. She'd even seen a bag of chocolate in the refrigerator just now.

"You look like you don't want to be alone." Blake popped some candy into his mouth.

"Isn't that the understatement of the year?" Cori laughed, finally, blessedly, feeling the effects of the beer in her system. "I don't have much choice, do I?"

"It's just a few minutes—"

Her second bout of laughter cut off his words.

And then it happened. The dam holding in her emotions cracked and she nearly drowned in a moment of panic as words came tumbling out. "It's not a few minutes. I'm not a part of this family anymore. Do you know what that means?" She couldn't bear him towering above her, so she swung her feet to the chilly flagstones and stood, which didn't help because he was still a foot taller than her. He was now far too near, and the world tilted for just a moment.

Not waiting for it to steady, she continued. "It means I gave up my life for my child. I go to work. I come home. We eat. We play games. We color. He gets a bath. I stay up and work. Alone. Not for a few minutes, Blake. Every day. Him and me. *Alone.*" Cori was so out of control, tears welled in her eyes. She took a tattered breath, then another sip of beer, determined not to cry.

"And you, of all people," she couldn't resist adding, although it was dangerously close to the wrong thing to say, "shouldn't feel sorry for me, because I love Michael. And I wouldn't trade him for anyone or anything."

Because Blake loomed so close and she suddenly felt incredibly foolish yammering on like that, Cori stepped around him to stand at the edge of the pool with her back to him and several feet between them.

"So, thank you for the offer of the company, but I'm used to being alone." *Please leave,* she added silently.

Blake expelled a breath. Then he came to stand beside her.

Cori refused to look at him. The smell of chocolate drifted her way. She kept her arms wrapped tightly across her chest, the beer still clutched in one hand, biting down on her bottom lip to keep her mouth shut. She'd already said way too much.

"I remember how hard it was with Jennifer at first. It seemed as if it was just me against the world."

His hand came to rest upon her shoulder. He gave her a gentle squeeze, then his hand moved across and down her shoulder blades, up, across and down. Warmth seeped through her sweatshirt into her back and it was all Cori could do not to lean into his hand or settle against his side and tell him the truth.

"You have family. That's more than I had. This is a rough time for everyone."

Cori refused to acknowledge his words. To deny them was to betray her family further. To agree was to belittle her love for Michael. His hand dropped away and the cold bite of evening air shot through her. She shivered, telling herself it was from the chill.

"Thank you." Now if Blake would just leave…

"Don't say that."

Cori turned to look up at Blake. He stood close enough for her to curl her arms around his neck and pull his lips down to warm hers.

"You're always thanking me for something, as if I'm some kind of…of…busboy or something," he said, looking down at her with narrowed eyes.

Cori blinked in surprise. She'd relied on good manners for too many years to count. Her smile and a few kind words had ironed over many a difficult situation.

"Half of the time I know you don't mean it. It's just something you say to fill the air."

"That's not true. That's—"

"Bull. You know exactly what I'm talking about. I'd prefer you were real with me like you were just now." His eyes blazed down upon her. "Ranting about being alone and all your responsibilities instead of pretending everything is okay."

''But—''

''That's how you were that summer.'' Blake's hands landed on her shoulders. ''Anytime I told you to get lost or ignored you, you were polite beyond belief. I don't think nuns were as polite as you.'' He gripped her shoulders tighter, then shook her gently. ''It drove me crazy then. It drives me crazy now. Just stop.''

His hands fell away as if he'd just realized he was touching her again. Cori fought to fill her lungs.

''At first, I didn't think you had anything beneath all that blond hair and lip gloss. Then for a while, I thought I knew the person beneath all that.'' He inhaled sharply. ''Now, after hearing you rant and rave like a real person…'' Blake looked out at the fog-enshrouded vineyards and paused.

Cori waited to hear what he had to say next, hugging herself against the crisp night air, against the painful knowledge that she'd hurt him.

''Whatever happened, whatever it is, you can tell me. I'll understand.'' He looked down into her eyes, saying the things Cori had always dreamed he'd say to her.

She opened her mouth to tell him they had a beautiful child and to lay her fears about Michael's future at rest.

And then he ruined it.

''Tell your family, too. Things will be better for everyone.''

''No.'' Cori stepped back. The truth wouldn't make things any better for Blake, not if her grandfather knew. In this case, the truth wouldn't set anybody free.

''What if they don't want to hear the truth?'' she choked out, spinning away, escaping to the house before she gave Blake what he asked for.

HANDS THRUST IN HIS jacket pockets, Blake trod through the vineyard in the gray misty light of predawn, wishing that his life were as straightforward as the rows he walked between. Since he'd started caring for Sophia, he'd fallen behind in some of his duties for Salvatore Messina. And it didn't look like Cori was going to be able to provide as much help as he'd expected.

A crew of pruners was scheduled to trim back the kicker cane on the vines this week and a shipment of new vines that needed to be grafted to existing rootstock required inspection for pests and disease—transmitted too easily on delicate grapevines, attacking tender spring growth. Nonstop vigilance by the field manager was required to keep a vineyard healthy and productive. Blake was giving the Messinas spotty vigilance while trying to make sure Sophia was comfortable.

After tossing and turning in bed all night, Blake gratefully greeted the alarm clock and a return to the vineyards, where he had at least some control over his life. Heaven knows, he was failing Jennifer, with her fluctuating moods and impossible expectations. Even his parenting books weren't helping. There wasn't much else he could do for Sophia, besides be there for her. And, although he didn't know what was wrong, Blake's eyes were sharp enough to catch that Mr. Messina wasn't in the best of health, either. It seemed as if all Blake did lately was worry.

Blake had worked hard to create something that resembled a family here, and now it was disintegrating. Jennifer wasn't totally correct. They'd still be welcome in the Messina mansion after Sophia passed. It just wasn't going to be the same without her.

Then there was Cori. He didn't want to think about Cori, yet he couldn't seem to stop. Something was eating Cori up inside. Something more than worry for her mother. Blake could see it in her shadowed eyes and guarded expression, hear it in the frustration bolstering her words.

Unreasonably, Blake wanted to know what burden Cori carried. Did the boy's father give them trouble? Was she unhappy living in L.A.? Would her life these past few years have been different if Blake's pride hadn't forced him to let her go?

Straightening his shoulders, Blake strode purposefully out of the row onto the gravel road. Rusty, dented trucks lined the drive. A nursery delivery truck parked farther back. Hispanic men in worn flannel, blue jeans and scuffed boots tumbled out of doors at his appearance, anxious to receive instructions and start the day's work.

Before he could reach the crews, they parted for a sleek black limousine. The car pulled up next to Blake. Silently, the window opened to reveal Salvatore Messina. He'd taken to using a limo, claiming it allowed him more time to work, although Messina Vineyards' headquarters was only a fifteen-minute drive from the main house. Blake suspected the limo had something to do with Mr. Messina's health problem, but he respected the old man's privacy enough not to ask what was wrong.

"Good to see you out early," Mr. Messina said, craning his neck to survey the workers and the trucks.

With Cori still on his mind, Blake nearly asked Mr. Messina if he knew what was bothering her, not that his boss would answer even if he knew.

Blake pushed out a heavy breath. He couldn't be content worrying about Sophia dying, Jennifer's teenage angst and Salvatore Messina's increasingly mercurial moods and failing health. Nope. He had to add an obsession with the unknown problems of the woman who'd refused his love.

"Did you hear me?"

"What?" Blake quickly recovered, shifting his weight and forcing his attention back to his scowling employer, who had every right to be irritated. "I'm sorry. Say again."

"I said, who's grafting those new vines?"

"Robley and his crew. I've got Villalobo's bunch pruning." Most of the crews had worked on the Messina property before. They were well acquainted with the plants and Blake's preferences. They knew the land so well, they pruned and planted almost instinctively, without much direction from Blake. Just what he needed this year.

Mr. Messina stared at Blake in silence. With Mr. Messina, silence usually meant one of two things—intense displeasure or withheld information. In this case, Blake suspected Mr. Messina's displeasure about his choice of work crews, based on the way his employer's silver eyebrows sank.

"Go over each leaf. Carefully." Salvatore Messina eyed Blake speculatively.

"Yes, sir." Blake hid his frustration behind a neutral expression. He suspected it didn't matter who he'd chosen to graft, but in Blake's rush to get back on top of things he had irked Mr. Messina by not including him in the decision.

Under the circumstances, Blake was doing pretty damn well, running the vineyards while fulfilling Sophia's wish to be taken care of by those she loved. Still, disappointment swelled in him. Blake usually prided himself on exceeding Mr. Messina's requirements. Lately, he'd had trouble meeting his employer's minimum expectations. If there was ever a time Blake deserved to be chewed out by the old man, it was now.

Mentally preparing himself, Blake met his boss's dark stare evenly.

Surprisingly, instead of issuing recriminations, Salvatore Messina rolled up the limo window and drove away.

With a sigh of relief, Blake glanced at his watch, then hurried over to give instructions to each foreman. He needed to hustle if he wanted to have breakfast with Jennifer before school and help Sophia through her morning rituals.

"WHAT'S THE BIG DEAL, Cori? It's just one day."

"Sid, this is nonnegotiable. I can't go." Cori wasn't leaving her mother to fly down to Los Angeles for a business meeting with the new Bell-Diva vice president of marketing. She'd decided last night to try to mend things with her family without letting her grandfather know who Michael's father was. She was determined to make this super-mom thing work—her job, parenting, taking care of Mama. Today it was all coming together.

She finished grating cheese for a cheese and bell pepper omelette. Unfortunately, omelettes weren't something Cori made frequently. Okay, ever. The closest she'd come to cooking eggs was when she added them to the boxed cake mixes she sometimes made. But Cori felt confident she could improvise successfully.

"You know how important this account is, Cori. Abe Monroe asked for you by name, for crying out loud. Think of how happy Adam Parker's going to be to hear about this."

"Take a breath, Sid." Cori added the cheese to the eggs and milk she'd already mixed together. Behind her, Michael ignored his toasted waffles while he watched cartoons on the small television on the counter.

"Take a breath? Take a breath, she says," Sidney griped, then proceeded to rant incoherently about lost opportunities, ungrateful employees and how easily they could be replaced.

Cori knew Sidney's threats were only half real. It was the half about losing her job that was a little frightening.

Ignoring her fears, Cori set her cell phone down on the forest-green kitchen counter, knowing that Sid would take at least another minute to wind down. She poured the mixture into a pan, then added sliced green pepper. Satisfied when the omelette sizzled upon contact, Cori picked the cell phone back up. Sidney was gasping for breath—a sure sign that she was almost finished.

"Mommy, I need more syrup."

Cori retrieved the glass syrup pitcher from the cupboard, then set it in front of Michael. Maybe after he drenched the waffles in syrup, he'd eat something.

"Sid, can I have a word? Please?" Cori watched Michael carefully dribble maple syrup over his waffles.

Sidney huffed in Cori's ear.

"Why don't you have the team come up to Sonoma for a relaxing weekend in the wine country?" Cori turned to check on the omelette, only to discover that the frying pan had practically disappeared behind a billowing cloud of smoke. Frantic, she turned on the fan over the stove.

Before the smoke cleared, glass shattered at Cori's bare heels, stealing her breath.

"It wasn't me." Michael's standard disclaimer.

Her entire body tense, Cori didn't have to look down to know syrup was splattered all over the kitchen. It was plastered to the back of her bare ankles.

''I've got to go, Sid. Tell them I can meet to discuss my ideas over breakfast on Sunday, if they decide to spend the weekend.'' She hit the end button and tossed the phone onto the counter.

''What are you doing?'' Blake's irritation cut through the hum of the kitchen fan.

Cori flinched. Of all the people on the property, only her grandfather would be less welcome at that moment than Blake. ''I'm making my mother breakfast.''

''Damn it, Cori, you'll stink the whole house up.'' Blake hopped through the syrup swampland to turn off the burner, then headed for the sink with the still-smoking pan.

''Start fanning the kitchen door, boy,'' Blake ordered as he passed Michael, who was slouched over the kitchen table, his attention still on the cartoons.

''P.U. What stinks?'' Jennifer walked into the kitchen with all the disdain of a teenager, her backpack slung over her shoulder. ''Tell me that's not syrup on the floor.''

''His name—'' Cori was right behind Blake ''—is *Michael.*'' After all she'd done for Blake by keeping her secret, the least he could do was call his son by his given name.

''Hello-oo! Anybody home?'' Jennifer waved a hand in front of Michael's face.

Other than tilting his head slightly to the left, Michael remained unfazed. Such was the behavior of a four-year-old feigning innocence.

''Jen,'' Blake admonished his sister. ''Aren't you supposed to be waiting for the bus?'' Blake stopped abruptly in front of Cori, so that she almost ran into his broad back. She backpedaled. He punched the power button on the television and tried again. ''Open the kitchen door. Now.''

Michael blinked once and hopped out of his chair.

Blake began scraping the egg mess into the sink, then blasted the pan with water.

''His name is Michael,'' Cori repeated, grabbing a sponge and thrusting it under the water, splashing her red T-shirt in the process. "And I spent a lot of time on that omelette. Now you've ruined it."

"Saved somebody's life is more like it," Jen observed dryly.

Blake looked over his shoulder at his sister. Cori crouched down on the floor and began making small lakes of maple syrup with glass shard islands, relieved that Blake's ire was momentarily directed elsewhere.

Jennifer tossed up both hands. "You're right. I've got a bus to catch. Just need a signature on this before I go." She waved a paper at Blake.

"Fan the door, kid." Blake made a push-pull motion with his arm until Michael did as he was asked.

"Michael," Cori muttered, rolling her eyes, marveling that Blake could keep track of all the goings on and hold more than one conversation, yet not remember Michael's name.

Blake snorted in response. "You Italians give everybody these formal names that only mothers use. Corinne? Lucas? Nobody but your mother and grandfather call you that. Did you think when you named your son that all his school friends would call him by that mouthful of a name? Do you think his drinking buddies are going to call him *Michael?*" Blake turned the pan around and scrubbed vigorously. "You ruined this omelette when you forgot to grease the pan." He left the pan to soak the remaining difficult pieces and dried his hands on a dish towel.

"I didn't forget," Cori said defensively. She hadn't known. Wasn't it a nonstick pan? She didn't cook much. You could buy so much good take-out in L.A. that she'd never learned how to cook from scratch.

"How about I sign this for you?" offered Jen.

Stretching out a hand toward Jennifer's paper, Blake lowered his chin and peered down at Cori. "You were distracted enough that you didn't notice all the smoke. Maria's due any minute, and she'll be pissed that you even touched her pans."

Cori looked around. The kitchen was really smoky. Cori opened her mouth to thank him for helping her, but he cut her off.

"Don't say it." Blake held up a palm. "Jen, grab that mop in the pantry, will you?" He took the paper from Jen and then picked up a pen near the kitchen telephone. "What's this I'm signing?"

Cori gave up on the sponge and tried paper towels. When she realized Blake and Jen hadn't spoken for an abnormal amount of time, she looked up from smearing syrup. Blake studied the paper, his expression boding ill for someone. Jen gripped the mop so hard her knuckles were white.

"What's wrong?" Unlikely as it was, Cori feared the paper had something to do with Mama.

"When were you going to tell me about this?" The ice in Blake's tone seemed to cool the kitchen ten degrees.

"It's no big deal. Just a midterm progress report."

If Jen weren't standing so stiffly, Cori might have believed the girl didn't care.

"*F* as in fail is a big deal." Blake shook his head in disbelief, his fist wrinkling the paper. "There are two of them."

BLAKE NOW TURNED HIS full attention on his sister. Looking at her progress report tore him apart. He wanted to shout his frustration, blame himself, blame her. Jen never brought home a grade worse than a *B*. He drew a steadying breath. "I thought you were doing your homework with Sophia."

"I do," she lied, her pink cheeks giving her away. "I'm going to miss my bus if you don't sign that thing."

"To hell with the bus. I'll drive you to school today. It says you have missing assignments. What's that all about?"

"I want to take the bus," she protested, albeit weakly.

"I'm driving you to school."

Tears filled Jen's eyes. Blake forced himself to be firm with her. He was responsible for her. He'd have to straighten her out, no matter how weary he was.

He jumped as Cori's fingers moved lightly over his skin before stopping on his biceps. Unwanted longing curled in Blake's belly. He hadn't felt such peace and completion, such hurt and loss, since the night they'd made love. He should have shrugged away her touch, not endured it, not reveled in the heat of her skin on his.

"What's Mama supposed to do for breakfast now?" Cori asked.

Blake fought the urge to snap at Cori, and lost, pulling away from her. "She can't keep down much more than water."

Rather than wilt at his tone, Cori just swallowed. "What's she been living on?"

"She had an IV tube in the hospital."

"And lately?"

"Water. Broth. A little bread soaked in milk. We tried those energy drinks, but they don't stay down."

"That can't be enough..."

"It's not." Blake hardened his expression against her. Cori was soft. She'd always been soft. Blake couldn't handle taking care of another weak female right now. He didn't need to know her secrets. Suddenly, he wished she'd just disappear as she'd done nearly five years ago.

"Thank you for telling me."

Blake spared Cori another glance. Her brown eyes didn't waver from his. Soft? Cori? Not at the moment. Why was Sophia keeping the details of her health from Cori? Rather than rebuke Cori for thanking him, again, Blake gave her the briefest of nods.

"If you're going to drive me, we need to leave now," Jen wailed.

"Mommy, my arm hurts. I need to stop," the kid whimpered.

Blake considered whining a little himself.

"I REALLY REGRET MISSING the Mustard Festival this year. We've had such a mild winter that the wildflowers must be spectacular." Mama smiled at Cori, who sat ramrod straight in a chair next to her mother's bed.

Cori struggled to hide a yawn. The Mustard Festival in nearby Napa celebrated spring with blooming wildflowers between rows of grapevines. Attending black-tie events and driving through the scenic area was an indication to those in the business that spring had arrived in the wine country.

Michael slept in the window seat across the room. Mama had been talking for hours, bringing Cori up to speed on friends in the wine industry and people living in the area. Her drawn face showed fatigue, but she seemed reluctant to rest.

Despite the length of time they'd spent together, Cori was disappointed that none of the topics her mother brought up were personal. Although she'd tried to talk about her mother's needs, Mama deftly switched topics. Her mother could have held these conversations with anyone, including a stranger. The only real conversation they'd shared was that first night when Sophia had been half asleep.

"Mama, don't you want to rest?"

"You're my guest, dear. I can't just go to sleep while you're here."

You're my guest. The words pierced Cori's heart. She'd never be part of her own family again. Perhaps that was why Mama kept up the idle, tedious chatter about nothing.

"You think I'm a guest?" Cori struggled over her mother's words.

"Well, not a guest. That's not a pleasant word to use with family. And you are family, even if you've felt you've had to live away from us."

I had no choice. Cori tried to compose herself. She couldn't possibly tell her mother that now. She'd kept it from her all this time.

"Thank you," Cori finally said. She wished Mama would treat her more like family. Then Cori would be able to slouch in this uncomfortable chair instead of sitting bolt upright with an aching back. Of course, Cori never talked about personal subjects with family, much less slumped, since she'd learned at age eight that life wasn't that way in the Messina household.

"I want you to be comfortable, dear," Mama said.

Cori thought of Blake and his admonition that she should be honest. Maybe it was that simple. Maybe all Cori had to do was let down her guard and her mother would let down hers.

"Well, if you're not tired, would you mind if I slipped out to take a nap in my bedroom? Michael will be all right over there. He should sleep for another hour." Okay, so she'd resorted to a little reverse psychology. Cori suspected her mother would sleep if she left the room. Michael was fine and didn't really need watching over, and letting Mama believe she was caring for Michael might give her ego a much-needed boost.

"If you need to rest, I'd be happy to watch him."

It worked. Holding in a smile of joy, Cori stood, turned to go, then stopped. She couldn't leave without pushing Blake's advice a little further. "When I come back, I want you to talk to me like family," she said in a shaky voice. "No more of this drivel about being a guest."

Mama gasped dramatically. "I don't talk drivel."

"You can drivel with the best of them." Cori leaned over and kissed her mother on the cheek. "Take a nap. I'm sorry I didn't realize earlier how tiring this was for you."

Mama placed her palm against Cori's cheek, her eyes suddenly misty. Cori held back tears of her own. Maybe Blake was right about being truthful. At least, with her feelings.

"I used to kiss you on the cheek like that when I came to tuck you in."

"I remember, Mama." It was one of Cori's fondest memories, brought back when she kissed Michael each night.

"You'll take a rest and not work?"

"I believe you've bored me to the point where a nap is necessary, yes," Cori fibbed. She needed some uninterrupted work time.

Mama smiled. "I must not have taught you the fine art of conversation."

"*Au contraire.* You taught me much too well." According to Blake, that is.

BLAKE REMOVED HIS muddy boots at the kitchen door of the Messina mansion, grabbed a handful of M&M's from an open bag in the refrigerator, and then took the back stairs to the second floor. He needed to check on Sophia.

He pushed open the door to Sophia's room and peeked in. Sophia slept peacefully, her chest rising and falling in a regular, if shallow, rhythm. Movement by the windows caught Blake's eye and he saw the kid snoozing, as well, his back to the door. Cori's child fit snugly into the window seat. Still, one wrong move and the kid would tumble from the padded bench onto the floor.

Telling himself he was only ensuring Sophia's continued rest, Blake slipped into the room. He placed the flowered ottoman from Sophia's love seat next to the window seat. If the kid rolled off, he wouldn't fall far.

Where was Cori?

Unable to stop his curiosity, Blake took a few steps down the hall, then pushed open the door to the pink room. Cori lay on the bed, a fuzzy pink afghan covering her torso, a pile of papers next to her head. She'd been wearing shorts today, taking advantage of the warmer than normal early spring weather, and her legs lay in glorious exposure on the pink comforter. He couldn't help but stare at her. Cori's face was relaxed, making her look more like the young woman who'd wrapped herself into his heart several years earlier than the worried mother he'd been watching over these past few days.

"I'm not asleep this time, either," Cori said with a yawn. "Just resting my eyes."

Blake didn't react, didn't budge from the door frame when he knew he should have excused himself and returned to his duties. He was too focused on Cori's casual reaction to being caught in bed. Rather than jerk up, she rolled onto her back and stretched her arms over her head, no more bothered by his presence than when he'd been her lover. He couldn't take his eyes off the curves she presented.

"Rough day?" She pushed herself to a sitting position, her brown eyes suddenly full of compassion. "Sorry I asked."

His jaw tightened as her question brought back all of his frustrations with Jennifer.

"Is everything okay?"

Compelled by Cori's genuine sense of interest, Blake took

two steps into the room and started dumping on her before he knew what he was doing. ''I spent an hour this morning talking with the principal and counselor at the junior high school. Given what's going on with Sophia, they all wanted to treat the situation carefully. I convinced them to be tough.'' He shrugged as if he fought with school officials every day. ''Starting today, I have to sign a homework planner Jennifer brings home every night.''

''Jen needs your understanding as well as your discipline.'' Cori sighed. ''I know it's hard for me to concentrate on work with all this going on. If I didn't have my boss breathing down my back, I'd gladly set it all aside. Just because Jen seems to be taking it in stride, doesn't mean she isn't as overwhelmed as the rest of us.''

Pearls of wisdom, his mother used to say when someone made things clearer. Damn if Blake's tension didn't ease just talking to her. Was he supposed to feel that way, with all the history between them? Blake rubbed the back of his neck. He didn't think so. He didn't want her trying to fix his problems. Then she'd discover just how many problems he had—among them, loneliness.

Cori's head tilted and Blake realized she was looking at his socks. He backed into the doorway.

''I noticed this morning that you made an appointment for work.'' He laced his tone with a hint of disapproval.

Cori's brown eyes hardened and she leaned back. There. That's what he wanted, wasn't it? To put some distance between them?

''It's important to our agency. To my boss. To my survival.'' She reached for the pile of papers on the bed and began straightening them, upright and substantial as a shield. ''Besides, it's just tentative.''

''More important than Sophia?''

Cori glanced down at his legs and clamped her mouth shut. Small hands brushed Blake's knee as the kid stepped past him, carrying a blue book.

"'Scuse me." The boy wobbled over to the bed and climbed into his mother's lap.

Cori tossed the papers to the floor, tucked the kid's book behind her, wrapped her arms around him and kissed the top of his little head. As she rocked him gently, the kid's eyes drifted closed, shutting Blake out. The boy didn't look much like Cori. Oh, he had the brown eyes, but his hair wasn't blond like Cori's or black like the others in the Messina clan. He must have gotten his brown hair from his dad. And his features. Blake couldn't see any of Cori in his features, either. Dumbo ears waved on either side of the kid's head. Blake remembered the pain of growing into ears like that.

"Does his father spend much time with him? Has he even seen him?" Blake voiced the questions he'd been asking himself over the past few days. Immediately, he wanted to take the words back. It was none of his business. He and Cori had shared something brief and physical. She'd left for school the next day without even saying goodbye. It was only idle curiosity that made him ask.

Regardless of the reason, Blake studied Cori carefully as he waited for her answer.

"Once," Cori said quietly, then kissed the top of the boy's head, leaving her face tucked above her son's and averted from Blake.

Once. Her faint answer reverberated through Blake, her pain nearly palpable. What could have happened to hurt her?

The doorway to the bedroom may just as well have been a solid wall between them. Blake, who'd been struggling with Jen's independence and absence of hugs, suddenly felt very alone.

Silence blanketed the room until Blake realized that if he barely breathed, he could hear Cori humming. The boy looked so right, cradled in her arms. Cori loved that boy.

Blake, who'd lost so many loved ones in his life and was on the brink of losing more, what with Sophia passing on and Jennifer striving for independence, realized what he was feeling.

He envied the boy that security.

LATER THAT AFTERNOON, seeing no one around, Jen slipped into her room, closing the door behind her and dropping her backpack on the floor. With a sigh, she settled her rump on the edge of the pink bed before flopping onto her back. This had been her room before Cori and her brat showed up. Jen felt special in this room, as if she were somebody important.

Jen rubbed her stomach in a vain attempt to ease her discomfort. She was getting used to feeling bad all the time. Life sucked. She was invisible to most kids at school. Her teachers rode her about her schoolwork. Blake couldn't look at her without snapping. On top of everything else, Cori and her little monster were camped out in her room.

She kicked the blue sleeping bag on the floor with her foot, sighed and stared blankly at the wall.

It took her a moment to realize that a kaleidoscope of color sparkled across the far pink-and-white striped wall. Jen admired the beautiful display before looking around to find what was reflecting the afternoon sunlight. Diamond earrings glittered on the desk. These weren't chips like the ones Blake had given her for Christmas last year. These suckers were each as big as a pencil eraser. They were so big, they had to weigh down Cori's ears.

Jen found herself standing in front of the desk, looking at the stones. Of its own accord, her hand reached out to one earring; she picked it up gently with her thumb and forefinger, rolled it across her thumb. Ronnie Anderson couldn't possibly miss these things. That would show her that Jen was more than just a farmhand. And maybe they'd catch Devon's attention.

Jen picked up the other earring, then slipped both into her pocket. She'd wear them one day and Cori would probably never know they were missing.

CHAPTER FIVE

"HAVE YOU SEEN my diamond earrings, Mama?" They were missing, and although Michael denied any involvement, Cori suspected he'd managed to lose them in some cranny where she'd never find them again.

"No, but I don't get around much. I'm sure they'll turn up," Sophia replied. "Do you see Blake outside? If you look out the window, you'll probably see that old work truck of his. Maria tells me he's been staying close to the house lately."

"Tell me what you need, Mama. I'll get it for you." Another day had passed and Cori still hadn't been able to break the wall between her mother and herself. Mama preferred Blake when she needed something.

"It's nothing." Noticing Cori's doubtful expression, her mother added, "I'm fine."

With a sigh of resignation, Cori walked over to the windows, pulled aside the heavy, rose-colored drapes and looked out on the straight rows of the vineyards. It took her a few moments to spot a truck. When she recognized the faded brown vehicle, she paled. "He's out there."

"Oh?"

Cori swallowed her disappointment. "Do you want me to get him for you?"

"No, dear. I'm sure he'll pop up to check on me soon."

It was clear that Mama needed something and wasn't going to ask Cori. The best way for Cori to help her mother was to bring her someone else. "Then, I'll go get Blake."

"That won't be necessary." Mama's hopeful expression belied her words.

"Yes, it will." Cori forced herself to walk steadily out of the room and down the stairs. Outside, she blinked in the bright sunshine, wishing for a pair of sunglasses to shade her eyes, to hide her feelings.

So, Blake still drove the same old truck. She'd begged Blake to make love to her in that jalopy.

Moving briskly on the packed dirt road, Cori sidestepped a few puddles still resisting evaporation from last night's showers. The crisp air gave her bare arms goose bumps. Short sleeves were fine inside the house, but she'd forgotten how sunshine didn't mean warmth in Northern California, the way it did down south at this time of year.

Amidst the neatly tended rows of grapevines ready to burst forth with life, Cori relaxed a little, breathing deeply the scent of wet earth and spring growth. She'd missed these signs of nature that foretold the changing of the seasons. It was cruelly ironic that the vineyards were ready to come out of hibernation while her mother was nearing death.

Cori rounded a bend in the road and spotted the truck ahead, but there was no sign of Blake. Cori walked past the truck, but she couldn't see Blake's tall, familiar figure anywhere. Frustrated, she returned to the vehicle and climbed up into the truck bed. The added height gave her a better view of the area, but still Blake wasn't to be seen. He could be anywhere, even in another section of the vineyard. For all she knew, his truck could have died here days ago.

She called for him, then hopped down and honked the horn, leaning in the open window and trying not to look at the vinyl bench seat.

"What's wrong?"

Cori turned to see Blake come running out of a row of grapevines over a rise near the river. Blake's stride was fluid and graceful, despite his jeans and work boots. Everything about him stood out sharp and clear in the bright spring sunshine. Cori leaned against the old truck for balance, its warmth seeping through her blue jeans and the thin cotton of her T-shirt. He was beautiful, and he took her breath away.

The memories tumbled back. Blake had been aloof, yet seemed so mature. Much more seasoned than the boys her grandfather arranged for her to go out with. She could look into his eyes and see there was depth. This was a man who'd lived, who'd faced life's challenges head-on, without benefit of a safety net. At Christmas, those gray eyes warmed when they looked at Cori. And the heat in his eyes lit a fire between them at spring break. Nearly five years later, his face was less gaunt, his body filled out with muscle, yet when his eyes met hers, she still recognized the man she'd fallen in love with.

''What's wrong?'' he repeated, stopping a few feet in front of her, not even winded.

Cori got winded just walking up the stairs. It took her a moment to catch her breath just from looking at him. She collected herself enough to say ''Mama needs you.''

''Hop in.'' He opened the driver's door.

Cori hesitated; her eyes flew up to his and then away. Aeons ago, in what seemed like someone else's life, he'd opened the truck door for her and she'd slid onto the center of the bench, just far enough to the right that he had to sit next to her. Thigh to thigh, shoulder to shoulder. He'd rescued her that night. Half a year later, she'd helped him steam up this truck's windows down by the Russian River and nearly lost her virginity in acrobatic style.

This time, Cori slid all the way across the bench seat, letting her arm dangle out the open passenger window.

Blake hesitated, then climbed behind the wheel. Revving the engine a few times, he backed the truck around and headed toward the house.

''Has there been any change? Is she feeling all right?''

They both knew Sophia wasn't feeling all right.

''She just asked for you.''

HEART POUNDING, Blake ran ahead of Cori, making it to Sophia's bedroom first.

''What's my favorite socialite need?'' he asked in what he hoped was a charming, unconcerned voice.

Sophia looked past him toward Cori, panting in the doorway. ''Corinne, can you go check on Michael? I sent him downstairs for cookies and milk.''

''I know. Maria's with him. We came up through the kitchen.''

''Have you helped her to the bathroom yet this afternoon?'' Blake asked Cori, suddenly suspicious of Sophia's motives. Why wasn't Sophia being honest with Cori?

''No. I didn't know she needed help,'' Cori admitted with a hurt look on her face.

''I can make it on my own,'' Sophia protested.

''This ends now.'' Blake gave Sophia a chilly look before turning to Cori. ''With her arthritis, Maria is barely strong enough to help Sophia up. Sometimes Maria has trouble getting upstairs, particularly when it rains. Let's hope you've built up some muscles carrying that kid around.''

''Don't tell Corinne things like that. I get up all the time.''

''Liar.'' Blake towered over Sophia, giving the woman his best no-nonsense look. ''Your daughter is here to help you. She's going to learn right now what's best for you. And you're going to tell her when you need something. Agreed?''

''That's right, Mama.'' Cori stepped next to Blake.

Sophia rolled her head away. ''You have a child to take care of.''

''He's potty trained.''

''And I'm not.''

Her words sounded as if they were in jest, but Cori took them seriously, nodding and moving into her mother's line of vision. Blake admired Cori's perseverance. For whatever reason, Sophia didn't seem to want Cori involved in the less pleasant aspects of her care, yet she shunned the idea of a nurse.

''Much as I'd love to stay and hear you two spar with each other, I have work to do.'' Blake gently nudged Cori aside with his hand.

''I'll show you how to do it this time. She might need another break close to dinner.''

Sophia looked chagrined. ''You're taking away my dignity.''

Blake laughed as he helped her up. "You can say that after having stayed in a hospital and being wheeled around with a gown that didn't hide anything in back?"

Sophia gasped. "You never told me that."

"Didn't you feel that draft? Didn't you notice all the men in the hall turn and stare at your backside when the doctor made you get up and walk the hall?"

"You're shameless."

"Maybe," Blake allowed, glad that Sophia could still joke with him. She'd become a featherweight over the past few weeks. He doubted she weighed one hundred pounds. "It's best if you make her walk a little to keep her strength up," he said to Cori, who dogged them every step of the way.

Blake made sure Sophia was settled right in front of the commode before he turned and left the room. "I've been giving her some privacy, but I've known plenty of girls to travel in pairs to the rest room."

"I'll manage on my own, thank you," Sophia pronounced haughtily as Blake shut the door behind him.

"She won't be able to do it herself much longer," Blake whispered to Cori, whose eyes were trained on the door. "I've ordered a wheelchair and a bedpan."

"I've changed quite a lot of diapers. And I was with her the first time she had cancer, although she was always sending me away then, too." Cori paled, but she looked up at him with determination.

He liked the strength in her eyes. Maybe a little too much. Keeping his features neutral, he nodded and proceeded to tell her what he felt she needed to know.

"When she first came home, I tried those energy-boosting drinks on her, plus some yogurt and pudding. Anything I thought she might find palatable enough to eat. It all came up. She's not too concerned about eating now, but you should try to get something down her every hour. Even if it's only a sip or two of water."

Cori swallowed. "It's that bad."

He gave in to temptation and rubbed her shoulder. He could imagine the smoothness of her skin beneath her T-shirt.

''Don't let her fool you, Cori. Your grandfather and Luke...'' Blake paused to look out the window at the vineyards that he loved so passionately, wondering how much he could say to Cori, finally deciding the time for pulling punches had passed. He swung around to look into her trusting eyes. ''It's like they're waiting for someone to tell them this is it. And Sophia is playing things the same way. She won't ask for anything that will take them away from the business.''

The toilet flushed. His hand fell away, tingling from the absence of contact.

''If you two are through with your secrets, I'm ready to sit on something a little softer.''

Blake stepped toward the door, but Cori stopped him, her hand on his forearm. Her touch comforted him, making Blake want to stop running so hard, sit down and forget about all the turmoil around him.

''Wait. I'll get her.''

Blake nodded, pleased that she was willing to step right in.

''I'll tell the kid to come up here when he's done eating.''

She murmured the boy's name with a shake of her head.

When Blake would have turned away, Cori's hand remained. He'd forgotten how powerful her touch was. It used to reassure him she cared. Now he had to remind himself that she'd left him.

''Thank you.'' She gave his arm a gentle squeeze, her brown eyes easily meeting his. ''Thank you.''

Damn, if she wasn't thanking him again. Only this time, he didn't feel like a busboy.

''WHY DID YOU WANT ME HOME if you weren't going to let me help you?'' Cori asked her mother while walking her back to bed. Cori was finally communicating with her mother, and she owed it all to Blake. Her heart warmed to the idea.

''You have been helping me,'' Mama protested weakly.

''If you call sitting on my duff and listening to you all day 'helping,' then I suppose that's what I've been doing.'' She guided Mama into bed.

''I've enjoyed visiting with Michael. And you.''

''That's fine. But I want to know what's going on. If you need to go to the bathroom, let me know.'' A fool. That's what Cori was for not realizing her mother couldn't get out of bed. Enter Blake and his honesty, straightening things out again.

''That won't be necessary.''

''Yes, it is. When was the last time you changed your nightgown?'' No nurse, Maria barely able to climb the stairs, and only men taking care of her? Cori suspected Mama had worn the pink nightgown for a long time.

Her mother blushed but didn't respond.

''Let's change it now.'' Cori walked over to the dresser where her mother kept her lingerie.

''That won't be necessary,'' Mama repeated.

''Well, if you want to smell like overripe fruit, that's up to you.''

Mama's gasp would have been audible down the hall. Cori looked back at her mother, the pale pink nightgown hanging in loose folds around her bony shoulders.

''Not that you smell bad now, but I haven't seen you in a different gown since I came. What if someone comes to visit?''

Some of the spark came back to Mama's features, a slight tinge of pink touched her cheeks. Cori remembered her mother's unexpected words the other evening about John Sinclair. Did she still dream of his return?

''This is the thanks I get for making you wear that gown to the prom, isn't it?'' Mama asked.

''Good heavens, no. I haven't ever come up with a good revenge strategy for that one.'' Cori shook her head as she pulled out a blue silk nightie. ''You made me wear a burgundy dress with a poof skirt and puffy sleeves to the prom. I looked like a grape ready for harvest. There is no punishment to fit that crime.''

''You looked adorable.''

"Mom, I was sixteen. I had braces. How much more could you humiliate me?" Cori came back to the bed.

"I made you go with Langston Bixley."

Cori groaned dramatically, dropping her head back and rolling her eyes to the ceiling. "The biggest nerd in school. He wore a pocket protector in his tux." Cori didn't mention that Langston refused to dance even one dance with her. She'd spent the entire evening glued to the wall watching Nick Higgins, the boy she had a crush on, dance the night away with his date.

"Langston went on to become one of the brightest stars in Silicon Valley, now worth several million dollars. And his business didn't even waver when others were going bankrupt."

They grinned at each other. Cori reached down to take her mother's hand. She hadn't realized how much she'd missed her mother's sense of humor. Cori's throat worked itself into a vise and her eyes misted.

"Why did you want me home, Mama?"

Mama looked to be fighting tears herself. Cori couldn't remember the last time she'd seen her mother cry. The realization lurched her heart into her throat, and Cori's breath hitched.

"Because you're a part of this family. A part of my life. And I want you to know it. I just didn't want you to see me helpless."

Cori fought the onslaught of tears. "You sent me away last time. I remember taking trips with Luke and Grandfather on the weekends and worrying about you."

"I was vain enough that I didn't want you to see me unable to get out of bed. I guess I still am. And as much as I love Blake and Jennifer—" Mama's voice wavered "—I'm selfish enough to want my own daughter here with me when I go."

Tears spilled over Cori's cheeks.

"I was there for my mother, listening to her stories, her triumphs, her regrets. I wanted the same thing."

"It's not fair." Cori used one of Michael's favorite gripes. "You beat the cancer once."

"No, it's not fair. Maybe I should have gone to the doctor

sooner. I don't know if it would have helped. All I know is that I can't fight it their way anymore—with needles, drugs and no dignity. This has been the toughest thing I've had to do. I guess that's why God saved it for last.'' Mama squeezed Cori's hand. ''But I can face it with my little girl beside me.''

''I'll be here, Mama.'' Cori grabbed some tissues and they both blew their noses.

CORI LAY AWAKE IN BED later that night, staring at the ceiling and attempting to come to terms with mortality. She could deny it no longer. Her mother was dying. With that grim acceptance came fear. Breast cancer had taken both her mother and her grandmother. There could be cancer growing in Cori right now. Or she could get hit by a truck and die tomorrow. Either way, she needed to make sure Michael was taken care of.

Michael rolled over in his sleep, his arms skimming the polyester sleeping bag with a startling *hiss.* Who would kiss his cheek at night if she died?

Her brother, Luke, was too dedicated to the winery. He didn't have time to devote to a little boy. And there was no way her grandfather would take him. There was Sidney, her boss, who didn't know a thing about kids and wasn't likely to learn.

That left Michael's father. In her mind's eye, Cori saw swirls of brown hair on the crown of two heads, father and son. She saw Blake standing in the doorway of the pink room with an odd look of longing on his face as he watched her cuddle Michael.

Did he want a child of his own?

The night they'd created Michael had started out so magically. She'd come home at spring break wanting to make love with Blake. In her heart, she'd known it wasn't the right time. Cori didn't plan to come home after graduation except to visit. It wouldn't be fair to Blake. But she'd lasted five days before she snuck down to the river to meet him. They'd ended up in his bedroom, holding on to each other as if they couldn't get close enough.

The evening was perfect, until Blake asked her to move in after graduation. All the time they'd spent together, sitting at the river under a blanket of fog, talking on the telephone. Didn't he know Cori better than anyone? She'd thought he understood how important it was for her to get away from her family and make it on her own. But he hadn't. Worse, when she tried to explain her need for independence, he thought that she wanted to sleep with other men.

But her return home wasn't about her relationship with Blake.

Cori jumped up, pulled on her jeans and her red Stanford sweatshirt, and laced her tennis shoes without socks. She'd tell Blake. She'd tell Blake and no one else, for Michael's sake. What she and Blake had shared and then broken didn't matter. Michael's future had to come first.

Panicky steps took her down to the river through the fog. She knew the land intimately, had been sneaking down to the riverbank in the dark since she was twelve. Cori was panting more from adrenaline than from muscle strain when she got there. She couldn't outrun her need to protect Michael.

The Russian River flowed by dispassionately in near silence. Blake wasn't there.

She should go back. This was madness. She'd draw up a will for her own peace of mind and no one need ever know until she was ready to tell them. Unless it became a necessity. Then she'd have to rely on someone, maybe a stranger, being smart enough to find the will and follow her wishes.

Cori paced back and forth at the edge of the river. The fog's embrace was cool and comforting, but she was still restless. Michael's future needed to be secured.

She'd paced maybe a total of thirty seconds. She couldn't stand it anymore. Cori took off down the road along the river.

The road leading to Blake.

"I FINISHED TODAY'S homework. How much more of this old stuff do I need to do?" Jennifer snapped at Blake without lifting her head. She was bent over the kitchen table, nubby pencil gripped tightly in her fingers, red after hours of homework.

''Five more minutes.'' Blake pretended to be totally focused on the muted weather channel, masking his irritation with his sister as best he could. Every few minutes, he popped a peanut M&M into his mouth and sucked on it in an effort to keep a handle on his emotions. He was more than a little mad at himself for allowing Jen to slip this far. He should have known something was wrong when she'd started her Jekyll and Hyde mood swings about the same time Sophia had fallen sick.

''There's a weekend coming up, you know.''

''Yeah, well don't be planning anything with Shelly. You're grounded.''

''You only said that twenty times already.''

''A little less talk and we'd be done by now.''

''I can finish on the weekend. It's not like I'm dating.'' Her voice sounded wistful.

Did she like a boy at school? Blake opened his mouth to ask her, but the awkward question stuck to the chocolate coating his throat.

''What was that?'' Jen looked to the front of the house.

''Just finish the page,'' Blake said wearily. It was nearly eleven. If he crashed soon, he'd have about five hours' sleep before he needed to get up again to meet the field workers at first light.

''Something's out there. Didn't you hear it?''

''Jen,'' Blake warned at the same time that he heard it, too. Someone was knocking on the front door. No one ever knocked at their door, particularly at eleven o'clock at night.

Blake hurried to the front of the house, his mind latched on to the unpleasant possibility that Sophia had passed away. *Too soon,* he thought. His heart stalled when the door creaked open to reveal Cori, looking as if she'd just rolled out of bed—and not in a good way. Her hair was flat on one side and damp from the fog. Wild eyes and red cheeks, along with her shallow breathing, led him to believe she'd run over here. She looked terrible.

Who was he kidding? She was a beautiful damsel in distress, he thought guiltily, unable to think straight. Despite everything she'd put him through and everything he'd convinced himself she was, in the past twenty-four hours he'd recognized the strength and dignity of the woman he'd fallen in love with in the woman standing in front of him. Or maybe it was just that he wanted to remember and relive the feeling of excitement and intimacy of being with Cori. Either way, the sight of Cori filled him with the kind of anticipation he shouldn't have been feeling when expecting bad news.

"You're still awake." She stood awkwardly on the wooden porch, moving from side to side. "I saw the lights on."

Blake stepped outside into the chilly evening and closed the door behind him. He didn't want Jennifer to overhear what Cori had to say.

"Is something wrong? At the house?" How else could he ask Cori if her mother had died? Should he risk taking her in his arms when she told him?

"No, no." Cori shook her head and backed away, her eyes on her feet. "I'm sorry to have disturbed you. I just had to get away."

She looked it. The need to keep her talking and to find out what was wrong propelled him a step closer.

"I told you we were awake. Does Sophia need me?" *Do you?* He couldn't stop the thought.

Cori shook her head and hugged herself in silence. Why had she come in the middle of the night?

"Do you want a cup of coffee? I was just helping Jen with her homework." This was lunacy. Cori stood on his porch in the middle of the night, a magnet he was drawn to. Why couldn't he have gotten over Cori the way he'd convinced himself he had?

"Jen's lucky she has you to keep her on track."

Her praise seemed undeserved, given Jen's current predicament. "She hit twelve and became this being I swear I didn't raise. She takes all my energy and then some." He rubbed the back of his neck, admitting, "I could barely keep myself from yelling at her every time she gave me attitude today. I don't know how people raise more than one. Jen seems to be my limit.''

''Oh.'' Cori found it difficult to hide her disappointment.

The cold seeped through the porch boards, through his socks and into his toes, which were rooted a yard from hers. He realized she still hadn't explained the purpose of her visit.

''What was it you needed?''

Cori's eyes darted away from his. ''I...I just wanted to say...'' She shivered as she hesitated, then started again. ''What would you do if you had another child?''

Blake laughed once, a weak attempt to cover his confusion. ''That's not going to happen. Jen is my first priority. I don't even date anymore.'' Not since Cori and their major crash and burn.

Cori swallowed and looked at his socks. A raw silence settled between them. A foreboding thought crept unpleasantly into Blake's head as he waited for Cori to say something.

And then he knew.

Blake started to shake his head in denial even before Cori looked up at him and confirmed his suspicion.

''You have a child. *Michael.*''

''No.'' The first wave of shock shuddered through his system, followed by the numbness created by a lack of oxygen. The kid was too young, too small. Blake staggered back to the door, leaning on it for support as he drank air in deep, quick breaths.

Cori hugged herself tighter than before as she stared at him with those big, dark, lying eyes.

''I seem to recall using a condom.'' The anger crashed through him as the initial shock of her statement wore off.

''Condoms aren't one hundred percent effective.''

He made a derisive sound, one he'd learned from Jennifer.

She cleared her throat, her gaze sliding to the window to his left. ''My doctor wasn't sure if I was incredibly fertile or if you were one of those men with really potent sperm that can get a woman pregnant even if you use a condom, or if you were at the gate, so to speak, without one. Or it could've been both you and me combined.''

Her words brought back the memory of that one night in all its Technicolor glory. Burning for each other, they'd almost made love in his truck. He'd touched her before he remembered the importance of protection. They'd rushed upstairs to Blake's bedroom and a box of condoms.

The kid couldn't be his.

An image of the boy's ears sticking out came back to him with painful familiarity. Why hadn't he suspected anything before this? Because the kid's size made him seem too young to be Blake's? Because he was preoccupied with caring for Sophia? Because Blake hadn't wanted to consider the possibility Cori would raise their son without him?

Blake swore and rubbed his stiff neck. ''What makes you so sure it's mine?''

''You're the only one.''

''I recall you dumping me because you needed to be free.'' He would have married her. Hell, he would have married her and she hadn't even told him she was pregnant. Was he so far beneath her that he hadn't mattered enough for her to tell him?

''There was no one else,'' she said, holding herself stiffly. ''I couldn't come back here. I told you that. Several times. You wanted to stay.''

''I needed to stay for Jennifer.'' During all their conversations, he'd thought Cori had meant being away at school when she'd talked about her freedom—not leaving forever. Could that have been just wishful thinking on his part?

''And I needed to go.'' At his deepening frown, she tossed up her hands. ''Don't sweat it. My family misunderstands me all the time.''

Blake swore again. Louder. ''It's clear to me that I've never understood you.'' He tilted his head back and pretended to look at the cobwebbed porch rafters. ''Why are you telling me this now?''

When Cori didn't immediately respond, Blake dropped his chin to his chest and gave her a hard look. She wasn't mad, which meant she was holding something back with her Messina silence.

"You deserve to know," she said finally.

"Yeah, right." Blake blew out a frustrated lungful of air. "I deserved to know the day you suspected you were pregnant!"

"I was young and under a lot of pressure." Her face crumpled.

"Don't you dare cry." Blake took two quick steps toward her, forcing her to the edge of the porch. "Pressure, my ass. I wasn't good enough for you." He flexed his fingers to keep from grabbing her and shaking her into confessing her child wasn't really his. "Does anyone know? Your mother? Grandfather?"

"Mama guessed."

He recognized panic in her eyes. She didn't want anyone to know. Despite managing all of Messina's vineyards, millions of dollars' worth of property, he still wasn't good enough for her.

"Fine." He spoke tightly. "You've kept your little lie this long. Give me some time to get used to it before you tell anyone else."

"Thank you," she whispered, deceptive eyes full of unshed tears.

That was almost too much. "Hell, Cori, I don't know why you're thanking me, unless it's for my sperm donation."

CORI PEEKED into her mother's bedroom. In the dim hall light, she could just make out her mother's frail frame beneath the bedspread. Cast in shadow, the room offered no comfort to Cori this evening. The house, too, stood in oppressive silence.

She'd done the right thing for both Michael and Blake. So, why did she feel so lost? Because she couldn't tell Blake everything and he thought she was a selfish bitch.

Movement in the shadows startled her. Luke rolled off the couch with a grunt and padded toward Cori in socks and a pair of sweatpants. He gently took her by the shoulders and prodded her out into the hall, shutting the door behind them.

"What's wrong?" he whispered, peering down at her.

Cori rubbed her arms, shivering with the knowledge that she'd promised Blake she wouldn't tell anyone else.

"Have you slept here every night since she came home?"

Luke nodded with a grim smile. "I have a permanent kink in my spine." He arched his back with a groan. "Blake used to take the day shift, with Jennifer and Grandpop on afternoons and evenings. Maria's our reliever. Your being here has helped a lot."

Blake's watching her mother during the day must have made it impossible for him to finish his duties. Suddenly, Cori knew the source of some of Blake's sharp remarks. He had to have been relying on Cori to care for Mama so that he could do the job he was paid for. It must have been extremely annoying to hear her excuses—her own work. She'd probably disappointed Blake tremendously, for he wasn't normally a bitter man. Now she'd sunk even lower in his esteem. The realization that he'd resent her for what she'd hidden from him filled her eyes with tears.

"Did you and Blake fight?"

Cori looked pointedly at Luke. *Did he know?*

He shrugged. "Just a guess, but whenever you snuck out, it was down to the river. I've found Blake down there a lot over the years."

"You used to sneak into town," she countered without answering directly. Luke was more a prowler than she was, going into town and looking for girls, beer and fights. The sheriff had often escorted Luke home during his high school years, much to their grandfather's chagrin.

Luke rubbed the top of her head as if she were Michael's age. "Always the golden girl, staying out of trouble."

"Hardly." She hugged Luke tight, no small feat when he towered over her. "I've really missed you."

''Me, too, munchkin,'' Luke said. ''You know, I think it would have been great if you and Blake had worked out.''

Cori stepped back so that she could see Luke's expression, but he didn't wear a brotherly smirk, only a look of concern. ''Did he say anything to you?'' She wasn't sure if she meant now or back then.

''Blake?'' He shook his head. ''Didn't you know? He's part Messina. Doesn't say a word or ask questions about things that don't concern him. Grandpop loves him. It'll kill him if Blake ever leaves.'' Luke rubbed a hand over his face. ''Not that I think Blake plans to leave. He's too loyal to Grandpop.''

''He fits right in.'' Her grandfather would be crushed by what he would certainly consider Blake's betrayal.

Luke touched her shoulder with his fist in a playful punch. ''Just like Mama. You worry too much about everybody but you.''

HE HAD A SON.

Blake wasn't sure he was ready to accept it. He hadn't told Jen anything. Who knew how she'd take the news. Hopefully, Cori would keep her word—as good as that was—and not tell the rest of her family until Blake had time to get used to the idea.

There was no sign that Cori and the kid had been downstairs this morning. That didn't mean Blake wanted to see them. He especially did not want to see Cori. He wouldn't have thought that she could break his heart again, but she had. What little respect and rejuvenated love he'd held for her was buried beneath the oppressive weight of her duplicity.

He climbed the kitchen stairs to Sophia's bedroom, slowly for once, despite the fact that he had little time to waste.

It was early, with the sky still a soft shade of blue-gray. When it was light enough, Blake and his crew were going to begin the trellising. In this first phase, they made sure the recently pruned plants were still adequately attached to the trellising system. Like all vines, if not carefully monitored, a vine would grip itself or a neighboring vine, making harvesting exceedingly difficult.

Blake's pace quickened as he passed the pink room. He longed to see his son, but at the same time, Blake didn't want to face the kid. How was he supposed to treat the boy? All was silent behind the door and he passed it without incident, without relief of his tension.

He wondered how Sophia would treat him once he told her he knew about the kid. He didn't trust himself to say anything yet. Every time he mentally broached the topic with Sophia, he couldn't keep from condemning Cori. Blake could just hear him telling Sophia he didn't want anything to change between them, but her daughter was trying to ruin his life. Wouldn't that go over well?

Blake tapped on Sophia's door before stepping in.

"Good morning, sunshine," he said with false cheer.

Someone tugged the curtains open, spilling gray light onto a chipper Sophia propped up in bed. Cori stood awkwardly next to the window wearing blue capris and a short orange sweater that seemed to fit her like a second skin, stopping an inch shy of her navel. The combination revealed smooth skin across her softly rounded abdomen.

His child had grown inside that belly.

Cori lowered her eyes and disappeared into the bathroom, taunting him with a strip of bare skin at the small of her back. She didn't close the door. He could hear her moving things around, setting things down on the counter and pulling out drawers.

"Good morning, Blake." Sophia smiled in welcome.

Blake felt anything but welcome. With leaden feet, he moved to stand next to Sophia, the guilty defendant prepared to receive his sentence.

"Ready for your morning break?" His voice sounded coarse to his ears. Sophia knew what he'd done. Bless her heart, she hadn't held it against him, although she had every right to. Did Sophia know Blake had been kept in the dark all this time? He wanted desperately to ask her.

Cori pulled out another bathroom drawer. He wondered what she was looking for.

"I've already visited the rest room." Sophia's eyes twinkled. She raised her shoulders in delight. "Corinne and I managed."

An irrational pang of jealousy froze Blake in place. The only way he could pay Sophia back for all she'd done for him was to help her through this. Hard as it was on him, he should be happy someone she loved was here for her. Yet, this was usually his time alone with Sophia and he couldn't help resenting how Cori had so quickly replaced him.

Blake swung his head toward the bathroom in time to catch Cori framed in the doorway. Barefoot, the Barbie-pink of her nail polish was all the testimonial he needed to cement the frown on his face. Any chance of asking Sophia about the situation with Cori vanished.

If she thought he'd accept her declaration at face value, she could think again. He'd demand a blood test, ears be damned. Any kid could have big ears.

Cori worked her fingers nervously across the comb in her hands. The need to deny her claim bubbled dangerously close to the surface. Feeling as if he'd shatter if he held it in any longer, Blake turned to go.

"You can read the newspaper to me," Sophia offered. "If you have time."

Time. If he believed Cori, Blake had been robbed of time with his son. He tried to slow the quick, angry rhythm of his breathing, refusing to look at Cori. Time was something Sophia had little of. Her eyesight had weakened lately. She still liked to hear about the local news and have someone read to her. And he still cherished Sophia's company.

With a curt nod, Blake walked woodenly to the chair next

to Sophia's bed, then sat, the flowery fabric cool and unwelcoming beneath him.

"You'd better finish my hair before that rascal of yours wakes up."

Blake stiffened, trying not to watch Cori walk around to the other side of the bed. She climbed up on the mattress and sat next to her mother, legs folded beneath her.

Blake spent a few minutes trying to read the *Healdsburg Tribune.* His eyes scanned the words but nothing made sense. Finally, his brain recognized a headline.

"They found another sharpshooter in Napa."

Sophia made a sympathetic noise.

The glassy-winged sharpshooter was a large variation of grasshopper that was spreading Pierce's Disease through the vineyards, orchards and forests of California. The disease dehydrated plants, such that, once infected, essentially they died of thirst. Sharpshooters carrying the disease through California's Central Coast region had already destroyed billions of dollars worth of grapevines. There'd been some infestation in the Napa Valley, but none had yet been spotted in the Sonoma area. It was every grape grower's worst nightmare.

"Which winery?" Sophia asked.

"Heart's Glen."

"Tom Potiglia's place," Cori added, intent on brushing her mother's hair with delicate strokes. "Down by the river. They like water."

The unspoken thought being that Messina Vineyards was in danger, positioned as it was, close to the water. It was Blake's job to make sure that didn't happen.

"Any news on whether or not the wasps made it through the winter?" Sophia asked.

"No," Blake answered.

Tiny wasps had been released in several high-risk vineyards last spring, including the Messina property. The wasps ate the sharpshooter eggs, but scientists weren't convinced the wasps were hardy enough to make it through the brisk Northern California winter. Blake hadn't seen any since their release last year.

Silence crept through the room while Blake looked for other news that would interest Sophia.

''Says here Elizabeth Hurley stayed at the Madrona Manor last weekend.''

''Pretty woman. Bad luck with men,'' Sophia commented with her eyes closed.

''She has too many responsibilities to make a relationship work.'' Cori didn't look up from her task.

''That's no excuse,'' Blake blurted.

''It's not an excuse. It's reality.''

''Maybe she has all these men bedazzled.'' He'd never seen that movie of Ms. Hurley's, but he'd heard about her devil role from Jennifer.

''Maybe every man sees only what he wants to see,'' Cori replied.

Sophia frowned and opened her eyes. ''Is there something going on here that I don't know about?''

''No,'' Blake and Cori both denied emphatically.

Sophia looked doubtful, so Blake raised the newspaper between them. A soft sound at the door caught Blake's attention.

The kid—his son?—wandered sleepily into the room. If Blake's calculations were correct, he'd be about four, not three as he'd originally assumed. Wearing character pajama bottoms that didn't match the pajama top, the boy walked over to Sophia's bed and stood next to it, resting his head on the mattress.

''Come on up with Grandma.'' Sophia patted the bed invitingly.

The kid climbed up, then stretched out next to Sophia on his side and closed his eyes again, slipping his thumb into his mouth. His right ear jutted away from his head and pointed toward the ceiling. Lots of kids had big ears. Lots of kids sucked their thumb. Blake and Jennifer both had.

He's always been a good sleeper. Hadn't Cori said that to him a few days ago? Jennifer had been a good sleeper, too.

Cori reached across her mother and gently rubbed the kid's back. Her eyes met Blake's, and he glowered at her because he knew.

The minute he acknowledged the kid as his own, he'd have to abandon the relationship he had with the Messinas, perhaps even find another job. He could just imagine Mr. Messina's outrage and feel Luke's disappointment. They'd all side with Cori, blaming him for her predicament, for surely he was the reason she'd stayed away, although he hadn't known a thing. Damn, if he wasn't a fool who deserved what he got. Booted out of a job, banned from this family he'd come to love.

With Jen clawing for independence, he'd be alone once more.

CHAPTER SIX

"DO YOU EVER LOOK BACK on your life and wonder where it all went wrong?" Cori asked, sitting on the floor in the dark next to Luke, who sprawled across Mama's couch. They were whispering so as not to disturb Mama, and had been doing so since eleven. The clock downstairs had long since struck midnight. As best Cori could recall, it was the longest conversation the two siblings had ever shared.

"You're twenty-five, not eighty-five. Get a grip, Cori."

"Spoken like a man who hasn't had children."

"At least, none that I know of," Luke replied with a yawn.

Cori straightened. It was a perfect opening for a discussion about the decisions she'd made. "Would you want to know if you had a child?" She held her breath as she waited for his answer.

Luke continued to stare at the ceiling. "I don't know. I never thought about it before. Part of me is like, eh, I'm not that protective of my genes, so I don't need to know I made a little Tom or Susie as long as someone loves the kid. And then this other part—and this may come from living in this house too long—the other part of me says I've got to marry the woman and provide my kid with a real home." He yawned again and rolled onto his side, his sleepy gaze resting on Cori's face. "You know, that's not a question I can answer. Maybe you can answer it for me. How did Michael's dad feel about knowing he created a little rug rat?"

"I didn't tell him until recently." Cori tried not to squirm. The words sounded like an admission of guilt.

"Why? Did he beat you or something?" Luke sat up, suddenly alert, immediately ready to defend her.

"Why does everyone assume that?"

"Well, hell, maybe because the kid is dying for some male attention and as far as I know he never gets a visit from his own father. When you look at it that way, it seems like you should have a good reason for not telling the guy he's a father. I don't know of any other reason not to come clean."

Cori bit her lip. The only way to be judged fairly was to tell Luke the truth.

So she did.

"You really know how to screw yourself, don't you," Luke commented later in true brotherly fashion.

"Oh, that's very helpful." She hadn't told Luke so that she could be made fun of.

"Okay, okay. Blake's as good of a guy as they come. You did the right thing by protecting him and Jen. But if I were him, I'd be ticked that you took the decision out of my hands."

"He is upset about that," Cori grimaced.

"Does Grandpop know?"

"Not yet, but he will." Cori dreaded telling him yet knew she'd have to someday.

"You know, I feel for you, Cori. It hasn't been easy on you and it's not going to get any easier. I wish you had told me sooner."

"Thank you. I don't think it would have made much difference in where I ended up." She was in this alone.

"Maybe. Still, I'm glad you told me." Luke pushed her shoulder, then lay back on the sofa, pulling a blanket over much of his body. "Much as I love playing Dear Abby, it's after one and I need to get up early tomorrow. Go to bed."

JEN HURRIED across Healdsburg Junior High's nearly deserted campus. She hadn't gotten on the first bus after school because Devon Hamlisch had asked her to meet him out by the track. The earrings had worked. Fast.

Take that, Ronnie.

Jen straightened as Devon's dark head appeared at the corner of the building that housed both the gym and the band room. Heart pounding with excitement such that she barely paid attention to her upset stomach, Jen jogged the last twenty feet to the corner, her backpack bouncing on her back.

It was just like in the movies. Propped against the wall of the building, Devon looked so cool in his baggy jeans and Nike T-shirt. His dark hair was spiked and he wore a shell necklace. Despite the earrings glittering in her ears, Jen would have felt most uncool in her jeans and thin sweater untucked over her hips, if she hadn't been the one Devon had asked to meet.

He crooked his finger toward her and Jen thought she'd faint.

"Hi, Devon," Jen whispered in her best breathy imitation of Britney Spears, daring a glance up into Devon's face as she stepped within three feet of him. This was the closest she'd been to him since they'd been in the same reading group in fifth grade.

"Hi, back."

His dark eyes slid over her body, making her all jiggly inside, despite the fact that she didn't have anything to jiggle. He likes me, she thought, mirroring his relaxed position against the wall.

"Do you wanna make out?"

Jen almost fell over. "With you?"

He laughed, taking a step closer. He was a few inches taller than she was, so her eyes stared directly at his mouth. His lips were beautifully shaped and they moved. It took her a moment to register what he'd said.

"With me." He took another step closer and entwined his fingers with hers.

A jolt of electricity shot through her. Devon Hamlisch was going to kiss her. He was holding her hand. He wanted her to be his girlfriend. With the warm sun on her back, life had never been so good.

He leaned forward and, after a moment of hesitation, she tilted her head up. Jen closed her eyes as his hot lips covered hers. His hand nearest the wall settled on her hip. His head moved from side to side, just like in the movies. She let out a tense breath and stepped closer. His tongue pushed into her mouth.

Eeww, weird. Jen almost pulled away. She hadn't expected to feel the bumpy texture of his tongue. He'd been eating potato chips and she tasted them, too. If she could tell all that about him, there was no way she was putting her tongue in his mouth.

Then she was distracted by his hand creeping up underneath her sweater, fingers splayed across her skin and edging toward her white training bra. And there was nothing for him to find in her bra. She should tell him to stop. Now. But his tongue was practically down her throat. How could she say anything?

She put her free hand over his and gently tried to push it away. Devon emitted a noise deep in his throat that vibrated against her mouth. He kept moving his head from side to side and polishing her teeth with his tongue. His hand moved upward again, resisting her subtle message.

''No.'' Jen managed to break free of his suction lips. His saliva lined the outside of her mouth and she longed to wipe it away, but didn't dare let go of him. ''I'm...I'm not ready for that.''

His beautiful mouth curved into a sneer. ''Then, why'd you come?''

''I thought you wanted me to be your girlfriend.''

Devon laughed, not such a friendly sound this time, and Jen felt like a loser.

''We're here to have some fun.''

Jen's heart fell through her toes, taking the power of speech with it.

''Hey! What are you doing?'' Ronnie shrieked, rounding the corner with Kitty.

Skyler followed a few steps behind them.

''Oh God.'' Jen jumped behind Devon and discreetly wiped all traces of him from her mouth. She could hear them descending upon her, their footsteps a cadence of doom. ''Say something,'' she hissed at Devon.

"We were just talking," Devon said, but he was clearly not serious.

"You don't talk to *her.*" Ronnie ran past Devon and pushed Jen hard.

Jen's head bounced once against the stucco wall. Stars momentarily blinded her.

"Don't."

Someone moved next to her, almost on her toes. It didn't sound like Devon.

Jen's vision cleared. All she could see was Skyler's back.

"Run," he whispered over his shoulder.

Jen didn't wait for a second invitation. She exploded from behind Skyler and raced all the way to the bus stop, ignoring the shouts behind her, waving her arms at the bus driver so that the woman wouldn't drive away without her. Jen leaped up the steps without daring a backward glance. Then she sank into a seat on the far side of the bus so that Ronnie and Kitty wouldn't see her, even if they had followed her all the way across campus.

"I WAS LULLED into thinking I was safe. I don't remember ever being blindsided like this except by your father."

Cori, who'd been playing checkers on the floor with Michael, looked up at Mama's words. Since their talk the previous afternoon, they'd been more relaxed and candid with each other. Nevertheless, no one in the Messina household talked about John Sinclair. Just as, Cori realized, no one had probably talked about her these past few years. Here was an opportunity she'd longed for.

"Did he sweep you off your feet?"

"Oh, you don't want to hear about that."

Mama's cheeks seemed to have more color. Cori studied her mother more closely. Was she blushing?

"Yes, I do," Cori reassured her. She couldn't count the number of times she and Luke had asked about their father and been rebuffed when they were kids. They'd speculated about him, this man they barely remembered, but soon the unanswered questions had stopped.

Mama closed her eyes, and for a few moments, Cori thought she wasn't going to discuss John Sinclair, after all.

"He was a wonderful dancer. Did you know that all the women on my mother's side of the family fall for great dancers? Except for my poor Aunt Francesca. She died a spinster about ten years ago."

"I didn't realize dancing was a criteria I needed to judge men on."

"It's a weakness you should try to avoid. Good dancers don't generally make the best of husbands."

Cori chuckled.

Michael moved his checker sideways rather than diagonally and swept the last two of Cori's red pieces off the board. "Check," he said with a broad smile. "I win." He wiggled onto his tummy and began to roll the checkers like wheels across the carpet.

"John had this gorgeous blond hair that he combed back, but it had waves in it that gave me the impression that he was a little wild."

Cori ran her fingers through her own blond curls. "So it was love at first sight?"

"Oh, heavens no. It was more like lust…on my part, not his. I chased him all over the college campus. It took him a year to realize he loved me." She sighed, a smile coming over her features that lessened the toll of her illness.

"Why didn't it work out between you two?" Cori thought she knew the answer, but she had to ask, anyway.

"I was young. He was young. My father wasn't." Mama's smile faded. "John made me choose between him and my family. Unfortunately, he made the ultimatum when my mother was diagnosed with breast cancer. I couldn't leave and he couldn't stay."

"You never told me that before." Cori didn't remember her father leaving. Her memories of him living with them were vague and fuzzy—a tall man with a loud laugh who gave her airplane rides and chocolate treats. She couldn't recall any fights between her parents.

"I thought it made your grandfather look bad. Papa meant well. He just didn't understand I loved John." Mama's eyes drifted toward the window, making Cori wonder if her mother realized Salvatore was behind John's leaving.

"I want you to do something for me, Corinne."

Cori reached for her mother's fragile hand. "What is it, Mama?"

"I want you to find John for me."

"Find him?" Cori had to wonder if John Sinclair wanted to be found.

"Yes. I want him to know I made a mistake when I let him go."

"Oh." Cori didn't know the first thing about finding someone. She'd heard about people doing searches on the Internet and she'd seen private detectives on television, but that was about it.

"Of course, John should never have given me the ultimatum in the first place, but I'll forgive him the impetuousness of youth." Mama looked over at Michael, making sputtery engine noises as he rolled his wheels. "You know a little about impetuousness, don't you, dear?"

An image of Blake kissing her years ago wafted in her mind's eye. The memory shifted, updated itself. She saw Blake's leaner face approach hers, his gray eyes warm and welcoming. "Not anymore."

"I take it from the discussion this morning that you told Blake about Michael."

"He's hurt." Cori thought about the fierce looks she'd received from Blake. She'd have to hold on to her memories, because he'd never forgive her. "And angry."

"He has every right to be both."

"I suppose," Cori admitted, not liking that her mother wasn't sticking up for her.

"It's funny, isn't it, how family shapes the choices you make in life." Mama closed her eyes. "Promise me you'll find him."

"I'll do what I can." Unfortunately, Cori had no idea where to start. And she was certain time was running out.

"I WANT A TURN."

"Michael, I told you I'd let you check out the Disney site as soon as I find what I'm looking for." Cori tried to cover the helpless feeling of frustration welling inside her heart. They sat in the pink bedroom with Cori's laptop on the desk. Mama was napping.

Cori had tried several different search engines on the Web and found more than three hundred John Sinclairs across the United States. Unless she sent out e-mails asking each one if he was her father, Cori was at an impasse. She'd have to talk with Mama to whittle down the potential list. And Luke. Luke might know what to do.

Temporarily defeated, Cori typed in the address for the Disney site and helped Michael play with it for a while. She could just call a private investigator, but if her grandfather found out, he'd undoubtedly be furious. Salvatore Messina believed anything even remotely capable of becoming a scandal was to be avoided. On the other hand, if Cori asked her grandfather to find John Sinclair, he'd probably laugh in her face. There was apparently no love lost between the two men. She should have known there was a reason no one talked about her father.

Whatever Cori did, she'd have to do it quickly. For Mama's sake.

"Too tight." Michael squirmed to free himself from her embrace.

"Sorry." Cori eased her hold.

"Blue, Mommy." Michael pointed at the blue cartoon bug on the screen. "This room is pink. When are we going to make it blue?"

"Like, never."

Cori looked up to find Jennifer standing in the doorway, backpack slung over one shoulder, a disdainful frown on her face. Her sweater was pulled out of shape, sagging on her chest, probably stretched from her backpack, except that it was on the side opposite the strap on her shoulder. Jennifer's frown deepened when she realized where Cori was looking.

"Excuse me?" Cori asked sharply, forgetting for the moment that this was a girl suffering through more than the normal hormonal angst.

"You guys aren't staying, so you've got no right to change a thing in this room."

"Mommy promised," Michael wailed, shoving the laptop in frustration. He stomped to the bed and picked up his baby book. "It's not fair. I want to go home."

Cori stood and placed herself between Michael and Jen. "If I want to change anything in this room, I will."

"It's not like anyone needs you here." Jennifer's face flamed. "We were fine before you came and we'll be fine after you're gone." The girl spun around and walked away, her footfalls on the wood floor echoing her displeasure.

Cori turned and opened her arms to Michael, needing a hug just as much as he probably did. He flung himself at her. How would Jennifer react if she knew Michael was her nephew? Probably with more spiteful jealousy. Hadn't Mama mentioned something about Jennifer staying in her old room? Could it be that Jennifer considered the room her own? Yet, how could she, when all of Cori's childhood collections were here? Cori looked around and tried to see her bedroom through the eyes of a twelve-year-old. The doll collection. The frilly pink accessories. It didn't appeal to her anymore, but it might to Jennifer.

Cori sighed, vowing to be more patient with the girl.

"Too tight, Mommy." Michael wiggled with a sniff. "I hate it here. I want to go home." He hopped down and looked out the window.

"Don't you want to spend more time with Grandma?" Any time spent with her mother was precious to Cori.

"No. I want to go swimming." The pool outside of Cori's window had obviously caught his attention.

"It's still too cold to swim." Not to mention, he'd sink like a stone since he couldn't swim a stroke.

"That's not fair!" Michael stomped his sneaker on the carpet, then sighed, his voice suddenly calm and sweet. "Can we go outside?"

Cori chuckled at his ability to control his moods at such a young age. No doubt, he'd make a great lawyer one day. "Let's go, Peanut."

EVERYTHING WAS BETTER before Cori and that *thing* got here, Jennifer thought once she got to Sophia's door. Sophia seemed to be getting worse every day since Cori and her little mongrel had shown up. And Jen's room! She looked back down the hall toward the room she'd always stayed in when Blake was gone. They planned to destroy *her* room.

In that room, she'd dreamed of living in a perfect house in a subdivision where she could walk to Shelly's house. She'd dreamed of riding a bike down a paved road rather than a gravel driveway. She'd dreamed of Christmas with presents under the tree wrapped up beautifully like Sophia did them, instead of hastily with cheap paper and a small, store-bought bow. In Jen's pink room, those dreams seemed a little closer.

She'd never have those dreams again. And it was all Cori's fault. Jen stomped into Sophia's room.

Sophia blinked awake, startled. That was Cori's fault, too.

"Sorry," Jennifer mumbled as she stumbled to the desk by one of the windows.

"Problems?" Sophia's throat sounded dry.

Jennifer changed directions and held the cup and straw for Sophia, not answering. Jen avoided looking too closely at Sophia's pale face.

"It must have been something awful, right?"

How could Jennifer tell Sophia that she'd been humiliated after what was supposed to have been the most romantic moment of her life? She'd practically been groped during her first kiss, and the guy didn't even like her.

And once Sophia was gone, Jen wasn't going to be allowed back in this house. She'd have nothing. No cool room, no boyfriend. Nothing. Why did everything have to happen to her? This was the worst day of her life.

Sophia dribbled water down her chin and Jen automatically moved to wipe it off with a tissue.

"Is it so hard to see me this way?"

Jen blushed and shook her head, embarrassed that she'd been lost in her own problems, horrible as they were, when Sophia was dying.

"You don't have to come every day. I know the end is getting closer."

To her horror, Jennifer choked up. First Devon's betrayal, then the room. She just knew Cori had noticed that her sweater was stretched. And now Sophia talked about dying.

"You can't die." Jen found herself sobbing uncontrollably. "It's not fair."

"If life was fair, we'd live forever." Sophia reached up with a trembling hand to stroke Jennifer's hair. "I'm glad that my memory will live on in your heart, even if my body can't go on."

"Don't say things like that. You've given up." She hiccuped. "I thought Messinas never gave up."

"I haven't given up. I'm enjoying what little time I have left."

Embarrassed beyond measure that she was crying in front of Sophia, Jen pushed herself away from the bed and ran to the desk by the window, fully intending to grab her backpack and escape. If Jen was lucky, maybe she'd be beamed up to the *Enterprise* for a ride with Captain Picard like they did on all those repeats Blake made her watch. Then she wouldn't have to face anyone she knew on Earth ever again.

"Please, don't go, Jennifer." The words were weak and hard to make out, but they were more effective than any order.

Jen wiped her cheeks and took refuge in the bathroom. Her stomach hurt so bad that she thought she was going to be sick. It was a long time before she was able to come out, and then she only pretended to do her homework.

"WOW, BIG CAR, Mommy. Who's going for a ride?" Michael ran toward the elegant black limousine that was parked in front of the Messina home. He pressed his face and hands to the tinted glass at the rear door, trying to look inside.

"Can't you control that boy?" came her grandfather's surly voice from behind Cori. "I'm not going to arrive at the art gallery with those fingerprints on there."

Cori hurried over to Michael and pulled him away from the car before her grandfather said anything to hurt him. "Sorry." She tried to wipe the smudges off with the heel of her hand, but they just smeared more.

"What are you wearing? This is black tie." Her grandfather stepped up behind her. "You didn't expect to go looking like a hooker, did you? What would people say about us, then?"

The scathing remarks brought tears to Cori's eyes. The orange sweater was a mistake, just like the red dress. Still, what did it matter how she dressed? Why couldn't he see who she was inside?

"I wasn't planning on going," Cori finally managed to mumble.

"Come on, Mommy." Michael, her little guardian, tugged her hand, frowning at his great-grandfather.

The driver trotted around with a rag in his hand. "It'll clean right up, Mr. Messina." He wiped the window clean, and then opened the door for her grandfather.

Salvatore climbed in stiffly, almost gingerly. Cori's brow wrinkled. Something was wrong. Michael tugged Cori farther away and, unable to determine what bothered her, she reluctantly started to follow him.

"Luke, let's go," Blake called from behind her.

Cori turned. Blinked. Stopped in her tracks. Blake strode toward her in a tuxedo that was obviously tailored to fit him. Perfectly. Her hand nearly reached out to touch the fine black fabric covering his shoulders.

"You're going tonight?" Cori asked stupidly. She'd heard Luke tell Mama that he and her grandfather were going to an art gallery opening. She'd never imagined Blake was going, too. But looking at him, she knew he'd fit right in. Blake looked delicious in black. The society women were going to melt at his feet. Cori's own knees weakened from wanting his attention, craving his touch.

"Hard to believe the farmhand can mix in with the big guns?" Icy gray eyes challenged her.

The sweet scent of chocolate reached her. She swallowed, remembering how Blake tasted after eating that treat, how safe she'd once felt with his arms around her.

Cori's gaze dropped to the ground. She wished Blake didn't have the power to wound her so easily, but his anger was her fault. What could she say?

Michael tugged her hand again.

"Okay, baby," she said. "Let's go walk down by the river."

Blake leaned over her and pitched his voice low. "He's not a baby, Cori. Stop treating him like one."

Michael yanked on her arm. Clearly, he'd heard Blake's rebuke and wanted to leave. What kind of role model was she to let everyone talk down to her in front of her son?

"He's my baby. I can call him whatever I want." That ranked with one of the stupidest comebacks Cori had ever uttered, but at least she'd said something. She knew Blake was hurt by her news, but he had to stop lashing out at her.

Blake's brows lowered. Cori cracked his chilly stare with a heated glare of her own. Blake didn't say a word, at least not with his lips. The look he gave her spoke volumes. He'd never forgive her for keeping his son from him. Then he, too, disappeared into the limo.

"Hey, Sis." Luke ruffled Michael's hair as he passed the pair on his way to the limousine.

Cori stood indecisively in the walkway. She needed to ask Luke about finding their father. Just not in front of her grandfather.

Luke passed Cori with a smile and then leaned into the open limo. "Blake, did you see the highlights of the Kings game? Remember when we saw them play the Lakers last year?"

Cori opened her mouth to ask Luke if he could spare a minute.

"Get in," her grandfather grumbled.

With a tight smile, Luke did as he was bid. The door closed behind him with a soft *thud,* shutting Cori out.

A familiar pang of rootlessness caused Cori to trip as she and Michael skirted the walls of her family's home. Cori used to be the one Luke took to ball games. She used to go to art gallery openings with her grandfather. She used to be the one Blake smiled at. Suddenly, Cori felt like Cinderella, left behind as the others went to the ball.

Choices. Life was all about choices, she reminded herself. Cori had chosen life for Michael and security for Blake in a way that presented her with much-longed-for freedom. She couldn't possibly regret that. She couldn't possibly miss dressing up in those beautiful, too-tight-to-breath clothes and having her hair sprayed until it was stiff as a board. The bad food and good wine she couldn't stomach. The air kisses. The pressure from her grandfather to be perfect.

"You know what, Peanut?"

"What, Mommy?"

"I need a big kiss."

She lifted Michael up for a hug and a smacking good kiss. He giggled, his arms squeezed her tight. This was real. Her little boy was worth everything she'd gone through. Anyone who couldn't see that was living in the wrong world.

Looking down at her comfortable tennis shoes as she carried Michael out toward the neat rows of grapevines, Cori knew she'd chosen the right path.

Then, why was her heart just a little empty at the thought of everyone but her stepping into that limousine?

SALVATORE MESSINA LET the cool leather of the limousine envelop him as he waited for the pain in his hips to subside. He squinted, as much from the torment as the bright sunlight streaming through the limousine's open door.

"Get in," he grumbled at Lucas, impatient for them to leave. Art gallery openings stretched on forever. Salvatore Messina hoped he could find a chair. He'd gotten to the point where he couldn't stand long. Couldn't sit long, for that matter.

How had it come to this?

Blake sat opposite Salvatore, his back to the driver.

"Did you walk the vineyards today?"

"Yes, sir. Buds are about to break," Blake replied.

Salvatore nodded, satisfied. The boy was a good employee who knew his place without being too impressed with himself, and he was faithful to a fault. Salvatore appreciated that. Blake had filled Corinne's place by his side, but couldn't fill the hole left in Salvatore's heart made by Corinne's absence.

Lucas slid into the car and onto the seat next to Salvatore, sending a wave of air underneath the leather seat, jostling Salvatore's hips. He clenched his jaw against the javelin of pain that speared through his body. Then the pressure of the car's momentum as it pulled away from the house pressed Salvatore into the cushion.

It didn't help his mood that Lucas was no longer devoted to Messina Vineyards. That had been a shock. He'd thought he could rely on Lucas until the end. Salvatore stared out the tinted window rather than at his selfish grandson. The boy had the look of Anna and Sophia, but lacked their unwavering dedication.

Even after John Sinclair left, Sophia hadn't tried to talk to her poor excuse of a husband or mention his name to Salvatore again. No. She'd dutifully taken her place at her father's side, helping him fulfill the promise he'd made to her mother. Sophia had never complained and never let him down. Until now.

Now everyone in his family had either betrayed him or was abandoning him. In his mind's eye, Salvatore watched Corinne's little bastard skip lightly to the limousine and imprint his grubby hands on the glass. Corinne stood next to him, looking like common trash. He'd never imagined things would end this way. Salvatore was supposed to have many heirs to choose from—all of whom shared his vision and dedication to keeping the winery prosperous and alive.

Instead, he was painfully alone.

BLAKE STOOD IN THE chilly evening air outside of the Messina mansion, only half listening to Luke and Mr. Messina. Consumed with the need to tell his employer he was the kid's father, yet dreading the worst, Blake had been unable to concentrate on anything all evening. Good thing they'd been attending an art gallery opening where people drifted around all evening. If they'd attended a dinner, Blake would have been hard-pressed to hold an intelligent conversation with anyone.

''I'm taking Peter O'Bannon to dinner in the city tomorrow,'' Luke was saying. ''He'll need a tour of the vineyards the next morning. What time should I tell him, Blake?''

It took Blake a moment to realize Luke had asked him a question. ''Sorry, um, eight o'clock is fine.''

Mr. Messina snorted.

''Since when have we known wine critics to be early risers?'' Luke rolled his eyes at Blake.

''Pick a time, then,'' Blake said, nearly gritting his teeth in frustration. Wine critics seemed so inconsequential compared to fatherhood. Pulling his tuxedo jacket tighter against the cold, Blake looked up at the darkened windows on the second story and tried not to wonder if Cori was awake.

Luke looked strangely at Blake, then turned to Mr. Messina. ''Any hope Cori might do the tour?''

''Cori?'' His attention drawn back to the conversation, Blake felt suddenly inadequate at having Cori preferred over him.

''Sure.'' Luke shrugged, giving Blake another strange once-over. ''She used to do them all the time. People love her.''

Blake felt Luke put a little too much emphasis on the word *love*. However, Luke didn't say anything else. In the meantime, Mr. Messina scowled and shook his head.

''How about I see what time Pete wants to get up in the morning and I'll call you,'' Luke offered. ''We'll do it together.''

''Fine.'' Only, Blake was feeling anything but fine.

CORI WAITED IMPATIENTLY for Luke in Mama's shadowy bedroom. She'd heard the limo pulling up and then muffled masculine voices outside. After what seemed like hours, the front door downstairs had opened and closed, followed by the sound of footsteps on the stairs. Cori stepped out into the hall, relieved to see it was Luke and not her grandfather.

''Where's Grandfather?'' Cori didn't want to be interrupted when she asked Luke to help her find their father.

''Downstairs in his office. He doesn't usually come upstairs right away.''

''Mama wants to find John Sinclair.'' Wasting no time, Cori quickly recounted what she knew of their parents' ill-fated marriage. ''Should we hire a private detective?''

''Without more to go on, like a social security number, it'll take a while.'' Luke shook his head, a grim expression on his face. ''She doesn't have that long.''

Cori didn't want to bicker over the proximity of Mama's fate. ''We need to do something.''

''Ask Grandpa. He'll know where John Sinclair is, or at least how to find him.''

''Can you ask him?'' Cori dreaded the thought of having to ask her grandfather for anything. Despite wanting to create a stronger relationship with her family, Cori didn't know where to begin with her grandfather. She'd been avoiding him these past few days, eating dinner early in the kitchen with Michael and making herself scarce when she thought he might visit Mama.

Luke glanced downstairs, then looked at Cori. He shook his head.

''Why not?'' Luke was the logical one to do the asking. He was obviously in her grandfather's good graces.

''He knows I'm buying some property.'' Luke looked a little shamefaced. ''He's going to go on forever, and I need something of my own.''

Cori's jaw dropped. ''You're starting your own winery?''

Luke removed his cuff links with precise movements, his eyes darting down the staircase. ''You had the right idea years ago. He won't let me make even the smallest decision on my own.'' He rolled the black onyx studs like dice in his hands before looking at her again. ''I'm thirty years old and he still treats me like I'm twelve. I want to make wines my way. I need to prove to myself that I know what I'm doing.''

Cori couldn't believe it. Leaving the family fold voluntarily was far worse than being cast out. Her grandfather would consider Luke's starting his own winery the ultimate betrayal. But she understood her brother's need to prove himself, and how that need could eat away at you.

''He'll never forgive you.'' She spoke from experience.

''Yes.'' Luke's expression was grim. ''So you see, if you need to find John Sinclair, it's up to you to ask Grandpop.''

VOICES FROM DOWNSTAIRS announced visitors. Cori stepped out of her mother's room and into the hallway. She wasn't familiar with the woman talking to Maria at the bottom of the stairs, but she knew immediately by the black bag she carried that the woman was a nurse.

Apprehension knotted Cori's stomach. It wasn't that the nurse intimidated Cori. It was that the nurse held answers Cori would rather not have. She looked friendly, with laugh lines creasing her face, soft blue eyes and long black hair streaked with gray. She introduced herself to Cori simply as Nellie from Hospice and proceeded to give Mama a brisk exam, asking her about the effectiveness of her pain medication.

Mama's answers were curt. Her eyes shuttered away from Cori. Suddenly, Cori wanted answers.

After the exam, Nellie didn't comment, but patted Mama's arm and bid her farewell. After a moment's hesitation, Cori followed Nellie downstairs, feeling Mama's eyes upon her.

''Corinne, can you get me some water?'' Mama called after Cori, a note of desperation coloring her words. It was clear Mama didn't want Cori talking with the hospice nurse.

''In a minute.'' Cori wouldn't be put off anymore. She needed to know the truth about her mother's condition, even if she didn't want to hear it.

"Please." Cori caught up to the nurse in the foyer. "How is she? Really?"

Nellie turned, both hands clasped over the handle of her bag. She assessed Cori clinically. Cori recalled a similar look, almost, but not quite, pitying, when her doctor had told her she was pregnant.

"Her system is beginning to shut down. It won't be long now." Nellie spoke without emotion.

Cori had noticed her mother's skin had lost more elasticity just since she'd arrived. Sophia's stomach was swelling and her complexion was turning yellow, but Cori hadn't wanted to believe this was the end.

"When?" Cori managed to choke out.

"That I can't say. The body can hold on a long time with a willing spirit." Nellie reached out to briefly clasp Cori's cold hand. "Sophia's in a lot of pain, but she hasn't given up yet."

"She's waiting for something," Cori whispered half to herself.

"Perhaps," Nellie allowed, tilting her head to one side as she considered Cori's words. "Or perhaps she's holding on because you're here. In either case, get her to drink as much as you can, even if it's only a few drops sponged on her lips. But don't force her. Nothing will make much difference now. It's all up to her."

I have to talk to Grandfather.

CORI SAT UP GROGGILY in bed. Shadows hung like shrouds about the room. She peered through the darkened bedroom toward Michael's sleeping bag, wondering what had awakened her. She could just make out Michael's small form sprawled on top of his bag and hear his steady breathing.

A muffled male voice carried down the hall.

Cori bolted out of bed, tugging her sleep shirt down over her hips. She ran to her mother's room. Her hand wrapped around Mama's door handle, but someone spoke again and Cori hesitated.

"John, you've changed your hair." Sophia laughed. "Why would you dye your hair?"

"It's me. Lucas."

Cori opened the door. Luke stood next to Sophia's bed in his sweats and a T-shirt, his face drawn and unsmiling.

"I don't know any Lucas." Sophia eyes crumpled in confusion. She turned her head to look at Cori. "Do I?"

"Mama?" Cori gripped the doorknob, unsure of anything.

"I don't know either of you." Sophia's eyes began darting around the room. "Where am I? Who are you?"

"Mama..." Cori couldn't keep a matching note of hysteria out of her voice.

"Don't say anything to upset her," Luke warned, his eyes on Mama. "You're home."

"It's me, Mama. Corinne." Cori stepped forward.

"What's going on here?" Her grandfather paused in the doorway, dressed in a blue silk robe and pajamas.

"Papa?" Mama whispered fearfully.

"Yes, *cara?*" Cori's grandfather moved with measured steps across the room, pushing past Luke and blocking Cori's view of Mama.

"Who are these people? What are they doing here?"

Salvatore looked sharply at Luke. "Get out."

In two strides, Luke grabbed Cori by the elbow and swung her out the door, closing it behind them. They stood frozen in place, both trying to decipher her grandfather's soothing words. Cori could hear only the gentle timbre of his voice.

Hugging herself, Cori stepped back. "What's happening?"

Luke's eyes were still fixed on the door. After a moment, his gaze dropped to the floor. Then he smiled ruefully. "I can't remember the last time you and I were both barefoot." He rolled his head around with a sigh. "She's just a little lost. It happens every once in a while when she gets tired."

"She didn't know me." Cori shivered.

Luke leaned against the wall, looking weary. "No."

How could he be so calm? She rubbed her arms. "My own mother didn't know me."

''She didn't know me, either,'' Luke said softly.

''I didn't mean to sound like a selfish heel.'' Her brother had been hurt, too, and it sounded like he'd been through this before. How many times would Cori have to go through this?

Perhaps sensing Cori needed reassurance, Luke gripped her shoulder and gave it a squeeze. ''She might recognize you in the morning.''

If Luke's words were meant to calm her, they had the opposite effect. ''Might?'' These past few days had been bad. If her mother didn't recognize her, Cori didn't think she'd be able to hold herself together. What if Mama didn't remember Michael? How would Cori explain that to him?

''The closer we come to the end, the less lucid she'll become.''

''We are *not* near the end.'' Cori hadn't even asked her Grandfather about finding her father.

Luke stared at Cori in disbelief.

''I have to find John Sinclair first. I promised her.'' Cori couldn't hold Luke's gaze. She strained to hear what was going on in the other room, but there was no sound.

The grandfather clock in the hallway downstairs chimed the half hour.

''What time is it?'' she asked.

''Time for you to realize you may not be able to provide her with a fairy-tale ending. You think John Sinclair is waiting to hear from us? No way. There's a reason he doesn't keep in touch. And I, for one, don't want to know what that reason is.'' Luke didn't pause long enough for Cori to defend herself. ''This isn't some carefree visit. She's given you a couple of good days. Things are only going to get worse. The last thing we need is for you to delude yourself about what's happening here.''

Cori shook her head, unwilling to believe her mother's mind wouldn't clear. ''She's strong. She'll hold on until I find John.''

''She's dying. She won't wait for you or anyone.'' Luke's

eyes burned black in the dim hallway, his expression staunchly grim.

"Stop it!" She knew Mama was dying. Did he have to throw it in her face? "You say that and yet you go about your work and the social rounds, anyway? How can you?"

"Do you think it's easy? That Grandpop and I are heartless?" Tears glistened in his eyes. "She wants us to go on because she knows the situation we're in. We need every contact, every sale and every promotional opportunity. Grandpop's invested so much internationally that we're short on cash flow. Not that he'll pull back and listen to reason. This is another bumper crop year, which is going to drive down prices for the second year in a row, which means fewer profits again." He rubbed his eyes and then pulled the grim expression back in place. "So how exactly did you want me to behave?"

She saw their predicament clearly now—follow your heart and stand vigil at Sophia's bedside or attempt to save your life's work. Had Mama been faced with the same choices when her mother was dying and John Sinclair gave his ultimatum?

Cori sighed. "And you're leaving him." Poor Grandfather. "Your timing sucks."

"Hey, don't judge me. I'll work both places as much as I can." He swallowed. "Or as much as he'll let me. We both know this is his show. But when Mama's gone, I'll have nothing to keep me here." Luke stared down at her, his eyes shining with regret. "And neither will you."

CHAPTER SEVEN

SATURDAY DAWNED with a bleak sky that matched the frost of disappointment wrapped around Blake's heart. The detour Sophia had made from reality seemed more permanent this morning than during any of her previous episodes. To protect his daughter's peace of mind, Salvatore Messina had banned everyone but himself from Sophia's bedroom.

Since hearing the news, Jen had sulked over her homework at the kitchen table, limiting her communication with Blake to monosyllables.

Unable to shake the feeling that the end was near, Blake drove down by the river and parked, watching the water flow dispassionately past, while the sky filled with clouds to bursting. Some storms swelled the river from a lazy waterway to a powerful torrent, until the banks couldn't contain it in places. Blake had seen other properties flooded with brown murky water. Although it hadn't happened to the Messinas yet, just the thought that it might happen troubled Blake.

Usually, time down by the river cleared his head. Not today. Blake had more than enough to think about.

He'd never made his peace with Sophia. He regretted that immensely. And he couldn't seem to shake his ambivalent feelings toward his son. Could he learn to love the boy? If he did, he didn't think he could keep it a secret, as he'd done with his feelings for Cori. His honor demanded he tell Mr. Messina. Soon.

Blake was considering wading into the river and dunking his head in the hopes he'd find some clarity, when Cori and Michael appeared on the road that paralleled the river. From where he'd parked behind a large clump of blackberry bushes, Blake could just see them through a hole in the bushes, rounding the bend and coming closer. They each wore clear plastic rain slickers.

Unexpected yearning coiled in Blake's heart as he watched Cori run her hand over his son's hair. The murmur of voices drifted closer, unable to clearly penetrate the truck's insulation. Blake cracked open his window.

"No worms," the boy commented with a frown, crouching down to examine the dirt beneath a grapevine with a crumple of his dry slicker. His slicker was large, coming down to his knees, with sleeves cuffed several times.

"Not until it rains, Peanut." Cori's soft endearment carried her affection for her son.

Pit, pat. Pit, pat. Large, fat drops came down slowly, landing on leaves, dirt, the two of them, and Blake's windshield. *Pit, pat.*

The boy giggled, then began twirling about with his arms flung wide and his tongue stuck out to catch the rain as it gained momentum. Blake closed his eyes against a wave of isolation. Mr. Messina wasn't the kind to abide those who broke his trust. Admitting Blake had fathered Cori's child would shatter that trust. Sophia would die, Cori would tell Mr. Messina about Michael, and Blake would lose this place he'd grown to think of as home. Then Cori would return to Los Angeles and he'd never know the boy she claimed was his son.

And he was curious about that boy. Cautious, but curious.

The kid stopped spinning and staggered dizzily until Cori grasped his arm just in time to save him from plopping his bottom onto the soft, wet earth. Cori laughed and hugged him tight before pulling him behind the bushes and out of sight. Blake's heart was tight with yearning. He longed to experience that closeness with his son, to see the boy's face light up with laughter and love when he looked at Blake, to be able to hug his son.

"Wait until you see the river in the rain, Michael. It's awesome."

Unable to resist, Blake stepped out of the truck and into the now-steady rain. The only protection he had against the shower was a beat-up baseball cap and a red flannel shirt over his black T-shirt. He hadn't anticipated being in the rain, but the thick canopy next to the river sheltered him.

Blake found them perched beneath a spreading oak tree, sitting on a gnarled top root. They watched the rain bounce across the river.

Cori leaned her shoulder into the kid's, just one more act of love Blake couldn't indulge in. "Didn't I tell you it was awesome, Peanut?"

The boy nodded reverently, craning his neck to look down river. "Where are the boats?"

"No boats when it rains," Blake said from the other side of the tree.

Cori nearly jumped out of her skin. She recognized him, then turned crisply away, obviously still smarting from the harsh words he'd tossed at her lately.

Too damn bad. He wasn't the one who'd lied all these years. He turned his gaze completely on his son. The kid regarded Blake just as carefully.

"Do you like the rain?" he asked the boy.

Michael nodded cautiously. His previous experiences with Blake hadn't been easy ones. Perhaps sensing Blake's need to make contact with him, Michael added, "I like the water. I'm a good swimmer."

The tightness in Blake's chest eased.

Cori shook her head.

Michael noticed and frowned at his mother. "I can swim."

"You sink," Cori said, softening the words with a smile.

"I don't sink!"

She laughed, the tender sound tingling through Blake's veins.

"I mean, you haven't learned to swim across the pool yet, Peanut."

The warmth of their conversation crept into Blake's heart,

easing the loneliness. It was almost as if they were including him in their intimacy. A trio, not a pair.

''This summer. Miss Wendy is teaching me.'' The kid spun around to face Blake squarely. ''Can you teach me swimming? Grandma has a pool.''

Blake's throat worked. He'd loved teaching Jen the basics of swimming, fishing and playing catch. Would he have that chance with his son?

''Michael, I've told you that pool is too cold and we didn't bring a suit.'' Cori's words were firm.

''I can teach you someday,'' Blake offered.

''Today?'' Michael smiled brightly, hope bubbling in his brown eyes.

Blake shook his head. ''Not today.''

''Never,'' Michael huffed and turned back to the river. So young, yet he already seemed able to identify pipe-dream promises made by adults.

''We need a sunny day.'' With effort, Blake transformed his voice into a pitch that might interest a small child. ''A warm sunny day when the wind doesn't prickle your skin.''

Both Cori and Michael swiveled around to look at him. Cori seemed just as mesmerized by Blake's tone as Michael was.

''That day, you know, before last night. It was sunny,'' Michael said.

''*Yesterday* was sunny.'' Blake nodded, completely in sync with his son. ''But it was *brrr* chilly without a sweatshirt, wasn't it?'' Blake rubbed his arms for effect.

''No. Mommy wore shorts.''

Blake's eyes darted to Cori. She'd worn that skimpy sweater, too, taunting him with glimpses of that glorious bare skin. Anger colored his words. ''Your mom shouldn't be wearing shorts in February.''

''We can't all be perfect,'' Cori replied lightly, as if he hadn't just attacked her verbally.

''She wore shorts at Christmas,'' Michael said defensively. ''Even Santa wears shorts. I've seen him.''

Blake rolled his eyes. He supposed in sunny Southern California, Santa did make appearances in shorts. ''It's hard to fight that kind of logic, except to say it's wrong.''

Michael regarded him silently for a moment, his little face scrunched into a frown. ''That wasn't very nice,'' he said. ''You should say sorry.''

Had he gone too far? The rain continued to drum around them while Blake's conscience wrestled with his hurt. Cori looked out at the river, leaving Blake to deal with his comments and his sensitive son.

''Sorry.'' The apology sounded as reluctant as it felt. Yet, Blake was humbled by his son's sense of what was right and his courage to speak up for his beliefs.

Michael's hand settled into Cori's. His vote was cast. ''Can I finds worms, Mommy?''

''Find,'' Blake corrected before Cori could.

Michael kept his eyes on Cori. ''Can I?''

''Let's look for a good patch.'' Cori stood and scanned the area through the downpour, presumably for a good worm-hunting ground. Her gaze kept coming back to a patch of wild grass beyond the oak's branches.

''You hunt for worms?'' Blake asked.

Michael nodded solemnly.

My son is a geek. Blake sighed. Could things be any worse?

''Over here.'' Cori led Michael out from under the oak's protective umbrella with a crinkle of plastic.

Already soft, the dark brown soil sucked at their feet as they walked, making a light *whoosh* with each step they took. Michael giggled, drawing a smile from Cori. Blake was definitely the odd man out.

''He's getting wet,'' Blake observed sourly from underneath the tree.

''Just his shoes,'' Cori called back cheerfully, setting Blake's teeth on edge.

Didn't she know that responsible parents didn't let their kids get wet?

The two circled the patch of grass, peering through sheets of rain, while Blake waited underneath the tree. Wind ruffled

Cori's hood back and rain landed on her face. She yanked the plastic forward, then leaned down to do the same to Michael's hood.

The boy waved her hand away. "Where are they?"

"I don't know. It's certainly wet enough."

Michael squatted for a closer look. Michael's slicker was so long that it protected his bottom from the backs of his heels.

Still, Blake felt compelled to watch out for him. "Careful of the mud on your shoes."

Neither Michael nor Cori dignified that comment with a response, further increasing Blake's feeling of separation. A return to the pair.

Cori leaned over the grass, parting it with her fingers. "It's a rare treat to be searching for worms in the open. Usually, we rush out to save the ones that crawl from the lawn sprinklers onto the sidewalk, don't we." Cori ran her fingers over the grass again.

"No worms?" Michael asked.

"Maybe it's raining too hard, Peanut."

"I'll wait." His knees dropped forward onto the grass, still protected by his long slicker.

Blake believed the boy was willing to wait out the downpour. And it looked like Cori didn't care. What parent encouraged her child to hang out in the rain?

"Unbelievable." Blake grabbed a stick off the damp ground and launched out from under the tree. He wasn't going to let his son stand out in the pouring rain all day waiting for worms.

As if on cue, the rain came down vehemently. Almost immediately, Blake's shirt and jeans were plastered to his body. His frustration burst into anger when he noticed Cori trying not to smile.

"You need a jacket." Raising his voice to be heard over the downpour, Michael stood and looked up at him.

Blake poked around the grass with his stick, wet material clinging to his every crease. "One worm? That's all we have to find?"

"Okay," Michael said, watching Blake with interest.

It didn't take long.

"Here." Blake bent the grass down on either side so that Michael could see it. The worm was a prime specimen, nearly five inches long, very fat and obviously upset at being exposed. It squirmed and twisted, trying to dodge the fat, cold raindrops that hammered its body.

"You did good," Michael said. "He's a beauty."

Blake's anger cranked down a notch at his son's praise.

"Now can we get out of the rain?" Blake looked up at Cori with an icy stare. Water ran down the sides of his face. Water seeped through his baseball cap. They, on the other hand, were dry. Instead of conveying the derision he expected, Cori smiled at him as if he'd done something wonderful.

"Can't we find more?" Michael asked.

"No." Blake tried, because of Michael's praise and Cori's smile, to keep his tone even. "You're wet. It's cold. You'll get sick if we stay any longer."

"Goodie! Let's stay." Michael clapped wet hands. "We stay home when I'm sick. And I wanna go home." The kid chucked off his hood and tilted his face to the heavens.

"Not acceptable." Blake straightened abruptly at his son's desire to leave, startling the other two enough that they stumbled back. Where did that kid come up with his ideas? "Come on. I'll give you a lift to the house."

"But I'm not done," Michael protested.

"Yes. You are."

Michael turned to Cori, pleading his case. "Mommy?"

She sighed, and Blake could tell by the way she looked at him that she hated to admit he was right. "It's raining too hard. Even the worms are hiding." She took Michael's hand.

Blake spun away, soggy and anxious to escape the deluge.

Behind him, Michael began to whine. A glance over his shoulder revealed the boy trying to twist his hand out of Cori's grasp.

After a few seconds, Blake took a step back toward them, intending to make his son behave.

"Don't," Cori warned softly.

Blake's foul mood deepened, but he turned his back on them, assuming they'd follow. If she was willing to live with Michael's tantrums, that was her problem. Forget the terrible twos. From what Blake had witnessed, Michael was in the frightening fours.

BLAKE DROVE BACK to the main house to the backdrop of whining child. It made him appreciate Jen's silences all the more.

Cori did nothing about the kid's gripes. She sat next to the window and ignored them both, either from anger or the patience of a saint, Blake didn't know which.

As they approached the house, Michael was down to an exhausted mantra: ''Not fair, not fair.''

Blake parked and led them into the kitchen. ''Slickers off. Shoes to me. Let's go.''

Cori opened her mouth to protest, but Blake shook his head. ''Both of you. Now.''

''Why does he want my shoes, Mommy?'' Michael gaped at Blake.

''They're muddy,'' Blake answered before Cori could. ''As soon as you take them off, you go upstairs and take a bath.''

''I took a bath already.''

Jen had never argued with Blake when she was four. Blake turned on Cori. ''Don't you use any discipline on him?''

Cori wouldn't look at Blake, much less answer. He could sense her disapproval, possibly as easily as she seemed to sense his. Cori shed her slicker, peeling it up over her head. Drops fell onto her T-shirt, dotting her breasts. She knelt to take off her shoes. Blake did the same rather than stand like an idiot and watch her. Wet denim constricted unpleasantly against his skin. He couldn't wait to go home and change.

Seeing that both adults were taking off their shoes, Michael stopped arguing and began fumbling with his own. He stood and stomped his feet. ''I can't get them off.''

With a sigh, Blake moved in front of the boy. He tossed up

his hands when he saw the kid's shoes. "Tie shoes?" They were double-knotted. Wet double knots.

"All the big kids have them," Michael said, puffing out his lower lip.

"Until you can tie and untie them yourself, you should only have Velcro shoes." Blake didn't know what Cori was thinking to have bought the boy tie shoes.

"Thanks for cleaning up." Cori's tennis shoes landed with a soggy splat next to Blake's knee. "I'm going upstairs. Michael, you come right up when you're done."

Blake's fingers tugged on the blasted knots. He was wet and tired. Now he was alone with the kid and he wasn't sure how he felt about it.

"I only found one worm," Michael said.

Irritated. That's how Blake felt. "One worm looks just like the rest in the rain."

"You're not the boss of me." Michael crossed his arms over his skinny chest.

With effort, Blake remained silent.

"My mom tells people what to do. You're not the boss of me."

Blake attacked the knots with renewed vigor.

SALVATORE MESSINA NOTICED Corinne peek into Sophia's bedroom. He sat in a chair next to the bed. Sophia slumbered peacefully, still lost in the past.

"How is she?" Corinne whispered.

"She's not back yet."

Corinne paused, seemed to blink back tears. "I need to speak with you."

Hope taunted Salvatore. Was she going to apologize for her behavior all those years ago and open the door for him to do the same? He'd missed having Corinne by his side. He could use her business acumen.

"Outside," she added, snatching hope away with her serious tone.

Salvatore scowled at her. He wasn't about to let her see him struggle to stand, but his granddaughter wasn't budging. After several strained seconds, he said, "Give me a minute."

Corinne withdrew to the hallway.

Salvatore lumbered out of the bedroom and pulled the door shut behind him. He met his granddaughter's gaze expectantly.

She didn't waste any time. "I need you to find John Sinclair."

The request took Salvatore by such surprise that he harrumphed before he could halt the reaction. The pain in his hip and his heart were making it hard to control his emotions lately, he rationalized.

"Feeling the need to search out your roots?"

She tried to scowl at him, but Corinne had never been good at hiding her emotions. She was upset. Near tears. "Mama wants to see him." She swallowed. "Before."

Her words hit him harder than he would have liked. He needed to talk with the doctor about his medication, because it obviously wasn't working. The pain hit him with dizzying speed. The need to curl up, give in, was almost overwhelming. And he couldn't do that. Not now. Not ever.

He drew himself up, ignoring the sharp pain in his hip and the ache in his heart.

"This family doesn't need John Sinclair." He'd bought off his daughter's mistake more than twenty years ago. He wasn't about to open the door to that swindler again. Sometimes he looked at Corinne's blond wavy hair and saw too much of John Sinclair for his liking.

"But Mama does," she said.

Silence dropped between them.

If Sophia came out of it, he'd have to speak with her, remind her why she didn't need John Sinclair in her life. Perhaps even tell her a little about the kinds of things John Sinclair had done with the money he'd bought him off with.

"We'll make a deal."

Salvatore laughed. Even to him, it sounded hollow. "You don't have anything I want." He wanted his daughter to outlive him. He wanted his winery to go on forever.

"I'll tell you who Michael's father is."

Salvatore peered at Corinne more closely. Things were getting interesting. In fact, if he thought about it, this was good. Finally, he'd be able to make the cowardly bastard pay and set things right with Corinne.

"Yes?" he encouraged.

But Corinne only shook her head. "You produce John Sinclair, help Mama make peace with him, and I'll complete Michael's birth certificate."

"How do I know you'll keep your end of the bargain?"

"You know I will."

And looking into her brown, tear-filled eyes, he did.

WITH EFFORT, Salvatore returned to Sophia's bedside, lowering himself into the chair with most of his weight supported by his arms. If Sophia's mind returned, he had to find a way to broach the subject of John Sinclair. He wasn't about to let that charlatan into their lives again. There might just be a way to convince Sophia she didn't need to see him *and* finally achieve justice for his granddaughter.

"You should be taking your medication."

The words surprised him, coming as they did from Sophia. She'd come back to him. He wanted to weep with joy. But he didn't. He frowned, instead.

"What medication?" Salvatore thought he'd been successful in hiding his weakness from Sophia. The last thing he wanted was for her to worry about him.

"I don't have enough time, Papa, to play games." She paused, struggling for breath. "Tell me what's wrong."

"There's nothing wrong with me." But he wouldn't meet her drawn, dark eyes.

"Mama always said you were stubborn."

A lump formed in his throat at the thought of Anna and Sophia both alive, laughing and talking about him.

"She said you needed strong people to love you."

He looked at his hands, scarred from hard work and spotted

with sun damage, not knowing what to say. It was true that Salvatore had no patience for māma's boys or whiners.

"I'm sorry I haven't been strong enough, Papa."

His head shot up and Salvatore met her gentle brown gaze. "Whatever gave you that idea?"

"I can't help you anymore." Her voice sounded small, like a young girl's. "Mama told me how important the winery was to you."

"I built it all for her."

"All she cared about was your love."

Salvatore scowled, refusing to acknowledge that he might have disappointed his beloved Anna. "All this is for her."

"You could have been a ditchdigger and she would have been happy."

"Not true." He denied the notion hotly, fighting the old insecurities. "Her family thought I was worthless."

"She didn't."

"Respect and reputation are important."

"Not as important as love." She sighed. "Love brings everything you need." Her voice slowed. "Richer or poorer. Better or worse."

Salvatore knew she was thinking of John Sinclair, of the vows Salvatore had forced John to take because Sophia was pregnant and foolishly in love with him. By mutual silent agreement, they never talked about that part of their past.

"You don't need him."

"I want to make my peace, that's all. We have no future together." Sophia paused, her eyes tearing up. "Can't you do this one last thing for me, Papa?"

"No." The gruff word barely escaped him. He wanted so much to please his daughter. He'd give her anything. Anything but John Sinclair.

"JENNIFER?"

Jen's heart clenched at the sound of a boy's voice on the other end of the line. She hadn't wanted to answer the telephone, except that Blake was out and she knew he'd go ballistic if she didn't answer and it was him. She never wanted to go to Healdsburg Junior High School again. She could hang up now, claim it was a wrong number, or succumb to curiosity and more degradation. Curiosity won out.

"Yes?"

"It's Skyler."

Dread filled Jen's spirit.

"Jen?"

"I'm here." Bring on the humiliation, she thought, closing her eyes. Heaven knows, she deserved it.

"You know what happened yesterday?"

"Yeah." How could she forget? Her first kiss had been publicly humiliating.

"I think you got caught in a fight between Dev and Ronnie."

The situation just kept getting better and better. So, Devon had used Jen for more than an after-school grope. He wanted to get back at Ronnie for something, and Jen was gullible and conveniently available. What did you say to that? Paint a big *L* on Jen's forehead for *loser?*

"Jen?"

"Yeah?"

"It's not so bad."

Jen rolled her eyes to the ceiling and blinked to keep the tears at bay. "How could that possibly be?"

"Well, when people talk about it, you're gonna look like you came between them. You know?"

"Oh." Now, that was cool. Jen wrapped herself around the thought that she was a home wrecker. Not bad for a girl still in her training bra. If it were true. "Skyler?"

"Yeah?"

"Why are you telling me this?"

Now it was his turn to be silent. If Skyler was putting one over on her, Jen would kill him.

"There's one of those craft shows out at the square tomorrow. Are you going?"

"Doubtful. I'm, like, grounded until I'm twenty. Besides,

why would I want to go to one of those?'' They were so uncool, with all the tourists and everything.

''My mom runs a booth and I have to help her. I was just wondering if I'd see you.''

This was one of those *X-Files* moments where you couldn't believe what was happening to you. In the past twenty-four hours, one of the most popular boys in school had tried to feel her up and now another was either looking for the same thing or actually liked her.

Jen recalled how Skyler had stuck up for her at the library and then shielded her from Ronnie yesterday. Could it be?

Naw.

''You aren't asking me there because you think I'm easy, are you? Because if you are, well, you just better not.'' As threats went, it was pretty lame, but it seemed to work.

''No, no, no. I...''

Someone in the background told him to get off the phone.

''...I think you're cute,'' he whispered right before he hung up on her.

Jennifer carefully placed the receiver in its cradle. This was definitely weird. She needed to call Shelly and spill her guts about the whole episode. And somehow, she'd need to twist Blake's arm to break out of this prison tomorrow.

Or not. It would be safer to stay at home.

Still...

SALVATORE HOBBLED into his home office, completely drained. Sophia's battle was nearing its end. Mentally, she'd returned to him, her mind tentatively back in the present with no recollection of the scare she'd given them all. Corinne sat with her now.

With heavy heart and painful limbs, Salvatore focused on the one thing that could help him through this. Work.

Outside, the rain continued to pelt the vineyards with moisture that would bring the vines out of their winter hibernation. The dark gray skies blocked the sun, making his downstairs office seem dark and depressing.

Carefully, Salvatore lowered himself into his chair behind the massive cherry wood desk Sophia had given him for Christmas one year. With a minimum of movement, he booted up his computer and flicked on the desk lamp. Several minutes later, he surfed the Internet to catch up on the latest vineyard news.

Salvatore was reading about the glassy-winged sharpshooter sightings when something bumped against his knee. The reflex sent tremors of pain up his spine.

"That's a cool hopper," Michael said, leaning trustingly against Salvatore's leg.

Salvatore glanced up sharply, but Corinne wasn't in the room. "Where's your mother?" he asked the boy.

"She's upstairs with Grandma." His big brown eyes were glued to the computer screen. "Do you like bugs? I do."

Salvatore looked at the screen and then back at his great-grandson, battling a reluctance to show even a hint of acceptance—since that would mean Corinne won—with a true curiosity and interest in the boy.

"Not this one," he said finally. "It's a bad bug."

His little eyes blossomed and focused on Salvatore's face. "Does it kill people?"

"No." Salvatore clamped his jaw together as Michael leaned more of his small frame against his leg. "It kills plants." The boy was amazingly affectionate considering that Salvatore had been so cruel to him. Perhaps the boy had Corinne's and Sophia's ability to forgive and love people as unlovable as Salvatore.

"Oh." Disappointment dragged the word out. He looked back at the computer screen. "Then, can I have a turn?"

Or perhaps the boy was as cunning as a true Messina. Salvatore laughed openly for the first time in months.

Hope had returned to the Messina family.

LUKE STEPPED into Mama's dimly lit bedroom, vigorously tugging his tie loose.

Sitting in the chair next to Mama's bed with her feet propped up on the mattress and her eyes heavy with the need for sleep, Cori didn't move more than to turn her head in his direction.

''Rough night?'' Cori asked in a whisper so as not to wake their mother.

''Hundreds of wine critics in this world and I have to get the one who thinks he knows how to make my wines better.'' Luke whipped his tie off and pitched his voice into cultured nasal tones. ''You Messinas have been making the same style of wine for years. Isn't it about time your wines came into the next century?''

''Peter O'Bannon?'' Cori guessed.

Nodding miserably, Luke continued his lament. ''He could tell Coca-Cola how to improve their formula. It was on the tip of my tongue to tell him I've proposed style changes for years.'' He sprawled onto the sofa, long limbs everywhere, eyes cast to the ceiling as if searching for relief. ''You don't know how bad I want out of here, to have the freedom to create wines my way.''

Cori nodded sympathetically. Messina Vineyards was built on making a consistent style of wine that their grandfather had perfected years ago. Those familiar with their wines knew what they were getting with every bottle.

''I've got to take him to breakfast tomorrow and then on a tour.'' Luke groaned. ''How do I defend what we do convincingly when I don't agree with it? Humiliation with no recourse. There's a fate worse than death.''

Cori slumped deeper in the chair. ''You tell him the truth, that Messina wines have been built on a consistent taste that consumers come back to. We're not about to become a flavor-of-the-month winery.''

''Oh man, I should have thought of that. Instead, my eyes glazed over. Can you think of some more comebacks for me?'' Suddenly, he sat bolt upright. ''Or better yet, go in my place.''

Being active in the wine industry again. Not only that, but doing something for Messina Vineyards, for Mama, really, who used to handle interviews like this. The idea beckoned with unreasonable strength. It was what she longed for and what her grandfather had forbidden her to do. Rolling her eyes, Cori turned him down. "I'm sure Grandfather would freak out."

"No, he wouldn't. Nobody charms the masses like you do. He knows only good can come of it. Between the two of you—"

Reason returned. "Sorry, I signed a noncompete contract with Bell-Diva. I can't work for any other alcohol beverage companies while I handle their public relations. And I canceled a meeting with them this weekend because of Mama, so I really shouldn't even stretch their goodwill." She'd called Sidney first thing Saturday morning to cancel her meeting with Bell-Diva.

"We don't compete with beer." Luke looked at Cori as if she'd lost her mind. "Besides, who's to know?"

"What part of *no* don't you understand?"

Luke continued as if she hadn't protested. "This is perfect. Peter won't know what hit him. And we really need a good spin on his review."

"Not happening." But Cori was smiling. It was a challenge and, therefore, tempting.

"Maybe you can feed him that story about how we ended up growing Pinot Noir instead of Cabernet Sauvignon."

She tried again. "Who would sit with Mama in the morning?"

"Details. Maria's here. Jennifer's always around." He walked over to her chair and knelt beside her. "Tell me you don't want to go even a little bit and I'll let you off the hook."

"Uhhh," she hedged.

"You don't really want to hear about me losing it in front of Peter O'Bannon, do you? Besides, Grandpa would be impressed to find you haven't lost the magic touch."

Cori chuckled. "This is so *not* a good idea."

BLAKE NEEDED TO GET some sleep so he'd be sharp for his morning meeting with Peter O'Bannon. But he continued to sit in the cab of his old truck down by the river. Parked behind the blackberry bush, his view of the bend in the river, of his spot, was partially blocked by oak trees and wild vines. Stars glowed brightly against the dark sky. The storm had passed, leaving behind a robust and muddy river and the pungent smell of wet earth. A light breeze rustled the leaves above him. An open bag of M&M's rested on the dash.

Sophia had recognized Blake earlier that evening, but the episode was the longest she'd had yet—nearly twelve hours. That couldn't be good. Earlier, Jennifer had listened to the news with nearly adult composure, then retreated to her room and her music.

Footsteps approached.

Cori. Blake knew it was her without looking, by the way his pulse raced.

"Can I come in?" she asked through the open passenger window.

"Why not?" She'd horned her way into every other part of his life.

Her shadowy expression solemn, she opened the creaky door and climbed in, bringing her flowery scent with her. He looked out the windshield, silently containing his turmoil.

A tree branch above the truck wavered and creaked, then settled into silence. From overhead, an owl filled the night air with his eternal question, echoing Blake's frustration. Questions for Cori stuck to the roof of his mouth. If he asked Cori about Michael, he'd be letting his interest in the boy override his wounded pride at being deceived. Blake wasn't at a point where he could let what he knew was right guide his actions. The wound created by Cori's betrayal was still too raw. For now, frustration, hurt and anger, tinged with the doubt of denial, were in control.

"Would you baby-sit for me tomorrow morning around nine?"

It was the last thing Blake had expected her to say. And it drew his eyes crashing into hers. Her gaze held his without hesitation. She was serious. Blake's heart shifted into high gear at the chance to get to know his son.

"It'll give you some one-on-one time with Michael. If you want it."

Momentarily rendered speechless by her generosity, Blake finally managed to nod. They both turned back to the windshield. Blake knew he hadn't been able to control his frustration around Cori. His life was spiraling out of control and Cori received the brunt of his resentment. Better her than Jennifer or Sophia. At least he knew Cori could take it.

Cori shifted toward him suddenly as if sensing his thoughts. "I thought you needed the chance to lay into me."

"What?" He didn't think he'd heard her right.

"I'm letting you clear the air, under the condition that you stop belittling me in front of Michael. He's bright and he's already noticed the tension between us. If you want to be a part of his life..." She pushed her hair away from her forehead. "Well, I'd pick a different way to go about it."

Their eyes locked again while Blake wrestled with his harsher emotions. And lost. He'd love to spar a few verbal rounds with her.

"You lied to me." He slammed the hard plastic steering wheel with his palm. "You kept my son from me for four years. I don't even know his birthday." Blake was horrified to find himself choked up.

Cori clasped her hands firmly in her lap, not letting her gaze waver. "January fourth." She paused. "Nine o'clock in the morning. Seven pounds, four ounces."

Blake lost himself in the image of the delivery room. Never having been in one himself, he used what he'd seen on television. Was it an easy delivery? He couldn't bring himself to ask, yet he longed to know how his child had greeted the world. Anger pushed past the curiosity once more. Blake could count on one hand the things he knew about Michael—a good sleeper, a thumb sucker, liked worms, and clung to his mom as if he had no one else in the world.

And he had a dad waiting to love him.

"When are you going to tell your grandfather?" Once the old man knew what he'd done, that would be the end of Blake's time at Messina Vineyards. Salvatore Messina would probably assume he'd refused responsibility for his child. He'd believe

Cori before he'd take Blake's word, and he'd make it difficult for Blake to establish a relationship with his son.

Her hands flexed, the only indication that her veneer of control wasn't deep. "Not yet. I want to wait until...after."

She didn't have to say after what. They both knew. He'd lose more than his job once the news got out. He'd lose his mentor, possibly his friendship with Luke, as well. Blake tilted his head from one side to the other in an effort to relieve the tension in his neck. "I want to be there when you tell him." May as well stand up, face the music and fight for his job, Jen's home. She'd be a bear to live with if they lost their place here with the Messinas. Blake wouldn't be all that jolly, either. There was something about the sense of family permanence here that Blake loved, perhaps because he'd lost his parents too soon.

"I don't think you should," Cori said in a small voice.

Blake laughed harshly to let Cori know she couldn't snow him that easily. Their versions of the truth might differ, but Blake stood a better chance if his version was told. "I want to make sure Mr. Messina hears my side."

In the tree above them, the owl nagged the night, the sound filling the truck.

Frustration roared through Blake's veins. "What's his full name? You didn't name him something lame like Francis, did you?" He was practically yelling now.

"Michael Messina Sinclair."

She'd given him the Messina name. No Austin or Blake. That hurt so much that he had to lash out again. "He's a spoiled brat." There. He'd said what had been bothering him for days.

Cori didn't defend Michael, so Blake turned the tap on. "He talks back. He whines. He doesn't obey any rules. He's out of control. How could you let him turn out like that? Jennifer can't stand him. I don't know how I'm going to tell her and survive. She's already giving me the silent treatment."

"Michael's out of his comfort zone. Nothing is familiar to him here. The house isn't childproof—"

''Jennifer never had any problems.''

''Jennifer was older when she came here and she didn't live in the main house.''

''Jennifer obeyed the rules.''

''She probably won't much longer.''

Anger flamed, requiring a deep breath to contain. Blake spoke carefully, defining territories. ''We're not talking about Jennifer.'' She was off-limits. ''This is about you and your kid. I can't believe you kept this from me for nearly five years. Why?''

Cori didn't answer, just stared down at her hands. How could she just shut off her emotions like that?

''You got your thrills with me and paid the price.'' Purposefully, he pushed. ''What? I'm not even good enough for an explanation?''

Her head shot up, eyes shadowed in the moonlight. ''Good enough?''

''Don't pretend. I was just the field hand to you. A distraction you couldn't tell your family about.'' He struggled to slow down, but the words worked their way out, anyway. ''Was it fun to slum around? Was it thrilling enough for you? Was it?'' Blake grabbed Cori's shoulders, needing her to admit she'd used him. ''Are you ready for another dip on the wild side?''

Instead of waiting for her answer, he crushed his mouth upon hers, wanting to punish Cori. Instead, his tongue plundered into familiar territory and short-circuited his brain. Everything about Blake's life was unraveling, spiraling out of control. And so was Blake, until Cori's lips parted beneath his.

Not like this.

His grip loosened. His hands glided up to cradle her face, encouraging her response. Comfort crept into his system, taking the edge off his anger, soothing the wounds to his pride. Until her startled breath mingled with his.

Immediately, Blake jumped back to his side of the truck.

What had he done?

"Get out," he commanded as he turned the key in the ignition and brought the engine thundering to life.

The order was unnecessary. Cori had already fled, leaving the passenger door hanging open.

CHAPTER EIGHT

"I'M GOING OUT to a meeting. Can I get you anything before I go? Bathroom? Water? Food?" Cori looked down at her mother's drawn face as she smoothed her gray sweater over the butterflies in her stomach. She was having second thoughts about meeting the wine critic, yet she wanted to do something positive for her family's business.

Sophia shook her head. "You run along. I'll be fine."

The sun streamed through the bedroom window onto Michael, who was playing with an action figure at the foot of the bed, the swirling pattern on his crown a reminder of his father.

Facing Blake today promised to be uncomfortable at best. Letting Blake blow off steam last night had seemed like a good idea at the time. Blake deserved a forum for his unsteady emotions. She'd held up well against his onslaught, until he'd gotten personal and insulted Michael. Repeatedly.

She'd blown her stack, he'd blown his, and they'd somehow ended up lip-locked with her tongue in his mouth. The truth was that she'd been willing. After the initial shock of the moment had passed, she'd melted against him as his hands reacquainted themselves with her body. Once again, she looked the fool.

"Blake should be here any minute to watch Michael." Michael was a sweet handful. So far, Blake had only been exposed to the handful. The more time he spent with her son, the better. Cori was convinced that letting the two get to know each other gradually, without her around, was for the best.

"We're here." Blake stepped into the room, avoiding Cori's

gaze. He was followed by a sour-faced Jennifer toting her backpack.

Cori could sense the tension between the siblings just as solidly as the tension between Blake and herself.

Recalling their kiss made her lips part. During the night, Cori had realized Blake meant to punish her with that kiss, for thinking poorly of him. Where Blake had gotten the idea that he wasn't good enough for her, she had no idea. What had started out so angry and rough had shifted subtly into tenderness. That was the piece of the memory she couldn't let go of. What she wouldn't give to have Blake show her tenderness instead of contempt.

"What a pleasant surprise." Sophia smiled kindly at the pair, her fondness evident in her expression. "More homework, Jen? On a Sunday? They're working you too hard at that school."

"In addition to my homework—" Jennifer tossed Michael a look of disgust "—I'm here to baby-sit."

This was not at all what Cori had asked for the night before. She gave Blake a sharp look. Was he crazy? Michael and Jennifer were as combustible as nitro and glycerin. He avoided her gaze.

"Baby-sit me or Michael?" Sophia asked good-naturedly, ignoring Jen's bad mood.

"The little master destroyer." Jen rolled her eyes. "And I'm not even getting paid. But if I do this, I get to go to the festival later today. Blake's taking me and the kid."

Blocking the memory of Blake's lips on hers, Cori lowered her voice as she stepped closer to him. "I thought you were staying with Michael."

"I forgot I have an appointment with a wine critic this morning." He shrugged, his gaze sliding around the room, everywhere but over Michael and Cori, as if he'd never seen the rose drapes and Queen Anne furnishings before.

"Peter O'Bannon?" She was going to kill Luke for not telling her Blake was meeting with him, as well. She might be suspicious of Luke's motives if she didn't know how absent-minded he could be. ''I suppose it's too late for one of us to cancel? Especially if Luke told him we were both going to be there.''

Blake gave her a sidewise glance, looking just as unhappy as Cori was that they were going to be breakfast companions.

Picking up the gist of the conversation, Michael's face scrunched up. ''I'm going with Mommy.''

''Your mom has some work to do,'' Blake said evenly.

''Noooo.'' Michael leaped from the bed and ran to Cori, latching on to her jean-clad leg. ''I'm going, I'm going,'' he wailed.

''No, you're not,'' Blake said. ''You'll stay here with Jen and Grandma Sophia. If you're good, I'll come by later with a surprise for you.''

''I'm going, I'm going,'' Michael repeated.

''I'm trying to work here,'' Jen snapped, unpacking her backpack.

Crocodile tears spilled from Michael's eyes as he shook his head. Cori couldn't leave Michael here like this. One hour with Michael and Jen would be as volatile as Mount St. Helens when it erupted. How restful would that be for Mama?

Cori capitulated. ''Okay, I'll stay.'' It was for the best, anyway, given her contract with Bell-Diva.

''He'll be fine,'' Blake protested, trying to take Michael's hand without touching Cori.

His efforts seemed to upset Michael even more. He dodged Blake by circling Cori's leg. Blake finally looked at Cori, his expression full of disapproval. No doubt he was cursing her parenting skills again. When he spoke, though, his tone conveyed none of his apparent frustration.

''I was going to take Michael to McDonald's for lunch and then to the festival in town. They'll have face painting, games and ice cream.''

His offer stopped Michael in his tracks.

''I thought you had a ton of stuff to do today,'' Jen said, studying her brother closely.

''No problem. Plenty of hours in the day.'' Blake smiled at

Sophia, but Cori could sense the tension in the set of his shoulders beneath his blue T-shirt.

Despite his casual demeanor, Cori knew the field manager's job was endless, not limited to the amount of light in the day. Worse, if Blake did resent Cori for working when he couldn't, this situation wouldn't help smooth out the relationship they needed to parent Michael together.

Cori finally found her voice. "No. I'll stay."

Blake's gray eyes challenged Cori's authority, before he knelt down next to Michael, who still held Cori's leg. The position exposed her to the matching swirls of brown hair on their heads.

"You want to go to McDonald's, don't you?"

"Is there a playland?" Michael asked cautiously.

Blake nodded. "Do you want to go or not? Because the only way you're going is if you stay here while your mom and I go to this meeting. Deal?"

Michael nodded, and quietly walked over to sit down by the window.

Blake looked up at Cori expectantly. She supposed this was where he wanted her approval.

"That's so out of line." Cori pushed her hand underneath the hair on her forehead. She wanted Blake and Michael to spend time together, but she didn't want Blake to bribe him. Darn her son's stubborn streak.

"Let's go. You don't want to be late, do you?" Blake smiled at her. It was that rare, playful smile that did wicked things to her insides.

Checking her watch, Cori realized she didn't have any more time to argue. Blake stood, clearly knowing she'd seen things his way.

"Only if you promise to behave." She used her most severe tone.

"I will, Mommy. I'm a good boy," Michael said solemnly.

"I know you are, Peanut. I meant Blake," Cori flung over her shoulder as she hurried to collect her purse.

"Halle-stinkin'-lujah," Jen said. "Finally, I'll get some peace and quiet."

Sophia chuckled, the sound temporarily lifting Cori's spirits.

CORI HAD TO BE THE BEST public relations guru Blake had ever seen in action. And the most beautiful. They sat across from each other at a table in the Madrona Manor, the fanciest bed-and-breakfast in the area. The place was bustling with business—the buzz of muted voices mingled with the clink of serviceable china.

Parked in the power seat at their table, Peter O'Bannon had the blustery temperament of his receding red hair, which he wore in a comb-over. Full of stale, hot air, he kept pushing up his sleeve to reveal a fancy gold watch, until Cori took the bait and complimented him on it.

They'd finished eating and exchanging pleasantries, and Blake had the feeling Peter was building up to what he considered the hot questions. Blake gestured for the waitress to refill his coffee cup, hoping the caffeine boost would keep him sharp. He was running on too little sleep.

"So, you see, Messina Vineyards has always been a family-run winery, with each of us dedicated to it in some way, which probably explains its longevity."

Cori spoke smoothly, appearing confident and professional, except for an occasional, haphazard glance exchanged with Blake, in which he could read a hint of discomfort. He couldn't tell if she was uncomfortable with him after last night's kiss, or with Peter O'Bannon, who appeared to personify the term "wine snob."

Blake's gaze lingered on Cori's mouth. That kiss had been something once he'd gotten past his frustration. In it, there was a spark of hope that made him believe he shouldn't give up on her. Would he have felt this anger and frustration if she'd shown up on his doorstep when she'd learned of their pregnancy and expected him to marry her? No way. He'd have welcomed her back with open, if cautious, arms. So, what was the difference?

The difference was that she wasn't offering marriage as part of the parental package. Blake still wanted her to care for him on some level. They had nothing between them but a desire for each other. And desire was empty without friendship, respect and love.

Blake's attention reluctantly returned to Peter's haughty questions.

"Wouldn't you say Messina Vineyards has had trouble drawing in younger wine drinkers, say, in their twenties?" Peter's smile was as slick as oil.

With a guileless smile, Cori rolled her eyes. "It seems every winery wants to attract those twenty-somethings who think wine is intimidating and who drink beer, instead. Wine Brats was formed by second- and third-generation wine family members in their twenties because they wanted their peers to know what they were missing."

"Are you a member?"

"Of course."

Peter turned on Blake. "And how about you?"

"I am, too." Only because Mr. Messina had insisted he join. But suddenly, Blake was happy he'd done so, given the way the wine writer asked questions as if he were waiting to spring a trap on Cori and Blake.

"The fact is," Cori continued patiently, "wine is more a life-stage beverage. It's a slower drink that you sip, relax and enjoy, while beer tends to be consumed more like soda, quickly and for refreshment."

Peter pursed his lips, jotting something in a little notepad he'd placed on the table. It was hard to tell if Peter was satisfied or frustrated with the way the interview was going. Blake glanced at the notebook, but apparently Peter knew shorthand, since Blake recognized none of the characters on the page.

Flipping back a few pages, Peter studied his notes before shooting Cori a Cheshire cat grin. "I happened to taste a bottle of Messina Vineyards Chardonnay several years ago and saved my review. Luke and I tasted one of your more recent vintage Chardonnays last night." Peter sniffed and looked at his notes again. ''I must say, I didn't need to take down anything new. Both wines wove together complex vanilla, ripe pear and forward fruit with citrus notes that lingered.''

Cori beamed at Peter, seemingly ignoring his attack. ''Excellent.''

Sensing the direction Cori was going, Blake jumped back in the fray. ''I can't tell you how hard we strive for consistent quality in our grapes to deliver consistent quality in our wine. Among other things, we carefully select new rootstock and utilize the same pruning techniques. Barring any major aberrations in the weather, such as the extremely wet year we had from El Nino several years ago, our winemakers can rely on the same level of grape quality year to year.''

''I'm sure Luke talked in-depth about our wine-making process.'' Cori picked up the thread of conversation. ''Peter, have you ever invited people over for dinner and been unsure which wine to serve with the food?''

Peter looked almost horrified that Cori would suggest he was unsure of anything. ''I entertain quite often, but I like to experiment with different wines.''

''We want our wines to be the trusted friends our consumers reach for. There may be some people that want to experiment every day, but they're outnumbered by those people who drink wine to relax and want a taste they know they'll enjoy.''

''Surely you must feel a little stagnant after all this time? The same wine, over and over.''

''Let other wineries take on the role of providing a new taste adventure. There are tens of thousands of wine options available at grocery stores alone and new ones being introduced all the time.'' She smiled at Peter. ''We believe that no one wants to experiment all the time.''

Man, she was good. While Peter was occupied with his notebook, Blake grinned encouragingly at Cori. In her returned smile, he saw none of her earlier discomfort. Instead, in that moment, they seemed to share something beyond a child. They shared a bond of mutual respect.

It wasn't earth-shattering, but it was a step in the right direction.

Cori glanced at her watch. "Peter, we need to get started on that tour. I know Blake has an appointment later."

With their son.

Blake stood. "I'll take care of the check and pull the truck around." He strode across the room.

"Blake Austin, what are you doing here?" The words came from another winery's field manager.

"Steve." Blake stopped at his table and shook the older man's beefy, calloused hand, recognizing his companion, a local tractor salesman. "Dale."

"We never see you out this late in the morning," Steve commented.

Dale gripped Blake's hand solidly. "We never see you out, period. Field managers don't usually brown-nose it with the owners like you do."

Blake bristled at the implication that he was different from these men. They had college degrees validating their qualifications, Blake only had the sweat of his efforts. Was he to blame that Salvatore Messina had faith in his abilities to represent the winery as well as manage his vines? All he wanted was to gain the respect of his peers, yet each new success was met with envy rather than the esteem he sought.

"Is that Cori Sinclair?" Dale asked. "Haven't seen her in a while."

While Blake mumbled a response, someone at the table behind Dale spun at the question and looked in the direction of Dale's gaze. The man's appearance screamed success on vacation, from his trim brown hair to his soft, unscarred hands and designer polo shirt.

"We're here with a wine writer. Peter O'Bannon. He's doing a piece on Messina Vineyards."

Steve pulled a sour face. "My sympathies."

"You know Peter?" Blake asked, keeping one eye on their curious audience, who continued to stare at Cori.

"Oh yeah. He did a piece on us for the *Wine Spectator* last year. I hear he's launching a new wine magazine and sees himself as the next Marvin Shanken.'' Steve shook his head. ''If you're taking him on a tour, make sure he gets plenty of pit stops. The man can't hold a cup of coffee.''

''CORI SINCLAIR?''

Cori had been about to follow Peter out the door when she heard her name. She turned to find an attractive, tall, well-dressed man bearing down on her.

''I'm Abe Monroe from Bell-Diva.''

Bell-Diva's new vice president of marketing. Cori's insides went cold. She'd forgotten that she'd invited him to breakfast this morning, or that she'd originally suggested to Sidney that the Bell-Diva team stay here. She'd assumed they'd canceled the trip when she'd told Sidney first thing yesterday morning that her mother had taken a turn for the worse. She'd also told Sidney she needed at least a week off. She'd turned off her cell phone and packed away her laptop. Mama was more important than any job.

Belatedly, Cori extended her hand, plastering a smile on her face. ''Mr. Monroe, it's so nice to meet you.''

He didn't waste any time on pleasantries, smiles or gestures. Even his handshake was brief. ''I didn't expect to see you here this morning.''

''I hadn't planned on being here. My mother—''

''Yes, how is your mother?'' There was no trace of compassion in his voice. In fact, his words were loaded with suspicion and his eyes regarded her harshly.

Startled, Cori managed to say, ''We had a rough day yesterday, but she's better now. Thank you.''

''Sidney mentioned you were so upset that you couldn't leave her side. Imagine my surprise when I find you here with a wine critic, enjoying a Sunday breakfast.''

She knew she shouldn't have come. Cori fingered her purse strap. ''I apologize, Mr. Monroe. Circumstances—''

''Were you here on behalf of a winery?''

''I came as a favor to my brother.''

"For a winery?" he prompted.

Cori realized she and Abe Monroe would never be able to work together, even if they hadn't had this unfortunate experience. He was too domineering.

She lifted her chin. "My family owns a winery, yes. It was the topic of conversation, if that's what you're getting at."

"Which means you are in breach of contract, Ms. Sinclair." He started to turn away, but Cori stopped him.

"I suppose *you* would see it that way." She wouldn't lose the Bell-Diva account without a fight. She owed Sidney that much. Besides, his attitude galled her.

Mr. Monroe stepped back toward her, an impatient expression on his face.

"My mother," Cori began, blinking back tears, "devoted her entire life to my grandfather's winery. She's bedridden, weak and feeling useless. If I can have breakfast with someone, recount a few family stories and generally make this time easier for my family, I will." She took a deep breath and willed her voice to stay steady. "If you were looking to break your contract with Collins & Co., why didn't you just do it? You don't need to dangle Adam Parker in our faces. You don't need to make needless demands on our time. Just do it. Just do it, Mr. Monroe, and be done with it. I, for one, don't have time for your games."

BLAKE POINTED THE TRUCK toward home after he and Cori dropped Peter O'Bannon at the Madrona Manor. They'd taken him on a tour of the vineyards and winery facilities, given him a case containing twelve different bottles of wine and a souvenir polo shirt from the gift shop. For all his digging about old wine style, Peter didn't refuse the wine. In fact, he seemed cautiously pleased.

The ride into town in the morning had felt silent and awkward. The trip to and from Messina Vineyards with Peter had been filled with questions, answers and stories from both Blake and Cori. Now Cori fell silent again. Blake had sensed a change in her mood after breakfast. He'd seen her stop and talk with the interested stranger. A former boyfriend, perhaps?

"That went well," Blake commented, wishing he could recapture the friendship they'd once had, the easy camaraderie.

"There's no pleasing guys like him," Cori commented flatly, effectively ending the conversation.

The silence between them lengthened.

"Be careful with Michael today. He can be a handful when he doesn't get the attention he wants." She added softly, "Things break."

"Thanks." Blake glanced at Cori, surprised at her unexpected piece of advice. Slouched in her seat, she looked up at the skyline, arms crossed over her chest.

"He must have lots of toys at home to break." Blake laughed, hoping to take the sting out of his words. He had no idea how Cori coped with Michael. If Cori was saving for a house, would she splurge on toys? Would she toss Michael one when she needed to put in extra hours at home or did she have a baby-sitter she relied on?

"Jen had more." Cori released a breath and rested her elbow on the truck's center console, apparently not offended by his probing.

His son had fewer toys than Jen had? What else did his son lack? That car Cori was driving was dented, with an interior that was falling apart. The more he learned about Cori and Michael, the more Blake realized they needed him. With just a slight effort, Blake's hand could clasp hers, showing her his willingness to care again. Would she shake him off or squeeze his fingers in return? Probably she'd reject him, prefering someone exuding success like the guy he'd seen her with this morning.

"Who was that guy you talked to this morning in the restaurant?" He silently cursed his unending curiosity where Cori was concerned.

Cori's arms refolded over her chest. "That was a former client of mine."

Relief that the man hadn't been a former boyfriend allowed Blake to breathe easier. "What a coincidence to see him here."

"No." Cori sounded irritated. "I was supposed to meet him this morning and I canceled at the last minute."

"I don't get it."

"He was my client up until this morning, when he realized I'd broken the terms of our agreement. I'm not supposed to do any promotional efforts for any other alcohol beverage, including wine and Messina Vineyards."

Blake caught a side view of her tight features before returning his attention to the road. "You were fired?"

"Yes. I was canned."

"You weren't doing anything." Oops. "I mean, you were awesome, but it wasn't like you were working or anything."

"I was working. Maybe it didn't look like work, but believe me, PR is not an easy job." Cori sounded defeated. "I've been doing things like this for so long, I can't remember not doing it. Where do you think I learned how to network and do public relations? I probably started when I was Michael's age."

"Really? But you were just a kid. Your family wouldn't use you like that."

Cori's voice trembled. "You know nothing about me or this family that my grandfather doesn't want you to know."

"I know they care for you," he said after a moment. "They'd do anything for you."

"That's *so* not true." Cori's voice shook with such anguish that Blake turned to look at her. Tears gathered in her eyes. "My grandfather supports people that do exactly as he says. Don't be fooled, Blake. The minute you let him down, he'll drop you like *that.*" She snapped her fingers.

"You can't believe that. Sure, the old man's tough, but he wouldn't treat his own family like that." Could that be why she'd left? Because she felt as if her grandfather didn't love her?

"I'm living proof. I made what he considered a mistake and that was it. No second chances." She sniffed. "I know my mother and brother love me. But the most important thing in that house is Messina Vineyards and the goals my grandfather sets for it.''

Had Michael been her mistake? Blake didn't want to believe that.

''Have you ever been inside a house that doesn't have a picture of their children or grandchildren up somewhere? On a mantel? Desk? Refrigerator? There's not a picture in that house of Mama, Luke, Michael or me. Admit it. You hadn't heard of Michael's existence until I showed up with him.''

Although it was true that Blake hadn't known Michael was her son and not her boyfriend, he couldn't admit anything. If he did, he'd have to believe the worst. If Mr. Messina treated his granddaughter so coldly, what hope did Blake have of keeping his job and Jen's home when his employer learned the truth?

''YOU *WHAT?*'' Sidney screeched into Cori's ear.

Pacing the pink room, Cori grimaced and thumbed the volume on her cell phone down several notches. ''I went to breakfast with a wine critic and ran into Abe Monroe.''

''A wine critic? Why on earth would you do that? You know the details of the contract as well as I do. It's noncompete, plain and simple.'' She exhaled heavily into the telephone. ''Never mind. Tell me you talked to Abe.''

''I talked to him,'' Cori allowed. She had dreaded telling Sidney what happened, but she couldn't put it off. Once Blake and Michael had set off for McDonald's, Cori had retreated to the pink room to make the call.

''Oh, that tone in your voice doesn't reassure me, Cori.''

Sidney's tone of voice wasn't reassuring Cori, either.

''I didn't like him. I don't think his style would mesh with mine.''

''Damn it, Cori, think of the bottom line,'' Sidney huffed. Everything came back to money for Sidney. ''I don't care if you liked him or not. He's balls-to-the-wall blunt and plays by the rules. He won't overlook this kind of thing.''

Cori had to agree with Sidney's assessment. ''No, he probably won't. He's new at Bell-Diva and is just looking for a reason to replace us with someone he's used to working with.''

''Adam Parker.'' Sidney was oddly speechless for several seconds. ''Listen, I know you're going through a tough time. I'll do what I can, but if we lose this account, I'm going to have to...well, we'll talk about that later.''

Cori knew what Sidney was going to have to do. Fire her. She sank into the desk chair. ''I'm sorry, Sidney.'' Not that it helped the situation, but it made Cori feel better to apologize. ''Let me know if there's anything I can do.''

Cori disconnected the call and cradled her head on her arms, willing herself not to cry—

''I couldn't help but overhear.''

Cori sat bolt upright and turned to face her grandfather. He stood in the doorway, leaning on the door handle. She'd kept the door open in case Mama called her, thinking that everyone else was gone.

''Trouble at work?''

Cori drew in a deep, controlling breath. She would not break down in front of him. ''Nothing I can't deal with myself, thanks.''

He nodded slowly, studying her face. ''You work with Bell-Diva?''

''Yes.'' How long she'd be working with them was another story.

''They import beer?''

''Six different brands. Nightshade is their current leader.'' Pride raised her spirits. She'd done a lot to make that brand popular. If Abe Monroe wanted to play the good ol' boy network, let him. It was his loss. ''I got them a spot on the *Today Show*. Sales skyrocketed that weekend.''

''The *Today Show*. Impressive.'' He scratched his chin. ''They must be happy to have you on the account.''

Oh, yeah. They were really happy with her. Cori looked out the window.

''Lots of companies would be happy to have you on their team,'' he said evenly.

Cori snapped her gaze back to her grandfather, but he'd already turned and started walking away. She pulled her knees up to her chest and wrapped her arms around her knees, trying to hold the unexpected compliment close to her heart.

MICHAEL SUCKED THE SALT off his french fries while Blake watched. The kid smiled up at him. No doubt, the little manipulator was happy things had gone his way. He'd just spent ten minutes climbing, sliding and lobbing balls at other kids in the playland. Despite Blake's brutal criticism last night, he did believe Michael was bright. He just lacked a father's influence.

The little guy wasn't so bad as long as he was occupied. During the twenty minute ride south to Santa Rosa, Michael had babbled on and on about bugs, playing soccer, and his friends at preschool, sharing their adventures in a disjointed way that made Blake's head spin in confusion. Jennifer had never been so talkative.

"Mister?"

It took a moment for Blake to realize Michael was talking to him, calling his father "mister," as if he were a stranger.

The boy wrapped his sticky fingers around Blake's forearm, his brown eyes earnest. "Do you have a daddy?"

An image of Kevin Austin, smiling, brown hair shining above golden hay fields came to mind. Blake's adopted father had won Blake's love and respect and instilled in Blake a love of the land. And Blake hadn't been an easy sell for a new father. He remembered how Kevin had waited out the outbursts of an insecure teen who was afraid his mother wanted to replace him in her heart with her new husband. His parents had been gone for eight years, and Blake had yet to fill the hole their absence created in his heart.

Blake shook his head, driving away the unexpected tears. The little guy let go, leaving wet fingerprints on Blake's arm. If Blake flexed his fingers, he could feel the warm imprint of his son's hand on his skin. His breath caught in his throat.

"Me, neither." The boy sighed dramatically, rubbing the hair at the back of his head until it stuck straight up. "Mom says we can't have one. What do you think?"

Blake imagined the kid's tone was the same one he used when diplomatically trying not to ask for an ice cream. Rather than feeling his usual irritation and anger at the boy, Blake now felt pride, and almost smiled. Michael was a bright kid when he wasn't demolishing things.

"I'd like to have one." Michael picked up a french fry carefully, avoiding looking at Blake directly.

Blake chuckled, surprised at the unexpected way Michael had charmed him. He was heartened, too, that Cori hadn't been considering other men as father material.

"My mom used to tell me we couldn't have a puppy," Blake whispered conspiratorially, leaning closer. It was an ancient memory of his life. "But my dad found me one, anyway."

"Oh." The boy's eyes grew wide. "I can't have one until I'm five. Mommy is saving for a yard. She says we can have one when I'm five."

"A yard?"

"Puppies need yards, not 'partments."

Somehow Blake hadn't pictured Cori living in an apartment, although maybe it was something trendy and fashionable. Of course, that had to be it.

"Mommy and I share a room while we save." He popped a bite of pancake in his mouth, not that it stopped him from talking. "She has a regular bed. My bed's a race car."

Blake couldn't believe Cori lived in a one-bedroom apartment. And yet, it made sense, with what Blake had heard about the cost of living in Los Angeles and what he'd seen of Cori's lifestyle. An old, dented car, suitcases that weren't designer, her concern over keeping a steady paycheck.

None of which boded well for Blake's future at Messina Vineyards when Mr. Messina learned the truth.

JENNIFER ENJOYED THE small fair held at the plaza in downtown Healdsburg. Her stomach still hurt, but not near as bad as it had Friday night. The plaza was filled with booths offering food and local crafts. The sun sparkled, doing its best to chase away the morning fog.

Blake had invited Michael for some wild reason, and Cori had insisted on coming along, too, muttering something about controlling breakage, since Luke had offered to stay at home with Sophia. Their coming would have pissed Jen off more if Blake and Cori actually talked to each other. The last thing she wanted to discover was that Blake had a crush on Cori. Luckily, Michael wasn't whining, for once, and Blake wasn't treating Jen like a child. Cori spent a lot of time walking apart from them.

Feeling attractive in her white shorts and ice-blue T-shirt, Jennifer laughed louder than usual at Blake's jokes and even let little Michael hold her hand once, all the while looking for Skyler.

Skyler thought she was cute.

After a soda, a hot dog with the works and a cotton candy, Jennifer wasn't feeling so good. She pulled her hand away from Michael when he tried to slip his sticky fingers into her palm, and complained to Blake.

''My stomach hurts.'' This was different from the discomfort she lived with every day. This was a fist squeezing her abdomen.

''I'm not surprised, after what you've been chowing down on.'' Blake smiled as if he didn't truly believe her stomach hurt.

''How about a water?'' Cori suggested, pointing to a vendor ahead.

Jennifer appreciated the sympathetic tone, and accepted the offer. It was nice to have someone nurture her, she decided, even if it was Cori. Since she still had Cori's earrings, Jen couldn't quite look her in the eye.

A little while later, Jennifer complained again. ''My stomach still hurts.''

Blake felt her forehead. ''Not hot.''

''Maybe we should sit down and rest a minute.'' Cori came through again, pointing out a bench behind a row of booths.

So they sat. Michael played hopelessly with a yo-yo Cori had bought him. It was a sparkly red one that the boy just had to have. Unfortunately, Michael lacked the coordination needed to snap the thing back once he'd thrown it out, so someone—usually Blake—wound it up for him every time. Jennifer shifted on the bench, trying to get comfortable and not succeeding. She felt like she needed to go to the bathroom.

"Maybe we should leave," Cori suggested, looking at Jennifer closely.

"Not yet," Jen said. She hadn't even seen Skyler.

"It's been over an hour. I'm sure Luke is champing at the bit," Blake conceded, looking in the direction of his truck, nearly half a mile back through town. "If he's still there," he added under his breath.

"He'll be there." Cori came to her brother's defense, but Jennifer noted she didn't look all that confident.

Jennifer had been around the Messinas long enough to know that anything work-related took precedence over family matters.

Blake started down the sidewalk. Jennifer and Cori stood to follow. Michael sat at the end of the bench.

"Red," Michael said.

Jennifer turned to look back at him. "Yeah, your yo-yo is red. Come on. Let's go." The kid wasn't the brightest bulb on the tree.

"So're you." And the little brat pointed toward Jennifer's butt.

"What?" Jennifer turned and attempted to look at her behind, but she couldn't see anything past her hips.

"Red," Michael repeated.

Blake came back a few steps.

"Did I sit in something?" Jennifer demanded angrily, turning her back on Cori and Blake. The shorts were new and they were white to boot. She never should have sat on that stinking bench.

Cori gasped. Blake's face flushed.

"What?" Jennifer had a sinking suspicion the news wasn't going to be good.

"She hasn't started..." Cori looked at Blake.

''Not that I know of.'' Blake looked uncomfortable.

''Please tell me this isn't happening to me,'' Jennifer pleaded. Lacking any other way to cover herself, she retreated to the bench. What a way to cross the bridge between being a child and a woman. Other girls waited expectantly for their period, and Jen had thought she had indigestion.

''The important thing is to get her home.'' Cori took charge just like a Messina. ''Why don't you bring the truck around and pick us up over there?'' Cori gestured to the road a block behind them.

''Hurry,'' Jennifer pleaded, watching Blake walk away. She hid her head in her hands, unable to face Cori. She'd never be able to look Blake in the eyes again. *I started my period in public. In front of Cori. In front of Blake.* She groaned. ''I cannot believe this is happening to me.''

''I guess you've learned that there is a risk to wearing white shorts.'' Cori pulled Michael up into her lap.

Jennifer glared at her, but Cori only shrugged. ''Best silver lining I can come up with on short notice.''

''She's red like my yo-yo,'' Michael observed with an innocent smile at Jennifer.

''Shut up,'' Jen snapped.

''Jen,'' Cori admonished her. ''Be grateful he pointed it out before you walked into a group of your friends.''

As if on cue, a large group of junior high school kids walked across the street toward the bench where they sat. It was a rare mix of popular and borderline-popular kids, including Shelly and Skyler. Jen crossed her legs tightly in front of her. Thank heavens Devon and Ronnie were nowhere to be seen.

''Hi, Jen. We're going to walk down the other side of the festival. Want to come?'' Shelly asked, then whispered, ''Look at Kitty's hair. She put in highlights.''

Jennifer looked. Kitty had, indeed, highlighted her hair. Purple highlights. Jen thought she'd choke with envy. Some girls had all the luck. Good luck, that is.

''No, I...'' Jen floundered. What could she say? Skyler was looking right at her. Jen blushed and looked at Cori for help.

Cori lifted Michael up and onto Jen's lap. Instead of whining or slipping off, miracle of miracles, he settled against Jen.

"Sorry," Cori said with a sunny smile, as if nothing in the world were wrong. "But Jen's baby-sitting today. Maybe some other time."

"JOHN SINCLAIR?" Salvatore's voice came out gruffer than he would have liked, as if even his vocal cords didn't want to have this conversation. His words echoed hollowly in his office at Messina Vineyards headquarters.

"You've got him."

It was him, all right. Salvatore recognized his cocky tone of voice.

His heart sank. He'd been dreading this conversation with his former son-in-law, but Sophia had scared him this weekend. Her request wouldn't let him sleep. Finally, he'd risen with the dawn, found John's telephone number and sought the privacy he couldn't be assured of at home.

"This is Salvatore Messina."

"What's up, old man? I'm pretty busy. So many women, so little time. Ain't that right, baby?"

A feminine voice cooed in the background.

"I'll get right to the point." Before Salvatore hung up the phone in disgust. "My daughter wants to see you."

"After all this time she's come to her senses?"

How Salvatore hated this man. "No. She's dying."

That shut him up. The ticking pendulum of the cuckoo clock Salvatore had purchased on a trip to Germany last year filled the silence on Salvatore's end.

"Well?"

"I can be on the next plane if you buy me a first-class round-trip ticket and wire me ten thousand dollars."

"What?" He didn't have the money to spare and wouldn't give that much to John Sinclair, anyway. "Have you no shame?"

"Have you forgotten, old man? I may make deals with the devil, but I don't bargain."

Salvatore listened to the dial tone long after John hung up on him. There had to be a way around the man's price.

JEN SNUCK INTO THE pink bedroom after school on Monday. Her tennis shoes dragged on the thick pink carpet as she walked toward the desk. The diamond earrings burned in her pocket. She needed to return them.

Cori had bought Jen a variety of items for her period, including a book about the changes that were happening to her body. The book even said that some girls didn't develop breasts before they got their periods. She was normal. What a relief.

If she didn't return the earrings, they'd likely land her in trouble. She couldn't repay Cori like that, no matter how much her presence here upset Jen.

She stopped in front of the desk and pulled the earrings out of her pocket. They were awesome pieces of jewelry, and she felt grown-up wearing them. Although they hadn't helped today with Skyler. He'd passed her twice in the hall and said nothing more than a reserved "hi."

With a sigh, Jen set them on the desk next to a blue baby book. She'd been in the room several times, but had never seen the book before. Because Jen didn't want to leave the earrings just yet, she flipped open the baby book about midway. It wasn't like you needed to start from the beginning with one of those things.

Yuck. A lock of blond hair. What looked like fingernail clippings. Something black and shriveled in a plastic bag. Jen closed the book so fast it tumbled to the floor, landing with the first page open.

Mother: Cori Sinclair.

Father: Blake Austin.

Jen's stomach rolled. The brat was Blake's? That couldn't be. The kid was so…so…irritating. Besides, Blake would have told her something like that, wouldn't he?

Jen recalled all the parenting books she'd seen around the house lately and the way Blake seemed unable to look her in the eye. Jen's stomach knotted further. Blake was studying to be a parent to that thing. And Blake could barely stand Jen anymore. What was going to happen to her?

They were all lying to her. And now…now she was going to be pushed aside to make room for the brat. Everything became painfully clear. The boy was in and she was out.

Jen dropped the book onto the desk and snatched up the earrings. Shc deserved those earrings. When Blake abandoned her, she'd sell the diamonds and buy a ticket out of here.

CHAPTER NINE

BLAKE PAUSED AT THE DOOR to Sophia's bedroom. Cori sat at the desk by the window, wearing her khaki capris and clingy orange sweater. She'd avoided speaking to him all day. He moved to her side and knelt beside her, not allowing his eyes to stray to her bare toes. She didn't look at him. In fact, she stared out the window, her features pinched tightly as if she was trying not to cry.

''What's wrong?'' Blake asked, glancing back at Sophia.

Cori dabbed at her nose with a tissue. ''I keep waiting to hear if I've lost my job. I think Sidney's going to fire me.''

Fantastic! Blake felt as if a two hundred pound weight had just rolled off his chest. He could breathe easier. She'd have no reason to return to Los Angeles. Another glimpse of her tense, worried features prompted Blake to say, ''I'm sorry about that.'' It must hurt to have your job yanked out from under you. Then, he felt a nagging sense of foreboding. He could no longer deny Cori's concern that Mr. Messina would fire him when he learned the news. How could Blake believe his job would be safe when Mr. Messina had cut off his own granddaughter? Which made the reason he'd sought Cori out that much more important.

''I want joint custody.'' He'd thought about it a lot. Much as he resented the way Cori had handled things, he couldn't turn his back on his son. And he didn't want to turn his back on Cori. Fool that he was, he still wanted to be with her. It wasn't clear to Blake if the wanting was lust or love. At this point, it didn't matter. He was set on building a family. Sure, they'd be dysfunctional at first. Blake was used to dysfunctional. But he believed that painstaking work and commitment would make a family out of Michael, Jen, Cori and himself.

Cori looked up at him with a blank expression.

''And a say in how he's raised, how we discipline him.''

''That would require us to talk without jumping down each other's throats,'' she whispered, still looking straight ahead.

Her words brought to mind Blake's tongue inside her mouth the other night and how, after a mutual, initial shock, she'd melted against him. He shifted his weight. She'd kept his son from him and lied when he'd asked who the father was. Yet, on many levels, he respected her.

She'd taken on motherhood alone and done all right. Cori was generous and caring, having made some bargain with her boss to guarantee her paycheck while helping her mother. Despite Jen's smart mouth and bitter sarcasm, Cori had helped his sister through her first period. They needed to create a platonic relationship. For Michael's sake, Blake would conquer the longing he felt for Cori until they'd rebuilt the nonphysical connection between them.

''I think I can do that. I did it yesterday, didn't I?''

She rubbed her arms and said stiffly, ''We live in Los Angeles.''

Blake wondered if her desire to return to L.A. would change if Cori didn't have a job to go back to. He hoped so. ''He's my son.''

Cori turned to face him, staring sadly down on him from her seat above. ''You can't even call him by his name.''

Blake let his knees fall to the floor. She'd noticed. He shouldn't have been surprised. Blake was having a hard time adjusting. But he was trying. Wasn't that the important thing? Could he help it if he felt awkward saying ''Michael'' when he'd had no say in naming the boy?

''I'm not going to let you punish Michael because of a mistake I made.''

Before Blake could answer, Jen stepped into the room, as sullen as ever and glaring at Blake. ''What are you doing here?''

Blake mentally cursed Jen's bad timing, while simultaneously wondering about her sour mood. He looked back at Cori. "We'll talk about this later. Tonight. Be there." She'd know that he meant he wanted to meet down by the river. They seemed to communicate better in the dark, anyway.

"You're in my spot." Jen tramped across the thick carpet to stand beside Cori. "I need to do my homework."

Without a word or even a smile, Cori moved to Sophia's side, dropping into the chair as if she lacked the energy to stand.

"Lighten up," Blake cautioned his sister.

Jen rolled her eyes.

Michael stirred, rolled over in the bench seat and blinked sleepily at them all. Fascinated, Blake watched his every move.

"Does he have to be in here?" Jen asked, gesturing to Michael.

Blake looked irritably at Jen. "Rough day at school?"

She ignored him, unzipping her backpack and retrieving her books. Her eyes seemed red. Was everyone hormonal around here?

Michael ran over to Cori. "Mommy, I'm hungry."

Without another word, Cori picked up his son and carried him out. Blake followed.

"Of course," Jen commented acerbically, as Blake followed the pair into the hall.

Cori's assessment was wrong. The tension in the house wasn't just upsetting the kid. It was also upsetting Jen. Blake realized he needed to spend more quality time with Jen to help her through this difficult time, which, he hoped, would also help her accept Michael as her nephew and not just as a pest she thought was going to disappear from her life.

"What shall we have today, Peanut?" Cori's arms supported the boy's bottom, his spindly short legs dangled on either side of her hips. His head rested on her shoulder.

What would his son feel like in Blake's arms? He was dying to know.

"Cookies."

"How about some apple slices?" Blake said.

"No." The boy pouted before turning his head away, making Blake wonder what had happened to break the fragile relationship they'd started yesterday.

"Cookies are fine," Cori said.

Blake moved in front of them, opening the pocket door to the back stairs and taking the stairs first, in case Cori stumbled.

"Good food means he'll grow." The kid needed all the nutrition he could get. Blake didn't want his growth to be stunted.

"I don't want apples."

"You'll have two cookies," Cori said, attempting to reassure the boy as they entered the kitchen.

Blake picked a shiny red apple out of the refrigerator and started slicing.

"Cookies." Eyeing Blake, Michael started to cry, small sniffles and big tears.

Cori lifted the milk carton out of the fridge with his son still strapped to her chest, then poured him a glass. She chose two of Maria's homemade chocolate chip cookies, then set him down at the counter with the cookies on a napkin.

Blake felt extraneous, irritated that Cori wasn't respecting his wishes. He sliced and pared with sharp movements. When he was done, Cori surprised him by whisking the pieces onto another napkin and in front of Michael. Blake breathed a sigh of relief. He could make this work.

"No!" With the back of his hand, Michael flung the apple slices off the counter. They bounced off the logo on Blake's T-shirt, then scattered across the floor.

Blake rubbed a hand over his chest. Would he never be more than a nuisance to his own son?

"WHY DON'T YOU HAVE any pictures of Michael around?" Cori asked of Sophia later that evening. "I sent you lots of pictures." She sat with Mama to avoid going down to the river. Cori needed to slow Blake down. He constantly pushed her, criticizing her parenting decisions, scowling at her, then doing a reversal and playing the concerned dad role. Didn't he realize that four-year-olds tended to dig in their heels if pushed? And that his ever-changing moods confused Michael just as much as they did her?

Cori didn't want to admit Blake sparked nervous excitement in her whenever he came near. She didn't want to consider that his kiss could mean he still wanted her on some level—a level buried far beneath the hurt she'd caused. Cori didn't know what to expect from him next, so she couldn't prepare any defenses. Coward that she was, she cocooned herself in the safety of Mama's bedroom instead of meeting him down by the river as he'd asked.

"I keep those in my bedside table, along with every picture Michael ever made for me."

Cori pulled open the drawer. Sure enough, it was brimming with snapshots and inexpensive portraits of Michael that Cori had sent over the years. Interspersed between the photos were finger paintings; drawings that were no more than scribbles of color and watercolors.

"You don't put any of them up." She ran her thumb over the thick trail of blue paint that Michael had made with his thumb. "You never put any pictures of Luke and me up, either."

"I'd rather hug family than stare at a piece of paper, wouldn't you?"

Cori nodded numbly, blinking back the tears. "Was I a good kid, Mama?" Cori couldn't resist adding, "Are you proud of me?"

Mama reached for Cori's hand, her grip cool and lacking strength. "I am so proud of you, dear. To go off and make it on your own is fantastic. I also thought you were a wonderful child. Until your grandfather spoiled you rotten. In his eyes, you could do no wrong."

Cori recalled her grandfather's stormy expression that day in her dorm room. "He found out I wasn't perfect."

"It's hard for men to let their little girls grow up."

Cori wouldn't tell her mother how horrible her grandfather still was to her.

"Have you found him yet, Corinne?" Sophia asked, changing the subject.

"I haven't." She'd gambled all her hopes for finding John Sinclair on her grandfather, who was away at a conference in San Francisco.

"I wanted to see him before… Well, I guess you can't always get what you wish for."

Cori squeezed her mother's hand, wanting to give her hope. "We'll find him."

"Thank you. Could you open that bottom drawer?" Sophia asked. "And hand me the papers?"

Cori did as she was asked. "What are these?" They appeared to be legal documents, signed by her mother, the family's lawyer and her grandfather.

"When my time comes, I don't want to be revived. I don't want my body to be kept alive on a machine after my soul departs."

"But Mama…" How could her grandfather have signed such a thing?

"Corinne, I'm in pain. All the time. I take a few pills but they upset my stomach. I know the end is coming. Promise me you'll honor my wishes."

"But Mama…" Let her mother die?

"Corinne, you sit next to me now and I talk to you. If it comes to this, I don't want you sitting next to my body when I'm not here." Mama tapped her temple, then her chest. "Or here. Do you understand?"

Carrying out her mother's wishes challenged everything Cori believed in. With the superior medical technology that doctors had nowadays, they could keep her mother alive longer. But looking down into her mother's worn features and sunken brown eyes, Cori didn't know how she could be so selfish as to deny her mother relief.

"HEY THERE, BUDDY." Blake stepped into the pink room after having stood in the doorway watching his son play with action figures, complete with spittle-spurting sound effects. "I thought you might like to play some soccer." He held out a brand-new soccer ball.

"No, thanks." Michael looked at Blake with a careful lack of interest that reminded him of Mr. Messina.

His reaction might have sent Blake packing, except that Blake remembered how patient Kevin Austin had been with him. And he noticed that the boy's gaze lingered a little too long on the ball. The boy returned his attention to the brightly colored plastic figures, but the sound effects were conspicuously absent.

"That's too bad." Blake spun the ball in his hands. "Because the vineyards were just mowed and we could dribble up and down the rows."

"I'd rather swim." Michael didn't even look up.

Blake smiled. The boy was one heck of a wheeler-dealer at age four.

"Your mom said yes to soccer. Swimming is still a big no. Besides, if we hurry, I'll have time to go for lunch."

Michael sighed dramatically, then stood, not looking at Blake. "If you want."

Blake wanted a lot more, but this was a good start.

SALVATORE SAT AT HIS DESK pretending to read over a contract with an overseas distributor that needed his signature. Instead of reading, he was listening for Corinne's voice as she returned to Sophia's room after dinner, and his great-grandson's footsteps as he snuck down the stairs for his nightly visit.

The door to his office, which normally would have been closed, stood ajar. His computer was on and connected to the Internet. Salvatore was ready for this stolen moment.

"Mama, I brought you some ice chips and some Jell-O." Corinne's voice drifted downstairs.

He could just barely make out Sophia's refusal. He didn't want to think about what his daughter's loss of appetite meant. Instead, he concentrated on listening to the sign that the most joyous part of the day was about to begin.

There it came! A soft *thud.* Salvatore allowed himself a brief smile. Michael almost always made noise on at least one step, as if he wanted to signal to Salvatore that he was on his way.

"Hi, Big Grandpa," he whispered from the doorway a few seconds later, anticipating Salvatore's request and closing the door behind him.

Salvatore looked up with a smile, taking in Michael's stained T-shirt. He sighed. If he had to guess, he'd say the boy had eaten spaghetti for dinner. "Is it your turn on the computer already?"

"Oh yes. I cleaned my plate, just like you said." Michael's expression was solemn.

There was hope for the boy. Salvatore had noticed that, after spending only a few short hours with his great-grandson. "You didn't have any of those chicken pieces, did you? Or french fries?"

"Not for dinner. I had them for lunch. Blake took me."

Wasn't that interesting? "He takes you out, does he?" Why would Blake do that?

Moving toward the computer, Michael shrugged, a nonanswer that irritated Salvatore. There was still work to be done here to polish the boy. What he lacked in manners, however, he more than made up for in brightness.

When his great-grandson touched the mouse, the screen saver disappeared, revealing a close-up photo of the glassy-winged sharpshooter.

Michael giggled. "I knew it."

Salvatore always made sure he talked with Michael about the insect that threatened the California wine industry before they did anything else. Michael liked worms and bugs, something Salvatore encouraged, useful knowledge that would serve the family well. Michael also liked cartoons and such, but Salvatore discouraged that idle business. In just a few short days, he'd learned of his great-grandson's desire for a puppy, a handheld video game and a father.

Once Cori disclosed the name of Michael's father, Salvatore

planned to make sure Michael got the most useful of his wishes, as long as the man wasn't a liar and a cheat like John Sinclair.

CORI SLOUCHED IN A CHAIR next to a sleeping Sophia, while Jen did her homework at the desk. The faded afternoon sunlight wasn't enough to illuminate the room. Jen used a lamp. Cori preferred to hide from her fears in the shadows. It was easier to bide the time in the darkness with her dark thoughts, waiting for the inevitable.

On a bright note, Blake didn't cut into Cori every time their paths crossed, although that might have been because she was avoiding him. When they were together, she often caught Blake looking at Michael with guarded longing, yet she still hadn't heard him call Michael by name. Jen, however, was surlier than ever. The brief truce they'd experienced during the fair on Sunday hadn't lasted past Monday night.

It was Michael's attitude toward Blake that tested them all. Her son could be charming or maniacal. It was impossible to predict.

A tumbling crash reverberated down the hall. Sophia stirred but didn't waken.

Cori sprang from the chair and sprinted to the pink room, but not before registering the look of disgust on Jennifer's face.

Michael sat in the middle of the bedroom. The shelf on the wall that held Cori's china doll collection was tilted precariously. Dolls were cast about the floor, three porcelain heads shattered. A bit of Cori's childhood crumbled. How many times as a little girl had she carefully brought down a doll only to delicately place it back on the shelf, afraid that she would break one? Now her little boy had killed three of them in one blow.

"It wasn't me," Michael said, backing into the far corner of the room.

"Michael." Cori looked at the mess with tears of disappointment in her eyes. They weren't her most precious possessions. He was. She just expected too much of him for a four-year-old. "It's okay."

"It's not okay." Jennifer stepped into the room, gray eyes

blazing. ''He broke those dolls. Do you know how rare those dolls are?'' Jennifer gestured angrily at a crushed skull. ''Hundreds of dollars.''

''Jennifer.''

''Destroyed by your grubby little hands.'' Jen pointed accusingly at Michael.

Michael ran to Cori and latched on to her leg. ''It wasn't me,'' he cried.

''Jennifer, please,'' Cori said.

''It *was* you.'' Ignoring her, Jennifer leaned over Michael, her expression almost feral. ''You've destroyed them just like you destroy everything you touch.''

''Get out!'' Cori couldn't stand it anymore. If anyone was going to discipline Michael, it would be Cori. And she'd do it without humiliating him. ''This isn't your room. These aren't your things.'' *This isn't your family.* She barely bit back the words. It hardly seemed fair to even think them, when Cori so obviously didn't fit in, either.

Jennifer pulled back, as if readying herself for an argument.

''Jen, do as she says.'' Blake appeared in the doorway, his icy gaze on his sister. He'd left his work boots downstairs again. His white socks sported dark brown marks on top from dirt getting through his bootlaces.

Simmering with anger, Jen spun around and stomped out of the room.

Regret raced through Cori. She needed to apologize to Jennifer. But first, she needed to clean up the room.

''Sit up on the bed, Peanut, so I can clean this up.''

''I didn't do it, Mommy.'' Michael clung to her leg with no signs of weakening his grip.

''Yes, you did,'' she said calmly, gently trying to pry Michael loose from her leg.

''There was this spider and I tried to kill him with my pillow.''

Cori sighed. She saw the blue pillow on the desk below the shelf. Chances were the spider was still alive and vulnerable to another attack.

''IS THAT HOW YOUR MOTHER kills spiders?'' Blake tried to soften his words but didn't quite succeed in covering his irritation. Cori hadn't shown up at the river any night this week. He'd waited Monday night in the cool darkness and then gone home and kept vigil by his window until he was sure she wasn't coming. Every time he'd seen her since, she'd used Michael or Sophia as an excuse not to talk. He'd spent more time this week with Michael than with Cori. Not that he was complaining about time spent with his son. But Blake's plan was for a family that included Cori. He wanted to win her back. He couldn't do that if she wouldn't even talk to him.

"No," Michael finally replied in a little voice.

"Did you know those dolls were breakable?" Blake stepped closer to Cori and the kid.

"I didn't do it." The boy turned his face away.

"Blake," Cori said in a warning tone, a mother defending her cub.

Blake raised his eyes from the kid to Cori, then shook his head with a frown. "Let the boy answer."

When Michael kept his lip buttoned mutinously, Blake repeated the question. "Did you know those dolls were breakable?"

"He's four years old." One hand came up to warn Blake off, the other curled protectively around her son's head, pulling him more securely against her.

One more step and her palm would be flat against Blake's chest, her warm flesh over his heart.

"He won't learn to tell the truth or use better judgment if you let him get away with things like this."

"If you're questioning my parenting skills…"

"I know you'd never spank him, but you didn't even tell him to be more careful when he broke the syrup pitcher."

Brown eyes flashed. "The kitchen was practically on fire. I hardly think that's the time—"

"And the vase that's missing in the hall? Did he get a time-out for that?"

Her hand dropped to her side.

"I thought not." Blake crouched down to the kid's level. "Look at me."

Michael kept his head turned away from Blake, his chin tucked to his thin chest. At this angle, with his short haircut, Blake couldn't miss that his ears stuck out a lot.

"You're going to sit on that bed until your mom cleans up this mess. No toys. No TV."

Michael's lower lip trembled.

"You're going to tell your mom you're sorry you broke her dolls. Then you're going to tell Grandma Sophia that you're sorry you broke her vase. No TV until that's done."

Michael sprang onto the bed, threw himself facedown onto the bedspread and began to wail. Luckily, pillows muffled most of his tantrum.

Blake unfurled himself and stared down at Cori.

"Thank you," Cori said, her face tightly drawn and eyes studying her toes.

They stood without speaking, barely a foot apart. Divergent opinions on discipline wasn't the only thing separating them. Why was she avoiding him?

"We're back to that." Blake shouldn't have expected anything but her thanks. He had to figure out a way to break through the defenses of her good manners and return to the candid relationship they'd once shared.

But Cori surprised him. She squared her shoulders and regarded him defiantly. "I'm polite. Sue me."

Brown eyes sparked the tinder he'd been hiding for so many years in the cave he called a heart. Suddenly, Blake felt incredibly alive. Twice in a week, he'd pushed Cori past the exterior layer of Messina polish that she maintained, mining the real emotion beneath, getting a reaction out of her. The Cori he'd first met was beneath the facade of the ice princess.

His mind hadn't been tricking him by keeping her in his thoughts. It just hadn't allowed him to let her go because he still loved her. And he was growing to love their son, as well. How could he not, when they'd created Michael out of the very act of love?

Thin, dark eyebrows arched over her brown eyes when he didn't immediately respond. But Blake was momentarily distracted. *He loved her.* Blake wanted to laugh at the joy welling inside of him, because he knew everything was going to be all right.

He wanted to share this discovery with her. He wanted to run his hands over her soft skin, but repeating Saturday's blistering kiss wasn't an option, because eventually, job or not, Cori would return to her life in Los Angeles, taking Michael with her, unless Blake rebuilt the bond they'd shared when Michael was conceived. He'd have to proceed carefully, and rediscover the key to her heart. For the first time in days, since he'd learned he was a father, Blake allowed himself to hope.

Cori held herself still, despite a wailing kid in the background that grated on everyone's taut nerves. Many other mothers would have cracked by now and been flaying Blake alive for butting into her life. Blake nearly puffed himself up with pride. She was really something. And she was his.

''You're pissed off. Wouldn't you like to just tell me off?''

''Yes.'' Her eyes smoldered.

Blake laughed. ''What's stopping you?'' He gestured to Michael. ''He's not paying attention. And nobody could hear you over him.''

This close, Blake could sense Cori's frustration. Her jaw worked and her eyes narrowed. He could see her temper ignite. Her body trembled with it. He couldn't wait to see what would happen next. And then she exploded.

''You want to hear that you're right? Well, fine. You're right!''

She was beautiful when she cut loose. No woman could match her blazing eyes and fiery cheeks. Blake wished the light had been better that night at the pool so he could have seen her like this.

''I've been trying to get Michael to tell the truth rather than punishing him. So, this is good. I'm punishing him.'' She crossed her arms over her chest and cocked one hip.

''Wrong. *I'm* punishing him.''

She tossed her hands. "That's so like you to think you know everything about him. And me. We've been here, what? A little over a week? Wasn't it just a few nights ago you said you never knew me?"

Blake should leave. Heaven knows, he had enough work to do. Workers were still grafting new vines on the south acreage, work that should have been done weeks ago. There was Jennifer to talk to, Sophia to check on. But he just couldn't keep from looking down on Cori's flushed face or stop thinking about how much he loved her. Then he made one of the biggest mistakes of the day.

He smiled at her.

"Don't you dare find anything amusing in this situation," she warned, but her lips twitched suspiciously.

The goofy smile, the one he reserved for days when Jennifer did something he couldn't help but be proud of, wouldn't cease. Cori Sinclair was mad as hell at him, his son was exercising his lungs as if practicing for the opera, and Blake couldn't stop smiling because he suddenly realized that he hadn't done more than exist to pay bills and provide for Jennifer in years.

"If you laugh, I'll place the curse of the Gypsies on you."

He chuckled. "I'm sorry," he said at the narrowing of her eyes.

"No apologies or thanks, remember. The curse of the Italian Gypsies. On your head." Cori reached up with two fingers and pushed him gently on the forehead. Then she sidestepped him and made her escape, leaving him with a throbbing spot above the bridge of his nose and one at the base of his heart.

"AHH-AH."

Cori froze in the library at the cry of pain and glanced out the door. Her grandfather was down on one knee, groaning about one-third of the way up the stairs.

Cori's fingers tightened on the cool leather of the old book her mother had sent her to find. Was Grandpa dying, too?

While she watched, he hitched himself to his feet and, with a death grip on the banister, hauled himself slowly up the stairs.

"Are you all right?" Cori asked, moving quickly up the steps behind him.

Grandpa almost fell over again at her words. Cori held his arm to steady him. It was thin beneath his jacket. The idea that Salvatore Messina was weakening with age was not one she'd ever considered.

"Where did you come from?" There was no frailty in his tone. It cut sharply enough to make her drop her hand and step back in confusion. Then she recognized the look in his black eyes. It was the same she saw in Mama's every day—a quiet resignation.

"I might ask the same of you." Cori straightened her shoulders. "It's the middle of the afternoon. You're never home this early."

Her grandfather looked away and moved up the stairs meticulously. "I have to get ready for a dinner tonight. The annual winemaker awards are this evening. I'm receiving an award."

Cori watched him struggle with detachment. "When is John Sinclair coming?"

"He won't come."

"You didn't ask him," she accused, frowning.

"I asked." He struggled up another step. "He's just not the type of man to do what's right."

The need to help him, this man whom she'd respected and loved as much as he'd let her, warred with the feeling that he was getting what he deserved. Her grandfather wanted to control everything. Until Cori's rebellion, John Sinclair was apparently the only other thing he hadn't been able to control. How would he handle Luke's leaving?

"Prove it."

Her grandfather stopped and angled his head around to look at her below him. "I'll expect your information, as agreed, and then you'll stay out of my business."

Why was he so bent on retribution? "So. You still plan to get your revenge, even if I don't feel you need to?"

"My family has been wronged. I have to take action."

"No, you don't," Cori stated firmly. "Our agreement was for John Sinclair to come out and make peace with Mama. Revenge wasn't part of the deal."

"I'll give you his number and you can talk to him yourself. Don't romanticize him. There's a reason we don't stay in touch." He straightened and took a deep breath. "Then you can consider our bargain complete." Continuing up, her grandfather took each step slowly, moving one foot on a riser, then with deliberate care pulling himself along with a tight grip on the banister.

Cemented in place, Cori watched the man she'd never credited with a weakness fight his body upstairs. How long had this gone on? She'd never known her grandfather to be sick.

When it became apparent her grandfather was heading toward Mama's room with its closed door, Cori moved quickly, easily passing him in the wide, planked hallway and opening the door for him. She held on to the cool metal of the doorknob and stepped to one side.

His black eyes dropped to her hand with a frown.

The memory returned of her grandfather coming into Mama's room the week before. This time, Cori made the connection that he'd leaned on the doorknob for support, the same as he'd done on Sunday when he'd given her a nugget of hope after she'd admitted her blunder to Sidney. Her hand fell away from the knob and she backed up a step, dropping her eyes. Still, she caught her grandfather's silver eyebrows lowering ominously.

"What a pleasant surprise." Mama spoke slowly and softly, as if she couldn't spare enough breath to speak.

"I'm still allowed to visit, aren't I?" her grandfather said gruffly, placing his hand almost casually on the doorknob, then gradually leaning his weight upon it. "I'm going out tonight."

Cori walked to her mother's bed and gave Mama a smile, placing the book on the nightstand. She'd read it to Mama later. She was convinced that with this pain, her grandfather couldn't go out tonight. Cori wasn't even sure how he'd made it to the conference in San Francisco.

''Oh, the awards. I'd forgotten.'' Mama looked at them in turn. ''Why don't you take Cori tonight?''

''What? Mama, I don't want to leave you,'' Cori protested.

''It's always a lovely dinner, and I'm sure Papa would enjoy having you there.'' Mama panted after the long-winded speech, a slight frown on her face. ''In fact, I insist.''

''Mama,'' Cori began. She shouldn't be caught anywhere near a wine industry function, not after what had happened on Sunday.

Coal-black eyes landed upon Cori, halting her argument, reminding her that every request of Mama's should be honored.

''Maybe you should go, Corinne.'' The steel was back in her grandfather's voice. As invitations went, this one was cold as ice. ''I could use your help.''

''What about Michael? I can't take him.''

''We'll see what we can do, won't we, Papa?''

''Of course.'' His smile was all for his daughter. The chilly rebuff churned in the pit of Cori's stomach.

''It's so nice to be surrounded by family.'' Mama smiled, probably thinking they were mending the rift between them.

Cori experienced a twinge of guilt. They weren't anywhere near reconciliation. She practically hid Michael from her grandfather to avoid any unpleasant scenes like the one they'd experienced that first day back. They ate early in the kitchen to avoid him. Much as Cori wanted to close the gap between them, she didn't know how.

''I just need that telephone number from you before I go. So I can make that call.'' Cori met her grandfather's black eyes. Where her mother was concerned, she'd do almost anything, even brave her grandfather's wrath.

''Tonight,'' he said bluntly, his brows pulled low.

BLAKE SHOWED UP LATE at the awards dinner. He'd spent too much time walking the fields with a new employee. Then he'd wanted to make sure Sophia and Michael were settled in with

Maria and an angst-ridden Jennifer. He'd raced over to the Sonoma Mission Inn in the new truck, his tux on, but his hair still wet.

Even amidst the throng of tuxedos and sequined dresses, Blake easily located the Messina group. There was only one seat left at their table. Next to Cori. When had she been invited? It didn't matter. Blake couldn't believe his good luck. Facing the door, she glanced up and briefly met his gaze before returning her attention to someone sitting across from her. He recognized the expression on her face immediately, pleasant but impersonal, the Messina game face.

Just looking at her stole his breath and took him back to that first summer they'd met. Her black dress seemed to sparkle, making her slicked-back blond hair shine and her dark eyes seem large. As he drew nearer, her deep red lips caught his eye. Diamonds sparkled at her throat but not her ears. She was the epitome of understated elegance.

Blake sat down and received Salvatore Messina's withering glance. His employer hated anyone to be late or to bring undue attention to the winery. Luke, on the other side of his grandfather, gave Blake a half grin.

Cori turned and said something to her grandfather, and Blake's eyes widened. The entire back of her gown was missing, the front held up only by a thin strap around her neck. Her skin, smooth and tawny, beckoned for his touch. Blake tugged at the tight knot of his collar. Mr. Messina caught his expression with a reproachful frown.

''Your dress,'' Mr. Messina began, tilting his head toward Cori.

''Was in my closet,'' Cori said with a shrug.

If that dynamite dress had been in her closet, where had she worn it before? The thought had him reaching for his water glass.

Salvatore Messina took a deep breath and returned to the discussion of the potential ramifications of the wine glut that was hitting the market. The abundant supply in the United

States, combined with the rise in imported wines from Chile, Italy and Australia, was driving prices down.

"What I'd like to know is, will consumers stay with the brands they buy now and enjoy the lower price, or trade up to higher quality brands now that they're more affordable?"

As someone offered an answer to his question, Salvatore Messina leaned over to Cori. "Make sure Congressman Lyle talks to me after his speech."

"I will."

"Now."

"They're just serving dinner."

Salvatore Messina gave her The Look before returning to the discussion. Blake was used to The Look. It meant move your butt quickly, no questions asked.

"The number?" Cori asked, perhaps misunderstanding the meaning of The Look.

Salvatore Messina turned slowly back to Cori. "Not now. Now you need to talk to Congressman Lyle's people."

Cori stood, possibly a little less gracefully than usual, as their chairs were all crowded closely around the circular table. Her hip brushed Blake's arm, and when he turned his head, he came face-to-face with her chest. The material strained around her breasts, curves that had increased since she'd last worn that dress, he was sure.

Blake looked at his salad, focused on the various green textures and tried not to notice the plump cherry tomatoes peeking between the leaves. He took a drink of water and forced his eyes on the bread bowl, willing himself not to think about Cori slipping back into her seat. It was important to Blake that he take things slow, to reestablish a level of friendship before he touched her intimately again.

Cori returned a few minutes later. Blake wasn't sure if she was trying to avoid him or not, but she slid into her seat using the space next to her grandfather.

Blake sighed, but he wasn't sure it was in relief. He took a sip of the wine, savoring the liquid on his tongue before swallowing. It was a competitor's and very good. A subtle blend of oak and spices. Not as good as Cori tasted, but just as complex.

Blake snuck a look at her. She was sexier than hell tonight. Temptation personified. It appeared he carried the same weakness for Cori Sinclair that he did for chocolate, only it wasn't stress or sadness that made him want Cori.

Conversation. He needed to start a conversation with her. Something they wouldn't argue about. His gaze landed on his wineglass.

Blake turned to Cori. ''I really like the w—''

''Corinne, see if they have a different wine. This is unacceptable.'' Salvatore Messina cut Blake off, gesturing to his Chardonnay.

Blake clamped his mouth shut, waiting to see how Cori would handle her grandfather's request and wondering if she'd need his help.

''Did you donate the wine, Grandpa?''

''No.'' Mr. Messina chuckled. ''I gave him money.''

''Next time,'' Cori said under her breath, ''donate the wine, as well.''

Salvatore Messina glared at his granddaughter. Blake ducked his head, angling his face away from his employer to hide his smile, but not before catching Luke's conspiratorial grin.

Unable to quit when she was ahead, Cori gestured to the glittering ensemble. ''Every wine drinker in this room is sipping this wine and looking at the bottle on the table.''

Salvatore Messina's face reddened. His fingers drummed on the tablecloth. Cori might be brilliant at public relations, but she wasn't so smart when it came to her grandfather. You didn't want to go head-to-head with the old man every minute. He'd wear you out first. And if you gave him attitude, he'd shove it back down your throat.

''Why didn't you suggest that sooner?''

''I'm sure they asked you months ago, before I even came home.'' She changed her tactics and smiled sweetly. ''The number?''

''I'll have none of your impertinence.''

Blake would have thought Cori was unfazed by her grandfather's behavior, except that her right leg bounced nervously next to his knee. His hand itched to reassure her with a touch, but that tempted danger on all fronts.

Luckily, the waiter interrupted, taking salad plates and silencing Mr. Messina. Blake wondered why Cori wanted this mysterious number she kept asking for. The founder of Messina Vineyards took one look at the plate the waiter set down in front of him and turned toward Cori again.

''Corinne, go request a rare steak. This is medium.''

''They cook these things by the hundreds and let them sit. Nothing's going to be rare,'' Blake interjected, giving in to temptation and placing his hand over the shimmery black fabric covering Cori's bouncing knee. She didn't jump at the contact, but swung her dark brown eyes to him. Blake pulled his hand back slowly, holding her gaze all the while, backing it up with a reassuring smile. He was pleased to see heat spark in her eyes.

Progress.

''Well?'' Salvatore Messina stabbed at Blake with a disapproving frown.

Cori didn't argue. She backed her chair awkwardly away from the table and stood without acknowledging Blake or his attempt at buffering.

No one at their table ate. They all waited for Salvatore Messina to be served. Awkward conversations started and stopped until Cori returned with her grandfather's plate. As rare steaks went, it was a tad brown.

Later, after accepting an award for helping pioneer the Sonoma wine industry, Salvatore Messina talked amidst a group of well-wishers, including Cori and Blake. An excellent statesman, Mr. Messina knew how to keep conversations rolling and spar with Cori without drawing attention. Blake wouldn't have noticed the tension between the two if he hadn't been protecting Cori's back. Every man in the room over the age of eighteen maneuvered for a look at her in that dress. Blake guarded it zealously.

Cori thought her grandfather should talk with a reporter from a San Francisco newspaper. Salvatore Messina didn't. She thought he should discuss new wine-growing practices with Robert Mondavi, one of California's wine-making kings. Mr. Messina changed the subject. She suggested he sit down. He just sniffed and ignored her. Luke, on the other hand, listened intently and took her suggestions. And so it went. Through every conversation, Cori doggedly asked for "the number."

Upon Luke's return to the circle, Blake bumped him with his elbow and gestured to Cori and her grandfather. "Always like this?"

"Never this bad. She's gotten more persistent." Luke listened to Cori's advice, this time to talk with the grower representative, which was once again ignored by Mr. Messina. Luke smiled at Blake as he targeted the grower rep. "Better, too."

Admiring Cori's bare back, Blake privately agreed.

Poor Cori. Most of what she said made sense, yet the old man still stubbornly refused her advice.

Music started behind them in the ballroom. Blake hesitated only a half second before taking Cori's hand in his and pulling her away from Mr. Messina.

"Dance?" he asked.

With her heels on, the top of her head made it to his nose. Just the right height for a slow dance.

She tilted her head and looked at him, then back to her grandfather. "Maybe later." But her hand was still cradled in Blake's.

"There is no later. It's nearly ten o'clock and I have to get up at four in the morning. I need a dance now before I turn into a pumpkin." He gave her what he thought was his most charming smile. "Please?"

"One dance." But her eyes sparkled and she was smiling.

"We'll start with one dance." Blake led her out onto the dance floor and held her tenderly in his arms. They moved harmoniously, with a respectable distance between them.

"Why haven't you come down to the river?"

She tilted her head up to look at him, then closed her eyes. ''I can't stand the waiting. My job, my mother, you. I can't decide anything until I know whether or not I have a job or how long I'm going to be here.''

''Would you like to stay?'' Hope made Blake's heart beat faster. ''It's a good place to raise kids.''

Cori opened her eyes, looking at something beyond Blake's shoulder, looking sad. Blake wished he could make her smile again.

''Staying isn't an option open to me.''

''I didn't ask you that. I asked you what you wanted.''

''Let's not talk. Let's just dance.'' Cori sighed and snuggled closer, which was great, except—

''Ouch!''

Blake had stepped on her foot. ''Sorry.''

''Oooh.''

Blake's foot snagged the hem of her dress. ''Sorry.''

''You're a horrible dancer.'' Cori laughed when she said it, taking the sting out of her words because there was joy on her face, lighting her eyes.

''Yeah, Sophia's lessons never took.'' She'd tried several times to teach him how to dance, but Blake had two left feet.

''Hang on. Grandfather's trying to get my attention.'' Holding his hand, Cori dragged Blake back over to Mr. Messina.

Blake was more than happy to follow her wherever she wanted to lead him.

''What do you think you were doing out there?'' Mr. Messina snapped, handing Cori a slip of paper and glaring at Blake.

''Dancing. Isn't it great?'' Cori placed a quick kiss on her grandfather's leathery cheek, grabbed the paper and disappeared into the crowd, leaving Salvatore Messina behind, openmouthed.

CHAPTER TEN

JENNIFER SAT ON THE BED while Michael lay on the floor. She'd been recruited to baby-sit her nephew. Jen couldn't believe no one had told her she was an aunt yet. What were they waiting for? Her to get her driver's license? She'd much rather be down the hall with Sophia, but Maria was adamant that Jen needed to be with the brat.

"You can come down here with me," Michael offered, patting the carpet next to him.

"No, thanks." He apparently hadn't understood that she couldn't stand him. Ignoramus.

A television commercial came on featuring a blond teenager playing with a football. He reminded her of Skyler. She wished she could have hung out with him on Sunday. But no. She'd had her period and missed her opportunity. Now Skyler wasn't talking to her.

At least Devon hadn't spread any rumors about her. Ronnie gave her dirty looks, but hadn't said a word to her. Skyler was right. Jen was going to be okay.

Why wasn't Skyler talking to her? Maybe she'd work up the nerve to call him later.

"Want to look at my book?" Michael hauled out his baby book, of all things. She'd already learned what she needed to from that book. As if she wanted to know when he'd pooped his first one.

"This is all about me," he said proudly, pointing to the title and climbing up onto the bed without waiting for her answer.

Michael flipped a few pages in. "Here's me as a baby." He giggled and pointed.

Inextricably, Jen's eyes turned to the book. She hadn't seen that photograph the other day, not that she'd missed anything. It was a typical baby picture. His eyes were screwed shut, his face red and his fists tightly knotted on either side of his head. Jennifer had one like it at home, minus the fists.

"This is my hair." He pointed to a piece of hair stuck to the page with clear tape.

Jennifer suppressed a shudder. Ick. Obviously, this "admiring body parts" was a boy thing.

"My first toenail."

"Oh, I almost forgot." He flipped to the front of the book. "My birthday." He passed his palm over the page. "When is my birthday, Jen? I forgot."

With a sigh, Jen pulled the book closer, hoping there wasn't anything grosser in the book about to fall out in her lap.

"Michael Messina Sinclair." Figures they'd fit that name in. Get a grip, Cori. It's not like the Messinas were movie stars or something. Sheesh. "Born January fourth."

"That's right." He brightened. "And it says my mom's name, too." He added a little sadly, "I don't have a father."

Jennifer gave him a you're-a-moron look and scrambled off the bed. "What do you mean?" Hadn't they told the kid? Then Jen realized they couldn't tell him. He was just a baby. He'd blab to everyone.

"I don't have a dad and I want one. Other kids have dads."

"I don't."

"Oh, that's sad. Are you sad?" He hopped down off the bed and took her hand.

Sappy kid. But she admitted, "I'm okay with it now. I have Blake."

"He's your dad?" He dropped her hand and stepped back, assessing her. "Is he a good one?"

She laughed despite herself. "He's not my dad, you dork. He's my brother. He took care of me when my parents died."

"He can be mean."

"Not always. He bought you a soccer ball, didn't he? And played with you?"

Michael shrugged, seemingly unwilling to give in. ''We play sometimes.''

Blake was strict, but he wasn't mean. Suddenly, she wondered how her brother felt about being a father, particularly when Michael didn't seem to like him much. Were Blake's feelings hurt? For the first time in a long while, Jen worried about someone's feelings other than her own. Blake had sacrificed a lot for her when their parents died. Maybe there was a way she could pay him back.

CORI EXCUSED HERSELF and managed to make it outside the hall. The place was packed. The throng shifting through the main hallway into the ballroom was reluctant to let her through. Once outside, Cori placed a call on her cell phone to a number from an unfamiliar area code.

''John Sinclair?'' she asked, when a man answered groggily.

''You've got him.'' His words were smooth and cultured.

Cori immediately doubted her grandfather's appraisal. This wasn't the voice of someone you couldn't trust.

''This is Cori Sinclair. Your daughter?'' She sounded like a teenager. Where was her cool business persona when she needed it?

''Well, this is a surprise.'' His voice carried a note of sarcasm that Cori attributed to her grandfather's previous call. ''Did you turn out as pretty as you started? Or did you take after your grandfather's side of the family?''

Cori didn't know how to respond to that, so she got right to the point. ''I'm calling for Mama. She's sick and she's been asking for you.'' She didn't say Mama was dying.

''Did your grandfather tell you to call me? I've already told him my price for a visit.''

''Price?'' Cori's high heels suddenly launched her to a dizzying height. She swayed slightly.

''Ten thousand dollars. Plus travel, first-class. Nonnegotiable.''

''What?'' There had to have been some mistake. Perhaps her

grandfather had hired someone to play this role. "You're not really John Sinclair."

"Oh, I'm John Sinclair, all right. You were there at the river the day I left. You cried when I got in the boat and Luke had to pull you back from the water."

The unpleasant memory came rushing back. They'd followed him down to the river. Her father shouting his goodbyes over the sailboat's motor as he headed downstream. Luke holding on to her by the arms as she sobbed for her daddy.

"I thought you might remember that, Peanut," he said in response to her silence.

Peanut. Cori's stomach whirled unpleasantly. Her grandfather was right about John Sinclair. She'd never call Michael "Peanut" again.

"You're not coming," she whispered.

"I loved your mother once." His voice sounded gruff, although it could have been her cell connection. "But there was only one man she'd do anything for and it wasn't me." He laughed mirthlessly. "I've got my pride and my price. Since it doesn't sound like you're going to pay it, either, if you're ever in Atlantic City, look me up."

"HEY, I'VE BEEN searching for you." Blake stepped in front of Cori as she made her way numbly back into the hotel. "I know I'm no Fred Astaire, but I'd love another dance."

Cori stood rigidly. She could hold it together. She was a Messina. Then her eyes found the compassion in Blake's gray eyes and all her defenses crumbled. She couldn't honor Mama's last request. She'd failed.

Cori spun away from Blake, weaving an intricate pattern through the throng until she reached a side door and burst back out into the night.

Blake was right behind her, then at her side with a comforting hand under her arm. If his touch had been firm and demanding, Cori's defenses might have been shored. As it was, she broke down, spinning around to burrow into his chest. He enveloped her in his sturdy embrace.

"Hey, what's wrong?"

She sobbed silently, trying to regain control, but it was no use. She'd let her mother down. In the face of her defeat, Cori allowed herself to sink deeper into the warmth of Blake's touch.

"He's not coming," she managed to snuffle.

Blake pushed her away, holding her upper arms. "Who?"

"My father. Mama wanted to see him one more time."

"I'm sorry, Cori. I didn't know." He cast a quick glance back inside. "Do you want to go home?"

Cori nodded. That was the nice thing about Blake; he seemed to know what she needed. Often, he knew what Michael needed, too, she admitted to herself.

In no time, she was in Blake's truck heading back to the house. Cori spent much of the ride in silence, staring blindly out the passenger window. Now she knew why she looked at the Russian River and felt the urge to escape. Her father had planted that seed long ago. So much time wasted at the river's edge.

As they turned into the driveway, Blake unexpectedly gunned the truck forward with a curse, sending gravel spitting everywhere.

Cori looked up and saw the flashing lights in front of the house.

"JEN?" Fearing the worst, Blake bounded up the stairs three at a time, Cori a few steps behind him. "Maria?"

"Are you all right?" Blake asked, as Jen flew out of Sophia's room and into his arms.

Jen was sobbing uncontrollably, her face red and streaked with tears.

Cori swept past the pair and into her mother's room. "Mama?"

Blake pulled Jen near the doorway so that he could see inside but she couldn't.

Two paramedics huddled next to the bed in a whispered conference. Sophia's eyes were slits, barely visible above the oxygen mask covering most of her face. She looked spent and didn't react to Cori's voice. But she was alive.

"I was just about to call you. We think she had a heart attack," Maria said, placing an arm around Cori's waist. "She's a strong woman, your mama."

Blake set Jen aside with a stern look. "Stay here. Don't come back inside." He waited until she nodded before entering the bedroom.

Cori couldn't seem to take her eyes off her mother. She stepped nearer to the bed. "Did they have to revive her?"

"Did Jen see?" Blake asked, stopping next to Cori.

"No, no." Maria spoke softly, turning her back to Sophia. "About half an hour ago Mrs. Sinclair clutched her chest and I screamed." Tears filled the older woman's dark eyes as her own hand slid to her chest. "I couldn't help it. She startled me. Jennifer came running from down the hall, but by that time Mrs. Sinclair had passed out."

Cori looked shocked. Blake curled his arm around Cori's shoulders and drew her to his side. Rather than resist, she leaned into him and slid her arm beneath his tuxedo jacket. It felt painfully right to shelter her there. Somehow, they were going to mend things between them.

"I had Jennifer wait downstairs for the medics." Maria patted Blake's arm. "You take her home and give her a cup of hot chocolate. She's a brave girl."

Jen's snuffles were audible inside the bedroom. He hoped she had heard Maria's praise. Blake berated himself. He should have anticipated that Sophia might have an attack or die while Jen was with her. He'd probably scarred his sister for life. All this time he'd believed being together was good for both Jen and Sophia. Like it or not, Jen wasn't coming into this bedroom anymore.

"What's next?" Cori directed the question to the two paramedics.

"We've got her stabilized, so we're taking her to the hospital in Santa Rosa."

"I'm going with her," Cori said, straightening beneath

Blake's arm. She leaned back to look up at him. ''Can you watch Michael?''

''Can we take him home with us?'' He wanted to reassure Jen, and the best way to do that was to get her home.

''You'll watch him carefully?''

''Of course.'' Just the fact that she had to ask hurt his pride. He was Michael's father, wasn't he?

''Thanks.'' She stood on tiptoe and hugged him tightly, pressing all her curves against his chest, almost making up for her doubt.

He squeezed tighter, not wanting to let her go.

''I hope he behaves for you.'' Cori drew away from Blake.

His arms fell uselessly to his sides. He wasn't supposed to feel this way about Cori at a time like this, as if he needed to keep her by him forever. Or maybe that was just further proof of his love for her.

Cori moved to her mother's side and took her hand. ''I'll go with you to the hospital, Mama.'' She looked up at one of the paramedics. ''I have time to change, don't I?''

''It'll be a few minutes,'' he said. He was the younger of the two, with red spots on his face. When Cori smiled at him, he blushed.

The two paramedics went downstairs to get their stretcher, and Cori hurried down the hall.

''Maria, can you take Jen down to the kitchen and make her that hot chocolate before you go?'' Blake asked.

''Yes, sir.'' Maria walked stiffly out into the hall.

Blake moved to stand next to Sophia. ''You've given us all a scare this time.''

She blinked up at him over her yellow oxygen mask.

''Don't you do anything foolish now, like give up.''

Her cheeks lifted as if she were smiling beneath the mask. Sophia's good spirits almost brought him to his knees, he was so grateful she was still alive.

''They're taking you to the hospital again. You're going to have to show them some of that Messina spirit if you want to come back here.'' Cruelly honest words, but he knew Sophia would fight to come home.

Blake thought he detected a brief nod.

''That's my girl.'' Blake leaned down to kiss her forehead. ''Do me a favor and don't flash any men this go-round.''

He could see the corners of her smile this time.

When the paramedics came back, Blake left them to retrieve Michael. He walked through the open door of the pink room, right into Cori pulling on her blue jeans.

''Sorry.'' He whipped around. Her back was to him, but he had caught sight of her red sheer panties and a slender bare back.

''Don't worry about it. I'll just be a second, once I find my bra.''

Blake squeezed his eyes shut against the image of her walking around in tight blue jeans and nothing on top. The backless dress was bad enough.

''I need to get him,'' he managed to choke out.

''*Michael.* He's still asleep.'' He heard her rustling through clothing. ''There.'' *Snap.*

Blake contained a groan. Family crises were supposed to be a solemn time, yet all he could think about was touching Cori's bare skin with his mouth. He started to turn toward Michael.

''Just need a shirt.'' Her tone was matter-of-fact, as if she didn't realize she was killing him.

Blake spun back to the hallway, strangulation on his mind—hers. Was she driving him crazy on purpose? ''Let me know when you're dressed, will you?'' he grumbled.

''I'm decent.''

He didn't turn right away, but scrubbed a hand over his face, trying to wash away the image of her naked body beneath his. When he did look back, Cori was on her knees next to their son.

''Michael, wake up, baby. You're going to have a sleepover at Jennifer's house.''

The kid mumbled. It sounded like ''I'm too tired,'' punctuated by a yawn and a sprawling of limbs.

"You be good and I'll see you in the morning." She kissed his cheek and stood. When she looked up at Blake, he could see tears filling her eyes. Unexpectedly, she rocketed into his arms, knocking him back a step.

"You've always been there for me." Her words were muffled against his shoulder. "Take care of my baby."

She stepped around him, picked up her tennis shoes and was gone. Her footsteps on the hardwood floor slowed to a stop at the end of the hallway. With a sniffle, he heard her walk into Sophia's bedroom.

"Ready for a road trip, Mama?"

Blake looked down upon the boy that he'd unwittingly helped to create. Cori was right about so many things. Could he have been blinded by love back then and turned a deaf ear to what she really needed?

He wondered who the real Cori Sinclair was. Spoiled socialite. Good mother. Selfish liar. Loving daughter.

Did it really matter?

Blake had to face his own truth. Regardless of who she was, he wanted to be the one Cori leaned on. She'd broken his heart twice already. He was willing to risk it a third time.

BLAKE WOKE UP to Michael screaming for his mommy. Blurry eyes tried to focus on the miniature maelstrom wailing inches from his face.

"Where's my mommy? Where's my mommy?" he kept repeating.

"It's okay. She's coming soon." Blake tried to reassure the boy, but he was inconsolable.

Blake sat up in bed and looked at the clock. Six-thirty. He'd gone to sleep around three o'clock. "Come here." Blake extended his hand with the intent of pulling the boy into his lap. At least then the noise would be directed away from his ears.

Michael backed away quickly, stumbling on his sleeping bag and falling on his bottom. He cranked the wailing up a notch, and then hit a fever pitch when Blake reached out to help him up. Immediately, Blake sank back onto the bed.

Jennifer appeared in the doorway wearing the same jeans and T-shirt she'd gone to bed in, hopelessly wrinkled now.

"What the…?"

"He's a little upset," Blake yelled above the noise. "How about if we call your mom?"

Michael's face was red and tear-streaked. He shook his head vehemently. "Where's my mommy?"

"Hey, little guy. What's wrong?" Jen approached the banshee with a soft voice.

Michael took one look at Jen and slammed into her leg, wrapping his arms around her appendage just the way he did to Cori. He stopped screaming and dropped his voice to a constant moan.

Blake's ears were ringing. He pointed to Michael and glared at Jen accusingly. "When did that happen?"

"We bonded last night." Jen grinned at Blake.

Shaking off the unexpected jealousy of seeing Jen comforting his son, Blake reached for the telephone. His sister, who'd been impossible to live with the past six months, had suddenly decided to befriend the boy she called the Master of Disaster? Unbelievable.

Blake swung his legs over the edge of the bed and onto the child's blue sleeping bag as he hit redial for the ward at the hospital where Sophia was staying. A few minutes later, Blake learned Sophia's condition was still stable and that Cori was sleeping in a chair by her bedside.

"How about pancakes while we wait for your mom?" Blake tried to make his voice sound nonthreatening and optimistic, the optimistic part more for himself than Michael.

With his back to Blake, the kid shook his head. The moaning volume increased.

"I don't know, Mikey. Blake makes some pretty good pancakes. He puts chocolate chips in them."

The moaning halted for a heartbeat.

Aha, a fellow chocoholic. "Yeah, I'm going downstairs to make a big stack of chocolate chip pancakes and a lot of bacon. I'd hate to have to eat all that alone."

''Hey, what about me?'' Jen protested.

''And me.'' Michael didn't look at Blake, but it was progress.

Blake scratched his chin and grinned at Jen. ''I suppose I could share with those that set the table. Do either one of you know how to do that?''

Michael turned his tear-smudged face toward Blake. ''I know how.'' Then he hiccuped.

''You'll do...Mike. You'll do just fine.''

CORI WAITED next to Mama's hospital bed, rolling and unrolling a piece of paper. Mama looked so small and frail lying there with tubes and wires attached to various points on her body. Now Cori understood what Mama had meant about losing her dignity.

Movement in the doorway caught her eye.

''I didn't expect you to still be here. Who's with the boy?'' her grandfather said, leaning on the doorknob, looking impeccable in a pair of olive khakis and a gray dress shirt.

''Blake and Jennifer.'' She stood, feeling unpresentable in her wrinkled jeans, flat hair and stale makeup. ''Would you like to sit down?''

He nodded and stepped carefully over to the chair. He looked down on Sophia with a detached expression before carefully lowering himself into the seat. ''The nurse said she's stable.''

''Yes.''

''Has she spoken?''

''Not yet.'' Cori fidgeted with the paper. ''I talked with John Sinclair last night.''

His hand fiddled with his cuff button. ''And?''

''You were right about him. About how he is now.''

''Meaning, I was wrong about him back then.''

''I wasn't old enough to know if you were right or wrong then.'' With effort, Cori tamed the irritation in her tone. The last thing she wanted was to start a fight.

''Sophia agreed with me.''

Cori knew what her mother thought now, but held her tongue.

He eyed her expectantly. "I lived up to my end of the bargain."

Cori's stomach clenched. "I can't deal with your vendetta today."

After a moment, her grandfather nodded, surprising her when he added, "I've lost my taste for revenge lately."

They sat in silence for a few minutes, until Cori noticed her grandfather was unnaturally still, almost as if he couldn't bear to move. "When are you going to get a new hip?" Her first secretary had needed that particular surgery, holding off until the last minute when she could barely walk. It'd taken Cori a while to make the connection between her grandfather's symptoms and her former secretary's.

He scowled. "Doctors. What do they know?"

Mama's eyelids wrenched open a crack. Cori moved closer and touched her mother's arm above the IV tube. Her eyes opened wider.

"You gave us a scare last night." Cori smiled bravely. "I'm sorry I wasn't home."

Sophia didn't answer. She looked at Cori and then her eyes moved to Salvatore, then back to Cori and the paper in her hand. Cori unrolled the document and held it up so her mother could see what it was—her instructions not to be revived.

"Find the doctor," her grandfather ordered.

Cori ignored him. "I thought it better if we kept this with you." Cori took some medical tape and attached it to her mother's headboard. The look she exchanged with her mother was meant to convey the bonds of love. But her mother's eyes were dull and lacked awareness. Maybe her grandfather knew best, after all.

Cori swallowed her fears and tried to appear cheerful. "The doctor came by a while ago and said I could break you out of here if you woke up before lunchtime. What do you say?"

Mama's eyes remained empty. She said nothing, letting the

hospital white noise fill the tightening space in Cori's heart. Cori spun on her heel and ran for the doctor.

"I CAN'T REMEMBER the last time you made pancakes," Jen said, stuffing another bite into her mouth.

Blake couldn't remember, either. He associated the pancake griddle with slow Sunday mornings and afternoons where you slept off the haze of sugar before heading off to the movies or watching a game on television. And he'd about given up on Jen ever enjoying his company again.

Jen burped, eliciting a giggle from Michael. "We should do this more often."

Why hadn't they? Oh yeah. Miss Hormonal had something against hanging out with him. And, if Blake were honest with himself, he was reluctant to bridge the gap between them because he'd been beaten down so often. It was easier to do nothing, say nothing, than to risk an argument—or worse—a deejay episode like the one he'd experienced last week, hearing the same song over and over again.

"Have you had enough, Mike?" Blake asked. He'd already made his son a snake pancake and one shaped like an *M*. That was about as far as his culinary creativity went. When the boy didn't answer, Blake looked over his shoulder. The kid was sitting sideways in his chair, facing away from Blake.

"Done," the boy said with a smile at Jennifer.

It was a beautiful smile, similar to one of Cori's. Blake just wished it was directed at him.

SOPHIA CAME HOME later that afternoon, but the episode had taken its toll on her both physically and emotionally. Blake, Jen and Michael met the ambulance at the front door. Sophia didn't acknowledge any of them. She was home, but lacked awareness. Jen started to cry when she saw how distant Sophia had become. Blake sent her home with a promise to call later. He didn't want her last memory of Sophia to be like this.

Cori stepped out of the ambulance looking as drained as

Sophia. Blake moved closer, but before he could so much as touch her shoulder, Michael leapt into her arms and wouldn't let go. Cori hugged Blake briefly with one arm, eliciting a complaint from Michael as he was squished between them.

"You okay?" Blake asked.

Cori blinked back the tears, able to give only a brief nod.

They were down to bedpans, adult diapers and waterproof mattress pads. Privately, Blake held no hope for Sophia returning to the lucid state she had been in yesterday. Sophia was alive, but nonresponsive.

As soon as Sophia was settled in her room, a red-eyed Cori retired to the pink room with Michael. That left Blake alone with Sophia, as Mr. Messina wasn't back yet from the hospital and Luke was still at the winery.

The silence in the room was oppressive, hanging heavily on Blake's shoulders. After a time, he filled it.

"Do you remember that time Jen flung peas across the table at me, except they hit that stuffy wine critic?" Blake asked Sophia. "I thought Mr. Messina was going to explode. Luke and I could barely keep a straight face. You just looked around the room like a queen and commented how fresh the produce was that year, something about it just popping out of the pod."

Blake smiled at the ceiling, looking anywhere but at Sophia. He didn't want to carry this image of Sophia with him, either.

"Or how about that Christmas Eve when Jen wanted to help you cook dinner and you didn't tell her you didn't know how to cook? You canceled your gourmet dinner and tried to do it yourself. You let the turkey sit in the oven after it was done because you didn't want it to get cold while you finished preparing the rest of dinner, only it just dried up and got hard as a rock." Blake smiled. "We ended up eating Big Macs for dinner that year."

He rubbed his hands over his face and looked out the window.

"And that time you and Jen decided to surprise me for my birthday with a new pair of boots, only you couldn't read the shoe size in my work boots out back? So, you took them to the store to make sure you had the right size, while you thought I'd be busy with Mr. Messina and the winemakers talking about grape supply. Only, they decided to go out for lunch and I had no shoes.'' He managed to laugh past his choked throat. Hell, someone had to keep it light. Sophia was somber as a ghost. Blake finally looked at Sophia. Her open eyes stared dully at the ceiling.

Blake wiped the tears from his cheeks. He'd promised himself he wouldn't break apart like this, but he hadn't realized until she'd been wheeled off the ambulance that he hadn't ever thanked her for opening her heart to him. He couldn't leave things unsaid between them, no matter how hard it was to say the words his own mother and father had never said to him. He'd known they'd loved him. The Austins were just a family that didn't voice those three words.

''You made this seem like home for us. I can never thank you enough, except to say we love you...'' Putting it in the third person didn't seem right, so he added, ''*I* love you.''

''I don't know how long you knew about Michael, but I want you to know I plan to live up to my responsibilities.'' His voice tightened, coming out barely above a whisper. ''Not just financially. I want to give him a father's love.'' Blake bowed his head. ''I love her, too, even after everything she's done. But you probably already knew that.'' He rubbed his eyes, then rested his head in his hands. ''Watch over us from up there, will you? I think we're going to need it.''

Footsteps pounded up the stairs, bringing Blake's head up. Luke shot through the doorway. Late, as always, but with a tentative smile that made up for it. Or, at least, it would have if Sophia weren't dying.

''I'm going out for some fresh air.'' Blake stood, barely keeping it together. ''Call my cell if you need me.''

PAUSING AT THE DOORWAY to the pink room, Blake listened, but there was only silence. Blake longed to talk with Cori about how she was holding up, Sophia, and his experience with Michael. But it would have to wait until later.

He walked to the back stairs, slid the pocket door on its silent coasters into the wall and stopped. Cori sat a few steps down, hugging her knees. She quickly averted her eyes, but not before Blake noticed the tears. Close to tears again himself, Blake hesitated. Maybe she needed to be alone.

''Don't mind me. I'm just having a moment.'' Her words came out unnaturally high-pitched.

She needed him. Blake settled onto the top step and pulled the door nearly closed behind him, plunging them into semi-darkness so that he could just make out her golden curls.

''Rough night?''

She shook her head.

''Rough morning?''

Cori pulled her lips into a taut line, as if trying not to speak, until finally she expelled a breath. ''On top of everything else, I was fired this morning. The funny thing is, it seems so trivial, like it happened to someone else.''

Blake reached out and gently laid a hand on Cori's shoulder. ''Maybe it's for the best.'' At any other time, he'd be thrilled to hear the news, since it meant one more opening for him to convince Cori to stay.

''We're almost through this now.'' Blake hadn't realized how hard it would be to acknowledge aloud that Sophia was dying. He'd known there was no hope for months now. Seeing death so near shouldn't be so painful.

Cori's fingers entwined tightly around his as if she'd never let him go. How he wished that were the case.

''I should have come home sooner.''

What could he say to that? There'd been many a night he'd wanted to call Cori. In his mind, he'd asked her to come home to him. Maybe if he'd swallowed his pride and done so, she would have. They could have made a family, maybe even had another baby.

''Why didn't I come home sooner?''

That was the $64,000 question. She drew in a labored breath while he waited for her answer.

"I was too absorbed in doing what I thought was right. Maybe…maybe we were all wrong."

She spoke with notes of sadness and wonder threading her voice. Blake longed to hold her in his arms and comfort her, but he sensed she needed to work through her thoughts first.

"She's what I associate with home." She sniffed. "I'm losing the cornerstone of my home. What am I going to do?"

"We're all losing something, Cori."

She tilted her head up to the ceiling.

"It's not fair. We were just becoming friends." She turned and flung herself up the stairs separating them and into his waiting arms.

If it hadn't been such a gut-wrenching time, Blake's heart might have soared. She'd turned to him several times in the past twenty-four hours in search of comfort. As it was, tears rolled down his own cheeks. His hands made comforting circles on her back while she poured her heart out onto his shoulder in quiet sobs.

"It's not fair," he agreed. "But you'll get through it. We'll all get through it."

"I'm sorry. I forgot you lost your mother and father." She pushed herself up and wiped her nose on a wadded-up tissue she'd been gripping in her palm. "I lived through her cancer once before. I watched her go from a gorgeous cover girl to someone who'd throw up at the smell of her own makeup. And her hair—" She pressed the heels of her hands into her eyes. "One day I found her on the bathroom floor crying with clumps of her beautiful black hair clutched in her fists. But no matter how weak she got that time, she fought back."

"She's got the Messina strength, that's for sure."

"Part of me believed this time would be the same. I thought she'd fight it. I thought she'd make it." More sniffles. "And then when I realized she'd given up, I thought I was okay with that because she was still there, with me."

"She's not there now."

"No."

Blake drew her close again. After a heartbeat of hesitation, her body accepted the solace Blake offered. His own turmoil eased.

"It used to help me to think about how my mother would have wanted me to go on," Blake said. "I know it's tough now, but it'll get easier. We've got each other, plus Jen, Luke, Mr. Messina and...Mike to think about."

She backed out of his embrace and searched his features in the dim light, silently asking questions he tried just as wordlessly to answer. He didn't want her to leave.

"That's not his name," she said finally, tentatively.

"I want to talk to you about that. Michael is a mouthful of a name to give a kid to use on a daily basis." There. He'd all but said he wanted to be with them every day.

The door slid open above them, sending blinding sunlight from the hall window into Blake's eyes. He squinted up toward the hallway, trying to force his eyes to adjust.

"Mommy, I'm thirsty," Michael said, thumping down the stairs below Cori. He leaned closer to Cori's face, brushing her hair off her forehead. "Have you been crying, Mommy?"

"Just a little, Pea—baby."

Michael spun on Blake. "You made Mommy cry." He slugged Blake on the thigh, but his stringy arms lacked any power. It was more a symbol of possession, of one male's territory crossed by another. All the time they'd spent together and the tentative bonds they'd built walking the fields and kicking the soccer ball dissipated.

"Michael."

Cori's disbelief blew over Blake slowly, followed by the awareness that she wasn't correcting Michael in any way.

Cori needed to discipline their son. Why didn't she ever lay down the law? "We don't hit," Blake said angrily. "You know the rules. Time-out on the bed until you can say you're sorry."

"You're not the boss of me." Michael's little face contorted into a mask of rage. "Tell him, Mommy."

In that moment, Blake understood that he threatened Michael.

"Michael," Cori said again.

"He's not going to be my daddy, Mommy. Not him." He swung his head quickly from side to side.

"Michael."

Blake heard what he took for fear in Cori's voice. His gut tightened. "Afraid someone might hear him, Cori?"

"No, it's rude." But she didn't look at Blake and her voice came out barely above a whisper. "Michael, apologize to Blake now."

Blake wasn't buying it. Neither was his son.

"No." Michael crossed his arms over his little chest.

"That's it." Cori reached for Michael as she started to rise.

"No," Michael wailed, stepping back. But he hadn't considered that a step back was also a step down. He fell backward and down the stairs, tumbling and shrieking, tumbling and shrieking, until he stopped both.

Blake shot forward, while Cori screamed, frozen in place.

Please don't let him be seriously hurt.

Blake reached the boy at the bottom of the stairs. Michael's head had stopped on the last padded step before the kitchen's marble floor began. His little legs were sprawled on the steps above. Blake noted Michael's wide brown eyes, staring up at him seemingly in surprise, and the blessed fact that none of his bones stuck out at an odd angle.

"Are you all right?"

"Peanut, are you okay?" Cori stumbled down next to them and made to scoop Michael into her arms.

Blake held out his arm to stop her. "Don't move him." Just in case he had some kind of serious injury.

Michael started to cry. He got his elbows under his shoulders and lifted his head.

Blake sighed with relief at the sight. Cori gathered Michael into her arms.

"What's going on down there?" Luke asked from above.

"Michael fell," Cori called back. "He's okay, aren't you,

baby?'' Her arms cocooned Michael. Her cheek nestled against their son's hair. Both faced away from Blake.

Michael continued to cry while Blake sat apart and alone.

''HE'S OKAY,'' Blake told Cori half an hour later when they had returned to the pink room. ''Aren't you?''

Michael didn't answer.

Discounting Blake's assessment, Cori had called the boy's pediatrician down in Los Angeles. Blake knew Michael was fine. The kid had a way of looking at him sideways that he would never have managed had he really been seriously injured. Yet Michael clung to Cori and whined often enough for her to continue to lavish her attention on him.

Blake was jealous. Of his own son and the attention Cori gave him. Of the way Michael and Cori could hug each other any time they wanted. Of the way Michael had bonded with Jen. Anger tingled in his veins. Anger at himself. At Cori. At everyone. Blake controlled his emotions no better than his four-year-old son did.

''Cori, I need to talk with you.''

She looked at Blake as if he'd asked her to dance naked in front of the workmen, then turned away as if he was just a field hand and not the father of her child. She and Michael were on the floor watching television. The boy lay in the crook of her arm, snuggled against her.

It was easy to picture Blake lying on the other side of the boy, part of their family. Making that vision a reality was next to impossible. Yet, he had to try.

''I need to talk to you *now,*'' Blake said.

''I'll meet you later.''

Meaning, she may or may not come down to the river tonight.

''You'll meet with me now.''

Cori looked up into his eyes and frowned. ''Now?''

Rather than answer her, he walked out the door. Luke was down the hall and Blake didn't want him to overhear what he had to say. Perhaps sensing the urgency of his request, Cori followed. He heard the light tread of her bare feet behind him.

When he got down to the kitchen, Blake leaned against the sturdy oak table, watching her closely. Cori propped herself against the marble counter several feet away from him.

"I want to be a part of his life." *A part of your life, too,* he silently added. He couldn't risk saying that yet.

"I don't know what you said to him to make him dislike you, but he's not going to run into your arms if we tell him now." She looked tired, still wearing the same clothes she'd worn to the hospital last night.

"I didn't say anything to him. He's jealous of me. I'm guessing he's never had to share you before and he's upset that you weren't there with him this morning. He woke up crying for his mommy." The words came out more bitterly than he would have liked, so he softened it with "I made him pancakes."

"He's normally a very loving child." She couldn't back up her words with eye contact.

He spread his arms. "Hey, everybody loves me." Everyone except Cori. But Blake was going to change that just as soon as he fixed his relationship with his son. "Seriously, the kid needs a father."

Her eyes dropped. "Los Angeles is a ten-hour drive from here."

"Or a seventy-five-minute flight." If he had his way, they'd all live here in Healdsburg. She'd work for the winery while raising their son.

"You can't come." Cori crossed her arms over her chest.

"Excuse me?" Thirty minutes ago, he'd almost had it all. Now she was rejecting him. He pushed away from the table. Blake had known this wasn't going to be easy, but he hadn't expected to be refused even minimal contact outright.

"I mean—" she pushed the hair off her forehead with a sigh "—my grandfather won't like it if you take so much time off."

"I don't care what your grandfather likes." He spoke carefully, trying to hold on to his temper and disguise his hurt, probably not doing a good job at either one.

Her eyes met his, then broke away again. "Yes, you do. This job is important to you."

Sure, it was important, but his love for Michael and Cori was more so. "You're saying no?"

"I'm not saying no." She paused and looked into his eyes. They were dark and devoid of hope. They'd exchanged warmer glances on the stairs a half hour ago. "I'm just saying the timing isn't right."

"Like when you didn't think it was the right time to tell me you were pregnant, so you didn't tell me at all? Or the time you didn't think it was the right time to tell me I was a father? Families don't come with a timetable or wait for the right moment. What you're saying is it's not convenient for you." His breath came fast and his temper spun nearly out of hand.

Her eyes looked stricken. "Yes," she whispered.

The impossibility of the situation towered insurmountably over what little hope he had left. Cori wasn't going to let him see his son. Not on alternate weekends. Not ever. Being with her was out of the question. Any chance he'd had of making a family with her was gone.

Tears flowed down her cheeks. He couldn't take that. She played selfish games and she wanted his sympathy? He'd be damned if he'd give her any. He stomped toward the door, not trusting himself to speak.

"Wait." She reached out a hand to him but only took a small step in his direction. They were yards apart, but they may just as well have been at opposite ends of the pole.

"This whole conversation came out wrong," she said, brushing away tears. "What I'm trying to say is yes, he does need you. I just can't wrap my mind around the logistics of it all right now."

A small compromise, but one he was willing to accept. For now. Because believing her gave his foolish heart hope.

CHAPTER ELEVEN

"MOMMY, THERE'S A stranger." Michael said from his position on the window seat later that afternoon.

Dutifully, Cori walked over to the window to see. Michael often spotted workmen around the vineyard, so she was surprised to look down and see a teenage boy coming down the drive.

"Who is it?" Luke asked from the chair next to the bed.

"I don't know. It's a boy. Maybe it's someone for Jennifer."

"I'll go see," Luke offered.

"No, you stay," Cori said. Sitting with her mother in her catatonic state, she'd had plenty of time to replay the horrible way she'd handled things downstairs with Blake. If he never spoke to her again, she wouldn't blame him. Cori needed a distraction. Besides, Luke spent so little time with their mother, she wanted him to stay longer. "Come on, Michael." She held out her hand, and together they walked carefully down the stairs to the front door.

They opened the door, clearly surprising the teen, who stood hesitantly on the bottom step. Definitely here to see Jennifer.

"Hello. May I help you?"

"Does Jennifer Austin live here?" His discomfort was palpable from the way he fidgeted.

Cori recognized him as one of the teens that had approached Jennifer on Sunday. She couldn't sense any attitude in his nervous blue gaze and she approved of his short blond hair, although he could stand to lose the baggy shorts.

Cori made her decision. "Yes, she does. We'll take you to her."

He stepped forward just as she and Michael came out the front door and closed it behind them. The teen looked perplexed.

"She's at the house around back."

"Oh." He blushed, big rosy splotches that highlighted what little acne he had on his face. He fell into step next to them. "You don't have to take me, just point me in the right direction."

Cori smiled. "It's a little more complicated than that. By the way, I'm Cori and this is Michael."

"Skyler." His head bobbed a few times.

Intrigued by the teen's name, Cori debated whether he had yuppie or hippie origins. The people of Sonoma County were known for their hippie roots. The yuppies had gravitated to Sonoma in the nineties. He seemed comfortable enough with people that he could have come from either type of family.

"What do your folks do?" Despite the tension between them, Cori was a little protective of Jennifer.

"My dad's a lawyer for the Environmental Protection Agency and my mom makes arts and crafts."

Hippie roots, for sure. They walked around the house and picked up the back road toward the river.

"Are you Jennifer's mother?" He gave her a speculative glance.

Cori fluffed her hair. Did she look old enough to be a teenager's mother? "No, but you're lucky you asked me that question and not Jennifer. I'm..." Cori hesitated. She had been about to say "friend," but that didn't seem quite right. "...a family friend."

"How old are you, Mike?"

Cori didn't miss the fact that he shortened Michael's name even while she was impressed he'd remembered it.

"Four."

"My brother is four. You in preschool?"

Michael's head wobbled up and down. "I go to Academy. We practice ABCs."

"Cool. My brother goes to Toddler Town."

Cori hoped Jen would go easy on this one. From what she could see, he was a keeper. They continued with an easy stream of small talk all the way to Jennifer's house. Try as she might, Cori couldn't stop looking for Blake's dark head towering over the vines or his truck parked alongside the road. She dreaded seeing him again, to face his anger and iron out the details of his visitation rights. She wanted something else entirely, something out of her reach—a future with Blake. But they didn't see a soul and her hopes were left hanging.

"Hey, you were right. I never would have found this place on my own," Skyler said once they reached the house.

"I slept here. This morning," Michael said, proudly puffing out his chest.

"Last night," Cori corrected, wishing Blake could see their little man's behavior now.

"Last night," he repeated dutifully.

The trio stepped onto the front porch. Cori knocked. A few moments later they could hear the pounding of footsteps across the hardwood floor.

"Who is it?" Jen called out, irritation evident even through the door.

Cori and Skyler exchanged worried glances.

Jen flung the door open, then dropped her jaw when she saw Skyler. She wore a baggy, faded T-shirt that hung loosely over Winnie-the-Pooh boxer shorts.

"Aiyeeee!" She slammed the door in their faces and they could hear her footsteps pound away from the door.

Michael giggled, while Cori tried not to.

"I take it from her response that she didn't know you were coming," Cori said dryly.

Skyler looked apologetic. "She wasn't at school today, so I took the bus over here. She's been having a hard time lately." He ran his hand over his short hair. "I was worried."

"Someone we love is dying." Cori held back the tears with a deep breath. "It's hitting us all pretty hard."

"Oh man. I'm sorry. I should go." He stepped off the porch.

It was a shame, because Cori suspected he'd do Jennifer's ego a world of good.

"Wait. Why don't you and Michael play for a few minutes while I go talk to her?"

He looked back. "I don't know. My grandfather died last year and I felt pretty weird for a long time."

"Then, you'll understand what Jen's going through. She needs friends like that now." Cori looked down at Michael. "You'll play with Skyler for a few minutes while I talk to Jen, won't you?"

"Sure." It seemed Michael had found a new role model. If only he and Blake had hit it off as easily.

As Cori went inside, she heard Skyler say, "Do you know how to play Rock, Paper, Scissors?"

She walked through the living room and glanced into the kitchen. Although she'd never lived here, she'd baby-sat Jen a few times and was familiar with the layout of the house. MTV blared from a small television above the refrigerator. Meat defrosted on the counter. No Jen.

Cori headed upstairs, following the sound of melancholy music, and knocked on Jen's door. It didn't take long for her to swing it open. Red eyes and a deep scowl greeted her.

"Are you out of your mind bringing Skyler Wight here?"

"Jen, I—"

"Why didn't you call? You always have that cell phone of yours on."

Actually, Cori had turned it off at the hospital and hadn't turned it back on. It sat silently on the dresser in the pink room. "I—"

"I look like such a dork." She held out the bottom of her T-shirt. "I bet he took off fast after I slammed the door in his face."

Cori grabbed Jen's shoulders and gave her a little shake to disconnect her motor mouth. "Jen. He doesn't think you're a dork. He's waiting downstairs with this lovesick expression on his face."

"Really?"

The hope in her eyes was almost too painful to look upon. The girl needed some extra-special attention. Cori was going to make sure she got it, if she had to hog-tie Jen and drag her downstairs.

Jen's face fell. "I can't. I can't talk to him."

"Why not?"

"Because Sophia's sick." Jen's throat worked. "Really sick."

The pressure of tears clogged the back of Cori's throat. She placed her arm around Jen's shoulders and led her to the unmade bed. It said something for Jen's state of mind that she didn't immediately shrug out of Cori's embrace, although the girl's shoulders were tense beneath Cori's arm. Tossing the covers in the general direction of the pillows, Cori sat, patting the spot next to her. Jen sank down, keeping her distance.

"A long time ago, when Mama had cancer the first time, I told her I'd turned down an invitation to the prom because she was sick. I thought she was going to go through the roof, she was so mad. She told me clearly, loudly, and in a voice that said I shouldn't argue with her, that I was never, ever to stop living my life based on what was happening in hers."

Jen looked at her in openmouthed amazement. "What did you do?"

"The next day, I found Nick at school. I told him I'd changed my mind, only by that time, he'd already asked somebody else."

"Eewww."

"Yeah. I ended up going with the son of one of my mother's friends. Pity date. Major geek alert."

Jen giggled. "I can just imagine you with some four-eyed dork."

"Gee, thanks." First she was considered old enough to have a twelve-year-old, and then she was easily pictured with a geek for a prom date. Cori's self-image was getting quite a few knocks today. "I guess this is where I tell you to get your butt out there lest you end up in the same boat."

Jen shook her head. "I can't. I mean, he's seen me do some

incredibly stupid things lately. Besides, look at me.'' She pulled on her T-shirt.

''I don't think that matters. He said he came because he was worried about you. Still—'' She gave Jen the once-over. ''You could use a little polishing up. Do you have anything clean to wear? Something that fits you?'' Clothes seemed to be growing like twisted vines from the dresser. Nothing hung in her closet. ''Then a quick brush of hair and teeth, and *voilà,* you're ready for business.''

''Oh, crud. Do I have bad breath, too?'' Jen looked stricken.

Cori sighed. She may be in love with Blake, but at least she wasn't *young* and in love.

LEANING AGAINST A TREE, Cori watched the river flow past, shimmering under the full moon. As a child, she'd dreamed of taking a boat downriver whenever the pressure of being a Messina got to her. Now she realized that was just a four-year-old's way of dealing with the horror of seeing her dad disappear around the river bend. At twenty-five, she was going to have to learn how to deal with her mother's death, and she didn't think it would be as easy as it had been for her to let go of her father.

Cori didn't know how long she stood in the darkness pondering how her life had been like the river. She'd gone with the flow until she'd gotten pregnant. Then she'd gone with the flow again after she'd had Michael. Oh, she'd tried to steer herself in a specific direction to prove that she could, but when it came down to it, she was still drifting. If Cori wanted to be part of her family badly enough, she'd have to do something. She just didn't know if she needed her family as much without her mother in it.

But she did know she needed Blake.

She wanted the Blake she'd fallen in love with, the Blake she'd leaned on, then chased away. Could they make it work if Cori sacrificed her pride to be what her grandfather wanted her to be, to play the role left empty by Mama, the one he'd tried to make her play the other night at dinner? Cori didn't think she could do it. She'd tasted professional life, in the real world where people respected her opinion. At least, some of her clients respected her. Coming back to Healdsburg and not being a part of Messina Vineyards was not an option. She couldn't do that to her grandfather.

Cori wished she could forget all the secrets and crossroads she was facing for just a few hours of acceptance from Blake. Would it be too much to ask him to hold her one more time? No strings, no hidden agendas, no games and no fear of reprisals?

Why couldn't she? Because he despised her for keeping his son from him, that's why.

Didn't he?

Cori recalled how compassionate Blake had been to her these past few days before the scene on the stairs. Wary, but the white-hot anger and derogatory remarks were gone.

Of their own accord, Cori's feet turned and started off toward Blake's house. It was only eleven. He might still be up. But when she reached the house, it was dark.

Cori lowered herself onto the top porch step. She'd wanted to talk to Blake now. Her courage would most likely have deserted her by morning. Dejected, she wrapped her arms around her knees and sank her chin into the cradle she'd created.

A sound around the corner of the house had her shooting to her feet, reminding her how dangerous it could be outside at night. Vagrants sometimes traveled along the river, as did mountain lions and other wild animals. She moved back into the shadows of the porch, held her breath and waited.

It was a man, all right. Tall, broad-shouldered...Blake.

Cori sighed in relief. Blake stopped and looked toward her.

"Who's there?"

"Me." She moved onto the top step and into the moonlight.

Blake approached, not saying anything. He stopped at the bottom of the steps, doubt evident in his expression even in the darkness. Cori felt the most insane urge to lean over and wrap her arms reassuringly around him. Instead, she sank to the porch, her gaze taking in his flannel and jean-clad body before resting on her own tennis shoes.

''Why didn't you tell me? Were you scared of me?''

She didn't have to ask what Blake meant. She knew he wanted to know more about her decision back then. ''It's complicated.''

His gray eyes were as chilly as the night around them. ''Cori, I'm trying to understand your side, but these evasive answers don't help.''

''They don't help anyone, do they.'' Cori took a deep breath, bolstering her resolve to tell him most of the truth. ''You should probably sit down. This could take a while.''

BLAKE DIDN'T WANT TO SIT. He had too much pent-up energy to remain still, yet he had to sit if he wanted his answers. Blake lowered himself to the bottom step on the opposite side of the porch from Cori, and leaned his back against the railing. He rested one foot on the step and one on the ground.

''When I was twelve, my girlfriends were having a sleepover on the same night my grandfather was entertaining visiting diplomats. While my friends were scaring each other with ghost stories and talking about boys, I had to smile and be polite to these people who barely acknowledged my presence.'' She hugged her knees, staring out at rows of cloaked vineyard. ''In high school, I could never go to football games because it was harvest season and we needed every pair of hands. When we weren't tending to the grapes, we traveled or entertained. Actors, politicians, reporters, wine critics. My friends were experiencing their first kiss and hanging out with boys when I was having six-course meals with the president of the United States. By the end of high school, I had no friends here and no life of my own.''

''This has nothing to do with us.'' So growing up a Messina wasn't a bowl of cherries. Blake's childhood hadn't been rosy, either, not before Kevin Austin entered the picture. None of that was an excuse for what she'd done.

''It has everything to do with us.'' Cori leaned closer. ''By the time I made it to college and realized there was more to life than following orders, I knew I couldn't come back here after graduation."

"Your family would have understood. You didn't need to fit some mold. You could have done public relations for them here." They loved her. He loved her. Couldn't she see that?

"My grandfather wanted another Sophia Sinclair, someone willing to be the goodwill ambassador for the winery, someone loyal enough to stick by his side and make sure his needs were taken care of. He's never wanted anyone around with an idea and the guts to express it, particularly when their opinion contradicted his. I know he dogs Luke on everything, questioning every decision Luke tries to make without him. You've seen that in him, haven't you?"

Blake recalled Mr. Messina ignoring Cori's advice the other night, and how he'd questioned Blake's choice of grafting crew. Of course, that hadn't been the first time Blake's judgment had been questioned, but he wasn't going to be caught bad-mouthing his employer, particularly to his granddaughter. So he sat, seemingly absorbed in the shadowy view, waiting for Cori to continue.

"I came home that summer and met you." She ran her fingers through her hair, an enticing movement that reminded him how silky and alive her hair was to touch.

"You were independent and self-sufficient. I yearned for that. I'd always felt years older than my peers, but with you, it was right. We became friends, despite your best efforts." She smiled regretfully. "I went back to school for my final year feeling more focused than ever. I treasured those nightly phone calls with you because you'd proved to me that a person could make it without family. I hadn't possessed the courage to grasp that idea before meeting you."

Blake stared at the eaves. He'd been in love and she'd been motivated by him to move on?

"I knew by then that I wanted to work in public relations and I interviewed with some firms until I landed a job. In the meantime, my grandfather made plans for me without my knowledge. He had me scheduled to attend dinners, show visitors around, even take a group of wine critics on a tour of Europe.'' She turned and set her back against the railing, mirroring his position. ''I was getting a business degree from Stanford and he wanted me to play hostess? To continue smiling and hiding the fact that I had an opinion? I couldn't do it.'' She sighed. ''But I couldn't tell him, either.''

Blake replayed scenes from the awards dinner, recalling how Cori had continued to state her opinion despite being rebuffed by her grandfather. At twenty, would he have been able to accept that as his future?

''When I came home at spring break, I knew I didn't want to come back here in June—and the last thing I should have wanted was to sleep with you.''

''Great.'' Blake barely found enough air for the word. Everything fell apart. ''I thought what we felt was mutual.''

Cori winced. ''That didn't come out right. I…liked you. A lot.''

The ''friend'' speech. Hell, this wasn't getting any better. Blake ordered his heart to keep beating.

''But you were just starting out and building your career *here.* You were one more tie to this place I couldn't have.''

When he didn't respond, she added softly, ''I just couldn't resist you.'' Cori sighed heavily. ''I came home for spring break knowing I had to be with you at least once. It was totally selfish, but I had to have you.''

Balm on the wound, but she'd cut too deep for it to be healed that easily. Blake focused on the point, or lack thereof. ''That explains why you left me that night. It doesn't explain why you didn't tell me you were pregnant.''

Silence. The dreaded Messina silence. *Please tell me the truth.*

''It was a hard decision. I was…'' She hesitated. ''Alone.'' She rushed on. ''I'm not saying it was the right decision. It was just the only option for me at the time.''

Another explanation of what she'd done. Not why. Not the truth. Would she ever tell him the whole truth? Convinced his lower status in life played a hand in it, Blake's spirits hung around his bootlaces.

"So here we are," Blake said awkwardly, wondering where that left him. But he knew. Alone. With no easily attainable parental rights. And no Cori.

She moved down a step closer to him. Her feet tucked below her. Her dark eyes riveted on him.

"Can you ever forgive me?"

There was a part of him that already had and there was a part of him that never would. She continued to wait for his answer.

"You haven't told me why."

She looked hurt and rubbed her bottom lip over her top one. Her mouth absorbed his attention for a moment. Or two. Not the time, he told his suddenly alert body. Not ever again.

Cori hung her head. "I thought if you understood what brought me to that point, you'd realize why." Her voice sounded small. Remorseful.

"I think I know why," Blake finally admitted, moved by the pain in her voice. She had wanted out and he hadn't been good enough to make it worth staying. "And somewhere inside me I think I can forgive you…someday." What a fool he was for opening himself up to more hurt. The smart thing to do would have been to say no.

They sat staring at each other, he mooning stupidly, and she with an unreadable expression on her face. If there had been more light, Blake might have pinpointed it as longing, unbelievable as that was. Yet, they continued to stare mutely at each other.

Maybe it was longing. What the hell did that mean?

Just take her into your arms, you dummy.

While he debated his internal voice, she blinked, seemed to realize they were having an awkward moment and stood. Blake shot up, too, both feet firmly planted on the ground. With Cori on the second step, they were almost on equal footing.

"I guess I should be going. Luke said he'd stay with Mama, but you never know what he'll do."

Blake wanted to say, don't go. ''I'll walk you home'' came out instead. In his mind, they were lip-locked, his hands roving across her back, while he wondered what color panties she had on.

She held up her hand. ''It's all right. I know the way.'' Only, instead of lowering her hand to her side, it managed to land on his chest. She blinked, almost as if she were as surprised as he was at the contact.

Warmth seeped through his shirt, seemingly into his heart. He covered her hand with his, pressed it against his chest and drew in a ragged breath. She took a step closer.

''You're not going to do this to me again, are you?'' The last bastion around his heart made him ask.

She reached up and curled her hand around his neck until her fingers were threaded in his hair. Then she drew him down to her mouth. ''Make love to you?'' she asked before their lips touched.

Blake groaned over the images her use of the word *love* conjured up. Definitely up. Upstairs to his bedroom and a couple of condoms. Her touch heated him more than the memories of her ever could. Lip-locked, his hands glided across her back, while his mind wondered persistently what color panties she wore.

Her flavor burst inside his mouth as their tongues danced. She was sweet and warm, just as he remembered. He was home. He left her mouth to taste and nibble his way down the side of her neck, rejoicing in the familiarity of her smell, of her feel against him, the fact that she was in his arms.

''You do forgive me?'' Cori whispered across his ear.

Would he forgive her? ''Only if this isn't just for one night.''

Cori cradled his head in her hands and gazed at him with eyes brimming. A tear rolled down her cheek. He brushed it gently away.

''None of that. I'm the one who should be crying. The last time I said something like that to you, you hightailed it out of town.''

''I love you,'' she said, so sincerely that he thought she believed it.

His body clamored for him to trust her. His head wondered how long it would be before she left him.

He bent his head to kiss her again, then scooped her into his arms and wobbled up the stairs to the front door. He set her down and turned the knob, only to find it locked. He groaned. ''I only have a key to the back door.''

Cori smiled against his lips and moved her hands teasingly over the placket of his jeans.

''What now?''

''We go to the back door.''

He slid his hands over her firm cheeks and lifted her to him, needing her closer now, not thirty paces and fifteen stairs from now. She wrapped her legs around his waist and her arms around his neck. All he could think about was carrying her upstairs, taking a brief appreciative look at the thong he'd felt beneath her jeans and burying himself inside her, finally recapturing the peace he'd felt that one night so long ago.

''Wait a minute. Before I take the steps again I need some sustenance.'' He slid a hand beneath her Stanford sweatshirt, splaying his palm over the smooth skin of her belly. He closed his eyes for a moment, imagining his son—Michael—growing inside of her. She must have been scared half to death, alone and away from her family. Away from him.

The tops of his fingers brushed satiny material, and he drew his hand farther up her body to cup her breast. He circled it with his palm, testing it against his memory of her from years ago.

''You've grown.''

She chuckled, her head tucked into his neck. ''I've gained weight.''

''Only in the right places.'' His hand over her fullness, he made a circle with his fingers and thumb, then pulled her breast, bra and all, through it.

Cori groaned and gave his ear a little nip of approval.

''We've got to get upstairs.'' He hitched her up higher and

navigated the steps, then the dimly lit side yard to the kitchen door, never wanting to let her go. Never wanting her to stop touching him.

She lightly brushed her fingertips over his scalp while she sucked at his neck.

"Hey, no love bites where they can be seen," he halfheartedly protested.

She laughed, pressing a light kiss to the spot.

Blake hopped up the back steps, then stopped, gazing into her eyes. "Last chance to back out."

"Not on your life, Austin."

He kissed her because he loved her, because she'd come back to him. Although he couldn't say it yet. *Don't break my heart.* Damn, he kissed her harder and told his internal security system to take the night off.

He set her down. "No funny business until we get upstairs. Quietly."

She was already leaning over to take off her shoes. "I know the drill."

"Interesting analogy." He watched the tantalizing curves outlined by her movements. "Are you on the pill?"

She straightened as if she'd been struck by lightning. "No."

"No?" he echoed stupidly. "No diaphragm?" Potent Sperm and Fertile Myrtle II. It sounded like a bad movie.

"No." She sagged against the wall. The energy drained out of her.

He commiserated. He wouldn't mind having more kids with Cori. He just wanted to lay the foundation of their relationship first.

"You could use double coverage," she offered brightly.

The thought wasn't immensely pleasing for Blake.

"We could do other things," he countered, sincerely hoping he'd be able to stop at those other things.

She looked despondent, which helped his ego immensely. "If you're sure."

He leaned down to buss her quickly. "There'll be time

later.'' Meaning the rest of their lives, but he wasn't about to scare her off like he had the last time.

IT SEEMED TO TAKE FOREVER to sneak up the stairs past Jennifer's room and into Blake's bedroom. Cori's hand was nestled within his the whole way. She hadn't been this sure about anything in a long time, nearly five years. With only one sexual experience to draw from and the ten extra pounds she knew made her look different without her clothes on, she'd agreed to come upstairs for some intense foreplay. If it had been anyone else but Blake, she would have given in to her insecurities and run home. But this was Blake, and in her heart, he meant home.

He turned on some music while she walked over to the window. The pane was open and the breeze made the cream-colored sheer curtains dance on either side of her as she looked out. The brisk air prickled her skin. She couldn't wait for Blake to warm her up.

''I can see the river from here.'' More specifically, she could see their stretch of the river. That explained how Blake usually found her there all those years ago. With a low carpet of fog, on a moonlit night like tonight, Blake had a breathtaking view of the valley in which Messina Vineyards was nestled. Moonglow lit the bedroom softer than any candle.

''I've been wondering what kind of underthings you're wearing.''

She turned to him with a seductive smile. ''Really? What did you guess?''

''Black.''

Cori shook her head. ''Not very imaginative.''

He looked hurt. To lighten the mood, she slid her hands beneath her sweatshirt, palms out, and waved them around in front of her chest. ''It's purple today. Do you like purple?'' She hoped so.

Blake nodded. Smiled.

''I can't believe I waited this long for you,'' she said, laughing self-consciously as her hands dropped to her sides. "I'm a little nervous."

"Me, too." His eyes seemed to devour her, but more than five feet still separated them and the air from the window definitely had her chilled now.

Cori shook her head in disbelief. "Men are never nervous."

"That's not true. Men worry about the same things women do. Can I please her? Will she laugh when she sees me naked?"

"You don't." Cori grinned, grateful that he was taking the time to put her at ease.

"We do. Want me to tell you what I'm thinking right now?"

"Yes," she breathed.

His eyes roamed her fully clothed body. "I'm remembering how soft your skin felt beneath my hands. How you sounded when I touched you. How right it felt when you were in my arms."

Wow. "That's really…really…" Cori struggled for a word to describe how he made her feel and came up with several. "Sweet. Poetic. Hot." She'd do anything for this man she loved.

"Yeah, well. What can I say?" He closed the distance between them. "You inspire me."

For the next few hours, they inspired each other.

CHAPTER TWELVE

"I'D BETTER GET BACK." Cori sat up in bed, pulling the sheet up to cover her breasts.

Blake hadn't expected their interlude to last this long or to end this quickly. They'd just shared what seemed like a marathon experience of pleasuring each other. Gazing up at her with his head resting on his hands, he clenched his fingers so he wouldn't reach for her again. "I'll walk you back."

She leaned over and touched her lips to his. "I'd like that."

A few minutes later, they stepped out onto the back porch and into the brisk night. Cori moved next to Blake and lifted his arm around her shoulders with a smile, keeping her hand clasped around his. They started walking at a leisurely pace. Blake drew her closer, reveling in the warmth and intimacy, something he didn't dare call the bond of love, because that would mean he and Cori had solved all their problems.

"I don't want this night to end." Blake leaned to press a kiss to her crown.

Cori squeezed his hand. "I know. Tonight was magic."

"Oh, I wouldn't call it magic. Magic implies it was all an illusion. Which would mean the past couple of hours only existed in our minds." He caught her smiling. "Then I'd never experience that thing you do with your lips again."

Cori laughed softly. "That was real, and, despite what you say, magic at the same time. What comes next won't be as easy or pleasant."

The hairs on the back of Blake's neck prickled. "What do you mean?"

"It's obvious, isn't it?" She paused, perhaps waiting for him to answer. Since it wasn't obvious to Blake, he kept his mouth shut, wishing she'd trust him enough—no, love him enough—to speak plainly. "When my grandfather finds out, he's going to make sure he can control you," she finally told him when he didn't comment.

"Control me? He already bosses me around." That was the least of Blake's concerns. Fire him, take away his home. Those worries were more pressing.

"You don't understand." Cori's hand released his. The same hand that had loved him so intimately such a short time ago. "He'll push you harder, expect more, and if you don't live up to his standards, he'll get rid of you."

"Why would that matter if we're together? Cori, that's ridiculous."

"As ridiculous as him paying off my father to get him to marry my mother, and then later to get him to leave? My mother says they were in love, too."

Blake shook his head. "He didn't. He wouldn't."

Cori marched along the road in silence. Finally, instead of arguing, she asked, "Are you willing to swallow your pride for this job? To stick it out?"

"It won't come to that." Blake couldn't believe Mr. Messina would do that to him. Fire him, yes. Make him a monetary offer to leave, no.

She turned to face him, wrapping her arms around her chest. Her chin jutted out. A solitary tear tracked across her cheek.

In two steps, he enfolded her in his embrace. "Oh, baby, don't cry."

She pushed her small hands against his chest, dropping her head back so she could see his face. "I need you to be sure. I love you."

Sure of what? His love for her? That was unquestionable. But did she love him enough to make this work? If he doubted anything, it was her commitment and ability to stay.

Her eyes searched his, found the doubt. She squeezed her eyes shut tight and dropped her head so that he could no longer see her expression.

"Don't...don't tell him, then." This time when she pushed, she freed herself. Cori walked quickly away from him.

"I didn't say I wasn't sure." How did her short legs manage to keep ahead of him?

"You didn't have to say anything."

"Cori, this is crazy. You're overdramatizing. If you don't want me, if this is some game of yours, there are easier ways to discourage me than this."

She spun around and slapped him. Blake's cheek prickled like frostbitten skin. Cori stood trembling before him, flexing her hand as if it hurt, as well.

"If you can't see I'm trying to protect you, then you can't see. If you want to stay in Sonoma, I have to be a part of Messina Vineyards again. I don't want you to hate me when he makes it hard for you."

She pivoted and headed for the house again. "I don't know what you want from me."

Couldn't she tell? Blake's heart held together by sheer force of will. "I want us to have a life together. To raise our son together."

Blake reached out and desperately turned her to face him. They were on the other side of the swimming pool now, within shouting distance of the mansion. He could feel her slipping through his fingers, his dreams of family drifting away with the mists of the night.

"Maybe I'm confused. Maybe I'll keep playing catch-up until you tell me exactly what's going on." Blake lowered his voice. "You must know how I feel about you."

"Do I?" She shut her eyes and took a breath, then snapped her gaze back on him. "I get that you don't trust me, but you've always jumped to the wrong conclusions, and you certainly never said a word about *love*." Her voice faltered.

"Maybe I'm not as free with my words as you are, but I'm trying. Remember, I'm the one who keeps getting lied to and still comes back." He'd told her he'd forgiven her, hadn't he? How much more did she want from him? Didn't what they had just shared count for anything?

"If that's the best you can do, I don't know if I want you to keep trying." Tears filled her eyes and her lower lip trembled.

God, he'd really screwed up. He was back where he'd started hours ago, days ago, years ago.

She released a shuddering breath. "I won't stand in your way if you want to see Michael, but you can't tell him you're his father. Not yet."

"Thanks," Blake mumbled, grateful that he'd made some kind of progress, despite the fact that his heart had been tossed away yet again. She'd been right. It had been magic between them—an illusion that couldn't last.

"WHY DON'T YOU GO ON to bed." Cori gently shook Luke awake where he slept on the couch. "I'll stay with Mama tonight."

"You don't have to tell me twice." Luke stood, stretching his lean body to the ceiling before stumbling out to the hall.

Cori sank into the chair next to her mother and waited until she heard Luke's bedroom door close. In the soft light from the hallway, Cori could see Mama's chest rise and fall weakly. She pulled the chair closer to her mother's bed. Mama slept peacefully, not that it would have mattered. Awake, only Mama's eyes gave away the secret that she still lived.

"I made a terrible mistake, Mama." She smoothed her hand over the satin bedspread. "I thought he loved me. I thought if I explained, he'd understand."

Leaning both elbows on her mother's bed and clasping her hands as if in prayer, Cori examined Mama's face. "I really wish you could hear me because I need your advice. My pride says this has all been a bad case of lust and I need to move on."

Cori conked her head lightly with her knuckles, her cheeks heating at the memory of how she'd exposed herself to Blake earlier. Physically and emotionally. "My heart, on the other hand, can't seem to let go. Pretty sad, huh?"

Her mother's face remained blank. Cori sat up straighter,

shamed by the thought that she was being a whiny, self-centered daughter. Her mother was dying and all Cori could think about was her broken heart?

"Did I tell you I talked to John Sinclair? I can see why you fell in love with him, he's quite a charmer." Cori choked on the lie. Thoughts of her conversation with her father gave her the willies. Still, Cori couldn't bring herself to tell her mother her ex-husband wasn't coming.

"I miss you, Mama." Cori settled her head on her arms and closed her eyes against the tears.

HE'D LOST HER.

Blake sprawled on the living room couch and stared at the cracks in the ceiling while he waited for the coming dawn. No point in sleeping now, with sunrise just a few hours away. He may as well use the time to decide how to straighten out the mess he'd made of his life.

It sure beat remembering the lovemaking they'd shared.

The Messinas took misdirection to an art form, which made Cori's declaration of love that much more painful. Had it been a rare statement of truth? He didn't want to believe anything else. Yet, it was hard to believe. If she loved him, why had she left him years ago? How could her need for independence have overruled her love for him? And later, the welfare of their child?

Blake had to face facts. He was insecure when it came to Cori. Every time he started to open up to her, she broke his trust, shattered his heart by putting herself first. But love wasn't something you questioned. If he wanted Cori and Michael permanently in his life, he had to trust her and try to understand her fears about Mr. Messina, even if he didn't put as much credence in them as she did. Her fears were affecting their lives.

He had to try harder to be Mr. Sensitive. She'd slapped the hell out of him when he'd accused her of being paranoid. He rubbed his cheek, still feeling the sting of her blow. Gophers had more brains than he did. At least they knew when to duck for cover.

CORI AWOKE TO FOOTSTEPS and the smell of fresh flowers. Maria carried a large bouquet over to the window with stiff steps. Cori lifted her heavy head, only to have Mama's hand slide off her crown. That was impossible. Mama hadn't moved on her own since she'd woken up in the hospital.

"Mama?" Was she conscious? How else could her hand have gotten on Cori's head?

But Mama lay inert and unresponsive. Cori ran her fingers through her hair as if to tease out answers. Maybe Cori had held her mother's hand close during the night and somehow managed to position it over her head. Cori didn't remember. With a sigh, Cori chose to think Mama had comforted her, no matter how unlikely that was.

"Maria, you shouldn't have brought those upstairs. I would have carried them for you," Cori said.

"I wanted to bring Mrs. Sinclair something to cheer her up." Maria brought the card over to Cori, blinking back tears. "Michael is downstairs having breakfast with Blake and Jennifer."

"Oh." Cori self-consciously pushed her hair out of her face. She needed more time before facing Blake again, possibly another four to five years. "Can you sit with Mama while I take a shower?"

"Certainly. I'll get the flowers water." Maria trundled slowly into the bathroom.

"Thank you." Cori looked at the small sealed envelope. It was addressed to Sophia Sinclair. Maybe her grandfather had sent the flowers. Cori opened the card and read in wonder, her eyes glistening by the time she realized who the flowers were from.

"Mama, listen to this." Cori took her mother's hand. "'My dearest Sophia, how did we two thorny weeds manage to produce two such beautiful roses? All is forgiven. Forever yours, John.'"

Her father wasn't totally heartless. When Cori looked up,

Sophia's eyes were open but she didn't look as if the news from John Sinclair had even registered.

"He still loves you, Mama. He sent this beautiful card and a gorgeous bouquet of flowers, see?" She pointed toward the window. For a moment, Cori thought she caught Sophia's eyes drifting to the window. But then Sophia's eyelids closed.

Cori patted Mama's hand. "He loves you." With a sigh, Cori went to take a quick shower, comforted to discover her father wasn't totally abhorrent, after all.

"HOW ABOUT SOME CEREAL or toast?" Blake asked Michael, standing like Vanna White at the Messinas' pantry, trying to entice the boy to eat something. Anything. Blake's eyes kept drifting to the sliding pocket door leading to the back stairs. Cori had yet to make an appearance this morning. He couldn't wait to see her so that he could try to repair last night's damage.

Sideways in the kitchen chair, Michael sat with his back to Blake. "I like pancakes. With chocolate."

"Saturday and Sunday are pancake days. Jen's got school this morning."

"Yeah, I'm going to miss the bus if you don't hurry. Blake's driving me out to the highway bus stop in, like, two minutes." Jen supported Blake with a grin. She'd been uncharacteristically helpful the past few days. "Want to ride along?"

"Okay." Michael gave her his full-wattage smile. He doted on Jen. Blake wished he could say his son felt the same about him. They were still two dogs fighting over the same bone. Blake found his gaze on the stairway door once more. So far, Michael wasn't sharing his mom with anyone.

"Great, you can ride back with Blake." Jen's tone sounded forced and too chipper.

Michael lowered his head to the table with a small "Oh."

Blake's heart tore a little. Clearly, Michael didn't want to go now that he knew he'd be alone with Blake. The stairway door slid open. Blake's heartbeat accelerated. He straightened. Maria lumbered into the room and closed the door behind her.

Blake slumped against the counter.

"Miss Cori is taking a shower. I'm going back upstairs to sit with Mrs. Sinclair," Maria announced, making a beeline for her coffee cup.

Blake hid his disappointment behind a determined smile, shut away the image of Cori in the shower and turned his attention to the matter at hand. His son. The only weapon he held in his arsenal was bribery. And he wasn't above using it.

"Well." Blake closed the pantry door. "Let's take Jen to school, and on the way we'll swing through someplace quick for breakfast."

"Cool." Jen popped out of her chair. "I hope you're hanging around a while, Mikey. Breakfast is usually cereal and granola bars when you're not here."

Michael smiled happily, scooting off his chair and following Jen to the door, ignoring Blake completely.

"MIKE, CAN I TALK TO YOU? Man to man?" Blake and Michael sat at a table in McDonald's. Blake nursed his coffee while Michael devoured his pancakes and sausage. In the end, it had taken them so long to decide what to have for breakfast that Jen had no time to even drive through a fast-food restaurant before class started. Rather than complain, she'd pulled a granola bar from her backpack and disappeared into the throng of junior high school students with a smile and a wave.

"Sure," Michael said, his mouth full of pancake.

Blake resisted smiling at the endearing sight or pointing out it wasn't polite to speak with your mouth full. "You have a lot of friends here, don't you."

The boy nodded, spearing another drippy forkful. "Jennifer's my friend. And her boyfriend, too."

Since when did Jen have a boyfriend? Curiosity almost beat out Blake's purpose, but he stayed focused on the task at hand—winning over his son. "How about Luke?"

"Uh-huh."

"And Grandma Sophia?"

"Kind of. She's sick."

"Who else?" Blake hoped he numbered among Michael's friends, and waited to hear him say it.

Michael chewed thoughtfully. "Big Grandpa," he finally offered. "We talk about stuff and he lets me play on his computer after dinner."

Coffee churned in Blake's stomach as envy reared its ugly head. Even tough, old Mr. Messina had found his way into the kid's heart. He kept his voice light and easy. "You like that, do you?"

Michael bobbed his head and slurped his milk.

"Anybody else?" Blake stared into his coffee cup, expecting the worst.

"You," he added a little sheepishly. "Sometimes."

Blake blew out a breath of relief. Thank heavens Michael was so honest and sensitive. Another kid may not have admitted as much. "Your mom and I are friends."

Michael's head bowed. He pushed his pancake piece around the plate, mopping up syrup, before lifting doubtful eyes to Blake. "Are you sure you and Mommy are friends? You fight a lot."

It was Blake's turn to look away. When he was hurt, he'd behaved badly, venting his pain on Cori. Forcing himself to meet his son's gaze squarely, he answered, "We used to be best friends when she was in school. Have you ever fought with your friends?"

"Sometimes."

"It's hard to get along after you argue with someone, isn't it?" Pride had kept him from calling Cori right after she left, even though he'd missed her like hell. When Cori hadn't called after a few weeks, Blake's mind had created several unpleasant scenarios, all of which ended with his heart broken. So he hadn't called. He'd followed the path of least resistance instead of putting his heart on the line one more time. And look at what he'd lost.

"You have to say you're sorry," Michael said solemnly, understanding dawning in those bright brown eyes.

Blake nodded. That was exactly what he planned to do.

"And mean it," Michael added.

"I'm going to say sorry, I promise. I'll make sure I say it right, because I've missed being your mom's best friend." Blake swallowed, his throat suddenly tight. "I wanted you to know that your mom loves you an awful lot, more than anything. Nobody, not even a friend like me, could make her love you any less."

"I know how you can be better friends." Michael stabbed his last large bite of pancake, stuffing it into his mouth with his fork upside down.

"How?"

Michael removed the plastic fork with flourish, sucking it hard to get every last drop of syrup. He tossed it on the plate, licked his lips and leveled Blake with a stern look. "Don't make her cry."

CORI TOOK ADVANTAGE of Luke's presence and the sunny afternoon to take a walk with Michael out in the vineyard. The air was just warm enough to be comfortable in the sun, with a light breeze that ruffled Michael's soft brown hair. Her little angel needed some exercise to shake his sillies out, in order to prevent another of his little accidents.

Cori led Michael down a row of the vineyard that trailed from the house up to the main road. The plump buds that held new growth were just starting to open on the vine.

"Do you see this, Michael?" she asked, pointing to a small leaf that was partially unfurled. "This round piece is called a bud and it's breaking open, see? Soon it'll grow into a leaf."

Michael squinted his eyes up at the cane tied to the trellis nearly two feet above him. "I can't see."

Cori lifted him to her hip and pointed to the leaf again. She'd always wanted to share her love of the vineyard with her little boy. His shoes bumped the edge of her khaki walking shorts, undoubtedly leaving dirt tracks, but she didn't care. They wouldn't be here much longer. And then they'd be back in the city and their little apartment.

"This time of year is called bud break because it's warm

enough for the buds to open and start growing. In a few weeks, these vines will be covered with leaves and, soon after that, clusters of tiny grapes.''

''I like grapes,'' Michael said solemnly, lightly fingering the bud.

Out of habit, Cori tested the tension of the trellis wire, satisfied when it didn't give to the pressure of her fingers. Grapevines needed lots of support.

Michael mimicked her and tugged on the wire.

''Gently,'' she cautioned. Weathered wires had been known to snap with whiplike speed, carving scars into vines, earth and flesh that was unlucky enough to be in the way. These wires were gray, without any noticeable rust, but Cori wasn't taking any chances. As a field manager, one of Blake's jobs was to make sure the trellises were sturdy enough to support the clingy vines and heavy clusters of fruit later in the year. It was clear that Blake took good care of the vineyard.

She set Michael back on the ground and they continued walking up the row toward the road. She'd seen workers transplanting new stock at the corner of the drive the other morning and she wanted to see them herself. She loved acquainting herself with the vines. It made her feel a part of the land, a part of her family's winery.

''Stretching your legs?'' Blake asked from a few rows over and behind them. He towered above the winter vines, his burgundy T-shirt taut across his broad chest. The sun caught the red highlights in his hair, almost making it seem on fire.

Startled, Cori stood as still as the vines around her and looked at him. Words about her day, about things she wanted to share with him backed up in her throat until her pride took over and she realized she had nothing to say to Blake Austin. Cori looked away, toward her son.

Michael crouched next to a grapevine and peered at it with interest. As Cori watched, he grabbed on to the slender trunk of a grapevine and shook the plant.

''Michael, don't do that,'' Blake rebuked firmly, before Cori had even opened her mouth to reprimand him similarly.

Michael hopped back a few steps, his eyes on Blake, his lips trembling.

Blake ducked under several trellises until he was in the row with them. Instead of lambasting Michael for tampering with the vines in his care, Blake knelt down by a grapevine halfway between Cori and Michael, resting a knee on the dark earth.

''This is a delicate plant. We just transplanted it a few days ago.'' Blake ran his hand gently up the thin trunk, then back down. ''These vines are just babies, only four years old. As old as you, right?''

Michael nodded.

From where she stood, Cori could see the swirling pattern of brown hair on top of Blake's head. ''You're a strong enough boy that you could almost break one, and that would kill it.'' Blake looked into his son's eyes earnestly. ''You wouldn't want to do that, would you?''

Michael shook his head and gave a mumbled ''Sorry,'' before trodding away from them toward the road. His sneakers kicked the dirt, but it seemed to Cori he did so more because he was disappointed in himself than because he was hurt by Blake's reproach.

''You have a way with Michael,'' Cori said. ''Not everyone would have explained it to him in a way he'd understand.''

Blake stood with his back to her, watching Michael walk away. Cori's heart lurched painfully. He'd be a good father if she gave him a chance. Yet, how could she when he thought so poorly of her? They stood for a few moments in silence.

''I'm sorry about last night.'' Without turning, he looked over his shoulder at her, then glanced up the row toward their son. His gray eyes turned to her again and swallowed. ''Don't give up on me yet, okay?''

Cori managed to nod, her throat clogged with hope. She hadn't expected an apology. Blake smiled grimly, then started walking toward Michael. After a moment, Cori followed.

Farther down the row, Michael started leap-frogging with an enthusiasm only a four-year-old could muster.

''What are you doing, Peanut?'' Cori asked, her heart gladdened at the sight of him having such a good time, before she realized she'd used her father's nickname for her.

"I'm a hopper, like that one." Michael didn't miss a hop, but pointed to one side, to a grapevine.

"Hopper?" Blake's voice was filled with apprehension.

Cori stopped midstride, but Blake charged forward. The grape growers referred to grasshoppers as hoppers, the most deadly of which to grapevines was the glassy-winged sharpshooter, or the B-52 Bomber as some had started calling it. The large grasshopper worked like a mosquito when it came to spreading Pierce's Disease to plants. There was no defense. Once infested, the vines were doomed to die from dehydration. Several wineries in the Central Coast region of California had fallen into bankruptcy because of Pierce's Disease.

"Where did you see the hopper?" Blake kept his voice even as he stopped near where Michael had pointed, where Michael had started imitating the bug.

"Over there." Michael continued to hop away from Blake.

Cori didn't think she could hide her panic if she spoke. If Michael was right, if he had spotted a sharpshooter and it carried the infectious disease, the winery wouldn't survive. Never in her wildest dreams had Cori imagined her family's business could fail. Even when Luke had told her Messina Vineyards was in trouble financially, Cori knew her grandfather would find a way to go on. But how could he push on if the vineyards were destroyed?

Cori hurried to catch up to Blake.

"Does he know what one looks like?" Blake asked without sparing her a glance. He was crouched down on the ground looking carefully at the underside of the vine where a grasshopper could easily chew on the woody cane or lay eggs.

Cori nodded, searching the ground for any signs of a large grayish-brown grasshopper. "He's fascinated with bugs." Michael could tell a ladybug from a beetle and a black ant from a red ant. His fascination with bugs made Cori believe her son had seen a hopper. Apprehensively, she scanned the trunks of the vines, not wanting to believe the worst. If there was a hopper, if it was infected, the vines would die within two years. Even if they yanked out the diseased vines, it would take four years for new rootstock to mature into productivity. This section of the vineyard had been grafted, using existing rootstock to increase disease resistance and accelerate productivity.

''That doesn't mean anything. It could have been a plain old, everyday grasshopper.'' Blake continued to examine the vines.

''These vines were just grafted.'' Cori stated the obvious.

''I know.'' Blake's voice seemed strained.

Despite all vines being inspected before planting, most of the spread of the sharpshooter was through new vines grown in the warmer climate in Southern California. Unfortunately, the sharpshooter was more prevalent down south, where they laid eggs on new grape stock. The small eggs were sometimes missed during the agriculture inspection of shipping, and hatched in the warmth of the truck or under the mild spring sunshine—just as the vines were planted or grafted in the vineyards. It was Blake's job to inspect the stock. Blake would take the blame if sharpshooters had infested the vineyard.

''But this section's not too close to the river.'' Cori tried to sound optimistic. Sharpshooters liked areas close to the water, and the Russian River was on the other side of the house.

''Close enough. If it didn't come from the new grafts, it could have flown over.'' One of the characteristics of the sharpshooter that made it so threatening to agricultural crops was its relatively large wings, which could carry it farther than other pests.

''Michael, honey,'' Cori called, her voice tight. ''Come back and show us where you saw the hopper.''

Michael hopped from side to side and then turned back toward them.

Blake and Cori silently kept up their search. The spring air that had previously seemed so light, now seemed laden with sorrow. A school bus pulled into the driveway. Neither Blake nor Cori paid it much attention.

''They look the same,'' Michael said, looking first at one grapevine and then at another.

''What color was the hopper?'' Cori asked.

''Blue?'' Michael drew out the word uncertainly.

Cori pointed at the dirt, trying to control the panic that threatened to well up inside of her. Her family's livelihood was at stake. ''Brown like this? Or blue like this?'' Cori pointed at Blake's blue jeans.

''Brown,'' Michael said with finality, looking at the dirt. ''It was a sharpshooter. I've seen pictures.''

''What did Mikey lose now?'' Jennifer bent beneath trellises to reach them.

Cori bristled at the teen's nickname for Michael, but before she had a chance to formulate a reply, Blake spoke. ''Slow down, Jen. Look for a hopper.''

''You're kidding me.'' Despite the disbelief in her tone, Jen slowed and began scanning the ground, her thin back bent. ''Right? This is some kind of joke.''

''I wish,'' Blake muttered.

''Did you see one?'' she asked.

''I did,'' Michael piped up.

Jen straightened. ''Seriously? You have some sharp eyes, my man.'' She swung her backpack to the ground and put up her hand to give Michael a high-five.

Three things happened simultaneously. Michael pointed and shouted, ''There!'' Jennifer's backpack knocked into a grapevine. And a large, brownish-gray grasshopper leapt right onto Jen's face.

Screaming, Jen flailed her hands and leaned back in surprised defense against the small insect. Her hand slapped it down to the ground and she stepped on it with a shiver of disgust.

Cori and Blake scrambled over to see the crushed remains. Michael followed at a slower pace.

''Tell me that's not what it looks like,'' Cori said, watching Blake poke the flattened bug with a stick. She'd only seen pictures in the newspaper and on the Internet.

"Aw, you killed it," Michael said sorrowfully, squatting next to the remains.

Blake swore and flung the stick aside, giving Cori all the answer she needed. Her heart sank.

"Maybe it doesn't have the virus," Cori offered.

"Yeah. Even if it does, it may not have nibbled on any of our vines," Jen seconded.

Blake shook his head. Cori could tell he'd already accepted the worst.

"I've got to make some calls." Blake straightened, avoiding Cori's sympathetic gaze.

She knew one of those calls was going to be to her grandfather.

BLAKE STOOD WITH CORI at the secretary's desk outside of Mr. Messina's office at Messina Vineyards' headquarters, wishing for a piece of chocolate. The administrative offices were housed in a large building that looked like it had been transplanted from Tuscany, Italy, with peach walls and bright blue shutters. A hospitality facility with a large tasting room, delicatessen and gift shop filled the first floor. The administrative offices were on the second floor.

Blake had called several agencies on his way over to see Mr. Messina and left a crew going over the vineyards vine by vine. Blake should have stayed with the rest, but he felt he had to deliver the bad news in person. Maybe Blake was a glutton for punishment, but he couldn't use the phone to tell the man who'd been so fair to him that his business was in danger.

Blake didn't know why Cori insisted on coming with him, but he was glad she did. She'd held his hand in the truck on the way over and touched his arm reassuringly every few minutes while they waited. Jen had been left in charge of Michael, and Maria in charge of Sophia.

Cori spoke amicably with her grandfather's secretary. Blake noticed Cori had the woman talking about herself, deftly deflecting any personal questions the secretary asked without seeming rude. Was that how easily she'd managed him four years ago? He didn't think so.

The secretary answered her telephone, then hung up and indicated they could go in.

As Blake stepped inside, he was struck again by the darkness of Mr. Messina's office. The walls were paneled in dark oak, the floor carpeted with a burgundy oriental rug. A breathtaking view of vineyards sweeping down to the Russian River was the only warmth in the room. And even that was framed in darkness—floor-to-ceiling, heavy burgundy drapes hung on either side of the window.

Salvatore Messina sat in a large, black leather chair behind a sturdy oak desk. He gestured to the worn, red leather chairs across from him. As Blake and Cori took their seats, Mr. Messina's eyes watched them in curious silence.

Never one to stand on ceremony, Blake wasted no time. "A sharpshooter's been found in the vineyard."

This apparently had not been what Mr. Messina was expecting, for his face paled. Although Mr. Messina had been still before now, Blake swore his employer froze.

"Where?"

"By the front drive. We've only found one so far."

"The new vines?" Salvatore Messina had a keen mind for a man his age.

Blake nodded.

"I want the contact information for the company that sold us those vines forwarded to our lawyer." Mr. Messina's words were sharp.

Blake nodded again. What could he say? He was sorry? The company who'd sold them the vines was going to be plenty sorry.

"Who found it?"

"Michael." Cori spoke for the first time since entering the room. "Blake was teaching him about vines."

Salvatore Messina's expression wobbled. Blake almost thought he was about to smile, but it hardly seemed the reaction one would have to such news. Then Mr. Messina's expression darkened. He regarded Cori cynically. ''Are you here for a reward?''

''No, I thought...'' Cori's voice trailed off. She met her grandfather's eyes squarely before repeating ''No.''

She'd thought, what? She could witness her grandfather falling apart? Gloat in his misfortune? That didn't sound like Cori, although Mr. Messina seemed to think as much. Blake had never witnessed such an interchange between Mr. Messina and his granddaughter before the awards dinner. Was this the way he'd always treated her? Cori's need to be independent suddenly gained more credence.

''And you.'' Salvatore Messina's words cut into Blake's thoughts, even as his expression turned bitter. ''I trusted you to watch over my vineyards. Your attention has been spread too thin between your duties for me and what you've been doing at the house.''

Blake felt his employer's cold words wash through him. Despite Salvatore Messina's displeasure, Blake wouldn't stop helping Sophia when the end was so near.

''You'll keep focused from now on. I'll tell Maria you're not allowed inside the house anymore.''

''What?'' Blake couldn't stop himself. ''Sophia needs me. She won't let you hire a nurse.''

''She won't know at this point. If you can't manage to turn this around, I'll be looking for a new field manager.''

Mr. Messina's reaction was just as Cori had predicted. ''Let's wait and see what happens tomorrow before we jump to any conclusions,'' Blake advised.

''I don't need someone who waits around.''

''I'm doing everything to control the situation.'' Blake was finding it difficult to hold his temper.

''That's enough.'' Cori's severe tone stopped them both.

Salvatore Messina shot Cori a venomous look, then looked at Blake. ''I hadn't realized my granddaughter was such a distraction to you until now.''

Cori leaped out of her seat and stepped in front of Blake. ''Stop right there. Blake has been at Mama's side these past few weeks more than either you or Luke, and still works long hours for you.''

Blake couldn't see her face, but when he leaned a little to the left, he could see Mr. Messina's rigid features. The man had eyes only for his granddaughter. For a moment, Blake thought he read surprise on his face, then Mr. Messina's expression changed. Hardened.

Grandfather and granddaughter stared at each other in silence as seconds ticked by on the cuckoo clock behind them. Blake didn't know what was happening, other than that smoke was steaming out of both their ears. He decided it was time for him to leave.

''I've called several noted experts. They'll be inspecting the vineyard tomorrow.'' Blake tried to reassure Mr. Messina, but all he got for his efforts was a curt nod. Was Blake finally seeing what Cori had been trying to tell him? Or was this just Mr. Messina's unpleasant reaction to the stress of having discovered his vineyards were in danger?

Blake stood.

''Wait.'' Cori turned, raised a hand to stop him. ''It's time.''

CHAPTER THIRTEEN

''YOU LIVED UP TO YOUR END of the bargain. I'm keeping my word, as well,'' Cori said, looking directly into her grandfather's eyes. She took a deep breath. ''Blake is Michael's father.''

Blake jerked as if connected to a live wire. She'd given him no warning that she'd chosen this moment to tell her grandfather. Hadn't they had enough bad news for one day? Mr. Messina stared at Cori for a moment, then looked darkly at Blake. The cold hand of uncertainty clutched Blake's gut. This wasn't going to be pretty.

''I should have known.'' Mr. Messina looked from one to the other, his gaze landing sharply again on Blake. ''This explains why Sophia wanted to keep promoting you.''

Blake fell back in his chair as if he'd been struck. He'd been promoted quickly, but deservedly so. At least, that's what he'd thought.

''It certainly wasn't for your expertise. Look at where you've landed me now.''

''Nobody can protect you from the sharpshooter.'' Cori was quick to rise to Blake's defense, as well she should since she was the cause of his imminent demise.

''How do I know he didn't check the vines carefully? In my day, loyalty stood for something. Men didn't work your fields during the day and sleep with your granddaughter at night. It makes me doubt his skill.''

''You make it sound like I'm a piece of your property,'' Cori sputtered.

Numbly, Blake tried to follow the conversation, tried to

throw out a defense, but his brain stumbled repeatedly over something Cori had said.

"Could we slow down for just a minute?" Blake interrupted, leaning forward.

Both members of the Messina clan turned their attention on Blake.

"What bargain?" Blake asked.

Cori blushed and looked out the window.

"What? You only told your grandfather about me because of some deal you made?" Anger at Cori's betrayal charged bitterly through Blake's system. She was putting herself first again. "You never were going to tell me about Michael, were you?"

"Yes, I was—but think the worst, you always do," Cori responded weakly.

Cori kept her back to him and Blake found himself doubting her words once again. He looked to Mr. Messina. The old man said nothing.

"So now I get the Messina silence?" Blake shifted restlessly in the chair. His whole life was a sham. His job. His feelings. He had nothing to go on but gut instinct. "Which means you don't think I'm good enough to be told the truth."

Cori whipped around and opened her mouth to speak, but Salvatore Messina beat her to it.

"I had no idea your confidence was that shallow," Mr. Messina said.

"Don't," she admonished, although Blake wasn't sure whom she meant to curtail.

"Well, surely the boy knows I wouldn't hire an idiot, much less promote him." Mr. Messina tilted his head to one side and shrugged, his answer belying his previously indicated lack of faith. "How would I look with fools working for me?"

"Why does it always have to come back to you?" Cori said. "You claimed my pregnancy would weaken the winery."

"It did, didn't it? You left and we all had to step in to take up the slack," Mr. Messina snapped.

"You wanted to punish Michael's father, either by ruining

him or by forcing us into marriage and then paying him to leave.''

A chill thundered down Blake's spine as he realized that he'd been right. Cori hadn't returned to the winery at all after her graduation because of him. Yet, he couldn't believe the nerve of these two, playing with his life as if he were a chess piece. She should have told him.

Mr. Messina held up one hand. ''I've often regretted letting my temper get the best of me that day.''

''And the threats against Blake?'' Cori pushed, avoiding Blake's stare.

Deadly eyes took aim at Blake. ''That's still an option.''

''Wait a minute.'' Blake's anger burned his earlier apprehension to ashes. ''I haven't been involved in any of this.''

''Immaculate conception?'' Salvatore Messina asked, silver brows arched.

Control. Blake had to wrest control of the situation. ''Let's go back to the beginning where you threatened me behind my back.''

Salvatore Messina didn't even blink. ''I never knew it was you I was threatening.''

''Would it have made a difference?''

''Hell, yes. I would have fired you like *that.*'' Mr. Messina snapped his fingers crisply.

Blake and Jennifer would have been out on the street. Even though he'd suspected as much, Blake was furious with Cori for not telling him about Michael and about nearly losing his job and his home without even knowing why. He glared at Cori, but she seemed to have checked out of the conversation. He couldn't allow that.

''Why didn't you want to marry me?'' Blake cursed his voice for coming out rough and weak. ''I thought *love* was supposed to conquer all.''

She shook her head sadly and answered without turning. ''Because my grandfather would have made your life a daily hell and what little love we shared would never have been enough.''

"And the deal you two made…?" Blake prompted.

"I'd find John Sinclair and get him to visit. In return, Corinne would fill in your name on the birth certificate."

He'd been burned again by her hidden agenda. "I thought you said your father refused to come out here, Cori." Blake ground out the words.

"He did refuse. But he sent flowers to Mama this morning."

There was a pause, and then Mr. Messina admitted, "I sent the flowers."

"You?" Cori covered her hand with her mouth and shook her head, eyes filled with tears. "That's so wrong."

Blake silently agreed, but feigned indifference.

Mr. Messina shrugged, but his eyes lowered to his desk. "If it makes her happy, what does it matter?"

"Because I'll know." Cori moved next to the window, her back to them once more. She gripped the heavy burgundy drapes with one white-knuckled hand.

"I'm not the least bit remorseful," Mr. Messina said, baring his teeth at Blake.

"Don't look at me." Blake tapped his chest. "I didn't know I was the father until a few days ago."

Mr. Messina frowned. "You didn't think to call Cori when she didn't come home? You weren't man enough to make sure nothing happened?"

"Maybe in the back of my mind I assumed I'd be told if she got pregnant." He pointed at Cori. "Besides, she left me. Not the other way around. I've been lied to, many times, and now I'm being threatened."

Mr. Messina shrugged, his hands palms up toward Blake. "Taught a lesson. It's an entirely different thing."

"I'm sure my lawyer will think otherwise." Blake leaned back in his chair and crossed his arms. He wished Cori would argue with him and tell him she was sorry so he could hope. She'd always left him with that bit of hope.

"'Taught a lesson' is a family phrase, that's all." Mr. Messina smiled, but the expression lacked humor. "You should feel…uncomfortable."

"Like cement shoes?" Blake's eyes narrowed. "Have you been watching *The Sopranos* again?"

"Something like that." Mr. Messina's smile didn't change.

Certain that his boss was enjoying this too much, Blake tossed up his hands. "I've tried to be a good employee. I've tried to pay back the kindnesses you and Sophia extended."

Mr. Messina rolled his eyes.

"I've even tried loving her." Blake jabbed his finger in Cori's direction, wanting her to turn around and fight for their love. Maybe then he'd be able to rein in his temper. "And it's taken this to make me realize what a waste of time my tenure here has been. I'm giving my notice."

Cori kept her back to them, refusing to join the conversation.

"Don't get excited and say something you'll regret later," Mr. Messina warned with a quick glance at his granddaughter.

"You were going to fire me, anyway."

"I was not. You're family now. You and Corinne will get married and settle down, and provide my great-grandchild with a name."

"Didn't you hear a word I said? I can't stay here. I can barely bring myself to look at the two of you." He stood. "And you won't keep my son from me any longer. I'm hiring a lawyer and petitioning for my paternal rights."

Blake waited for Cori to say something, to turn around and argue or plead her case. She'd said she loved him. He clung to those words. Yet, she remained silently facing the window.

Finally, feeling the fool he was, Blake walked out alone.

CORI DIDN'T WATCH Blake Austin walk out of her life. Her tear-blurred vision saw only a watercolor vineyard. Blake had every right to be angry. She couldn't say anything in defense of what she'd done, other than that she'd done it to protect him. If he couldn't see that, if that wasn't enough, if he thought the worst of everything she did, it was only lust and they weren't meant to be together. She'd somehow manage to piece her heart back together and move on.

"That could have gone better." Her grandfather broke the silence.

How was she going to handle Blake's temper when he came to visit Michael? Cori gave in to her shaky legs and sank to the floor. She wanted to cry. Her grandfather would love that. Where was all that Messina strength when she needed it?

"Here, now. None of that," her grandfather said. She heard him struggle to rise from his leather chair. "He'll come back."

Shaking her head, Cori closed her eyes against the burgundy drapes. They were the color of hearts and deep, lasting love. Her mother was dying, her grandfather wanted her out of his life and Blake hated her. Love would forever elude her.

"Give him time. He'll come around." A large hand gently stroked her hair. Cori couldn't keep a sob from escaping. It wasn't fair. Her family was capable of such love and kindness, yet somehow they couldn't make it work.

There was a time when she'd have taken his words and actions at face value, believing she came before Messina Vineyards. That time had passed years ago. Cori moved her head to the side and stood, breaking away from her grandfather's touch.

"It's a little too late for comfort, don't you think?" Cori filled her lungs with air, hoping to bolster her strength, as well. She turned and faced her grandfather, taking two steps away from him, not wanting to see his frailties. "You can't force a family on anyone. It didn't work with my father. It didn't work for me. You got what you wanted, so just leave me alone—" Her voice cracked on the last word.

Cori's feet couldn't move fast enough across the oriental carpet to the door. It wasn't until she'd fled the building and was following a dirt road by the riverbank that she questioned whether it was her imagination or whether she'd actually heard her grandfather say "I can't do that," as she walked out of his office.

A SHORT TIME LATER, Cori slowly climbed the stairs to her mother's bedroom. She stood on the threshold looking at the bright flowers on the other side of the room. This morning they'd been a promise that everything was going to turn out all right. Now they were the banner proclaiming her grandfather still ruled everything.

Mama was alone. On the way up Cori had passed through the kitchen, where Maria was refreshing her coffee mug. Michael and Jen were also in the kitchen, wolfing down yesterday's homemade cookies.

Movement by the bed caught Cori's eye.

"Mama, are you awake?" Maybe something good would come of this day.

"I don't feel so good." Mama's face paled. "I think I'm going to throw up."

Cori grabbed the trash can by the desk and rushed to the bed, lifting Mama into an upright position with the can in front of her. Just in time, too. Mama vomited into it. The liquid was thick and dark, but there wasn't much of it.

Odd, Cori thought, that it would be that color, when all Sophia had in her stomach was a little water and nutrients from the IV tube at the hospital.

She settled her mother back on the pillows, then went to the bathroom for a wet washrag.

"I think I'm over the worst of it," Mama murmured as Cori gently wiped her face.

Not knowing what to say, Cori remained silent, grateful that her mother's mind was finally clear. She could use some good news.

"Do you think I'll be okay?" Mama asked.

"You'll be fine," Cori lied through threatening tears. Now that Mama wasn't throwing up anymore, Cori's spirits lifted. Her mother had returned.

"I've seen you and Blake together. More lovely grandchildren for me," Mama murmured weakly.

Cori didn't comment. Remembering how Blake had left her earlier, she knew that wasn't going to happen.

"Poor Luke and Papa are in for a bit of trouble." Mama

sighed, barely a wisp of air. ''I'm so tired.'' She closed her eyes. ''It's okay, though. Eventually, everything will be okay.''

Cori cradled Mama's hand within hers. She rubbed her right hand over Mama's wrist and forearm. It took her a few minutes to notice Mama's chest wasn't moving. Placing her thumb at Mama's wrist, Cori felt for a heartbeat.

''Mama?''

Nothing. Cori's hands started to shake, her stomach convulsed.

Cori's eyes strayed to the telephone on the bedside table. She reached for the receiver. Then the paper with Mama's wishes resting next to the phone caught Cori's eye and her hand hovered midair. This was the way Mama wanted it. She had to honor her request, no matter how wrong it felt. Didn't she?

Muffled footsteps sounded behind her. Cori twisted around in panic, speaking before she saw who it was.

''Help me. She's gone,'' she choked out.

Blake rushed to the bedside, stepping between Cori and her mother. ''Sophia?'' He checked her pulse. Cori leaned past him to watch. After several seconds, Blake lay Mama's hand gently down on the bedspread, then took a few steps back, his eyes never leaving Mama's face.

''Do something,'' Cori pleaded. Blake was always quick to speak, quick to react. Why wasn't he doing anything? Mama hadn't drawn a breath in over a minute.

Blake regarded Cori silently with red-rimmed eyes.

''Please.'' Tears spilled over Cori's cheeks. ''She was just talking to me. She's back. She came back....'' Her voice trailed off as she realized Blake's attention had shifted. He was looking at the paper next to the telephone. Cori found herself looking at it, as well.

Yes, Blake always knew what to do. Cori felt ashamed for wanting him to go against Mama's wishes. Keeping vigil at her bedside hadn't been the same since Mama had come home from the hospital.

Cori swallowed her grief and reached for the telephone. The plastic was cold and hard in her hand.

Footsteps pounded on the back stairs. The steps were too quick to have been Maria's.

"Michael," Cori whispered. She didn't want him to see his grandmother like this. "Could you..." She couldn't look at Blake, could only stare at the phone. Cori sniffed and tried again. "Could you take Michael to your house? I don't want him to see this. Jen, too."

Not waiting for his answer or to watch him leave, Cori punched the three digits for emergency services. When the operator came on the line, she somehow managed to speak.

"My mother just died."

When Cori hung up the phone a few minutes later after also calling Luke and her grandfather, she stared down at her mother, smoothed a stray lock of gray hair into place and then kissed Mama's cheek.

"Everything's going to be okay, Mama."

CORI STUMBLED DOWN the hallway in her nightshirt to her mother's room, half expecting to find her mother resting in bed, ready to be helped to the bathroom, yesterday's events all part of a bad dream. Instead, she found Luke, sprawled across the small sofa, illuminated by the gray light of dawn creeping into the window. A quick glance to the empty bed, bedspread pulled up, pillows plump in their shams, confirmed her worst fears.

Mama was gone.

Luke stirred, stretched and groaned. Cori turned to find his heavy-lidded eyes upon her.

"You could have slept in your own bed last night," she commented, fighting the tears.

"It just didn't seem right." He pulled himself upright, only to slouch beneath the blanket, tilting his head to the ceiling. "Nothing seems right."

"We were there for her at the end. It's what she wanted."

Luke shook his head. "You were there for her. I was working, like always."

A sound at the door drew Cori's attention. Her grandfather stood in the doorway, leaning on the doorknob and staring at

Mama's bed. He looked worse than Cori had ever seen him, pale and drained of energy. His clothes were wrinkled, as if he'd slept in them.

"No one goes to work today," Cori found herself saying sharply, blinking back the tears.

Her grandfather looked at her through misty eyes. She'd never seen him cry.

"No one goes to work for the next few days," Cori repeated.

Her grandfather gave a quick nod, swaying from the movement.

Cori feared he would fall. "Luke, help me put him back to bed."

Fully expecting indignant protests, Cori was surprised when her grandfather said nothing. They each draped one of his arms over their shoulders, guided him back to his bedroom and then helped him into bed.

Cori wondered if this would be the tragedy that finally broke him.

SALVATORE DID NOT WANT to be in the Sonoma Hills Mausoleum. The floors were white marble, the walls were white marble and the urns were brass. Everything was starkly cold. Why had his darling Sophia wanted to spend the rest of eternity here?

Salvatore sat in a folding chair facing the urn holding Sophia's ashes. They should have spent more time together. But the business.... He lowered his head and blinked back his tears.

Show no weakness.

The pain was easier to bear when Salvatore lost himself. The priest's voice droned oddly over him, his words hard to follow as they echoed through the place, weaving in and out of the fake birdsong that was piped in.

Finally, the service came to an end. Salvatore shuffled into the receiving line, mumbling thanks to those who tried to speak to him. Their faces became a blur of white, held upright by stiff black tree trunks. He couldn't begin to remember who had attended and who hadn't. Perhaps, he thought in a moment of detachment, he shouldn't have taken two pain pills at one time. Things might have seemed clearer then. More painful, but clearer.

"I'll get the car," Lucas said from Salvatore's right.

Blake stood to Salvatore's left. Corinne had been standing next to Lucas. She and Jennifer each held a hand of his great-grandson. Fine boy, that one. Truly a surprise.

Salvatore swayed as he tried to focus on the small blur in black. What was the boy's name? Matthew? Martin?

Someone gripped his left arm. "Just a little longer," Blake said. Such a steadfast, dependable man.

Salvatore's eyes drifted toward Corinne. He remembered a trip they'd taken one year to an event in San Francisco. The lights and decorations had been no match for the promise of Corinne's beauty. A shame she'd chosen to leave the family. He could certainly use her strength and spirit now. Why was it she'd left? He couldn't remember. It didn't matter. She was family and should be home.

He tried to tell her that, but his words sounded funny. Slurred.

"What's wrong with him?" Corinne stepped closer.

"Nothing." Salvatore waved her away, only to list to the right. Salvatore tried to tell Corinne again to stay, but even though he was saying "I want you to stay," to his ears it sounded like he was saying "I wall you a play." He moaned in frustration. Why couldn't they understand him?

Corinne steadied his other arm. "We need to call the doctor. Jennifer, see that tall man with the gray hair? Ask him to come see me, please." Her voice rang out commandingly, just like that of a true Messina.

Salvatore knew what he needed, and it wasn't any doctor. He needed his family.

CORI STEPPED OUT INTO the backyard just as the night began snatching the last bit of daylight, chilling the air. Hugging herself in her black wool dress, Cori walked across the paving stones toward the pool and the cushioned glider, her heels clicking in meaningless elegance.

Upstairs Michael and Jennifer were watching cartoons in the pink room, while the last of the mourners quaffed their sorrows in the flower-filled living room. She'd left her grandfather sitting stony-faced between Luke and Blake, his apparent drug high wearing off. For all his threats about quitting, Blake had certainly rallied around her grandfather, rarely leaving his side during the past few days.

Cori sank onto the swing, slid out of her shoes and tucked her feet beneath her. The trees shadowed the rapidly darkening sky. In the distance, Cori heard engines turning over and car doors closing behind those who'd paid their last respects to Sophia Sinclair.

Cori leaned her head back and closed her eyes against the tears. Each of the past three nights numbed the pain of her loss a little more. Each morning she woke up thinking today it would be easier. And it was, until she'd read Mama's papers that first morning and realized Mama wanted to be cremated, not buried. According to her grandfather, all Messinas earned a plot of land to ground them in the afterlife. It was a family tradition. Cori never would have convinced her grandfather to allow it if Blake hadn't supported her.

Then yesterday morning she'd gone through Mama's address book and called her many friends and acquaintances to let them know today's schedule. Yes, Mama's suffering had been brief, she'd told them. They'd like donations to the Cancer Society in lieu of flowers. This morning, when she'd found her grandfather standing in Mama's doorway again, leaning on the knob with a sorrowful expression on his face, she'd almost collapsed to the floor. He was supposed to be the strong one.

The one bright spot was that Pierce's Disease had not been found in the vineyard. Yet. The glassy-winged sharpshooter they'd found was disease-free and no other hoppers had been found.

The back door clicked open, then closed, followed by slow, heavy footsteps. Cori assumed it was Luke or some mourner seeking the solace of the night, which was fine, except that the footsteps headed her way. Cori hoped it was Luke. She really didn't want to wear her gracious face anymore tonight.

Cori opened her eyes and lifted her head, tracking the footsteps as they walked on the other side of the tall hedge and rounded the corner, until the man was silhouetted from the lights in the house.

Blake. She'd recognize the outline of his frame anywhere.

He paused and her heart skipped a painful beat. They hadn't spoken alone since the day she'd told her grandfather Blake was Michael's father.

"How are you holding up?" he asked, walking closer.

As he neared, she heard the creak of new leather. Silly, she thought, that he could walk silently in his work boots and not in dress shoes.

"Fine." It seemed like hundreds of people had asked her that same question today and she'd given them that one-word answer, a reassuring smile and directed them to the bar or buffet.

Blake settled on the glider next to her, bringing the heat of his body into her space. She pulled her feet in tighter, while her heart told her to let them drift toward his warmth.

"You wouldn't tell me if you weren't okay, would you."

"No." She'd been trained to keep emotions inside. Public displays of affection were strictly forbidden. It'd been a tough battle to let her love for Michael show, to coo and cuddle her own baby in front of others.

"That's what I thought." Blake looked down at his hands. "Would it kill you to be honest with me? To share your feelings with somebody?"

There'd only been two people Cori had ever shared her emotions with—her mother and Blake. Now she had no one. She'd give anything to have a beer, or anything she could put in her hands to keep them occupied, to stop them from shaking and provide her with a social prop. "I have to hold it together."

"For who? I can see you're stretched to your limit."

"For *her*." The word nearly choked her. Quickly Cori

added, "She was always so perfect. She knew the right thing to wear, who to invite, what to serve, what to say. How can I live up to that?"

"You can't."

"That's right. Even you know I didn't do her justice today." She rubbed her long wool sleeves, trying vainly to warm herself up. "That eulogy. What was I thinking? Believing I had anything worth saying."

"Everyone was touched. You captured her warmth and humor by sharing those stories. I'd never heard them before and I felt it. People came away knowing you loved her, feeling your loss."

"I should have come back sooner." Cori sniffed and wiped away a pocket of tears in the corner of her eye with one finger. They both knew why she hadn't come back sooner.

He had nothing to say to that.

"All this time—" another sniffle "—I thought I wanted to come back here and be a part of this." She struggled to fill her lungs with air. "But it's really her. She was home. And now she's gone."

And then she was crying. Cori reached into the cuff of her sleeve for a folded tissue, blew her nose and dabbed her wet cheeks, noticing that Blake didn't offer her the solace of his shoulder or any words of comfort. The wedge of his rejection ripped her heart further. Suddenly, she wanted to hurt him.

"It looks like you're a part of the family now." Then she blurted, "We're leaving tomorrow morning."

"I want visitation," Blake retorted just as swiftly, as if he'd anticipated where the conversation was going.

"Fine." Cori slid her feet back into her shoes, then stood with her back to him, needing that distance to protect her heart. "Every other weekend."

"I want to tell him I'm his father. He'll take it better if we do it together."

Cori sniffed again rather than responding sarcastically to his phrasing. They were never going to be together. She'd always be alone. "We can tell him when you come down to L.A."

''Let's tell him now.''

''Not now. He's just lost his grandmother.''

''I can understand if you're not up to it tonight. We will do it in the morning.'' His tone rang uncompromisingly firm.

''Fine. Right after breakfast.'' Cori started to walk away, but paused at the hedge that hid her from the house, needing to set the record straight because her heart still yearned for his understanding. ''I just want you to know that I told you about Michael that night because I was afraid Michael would have no one if something happened to me. I didn't tell you because of any deal. I needed to know he'd be safe.'' She confessed it all with her back to him, because she was a coward and didn't want to see the contempt and disbelief on his face.

When he didn't immediately reply, she fled the night, back into the false security of the house.

''WE'RE GOING HOME today, Mommy?''

''Yes.'' Over the past few days, Cori had packed away the mementos of her childhood. Now, as she bustled about the room folding, rolling and tucking clothes and other items into their suitcases, the pink room looked rather empty. She'd even found her diamond earrings hiding in plain sight on the desk. She'd thought those were lost forever. ''When I'm done packing we'll have some breakfast, then get on the road.''

Luke had said his goodbyes an hour earlier before he'd left for work. She hadn't spoken with her grandfather since the argument days earlier about Mama's last wishes.

Someone knocked on the door.

''It's Jennifer.'' Michael hopped up to answer it. They'd become quite close over the past week. ''Oh, hello.'' Michael opened the door wider, a smile on his face.

''Morning. I made pancakes for our goodbye breakfast.'' Blake smiled down at his son, ignoring Cori. With circles under his eyes, he looked as worn out as Cori felt.

Michael looked at Cori expectantly, as if the invitation had included her, which it hadn't.

''I'm just finishing up. Michael, why don't you go down and

start?'' Cori didn't have an appetite. She'd promised Blake they'd tell Michael today, but she wanted to postpone the inevitable just a little longer.

Michael looked from one adult to the other. ''I don't like pancakes.'' Michael plopped back down on his sleeping bag, suddenly reluctant to go.

''Michael, that's not true,'' Cori said.

''You never eat pancakes with us, Mommy,'' Michael accused.

Blake held up a hand to stop Cori from answering. ''She'll be right down.'' Blake knelt next to Michael, who kept his eyes glued on the television.

''No, thanks, sir.''

Blake winced at being called ''sir.'' ''They're hot and the chocolate chips are melting,'' Blake tempted, not giving up, but looking far from happy now.

Zoop, zoop, zoop. Michael rubbed his feet over the sleeping bag, while casting a sideways glance at Blake. ''The good chocolate chips?''

''Oh, yeah,'' Blake said, brightening.

''Okay.'' Michael stood up slowly. ''But Mommy needs a goodbye breakfast, too.''

''YOU MAKE THE BEST pancakes,'' Michael said to Blake, his mouth full of his second one.

''I'd like to make you pancakes every weekend.'' It was true. He'd grown to love the little guy. It tore him apart to think he was leaving. Where Cori was concerned, he was numb, not letting himself feel anything. He'd given their love three chances. He couldn't let himself risk his heart again.

''Down in L.A.?'' Michael looked confused.

''Or here.'' They'd work out the logistics later, but Blake would see his son as often as possible. He'd take Cori to court to make it happen, if need be.

Michael took a deep drink of milk that produced a white mustache. ''We don't live here.''

Smiling, Blake handed him a paper napkin. ''I'd like you to. Jen and I are going to miss you.''

''We don't live here,'' he repeated patiently, as if Blake were the child and Michael the adult.

''What if your dad lived here?'' Blake was getting desperate. He knew Michael wanted a dad. Cori had said they'd tell him together this morning, but she'd told Blake a lot of things she didn't mean. Time was running out.

''Mommy says we can't have one.''

''I know, I know.'' What was taking Cori so long? ''But what if you could? What if…'' Blake hesitated. He should wait. He knew he should. But his need to be acknowledged as Michael's father outweighed his conscience. ''What if I was your dad?''

''You're not. You're my friend. Mom's friend.'' Michael frowned. ''Sometimes.''

''I am your father.'' Blake's heart sickened at the words, as if he were Darth Vader delivering the horrifying news to Luke Skywalker.

''That's not true. I don't have a dad,'' Michael said. He was breathing heavily and really working himself up. ''I'm telling my mom. Mom!''

''I'm here, baby.'' Cori stepped out of the stairwell and hurried to Michael's side, looking like a soccer mom, not an ice princess, in a pair of knit shorts and a pink T-shirt.

Blake shifted uncomfortably in his chair and studied his sock-clad feet. He should have listened to his conscience. Telling Michael he was his father was shocking enough without the one person Michael had relied on his entire life present. What kind of a father was he?

''He says he's my daddy. I told you I didn't want him for a daddy.'' Michael glared at Blake, looking most similar to his great-grandfather at the moment, despite the ears.

Cori pulled a chair close to Michael, her back to Blake, shutting him out again. This time, he deserved it.

''You know, Peanut, we can't choose who our parents are. God does that. Since we've lived so far away, you haven't had the chance to get to know your dad. That's all going to change.''

Cori was so much better at parenting than Blake was.

''You said we'd never have a daddy live with us,'' Michael wailed.

''He's not going to live with us. He's just going to visit. And stay in a hotel,'' she added—for Blake's benefit, he was sure.

Michael jumped out of his chair and leaned forward, yelling. ''Why did you have to pick him? He doesn't even like you. And I bet he didn't say sorry like he promised.'' Michael ran upstairs, slamming the door of the pink room, slamming Blake out of his heart.

Cori sighed and stood, keeping her back to Blake. She wiped her face. ''I asked you to wait for me.''

''I'm sorry. I should have. For some reason, I couldn't.'' What had he expected? That Michael would jump into his arms?

God, yes.

''Give it some time,'' Cori told him quietly before following her son upstairs.

That was it? No, *Blake, you bastard?* Or dire threats if he ever approached his son again? Blake deserved that much, at the very least.

SALVATORE MESSINA LEANED on his desk, waiting for Corinne and his great-grandson to come downstairs, ignoring the limo and driver waiting out front to take him to work. He couldn't sit down in a chair because he knew he might not be able to stand up in time to catch them before they left. He suspected Corinne was going to breeze out of here as fast as she could, taking his great-grandson out of his life forever.

She couldn't leave without resolving things between them. He'd tried to talk to her about Blake that day in the office. He'd make Blake marry her if that's what she wanted. Really, he admired the girl for holding the secret so long and so well. Salvatore needed people like that.

BLAKE STOMPED INTO THE kitchen without taking off his boots. Jen looked up from her cereal bowl with interest. Instead of blowing through the house and rushing back out again as he usually did during the day, Blake paced the kitchen, not wanting to be alone. His life was in ruins.

"You want me to make you some coffee?" Jen offered, staring at him questioningly.

"No." If one good thing had come of all this, it was that he and Jen were communicating again.

"Some pancakes?"

"Definitely no." Blake placed a hand on either side of the sink and dropped his head. "They're leaving." He hadn't thought their leaving would rip him apart like this. Hell, if it came to that, he hadn't truly believed they'd leave, despite the trouble he and Cori kept having.

"Oh, sheesh. Look at me. I'm not even dressed. Let me just run upstairs..."

Blake couldn't bear to turn around and face Jen. "They'll be gone by the time you change."

"I have to say goodbye to Mikey. Cori won't leave without letting me say goodbye, will she?"

Blake could hear the tears in Jen's voice and swallowed to keep his own at bay. "I don't know." Michael never wanted to see him again, with good reason.

He heard Jen's chair scrape back from the table. "Criminy, I wish you would have called me and told me sooner. Or, at least, told me he was ours. You could have trusted me that much."

"What?" Blake turned and followed her into the hallway. "You knew? Since when?"

"I don't know. Almost two weeks ago, I think." She leaped up the stairs.

"That long?" Blake counted back the days to when Cori had told him. Almost two weeks would mean that Jen had known about as long as he had. That explained the volatile temper, but not her acceptance of Michael. And who had told her? The only possibility was Cori. Why would she tell Jen?

Jen banged into her bedroom and slammed the door. Blake trotted up the stairs because Jen was still yelling at him.

''You think I'm a baby who couldn't figure it out? I mean, look at those ears.''

Blake stood close to the door. ''You figured it out? Cori didn't tell you?''

''No. It's in Mikey's baby book. He reads it all the time. Well, he doesn't read, exactly. He just has stuff memorized.''

Blake leaned against the door frame and called through the closed door. ''Am I missing something here?''

''Most likely. You are a little slow, plus you always think the worst.''

Cori had said much the same thing.

''Jen.''

She popped the door open, looking like she'd picked her T-shirt up off the floor and the jeans along with it. He was going to have to talk to her about the ironing board downstairs.

''Your name was written in the front of his baby book,'' Jen proclaimed.

''Oh.'' Was that all? Blake's heart deflated with disappointment. He'd expected something more mind-bending, some miracle to make him believe in Cori again.

''No, *oh.* Come on, you think she just wrote it there yesterday or something?''

''Well, yes.''

Jen rolled her eyes, then pushed past him. ''She wrote the whole book in this shiny, sparkly blue ink. Even your name. It's not the kind of pen you carry in your purse.'' Jen skipped down the stairs. ''He's a bright kid. Sheesh, by next year he'd be able to read the word *father* and then ask about your name.''

Blake sank down on the top step, overwhelmed by the implications. If Cori was willing to state his name in Michael's baby book and not on his birth certificate, she hadn't kept silent selfishly to achieve her independence. She'd kept her secret only to protect him and Jen. Why record the truth anywhere if she meant to keep it from him forever?

Suddenly, Cori's carefully worded answers and silences

made a whole lot of sense. She'd been walking a tightrope between his family and hers.

"I'm an ass." Who was about to lose the best thing that had ever happened to him. Two of the best things.

He bolted down the stairs and grabbed his truck keys off the counter. He ran past Jen, who was putting on her sneakers and ripped out the door. "You're a miracle worker, Jen. Love you!"

"Hey," she called. "Wait for me."

"Can't," he yelled, climbing into the old truck. He had to catch them, before it was too late.

BLAKE PULLED UP TO THE front of the Messina mansion with a sigh of relief. Cori's dented yellow Mustang sat in the driveway. Blake pulled in behind her but didn't get out. He needed the right words to win her over, yet he suffered from an acute case of brain freeze.

A limousine sat in front of the house. Its driver leaned up against the car. That meant Salvatore Messina was still at home. Cori was probably waiting to leave until the old man cleared the area. Blake could tell the tension between the two had gotten unbearable since Sophia passed away. They tried so hard not to look or talk directly to each other that they must want desperately to be together.

Suddenly slapped with a solution Cori couldn't resist, Blake hopped out of the truck and ran into the house. His new plan had to work. Precious minutes passed before Blake located Mr. Messina in his office.

"Cori's leaving." Blake closed the office door behind him.

The old man scowled from his perch on the edge of his desk, but didn't look up from the papers in his hand.

"I need you to stop them." More accurately, he needed Mr. Messina's help in making them a family.

Salvatore Messina's head jerked up and he gave Blake The Look. For the first time since Blake came to work at Messina Vineyards, he ignored it.

"That's right. You're going to stop them." Blake was willing to do anything to make them stay, but Cori wouldn't stay if her relationship with her grandfather wasn't mended. Blake began pacing the room.

"Damn foolish notion. Why would I want to do that?"

"Because you're alone now. Sophia's gone. I'm leaving—"

Mr. Messina cut him off. "I've got Lucas."

"Don't tell me you didn't know he closed escrow on that vineyard across the valley yesterday?" Blake scoffed, because he knew the old man knew. "Besides, I know you've been playing with Michael every night. You're probably the one who taught him about the sharpshooter."

Mr. Messina looked back at the papers in front of him, but Blake got the feeling he wasn't seeing anything. The man was stubborn as a mule.

"You're sick, too, aren't you."

Salvatore's dark eyes lifted to glare at him. Blake had never asked such a personal question before.

"The way I figure it, you have to apologize to Cori before she'll even consider staying. You both need family. Now more than ever."

Mr. Messina's head shot up, offense clearly taken. "I'm not going to apologize."

"Damn it, don't let your pride splinter your family into nothing!" Blake stopped pacing and planted his palms on the edge of the desk. They were wasting time arguing like this. Blake took a deep breath and tried reason again. "You don't relish being alone here, do you?"

The old man glowered at him. "Didn't I fire you?"

"Nope, I quit." Blake laughed, relieved. Mr. Messina was at his most reasonable when he was joking. Blake needed him reasonable.

"Damn well should have fired you when I had the chance." His employer's expression eased, but not completely, leaving Blake in doubt.

"You were bent on punishing me, remember?"

Mr. Messina smiled. "Haven't had the chance to do that yet. I've got some ideas, though."

Blake let out a relieved breath. ''I'd think working for you would be punishment enough. That, and...'' Blake drew himself up. ''Marrying your granddaughter.''

The old man's eyes lasered onto Blake, eyebrows raised.

''You heard me. I want to marry Cori. I love her.'' He swallowed because it was the first time he'd said it out loud. Maybe if he'd said it to Cori earlier and often, they wouldn't be in the mess they were in now. ''We'll live out at the house, close enough to keep an eye on you. But she won't do it unless you mend this thing between you.''

''She won't accept an apology.'' Salvatore Messina looked defeated. It was an expression Blake had never seen him wear before.

''The least you can do is try.''

''Let's go.'' Michael's high voice carried through the door. They were leaving.

''We've got one chance, you and I, so don't blow it.'' Blake opened the office door and stepped into the hallway to play their hand.

CHAPTER FOURTEEN

CORI FLINCHED when she heard the footsteps downstairs. It could only be her grandfather, which meant one last confrontation before she left. The suitcase banged awkwardly against her knee and she gripped Michael's hand tighter as she descended the stairs.

Blake stepped into view, a tentative smile on his face, no doubt trying one last time to make up with Michael. Except that he seemed to be smiling at her. That is, until he glanced over his shoulder.

Low grumbles announced her grandfather's presence.

Just what she needed, both Blake and her grandfather seeing her off. Her heart was already broken. What more did they want from her? Balancing the suitcase in one hand and her son in the other, Cori tried to take the stairs faster.

"Is that you, Corinne?"

Cori sighed as she reached the bottom step. Escape was out of the question now. She dropped the suitcase and turned to face the music. Michael stepped behind her and wrapped one arm around her bare leg. She was underdressed for this final confrontation, in her baggy knit shorts and pink T-shirt. Even the red dress would have been a better choice.

"It's Michael and me. We're getting out of your hair." Forever. God, she wanted to cry. How had everything turned out so wrong? Blake hated her and Michael hated Blake. Her grandfather couldn't care less about any of them.

"Leaving so soon?" Her grandfather stepped out of the shadows and into the light, looking pale, his eyes drawn with pain. He leaned on a table next to the wall, seemingly close to collapse.

Cori glanced at Blake, but he didn't notice her grandfather's weak physical state because he was staring at her. She had no idea what the stare was all about, since they'd parted on such rotten terms earlier. If he tried to talk about visitation now, she'd deck him.

"It's a full day's drive. We need to start early." She gazed down at Michael, who looked up at her with a worried expression. She smiled reassuringly. No one was going to hurt him anymore, if she could help it.

"We haven't discussed your mother's will," her grandfather said.

"Why would we need to do that?"

"Aren't you curious about your inheritance?" Her grandfather gave her a small smile.

Cori shook her head. She couldn't deal with this now. "Have Jasper Kraken call me." Jasper was the family lawyer. He'd be cold and impersonal, just the way a lawyer should be. Not a cold and impersonal family member. She leaned over to take Michael's hand.

"There are terms to the will." Salvatore Messina's words echoed in the large hall.

Cori immediately straightened. "What terms?"

"Trivial things, really." He waved his free hand. "About residency and such."

Cori's eyes narrowed. Something wasn't right. "Residency?"

"At the Messina Compound."

Cori was reminded of a time when she'd lived in this house and they'd played games like this for fun, trying to put one over on each other. "This is one of your games, isn't it?" Cori's eyes filled with tears. She didn't know if her grandfather was making a gesture toward reconciliation or just being cruel. How could he do this to her on the day she was leaving? She'd cry all the way to L.A. Cori didn't dare look at Blake and see his scorn. That would be her undoing.

"No." The word was spoken so innocently, she didn't believe her grandfather.

"You told me I wasn't getting anything. I'm okay with that." She reached again for Michael's hand. "Come on, Peanut."

"You need to stay." Her grandfather shuffled a step closer with a wobble. His legs didn't seem able to hold him steady.

"And you need to sit." With a brief tug of resistance from Michael, Cori rushed to her grandfather's side, lifting his arm around her shoulders and slipping her other arm around his back. "Help me," she said to Blake.

It took Blake a moment to react, but then he came to her grandfather's other side and together they helped him into a chair in the living room. Michael hid between the buttery leather couch and the long, dark blue curtains.

Cori stood back, hands on hips, her anger powerful enough to make her legs tremble. "I've never known anyone as stubborn as you. It's obvious you need surgery. You can barely walk."

"Stubborn." He snorted. "Nobody is more stubborn than you. Holding grudges. Staying away from your own family. Refusing responsibility."

"Protecting myself from emotional abuse. Leading my own life. Making it on my own."

"Selfish reasons."

"Personal goals."

He stood shakily, but with more balance than before. "You know nothing about goals. You worked for someone else."

"I worked for someone who values my opinion, who respects me and isn't threatened when I come up with an idea that's better than hers."

Her grandfather's face reddened. No matter how much she hoped, he'd never think of her as more than a little girl.

"Come on, Michael." Cori spun away, but Blake's words stopped her.

"Please, don't go."

"IT AMAZES ME that you're as successful as you have been," Blake said, scowling at the mess the old man had made of things. Didn't he understand this was their last chance? "I told you to apologize to her."

"You're fired." Salvatore Messina looked about ready to explode.

Cori narrowed her eyes at the two of them. Michael was nowhere to be seen. Blake's hopes were in shreds around his ankles.

"Great, I can collect severance pay." And Blake would, too, if only to make Mr. Messina mad.

"No, you quit already!" Salvatore Messina bellowed.

"Then, you can't fire me." Where had his son gone to? The poor kid probably thought his dad and great-grandfather were psycho. "Everything's okay, buddy. Your Big Grandpa is just upset because you and your mom are leaving, that's all."

"What's going on?" Arms crossed over her chest, Cori stood her ground, while her eyes darted to the door.

Blake stepped closer to Cori, needing her to believe him. He wanted to take Cori's hand in his, but one look at her deep frown and he kept his hand to himself. "It's National Apology Day. Isn't it, sir?" Blake gave Mr. Messina a warning look.

"When is Respect Your Elders Day?" Salvatore grumbled then caught Blake's expression, rolled his eyes and added weakly, "Family doesn't apologize to family. They understand."

The man was hopeless. "Like that's supposed to make up for threats? No wonder Cori stayed away so long. I can do better than that." Blake had to do better or Cori and his son would walk out of his life forever. He scanned the room quickly. Blake needed to reassure Michael. "Mike? Where are you? Come out here." Blake walked over to the couch and looked over the top. "Michael."

Cori gasped. Blake realized it was the first time she'd heard him call Michael by name.

Blake softened his voice. "I need you to come out so I can look at you and tell you I'm sorry. Remember how friends need to say they're sorry?"

Michael crawled out from behind the couch, then scooted forward just a hair. Blake knelt in front of him, reluctantly keeping his distance to avoid spooking the child. ''Do you remember when we met?''

Michael nodded, picking at the carpet and not looking up.

''Do you remember how mean I was to you that first day you came home? And you told your mom you didn't like me?'' It hurt just to remember that. ''I've said some things since then that haven't been very nice, either. Do you know why I did that?''

Michael shook his head. Jen appeared in the doorway, panting as if she'd run the entire way.

''I was mad at your mom because I loved her so much and I thought someone else was your father. So I was mean to you and your mom. We both know that being mean because you're angry is wrong, don't we? But I forgot.'' It pained him to admit he was an ass, but Blake wasn't going to keep his family without admitting his weaknesses. He could feel Cori's eyes on him, but he couldn't look away from Michael. If Cori couldn't forgive him today, at least he'd have mended things with Michael.

''Oh,'' Michael said in a little voice.

Salvatore Messina sank awkwardly into a chair. Blake prayed the old man would learn the value of an apology, or, at the very least, keep quiet.

''Then later, when she told me I was your dad, I didn't believe her.'' Man, Blake really sounded like a loser. ''So I was still mad. Pretty bad, huh?''

Michael nodded, eyes still on the carpet. His hands stilled.

''Then, just when I was starting to believe you were my son, I thought your mom only told me about being a dad because of your Big Grandpa. So, I was mad all over again, which is why I didn't wait for your mom this morning when I told you I was your dad. I'm one hundred times sorry for doing that. I should have waited.''

''You're mad a lot,'' Michael said, risking a glance at him.

''Not all the time. Just lately,'' Jen observed.

Blake tossed her The Look. ''You're not helping.''

Jen shrugged, but she was grinning.

''What I'm trying to tell you is that I was so busy being mad, I missed the fact that your mom loved me enough to have you. I was wrong. So wrong.'' Blake shook his head and blinked back the tears, not daring to look away from Michael. At this point, he needed his son's acceptance as much as he needed air. Only the fact that Blake's adopted father had had the patience to win Blake over gave him the courage to keep trying. He could do this.

''I love you, Michael,'' Blake said raggedly.

''I'm mean to you sometimes,'' Michael allowed.

''I think you owed me some.'' Blake reached out and tugged one little ear, instead of following through on his need to hug him. He wanted desperately to feel the little guy in his arms. ''You and I are learning a lot about each other, and we may not always agree on how to do things. But one thing I do know. You always love your family, no matter what. You can get mad or frustrated with someone in your family but you'll always love them.'' Blake risked a glance at Cori. Tears rolled slowly over her cheeks and her nose was red. She looked a mess, but Blake loved her, anyway.

''Well said,'' Mr. Messina whispered.

Cori glanced at her grandfather and then back to Blake. A sprig of hope swelled within Blake's heart at the wonder he saw in her eyes, but he wasn't finished making peace with Michael yet. He turned back to his son.

''Do you know what I love about you already, Michael?''

Michael shook his head.

''I love how your ears look just like mine when I was a kid I love playing soccer with you in the vineyard. And I love how smart you are. You know all about bugs.''

''And worms.'' Michael's brown eyes finally raised to Blake's, wide and accepting, answering half of Blake's prayers

''And worms.'' Blake nodded. ''So I'd like you to reconsider having me for a dad, because you've taught me that I can't be mad all the time. And that I need to say I'm sorry when I hurt somebody's feelings.''

''You still want to be my dad? After what I said?'' Michael actually looked surprised.

''With all my heart.'' Blake smiled and held out his arms. 'Please?''

There was a moment when Blake doubted Michael was going to accept him. In that moment, Blake's heart seemed to stall and his breath catch. And then the little guy flung himself into Blake's arms and wrapped himself tightly around Blake's neck. They both drew in ragged gulps of air. Tears stung the back of Blake's eyes. He finally knew what it felt like to have his son hug him.

Wonderful.

Michael smelled of baby shampoo and fresh-washed clothes. He was a warm, soft bundle with a strong grip and a heart that was willing to forgive and teach a dad how to love. Blake pressed a kiss to the silky hair on top of Michael's head in thanks and love, not letting go of his son.

When Blake met Cori's gaze, he saw she was still crying. A tear slipped over his cheek, but he didn't care. His dream of family was going to come true.

Blake whispered to Michael, ''Can you keep a secret?''

Michael nodded.

''I'm going to marry your mom.''

Michael giggled and bounced twice in Blake's arms.

''I just need to ask her, so I'm going to put you down for a minute. But then I'm going to want you right back, okay?''

Michael grinned and practically sprang out of Blake's arms. He clambered onto the couch and bounced his bottom against the back over and over again, a huge smile on his face.

With a deep breath, Blake turned to Cori, well aware that he still had his audience. He needed to tell Cori he loved her, too. But first, as with Michael, he had to clear the air.

''Thank you,'' Cori said quietly, wiping the tears from her cheeks.

Blake shook his head. "Again with the good manners. I think I've always envied your poise." True enough, even when he felt it drive a wedge between them.

"You said it makes you crazy."

He took Cori's arm and led her out the front door into the warm spring sunshine, leaving everyone else inside. "I think what drove me crazy was the way you told me just enough of the truth to be honest, yet withheld just enough of the truth to protect yourself. Eventually, it was my downfall, because I didn't know what to believe, so I thought the worst, just like you said."

As soon as he let her go, she stepped away, putting distance between them. It wasn't a good sign. With effort, Blake held on to his smile, but inside he faltered.

"You're beautiful."

Cori glanced down at herself and then cast a doubtful gaze on him.

"Inside and out."

Cori tugged on her pink T-shirt, shifted her feet and tried to redirect the conversation. "Did you want to schedule your first visit?"

"I'm not scheduling any visits." They were going to live together as a family. Blake wouldn't let go of that goal. He needed to experience the world through the joy and wonder of his son, and he needed Cori's warm, giving spirit by his side.

"Oh." Cori's face fell. "But…"

"I want you to stop breaking my heart." Blake's voice sounded like gravel crunching beneath his feet, because he was again giving Cori the power to wound him. This time, he was pretty sure she wouldn't crush him.

"What?"

Hope flitted briefly across her face. Blake saw it in the sparkle in her eyes and the upturn of her beautiful mouth.

"It's getting to be a habit with you." He allowed himself small smile. Blake wanted to enfold Cori in his embrace and never let her go. But there was the risk of not clearing the secrets away.

After a moment of consideration, Cori waved her hand dismissively. ''I'm sorry you feel that way, but you shouldn't punish Michael after the progress you've made.'' Her words had an angry edge.

''He won't be punished.''

Cori looked confused.

Michael popped out onto the porch. ''Did you ask Mommy to marry you?''

Blake laughed. ''Nope. Go back inside.'' So much for his son's ability to keep a secret. He'd have to remember that come Christmas.

''He didn't ask her yet,'' Michael yelled, running back inside.

Cori's eyes flashed. ''If this is some scheme of yours and Grandfather's, you'd better think again.'' She pushed past him into the house, heading for her suitcase. ''I won't let him buy you.''

''Wait a minute.'' Now who was thinking the worst? He'd been so close. He couldn't lose Cori, now that he had Michael's love and support.

Cori yanked up the suitcase handle and stomped back toward the door, wheeling the black bag behind her, bouncing it off the steps, and seemingly over his heart. Blake needed to convince her this wasn't a joke. Groveling seemed the best route.

''I admit, I asked your grandfather to mend things between you two. I suggested he apologize.'' Blake stood in the entry, watching Cori practically race out of his life. ''But what goes on between the two of us doesn't concern anyone else.''

Cori's sandals slapped angrily on the paving stones.

''Everything I said to Michael applies to you,'' Blake called before launching himself down the steps after her. ''I've been an ass.''

''Understatement of the year,'' Cori tossed over her shoulder.

''I know I'm not good enough for you, but I'm going to take care of you and Michael, I promise.''

''I don't know where you hooked this inferiority complex

of yours, but I'd throw it back. Grandfather told you he doesn't hire idiots.''

Blake's frustration snuck past his best intentions. ''Fine, Cori. I'm the best damn thing that ever happened to you and if you don't listen to me now, I'll just follow you to L.A. and prove it. I suddenly have a lot of time on my hands.'' He wasn't about to let her leave him again, not without a fight. He stopped next to her at the Mustang's trunk.

Cori struggled to put the suitcase handle down before giving up and tossing the bag in the trunk with the handle extended.

She'd reverted to the Messina silence. Blake took a deep breath, reaching for humbleness. ''Please. I couldn't trust you before. Every time I did, you crushed me by not telling me everything.''

She kept her face averted. ''And what happened in the past hour to change your mind?''

''Michael's baby book.'' Blake reached past her and slid the handle home.

She spun on him. ''Did you call a psychic hotline? You've never seen Michael's baby book.''

''No, but Jen has.''

Cori tossed her hands and headed back for the house, huffing dramatically as she stomped around the back of his truck. Blake dogged her, then swung Cori around to face him before she reached the steps.

''Why did you write my name in his book? You owe me that much, at least,'' Blake paused. ''No. That's wrong. I owe you. My career. My livelihood. A home for Jen.''

Some of the fight in Cori's eyes dimmed. She looked away, opened her mouth to explain, and closed it. Then tried again. ''I couldn't bear the thought of Michael thinking the worst of himself. Of me. Of his father. Since I couldn't risk writing his name on the birth certificate, I had to find a place where I could be honest.''

''You gave up everything to protect us.'' Even though Blake had assumed that was the truth, hearing it from Cori caused his heart to swell into his throat. She had loved him once.

Cori nodded. ''But the book was personal. Something just for Michael and me, so that I could tell him one day.''

''And me. You kept so much from me that I couldn't trust you, no matter how much my heart wanted to.'' Blake's hands slid down Cori's arms to her hands. He gave them a gentle squeeze. ''It was that one bit of honesty hidden in plain sight that made everything clear to me. You wanted everyone to know the truth. That's why you brought the book here.''

For a moment, Cori looked at Blake in wonder. He could see the truth in her deep brown eyes. Her love was still alive. Then she regained her composure and tugged her hands. But he wasn't letting her go.

Cori lifted her chin. ''Michael brought the book. I didn't want him to.''

''Ouch.'' He'd been the one to want honesty. ''You know what? That doesn't matter. Marry me,'' he said, dropping to one knee. He sensed it was all or nothing, and he wouldn't settle for nothing. ''On one condition. Complete disclosure. No more secrets between us.''

She shook her head. ''I can't tell you what a burden a secret like that is. I've had to keep things to myself before, but—''

''No more secrets,'' Blake repeated desperately. He wasn't going to lose her.

She sighed. ''Don't feel like you have to marry me just because we have a child together.''

''I want to marry you. I'm going to be miserable for the rest of my life if I don't marry you.'' Blake tried to look at her with all the love in his heart, but, hell, he hadn't had much practice, so he forced out those preciously guarded words, baring his vulnerable heart to her once more. ''I love you.''

Cori studied him, doubt shadowing her eyes. ''The other night, you never said anything about love.''

''I was an idiot, trying to protect my heart because I was sure you'd leave me, because I didn't understand why you kept Michael a secret from me. And because I always think the worst. But now that I know I'm good enough for you, I'll make it up to you. I love you.'' He stood and cradled her face in his hands, then placed a tender kiss on her lips. ''You'll hear those words about a million more times if you marry me.''

''Just say yes,'' Jen yelled from the front door. ''Don't leave him to raise me alone.''

Michael giggled, standing in front of her.

Cori smiled. ''How could you even think you weren't good enough for me?''

''Because I'm slow and insecure.'' He knew his answering smile was goofy, but he didn't care.

''You're not either. Look how far you've come on your own.'' Cori's smile faltered. ''My job. Your job.'' She looked toward the living room windows, then back to Blake. ''Him. How can this possibly work?''

It came down to her family. Nobody was smiling now. ''All we can do is try,'' Blake said, but his words lacked conviction. He needed a miracle here. Something to convince Cori their love would survive. An image of Sophia, before she became sick came to mind. She's always been able to make the old man see reason.

''Would it help,'' Salvatore Messina called from the front door. ''If I said I wanted you to stay?''

Cori gasped, her hand flying to her mouth. She looked up at Blake and then back to the windows. ''I never thought I'd hear him say that.''

Blake nodded, silently sending his thanks to Sophia. For surely, her influence was at work.

''We all want you to stay,'' Blake said, leading Cori away from the door and farther up the driveway in search of some privacy.

He had to ask for the words he hadn't yet heard from her today. ''You do love me, right?''

''You know I do.'' And the way her eyes met his without hesitation, begging him to kiss her, Blake knew she'd never stopped loving him. A love that strong could endure anything now that they were on equal footing.

He kissed her soundly, sealing the pact of love between them, taking her kiss as his answer.

•

"We'll start planning the wedding then," Mr. Messina called.

"Do you think I could be in it?" Jen asked.

"Me, too?" Michael chimed in.

"I wouldn't have it any other way," Mr. Messina replied, already taking the helm.

Cori gently pushed away from Blake, laughing, to ask, "Do you think this is how our family is going to be? Everyone having their own say?"

"Yes, love. I don't think your grandfather will be the only one to speak his mind." No more Messina silences. "It's not going to be easy. Family never is. But this family has changed a lot in the past week or so, and I think everyone will be on more equal terms."

Michael flew down the steps and wrapped himself around Blake's leg. "Daddy!"

"Welcome home, love," Blake whispered against her cheek, one hand on his son's head, and one hand tangled in Cori's hair, happier than he'd been in years.

Keeping Faith

Janice Macdonald

Dear Reader,

As a parent or grandparent, we want only the best for our children and grandchildren. But conflicting opinions can result in a painful and emotional tug-of-war. In *Keeping Faith*, six-year-old Faith is the centre of a universe that includes her mother, Hannah, her grandmother, Margaret, and three aunts. All would do absolutely anything for her. And so would Faith's father, Liam.

In this book I've tried to explore issues of trust and boundary setting, and the complexities – and, of course, the numerous joys and rewards – of the mother-daughter relationship.

I love to hear from readers and try to write back whenever possible. Please visit my website at www.janicemacdonald.com and let me know how you enjoyed this book.

Best wishes,

Janice

To my mother, Dorothy, my daughter Carolyn
and my granddaughter Emily.

CHAPTER ONE

HANNAH RILEY HAD NEVER actually experienced a gun going off at close range, but when she opened the *Long Beach Press Telegram* Monday morning and saw Liam Tully's picture, she figured the effect would have to be pretty similar. Around her, all sound and movement ceased. Oxygen seemed sucked from the room. The picture blurred.

Liam Tully? It couldn't be.

It was. A little older than the last time she'd seen him—six years older, to be exact—but definitely Liam. Thin face, too thin to be conventionally handsome. Deep-set eyes. Terrific smile.

The caption beneath the picture read: *Liam Tully, lead singer for the Celtic folk group, The Wild Rovers. The group from County Galway will perform next Friday through Sunday at Fiddler's Green in Huntington Beach as part of a four-week California tour.*

Hannah read and reread the announcement. Stared at Liam's picture as though it might reveal something the caption didn't. Stared at the picture and saw herself as she'd been the last time she'd seen Liam. Twenty-five, pregnant and scared to death. Of everything. *God.*

Carefully, as though it might detonate, she set the newspaper aside and smiled up at the dark-haired woman who had just walked into her classroom. Hannah stuck out her hand and searched through her brain, suddenly gone blank, for the woman's name. *Becker.*

''Hi, Mrs. Becker.'' She glanced at her watch. ''You're a little early, but if you give me a minute, I'll find Taylor's assessment results.''

Four-year-old Taylor had flunked a mock prekindergarten screening test two days ago. The real test, in which he would be put through his paces—skipping, hopping, wielding scissors and filling in the blanks to questions like ''A bed is for sleeping and a table is for…''—was a few weeks away, but his mother had called to ask Hannah what could be done to improve her son's performance.

As she retrieved Taylor's folder, Hannah had an insane urge to propose to Mrs. Becker, a brittle-looking blonde in a black pantsuit, that Taylor be allowed to be himself. An easygoing child who delighted in running through the sprinklers on La Petite Ecole's manicured lawn and showed little enthusiasm for mastering the alphabet.

She resisted the urge. Parents who paid thousands of dollars a year to send their children to La Petite Ecole, who crammed their kids' schedules with extracurricular classes in early math and classical music appreciation, did so in order to crush the competition when it came time for kindergarten.

And, as Hannah continually had to remind herself, most parents—however misguided their motives might seem—really only wanted the best for their children.

Most parents.

She dragged her mind back to Taylor Becker's mother, who had just asked her a question and was waiting for an answer.

''Sorry.'' Hannah smiled at the woman.

"I was asking if there's anything else we can do." She hesitated, her face coloring slightly. "I bought him this darling T-shirt to wear for the test. I'm sure it sounds silly to you, but I started thinking that if he were dressed in a really hip shirt it might set him apart from the others." Another pause. "We don't want him to fail again."

Hannah looked at her for a moment. "If I can give you a piece of advice, Mrs. Becker, I would strongly suggest that you don't use the word *fail.* Especially to Taylor. And I'd also suggest that *you* try to relax. If he sees you're stressed, he'll get anxious and maybe not do so well. Children pick up on negative emotions."

IT WAS CRAZY, but all afternoon—ever since she had read the article about Liam—she'd had the fantasy that when she got home, Liam would be waiting for her. At one point the feeling was so strong she'd actually picked up the phone to make an appointment at the beauty parlor—this was not one of her better hair days. And then, remembering that he was probably still a few hundred miles to the north, she'd put the phone down and revised the scenario. There would be a message to say he'd called. She could still recreate the sound of his voice. Even after six years, she could conjure it up. *Let's get together,* he'd say in her fantasy. *Let's talk about what happened. I miss you, I still love you.* But as she opened the front door, Hannah knew Liam wouldn't be waiting inside and, as she stood in the kitchen doorway watching her daughter, she knew, too, that there had been no call.

Faith, a week shy of her sixth birthday, sat at a large wooden table in the center of the room. Brow furrowed, she was squeezing pink icing onto a row of cookies. A California girl, all tanned limbs and sun-bleached hair, worn now in a tightly controlled ponytail that set off her clear skin and blue eyes.

Liam's eyes.

Children pick up on negative emotions.

Most parents only want what's best for their children.

Liam wasn't most parents.

Hannah didn't need Liam in her life.

Faith didn't need Liam in her life.

Children pick up on negative emotions.

Hannah consciously slowed her breathing, stayed in the doorway, smiling now as she waited for either her daughter or her mother, who was on the phone, to look up and see her.

Her parents had moved into the large Spanish-style house a block from the ocean in Long Beach just after Hannah's first birthday and, of all the rooms in the house, the huge square kitchen figured most prominently in her childhood memories.

She'd learned to walk by pulling herself up to the cabinet edges, knocked out a tooth on a pantry shelf after roller-skating across the polished floor on a dare from her sister Debra. A large cast of dogs had eaten from various bowls that were always set out by the back door, and litters of kittens had taken their first breaths under the kitchen sink.

Nothing much had changed. After her father died, her mother had traded in the avocado-green appliances and ditched the old wallpaper with its repeating pattern of yellow kettles and orange teapots. The walls were peach now, or as Margaret insisted, apricot bisque; the refrigerator and stove stainless steel, but something was always in the oven or on the stove and, until last week when he'd gone to doggy heaven, Turpin, the family's elderly black Lab, had still been eating from the bowl by the door.

The henhouse, her mother called it these days. Hannah and Faith and Margaret lived there. Sporadically, Margaret's sister Rose and her own sister Debra came to stay. Helen, the youngest of Hannah's aunts, had her own coop, a guest cottage behind the rose garden, but always joined them for meals. Males were conspicuously absent.

"Who needs them anyway?" Margaret would say. "We're just a bunch of hens cooing and clucking around our baby chick."

So while Margaret's friends were dealing with the empty-nest blues and converting extra bedrooms into sewing areas, Margaret kept busy as she had all her adult life—cooking, cleaning and caring for her brood. "My family is my life," she'd say when Hannah or Debra would urge her to expand her horizons with a part-time job or volunteering. "This is what makes me happy. My daughters and my granddaughter. Why would I want to do something else?"

If there were times when Margaret's fussing and clucking made Hannah question the living arrangement, Deb made no secret of the fact that Margaret drove her nuts. Deb's biggest fear was that she'd turn out like Margaret. "If you ever catch me acting like Mom," she'd say to Hannah, "just shoot me, okay?"

And Deb in turn drove Margaret nuts. Deb was the problematic chick in the nest; prickly and demanding, always flying away only to return a few months later, torn and tattered but still defiant. Margaret had been thirty-eight when she gave birth to Debra and had once, in Deb's hearing, referred to her youngest daughter as "an afterthought." Debra had never forgiven her.

Still the relationship had a weird kind of synergy. Debra could tell herself that however screwed up her life might be, at least she wasn't like Margaret, leading some nutso June Cleaver existence, ironing sheets and baking pies while her husband cheated with women half his age as Hannah's father had done. And Margaret's tales about her problematic daughter always got a sympathetic hearing from the women in her Wednesday Weight Watchers group. "I give Mom a sense of purpose," Deb would say, only half in jest.

So, too, did Faith. In fact, Faith was so thoroughly the center of her grandmother's life that Hannah worried what Margaret would do if she and Faith ever moved away. Not that she had any plans to do so. She was happy. Sort of, kind of, basically. A job she enjoyed—well, maybe she would rather be a landscape gardener, but somehow that hadn't worked out. A guy she liked. Allan was sweet and thoughtful and if he didn't make her heart beat faster, so what? Chemistry wasn't everything.

More importantly, Faith was happy.

And if Liam didn't care that his little girl was just about to turn six, that was his loss. Hannah tiptoed into the room and came up behind her daughter. Arms wrapped around Faith's shoulders, she nuzzled her neck.

"Hey, baby. Who loves you more than anyone else in the world?"

"Ow, Mommy, you're squeezing too hard and don't call me 'baby.'" Faith wriggled away. "Look." She held up a large colored tin for Hannah to see. "Grandma bought me these cookie cutters. They have all the letters of the alphabet. See, I'm writing my name with cookies."

"Wow, that's terrific." Hannah pulled up a chair and

sat down next to her daughter. The cooking gene had skipped a generation, gone from her mother to her daughter. Both loved long days in the kitchen, Margaret's cookbooks spread out across the table, the KitchenAid whirring. Impulsively Hannah brought her face up under Faith's. "I'm the kissing monster." She puckered her lips. "And I won't go away until I get ten thousand kisses."

"Momeee." Faith pushed Hannah's head away. "I can't see what I'm doing." Up on her knees, she began fishing small vials of silver balls and candy confetti from the tin. "Look. Grandma bought me all these decorating things. We're having *so* much fun."

"I can tell." Hannah glanced over at her mother, still on the phone. Margaret, sixty, and the oldest of the three sisters, had wiry, gray-blond hair tied up with an orange scrunchy. From Margaret's careful tone and turndowned mouth, Hannah guessed that the caller was Deb and that the crisis du jour was gathering strength.

"God." Margaret carefully set the phone back on the wall holder, leaned against the sink and folded her arms across her chest. "I swear Debra will drive me to an early grave."

"No!" Eyes wide and troubled, Faith looked at her grandmother. "I don't want you to go to an early grave, Grandma."

"Oh, honey," Margaret laughed, and hugged Faith. "That's just one of those silly things grown-ups say. Grandma isn't going anywhere. She's having too much fun with you. Did you tell Mommy what a great day we had? We shopped and baked and talked girl stuff," she said, addressing Hannah now. "And next week—"

"We're making all the cookies for Grandma's friend's party." Faith sprinkled blue sugar onto a pink cookie and sat back to look at the results. "Six kinds. Chocolate chip, lemon bars and I forget the rest."

"Oh, all different kinds." Margaret started clearing the knives and spoons from the table. "Poor Bella, she's got the garden club coming and she's overwhelmed so I offered to make the desserts. Somehow I'll manage to squeeze it between the birthday cake I promised to bake for Rose's friend and…damn, I know there's something else. Please God don't let it be something I promised to do for Deb. She's already upset because I forgot to ask what happened with that job interview she went on…" Margaret wiped the table and waited until Faith had gone to watch cartoons, then slowly shook her head at Hannah. "Tell me where I went wrong with Deb. Why can't I do anything right for that girl?"

Hannah carefully set Faith's decorated cookies into a tin, resisting the urge to bite into an extra letter *A*. Deb was twenty-two and she was thirty-one, but to Margaret they were always the girls.

"So what's up with Deb now?"

"She says she's moving in with Dennis."

"The bartender who sells marijuana?"

"This isn't funny, Hannah."

"I'm not laughing, Mom." Actually she'd been wondering whether or not to mention the news about Liam. "I thought she was through with Dennis."

Margaret reached for a jar of hand cream on the windowsill and began massaging it into her elbows. Margaret was always slapping alpha hydroxy on her neck and face and complaining that everyone called her ma'am.

"I thought she was through with him, too," Margaret said. "Now she tells me she's moving in and when I start asking her about it, she accuses me of nosing into her business. I swear to God, I can't win. Either I'm not there for her—her words—or I'm nosing into her business.''

''She knows she can jerk you around and get away with it.'' Hannah reached into the cabinet for a box of chamomile tea. Easier to analyze her mother's problems than to figure out why she kept looking at the phone and willing it to ring. ''Listen, don't we need to get this chicken going?''

''I'll take care of it.'' Margaret removed plastic-wrapped chicken from the fridge and carried it to the stove. ''Rose said she had indigestion all night after that last thing you made.''

''Tuna casserole?'' Hannah looked at her mother. ''How could she get indigestion from that? I used the same recipe you always use.''

Margaret grinned. ''Well, doll-baby, no one ever accused you of being Julia Child. Faith made me promise that I'd never get old because she didn't know who would make the kind of food she likes.''

''Little brat.'' Hannah shook her head. ''I tried really hard with those potato skins she wanted.''

''I know.'' Margaret's smile turned conspiratorial. The chicken breasts flattened out on a cutting board, she began slicing them into strips. ''Don't worry, Hanny, you have plenty of other talents, my love.''

Feeling disgruntled now, Hannah resisted the urge to ask Margaret to name the other talents. She knew Margaret would list qualities like sweet and generous, which had never struck Hannah as much to crow about. They certainly hadn't been enough to keep Liam interested. Margaret was back on Deb again.

''...and she just didn't sound happy about Dennis, so all I said was I'd like to see her married and she immediately flew off the handle and went on and on about how she'll get married when she's ready and she's not about to do something stupid like...well, you know what I'm saying.''

''Yeah.'' Hannah put her teabag in a cup of water, put it in the microwave and stood passively, watching the seconds count down. She knew only too well. Something stupid like Hannah did when she ran off with Liam Tully, then compounded the foolishness by marrying him in a Las Vegas chapel, only to return home three months pregnant and on her own.

Debra could run off with an Elvis impersonator and set up housekeeping in a Ralph's supermarket parking lot and no one would be surprised. But not levelheaded, dependable Hannah. If she spent the rest of her life in chaste contemplation, she would never live down what the family referred to as her Liam Lapse. Her father's death from a heart attack had been blamed on it and Margaret, who had never previously touched alcohol, dated the start of her evening consumption of wine to that time. ''We all suffered,'' her aunt Helen frequently reminded her.

''Just talk to Deb, will you?'' Margaret asked. ''At least she won't yell at you.''

Hannah took her tea from the microwave. The temptation to remind Margaret that it was up to her to work out her problems with Deb blazed briefly, then died. Even feeling as she did right now, kind of let down and confused about Liam coming back, her inclination was not to cause an argument. Ms. Congeniality, Deb called her. The downside was that Hannah often did things she didn't really want to do. Like last Saturday, when she'd gone with her aunt Rose to the World's Largest Singles Mixer because Rose hadn't wanted to attend alone.

•

God, what a nightmare that had been. A guy with a toupee that looked exactly like a small furry animal napping across his scalp had refused to believe Hannah didn't want to dance with him. She'd stood her ground, though, and eventually he and his furry friend had disappeared into the crowd. It wasn't quite so easy to say no to her mother.

"I'll talk to Deb," she said. "This time. After that, you're on your own."

Lately, Hannah reflected, it seemed as if she and her mother had reversed roles. As a kid, Hannah had needed constant reassurance from Margaret that one day boys would pay attention to her, that the pimples would go away and that, as unlikely as it had seemed at the time, she would actually get breasts. Now *she* was constantly doling out reassurances to Margaret and monitoring her mother's wine consumption much as Margaret had once sniffed for signs of teenage drinking. She hoped to God that by the time Faith needed monitoring and reassurance, Margaret would need less.

She decided not to say anything about Liam.

AFTER THE GIG, Liam shoved the sweaty clothes and boots he'd worn during the performance into a duffel bag and joined the other musicians making their way to the bus. The equipment had been packed up and stowed while he and a few of the others had gone next door for a couple of pints. The mike stands, lights and speakers. The guitars and drums, the audio effects and mixing console, T-shirts and merchandise. Packed up, stowed away, ready to start all over again.

In the bus, he sat up front for a while chatting with some of the others, then made his way down the aisle to the lounge in the middle. Yawning, he stretched out on one of the couches, hands pillowed behind his head. As buses went, this one was pretty plush. Microwave cookers and hi-fi. Mood lighting and couches. A far cry from the VW van they'd use in the band's early days. That one had been reliable only for breaking down at least once a day.

But now they were touring internationally. The Wild Rovers, all eight of them. No chartered jets yet, but this wasn't bad. Three days out and, as always, he felt the rhythm beginning to develop. Another day, another town. Pile off the bus, pile onto the bus. Stopping sometimes in the wee hours to traipse into an all-night place in the middle of nowhere for hamburgers and chips. Blinking in the fluorescent lights, bleary-eyed and half-asleep. Then back on the bus, collapsing into the bunk to fall asleep, rocked by the motion of the road. Waking to blinding sunlight creeping in around the black window shades. On the bus, off the bus. Set it up, tear it down. Different day, different town. He loved it. If there was a better way to live, he didn't know about it.

Someone pushed his feet off the seat, and he looked up to see Brid Kelly, long red hair streaming down her back and skin so white that in the murky light of the bus she looked luminous. She had on jeans and a thin sleeveless top. If there'd been enough light, he knew he'd be able make out the outline of every bone in her rib cage. Brid could be a poster child for famine relief. He worried about her and not just—as she sometimes claimed—because he'd never find another singer who understood his music the way she did.

She was holding a large plastic bowl and a beer, which she held out to him.

"Thanks."

She smiled and dropped down beside him. "How you doing, Liam?"

"All right." He sat up and eyed the bowl. "Is that cabbage salad you're eating again?"

"It is." She waved the plastic fork. "D'you want some?"

He drank some beer. "Have you eaten anything but cabbage salad in the last three days?"

"I have." She grinned. "Yesterday, I ate a carrot and three radishes."

He shook his head. She'd nearly collapsed after yesterday's show and he hadn't bought her excuse that it was the heat. "You're a skeleton, already, for God's sake. You'll make yourself ill, the way you're going."

"Ah, come on." With a wave of her hand, she dismissed his concerns. "I'll be fine. Nice and slim for when I walk down the aisle with Tommy Doherty."

"Tommy Doherty." Liam swung his feet back up on the couch and over her lap. "You've been talking about walking down the aisle with Tommy Doherty ever since I've known you."

"This time I mean it. I've had it with all this." She dug her fork into the cabbage. "I'm ready to start making babies."

"Another thing I've heard at least a hundred times."

"Right, well, it's time now."

"I won't hold my breath."

"You'll see, Liam. I've had enough of it. On the road for weeks at a time. What kind of life is it anyway? Always away from your friends and family."

He didn't answer. He'd heard her sing the same song so many times he could recite it by heart. She'd get back to Ireland and insist she was through. They'd have to find a new singer. But then plans for the next tour would get underway, and he'd see her wavering. The truth was, the music was as much a part of her life as it was Liam's. She was every bit as addicted to the life.

''What about you then, Liam? You never feel like putting down roots somewhere? You don't miss being close to someone?''

With an elbow on the windowsill, he watched the road. ''If I do,'' he said, ''I take a couple of aspirin until the feeling goes away.''

Brid pushed his leg and he turned to smile at her, then went back to watching the white lines flash past. Only one time had he ever considered packing it all in. About six years ago now. A marriage, brief as a blip in time. She'd missed her family, hated the long absences and frenetic craziness of his life. Because he'd loved her, he'd seriously considered settling down. Until he'd found out what she'd done.

He'd channeled his anger into the music and the following year he made the UK charts for the first time. *Betrayed.* That was the name of the single. And now, in a nice bit of irony, his next gig was in her hometown, where it had all started.

CHAPTER TWO

THE DAY AFTER HANNAH read about Liam coming back, she was standing in the kitchen making a salad for dinner when her sister Debra announced that she was pregnant.

"Don't tell Mom," Deb said. "I haven't decided what I'm going to do about it."

"You're kidding." Hannah dropped into the chair opposite her sister.

"Well, God, you don't have to say it like that. It was okay for you to get pregnant but no one else can?"

Hannah held up her hand. She wasn't in the mood for Debra. "If you want to talk," she said, "we'll talk. Otherwise, you can take your damn attitude and leave."

"Zowee." Debra's eyes widened. "Chill out, Hannah. What are you so steamed up about anyway?"

"Nothing."

"Come on." Debra peered at her. "It's something. You had a fight with Allan? You had a fight with Mom? You got fired?"

"For God's sake, Deb." She got up from the table, filled a glass with water from the fridge dispenser and sat down again. "Tell me what's going on with *you.*"

"I missed two periods and I threw up twice this week at work. Dennis freaked when I first told him, but once he got over the shock he thought it was kind of cool. Now he's saying I can move in with him until the baby's born. After that, who knows?"

"What do *you* want to do?"

Debra shrugged. "Not what I'm doing right now, that's for damn sure. 'Hi, my name's Debra,'" she said in a mincing voice. "'And I'll be your waitress tonight.' God. I am so sick of that job. I just want to have a decent job where I'm making some money and I don't have some jerk telling me to push the desserts and smile more. At least if I have the baby, it's something different, plus Dennis is being a whole lot nicer since he found out."

Hannah counted slowly to ten. Where did she even start? She traced the moisture on her glass and looked up at her sister. "What's happening with your classes at State?"

Deb rolled her eyes. "The instructors were such a bunch of idiots, I swear I couldn't even listen to them. I mean, I could learn more from surfing the Internet."

"But you're not going to get a teaching credential that way."

"Don't start on me about that, I've already heard it from Mom."

"Deb." Hannah put her elbows on the table. "You hate working where you are now, you hated working at Marie Callender's, you hated worked at Denny's—"

"Shut up, Hannah." Debra jumped up from the table, stomped over to the pantry in her clunky black waitress shoes and emerged with a bag of Oreos that she ripped open. "You think you've got it all figured out, don't you?" A cookie in one hand, she regarded Hannah as though she'd suddenly recognized something that hadn't been clear before. "You think you're so damn perfect."

Hannah snorted. "Right."

"No, you do. And Mom does, too. I am so sick of hearing how hard *Hannah* worked to get her degree, how wonderful *Hannah's* job is, what a great boyfriend *Han-*

nah has. 'Allan's an *attorney,*'" she said, mimicking Margaret's voice. "'And he lives on Riva Alto Canal and he's just so wonderful and Hannah's so wonderful—'"

"Maybe that's your interpretation, but it's not the way I feel..."

"Yeah, whatever." Debra eased the top off a cookie and bit into the cream filling. "I don't give a damn. Maybe you've got it figured out now, you know damn well the whole reason you got pregnant was to keep Liam around."

"No, I don't know that." Her face suddenly warm, Hannah held Debra's glance. She heard Margaret's car pull into the driveway and lowered her voice. "Look, Deb, having a baby is a huge decision—"

"Well, *duh*..." Debra was up from the table again. "Like I don't know it's my decision, too? God, I don't even know why I try to talk to you. Just because Liam was a jerk doesn't mean all guys are that way."

"Whoa..." Rose walked into the kitchen just as Debra stormed out. "What's the matter with her?"

WHILE MARGARET WORRIED aloud about Debra all through dinner, Hannah thought about Liam. Twenty-eight hours since she'd seen the article. Twenty-eight hours of thinking about practically nothing else. She didn't know his schedule—except for next Friday—but he was somewhere in California and it was making her crazy. Thinking of him in Ireland was one thing, thinking of him maybe just an hour or two away was something else. He *could* call. Of course, he could have called from Ireland, too. But he hadn't called. And he wouldn't call.

"Dennis is not a good influence on Deb," Margaret

was saying now. "I mean a bartender, for God's sake. And he bleaches his hair. What kind of guy would do that?" Her brow furrowed, she dug a fork into the gooey custard on her plate. "What is it with my girls?" she asked, glancing at Helen. "Why is it they both seem to have this thing for irresponsible men?"

"Well, hey, bad boys are more fun, huh, Hannie?" Aunt Rose, in a loose black silk shirt printed with beer bottles from around the world, winked at Hannah. Rose, a cosmetologist, was divorced from her second husband and staying at the house just until she got her credit card bills paid off. She'd recently had her eyelids tattooed with permanent liner because, she confided to Hannah, she hated to wake up beside a man and look washed-out. Rose was absolutely certain Mr. Right would turn up one of these days—for her and for Hannah. Rose had her money on Allan.

Aunt Helen shot Rose a disapproving look. "I'm quite sure that Hannah has already learned her lesson with…immature young men and I have no doubt that, before long, Debra will, too."

The youngest of the three sisters, Helen was small, pink and fair with a large soft bosom and a similarly proportioned bottom. Faith, who adored Helen, once confided to Hannah that hugging Aunt Helen was like hugging a great big marshmallow. Helen taught junior high school and everything she said had a sweetly reasoned tone as if she knew that, even under the most obnoxious and intractable behavior, goodness was just waiting to shine. Helen's husband had died years ago in a freak lightning storm back in Missouri where they'd gone to see his mother. Afterward, Helen had moved into the small guest cottage on Margaret's property and decorated it with Laura Ashley fabrics.

"What about that nice attorney?" Helen asked Hannah now. "Are you still seeing him?"

Rose shot up her hand. "If you're not, I get first dibs."

"Rose," Margaret and Helen said in unison.

"Hey, I like younger men." Rose grinned. "And he lives on Riva Alto Canal. What's not to like? Do your old auntie a favor, Hanny. See if he has an older brother."

"Well..." Helen smiled as if to say that particular subject was over. She looked at Faith. "Listen, sweetie, if you'll go bring me my purse over there on the couch, I've got a little surprise for you." Faith darted across the room and returned with a large canvas bag. "Let's see what we have here." Helen reached into the bag. "*James and the Giant Peach* and *Sleeping Beauty*."

"Oh, wow." All smiles, Faith clutched the books. "My absolute favorites."

"I knew they would be." Helen dropped a kiss on Faith's nose. "Now why don't you run off and read them? The grown-ups want to talk about really boring things." She gave Faith a few moments to leave the room, then produced a newspaper clipping from the bag. "This is probably something we should discuss."

Hannah felt her stomach tense. She watched Margaret, who was sitting next to Helen, reach for the clipping. Waited for the shock to register on her mother's face. The room felt hot and still suddenly. Margaret carefully set the clipping down on the table. Fingers over her lips, she looked at Hannah.

"Did you know Liam was coming back?"

"I just saw the announcement in the paper yesterday." She drank some water. They were all watching her. "It's no big deal, Mom." She looked at Margaret. "Really, don't worry about it."

Margaret drank some wine. "You're not planning to see him, are you?"

"Of course Hannah doesn't want to see him," Helen said.

"Why would Hannah give a hoot about Liam?" Rose asked. "She's got this hotty attorney boyfriend. Liam's ancient history. Right, Hannah?"

"ANY PLANS FOR A WEEK, Saturday?" Allan asked Hannah Wednesday morning when he dropped off his son at La Petite Ecole. "I have symphony tickets."

"Saturday?" She'd been sitting at one of the small painted tables selecting books for the afternoon's story session and she stood so that he wouldn't tower over her. Actually, she could stand on a table and he'd still tower over her. Allan was tall. She wasn't. Flustered now, mostly because next Saturday was Faith's birthday party and she was wavering back and forth about inviting him, she tried to find a way around the question. "Saturday." She frowned as though trying to picture her extensive social calendar. "Let me think."

Allan smiled indulgently. Allan always smiled indulgently. It was one reason she had trouble picturing them walking into the sunset together. That, and he called her "Kiddo." On the plus side, he was thoughtful, patient and sweetly romantic. As her Aunt Rose would say, she could do a lot worse. And, as her mother would add, in a not-too-subtle jab, she already had.

Allan and his ex-wife shared custody of four-year-old Douglas, who was in Hannah's class. A fastidious little boy, Douglas disliked getting his hands dirty and insisted on using a straw to sip his milk because he worried about germs on the glass. She'd been talking to Allan about his son's phobias during a parent-teacher conference and then somehow they'd moved on from Douglas to foreign films and she found herself accepting Allan's invitation to a festival. Half a dozen or so dates later, he was talking about moving in together. She felt him watching her, waiting for an answer.

"Actually, next Saturday is Faith's birthday party," she finally said, because she couldn't think of any way around it. "If you weren't busy..."

His smile broadened. "I'll give the tickets away. I'd love to meet your family and get to know your daughter."

"Well, I'm not sure you'll have much opportunity to get to know her. At last count, I think there were about fifty kids coming."

"Hey, it sounds like fun," he said. "I'm looking forward to it."

She smiled back at him. He really was kind of sweet, even if he didn't exactly make her heart turn over. "Okay, but don't pay any attention to my mother and aunts. They have this thing about me getting married, so they'll start asking you pointed questions about your intentions."

His expression turned thoughtful. "Really?"

"Yeah, so tell them you're just out for a good time and the last thing you'd ever want to do is settle down."

"But what if that's not true?" His eyes searched her face. "What if I tell them you're exactly what I'm looking for?"

"Uh..." She felt her face go warm. "Please don't, okay?"

He smiled. "Are we a little gun-shy, kiddo?"

"Not a little, and Allan...please don't call me

'kiddo.''' She picked at a piece of skin on her finger. ''Look, I screwed up once. I'm not about to jump into it again.''

''Perhaps you just married the wrong guy.''

Hannah shrugged. Inviting him had definitely sent the wrong message, she could see that now.

''One bad apple doesn't mean the whole barrel is bad.'' Allan also mangled metaphors. ''Any man who could just turn his back on a daughter like Faith obviously has a severe character flaw. She's a wonderful young lady.''

''You've never even met her,'' Hannah pointed out.

''She's your daughter. How could she be anything but wonderful?'' With a quick glance over his shoulder, he kissed Hannah softly on the lips. ''And I've always wanted a daughter.''

AFTER ALLAN LEFT, Hannah couldn't get his words out of her head. *I've always wanted a daughter.* And he probably would be a terrific father to Faith. Attentive, conscientious. There for her. Everything her real father wasn't. With a sigh, she opened the book she'd selected to read to the kids. A story about a cow who decides to be an opera singer and moves to New York to take voice lessons from Placido Domingo. As she held up the book to show the kids the picture of the cow, all dolled up in a sequined evening gown and warbling an aria, she sneaked a quick glance at her watch.

Nearly noon. Right now, Liam was probably setting up the instruments. No, he'd be sleeping still. Liam always slept late.

''Timothy is picking his nose, Ms. Riley,'' Morgan Montgomery said. ''It's revolting.''

Hannah put aside the book to look at Timothy. He sat

cross-legged on the floor, hands clasped on top of his copper-colored curls, an expression of angelic innocence on his freckled face.

"He was, Ms. Riley. I think I'm going to vomit."

Morgan clutched her stomach dramatically. She had glossy brown hair, a heart-shaped face and, at four, was frighteningly precocious. Her parents were both psychiatrists and when they came to school to discuss Morgan's progress, Hannah always had the feeling they were analyzing her.

"He flicked it at me," she said.

"Did not," Timothy said.

Hannah watched Morgan pick up her floor pillow and move ostentatiously to the opposite side of the room, where she settled back on the floor with a flounce of her GapKids tartan skirt. After a moment, Hannah started reading again. She had discussed Timothy's nose-picking problem with his parents and knew she hadn't handled this latest incident very well. The La Petite Ecole method would have been to engage him in open discussion of social manners, but she felt distracted and irritable and in no mood for talk about boogers. Why the hell did she really want to see Liam?

At noon, she sat with Jen Bailey on the steps in the sun, eating a microwaved Lean Cuisine lunch and watching the kids wrestle around on the grass, hitting each other with paisley-patterned beanbags. Jen was the other teacher for the three-to-four-year-old group. She had cropped burgundy hair and a nose ring and lived in a funky apartment in Huntington Beach with her boyfriend who played in a band and designed surfwear. The only reason Jen was hired, she'd told Hannah, was her fancy degree in French Literature from Vassar.

Dr. Marberry, head of La Petite Ecole, was quite the

snob when it came to fancy academic degrees. She hadn't exactly sniffed at Hannah's Cal State Long Beach credentials but Hannah felt pretty sure one reason she was hired was that her father had, at the time, managed the bank where Dr. Marberry had her business loan.

"I'm thinking about doing something really dumb," she told Jen.

"How dumb?" Jen asked.

"Really, really." Hannah hacked at a piece of glazed chicken. "I want you to talk me out of it, okay?"

"You told Allan you'd move in with him?"

"Dumber." She mashed the back of her fork into the overcooked wild rice. "Faith's father is in Long Beach. He's playing at Fiddler's Green next week. I want to see him."

"Faith's father?" Jen turned to look at her. "I thought he lived in Ireland."

"He does. He's here on tour."

"Cool." Jen jumped up to stop Timothy from flicking a booger at Morgan. "Someone needs a time-out," she told him. "Please go and sit in time-out, Timothy, and think about why you need to do this." She dropped down on the step beside Hannah. "So he called you?"

"No, I read about it in the paper." Admitting aloud that Liam hadn't even bothered to call her made her stomach tense. "It's crazy, I know it. I mean, I can come up with a dozen reasons why I shouldn't, but I want to. Tell me it's a bad idea, okay?"

BUT JEN HAD THOUGHT a Friday evening at Fiddler's Green, drinking beer and listening to Irish music sounded like a hoot. In fact, she wanted to go, too. And Friday also happened to be Grandma's Night Out, a weekly excuse for Margaret to shamelessly indulge Faith with ice cream, movies, or whatever Faith wanted to do. Indulgence, Margaret always said, was part of the fun of being a grandma. Bottom line, it removed not having a baby-sitter as a reason to stay home and watch a cheesy movie instead of standing here in the Fiddler's Green washroom twenty minutes before the performance and feeling sick to her stomach with nerves at the thought of seeing Liam again.

Actually, Margaret hadn't even mentioned Liam as they all ate breakfast that morning. Hannah guessed that Debra's call, just as Margaret was pouring her second cup of coffee, had been a sufficient distraction. As soon as she heard Margaret utter the word *pregnant,* Hannah had gathered up Faith and made a quick retreat. Margaret and Debra could manage their problems on their own, she'd decided.

Damn. She looked at herself in the mirror. Why hadn't she worn something a little more hip than khakis and a white shirt? She rolled the sleeves up, undid another button, peered at her face. She screamed suburbia. Light brown hair cut in this wispy, tousled style around her face. ''Blow and go,'' said the girl who had cut it. Easy and practical.

It had been white-blond and nearly down to her waist the last time she'd seen Liam. She'd bleached it herself one night while he was performing. The girls who were always hanging around his dressing room and throwing flowers up on the stage all had long white-blond hair. He'd been furious with her for doing it. ''I thought you'd like it,'' she'd said.

It no longer matters, she told herself as she dug in her purse for a lipstick, dropping scraps of paper and grocery receipts and a stale Famous Amos cookie still in its crumpled foil wrapper into the washbasin. *You have moved on from Liam Tully. Way, way on. You do not care about Liam Tully. You have no emotional investment in Liam Tully. You have moved on. Look at me!* She looked at her reflection again. *You are attractive, you are well-adjusted and, Hannah, you are calm.*

Right. Deep breath. God, this lipstick was too dark. She grabbed a paper towel from the holder, scrubbed it across her mouth, dug around in her purse for a different color and knocked her compact off the edge of the sink. The mirror shattered into a cobweb of silver spikes.

Back at the table, she gulped down half a glass of wine. Their table was closer to the stage than she would have preferred, but the place was small and already packed when they arrived.

Liam would see her.

There was no way he couldn't see her. Maybe she should leave. On the other hand, maybe he wouldn't even recognize her. *What if he didn't recognize her?* She drained the glass and glanced at the door. Jen gave her a quizzical look.

"You okay?"

"I don't know. I'm thinking this wasn't such a great idea."

"You still have a thing for him?"

"No way." She picked up her glass, remembered she'd finished the wine and glanced around for the cocktail waitress. "How could I? I haven't seen him for six years. I don't even know why I'm doing this."

"How come you guys split up?"

Hannah picked at the edge of the coaster. "Jealousy."

"You or him?"

Hannah laughed. "What did he have to be jealous of? I was this mopey, insecure, basket case. Whenever I think about being married to him, all I remember is lying awake in some apartment or hotel room, watching the clock, waiting for him to come home. Then he'd come in smelling like perfume.''

''He cheated on you?''

''I never caught him, but…'' She traced the rim of her wineglass as she considered Jen's question. ''There was so much temptation all around, how could he not?''

''So how long did you know him before you got married?''

''Not long. I met him in Ireland.'' She smiled. ''God, I was so…smitten. We had this whirlwind thing and then I went back home. He told me all this stuff, he'd call, he'd write, but nothing. And then one day he just knocked at the door. I was blown away.''

''He came over just to see you?''

''Not just to see me. He was on a six-week tour of California, all these small clubs and college campuses up and down the coast. He asked if I wanted to go with him. *Did I want to go with him?* It was like this fantasy. I'd wake up every morning beside him and pinch myself to make sure I wasn't dreaming.''

''So who's idea was it to get married?''

''I can't even remember. Probably mine, but it was one of those spur-of-the-moment things. We just decided to do it. No thought about the future, or him going back to Ireland. It was all just in the moment. For a while, anyway.''

''So what went wrong?''

''I guess we didn't really know each other. Everything was fine while it was this big adventure, but then that started to wear off…. When I look back on it, it feels as though I woke up one day and the dream was over. He was totally into his music and I sort of tagged along. There were always girls fawning over him. I'd wonder why he was with me when he could have any woman he wanted. And then I found out I was pregnant and the dream really *was* over.''

''He didn't want to be a daddy, huh?''

''Well, it wasn't just him. He had to go back to Ireland and he expected me to go with him.... I mean, he wanted me to go, or I thought he did, but the idea of having the baby so far away from home terrified me. Plus, he didn't really seem ready to settle down—''

''Yeah, that's like Rocky.'' Jen lit a cigarette. ''I mean there's no way he's ready to do the family thing.''

Hannah nodded sympathetically, although she was pretty sure Jen wasn't in any hurry to go the kids-and-suburbia route either. The difference was that Jen and Rocky were in agreement. Jen understood what Rocky wanted, recognized his limitations. With Liam, she'd always had this idea that he would magically turn into a responsible father figure. She'd wanted it so much she couldn't see that it was clearly not what Liam had wanted.

''Everything probably turned out for the best,'' she said. ''Faith's really happy and well-adjusted, and...'' The lights dimmed and the crowd was looking expectantly at the stage. Her heart started banging so hard she felt dizzy.

Transfixed, she watched a slim dark-haired guy in black jeans and shirt walk slowly across the stage, his face caught in the white pool of a spotlight. *Liam.* Without a glance at the audience, he sat down on the stool, picked up a guitar and began to sing.

''Wow.'' Jen leaned close to whisper in Hannah's ear. ''What a babe.''

SOME SHOWS WERE MAGIC, Liam knew that. The energy of the crowd, the music, voices from the audience singing along, filling the room until it literally seemed they could raise the roof. Others never really got off the ground. Something was missing. He would go through the motions, sing the songs that had always worked, but the magic wasn't there. Before he'd finished the first set, he knew that tonight was one of those times.

"Thanks." He smiled out at the audience, acknowledging the subdued applause. The club was smaller than most they'd played on this tour, the crowd jammed against the far wall or seated at the small tables in front. Intimate, but the lighting made it difficult to pick out faces.

"It's good to be in California again," he said, trying to warm them up. "You've some very strange weather here. That hot wind as though the devil himself is breathing down your neck. We've nothing like it back home. Except for my dog's breath, that is."

Polite laughter. He glanced over his shoulder, nodded to Brid to join him. Worrying about her wasn't exactly helping things. Half an hour earlier she'd had another fainting spell and he'd thought they might have to cancel the show, but she'd insisted she was fine. As she came over to stand beside him, he felt the crowd respond to her as they always did. Smiling, he held out his hand to her.

"A few years back," he told the audience, "I met a beautiful woman who completely changed my life. Brid Kelly." This time the applause was much louder. From the back of the room, someone whistled.

And then they held hands to sing a song they'd written together. Face-to-face, bodies swaying. She had on a filmy white dress that he'd joked looked like the lace curtains in his auntie's parlor, but it swirled around her and her red hair streamed all over her back and shoulders and she looked as if she'd just floated down from a cloud to join him.

She smiled into his eyes as they sang and he knew that at least half the audience would decide they were lovers. The press back home had come to pretty much the same conclusion, which meant that whenever he was seen with another woman, he was accused of cheating on Brid. It didn't exactly make for long-lasting relationships. Brid found the whole thing hilarious. "You're like my brother, for God's sake," she'd say. Still the stories persisted. Finally, he'd stopped trying to deny them.

They did a couple more songs together and then he brought Brid's hand to his lips and the audience applauded enthusiastically. As they broke for intermission, he heard a crash from the side of the room and looked over to see what was going on. A woman in a hurry to leave the room had toppled one of the small tables, sending glasses crashing to the floor.

"Obviously not a fan," he said with a grin at Brid as they left the stage.

HER HEART THUNDERING, Hannah stood in the lobby, back against the wall, waiting for Jen to come out of the rest room. All she wanted now was to get the hell out. Forget the second act. She'd seen all she needed to see.

At that moment Liam walked through the swinging doors of the bar and looked straight into her eyes. Her brain froze. Had he recognized her? His eyes flickered and widened.

"Hannah?" He shook his head slightly. "Hannah. My God, I don't believe—"

"Hi, Liam." Suddenly she didn't know what to do with her hands. Liam. She was talking to Liam. Close enough to touch him. His hair was different. Shorter, trendily mussed on top. A few lines around his eyes that hadn't been there before. Wiry still, with the same street-smart look that used to excite her, even though she'd never seen him in as much as a scuffle. Her parents, sensing the same quality, had been less enamored of it. He wore a watch now—something he hadn't done then—with a heavy black leather strap. Other than that, he looked pretty much as he had the night she had told him she was pregnant.

God, she couldn't think of a thing to say. None of the dreams she'd had of what she'd do if she ever saw him again—what she'd say, how she'd look—had her just standing there, tongue-tied.

She found herself studying his mouth, something vulnerable about his upper lip that had always gotten to her; the lower lip she'd once taken in her teeth. How was she supposed to talk calmly and rationally to him? The bar was emptying, people milling around, talking in clusters. The red-haired singer and a couple of the band members drifted by, cast glances at Liam, then at her, and disappeared. Jen emerged from the washroom, started over, saw Liam and stopped. With a wave at Hannah, she made her way back through the swinging doors.

"So..." Liam nodded slightly. "It's been...how long?"

"Six years...thereabouts."

"I didn't recognize you at first." He kept watching her, as though he were cataloging the changes the years had produced. "The last time I saw you, your hair was down past your waist."

"It's been short for a long time now," she said. "Easier to take care of." He nodded again, his gaze fixed on her. Self-conscious under his scrutiny, she touched her hair, remembered how he'd always liked it long. All her old insecurities were bubbling away just below the surface. She'd been thinner then. Younger. Was he thinking that? Comparing her to the redhead? Damn it, what did it matter what he thought? Someone with a hell of a lot more going for him than Liam Tully wanted to marry her. That said something, didn't it?

"So why are you here?" Thumbs hooked into the pockets of his jeans, he rocked slightly on his feet. "You've developed a taste for Irish music you didn't have a few years back? Is that it?"

"I've always liked Irish music, Liam." Her face went warm. "That wasn't one of our problems."

"Right." His mouth hardened, then he glanced over his shoulder at the double doors to the bar. "Well, I hear the band starting up again. I'd better get back. Good to see you again."

Stunned, she stared at him. He looked so much like Faith, it was unnerving. His mouth curved exactly like hers so that even when they were serious, a smile always seemed to be lurking. The identical way they both held their heads off to the side, a little quizzical. The same dark, dramatic brows. A total stranger would immediately see the resemblance. How could he not even care enough to ask?

"Nothing changes, does it?" The words shot out before she could think about them. "Music always came first. Obviously it still does. Your daughter's doing fine, by the way."

He stared at her. "My daughter."

"Your daughter. Who will be six on Saturday. Probably just slipped your mind, huh?"

"You had an abortion," he said.

"An abortion?" She blinked. "What are you talking about?"

"Your mother told me you had an abortion."

"My mother?" Incredulous, she gaped at him. "My mother told you I had an abortion?"

"The day you told me you were pregnant," he said, his voice devoid of inflection. "You were more than a bit upset about it. Something about being too young for the responsibility, as I recall. We had a fight and you left. When you didn't come home that night, I went to see your mother. You'd gone away, she said, but she wouldn't tell me where. The impression she gave me was that you were off having an abortion somewhere."

"My God, Liam. I...I can't believe this. There was never any discussion about an abortion. Why would my mother tell you that?"

"Obviously that's a question you should ask her," he said. Then he turned and walked back into the bar.

CHAPTER THREE

AFTER THE SHOW, there was a party at a big house on the beach. The friend of a friend of a friend. Liam stood out on the deck drinking a beer and watching the palm trees and the play of lights on the water while the festivities roared on in the lighted room behind him. The music had turned Paddywhack Irish, a great deal of whooping and diddly-diddly dooing. Mick, the Wild Rovers' fiddler, had launched into ''McNamara's Band,'' a tune he would never deign to play sober, and the accompanying clapping and foot stomping was so enthusiastic, Liam could feel the vibration under his feet.

He had a daughter. He repeated the words to himself, trying to make them seem real. A daughter. And he didn't even know her name. Hadn't asked her name.

''I have a daughter,'' he told Brid when she came to see what he was doing out there all by himself.

''God, they're banging saucepan lids in there.'' She cupped her hand around her ear. ''You have a what?''

''A daughter.''

Brid looked at him for a moment, then disappeared and returned a moment later with a plate of carrots. With a nod, she directed him down to the far end of the deck, away from the noise. ''All right, what's this about?''

''That girl I was talking to tonight.'' He drank some beer. ''We were married for about a year. She got pregnant, and I thought she'd had an abortion. Tonight she tells me that wasn't so. Apparently, her mother lied to me."

Brid leaned her elbows on the railing, staring out at the water. "So this girl," she said after a minute, "what's her name?"

"Hannah." Actually, he'd always called her Hannie. Now he thought of her as Hannah. He eyed the plate of carrots. "You didn't eat any of the barbecue stuff?"

She wrinkled her nose. "The chicken had a sweet sauce all over it, and I don't eat beef. So Hannah didn't know what her mother was telling you?"

"That's what she claims." He forced his mind away from Hannah and her news. "Brid, you're worrying me with this food thing. There's enough in there to feed an army. If you don't like the chicken, find something else. Some bread or cheese or something."

"For God's sake, Liam." She tossed the carrot she'd picked up onto the sand. "What's it to you what I eat? You're getting on my nerves, always watching me."

"Who will, if I don't? You're not exactly doing much of a job yourself."

"I'm fine. Leave off, will you? I swear, you're like the bloody food police."

Liam said nothing. Inside, they were singing "The Belle of Belfast City" and someone yelled for Brid to join them. She glanced over her shoulder but didn't answer. Moments passed and then she put her arm around his shoulders, pressed him close.

"Sorry."

He shrugged. She was a grown woman and it wasn't his role to watch over her, but he couldn't help how he felt.

"Do you believe that she didn't know?" Brid asked.

"I'm not sure." His thoughts back on Hannah's

bombshell, he picked at a bit of peeling paint on the railing. ''You'd have to know her family. When one of them sneezes, the others not only know about it, they're there with hankies and cough mixture. Hannah was always close to them. I can't believe she didn't know all about her mother's conversation with me.''

''But she came to the club to see you,'' Brid pointed out. ''And she told you about your daughter. If she'd wanted you to think she'd had an abortion, why would she do that?''

Liam looked at her. Brid had a point. On the other hand, if Hannah wasn't in on it, why had she never tried to communicate with him? She'd never sent so much as a single picture. Nothing. A daughter—and he had no idea what she looked like.

''It sounds to me as though the mother was trying to get rid of you,'' Brid said. ''Probably thought the abortion thing would do it.''

He considered. It wasn't hard to imagine Margaret's thinking. The family—to put it mildly—had never been particularly fond of him. Being a musician was bad enough, being an Irish musician was worse. Easy enough to imagine their thinking. He would take Hannah back to Ireland, leave her barefoot and pregnant in an unheated shack while he traipsed off around the world drinking and womanizing. Maybe they'd thought rescuing her from him was their only option.

''Did you love her?''

He shrugged.

''Come on, Liam. It's me, Brid.''

''I used to.''

''Not anymore?''

''I don't know. It's been a long time.''

She laughed. ''You should see yourself. Furiously

picking the paint off the wood because this whole thing makes you squirm, doesn't it? Talking about feelings?"

"'Feelings,'" he sang, trying to distract her. There *was* nothing he hated more than rambling on about what was going on in his head. It was one of the things he and Hannah used to fight about. She was always trying to drag him into long, drawn-out talks. "Tell me what you're thinking," she'd say. "Tell me you love me. Why is it so hard for you to say it?"

He eased off another chip of paint, realized what he was doing and stopped. Hannah. He'd spent years hating her for what she'd done, or what he thought she'd done. Seeing her tonight was...he couldn't believe it. She looked different...great, really. Enormous green eyes and a wee little face. He used to pull her leg about looking like a kitten. Now she looked all grown-up. The way you'd expect the mother of a six-year-old to look, he supposed.

"What now, then?" Brid asked. "What will you do?"

"I don't know. I'm still trying to get used to the idea I'm a father."

"Does she know about you? Your daughter, I mean?"

"I've no idea what they've told her."

Brid lit a cigarette, waved out the match and tossed it onto the sand. "Want to know what I think you should do?"

He grinned. "Have I a choice?"

"No." She spoke through a cloud of blue smoke. "If you've any sense, you'll forget tonight ever happened. Getting involved will only cause trouble. The child's here. You're in Ireland. Music is your life. You spend half of it on the road and you know nothing at all about being a daddy."

"That's your opinion, is it?"

"It is. But from the look on your face, I've the feeling I might as well be talking to the wind. You'll regret it though, Liam. I'm telling you. You're not a daddy sort of fellow."

HANNAH STOOD OUTSIDE her mother's bedroom, trying to tell from the sounds inside whether Margaret was sleeping. The house had been in darkness when she got home from Fiddler's Green. A note from Margaret on the kitchen table said she'd dropped Faith off at a friend's house for a slumber party. Hannah raised her hand to knock, then stopped. Back in her own room, she sat on the bed. Maybe she needed to sort things out in her own mind before she spoke to Margaret.

Including why seeing Liam tonight made her want to run around locking windows and doors. She got up, went down to the kitchen and microwaved a cup of chamomile tea, carried it up to her room and set it on the bedside table. Fully dressed, she lay down on the bed. Even in the familiar security of her room, she felt shaky and anxious, as though the stability of her life had been physically threatened.

Jen had advised her to move out immediately. "Your mother lied to you, Hannah. She told Liam you'd had an abortion. There's no way you can go on living there."

Most parents really only want to do what's best for their children.

However misguided their motives. How many times had she had to remind herself of that when dealing with the parents of her students? But she hadn't been a child. How was she ever supposed to trust Margaret again? She picked up the phone to call Deb. Changed her mind and set it down. Swung her legs off the bed and wandered over to the window. Stared out at the dark night.

The room overlooked the rose garden her father had started shortly after she was born. There were something like thirty or forty plants out there. He would mark special occasions with a new variety. She'd lost count of all the roses planted for her and Deb. A pink Tiffany when she graduated from high school, a yellow one whose name she could never remember when she got her degree from Cal State. Three or four, all white, to mark Faith's various milestones.

The only occasion never commemorated with roses was her marriage to Liam. When she'd asked her dad about it, he'd said something about poor-quality roses that year, but she knew the real reason.

Liam. His music still played in her head, but the evening had already taken on a dreamlike quality. One minute he'd been there, close enough to touch. And then he was gone. Elusive as smoke.

It had always been that way with Liam. She'd met him during a trip to Ireland, a birthday present from her parents. He'd been playing in a Galway club that she'd wandered into one evening. During a break in the session, he'd come over to talk to her. He'd quoted poetry, made her laugh, hummed songs in her ear. Looking back, she knew she'd fallen in love with him that night.

Still, she'd left the club never expecting to see him again. The next morning her landlady had knocked on her door to say she had a caller. Barefoot, in a red tartan robe, she'd walked out to the top of the stairs. Liam stood at the foot, smiling in the pale sunlight, a bunch of daisies in his hand.

On her last day in Ireland, the countryside had bloomed with hawthorn hedges and primrose and the air had smelled of mowed hay and turf smoke. They'd taken a boat to Clare Island and stayed until dark. On the beach, with the moon beaming down on them, they'd made love. Afterward she'd looked up at the crescent of a new moon, like a fairy tiara in the dark sky; watched the silvery light on Liam's face. Felt the fine sand slip between her fingers.

They'd kissed goodbye at the airport and, despite all his promises to stay in touch, she'd again had the feeling that this was it. That as magical and wonderful as the whole experience had seemed, it wasn't quite real. Like trying to hold on to the memory of a dream. But, once more, Liam had surprised her. The day she'd opened the door to see him standing there had been as mind-blowing as opening the paper to see his picture. ''Come with me,'' he'd said.

In a celebratory mood after a show one night, they'd driven to Las Vegas. The wedding chapel was so hideously tacky, they'd both dissolved into fits of laughter. As they walked back out into the garish night, Liam had dumped a bag of silver paper horseshoes on her head. Her father had been incensed. Margaret had cried for days, a mini nervous breakdown, according to Helen.

After Liam went back to Ireland, the family quietly and efficiently fixed up the wreckage of her life. A family friend had taken care of the divorce. Helen had arranged the job at La Petite Ecole. The nursery, where Faith had slept until she was five, had been decorated by Margaret and her sisters who, when Faith decided she was too old for rainbows and kittens, had redecorated it to look like a tree house.

Liam's name was seldom mentioned and, except for Faith, it sometimes seemed to Hannah that she'd dreamed the whole relationship.

Until tonight. She got up from the bed, padded out into the hallway and tapped on her mother's door. Nothing. She started to knock again, then stopped. It was nearly one. Margaret would be groggy. Better to wait.

THE NEXT MORNING, Saturday, Hannah doubled her usual three-mile run. At the bottom of Termino, she glanced both ways at the traffic then sprinted across Livingstone Drive and Ocean Boulevard, past La Petite Ecole, around the end of the pier and the new Belmont Shore Brewery with its ocean-view patio; down along the footpath that paralleled the edge of the beach.

She'd started running soon after Faith was born, and her route never varied. A sprint along the beach then up the slope that led to the art museum on Ocean Boulevard, twice around Bixby Park where, as kids, she and Debra had been taken by their parents to hear Sunday afternoon concerts on the grass, then back down the slope for the return trip.

Helen and Rose had given her an expensive headset for her last birthday so that she could listen to music while she ran. She'd used it a couple of times, but preferred the natural fugue of ocean sounds: the steady crash of the waves, the screeches and coos of gulls and pigeons and the slap of her feet on the asphalt.

These morning runs were hers alone, a time to think. Anything, from musings on what she'd eat for lunch to more profound matters such as whether she really wanted to spend the rest of her life teaching overprivileged and precocious four-year-olds.

This morning, her thoughts were dominated by Liam.

When she jogged up Termino twenty minutes later, she could see her mother outside the house, down on her knees, using a trowel to dig around the bird-of-paradise plants along the steps leading up to the front door. Margaret saw her and leaned back on her heels, trowel in hand.

''Damn nasturtiums, they run wild.'' Margaret gestured with the trowel at the offending pale green tendrils. ''Every year I pull them all out, and every year they come back more than before. God knows why your father ever planted them in the first place.''

Panting from her run, Hannah looked at the pile of orange calendulas and green nasturtium leaves her mother had yanked out. Neither plant, in Margaret's opinion, was in keeping with the Spanish architectural style of the house and she waged an ongoing and futile battle to eradicate them. Hannah bent and picked half a dozen blooms. ''We need to talk, Mom,'' she said.

Still on her knees, Margaret glanced up. ''Debra called this morning. I guess you know she's pregnant.''

Hannah nodded. Dennis had refused to put Deb on the phone when Hannah called earlier.

''Now she's saying Dennis doesn't want her to have the baby. She's come back here with her suitcases.'' Margaret gathered up the discarded plants and dumped them into the trash can at the side of the house. She ran her hands down the sides of her sweats, brushed the back of her arm across her face. ''I don't think she has the vaguest notion of what she really wants—''

''Mom, I don't want to talk about Debra right now.''

Margaret eyed her warily.

''I saw Liam last night.'' Arms folded across her chest, she looked at her mother. Margaret's face was unreadable, her eyes hidden by the baseball cap she wore, but Hannah sensed that there was a battle brewing. ''I don't even know where to start,'' she said.

''Then don't, okay?'' Margaret's stance mirrored Hannah's, arms folded, feet slightly apart. ''I've got enough on my mind with Debra. I don't need you giving me a hard time about something that happened years ago.''

Hannah stared at her mother, incredulous.

''I know for sure I'm not paying for her to have an abortion,'' Margaret said, ''but she's so headstrong, I don't even want to think what she might try. Rose and Helen are in there talking to her now. I had to come outside, I couldn't listen to her anymore. This is my grandchild she's casually talking about destroying.''

''For God's sake, Mom. This isn't about you. It's about Debra and what she needs to do for herself.'' Hannah took some deep breaths. Debra could fight her own battles. ''You lied to Liam.''

Margaret looked at her for a moment. ''You know what, Hannah? I don't intend to discuss this with you. I've got enough on my mind.'' She started for the house. ''Helen put a coffee cake in the oven and it's probably done now. It's a new recipe she clipped from the *Times*. You mix up sour cream and—''

''Damn it.'' Hannah grabbed her mother's arm. ''You are not just walking off. I want some answers.''

''Why don't you tell me what's really wrong?'' Margaret jerked her arm from Hannah's grasp. ''I've never seen you so worked up.''

''You told Liam I'd had an abortion, Mom. That's what's really wrong. Do you even realize the consequences of what you did? By lying to him—''

''Okay, Hannah, we've covered the lying issue. Let's talk about the consequences of your going to see him last night. Let's talk about the fact that he now wants to take Faith back to Ireland.''

''What?''

''He called this morning while you were running.''

"He said he was taking Faith back to Ireland?"

"Not in so many words. He said he wants to talk to you. But it's like Rose was saying, he's a troublemaker. If he tries to get Faith... Well, Helen gave me the name of an attorney who specializes in this sort of thing. When you've calmed down a bit, we need to give him a call."

"Mom." Hannah held her hands to her face for a moment, then took them away. "I don't believe this, I just don't believe it. You lied to Liam, deprived him of his daughter. Deprived Faith of her father and *you're* talking about legal action?"

Rose called from the kitchen, and Margaret glanced up at the house. "I'll be there in a minute," she said. "Listen, Hannah..." Her voice broke, and she swiped at her nose with the back of her hand. "Don't make me the enemy, okay? Any of us. Helen, Rose—"

"So they were in on it, too?"

"Don't say it like that. We were out of our minds with worry about you. Your father, too, to the point that it killed him. Imagine how you'd feel if Faith's life was in danger. Wouldn't you do whatever it took to save her?"

"Faith's a child, Mom. I was a grown woman. It's not quite the same thing."

"We found you walking along the side of the freeway," Margaret said. "Distraught, irrational, talking about killing yourself. And for what? For a fly-by-night musician, a womanizing jerk who wasn't aware enough to recognize the state you were in."

"That still didn't give you the right to lie. To me, or to Liam."

"To hell with Liam." Margaret's voice rose. "Liam isn't my concern. You are. You're my daughter and I was scared to death for you. You were clinically depressed. That's the term the doctor used. Maybe it was wrong, maybe I should have stayed out of it and just thrown up my hands and said 'oh well,' but I couldn't do it. If you're mad at me, so be it."

"Margaret," Rose yelled from the doorway. "Hannie. Come and have some coffee cake. Debra has something to tell you." She winked at Margaret. "Good news."

"Come on, sweetie." Margaret touched Hannah's arm. "Please understand that this worked out for the best. You're happy now. You've got your life back together. Faith's happy. All of this other stuff is in the past. Just let it go. It's not important."

Hannah shook her head. What was the point? Her mother absolutely couldn't see the enormity of what she'd done.

"Hannie." Margaret peered into her eyes. "Please tell me you're not going to see him again. What possible good can come out of that?"

"Liam deserves a chance to know his daughter, that's all I know. And I'm going to see that he gets it."

THE DOCTOR IN THE E.R. had a high forehead and a pinched-looking mouth and he wanted to know if Brid was Liam's wife. Dazed and groggy from too little sleep and God knows how many black coffees, Liam shook his head.

"No, but I'm her best friend."

The doctor raised a brow. "Then you should have gotten treatment for her long before this."

Liam swallowed the words he'd been about to say. He didn't like this doctor with his condescending attitude. He was in a foul enough mood that it was all he could do not to pick up the little prat by the lapels of his starched white coat. He'd been on the phone with Hannah's mother when someone yelled out that Brid had collapsed. In an instant he'd dropped the phone and, ignoring Brid's protests, had driven her to the emergency room.

"What are you?" the doctor asked. "Some kind of band?"

"That's right," Liam said. "Some kind of band."

"She said you're on tour."

"She's right," Liam said. "How is she?"

"She needs treatment," the doctor said. "She has an eating disorder. I'd suggest you get her into some kind of program or she won't be doing much touring anymore."

"AH, THAT'S A LOAD OF COD," Brid said when Liam told her what the doctor had said. "I've let myself get a bit run-down, that's all. I'll start taking my vitamins again." She sat up on the narrow cot, reached for the tie at the neck of the cotton hospital robe. "Now, clear out of here, Liam, while I find my clothes. We've got a show tonight."

"The show's canceled tonight," he told her. "Probably the next few nights, too. No more shows until you're well enough."

"CANCELED?" Hannah stared at the bartender, who was polishing glasses in the dimly lit main room of Fiddler's Green. A couple of guys sitting at the bar looked her way then returned their attention to the televised basketball game. "But I thought they were supposed to be here for three nights."

"They were." The bartender picked up another glass. "One of them called a while ago to say the girl singer was sick. Strung out on drugs, or something, would be my guess. Anyway, tonight's going to be karaoke.''

Hannah bit her lip. Okay, this was a sign. A warning that maybe her mother was right. Maybe nothing good could come from seeing him again. Margaret had been crying when Hannah left the house. ''Think of what's best for Faith,'' Margaret had begged her. ''That's exactly what I intend to do,'' she'd replied.

Now she wasn't so sure. What was the point of having Liam breeze in and out of Faith's life? And why risk all the rebuilding she'd done of her own life? Why upset everyone and everything? Because she owed it to him. Simple as that. He'd been lied to and the least she could do was try to make some kind of amends.

''Do you have any idea where I can find him?'' she asked the bartender.

''Him?'' The bartender grinned. ''The singer? Liam something or other?''

She nodded and felt her face heat up. God, this was embarrassing. ''Look, it's not what you're thinking…''

''Hey.'' He flicked the towel across the top of the bar. ''I'm not paid to think. All I can tell you is what I told the other girls who came in asking about him. I think the band's staying at some place in Huntington Harbor.

Hannah checked the urge to ask, *What other girls? How many other girls?* Liam had always drawn girls. Well, so what? He could bed a different girl every night, and she wouldn't care.

''Do you have the address?'' she asked.

''Yeah…'' The bartender grabbed a napkin and drew a map of Huntington Harbor. ''There's a party there tomorrow, that's how I know where they are. Huge house on the water with a yacht the size of the *Queen Mary* on the dock outside. Some big cheese from L.A. owns the place. A record promoter, or something.'' He winked. ''Told me to invite hot-looking chicks.''

Go home, Hannah thought. You don't need this.

''Hell...'' With a sigh, he threw down the pen he'd been using and reached for another one. ''I should probably photocopy these damn directions.'' He handed her the napkin. ''You'll probably have to take a number.''

''BRID WILL BE FINE, Liam.'' Miranda Payton, the record producer's wife, sat next to him, feet dangling in a pool that had been built to look like a tropical lagoon. ''I sent my own daughter to Casa Pacifica when I realized she was spending half her life in the bathroom with her finger stuck down her throat. They straightened her out in no time. Quit worrying about her and enjoy yourself.'' She brought a frosted glass to her lips, eyed him over the rim and smiled. ''You could be in a lot worse places.''

Liam laughed. An understatement if he'd ever heard one. Beyond the purple bougainvillea-covered wall that separated the property from the private beach, he could see the Pacific Ocean. The sun was hot on his back, and Miranda had brought out a jug of something icy that tasted like rum and bananas. The exotic scent of it mingled with the suntan lotion she was massaging into her legs. If he had to take a week off in the middle of a tour, this definitely wasn't a bad place to while away the time. Certainly none of the band had complained. A couple of them were off taking surfing lessons, the others had gone to see the sights.

He'd thought about calling Hannah again. Thought constantly about his daughter, whose name he still didn't know. Off on a trip, Hannah's mother had said. Another lie?

"You're *soooo* serious." Miranda trailed one perfectly manicured fingernail down his arm. "Are you always this way?"

"Always," Liam said. "A right wet blanket, that's me. I cast a pall on any party I go to."

Miranda laughed with disproportionate enthusiasm. "I don't believe you. I think you're just deep."

"Wrong," Liam said. "Shallow as a puddle. Ask anyone who knows me." He reached for his shirt. Miranda was making him uneasy. She was about forty, thin, tan and attractive in what Brid would call a high-maintenance way. Lots of curly hair streaked in different shades of blond, plum-colored lips and nails. She was Bert Payton's third wife, considerably younger and obviously bored. Which definitely wasn't his problem. He got up and started for the house.

Miranda followed him. Her hand at the small of his back, they made their way through the open French doors into the blue-and-white living room just as a housekeeper was leading Hannah into the room through a door off the hallway.

Startled, they all eyed each other. Hannah's focus went from Miranda, who was clutching her bikini top as though she'd been caught in risqué underwear, to Liam's opened shirt and bathing trunks.

Hannah had on a short, sleeveless cotton dress patterned with small pink and orange flowers. Her hair was pulled back in a band and she looked young and a little uncertain. He wanted to tell her the thing with Miranda wasn't what she thought it was, which was a bit stupid because he had no idea what she thought and what difference did it make anyway?

He started to speak just as Hannah did, and then Miranda chimed in and there was a flurry of introductions. Hannah, he noticed, was avoiding eye contact with him.

''I wanted to talk to you.'' She addressed his left shoulder. ''If this isn't a good time...''

''It's fine.'' He looked at Miranda, who fluttered her fingers at him and disappeared. ''So...'' He waved at the cluster of wicker armchairs upholstered in blue canvas. ''Pick a seat.'' She did and he sat down opposite her. Music drifted in from somewhere in the house. Hannah sat with her knees close together, her hands in her lap. A silence hung in the air between them, thick with ghosts and recriminations. Hannah. Hannie. Hannah. Formal as a stranger now.

She cleared her throat. ''Look, I just want to explain—''

''What's her name?'' he asked. ''What's my daughter's name?''

''Faith.''

Faith. He said it again to himself. Then he looked at Hannah. ''Why? Where did that come from?''

''When I was in the hospital having her...everything seemed so hopeless. You'd walked out—well, I thought you had—and my world was falling apart. And then I saw her and...'' Her face colored. ''I know it sounds kind of hokey, but she gave me the faith to believe in myself again.''

He leaned his head against the high back of the wicker chair and stared up at the white-painted ceiling beams. So many questions were rattling around in his brain. Where to start? Finally he looked back at Hannah.

''Do you have any pictures with you?''

She pulled an envelope from her bag and handed it to him.

''She looks like me,'' he said after he'd studied the

first one. "A right little terror, I bet." He looked to Hannah for confirmation.

She smiled. "She can be pretty strong willed."

Slowly he leafed through the stack. Pictures of a baby Faith in a cradle, on a rug gazing wide-eyed at a Christmas tree. School pictures of a little girl, smiling obediently for the camera. A snapshot—recent, he guessed—of Faith riding a red bike. Laughing, the wind in her hair. Unable not to, he smiled at the image. God, how incredible to look at this child and see his own face reflected in hers. And yet, beneath the wonder, an old anger, smoldering now with new intensity. She'd been stolen from him.

He should have been there. He should have been the one teaching her to ride the bloody bike, not sitting here now looking at pictures. They'd stolen her from him, robbed him of her childhood. And then a voice in his head spoke up. *Ah, catch yourself,* it scoffed. *Can you really see yourself playing the suburban daddy? Bikes and kiddies and lawn mowers. Telly and slippers and "keep the music down, love, you're waking the baby." That's not you and it never will be.* Without a word, he returned the pictures to the envelope and held it out to Hannah.

"They're yours," she said. "I brought them for you."

He stuffed the envelope into the pocket of his shirt and felt her watching him as he did. In the first few weeks of their marriage, he'd come home one day and found her ironing his shirts. He'd started laughing. Never in his life had he worn an ironed shirt, and the sight of her carefully pressing the creases in the sleeves struck him as so touchingly funny, he couldn't help himself. Now he had an urge to apologize for hurting her feelings.

‘‘What does she know about me?’’ he asked. ‘‘What have you told her?’’

Hannah looked at him for such a long time that he thought she wasn’t going to answer. ‘‘She thinks you’re in heaven,’’ she finally said.

‘‘In heaven?’’

‘‘See, we didn’t think she’d ever see you and—’’

‘‘No…’’ He shook his head, no explanation needed. It wasn’t difficult to imagine the scenario. Given the lie he’d been told, he could well imagine that her family had believed they’d seen the last of him. Certainly his parting shot to Hannah’s father would guarantee he’d never be welcome in their home again. And truth was, it was probably kinder than letting Faith think she had a father who had no interest in her. But heaven. Of all the places to pack him off to. He felt a grin spread across his face. ‘‘My God, Hannah. Wouldn’t it have been more like them to tell her I was in hell?’’

‘‘Yeah, well…’’ She smiled back at him, clearly relieved by his reaction.

‘‘That’s no doubt where your da would consign me.’’

‘‘My father died,’’ she said. ‘‘A few months after you left. A heart attack. Needless to say, my mom was pretty devastated. The family were all there for her, of course, but she still gets lonely.’’

‘‘Sorry,’’ he said. ‘‘I had no idea.’’ He recalled meeting her father for the first time, the look of clear disapproval on the man’s face. A tall, imposing man, obviously accustomed to having control over most things, including his family. Which must have made it pretty tough when his daughter ran off and married a ne’er-do-well Irish musician.

‘‘You never tried to contact me,’’ she said.

"I was too furious with you. I thought you'd had an abortion. Why didn't you ever try to reach me?"

"Because..." She shrugged. "I just figured it was over. I didn't especially want to hear you confirm it. I'm sorry," she said after a moment. "For everything."

So am I, he thought. *For everything.* They sat in silence for a while. The memories were all coming back to her, he guessed, just as they were for him. The cheap apartment, the car that spent more time up on blocks than on the road, tins of beans and fried-egg sandwiches for supper. Happy enough until those last few weeks, or so he'd thought. One night he'd woken from a dream about Ireland, starving for the sort of lamb stew he remembered his gran making. He'd roused Hannah out of sleep, and at two in the morning they'd found an all-night market and spent all the money they had on the stuff to make it. By the time they'd got everything home, he was no longer in the mood for stew, and they'd made love on the kitchen floor instead.

"What happened?" he asked her now.

Hannah traced a bit of the wicker weave on the arm of the chair. "Short version?"

"Let's begin with that."

"I fell apart, and my family had me hospitalized. That's where I was when you came to look for me."

"Let's hear the longer version," he said.

She covered her face with her hands, took a deep breath then took her hands away. "Oh God, Liam, I don't know. I was such a mess. I hated your being gone all the time. I hated the clubs and the girls always hanging around. I was miserable, lonely. I missed having my family around me. Mostly I was terrified of going back to Ireland where I didn't know anyone. My life would have been tagging around after you, or staying home by myself.''

He looked at her, wanting to argue but resisting. He knew his version of what went wrong; he wanted to hear hers.

''Not that we didn't have some good times,'' she said. ''I don't mean that. It was just...I felt like I was disappearing. That last tour you had in San Francisco, I stayed home, remember? In our apartment, I mean. Anyway, I started going through the drawers in your dresser, and I found these letters from some girl...''

''God, Hannah—''

''No, let me finish. It's a chapter in my life that I'd just as soon never think about again, but I want you to know so you understand...about Faith and everything. I just went to pieces. Everything is a kind of blur. I guess I called my mom and she was on her way over to pick me up, but I'd already left. I don't even know what I was thinking. She found me walking along the freeway. At that point, she decided to take matters into her own hands.''

He thought of those last couple of months with her. He'd come home late from a gig to find her sleeping. She'd be sleeping still when he went off again the next day. When she wasn't sleeping, she was crying. For days on end it seemed she'd do nothing but sleep or cry. He'd alternate between racking his brain to figure out why she was unhappy and losing patience with her for doing nothing to help herself. ''For God's sake, snap out of it,'' he'd say. ''Stop feeling so bloody sorry for yourself.'' And then he'd blow money they didn't have on hothouse roses.

Her expression clouded, and she picked at the fabric on her dress. ''The thing is, my family still worries about me and Faith. My mom especially. Although lately, the tables have kind of turned and it seems I'm always worrying about her…'' She smiled slightly. ''Another story. Anyway, they all know how bad things were after we split. I mean if it hadn't been for them…''

If it hadn't been for them, he'd know his daughter today. On the other hand, he hadn't recognized the severity of her depression and they had, so maybe he didn't deserve to know his daughter. He stood, restless, fighting a barrage of competing emotions.

''I was a real mess,'' she said again. ''I couldn't even take care of Faith. So now, every time I feel smothered by my family, I remind myself of that.'' She laughed, a short, humorless sound. ''Or they do.''

''But you're all right now?'' He turned to face her again, studied her for a moment. There was a confidence and strength about her that she hadn't had before. ''You look great,'' he said. She smiled and he was reminded again of all the good times they'd shared. ''No, I mean it. Back then, a good wind would have blown you away. You've…filled out.''

Her grin widened. ''Are you saying I'm fat?''

''No, not at all. And I like your hair the way you have it now. It suits you.''

''You used to like waist-length, white-blond hair.''

''Ah, well, we all change.''

''Listen, Liam…'' She leaned forward in her chair. ''About Faith. It's her birthday next Saturday, a week from today. We're having a party for her. If there's some way you can make it…''

He looked at her for a moment, tried to imagine himself in a room full of six-year-olds, one of them his daughter. Tried to imagine what he would say to her. *Happy birthday! You don't know me, but I'm your daddy. Thought I was in heaven, didn't you? Well, surprise! Sorry I can't stick around to see you grow up. Nice meeting you though. Drop by if ever you're in Ireland.*

Hannah was watching him. He felt the tension, hers and his own, as she waited for his response. ''Listen, I um…'' He rubbed the back of his neck. ''Maybe it's better we leave things as they are.''

''You don't want to see her?'' A moment passed. ''That's what you're saying?''

''Right.'' He hardened himself against the look in her eyes. ''Thanks for inviting me, though.''

CHAPTER FOUR

LIAM HAD REJECTED HIS DAUGHTER. The thought lodged in Hannah's brain for the rest of the weekend and was still there Monday even as she sat through another session with Taylor Becker's mother, who absolutely could not understand why she wouldn't be allowed to sit in on her son's prekindergarten readiness test.

Hannah tried to keep her voice free of irritation. Her personal problems didn't belong in the classroom, but it just seemed so damned ironic that she was dealing with parents who made themselves crazy trying to be perfect while her own daughter had a father who didn't give a damn.

That night, she took Faith to see *Harry Potter*, a movie Faith had been clamoring to see since the day it came out. Afterward they went for Faith's favorite cheese-and-sausage pizza with extra mozzarella. Dairy Queen brownie sundaes, another of Faith's favorites, were planned for dessert. A splurge, but tonight Hannah wasn't dwelling on economics. *Liam had rejected his daughter.*

Hannah sprinkled hot pepper flakes onto her slice of pizza. Not that Faith knew anything was wrong, but it seemed important to compensate for Liam's lack of paternal interest. She smiled across the table at her daughter. *You don't need him anyway, sweetheart. I can love you enough for both of us.*

Faith, in a pair of sixty-dollar denim overalls purchased by Helen ''Just because she's our own little princess,'' grinned at Hannah across the table, a study in perpetual motion. Up on her knees to carefully pick up a piece of pizza, then down to a sitting position, her head swiveling to watch a man with two small children in the booth on the other side of the aisle.

And then her smile dimmed and the slice of pizza in her hand dripped a sticky stalactite of mozzarella. She lifted the pizza high above her head and opened her mouth wide to catch the cheese. Her expression contemplative, she chewed in silence for a while. Then she put the pizza down. ''Mommy, Grandma was sad today.''

Hannah sipped at a glass of Diet Coke, thought guiltily of Margaret's tearful entreaties not to be mad at her. ''My only thought was what was best for you,'' she'd said last night and again this morning. And then Rose had taken up her sister's cause. ''Give your mom a hug and tell her you love her,'' Rose had urged. ''Between Debra's pregnancy and your no-good ex-husband, the poor thing's going out of her mind.''

''People get sad sometimes, sweetie, for all kinds of reasons,'' Hannah told Faith.

''I was sad two days ago,'' Faith said.

''You were?'' Hannah thought back over the last couple of days to what might have made her daughter sad. Nothing came to mind. ''How come?''

''Because Beth wouldn't play with me. It made me feel sad.''

I hate Beth, Hannah thought. She reached for another slice of pizza, then decided she wasn't hungry. *I hate Liam, too.* She watched the man who had caught Faith's attention a moment ago bundle a small child into a sweater, watched Faith staring at him buttoning up the sweater. The child said something and the man bent down and kissed the end of her nose. Something squeezed at Hannah's heart, and she looked away.

"Maybe Beth just felt like playing with someone else that day, honey," she said.

"But *I'm* her best friend." Faith stabbed at her chest. "She's supposed to play with *me*. She hurt my feelings."

"Ah..." Not trusting her voice, Hannah reached across the table, and caught her daughter's face in her hands. "People do that sometimes, sweetie," she said as Faith wriggled out of her grasp. "They behave in ways that hurt and make us feel sad. We don't always know why they do it, but it's kind of how life is."

"I have another best friend now." Faith's expression cleared. "Her name is Tiffany."

"Tiffany's a pretty name," Hannah said. God, it was uncanny how exactly like Liam Faith looked right then. Serious one moment and then a smile like a sudden burst of sunshine dissipating the clouds. She banished his image.

"Don't be sad, Mommy." Faith leaned across the table, bringing her face up close to Hannah's. "Tiffany's only my friend. I still love you best."

"And I love you best." Hannah felt her voice crack and she covered with a wide smile. "You're my very best sunshine girl, and I love you better than anything else in the world."

"Better than three million chocolate bars?"

"Three million chocolate bars with almonds," Hannah said.

Faith grinned. This was her favorite game. "Three million and one hundred million chocolate bars and two million Little Debbies?" she asked.

"Well, now you're making it difficult." Hannah pretended to consider. "What kind of Little Debbies?"

"Raspberry Zingers," a voice behind her said. "Or maybe Pecan Sandies."

Hannah turned to see Allan holding the hand of a scowling Douglas. She smiled at the boy, then looked up at his father. "Someone obviously doesn't know his junk food," she said. "Raspberry Zingers are not Little Debbies. And, if I'm not mistaken, Pecan Sandies are actually cookies."

Allan grinned. "Hey, kiddo."

Hannah bit back the urge to remind him how much she hated the nickname.

"My mommy's name is Hannah," Faith chimed in as though she'd picked up on her mother's irritation. "And my name is Faith." She smiled up at Allan. "I know what your name is. It's Allan. Want to know how I know?"

"Because I'm wearing a name tag?" he suggested.

Faith gave him a scornful look. "I don't see any name tag."

"Then I give up," he said. "How do you know what my name is?"

"Because my mommy has a picture of you by her bed, except you're wearing a blue shirt in the picture and now you've got a..." Clearly stumped by the color, she frowned over at Hannah. "A green one?"

"Kind of green," Hannah said, sorry that Faith had told him about the picture by the bed. Allan had insisted that they exchange pictures. She'd left his on her dresser and forgotten about it until she noticed that the housekeeper had set it by the bed. She couldn't decide whether or not she was pleased to see him. Allan had what Jen referred to as a high irritation factor. Extremely solicitous, he always opened doors, pulled out chairs and held her arm as they crossed the street. Rose couldn't see how being polite was a problem, and she'd just rolled her eyes when Hannah complained that she felt smothered by him.

Still, as she kept reminding herself, he really was a nice guy. And definitely cute. Blue eyes like his son, sandy blond hair a shade or two lighter; sun-bleached from his hours on the tennis courts. Preppy in khakis and Top-Siders. She shifted her glance to his casual but obviously expensive shirt. "More olive, I think," she said, referring to the color. "Or sage, maybe."

She noticed the children casting wary glances at each other and made the introductions, aware as she did of Allan watching her. Her face felt warm. Maybe she needed to squelch this before she got swept into something she didn't want. Helen had once confided that she'd married her husband because the family liked him. By the time she realized she had some serious doubts, the wedding invitations were in the mail. Never underestimate the power of family pressure, she'd told Hannah.

"Hey, Dougie—" Faith slid out of her seat "—want to go play?" Douglas moved closer to his father, his expression doubtful. "Come on." Faith grabbed his hand. "I'll show you something really cool, but you have to take off your shoes."

After the kids had disappeared into a giant plastic tube through which other children were crawling, Allan slid into the seat Faith had vacated.

"Neat little girl," he said. "Lots of confidence."

"Thank you," she replied. "I'm kind of attached to

her.'' *Her father doesn't give a damn, but that's his loss.* She sipped her Diet Coke. ''Your week to have Douglas?''

Allan nodded, started to speak then stopped as the kids came running back. Breathless, her cheeks flushed, Faith addressed Hannah.

''Mommy, I invited Douglas to my party. And he wants to come.'' Her ponytail had come loose from the red scrunchie, which she was now wearing around her wrist. ''Actually, that's good because three other boys are coming.'' She pushed back a long strand of hair. ''Holden Baxter and Timothy Jones, except that Timothy might not come.''

''You said three boys,'' Allan pointed out.

''Oh, right.'' She thought for a minute. ''James Bowen, that's the other one. And his sister Michaela. Mommy, please fix my hair?'' She scooted into the seat next to Hannah and handed her the scrunchie. ''It keeps getting in my eyes.''

''Okay, sit still for a minute.'' Hannah pulled her daughter onto her lap and tied the ponytail. ''There you go.'' She grinned as Faith slid back out of the seat and darted across the room. ''Hey,'' Hannah called. ''Wait for Douglas.''

''Oh, right.'' Faith returned to grab the boy's hand. ''You know what, Mommy? He's just like my little brother. Come on, Dougie. Let's go check out this really neat video game.''

''Maybe a little brother would be good for Faith,'' Allan said after the kids had gone again. ''And a big sister would definitely be good for Douglas.'' He held Hannah's glance for a moment. ''Not to mention how much I would personally enjoy an expanded family. Or a wife. What you might call a win-win situation all around, don't you think?''

''Allan...'' *Tell him, for God's sake. There's no connection, no chemistry. We're not destined for togetherness.* ''Look, we've talked about this before. We've known each other, how long? A couple of months?'' It was a cop-out, but she couldn't bring herself to hurt him. ''It's way too soon.''

He smiled. ''For you, maybe. As far as I'm concerned, I knew the first day I saw you in the classroom.'' A moment passed and he gazed off toward the video area where the children were playing. ''I do worry about Douglas,'' he said. ''He needs to socialize with other children a little more.'' With a look of distaste, he glanced down at the congealing pizza on the table. ''Which is why we came here instead of going to Felippi's, where at least you get edible crust and a decent Chianti to wash it down.''

Hannah smiled. ''The pizza's okay. A little overpriced, maybe.''

''It's revolting.'' He smiled back at her. ''But, hey. No sacrifice is too great for my boy. Even plastic cheese and cardboard crust.''

Hannah started to speak, then realized she was on the verge of tears. She excused herself to check on the children. God, she was surrounded by models of fatherly behavior. Over there, a guy in blue jeans was hoisting a small boy up on his shoulders to give him a better look at the screen. Another man, down on his knees, was urging a tyke in a cowboy hat and boots to blow his nose. Allan, talking to Douglas now, was enduring cardboard pizza so that the boy could be around other kids.

Everywhere, reminders of what fathers were supposed to be and what Liam wasn't.

MIRANDA'S HOUSE WAS a nonstop party scene. Booze and, Liam assumed, pretty much anything else a person might want. Girls coming in and out at all hours. Twice over the weekend, he'd started to phone Hannah then changed his mind. That afternoon he'd finished the pitcher of banana rum punch that Miranda had made, then wandered up to his room and fallen asleep. When he woke up, it was dark outside and the party was going full swing downstairs.

He rolled over onto his back and held the pillow over his head, trying to block out the noise as well as the image of Hannah climbing into her little red car and driving away.

But nothing blocked out the noise or the thoughts. Hannah and Faith, hands extended, had even invaded his dreams. He stumbled out of bed, splashed water on his face and wandered, bleary-eyed downstairs.

Miranda spotted him immediately and thrust a cold beer in his hand.

"Party pooper." She wore black leather trousers and a black silk shirt, and her hair was piled up on her head, strands of it down around her neck and shoulders. "Where have you been, you naughty boy?"

"Escaping," he said.

"Escaping?" She gave him a pouty-mouthed smile. "Not from me, I hope."

"From me."

She laughed. "Why would you want to escape from you?"

"Because I'm a no-good, lily-livered coward." He'd heard John Wayne or someone say it on a Western. It seemed applicable. "A pathetic, quivering mass of indecision," he added for good measure.

Miranda laughed louder. "Oh my. Well, not to worry.

No-good, lily-livered cowards are my favorite type of men.''

Liam drank some beer. Through the windows on the far end of the room he could see the sparks from bonfires on the beach, glowing and sputtering like fireworks in the dark night. Miranda had invited half a dozen or so bands, including his own, and the music throbbed from everywhere in the house. He stared at a girl with long, white-blond hair, who was drinking tequila straight from the bottle. She looked very young, sixteen or seventeen maybe. A thought buzzed across his brain. Someone's daughter. Abandoned by *her* father, too?

''Okay, I'm dying of curiosity.'' Miranda smiled her sultry, insinuating smile, keeping her voice low so he had to move closer to hear. ''Who was that girl who came here to see you?''

''She used to be my wife,'' Liam said.

''Your wife.'' She took a step backward, her eyes widened. ''Oh my. I wouldn't take you for the marrying kind.''

''I'm not,'' he said. ''Which is why she used to be my wife.''

Miranda appeared to be absorbing this new piece of information. ''She's cute,'' she said after a moment. ''Although I wouldn't have thought she was your type.''

''How is that?'' he asked, genuinely curious.

''Oh, I don't know.'' Miranda's eyes narrowed as she considered. ''She seemed sweet and wholesome. A homebody. You strike me as a more adventurous type. Dark and mysterious.''

Liam laughed. ''Right, that's me all over. But terrible husband material.'' *Terrible father material, too. I have a daughter who is going to be six tomorrow. She's hav-*

ing a birthday party, but I'm scared to meet her. "My wife's lucky she got out when she did," he said.

"Oh, I think perhaps you're being a little too hard on yourself," Miranda said. "You're obviously concerned about Brid. That says something."

"All it says is I need her for the band. If it weren't for that, Brid could starve herself to death for all I care." It wasn't true, but he felt so bloody awful about himself at the moment, he didn't want Miranda, or anyone else, trying to make him into something he wasn't.

Across the room he could see Pearse O'Donnaugh, who sometimes sang backup vocals with Brid, talking to the girl with the white-blond hair. Pearse was also a virtuoso on the tin whistle and held the title for bedding more girls during a single tour than anyone else in the band. He attributed both accomplishments to exceptionally agile tongue and lips. He would have the blonde on her back before the evening was through. *Someone's daughter.*

Miranda was giving him one of those looks. "Sometimes, I'm not really sure where you're coming from, Liam," she said.

He gave a laugh. "That makes two of us, Miranda."

An hour later, he had Miranda drive him to a toy shop, some overpriced place in a shopping mall as big as a town. When they got back to the house, he almost stumbled over Pearse and the blond girl half-naked on the beach. Without thinking, Liam grabbed the whistle player and punched him.

"I don't know what's gotten into you, Liam," Pearse said as he staggered to his feet, "but I'd take something for it if I were you, because you're acting like a bloody nutcase."

"WHEN I WAS PREGNANT with you," Margaret was telling Debra. "I was sick all the time. Morning, noon and night, all I did was throw up. Not like with Hannah, I wasn't sick once with her."

Debra rolled her eyes. "Even in the womb, Hannah was perfect."

Hannah said nothing. Debra was clearly back in the fold, and Margaret was just as clearly glad to have her there. They'd been sitting at the kitchen table when she and Faith had returned from their evening out.

She'd put Faith to bed, then gone back down to bake the cake for the birthday party Saturday. By that time, Rose and Helen were also seated around the table; Helen busy decoupaging paper flowers onto a ceramic teapot, Rose with the Dating Opportunities page of the *Long Beach Press Telegram* spread out in front of her.

Someone had sliced a pound cake and set it on a plate, next to a tub of Cool Whip and a full gallon jug of Burgundy. Margaret and Rose were both holding wineglasses. No one mentioned Liam, but whenever Hannah looked up from decorating the cake, she'd catch one of them watching her, their curiosity almost palpable.

"So, what was it like with Faith?" Debra asked. "Did you get sick?"

"A little in the morning." A tube of chocolate frosting in one hand, Hannah stood back to inspect her handiwork. She'd cut and frosted the cake to look like a grandfather clock. When it was finished, six marshmallow mice, which she still had to assemble, would run up the sides. And then she'd freeze it until Friday night. She glanced at the clock over the microwave. Nearly ten and she wasn't completely satisfied with the way it looked.

"I only wanted chocolate milkshakes when I was

pregnant with you,'' Margaret told Hannah. ''Remember that, Rose? That time, I sent you out at two in the morning to look for a Jack in the Box that was open?''

'''Distinguished professional gentleman,''' Rose read. '''Owns own home.''' She looked at Margaret. ''Do I remember what? Oh right...two in the morning and I'm driving around looking for a goddamn Jack in the Box. All I could find was a McDonald's, so I bought one of their shakes—''

''You said it would taste just the same,'' Margaret interrupted, ''But it didn't.'' With a smile, she moved on. ''Hannah was *so* cute when she was pregnant with Faith.'' She looked at Hannah. ''What were you, sweetie, about three months along? You were craving carrot cake. I'd barely got it out of the oven and you were going at it with a spoon. You couldn't even wait for the frosting. Remember that?''

''Yeah...'' Hannah nodded. Eating carrot cake and being fed lies about Liam. She couldn't bring herself to meet her mother's eyes. Earlier, when she'd walked into the kitchen, Margaret had tried to hug her and Hannah had felt herself withdraw. Right now, she felt like a stranger in the middle of her family.

''How about this one?'' Rose circled an ad with a pink magic marker. '''Divorced, Dynamic and Dedicated desires to meet'...nah. Sixty-four, too old.'' She broke off a piece of the pound cake. ''This is kind of stale. I had some of it at breakfast.''

''Well, you shouldn't eat cake for breakfast,'' Margaret said. ''Your taste buds aren't set up for it.'' She cut a sliver and stuck it in her mouth. ''Okay, that's it for me. Next week I'm going back to Weight Watchers.''

''I made a pound cake last week with pureed prunes

instead of oil.'' Frowning in concentration, Helen dabbed glue on a paper rose. ''You wouldn't know the difference.''

Rose peered at Helen over her red harlequin reading glasses, a sly smile curving her mouth. ''An example of having your cake and losing it, too.'' She drank some wine. ''Nothing like pureed prunes to keep you regular.''

''I've tried that,'' Margaret said. ''The cake, I mean. They ran the recipe in the food section.'' She looked over at Hannah. ''You're kind of quiet, sweetie. Are you feeling okay?''

Hannah waited a moment. But the anger—simmering since the night at Fiddler's Green—flared. ''Yeah, Mom, I'm fine. Terrific.''

Margaret gave her a long look. ''You don't sound fine.'' She got up from the table, put her arm around Hannah's shoulder. ''Come on, sweetie. You're not still mad about...the Liam thing?''

''As a matter of fact, I am.'' Her hand shaking, Hannah dipped the knife into the bowl of hot water. ''I think it's great that you guys are all yakking on about cakes and pregnancies. To hell with the fact that you lied to me and you lied to Liam. I guess that's in the past now, not even worth discussing, right?''

''Fine, Hannah.'' Margaret sat back down and pushed her chair away from the table. ''I thought I'd explained already. What would you like from me now? You want an apology?''

''An apology for what?'' The decoupage brush in one hand, Helen looked at her sister. ''For acting in your daughter's best interests?''

''Your mother was worried sick about you,'' Rose told Hannah. ''Liam would have taken you back to Ireland and God knows what would have happened then.''

"You were a mess," Debra said. "You know you were. Mom just recognized you needed help. Which is a damn sight more than Liam did."

Margaret dismissed further comments with a wave of her hand. "We all know why I did what I did. Now I want to hear what Hannah thinks I should do next. You want me to talk to Liam? Explain why it all happened? Fine. Tell you what, why don't you invite him to Faith's birthday party?"

"Margaret," Helen and Rose protested in unison.

"For God's sake, Mom," Debra said.

"I'm serious." Margaret said. "Invite him. We don't have to tell Faith who he is. It'll be a learning experience for him. He'll discover that six-year-old children are so removed from the life he knows he won't be able to get away fast enough. Do you have a number where you can reach him?"

Hannah shook her head. "Forget it, Mom."

"No. Let's clear the air and move on. Give me his number."

"I already invited him, Mom." She heard her voice shake and waited a moment. "I gave him some pictures of Faith and invited him to the party." Her eyes filled. "He wasn't interested."

CHAPTER FIVE

EVERYONE HAD HUGGED HER after that. Told her they loved her; made hot chocolate, poured wine, plied her with brownies and assured her she was better off without a jerk like Liam anyway. After a while she began to feel a little better. By the time Margaret and the aunts had gone to bed, it was two in the morning. Hannah and Debra still sat around the table talking.

"To hell with Liam anyway," she told Debra. "Allan's looking better and better."

"Mom would be thrilled to hear that."

"I'm not about to marry him just to please Mom." Elbows on the table, face propped in her hands, Hannah decided it was time for a change of topic. "Are you really happy about the baby, Deb? This is what you want?"

"Yeah…" Debra mashed a cake crumb with her finger. "I am. I mean, I was kind of freaked at first, telling Mom and everything. But Rose and Helen and Mom were all so sweet. They love this little thing already and then they were talking about how much happiness Faith had given them and…"

Hannah looked at her sister for a long time.

Debra returned Hannah's look. "What?"

"You can't base your decision on what makes Mom or Rose and Helen happy. It's your life."

"I know that…" Deb folded her arms across her chest, stared down at the table cluttered with glasses and plates and brownie crumbs. "But nothing is ever really one person's decision. I mean, almost nothing. It's like…I don't know, we're all threads in this family tapestry. You can follow one thread, pull it out and separate it from the rest, but it's part of the design. If you remove one strand, you mess up the whole thing."

Hannah grinned. "Remind me to ask you about that theory when you and Mom are fighting and all you want to do is get away."

"Yeah, I'll probably say to hell with the design and yank the damn strand out." She yawned. "So is the birthday cake all done?"

"Except for the marshmallow mice. I can make them in the morning."

"No, let's do them now." Debra got up again and returned with a bag of marshmallows. "Cut them in halves? Or quarters?"

"Halves." They worked in silence for a few minutes, gluing pieces of marshmallow together with vanilla frostings. "So is it really all over with Dennis?" Hannah asked.

"His official name is now Dennis the Menace." Debra reached for another marshmallow. "I guess I wanted the relationship to work so much, I couldn't see what a jerk he was. You know, I used to wonder why Mom stuck with Dad when she knew damn well he was running around on her, but you make yourself believe what you want to believe." She looked up at Hannah. "Like you and Liam."

"Actually, my situation with Liam was different," Hannah said. "Maybe when we got married I kind of hoped that one day he'd turn into this family man, but deep down I never really believed he would. Liam's into his own world and there isn't room for anyone else. On some level I guess I've always known that, I just couldn't accept it before." She lifted one of the mice for Deb to see. "What d'you think? Are the eyes too big?"

Deb glanced over at the mouse in Hannah's hand and laughed. ''Kind of. Unless he's got thyroid problems. Maybe if you cut the chocolate chips in half.''

''I'll put them in the blender.'' Hannah squatted to remove the blender from the cabinet. ''It'll be quicker than trying to chop the damn things.''

''Can I say something?'' Deb asked.

Hannah dumped a handful of chips into the container and pressed the pulverize button. ''Go ahead.''

''I mean this is small-minded and mean and I know I'm going to be sorry I said it, but I'm kind of glad about what happened with Liam. You gave him a chance to see Faith and he turned it down, which means he's a jerk.''

''Yeah...'' Hannah looked at Debra. ''And...''

Head lowered, Debra pressed her finger into the ground-up chocolate Hannah had dumped on a paper towel. ''Sometimes I hate that everything always turns out well for you. After Liam, you went back to school, got your life together and it just kills me sometimes that mine gets so screwed up. If Liam had turned out to be this great father and you guys had just waltzed off into the sunset, I would have been so damn jealous.''

''God, Deb.'' Hannah shook her head, equally touched and stunned by what Debra had said. ''I really, *really* don't think I've ever had it all together. In fact, lately I've been wondering why I'm thirty-one and still living at home.''

''Because of Faith,'' Deb said. ''Mom and Rose and Helen are always here for her when you're at work, and there's no way you could afford to rent a place that's even half as nice as this.''

''That's what I tell myself,'' Hannah said. ''But sometimes I think maybe it's just an excuse because I'm too scared to be out on my own.''

''Nah.'' Deb dismissed the idea with a shake of her

head. "You're just putting Faith's welfare first, which is good because her father obviously isn't interested."

Hannah sighed. "Let's not talk about him anymore. He's like a tornado that blew into town and tore everything apart. Even though things with Mom are okay again on the surface, deep down, I'm still mad at her. I almost think I was better off not knowing about the lie."

"Listen, Hannah, no one gets under my skin like Mom does." Deb scooped some chocolate, dumped it into her coffee. "Sometimes she just looks at me the wrong way, and I yell at her. But in this case, she was only thinking of you. Screwed-up thinking maybe, but she was truly scared. Not that I knew what was going on at the time, I was only fifteen or sixteen." She grinned. "I thought Liam was cool."

"You and every other woman." Hannah picked among the bits of chocolate for eye-size pieces. "Well, he had his chance."

"Exactly. Hold on to that thought," Deb said. "By the way, I forgot to tell you, Allan called just before you got home. He wanted to know if there was anything he could bring to the party Saturday. Or if you wanted him to stop by early in the morning to help set things up."

"He came in with his son while we were having pizza tonight." Hannah ran warm water over her hands, melting the sticky frosting from her fingers. "After the kids went off to play, we sat there talking about this and that and it was…nice. The way parents are supposed to be."

"And?"

"And I kept thinking, why can't I just fall in love with a guy like Allan?"

"No chemistry."

Hannah sighed. "I tell myself what a great guy he is, thoughtful, considerate. A good father."

"Listen, if there's no chemistry, there's no chemistry,'' Debra said. ''If you don't like broccoli, covering it with cheese won't make a bit of difference. It's still broccoli and it still does nothing for you.'' She grinned. ''Kind of like Allan.''

ALLAN ARRIVED four hours early on the day of the party. Hannah was tying a bunch of multicolored ribbons to the mailbox, when his Volvo wagon pulled up at the curb. She watched as he walked around to the passenger side and opened the door for his son.

Douglas emerged slowly, his face solemn beneath a black felt pirate hat emblazoned with a gold skull and crossbones. A breeze filled the full sleeves of his white shirt, which was tucked into a pair of red-and-white-striped pants. The silver papier maché sword he held in one hand glittered in the sun.

''Hey, cool costume.'' Hannah bent down to hug him. ''And those boots are terrific.''

''They make my feet sweat.'' Douglas looked up at his father, then down at his black rubber boots. ''Do I have to wear them, Dad?''

Allan, who had been gazing at Hannah, turned his attention to his son. ''Would you rather wear your flip-flops?'' he asked.

''Did you wash them?''

''They weren't really dirty, pal.'' Allan moved to the car, produced the rubber sandals from the trunk and helped Douglas remove the boots. ''There,'' he said after Douglas had first inspected, then stepped into a pair of blue thongs. ''Better?''

Douglas nodded, the faintest trace of a smile on his face. ''I need to get the presents,'' he said. ''Okay, Dad?''

''I told him it wasn't a costume party, but he was determined to wear it,'' Allan said after Douglas went off into the house, his arms full of lavishly wrapped gifts. ‘‘He’s been so excited about seeing Faith again. It’s all he’s talked about.’’

‘‘Good.’’ Hannah smiled brightly and, suspecting Allan was about to take her in his arms, moved a few steps backward. ‘‘So. We need to find you a job to do.’’

‘‘Just a moment.’’ Once again, he opened the Volvo trunk and lifted out a paper grocery sack. ‘‘Ingredients for lunch. I thought you’d probably be too busy with party preparations to find time to eat.’’

‘‘Actually, we were going to order pizza.’’

Allan grimaced. ‘‘Well, I’m here to spare you. I have in this bag all the ingredients for a salad Nicoise.’’

Hannah looked at him. ‘‘That sounds kind of ambitious, Allan. I was thinking of something quick.’’

‘‘This will be. Quick as a wink.’’ The bag in his arms, he started up the path to the house. ‘‘Birds-of-paradise are blooming nicely,’’ he said as he passed the orange plants lining the driveway. ‘‘A few nasturtiums lurking, I see.’’

‘‘Yeah, they’re the bane of my mother’s existence. The more she pulls them out, the more they seem to come back.’’

‘‘You could use the leaves in a salad,’’ Allan said. ‘‘Only the new ones, of course. And the blossoms are quite nice, too. They impart a rather pleasant peppery taste.’’

‘‘I’ll have to try it,’’ Hannah said, knowing she was about as likely to add nasturtiums to her usual salad of chopped iceberg and grated carrot as she was to whip up a salade Nicoise. But Allan considered himself a master chef. He’d cooked dinner for her at his house once, an elaborate feast that he’d chopped and cut and sautéed for hours. She’d stood in the kitchen as he’d lovingly described everything he was doing and then given her a little tutorial on clarifying butter. Another time, he’d promised, he would show her how to butterfly lamb. *Right.*

One of the few things she'd had in common with Liam was their very basic approach to food preparation. They'd lived out of cans. Except for the time he'd gotten a crazy urge to make an Irish stew at three in the morning. After they'd bought all the ingredients, neither of them had wanted to make the stew. Instead they'd ended up making love. On the kitchen floor. She wondered whether Liam remembered that.

With Allan behind her, she took the steps up to the house. *Go away, Liam.*

"I COULD GET USED TO THIS." Brid pressed a button to open the sunroof of Miranda Payton's butter-colored Mercedes and tipped up her face to the sky. "Riding around in fancy cars, the sun all nice and warm. Maybe I'll find a rich American at the party."

"Tommy Doherty will be heartbroken." Liam craned his neck to read the green street sign at the intersection of Pacific Coast Highway. Second Street. He turned left. Everything felt familiar. The palm trees and oil derricks, the milky pale sky. Across a bridge now; a marina and boatyard on one side, on the other, a small stretch of beach where Hannah and her sister used to play as kids. She'd told him about the time she'd lost a little wooden dog in the water. A painted dachshund with red wheels that clacked as she pulled it along on a string. She'd been walking it along the edge of the sand and a wave had carried it away. He drove on through Naples, past a steak restaurant he'd gone to with Hannah and her parents. Over filet mignon, her father had once again made it clear that a Las Vegas marriage to a visiting Irish musician was definitely not what he'd had in mind for his daughter.

"I put some rice cakes in there, too," he told Brid. "And bananas."

"So you've said already," Brid reminded him. "Three times."

"Well, I don't think you should have checked yourself out so soon. Miranda didn't think so, either. She said her daughter was in there for nearly a month."

"Miranda's telling you that because she wants to keep you around."

Liam turned his head to look at her.

"I'm serious. She fancies you."

"Miranda has a husband who could buy and sell me a hundred times over."

"She's bored to tears with him. She asked me if the two of us had anything going. You and me."

"What did you tell her?"

"I told her we were at each other every chance we got."

Liam grinned. "Did she believe you?"

"She might have if I could have kept a straight face."

Without taking his eyes off the road, Liam reached for the bag in the back seat and tossed it onto Brid's lap. "Eat. It's not just me and Miranda who think you left the place too soon. The doctor said you needed at least two weeks."

"The doctor wants money. I'm fine, Liam. Stop worrying."

"Eat a rice cake then."

"Nag, nag." She put the bag on the floor by her feet. "Are you sure you want me to come along? You wouldn't rather go alone?"

"I want you to come, I already told you."

Brid brought her feet up onto the leather seat, and put her arms around them. "You just want to keep an eye on me," she said. "Force food down my throat."

"Not at all," he said. "It's your company. There's no one I'd rather be with."

She grinned and punched his arm. "Liar."

He turned on the radio and flipped through the preset stations. Miranda's taste ran to soft rock and easy listening. Billy Joel was singing "An Innocent Man." As they came into Belmont Shore, the traffic congealed into a slow-moving mass. Trendy little shops lined both sides of the street.

Liam thought of the pink stucco cottage Hannah had called her dream house. There'd been a strip of blue ocean at the foot of the street, the powdery dust of sand in the air. And flowers everywhere, the colors like a kid's box of crayons. Purple bougainvillea and red geraniums, bright blue daisies with yellow centers and pink-and-white-striped petunias spilling out of terra-cotta pots. "Could you see us living in a place like this?" she'd asked him.

"I think you should have phoned her first," Brid said. "It might be a bit awkward, just showing up."

"I'll take my chances." Second Street ended and merged into Ocean Boulevard. A street—whose name he couldn't make out—forked to the right. He waited at the stop sign, unsure which direction to take. A car honked behind him. Liam rubbed the back of his neck, let the clutch out too soon and killed the engine.

"You're nervous, aren't you?"

"Don't be daft." He craned his neck to read the street sign. There was a supermarket at the foot of Hannah's street, he remembered. They'd walked from her house to a long pier with a fishing tackle shop at the end. "Nervous about what?"

Brid laughed. "Come on, Liam, it's me you're talking to. I mean about seeing your daughter. You're scared to death.'' She reached over and put her hand on his arm. ''You don't have to do this, you know, Liam.''

''I can't remember the name of her street,'' he said.

''That's why you should have phoned.''

''I'll know it when I see it.'' To his right, he saw a street with large two-story homes winding up a hill. He craned his neck to get a better view. ''This is the one, I think. It's a big brown house with turrets in the front like a castle. When I used to visit Hannah, I'd half expect them to pull up the drawbridge.''

''That one?'' Brid pointed to a turreted structure several houses up the hill with long, narrow windows and a heavy wooden door. ''Looks like money,'' she said as Liam pulled up outside.

''They do well enough,'' he said. ''Or they did.''

''They must have been thrilled with you.''

He shrugged and stretched across Brid to peer at the house. Everything looked much as he remembered. The house was built on a slight incline so that it sat about six feet higher than street level. Sixteen steps led up from the street, made a turn, then twelve more ended in a meticulously clipped lawn edged with orange tropical flowers. Her father had been an avid gardener. Hannah had given him a tour of the old man's rose garden. Every rose, she'd told him, marked a special occasion in her or her sister's lives. She'd told him she'd argued with her father because he hadn't planted a rose for her marriage.

''Are we just going to sit here then?'' Brid asked.

''No.'' As he opened the car door, he could hear children's voices and laughter coming from the back of the house. A bunch of colored balloons bobbed from the mailbox on the street.

Brid put her hand on his arm. ''Liam…''

''It's all right,'' he said. ''I've come this far…''

BY THREE, the party was in full swing. Hannah watched her daughter, who sat at one end of a long trestle table covered with white paper. All around her, a dozen or so children with newspaper aprons were applying spots of black paint to cardboard dalmatians. Aunt Rose, sporting a pair of faux fur dalmatian ears, supervised the activity, regaling the kids with a tale about a dalmatian who'd managed to misplace his spots.

"Any ideas what he might have done with them?" Rose asked.

"Maybe they got dirty and he had to wash them off," Douglas suggested.

Hannah smiled and headed across the yard to where the food was being set up. A neighbor, in a tall white chef's hat and a navy-blue apron presided over the barbecue; Margaret and Aunt Helen were filling Tupperware bowls with chips and cheddar cheese goldfish. Smoke from the grill hung in the air and mingled with the laughter from the children. Margaret leaned over to say something to Helen, then all three turned and smiled at Hannah.

Her throat suddenly thick, Hannah bent down to adjust the strap of her sandal. The image of the picture-perfect happy family—something she'd seen countless times—suddenly seemed false. She could tell herself she'd forgiven her mother for lying to Liam, but something had changed. This house—filled with people who loved her—suddenly didn't feel like home.

"Hannah." Margaret waved her over, then smiled conspiratorially at Helen. "We both think Allan is a doll."

Helen smiled broadly. "Nice, too. Very polite and friendly."

"He said I looked too young to have a thirty-one-year-old daughter," Margaret said.

''That's all it needed for your mother to fall in love with him,'' Helen added.

''Not true,'' Margaret protested, pink-faced. ''I liked him the moment I saw him in the kitchen wearing my apron and whipping up a salad. I thought, there's the guy for Hannah. Now if only we could find someone like that for Deb.''

''Where is Deb?'' Hannah asked.

Margaret's happy expression faded. ''We argued again this morning, and she stormed out. I don't know if it's the pregnancy that's making her so touchy or what. All I asked was whether the baby was going to have Dennis's last name.''

''Maybe she thinks that's her business,'' Hannah said.

''I'm her mother,'' Margaret said. ''If she's living in my house, I think I have the right to ask a simple question without her jumping down my throat.'' She sighed. ''If you could have a little talk with her, I'd really appreciate it.''

''Where's that guy of yours?'' The man tending the barbecue waved a spatula at Hannah. ''Tell him to come and give me a hand. I could use a little break from women's yak-yak-yak.''

Margaret peered across the yard. ''I see him over there with his little boy. Allan,'' she called. ''Get over here. We want to put you to work.'' She smiled at Hannah. ''He is *so* cute.''

''Goodness.'' Tupperware bowl in hand, Helen stared out at the crowd on the lawn. ''Is that who I think it is? Over there by the steps.''

''Damn.'' Margaret exhaled loudly, then turned to look at Hannah. ''I thought you said he wasn't coming. I'll go and talk to him—''

''No, Mom.'' Hannah put her hand on Margaret's arm. ''I will.''

CHAPTER SIX

"I THINK THIS IS WHERE I go find the ladies' room or something," Brid told Liam. "Good luck."

As he watched Hannah approaching, Liam had an irrational urge to bolt. To drop the presents, wrapped by Miranda in silver paper with big yellow bows, and return to a place where he knew what he was doing.

Beyond Hannah, he could see a group standing around a barbecue. One of the women might have been Mrs. Riley, he wasn't sure. And then Hannah was standing in front of him, color flooding her face. She wore a short white skirt and sandals. Her pale pink lipstick was almost the same color as her sleeveless blouse. No smile.

"I didn't think you were coming," she said.

"Neither did I." The three square boxes were stacked one on top of the other, the top one brushing his chin. Hannah's brown hair curled around her face. She looked very young, hardly old enough to have a six-year-old daughter. The group at the barbecue were watching with undisguised curiosity. The woman in the blue dress was Hannah's mother, he was sure of it now. He shouldn't have worn a tie. Sweat trickled down the back of his neck, beaded on his forehead. He should have bought flowers, chocolates or something. "These are for…I don't know if it's the kind of thing she'd like. The girl in the shop had a little girl though…"

Hannah gave him a faint smile, then seemed to mentally shake herself. "Here, I'll take them." She reached for the boxes, held them against her chest, but kept staring at him as if she thought he might be a figment of her imagination. "I'm stunned, Liam. I don't know what to say. I haven't… Faith doesn't know. I mean, I haven't said anything. Why did you change your mind?"

"I don't know." He followed Hannah's glance to a long trestle table, where a dozen or so kids sat daubing black paint on paper and each other. He saw Faith. A little older than she'd looked in the pictures Hannah had given him, a pair of white fur dog ears on her head. Hands raised like claws, she was barking at a boy in a pirate's outfit. Liam grinned. *My daughter.*

"You spotted her," Hannah said. "Looks like she's getting in a little practice for a game of My Dog Says. It's like Simon Says," she added after Liam gave her a puzzled look. "But the kids bark and growl instead."

Liam watched Faith chase the pirate across the grass. Groups of adults in summer clothes stood around the yard, talking and watching the kids play. Hannah tapped his shoulder.

"I'm going to take these inside." She indicated the presents. "Do you want to come with me?"

He followed her into the kitchen.

"The wallpaper's different," he said. "It used to be little yellow teapots."

Hannah set the presents down on the table and looked up at him. "You remember?"

"And the cooker and fridge were green."

"Avocado," she said.

"And the fridge was covered with snapshots and newspaper clippings. You could hardly see the space between them."

"Yeah, well…" She gestured at the front of the current fridge, a pristine stainless steel, unmarred by even a magnet. ''My mom finally moved out of the sixties. Want something to drink? Soda? A beer?''

Liam shook his head and saw disappointment covered by a quick smile. ''Changed my mind,'' he said. ''A beer would be nice.'' He moved to the window and stared out at the kids on the lawn. Faith appeared to be issuing commands to the other kids who were tearing around the yard on all fours. As Hannah handed him the beer, he caught a whiff of something familiar.

''Your hair,'' he said. ''It still smells the same.''

She touched her hair, blushed a little. ''Same shampoo. I'm a creature of habit.''

''It's nice. Brings back old memories.'' Back in Ireland, after they'd split up, he would lie in the dark and think about her and remember exactly the way her hair had smelled, the way traces of the aroma had lingered on her pillow. Once, in a particularly low moment, he'd gone out and bought a bottle of the same shampoo she'd used. And then he'd felt like an idiot for moping over a woman who'd aborted his child.

He stayed at the window, Hannah beside him. Watching his daughter. *Their* daughter. With something that felt a lot like envy, he watched the pirate's dad come to the rescue of his son. Faith, he noticed, was now wearing the pirate's hat.

''Oh, God.'' Hannah, who had apparently caught the switch, too, started laughing. ''Faith's never been the shy type.''

''That's good.'' The surge of pride he felt surprised him. ''She goes after what she wants.''

''Yeah...'' She nodded, still smiling.

''Do you remember the last time we were at a birthday party together?''

"Yep," she answered. "The one you had for me. My twenty-first."

"And I forget to post the invitations so no one showed up."

"Yeah, but you made a great cake."

"If you like them flat as a pancake. And burned."

"Well, it was your first try."

"I'm not sure I'd have done any better after a dozen tries," he said. "You can't have forgotten the chicken?"

"The chicken?" Her expression puzzled, she looked at him for a minute. Then she clapped her hand to her mouth. "Oh, the chicken," she said, laughing now. "I remember."

He'd been trying to cook dinner for her. But he'd forgotten to look in the oven before he turned it on and hadn't seen the bags of potato chips she'd kept there to keep them from the mice that had overrun the apartment. After he'd put out the fire, he'd stuck the chicken back in—its innards still wrapped in plastic—and turned the temperature up high.

"God, the smell." Hannah was still laughing. "I mean, it would have been hilarious if we hadn't been so broke. I can still see you standing by the stove with this little tiny black thing the size of a sparrow."

"But the gravy was all right though. Nothing like a nice gravy dinner. Ah, well..." he said a moment later.

Hannah's smile faded and she stood looking out of the window at the children on the grass. A few seconds passed, and then she turned to him. "I'm glad you decided to come, Liam. It feels strange to be standing here with you, watching Faith. But it feels good, too."

"It does." He looked down at the beer can in his hand. "Strange but good."

"How long will you be around?" she asked.

‘‘It depends on Brid. My singer. She’s out there talking to the tall blond guy. She’s had a few problems. If she’s well enough to tour again we’ll leave in three or four days. We have a gig up near San Francisco next week. A big music festival. I’d like to make it.’’

‘‘So the band’s doing well?’’

‘‘It is.’’ He glanced at her. ‘‘We made the UK charts a couple of years in a row. And we’ve got a European tour coming up soon after we get back.’’

She smiled. ‘‘Fantastic. I’m happy for you, Liam.’’

‘‘Thanks.’’ Something in her eyes told him she meant it. ‘‘And yourself? Things are going well for you, too?’’

‘‘Yeah…pretty good. I teach in a preschool.’’

He caught the hesitation in her voice. ‘‘And you’re happy doing that?’’

‘‘Sure, it’s great.’’

He looked at her. ‘‘That’s not really what you want to do, is it?’’

She grinned. ‘‘No. I have this dream about doing landscaping design. Drought-tolerant plants. Rosemary, lavender, sage. Things that grow well in California.’’ Her face grew animated. ‘‘People are always surprised at how colorful that kind of garden can be.’’

‘‘So why are you teaching preschool if what you really want to do is grow plants?’’

She shrugged. ‘‘I don’t know, lots of reasons.’’

‘‘That’s a mistake, Hannah. You only live one life. Don’t waste it doing things that don’t make you happy.’’

‘‘That’s a nice thought, Liam,’’ she said, an edge to her voice now. ‘‘And it’s an easy thing to say, it’s just not so easy to do. Happiness isn’t always about just doing things for yourself. There are other people to consider.’’

‘‘You’re right,’’ he said. ‘‘As long as you don’t make

other people an excuse for not taking responsibility for your own happiness.''

''Well,'' she said brightly, after a moment of heavy silence. ''I guess I should get out there and do my hostess duties.''

''Right.'' Liam drank some beer and Hannah didn't move. They stood watching the children, queuing up for hot dogs. Brid and the pirate's dad were at the edge of the crowd, laughing about something. Faith had made her way to the front of the food line. He wondered what Hannah was thinking. He wondered if she was in love with the pirate's dad. He wondered if she'd had any thought of telling Faith that her daddy wasn't in heaven after all. He wondered if he needed his head examined. He decided he didn't care.

''Does she like…'' He started to ask, and then Hannah's mother walked into the kitchen, holding the arm of the pirate's dad. For a moment, they all stood looking at each other. Hannah's face was like thunder; Margaret's all flustered surprise—real or not, he couldn't be sure. The pirate's dad looked slightly amused and perfectly at ease. He had the kind of haircut that the men in the magazines Brid read all sported. In fact he looked a bit like someone in one of the ads—tanned and expensively dressed. Definitely a son-in-law candidate. Liam decided it was time to make his exit.

''OF COURSE I DIDN'T PLAN IT.'' Margaret held a glass of pinot noir as she moved around the kitchen, putting away bowls and serving platters. ''Allan suggested we all have dinner at Kelly's tonight, I'd told him I love the steak there, and we came to look for you to tell you about it. How would I know you were with Liam?''

"I wasn't *with* Liam, Mom. You make it sound like... We were *talking.*"

"Excuse me," Margaret poured more wine into her glass. "I don't think I suggested you were doing anything other than talking. I just said—"

"I know *what* you said. It was *the way* you said it." Hannah scooped leftover potato salad into a plastic container. What was the point of arguing? Margaret would continue to claim innocence and Hannah would continue to believe that her mother knew exactly what she was doing when she brought Allan into the kitchen. She put the container into the fridge and picked up a bowl of baked beans. "You want to save these? There isn't much left."

"Toss them," Margaret said. "Listen, I can finish cleaning up here, if you want to go and get ready. Allan said he'd be here at seven."

Hannah scraped the beans into the trash. Faith had gone home with Allan and Douglas. This had also been arranged while she'd been talking to Liam. Allan would return with the kids, pick up Hannah and Margaret and drive to Kelly's, where they'd meet Rose and Helen. In the span of one afternoon, Allan had become part of the family.

"Who was that woman with Liam?" Margaret asked.

"His singer."

"She was all over Allan," Margaret said. "Not that he was doing anything to encourage her. Actually the opposite, I think he was a little embarrassed."

"He'll get over it." Why *had* Liam brought Brid to the party? And what was his relationship with the singer? And why the hell did any of it matter? Once again, Liam had just walked away. Not a word about wanting to see Faith again or keeping in touch. Nothing, just that faint, inscrutable Liam smile and then he was gone—down the road in a yellow Mercedes. With another woman.

''I suppose he didn't say anything about wanting to contribute to Faith's support,'' Margaret said.

Hannah felt her pulse kick up a notch. The thought had occurred to her, but she didn't want to discuss it with her mother. If Liam chose not to support his daughter, it was probably because he didn't really feel he had a daughter and so felt no obligation. She could tell herself this, but Margaret's question brought all the disappointment and simmering anger to the surface. Anger at Liam, at her mother, at herself for being taken in, once again, by Liam.

''No, Mom, he didn't say anything about it,'' she snapped. ''Maybe he would have though, if he hadn't been cheated out of the first six years of Faith's life.''

''Oh, for God's sake.'' Margaret dismissed Hannah's comment with a wave of her hand. ''How many times are we going to play this same refrain? Okay, maybe I should have handled things differently, but I didn't. Get over it. It's time for everyone to accept what happened and move on. Liam knows he has a daughter now. What he does about it is his decision.'' She wrapped aluminum foil around a plate of sliced tomatoes and set the plate in the fridge. ''Does he want to see her again?''

''No.''

''Just no?''

''He didn't say anything, Mom. He just left. So, you can breathe easy again.''

Margaret turned to glare at her. Arms folded across her chest, blue eyes bright with anger. ''Sure, blame me for Liam's irresponsibility. What is it with you and Deb? Has she been giving you lessons in hostility? I'm tired of the two of you making me the enemy. How *should* I react to Liam? First he says he doesn't want to see Faith. Then he just shows up. And then he just leaves again. Who knows what the hell he's thinking?''

''Maybe he's confused about things,'' Hannah said. ''Maybe it isn't so easy for him to just move on and forget the six years he spent believing he didn't have a daughter.''

Margaret shook her head. ''Hannah,'' she said softly.

''What?''

''That's you, isn't it? Always giving him the benefit of the doubt. In your book it's poor Liam, the injured party.'' She refilled her wineglass. ''I worry about you, Hannah, I really do. One of these days you're going to have to stop making excuses for other people's failings and start paying attention to your own feelings.''

Hannah opened her mouth to speak, then stopped. Her heart thundering, she picked up the saltshaker. Studied the grains crusted around the chrome top as she thought about all the things she couldn't bring herself to say to her mother.

But maybe Margaret was right. Maybe it *was* time for Hannah to focus on her own needs and stop accommodating everyone else's. For starters, she should stop going to singles dances with Rose just because Rose didn't like to go alone. And she should stop worrying that Helen's feelings would be hurt if she quit her job at La Petite Ecole. And maybe she should stop running interference between Margaret and Deb. And, on the subject of Margaret, she should find a place for herself and Faith and stop worrying that her mother would drink herself into a stupor as a result. And Liam. She needed to know Liam's intentions regarding Faith. Either he wanted to be a part of his daughter's life, or he didn't. And if the latter, she didn't want to hear another word from him.

"I'M DEPRESSED." Brid stared gloomily into her glass of beer. "God, but he was a lovely man. And I thought he liked me, too."

Liam watched the play of sunlight on the water. They were sitting in green plastic chairs on the outdoor patio of Belmont Shore Brewery where they'd driven, although it was just at the bottom of Hannah's road, after the party. At the next table, a middle-aged couple was discussing the price of real estate in California. Shot through the roof in the past year, one of them said. Astronomical, the other agreed.

Brid grinned. "I mean, I was all but working out the colors the bridesmaids would wear. D'you think maybe he's gay? That could explain it."

"He has something going with Hannah," Liam said.

Brid gave him a skeptical look. "She told you that?"

"Not in so many words," Liam said.

"How do you feel about that?" Brid asked.

"It's her life."

She kept watching him. "I can't tell whether it bothers you or not. You're a difficult read, Liam."

"Probably because there's nothing there to read."

"So how was it? Seeing your little girl?"

"Strange. I told Hannah that. Good, but strange."

"And now you've seen her," Brid said. "What's next?"

"I don't know." He drank some beer. "I watched her today. The way Hannah's bringing her up...it's everything she needs, really. Loving family, all the material things, a stable life. It's the way Hannah grew up, but it couldn't be more different from what I had as a boy. What do I have to give her?"

"You're her father, Liam. That's enough. If every father wondered what he had to give before he made a commitment to his child, there would be a lot fewer fathers around, believe me."

"Hannah will get married again and whoever she marries will probably do a better job of being a father to Faith than I ever could."

Brid looked at him. "So drop it then."

"I should."

"What's stopping you?"

He shrugged, but had no answer to her question. "I'd want to be a good father," he said after a moment. "Not just someone who sends a birthday card and presents at Christmas. But if I can't be the kind of father I'd like to have had myself, I might as well walk away."

"Liam." Brid put her elbows on the table and looked into his eyes. "Let's back up a bit. You're on tour eight months out of the year, and when you're not touring you're recording. You live and breathe your music. Tell me how you'd find the time to be a good daddy to your daughter."

He shook his head. He didn't know.

"You need to make a choice, Liam. Right now, the band is the most important thing in your life. If you choose to keep it that way, then I'd say let Hannah find a new father for her daughter, because there's no way you can fill the role. But if you don't, if you really want to be the kind of father you're talking about, then you need to have a long talk with Hannah."

ALTHOUGH MARGARET HAD ADVISED Hannah to pay attention to her feelings, she'd still been furious when

Hannah opted out of dinner at Kelly's. But, as Hannah had pointed out, if her mother had consulted her before making the arrangements, she would have told Margaret that what she really wanted after the party was a quiet evening to herself. Which is exactly what she was having when Liam knocked on the front door.

"Liam." She raised a hand to her hair, which she'd scraped up into a scruffy ponytail after removing all her makeup. She'd also pulled on a pair of faded black leggings with a hole in the seam, an old red flannel shirt that had been her father's and fleecy gray socks. Her comfort clothes. "What…what's up?"

"I wanted to talk to you," he said.

She hesitated a moment, then motioned for him to come in. "Everybody's gone out to dinner. Faith included." She led him into the living room where he stood, arms folded across his chest, his expression hard to read.

"Have a seat." She moved the day's newspaper from the sofa, but he remained standing. He'd worn a tie with a gray cotton shirt to the party. The tie was gone now, the shirt opened at the neck, a leather jacket over it. It occurred to her that she couldn't remember seeing Liam in a tie and the thought of him putting one on for his daughter's birthday party tugged at her heart. She had a sudden urge to touch him.

"Want something to drink?" she asked instead. "Beer, wine, soda? I'm having chamomile tea, myself."

"A beer would be fine." He followed her into the kitchen, stood with his back against the counter, watching as she moved around.

"Did Faith enjoy her party?"

"She had a great time." Hannah opened the refrigerator. "Bud or Miller."

"Either."

She opened a Miller. "You didn't stay to see her open her presents," she said as she handed him a bottle.

"I know...your mother coming into the kitchen threw me off track a bit. I'd been about to suggest we take Faith to the zoo. I've heard there's a great one in San Diego." He opened the beer, drank some. "I thought tomorrow, if you were free."

Hannah had set a glass down for him, but she returned it to the shelf when she saw him take a swig from the bottle. "Why, Liam? What's the point?"

"I'd like to spend some time with my daughter."

"*You'd* like it. What about Faith?"

"It's been a long time since I was a child, but I think I would have been thrilled at the chance for a day at the zoo."

"What do we tell her about who you are?"

"We don't have to tell her anything. Tell her I'm a friend from Ireland. What's wrong with that?"

Hannah microwaved a cup of tea. What *was* wrong with that? Faith would certainly enjoy a day at the zoo. She'd been clamoring to go ever since she'd seen the baby koalas on TV. The microwave pinged and she removed her cup.

"So you take her to the zoo—"

"*We* take her to the zoo."

"Okay, we take her." Her face felt hot. *We. Don't read anything into it.* "What then?"

"I don't know."

She looked at him.

"I *don't* know, Hannah. I can't give you a definite answer. I'm still sorting things out. I just know that I can't walk away and pretend she doesn't exist." He picked up a copy of *Cosmopolitan* that Rose had left on the table, glanced at the cover and set it down again. ''I want to start paying toward Faith's support, no matter whether I'm involved in her life or not,'' he said. ''We can set that up later.''

She nodded, her mind still on the zoo. ''I just don't think taking her out for the day is a good idea,'' she said. ''Even if we don't tell her who you are, she'll be curious. Kids pick up vibes. It could be unsettling for her.''

''It isn't my fault she doesn't know me,'' Liam said.

''I know that.''

''Your mother didn't look happy to see me.''

''She wasn't.''

''She's lucky I didn't tell her exactly what I thought of her little ruse. I would have, except I didn't want to spoil Faith's birthday party.''

''Thanks, I appreciate that.''

''But I still deserve the chance to spend a little time with Faith. No matter how your family feels about me.''

Hannah felt herself wavering.

''If it weren't for your mother's intervention, we might still be together.''

She waited a moment before she spoke, disconcerted by the possibility that Liam might actually regret their divorce. Somehow, she'd always imagined him emotionally unscathed.

''There's not much point in that kind of speculation, Liam,'' she said finally. ''We were young and we hardly knew each other before we got married. Add that to all the time you spend on the road, and it's pretty much a recipe for failure, regardless of what my family did.''

''What's the situation with you and the pirate's dad? Are the two of you...?''

She shrugged, leaving the interpretation up to him. "Allan's a sweet guy."

Liam smiled.

"What?"

"Sweet guys are seldom the love of anyone's life."

Hannah eyed him for a moment. "You know that from personal experience?"

He grinned.

Flustered, she quickly drank the cup of lukewarm tea, dumped the bag in the trash and ran water into the mug. "Sometimes we settle for strength and stability over excitement and romance," she said, realizing that she sounded exactly like her aunt Helen. *Damn it, Liam. Go away, you're confusing me.* She turned to see him studying her. He held her glance until she looked away.

"Okay, I know that didn't come out right," she said. "I didn't mean 'settle.' What I'm trying to say is I'm happy with my life. I don't need a whole bunch of ups and downs, I'm perfectly content with…a more even pace."

"Except you'd rather be doing landscaping than teaching nursery school."

"Well, yes, that."

"And will Allan be a part of this even pace?"

"I don't know that yet. Maybe." A moment passed. "What about you?"

"No one. Is that what you're asking?"

She nodded. "Your singer?"

He laughed.

"What?"

"I don't know. For some reason, I thought you'd be the exception. Everyone suspects Brid and I have something going. The papers have had a field day with our supposed romance. We're the best of friends and that's it.''

''Oh.'' For some reason, the knowledge that there was no one in Liam's life gave her a little charge. They stood for a moment, faint sounds filtering into the silence between them. The hum of the refrigerator, a car driving by. She imagined herself with Liam and Faith driving down to San Diego for a day at the zoo. She'd pack a picnic. Maybe they'd take the coast route. And the zoo really was terrific. She could almost feel it, the sun warm on their backs as they made their way up the hill to the exhibits. Faith between them, holding their hands.

She searched for a reason to say no. And came up empty. Faith would be thrilled. But Faith wasn't really the issue. Faith had come along on a couple of dates before and had taken it all in stride. Her hesitation was for herself. Right now, standing here in the kitchen with Liam; watching his face, hearing his voice, his laugh. She could fall in love with him all over again. And she would if they spent any time at all together. And then, when it ended badly, as it almost inevitably would, she'd have to start the rebuilding all over again. Was it really worth the risk?

''What time tomorrow?'' she asked.

CHAPTER SEVEN

HANNAH AWAKENED around midnight to someone knocking on her bedroom door. She heard Rose call her name, the door opened a little and Rose stuck her head around it.

"You sleeping, sweetie?" she called.

"Not anymore." Hannah sat up in bed and flipped on the bedside lamp. "What's wrong?"

"Your mom." Rose sat down on the edge of the bed. She wore a leopard-skin print velour robe and her red hair was done up in a yellow banana clip. "I wanted to wait until she was asleep before I talked to you. Hannah..." Rose leaned a little closer, dropped her voice, clutched Hannah's arm. *"Your mother broke down at Kelly's tonight."*

Hannah looked at her aunt. Rose's hectic color and fruity breath suggested she'd had a few drinks; her breathless, exclamatory manner confirmed it. Rose had a way of conveying news that a glass or two of wine served to exaggerate. Sentences sprinkled with moments of prolonged eye contact as though she were waiting for the full import of whatever she'd said to sink in. Lots of touching. Deb did a wicked imitation of how a tipsy Rose could make the most banal pronouncement sound dramatic. *Hannah, the grass grows a little bit every day.* Deb would clutch Hannah's arm, stare into her eyes. *Every day, Hannah! Can you believe it?*

Still groggy from sleep, Hannah leaned her head back against the pillow. "What do you mean, she broke down?"

"I mean she broke down, Hannah." Rose engaged Hannah's eyes. "*Right in the middle of dinner.* She didn't even touch her filet. And she loves the way Kelly's does filets. They are *so* delicious." She licked her lips as though the taste still lingered. "Allan was wonderful with her, Hannah. *He is such a prince.* Why didn't you come? He was so disappointed."

"Yeah, I know, he called me. So tell me about Mom."

"Well, I ordered a carafe of burgundy." Rose smiled. "Allan took one sip of it and you'd have thought it was poison or something. *He's just used to better quality, Hannah.* You can tell that just by looking at him. Anyway, he orders this Chateau Neuf de something or other. Forty bucks a bottle. *I saw it on the wine list. Forty dollars!* I mean, it was good, but forty bucks for wine?"

"What about Mom, Rose?"

"That's what I was getting to. Well, we all had some of the wine Allan ordered, but then your mom also polished off the burgundy. *The whole carafe, Hannah.*"

"I know..." Hannah picked at a cuticle, to avoid eye contact with her aunt. "She's drinking too much. I'm going to have to talk to her."

"She is drinking way too much," Rose agreed. "*Way* too much. We were all talking so I didn't really notice how much she was drinking but then she started getting weepy. She thinks she's losing you and Faith, Hannah. And Deb, too, and she doesn't know what to do about it. *She was hysterical, Hannah.* Sobbing, mascara running down her face."

Hannah drew a deep breath. She had the clear sensation of a very large glass dome being placed over her head, a feeling she'd been getting quite often lately. "Deb's broken up with Dennis and moved back home," she said after a moment. "Why would Mom think she's losing her?"

"Because Deb's decided she's not moving back after all. She had a little tiff with your mom this morning and now she says she's going to move in with a girlfriend. *Hannah, your mother was so excited about having another grandbaby—*"

"Deb's not going to have the baby?"

Rose sighed. "That seems to be up in the air, too." She looked at Hannah for a moment. "You hungry?"

"Not particularly." She glanced at the clock by the bed. "It's after twelve, Rose."

"You know what I'd like? *Mashed potatoes.*"

"Mashed potatoes?"

"Mmm-mm. Yummy mashed potatoes. *With bacon bits, Hannah.*" Rose pulled back the quilt on Hannah's bed. "Come downstairs and talk to me while I make some."

"Rose..."

"I'll put sour cream in them."

"I don't want to eat mashed potatoes at midnight, I don't care what you put in them."

"Chives and cream cheese," Rose said in a wheedling voice. "Come on, Hannie, do it for your old auntie. What joy do I have in my life?"

"You've got plenty of joy." Hannah pulled on the red flannel shirt she'd worn the evening before over the knee-length T-shirt she slept in and stuffed her feet into a pair of terry-cloth mules. "Damn it, Rose," she protested as she followed her aunt out of the bedroom and down the stairs. ‘‘I promised myself I was going to stop this sort of thing.’’

‘‘Instant or the real thing,’’ Rose called from the pantry. ‘‘Ah hell, let’s make it easy. Instant’s okay when it’s fixed up.’’ She brought a box of Ore-Ida into the kitchen, held it at arm’s length while she read the directions. ‘‘Stop what sort of thing?’’

‘‘This.’’ Hannah pulled out a chair and sat down. ‘‘Do I want to be in the kitchen at midnight making stupid mashed potatoes? No, I want to be sleeping. So why am I here? Because you asked me and I couldn’t say no. I’m like that with everyone and I’m sick of it.’’

‘‘You have a gift, Hannah,’’ Rose said, still squinting at the box. ‘‘You are kindhearted, loving and a good listener. The world would be a better place if there were more people like you.’’ She took a gallon of milk from the refrigerator. ‘‘You think if I double the recipe, it’ll be enough?’’

‘‘You’re the only one eating,’’ Hannah said. ‘‘So Mom’s upset about Deb?’’ she prompted.

‘‘Not as upset as she is about you and Liam.’’

‘‘Maybe it’s time she realized Deb and I are both grown women.’’

‘‘She will always be your mother, Hannah,’’ Rose said. ‘‘And she will always worry. It’s what mothers do. God knows, I’ve tried to get her to do things with me, like that Single Sailors thing last week. She might have met a nice man with a boat, but it’s always you girls…’’

Wait until she hears Liam and I are taking Faith to the zoo tomorrow, Hannah thought. Her legs, bare below the nightshirt, were cold, and she scooted them up onto the chair, pulled the shirt down to cover them and wrapped her arms around her knees. ‘‘Liam and I are taking Faith to the zoo tomorrow,’’ she told Rose. Later, she knew, she would ask herself what misguided impulse had prompted this disclosure. The best answer she could come up with right now was that she needed to talk about it to someone. Even Rose. She saw the dismay on her aunt's face, watched as Rose set down the measuring cup into which she'd been pouring potato flakes.

"No." Rose shook her head sadly at her niece. "Please tell me you're joking."

"I'm serious."

Rose clutched Hannah's arm. *"Don't do it, Hannah.* Please. For your mother, for yourself, for all of us. *Don't do it."*

Hannah rested her chin on her knees. "But I want to."

"But I want to," Rose mimicked in a whiney, child-like voice. She picked up the cup again, measured out the potatoes and put them in a bowl. "That's a very selfish attitude."

"How is it selfish?"

"For one thing, it's going to worry your mother to death."

"So that's why I shouldn't do it?"

"No, not just that…"

"What then?" She knew she should probably stop. It wasn't as though Rose was going to come up with some compelling reason that would make her change her mind, but something perverse was making her press on. "Give me one good reason why I shouldn't go to the zoo with Liam and our daughter."

"Because…" Rose microwaved a cup of milk, poured it over the potato flakes, then returned to the refrigerator. "What has fewer calories?" she called over her shoulder. "Butter or sour cream? Ah, the hell with it." She brought a tub of sour cream and a stick of butter over to the table and looked at Hannah. "Because none of us want to see you waste yourself with Liam. Sweetie, we'd all feel so much better if you and Allan—''

''Just got married, moved into his house on Riva Alto Canal and had a couple more kids?''

Rose grinned. ''You are such a smart girl. Look, take it from your old aunt who's been married to two losers, there's nothing romantic about poverty. When the *va-va-va-voom* wears off with Liam, Allan's going to look a whole lot better. I'm telling you, he wouldn't hear of any of us paying anything toward dinner tonight. Can you believe that? And Kelly's isn't cheap. Just the broiled chicken is $16.95, which I think is ridiculous. *A piece of chicken,* Hannah. How much can—''

''I'm not marrying Allan, Rose.''

''Well it's early yet. Allan's not going to rush you. 'I know it happened kind of quickly,' he told us, 'but I knew from the moment I first saw her.'''

''He knows I don't want to get married. He's a nice guy, but I'm not in love with him.''

''Taste these.'' Rose shoved the bowl of potatoes at Hannah. ''Tell me what they're missing.''

''Rose…'' Hannah pushed the bowl away. ''I don't feel like tasting potatoes. I came down to talk about Mom.''

''We're talking about her.'' Rose held a spoonful of mashed potatoes out to Hannah. ''Come on, one little taste won't kill you. Butter? Salt?''

''Damn it.'' Hannah tasted the potatoes. ''Butter.''

''I thought so.'' Rose sliced a stick of butter in two and stirred one half into the potatoes. ''Hannah, your mother has always relied on you. You're the dependable one, she's always said that. Well, except for the Liam Lapse. Deb was the one who caused her problems, but now Liam's back and, honest to God, Hannah, I see her drinking more now and I think he's the reason why.''

Feeling beleaguered suddenly, Hannah stuck her elbows on the table, held her head in her hands. The whole thing with Liam was complicated enough without Margaret playing a central role in the drama. ''What about Deb? Mom's always crying to me about how she doesn't understand why she and Deb can't get along. And Deb's pregnant, for God's sake. Why can't Mom just give me a break and focus on Deb for a while.''

''Hannah.'' Rose looked at her niece. ''Your mom isn't worried about Deb, because she knows Dennis isn't taking Deb and the baby and running off to Ireland where she'll never see them again.'' She pulled up a chair beside Hannah, sat down and took her hand. *''Worry over Liam killed your father.''* Rose stared into her eyes. *''If you're not careful, your mother's going to drink herself into an early grave for the same reason.''*

''BUT I DON'T WANT TO GET UP,'' Faith grumbled when Hannah woke her at eight-thirty the next morning. ''I want to sleep some more.''

''Okay.'' Hannah sat on the edge of Faith's bed. ''Here's the deal. You can keep on sleeping, or you can go and see the koalas at the zoo.''

''The koalas?'' Faith rubbed her eyes. ''Like the ones on TV?''

''Yep.''

Faith grinned widely. ''I've been wanting to see the koalas forever. Now I get to. I'm *sooo* happy.''

''Well, good.'' Hannah selected a yellow sundress from Faith's closet, dug in the dresser drawer for a pair of matching socks. ''When you're happy, I'm happy.''

Which, she reflected, as she coaxed Faith into her

clothes, was exactly the sort of thing Margaret would say to her. *Not fair to put the responsibility for your own happiness on someone else's shoulders.* God, her neck was stiff with tension and the top of her head prickled. After the talk with Rose, she'd lain awake most of the night. Around four in the morning she decided that she couldn't assume all the responsibility for her mother's drinking. She was going to go to the zoo, because that's what *she* wanted to do.

Tonight she would talk to Margaret. Right now she wasn't in the mood for a confrontation.

A sweater for herself and a change of clothes for Faith bundled under her arm, she tiptoed down the stairs. The smell of coffee from the kitchen told her Margaret was already up and probably gearing for battle.

''Is Auntie Rose coming to see the koalas?'' Faith asked.

''No, sweetie.'' As they made their way down the stairs, Hannah eased Faith's arms into a white cotton sweater. ''Just you and me and...a friend of Mommy's.''

''Jen?''

''No, a friend you haven't met.'' God, she couldn't look at her daughter's face. Maybe this wasn't such a good idea. ''We'll talk about it in a little while, okay? Right now, I want you to go eat some cereal. I have to get dressed and make a quick phone call.'' She started back up the stairs. *Please don't tell Grandma where you're going,* she thought. *I'm not in the mood for a fight.*

Deb was not happy to be wakened by the telephone when Hannah reached her at a girlfriend's house. ''Jeez, Hannah it's like the middle of the night.''

''It's eight-forty-five in the morning. I've been up for two hours.''

"Well, good for you," Deb said. "Some of us like to sleep in."

"So what's the deal with you and Mom?" Hannah asked her sister. "Rose said you guys had an argument and now you're not moving back home. And what's this about the baby?"

"Jeez." Debra sighed noisily. "Of course I'm keeping it. Mom said something that made me mad, I can't even remember what it was now. Probably something about Dennis, and she was talking to me like I was a little kid and it pissed me off, so I told her I was rethinking the baby. Plus, she'd been going on and on about Liam, the whole doom-and-gloom thing and I was bored with listening to it."

Hannah stared at her reflection in the mirror and wondered if it was just the morning light that made her look as though she'd been up for three nights straight. "Do me a favor, Deb." She shifted the phone to her other ear. "Don't give Mom more stuff to obsess about, okay? I don't think I can take it. Rose said Mom got really plastered last night because she was so upset about us."

"About *you,* Hannah," Deb corrected. "Listen, can we talk about this later? How about I drop by around ten? Maybe we could go have breakfast."

"I won't be here," Hannah said. "Liam and I are taking Faith to the zoo."

"Liam! You've got to be kidding. *Why?*"

Hannah took a deep breath. "Because I want to."

"And *you're* telling *me* not to give Mom stuff to obsess about?"

Five minutes later—Debra's snort of disgust still ringing in her ears—Hannah walked into the kitchen to face her mother. Margaret's nostrils pinched in cold fury as she glared at Hannah. Obviously either Rose or Faith had broken the news. After Faith finished her cereal and went upstairs to get her backpack, Margaret turned on Hannah.

"Everything I've ever done for you and Debra, I've done because I love you and want what's best for you. The two of you have always been my first priority. Always." Her voice broke. "I can't believe you're throwing it all in my face."

"I'm not throwing anything in your face, Mom. This isn't about you." Hannah reached into the refrigerator and tried to harden herself to the appeal in her mother's eyes. Suddenly the outing seemed more trouble than it was worth. She could take Faith to the zoo herself and avoid all the anguish. "This is a day at the zoo. Period."

Margaret snorted. "Day at the zoo! You might be fooling yourself, but you're not fooling me. It's that man screwing up your life again. Not to mention confusing your daughter."

"His daughter, too, and he has a name." Hannah dropped a stack of paper napkins into a wicker picnic basket. "It's Liam. And I wish you would just accept this, Mom, because all you're doing is making it difficult for everyone."

"*I'm* making it difficult?" Margaret leaned her back against the counter. "*I'm* making it difficult because I'm concerned about my daughter and granddaughter? Why don't you open your eyes, Hannah? It's not going to stop with this, I'll tell you that right now. You might as well just go and buy the damn tickets to Ireland."

Hannah looked at her mother, suddenly weary of the argument. "Mom, does it ever occur to you that all of this is *my* problem? Faith's *my* daughter? Liam was *my* husband. Faith's *our* daughter. I appreciate you're concerned for us, but damn it, I have a right to lead my life without having to factor your reaction into everything I do.''

''No.'' Margaret shook her head. ''You're wrong, this isn't just *your* problem. You and Faith have lived in this house from the day she came home from the hospital. I was right here, in this kitchen, watching when she took her first step. Who picked her up from her first day at kindergarten? Who took her to swimming lessons? I could go on and on.''

''You did all those things because *you* wanted to do them, Mom. You begged me to let you pick her up from school. You think I wouldn't rather have done it myself?''

''Then you should have said something.''

''I know that now. Remember yesterday when you told me to start paying attention to my own feelings? Well, that's what I should have done. But I didn't, because you were always telling me how much you loved doing all these things and I decided it wasn't worth getting into an argument about it.'' She shook her head. ''But I've learned my lesson. I'm going to start doing what *I* want to do. And I want to go to San Diego with Liam and Faith.''

''*Liam.*'' Margaret said the name like a curse. ''You might have forgotten the state you were in when you were married to him, but I haven't.''

''How could I forget when you and everyone else reminds me of it on a daily basis? God, I am so sick of hearing about it. So I made a mistake. Big deal. Deb's made a few mistakes. Everybody makes mistakes in their lives.''

''But they learn from them and move on. All you're doing by seeing him again is compounding your mistake.''

"Liam deserves a chance to spend some time with his daughter," Hannah said. "It wasn't his fault—"

"You know what I'm sick of?" Margaret asked, her voice low and fierce. "I'm sick to death of hearing about poor Liam and his goddamned rights. Fine, do whatever you want, it's your life. If you're so besotted and foolish that you'll agree to whatever this idiot wants, there's not much I can do about it. I'll tell you this though, Faith's my granddaughter and if you think I'm going to let him steal her away, you'd better think again."

"Grandma!" Faith burst into the kitchen. "Look! I have five dollars and I'm going to buy you a present at the zoo."

"Oh, my goodness." With a visible effort to compose her expression, Margaret got down on her knees, wrapped her arms around Faith's waist and looked into her granddaughter's eyes. "That is *so* sweet of you. But you know the nicest present you could possibly give me?"

Faith smiled. "What?"

"Just be my little darling girl," she said, her voice breaking. "Grandma loves you very, very much. And you know what? When you come home tonight, Grandma will have a great big surprise for you."

HANNAH AND FAITH WERE WAITING outside the house when Liam pulled up in Miranda's Mercedes. Faith, in a yellow dress, was hopping on one foot and circling her arms like a windmill. Hannah wore a green sundress and looked as though she might have been crying. As he got out of the car and walked around to where they were standing, Liam realized his heart was pounding.

He smiled at Hannah, then squatted down so that he was eye level with his daughter. *His daughter.* Eyes exactly the same dark, almost-navy-blue as his own. Faith clutched her mother's legs and peered warily at him. "You must be George," he said.

"No." She shook her head.

"Fred?"

A glimmer of a smile suggested she was on to his joke. "Fred's a boy's name," she said.

"Ah, you're right. Let me think a bit. I know. You're Griselda."

She released her grip from Hannah's leg. "My name is Faith."

"Faith. That was going to be my next guess. Well, good morning, Faith." He held out his hand. "I'm Liam."

Her eyes briefly registered his hand, moved to his face. "Hi."

"Hi. Shall we shake?" Faith nodded slightly, and he took his daughter's small hand in his own. "Nice to meet you, Faith," he said.

She rewarded him with a broader smile. "Nice to meet you, too," she said.

He felt a little thrill of victory, glanced up and met Hannah's eyes. She was smiling, too. He looked back at Faith. "I don't know about you, but it seems awfully early to be up and around. I haven't even had breakfast. What about you?"

"I had cereal."

"Cereal." Liam pulled a face. "Are you all that keen on cereal, then?"

Faith looked up at her mother.

"He's asking if you like cereal," Hannah said.

"Not the kind we have now," Faith replied. "But Mommy said I had to eat it."

"And what kind is it you have now?" Liam asked.

"The kind that gets all soggy when the milk goes on it."

"There's nothing worse," Liam said. "Tell me though, what are your thoughts on doughnuts?"

"Doughnuts?" Faith grinned. "I love doughnuts, don't I, Mommy?"

"She's a huge doughnut fan," Hannah said.

"Could you eat two, do you think?"

"Three," Faith said.

"Three." He gave her a skeptical look. "Ah, come on."

"I can. If they're doughnut holes."

"Right then." He held out his hand again. "If you'll help me to my feet, I think we should go and find a place that sells doughnut holes."

They found a place as they headed south on Pacific Coast Highway toward San Diego. Faith had spotted a Dunkin' Donuts, and Liam made a show of slamming on the brakes and zooming up to the shop as though they were on a mission of great importance. Hannah had shot him a reproving look, but now as they sat across from each other at a plastic table by the window, watching Faith drop quarters into a video game, Hannah seemed relaxed and happy enough as she sipped her double nonfat latte, or whatever complicated thing she'd ordered, and he felt he could breathe a little easier. Only an hour into the day, but so far things were going well enough. He said so to Hannah and she smiled.

"Of course they are. You're buying her doughnuts and taking her to the zoo. What wouldn't be okay about that?"

"I suppose you're right." He drank some coffee from a paper cup. "You know, in my whole life, I doubt I've spent more than twelve hours with children. I never know what to say to them. I thought maybe she wouldn't like me."

She eyed him over her coffee cup. "Girls always like you, Liam."

"Big ones though. And even that's not always true."

"You're doing fine."

"Is everything all right with you?"

"Meaning?"

"Earlier, I thought you might have been crying."

"Yeah..." She shrugged. "My mother."

"Let me guess. She's not happy about my seeing Faith?"

"To put it mildly." She picked at the edge of her napkin. "We always seem to be fighting lately. I feel guilty for upsetting her and angry at the same time..." She paused, bit her lip and seemed to struggle for a moment. "My sister would just say to hell with her. She and Mom have never been that close. I don't know, maybe Mom just has a bad case of empty-nest syndrome, but I feel bad for her. Responsible."

"Your sister's not at home anymore?"

"Well..." She sighed. "It's a long story. Mom's never quite known where she is with Deb, but I think she figured somehow that Faith and I would always be around. Now she's scared to death you're going to take us away."

"The pirate's dad could do the same thing," he said. "How would she feel about that?"

"She'd miss us," Hannah said. "But..." She hesitated. "Allan's sort of won her over. Plus, she isn't afraid Allan will take us...Faith, I mean." Her face colored. "He won't take Faith off to Ireland where my mom will never see her again."

Liam watched Faith for a moment. Her ponytail had

worked its way out of the clasp and her shoulders tensed as she energetically steered the wheel on the video machine.

"It's strange really," he said, "all things considered. But I don't blame your mother for being concerned. I'm not sure how I'd feel if my daughter ended up with someone like me."

Hannah frowned across the table at him. "What?"

"Well, picture it yourself. Faith brings this boy home—"

"Years from now, of course."

"Of course. Years and years."

Hannah grinned. "Twenty at least."

"Let's say she's told you all about him, and you want to like him because she's so over-the-moon. And then you meet him and put him through the twenty questions rigmarole—"

"Like my dad did to you."

"Believe me, with your dad it was a lot more than twenty questions and he didn't like the answers to any of them. I wasn't close to being suitable. But you'll be that way with Faith, too. You'll want a boy who'll go on to college and become a doctor or something. Someone who comes from the same sort of family you do. Who doesn't eat his peas off a knife."

She laughed. "You never did that."

"Only because I could never get them to stay on."

And then they were both smiling, sitting there with a box of doughnut holes on the table between them, the smell of hot coffee in the air, watching their daughter shoot space aliens. Once, Faith turned to see them watching her, grinned, then went on with her game.

He looked down at their hands on the table. Hannah's nails were polished pink, and she wore a woven silver band on the middle finger of her right hand and something with a green stone on the index finger of her left hand. They'd both worn cheap gold rings when they were married. He would take his off before performances because it got in the way of the guitar strings. Hannah had clearly disbelieved his explanation though and looking back, it seemed that many of their fights had started around the same time every evening when he removed his ring.

"Liam..." She glanced up at him. "What you said yesterday about how we might still be together if my family had stayed out of our lives?"

He nodded. "Right."

"I was surprised, to say the least. Do you really think about it much?"

"I used to." His glance shifted back to Faith for a moment, then across the table to Hannah. "But I'd remind myself about the abortion and after a while...well, I came around to thinking that, all in all, it probably happened for the best. Like you said last night, we had a lot of strikes against us. In hindsight, I can see that you were in a pretty bad state. I think it says something about what a self-absorbed bastard I was that I couldn't recognize it myself."

"Self-absorbed? That's how you think of yourself?"

He shrugged. "Single-minded, intensely focused, tunnel vision. It all pretty much comes down to the same thing."

"You did used to get kind of wrapped up in the music. Especially when you were writing songs."

"Which was all the time." He laughed. "Remember when I nearly burned the kitchen down? What was it I'd done? Left a saucepan on the stove or something."

"A pot of chili. I came into the kitchen and there was

all this smoke billowing up and you hadn't even noticed.''

''Day-to-day survival sort of goes by the board when I'm really tuned in to what I'm doing,'' he said.

''Still?''

He nodded. ''Music at the cost of everything else.''

HANNAH KEPT REMINDING HERSELF of that as they drove down the coast to San Diego. Reminded herself every time she looked at Liam and pictured scenes starring the three of them. Seated around the dinner table, going on vacation together and, her favorite, grouped around a bassinet smiling at the newest addition to their family.

The fantasies both compelled and annoyed her. It wasn't as though she'd put her life on hold while she waited around for Liam to say he wanted them to try again. Besides, as she kept telling herself, this day wasn't about her and Liam. It was about Liam spending time with his daughter. Hannah was only along for the ride.

She'd tried to keep that thought in mind last night as she prepared for their trip to the zoo. After Liam had left, but before everyone else got home, she'd roasted chicken, made a green salad and Faith's favorite macaroni salad, defrosted a loaf of pesto cheese bread and baked a pan of chocolate brownies. Then shoved everything in the back of the refrigerator so Margaret wouldn't see it.

''So Faith…'' Liam turned his head slightly to address his daughter. ''I bet I know what you like best about the zoo.''

''What?''

''Uh…'' He furrowed his forehead, feigning deep

thought. "Wait, it's coming to me. I think it's...uh, right, I'm getting a picture of it. It's...the koalas."

"Hey." Faith kicked her foot at the back of his seat. "How d'you know that?"

"Because I know everything," he said.

"Everything?" Faith cackled. "Uh-uh."

"I do though. Ask me a question."

"Um. How many is nine hundred and forty-two million, million, million and six billion, million?"

Liam groaned. "Ah, Faith, how could you do it to me? That's the one question I don't have the answer to." He looked at Hannah. "You told her, didn't you? You told her to ask me that question."

"No, she didn't." Faith leaned forward in her seat to touch Hannah's shoulder. "You didn't tell me, did you, Mommy?"

"I never said a word," Hannah agreed.

"See! Mommy didn't tell me."

"But how do I know you and your mum aren't in cahoots?" Liam asked with a wink at Hannah. "How do I know you're not just sticking up for her?"

Hannah gave Faith's foot a little tug, resisted a sudden urge to reach over and give Liam a quick hug. She pictured it—her arm around his shoulders, the way he'd feel as she pulled him close. His quick look of surprise. They'd been studiously careful to avoid even the most casual physical contact. He'd apologized for accidentally grazing her arm as they left the doughnut shop. She'd leaned far back in her seat when he reached over to get his sunglasses from the glove compartment. A tacit agreement, it seemed, that this day was all about their daughter, not her parents.

The beach towns rolled by. Seal Beach, Huntington, Newport. In Laguna, as they stopped for a light, she watched three teenage girls in bikini tops and towels, wrapped sarong-style around their hips, saunter across the road, tossing glances over tanned shoulders. She'd only been a year or so older when she married Liam.

She shifted in her seat and brought her foot up under her, turning slightly so that she could see Liam without appearing to be watching him. His faded navy T-shirt had a small hole on the shoulder. His jeans were similarly worn, his feet thrust into a pair of battered brown sandals. Allan had an expensive and extensive casual wardrobe of color-coordinated shirts and pants. Once he'd complained that it had taken him two weeks to find exactly the right shade of cream shirt to go with a new pair of khakis. Everything was either too yellow or too beige, he'd told her. If she asked Liam what color shirt he was wearing, she knew without a doubt that he'd have absolutely no idea. The thought made her grin. A moment later, as though he'd read what she was thinking, he turned his head to smile at her. The physical impact was like a bolt through her body.

Blood rushing to her face, she turned to glance at the back seat where Faith had fallen asleep, her head bent awkwardly. Hannah unfastened her seat belt, kneeled up on the front seat and shifted her sleeping daughter to a more comfortable position. Back in her seat again, she sat with her knees close together, her eyes straight ahead, intensely aware of Liam's hands on the steering wheel; of his legs, his neck. They passed through Laguna, past massive Spanish-style homes that blocked all but brief glimpses of the ocean. Bougainvillea climbed white stucco walls, tumbled over wrought iron gates. Hands, legs, neck. Mouth. She shifted in her seat.

This day wasn't about her and Liam.

Her body hadn't quite got the message. Shoulders

touching as they'd stood at the kitchen window the day before. Mouth curved in a smile. Would he take her hand as they walked through the zoo? Kiss her when he dropped her off tonight?

Pay attention to what *you* want, Margaret had said.

CHAPTER EIGHT

SOMEWHERE BETWEEN the zebras and the monkeys, Liam made a decision. They'd been traipsing around for hours from exhibit to exhibit. Faith had liked the monkeys. She'd also liked the elephants, the zebras, the lions and the giraffes. And, of course, the koalas. Then it was a return visit to the lions, several trips to the petting zoo, a stop for the picnic lunch Hannah had packed and then a final ogle at the monkeys.

Faith's hand was warm and sticky in his as they trudged up the hill, past an enclosure of exotic birds. His shirt sticking to his back, Liam had looked down at her face, flushed with heat and exertion, her hair tangled and blowing, and known there was no longer any question of simply going back to Ireland and forgetting about her.

He wanted his daughter in his life.

Brid was wrong about it being either Faith or his music. There was room for both. In fact, by the time they'd packed up the food and headed over to the monkey exhibit, he'd worked out a plan that would have Faith spending part of every summer and every alternate Christmas with him in Ireland.

He stood with Faith and Hannah watching small gray monkeys dart from branch to branch. He would tell Hannah when they were back in Long Beach tonight. At the same time, they would also discuss when to tell Faith that he was her father. The thought excited him so much that it was all he could do not to rush them through the exhibits so that he could tell Hannah about his decision.

A daughter. He looked down at her. *My daughter.*

"Hey, Liam." Faith tugged at his hand. "Do you want an ice cream?"

"An ice cream?" He pretended to think about it. "Nah. What I'd really like is a nice big plate of brussels sprouts."

Faith's look said she was on to him. *"Uh-uh."*

"Sure. I love them. Great big green ones with lots of salt and pepper. I bet your mother likes them, too." He shot another look at Hannah. "Ask her."

"Mommy wants ice cream," Faith said. "Right, Mommy?"

"I think someone has already had more than enough sugar for one day," Hannah said. "How about an apple?"

"No." Faith's face crumpled. "I want an ice cream."

"I want an ice cream, too," Liam said.

Hannah looked at him long enough for him to understand that he'd made a strategic mistake. "On the other hand, an apple sounds good, too," he amended.

"Hey, Liam, you know what?" Faith smiled up at him. "Allan said when we go camping, we have to put bits of apple on the stick when we roast the marshmallows because if you eat too many marshmallows, your teeth will fall out."

Allan should go to hell, Liam thought. And, suddenly a cloud drifted across his horizon, colliding with all the sunny thoughts of the things he wanted to do with his daughter. Allan's role hadn't occurred to him. Allan—who would be there when he wasn't. Birthdays, outings, meals together. Liam couldn't stop Hannah from seeing Allan, or anyone else she wanted to see, but children's attention spans were short. He might have made a hit with Faith today, but in a week or so she'd hardly remember his name. She'd end up thinking of Allan as her real father and himself as a sort of fun uncle she saw a couple of times a year.

THEY RODE BACK to Long Beach in silence, Faith asleep in the back seat. Hannah had dozed a couple of times, woken to look at Liam, who seemed lost in his thoughts. It was a little after eight when they pulled up outside the house, the lights were on in the living room. The drapes twitched once, then the room went dark. Hannah glanced at Faith, still sleeping, then at Liam, his face shadowy in the dim glow from a streetlight. She hoped to God her mother and Rose weren't sitting at the kitchen table, waiting for a debriefing.

"It's been a nice day," she said. "Faith obviously enjoyed it. I did, too."

"So did I." Liam turned in his seat to look at her. "How long do you think Faith will remember me?"

"After today? I don't know." She felt, rather than saw, Liam's reaction and tried to soften the words. "Faith had a great time, Liam, but she's only six."

"She'll forget me," Liam answered his own question. "I'll be gone in a day or so, and she'll forget all about me."

Again, Hannah tried to think of something to say that would make him feel better. "I think you made an impression on her. I think she genuinely enjoyed being with you."

"Until the pirate's dad takes her camping, or back to the zoo, or whatever. And then what?"

She looked at him, unable to come up with an answer.

Or at least an answer that wouldn't hurt him. The truth was, he was right.

"I'll help you carry her inside," he said. "She'll be a dead weight."

Hannah got out, held the seat forward as Liam lifted Faith out of the car. Cradling his daughter in his arms, he followed Hannah up the driveway. As she unlocked the door, she felt her pulse speed up. From the kitchen, she heard a chair scrape.

"Okay," she whispered. "Let's take her straight upstairs."

He nodded. At the top of the stairs, Hannah pushed open Faith's bedroom door and stood aside for Liam to carry her in. Margaret called from the kitchen and Hannah tiptoed to the top of the stairs. "I'm up here, Mom. With Liam. We're putting Faith to bed."

When she returned to the doorway, Liam had removed Faith's sneakers and covered her with a folded blanket.

Seated on the bed beside their daughter, he turned around to look at Hannah. "She'll be out for the night, then?"

"Completely."

He smiled, his eyes taking in the room with its menagerie of stuffed animals and toys littered across the floor. "Well..." He stood. "I'd better be going. I've a radio interview in Los Angeles tomorrow early."

Outside Faith's room, they stood in silence for a moment, then Liam turned and walked down the stairs. Hannah followed him to the front door, opened it and stepped onto the porch, waiting for Liam to say whatever was on his mind. Her stomach suddenly felt tense with apprehension.

"I don't have this all worked out yet," Liam said. "But I want to be a father to Faith. A *real* father. I want to spend birthdays and Christmas with her, whether it's here or in Ireland. I want her to come to Ireland for her summer holidays. Before I leave, I want us to tell her I'm her father."

Hannah couldn't speak. Ireland. He wanted to have Faith with him in Ireland. *Exactly what Margaret had predicted.* "Maybe you're moving a little fast, Liam," she finally said. "You just said you don't have it all worked out. Maybe we need to think things through a bit."

"I want to be a part of her life. I want her to get to know me. I've already lost too much time."

"I understand that. But this isn't simply about what *you* want. It's about what's best for Faith. You've spent one day with her. There's a whole lot more to being a father than a day at the zoo."

"I'm sure there is," he said. "Until now, unfortunately, I haven't had the chance to find that out."

"Look, let me at least prepare her a little."

"Prepare her for what? The shock of hearing I'm her father?" He laughed. "Oh right, I forgot. She thinks I'm in heaven, doesn't she? I suppose that could be a bit of a shock..."

"Liam, come on, I'm not the enemy here. I'm concerned about my daughter...our daughter. If we do tell her, I want to be absolutely sure it's the right thing to do."

"You need to consult with your family first, is that it?"

"This isn't their decision, Liam. It's ours. Yours and mine." But even as she said the words, she recognized their fallacy. Expecting that her mother and the rest of the family would just quietly accept whatever she and Liam decided was unrealistic, to say the least. As if to underscore the point, the curtain in the living room twitched again.

"Let me ask you something." She studied his face for a moment, trying to read some indication of whether this was true commitment, or more of a spur-of-the-moment fantasy. "You're on the road most of the time. How can you devote any kind of quality time to her?"

"I told you I don't have all the details worked out."

"Maybe you need to do that before you make a decision like this."

"Really?" Liam asked. "And what then? If you approve, I can be her father? But if not, the pirate's dad gets the job? To hell with that." He turned as though to go, then stopped. "Your family decided once that I wasn't fit to be a father, they're not going to bloody well do it again. I'll be by tomorrow, about six. I want to see Faith before she goes to bed and then we'll talk."

HER HEART THUNDERING so hard she felt sick to her stomach, Hannah watched the Mercedes peel up Termino and out of sight. As she pushed open the front door, she heard footsteps in the hallway and then Margaret was peering anxiously into her face.

"Well?"

"Well what, Mom?"

"Well, how did it go?"

"It went fine." She pushed past her mother and headed for the stairs. All she wanted was to lie down on the bed and try to sort out her thoughts. Rose appeared from the kitchen. Rose and her mother were wearing matching purple fleecy robes trimmed with white piping. They'd seen them on sale at the May Company a month or so ago and, even though Margaret always sniffed that Rose had no taste when it came to clothes, both sisters liked the robes so much they'd each bought one. Rose had some sort of pale green mask on her face and her hair was pushed under a pink stretchy headband. Margaret's hair was pulled up into an elastic and she was holding a glass of white wine.

"Did he say anything?" Margaret asked.

Hannah stopped halfway up the stairs, looked down at her mother and aunt. "Anything about what?"

Rose grinned, sending bits of her mask fluttering to the floor. "Damn it, I need to get this stuff of my face." She looked up at Hannah. "Your mother's *terrified,* Hannah," Rose said. "She thinks he's going to take Faith back to Ireland,"

"Well, it's not exactly unheard-of, Rose." Margaret's voice was indignant. "Oprah had a show about parents who kidnap their own children. So don't act as though it's some outlandish thing I dreamed up."

"I tried to tell her." Rose addressed Hannah. "But Ms. Gloom-and-Doom always thinks the worst. I told her, no way does that guy want to be a daddy. He's a musician, for God's sake."

"Musicians *do* have families, Rose." Margaret looked at her sister as though she were talking to a slightly dim-witted child. "And he's Irish, no less. The Irish are big on family. Next thing you know, Hannah will be pregnant again—"

"And barefoot, Mom," Hannah said. "Don't forget about that. Barefoot, pregnant and living in a shanty."

"Don't be sarcastic," Margaret said. "I'm your mother. It wouldn't be natural if I didn't worry." She took a sip of wine. "So when does he plan on trying to see her again?"

Hannah watched her mother for a moment. "You

know what, Mom? I think you need to lay off the wine a bit. I'm worried about your drinking.''

AT SCHOOL the next morning, Jen threw a music magazine down on the table where Hannah was setting out little bottles of apple juice. ''Rocky subscribes to it. Your boy's got quite a photo spread,'' she said. ''Read the bit about the redhead.''

Hannah's eyes moved from the three pictures of Liam and Brid arranged around a center article. Liam playing a guitar, his face pensive. Liam, head bowed over a yellow notepad, a pencil in his mouth. Writing Songs, the caption read. The largest picture showed Liam on a city street somewhere. He wore jeans and a black leather jacket and stood slouched, unsmiling, against the plate-glass window of what looked like a nightclub. Visible inside, a stage with a microphone and band posters on the wall.

Beside him, Brid, with her chin on his shoulder, arms wrapped around his waist. She looked tiny and insubstantial, lost inside a heavily zippered black jacket almost identical to Liam's and, incongruously, a filmy white dress that came almost to her ankles. Just Good Friends, the caption read.

Hannah looked at Jen, who shrugged. ''So did you guys have a good time at the zoo yesterday?''

''Yeah.'' Unsettled now, Hannah forced herself to look away from the picture. *We're just good friends,* Liam had said. Not that his relationship with his singer mattered to her, anyway. ''Actually, it was pretty much Faith's show,'' she said. ''She had a great time.''

The kids started filing in for their snacks, and Hannah got very involved with handing out bottles of juice, aware of Jen watching her thoughtfully.

‘‘My mother’s a psychiatrist,’’ Morgan Montgomery announced as she took the juice from Hannah. ‘‘And she’s going to an important conference in San Francisco.’’

‘‘Great,’’ Hannah said. Liam was also going to San Francisco. Maybe she should go, as well. Grab a quick session with Morgan Montgomery’s mother and see if they could figure out why she kept having these totally unrealistic delusions about Liam falling in love with her and quitting the band to buy a tract home in Orange County so he could be a part of Faith’s life without taking her off to Ireland.

‘‘Are you going to see him again?’’ Jen asked after the kids had filed back out to the playground.

‘‘Tonight.’’

Jen grinned. ‘‘Cool. And…?’’ She wagged her head from side to side. ‘‘Sparks?’’

‘‘It’s not like that. He wants to see Faith.’’

‘‘And that’s it? There’s nothing else going on?’’

‘‘He wants to be…’’ She held up the first two fingers of each hand. ‘‘Quote, part of Faith’s life. That includes having her spend time with him in Ireland.’’

‘‘God.’’ Jen’s smile faded. ‘‘What are you going to do?’’

‘‘I don’t know yet. We’re going to talk about it tonight.’’

‘‘How did your mom take that?’’

‘‘She doesn’t know yet.’’

Jen shook her head. ‘‘Poor Hannah. I don’t know how you do it. If I lived with my mother, either I’d end up killing her or she’d kill me.’’

Hannah looked at Jen for a moment. ‘‘I think I need to move out.’’ Her face felt hot. Having said the words, it was as if she’d opened a box and released something that couldn't be put back. "I need a place of my own. Me and Faith. It's time."

"Because of all this..." Jen waved her hand at the magazine with Liam's picture.

"That and..." An image of Margaret and Rose in their purple robes waiting for her to come home flashed across her brain. "Just everything."

"CAN YOU BE READY in twenty minutes, Liam?" Miranda Payton's blond head appeared around Liam's bedroom door.

"Sure." Liam stood and stretched. The sky outside the window was the usual ceramic blue, and he could hear voices from the pool beneath his window. It sounded like Pearse. He set down the notebook he'd been using to jot lines for a song. His usual working position—crouched over the pages with the guitar lodged under one arm and a pen in the other hand. Spread over the floor were the pictures of Faith that Hannah had given him. Next to them, an old picture of Hannah he'd kept in his wallet.

Miranda's glance moved around the room; lighted on his guitar, the notebook, on a shirt he'd thrown over the back of a chair, lingered on the unmade bed and finally came to rest on the pictures on the floor. Liam waited for her to say something, but the silence lengthened, and finally she just looked at him and smiled.

"I don't mind driving up to L.A. if you've got something to do," Liam said. In fact, he would rather go alone, but Miranda had offered and since he'd be using her car, he couldn't think of a way to refuse without seeming rude. "I think I've got the hang of California motorways now."

"Freeways, Liam." Miranda revealed her perfectly

white teeth. She was wearing black. Trousers, skintight shirt and leather jacket. "Listen, cutie, there's absolutely no way you can talk me out of going. I am *so* excited. I've never been inside a TV studio before."

"It's not that exciting, Miranda." Liam dug through his battered gig bag for the list of media interviews Joel, his manager, had lined up. An interview with a reporter at a coffee shop on Sunset; a visit with a radio DJ who seemed quite enthusiastic about the band and a taping for a TV chat show. Not one of the big ones, according to Joel, but any exposure was better than none. "A load of blah-blah-blah," Liam said with a grin at Miranda. "That's what it really comes down to."

Miranda watched him for a moment. "That's what *you* say, Liam. I think there's much more to it than that." She bent to pick up the pad he'd left on the floor. "What's this? A new song?"

"Yeah." He reached for the notepad. "Let's have it."

She pulled it away, out of his reach. "'Faith,'" she read. "'Faith, faith, faith. Hope. Hannah. Faith. Love.'"

"Miranda."

"Sorry."

"Forget it." He stuck the notepad in the bag. "I'll go and see if Brid's got herself together."

"Wait, Liam." She caught his arm. "I'm sorry, really."

"It's nothing. Drop it."

"Kind of personal, huh?"

"I said drop it, Miranda. It's nothing. Just words. *Blah-blah-blah.*"

"MUSIC?" The landlord cocked his head slightly. "Yeah, I hear it. Thump, thump, thump. It's the kid next door. I've told him to keep it down, the walls are too thin for that sort of thing. Other neighbors complain, but—'' With a what-can-you-do-about-it shrug, he looked at Hannah. ''What d'you think?''

Hannah tried for something diplomatic to say. The duplex wasn't quite what she'd envisioned. ''I need to think about it,'' she said.

''Suit yourself,'' the landlord said. ''For what you want to pay, you're not going to get a luxury condo at the beach.''

True, but she'd hoped for something a little nicer. She followed him into a small hallway with scuffed hardwood floors. The faint smell of cigarette smoke and new paint filled her nose, and she tried to imagine bringing Faith home here. On either side of the hallway were two small bedrooms, painted stark white. Dusty, uncovered windows stared out like blank eyes onto the street. The largest room was half the size of the one Faith now slept in.

She felt her throat clog with tears. In a little over two weeks, she'd gone from being comfortably secure in the center of a warm and loving family to feeling suspicious, alone and slightly adrift.

''I've got three other people wanting to look at it,'' the landlord called. ''No skin off my nose if it's not what you're looking for.''

''Just give me a minute.'' She walked into the other bedroom and peered out the window. The view was uninspiring, but the window box could be filled with geranium cuttings. She turned from the window to look again at the room and thought about an ad for bed linens she'd seen in the latest *Redbook*.

The picture was exactly the way she'd like her bedroom to look. Shades of taupe, cream and off-white; muslin curtains fluttering in the breeze and a bed piled high with fluffy pillows and comforters. And—not shown in the ad, but materializing now in her brain—Liam on the bed, pillows propped behind his head. Wearing nothing but a faint smile as he watched her undress.

She slammed a door on the image. But took the place anyway.

THE TV HOST, Rachel something or other, was a skinny redhead with enormous black-rimmed glasses, crimson lips and the longest fingernails Liam had ever seen in his life. More like talons really.

He sat on a high stool on a set designed to look like a chic living room, listening to her describe his music as ''a touch melancholy, but also joyous and uplifting.'' Rachel sat opposite him on another stool, legs in sheer black stockings crossed at the ankles, her expression intense.

Ten minutes into the interview, Rachel had started to get on his nerves, tossing out idiotic questions that had little to do with music. Brid would have answered some of them if she'd been there; idiotic questions didn't bother Brid. But Brid hadn't been in her room when he'd knocked that morning. Hadn't been home last night when he'd got back from San Diego and, from her undisturbed bed, it appeared she hadn't been home all night. Anxiety about her wasn't doing much to improve Liam's mood.

''You've been quoted in the European press as saying you tend to live life on the edge.'' The interviewer leaned closer. ''What exactly did you mean by that?''

''I suppose that I'm bored when things get too predictable.'' He couldn't actually remember having made the remark, but it was the way he felt sometimes. ''Excitement, intensity, that sort of thing, make me feel alive. I'd be miserable going off to the same job every day, for instance. Coming home to the same house every night.'' *So how can you expect to be part of Faith's life?* Rachel was waiting for him to say more. He shrugged as if to say that topic was closed.

Rachel consulted her notes for a moment, then reeled off highlights from the band's history. ''Your second release, 'Betrayed,' made the UK charts a few years back,'' she said. ''And you've got a new release set for later this year.'' A quick glance at her notes. ''August. And Wild Rovers fans in this country can catch you…''

''In Santa Barbara next week, San Luis Obispo the next day, then San José and San Francisco.''

''And then?''

''And then back to Ireland to do an album and another European tour later this year.''

Rachel smiled. ''It doesn't sound as though you'd have time to be bored.''

''It's the way I like it,'' he said. *I want to be a part of Faith's life.*

Rachel leaned forward on her stool. ''What would you have been, do you think, if you weren't a musician?''

Liam thought for a minute. ''I don't know.'' He shrugged. ''An ambulance driver.''

''Really?'' She smiled at him. ''And why is that?''

''Danger,'' Liam said, improvising because he really didn't know why the hell he'd given her that answer. ''Catastrophe. Physical risks. All that sort of thing. I thrive on it.''

''Ah.'' Rachel's smile grew knowing. ''A man who craves intensity and stimulation, who abhors the dullness and meaningless of a mundane existence.''

''If you say so,'' he said, glad now Brid wasn't here

listening to this rubbish. She'd have hooted him off the stool. Except that it wasn't *all* rubbish. He thought of the guests at Faith's party, grouped around the barbecue in their color-coordinated golf clothes. The joker in the apron and a chef's hat. He'd die before he put on an apron. But he didn't need an apron to be a father to his daughter.

Rachel had another look at her notes. She held his glance for a moment before she asked the question. "You've been linked romantically with your lead singer, Brid Kelly."

He made eye contact with her. "I have."

"But you both deny there's any truth to it."

Liam folded his arms across his chest. "Right."

"Right you're linked romantically, or right there's no truth to it."

"The latter," Liam said.

"And is there anyone in your life right now?"

"There are a lot of people in my life right now."

"A special someone?"

"I don't discuss my personal life," he said.

HANNAH HAD GIVEN the landlord a check for first and last month's rent and, on her way home, she stopped to pick up a few things she'd need for the new place. Her fantasies called for linens and dishes from the Pottery Barn and Williams-Sonoma, but her depleted checking account dictated Wal-Mart. Outside her mother's house, she turned off the ignition, leaned her head against the back of the seat and tried to think. If she packed a little every night when she got home from school, she could move this weekend. Jen had offered Rocky's truck and his help for the cost of a couple of six-packs and a pizza.

First though, she had to get through this evening.

Liam's visit and—before or after, she hadn't decided—the little matter of telling Margaret that she and Faith were moving out. Her brain couldn't, wouldn't, deal with Faith spending her summer vacations in Ireland. The prospect was so unimaginable, it was easier not to think about it. Which was a little like trying to ignore an elephant in the living room. With a sigh, she opened the car door and started up the steps to the house.

Faith greeted her in the hallway.

"Grandma has a big surprise for you, Mommy."

CHAPTER NINE

"SHE DOES?" Hannah hauled Faith up into her arms, and grinned as her daughter's legs wrapped around her. "God, you're getting big," she groaned, setting her down. Grandma's big surprise for Faith yesterday had been an elaborate jungle gym, installed in the backyard while they were at the zoo. What Margaret's latest surprise might be she had no idea and didn't want to imagine. She nuzzled Faith's neck. "I have a surprise for you, too."

Faith pulled away to look at her. "You do?"

"Yep. Remember Liam? He went to the zoo with us yesterday? He's coming to see you tonight."

"He is?" Faith jumped up and down. "Yay. I like Liam. Hey, Grandma." She started up the stairs. "Guess who—"

"Faith." Hannah put her fingers to her lips. "Let's not say anything right this minute, okay?"

"How come?"

"Just because." *Great. This from a teacher at La Petite Ecole?* She drew a deep breath. "Where is everyone?"

"Grandma's upstairs working on your surprise and so is everyone else. I have to make you stay down here, because if you go up, you'll ruin everything. Wait here, okay?"

"Got it." Hannah dropped her car keys onto the small

wooden table by the front door, and leafed through the day's stack of mail. After she and Liam broke up, she used to make daily pilgrimages to this table, frantically searching through the mail for a letter from him. He'd never written. Or maybe he had, she thought now.

She sat on the bottom stair. A scent of baking apples wafted out from the kitchen, mingled with the Lemon Pledge polish her mother used. When her father was alive, the smoky vanilla smell of his pipe tobacco would drift through the house like a presence. Years from now, Lemon Pledge and pipe tobacco would still mean home. In her new place, she would use this organic polish she'd seen in Trader Joe's. Beeswax, or something. In *her* home.

More laughter from upstairs. On the wall above the hall table, a picture of herself at a year; ribbons in her hair and a frilled dress. Within the same frame, a picture of Faith plunging tiny hands into her first birthday cake. Other pictures ran gallery-style along either side of the wall.

Margaret had been obsessive about framing all school pictures, even the hated eighth-grade one. Zits and a mouthful of braces. Embarrassed and mortified by the picture, Hannah had removed it from the wall and hidden it at the bottom of her underwear drawer, praying her mother wouldn't notice it was missing. No such luck. The picture was back again the following day.

She looked at it now, thinking of all the dramas—major and minor—that had played out in this house. Now she was about to take her daughter to an anonymous place with no memories, no warm associations; a place where traces of other lives had been eradicated with a few gallons of semigloss.

"Hey, look who's finally here." Her mother appeared

at the top of the stairs. ''Hannah's home,'' she called out. Rose and Helen emerged from the spare bedroom; behind them, Joe Graves, the guy from down the road, his shirtsleeves rolled up to the elbow. They were all smiling.

''I get to put the blindfold on Mommy.'' Faith jumped up and down beside Hannah. ''Okay?''

''Here, honey, use this.'' Rose pulled off the red bandanna she'd worn around her hair and tossed it to Faith. It fluttered like a gaudy leaf and settled on the stairs. Hannah, slightly bemused, watched Faith scamper up to retrieve it.

''Okay, Mommy, bend down so I can tie this.'' Faith said. ''And don't peek.''

''I'm not peeking.'' Hannah felt Faith's small hands at the back of her head, tangling strands of hair into the knot she was trying to tie. After several failed attempts, Rose called out an offer of assistance, which Faith stoutly declined. Finally, with the scarf so loose around her face that she had to tense her neck to stop it falling off, Hannah felt Faith grab her hand and they started up the stairs. Eyes closed because she could see through the bottom of the blindfold, she laughed as she tripped on a runner. In her enthusiasm, Faith was practically dragging her up the stairs. ''Not so fast, sweetie,'' Hannah said, still laughing. ''I can't see where I'm going, remember?''

At the top of the stairs, they made their way hand in hand down the carpeted hallway. She heard a door open. Someone removed the blindfold.

''Ta-da!'' Her mother and Rose said in unison. Hannah could only stare in silence at the completely unrecognizable spare *room.*

"LOOK, BUDDY, she's made it pretty clear she doesn't want to talk to you," the bouncer from the club told Liam. "So why don't you do us all a favor and take a hike?"

"I will. After I've heard it from her." Liam stood in the litter-strewn alley outside the Hooligan, a club in downtown Long Beach where he'd finally tracked down Brid. Rock music drifted out on a wave of smoke filled air. The bouncer had a shaved head and a pierced left eyebrow. His shoulders filled the narrow doorway. "Let me talk to her, all right?" He made to push past the bouncer. "Five minutes, and I'm gone."

"I said beat it."

"Look, she's got problems—"

"No." The bouncer poked Liam in the chest. "You've got problems, buddy."

"She needs medical help, or she's going to die," Liam said.

"Yeah, well, we're all going to die one day," the bouncer said. "You, too. Sooner than later if you don't get the hell out of here."

Liam was considering his options when four girls in black leather strolled up. One of the girls had rings in her nose, purple hair and, it appeared, a suspicious ID. As the bouncer examined it, Liam slipped inside.

He saw Brid in the lap of a guy the size of a refrigerator. One arm wrapped around his neck, her long hair all over his face and shoulders, the other arm hanging loose at her side, fingers curled around an empty glass. Liam took the glass, set it on the table and tapped her on the shoulder. If she came with him without a fuss, he'd have just enough time to take her back to Huntington Beach before he went to see Hannah and Faith.

The blow to the side of his face knocked him off balance and he staggered slightly. Brid emerged from the guy's neck. ''Come on.'' Liam grabbed her arm and pulled her to her feet. Then he felt a thud to the back of his head.

BY FIVE-FIFTY, ten minutes before Liam was supposed to arrive, the tension in the back of Hannah's neck was so bad that she took Margaret's Advil from the cabinet above the sink and downed two pills with a glass of water.

Behind her, Rose, in her black hot-date pantsuit, lots of gold jewelry and bloodred sling-back heels, was telling Margaret not to wait up for her tonight because she had a feeling she was going to get lucky. Margaret in gray sweats and a harried look was clearly trying to pretend she wasn't watching the clock. Earlier, Deb had sent Margaret into a spin by announcing that she was off to see Dennis and maybe patch things up. Right now that was overshadowed by the Liam vigil.

''Nearly six.'' Margaret removed a half gallon of vanilla ice cream from the fridge and began spooning it onto dishes of apple crisp cooling on the counter. ''You're sure he's coming?''

''He said he'd be here at six, Mom.'' Hannah eyed the ice cream melting over the apples and wished that Margaret and Rose would go away so she could just gorge and not think about whether Liam was going to show or not show. God, her mouth was watering. She went to the sink and downed a glass of water. ''It's exactly six now.''

''Liam was always late,'' Margaret said. ''I remember you standing at the living room window, waiting for him to drive up in that old van of his.'' She dropped the spoon in the sink and returned the ice cream to the freezer. "I did tell you Allan called, right?"

"Twice." Hannah wandered over to the window. When Liam got here, they could sit outside. On the patio. Out of earshot. She ran upstairs, mostly to get away from Margaret and the apple crisp, but also because she'd decided the pink-striped shirt she was wearing was too…June Cleaverish. In her bedroom she stood at her dresser mirror frozen with indecision. Blue denim? White sleeveless? Cotton sweater? God, her hair looked ridiculous. She turned to check her backside in the mirror. Images of pencil-thin *Cosmo* models in designer jeans danced through her head, mouthing Liam's name as they laughed at her big butt. She thrust her arms in the blue denim, ran back downstairs.

"You changed your shirt," Margaret observed as Hannah reappeared in the kitchen. "What was wrong with what you were wearing?"

"I've decided to start living life on the edge, Mom. I want to be wild and crazy. I thought I'd start with this shirt."

"Don't be sarcastic." Margaret refilled her wineglass. "Maybe *I* need to get out of this house. I'm getting a little tired of your attitude lately, you and Deb. I don't know what I've done to make you girls so hostile. I really thought you'd be happy with our little surprise."

"I'm sorry, Mom. Really. It was a lovely surprise. I'm just…" She felt tears brimming and turned away so Margaret wouldn't see. While she'd been at school, Margaret and Rose had painted and papered the guest room. All her books had been neatly arranged in newly installed floor-to-ceiling bookshelves and, on the new computer station, in front of a new and ergonomically correct chair, was the latest Macintosh system. She'd wanted to cry then, too. The geometric-patterned wallpaper and sleek, contemporary chrome and glass furnishings were unlike anything she would have chosen for herself. And she was fine with her old computer which, she didn't have the heart to point out, wasn't compatible with the new Mac. Fine also with the cozy space she'd created in her own room. Brick-and-board bookshelves, a scarred old desk that had been her grandfather's and a rocker draped with afghans. Her place to retreat from the world.

With Margaret, Rose, Helen and Faith all eagerly awaiting her reaction, she'd just stared, dumbfounded, finally managing to stammer out a thank-you. They were all smiling and happy with this incredible gift they'd given her. A gift that had probably cost more than a year's rent on her new apartment.

"I know how much you wanted a place where you can keep all your books and papers," Margaret was saying now. "And we decided that right now was as good a time as any."

"It was either that or a trip to Acapulco," Rose said. "Which I personally would have preferred."

"Well, that's you, Rose," Margaret said. "Hannah's not the frivolous type. What about the wallpaper? I picked out the pattern. Helen wanted to go with that textured paint she has in her bedroom. Personally I don't care for it."

"Ralph Lauren," Rose said. "Twenty-five bucks a gallon."

"Ridiculous," Margaret said. "You're paying for the name. Maybe you should call Liam, Hanny. Maybe he's just held up by...something.

"He'll be here," Hannah said with far less conviction than she'd had ten minutes ago. Margaret was right,

Liam *was* always late. If he didn't arrive in the next half hour, she was going to put Faith to bed. *I want to be a part of her life.* She felt a hot surge of anger.

''Hannah, have some apple crisp,'' Margaret said. ''It's not fattening, I used honey instead of sugar and the ice cream's low-fat.''

''I don't want any, Mom.'' Hannah remained at the window.

''She's thinking about her weight,'' Rose said.

''No, she just likes that cherry filling better,'' Margaret said. ''Rose kept insisting it was apple you liked, sweetie, but I knew you'd rather have cherry. Ever since you were a little girl, you've loved cherry pie filling. It's Deb who likes apple. Hannah, it's ten after. You really should call Liam.''

''For God's sake, Mom—''

''Don't snap at me again,'' Margaret said. ''I'm getting a little tired of it. This is a different side to you, Hannah, and I can't say I like it very much.''

''Well, time for me to go,'' Rose said. ''Wish me luck. This guy is *loaded.* By the way, Hannie, the mini-blinds were my idea. How d'you like them?''

''They're great.'' Hannah turned to look at Rose. ''Terrific.'' Her head was killing her. She looked at the clock. Six-twenty. Where was Liam?

''BUT I WANT TO STAY UP and see Liam.'' Faith sat in the tub, splashing water with her foot. ''Please, Mommy. I want to show him the picture I made.''

''I know, baby, but it's after seven and you've got school in the morning.''

''Quit calling me baby,'' Faith protested. ''I'm not a baby.''

Despite herself, Hannah smiled at Faith's indignation. "But you're my baby."

Faith frowned, not entirely appeased. "Okay, but just don't call me that." She grabbed the red plastic bucket that contained all her bath toys, and held it under the surface of the water. "Will you call him and tell him to come tomorrow?"

"We'll see. Come on, before you turn into a prune." Trying for a calm she didn't feel, Hannah lifted Faith out of the tub and toweled her dry. After she'd tucked her daughter into bed, she used the phone in her own room to dial Miranda Payton's number. No answer.

Damn him. She stared at her reflection in the mirror; picked at a zit on her chin, brushed her hair, sat down on the edge of the bed, got up again. At the window, looking out at the dark of the backyard, she rehearsed what she'd say to him when he finally showed up. Then it occurred to her that he probably wasn't going to show up. She dialed Miranda Payton's number again. A guy answered. Irish accent, but it wasn't Liam.

"Haven't seen him," he said. "Hang on, I'll see if anyone else knows."

"Thanks." Hannah loosened her grip on the receiver. *It's not me you're hurting,* she imagined herself telling Liam. *Personally, I don't give a damn what you do. But I won't let you hurt Faith.* She could hear music and laughter and then the guy came back on the line.

"Someone said he went to a bar somewhere to look for Brid," the guy said. "I didn't get the name of it, but if you hang on I'll find out."

"Thanks, I don't need it."

"Shall I tell him who called?"

"No." Her hand shaking, Hannah replaced the receiver. God, she couldn't deal with this. *In a bar with*

Brid. While his daughter was waiting to show him the picture she'd drawn for him. She stood in the middle of the room trying to think. Why was she surprised? Had she expected anything more?

"Hannah," her mother called from the bottom of the stairs. "How about some tea?"

Hannah squeezed her eyes shut. Obviously Liam wasn't going to make it, so she might as well move on to the next item of the evening and break the news about the apartment. "I'll be down in a minute," she called.

Margaret was on the couch in the living room. She'd lit a fire and changed into her purple robe. The TV was on with the sound off and Judge Judy was admonishing a guy with a huge beer belly. Even voiceless, Judge Judy struck Hannah as formidable. *If you were stupid enough to be taken in by him,* she could imagine Judge Judy snapping at her, *you deserve what you got.*

"So Liam didn't show up," Margaret said.

"Sure he did, Mom," Hannah said, irritated at her mother's I-told-you-so tone. "He's sitting here on the couch. You can't see him?"

"Come on, Hanny." Margaret's glance drifted over to Judge Judy for a moment, then she patted Hannah's knee. "You're upset."

"I'm not."

"Yes, you are." Margaret reached for a glass of red wine on the coffee table. "I'm your mother, I think I can tell when my daughter's upset. I can see it in your face."

"I'm only upset because you keep telling me I'm upset, damn it." Hannah sat down on the couch, and picked at a worn spot on the upholstery. Okay, that wasn't entirely true. When she looked up, her mother was watching her. "I thought you were drinking tea."

''I was.'' Margaret smiled. ''Now I'm having a glass of wine.''

''I think you're drinking too much, Mom. Rose thinks so, too.''

''Oh, Rose should talk. She isn't exactly averse to a glass or two herself.''

''I'm talking about you, Mom.''

''Have I ever complained about a hangover? Ever not been able to get up in the morning? Ever got a DUI?'' Margaret brought her feet up on the sofa, and tucked her robe around them. ''Don't worry about me, Hannah. Worry about yourself. Worry about what Liam is doing to you. I knew he'd let you down. If you'd asked me before you invited him over, I would have told you.''

''Mom.'' Hannah caught her mother's hand. ''Sit down. I need to talk to you.''

''What is it? Bad news? You're not preg… Rose said she thought you'd put on a few pounds, but…'' She stood. ''Let me get the pie first. Do you want a piece?''

''Damn it, just sit down, okay?'' She waited until Margaret sat down again. ''I'm not pregnant. We're going to move out. Me and Faith. I rented a duplex on Tenth Street.''

Her mother's face froze. There was a moment of silence while she appeared to absorb the blow. Then, her expression stricken, she reached into the pocket of her robe and pulled out a tissue. She dabbed it at her nose. Moments passed.

''Tenth Street,'' she finally said. ''God.''

Hannah frowned, puzzled. ''What?''

''*What?* Tenth Street, that's what. I mean anything above Fourth is…I can't believe you're going let my granddaughter live on Tenth. I swear to God, this wouldn't have happened before Liam came back on the scene. There's no way you would have rented anything on Tenth Street. God—''

''Mom. Stop, okay? You're driving me nuts.'' The street numbers increased as they moved away from the ocean, and she'd forgotten about her mother's dictum that the only decent place to live in Long Beach was below Fourth. Preferably below Second. Tenth wasn't even on Margaret's geographic compass.

''What about Faith? What if she wants to play outside?''

''The neighborhood is perfectly safe, Mom. Or I wouldn't have rented the place.''

''I knew this would happen,'' Margaret said. ''I told Rose. I said, 'Just wait, he'll fill her head with all these ideas and the next thing you know she'll be moving out.'''

''Mom, this has nothing to do with Liam. I want my own place. I want Faith to have her own home. It's just time.''

''He's moving in with you, isn't he?''

Hannah took a deep breath. Her mother's lower lip was trembling. Guilt battled with irritation. And won. She put her arm around Margaret's shoulders. ''Come on, Mom. I know this is hard for you. I know you love having Faith around, but you'll still be a part of her life. Our lives.''

Margaret brought the tissue from her sleeve and dabbed at her eyes again. A tear splashed onto the lap of her purple robe. ''I can't imagine getting up in the morning and not seeing her little face when I come down to breakfast.''

''Mom.'' Tears prickled in Hannah's nose. She caught Margaret's hand, held it for a moment. ''Please try to understand. This isn't easy for me either…''

"So this means it's all over with Allan?" Margaret asked.

"This has nothing to do with Allan. I've just decided I want my own place."

"I know what it is," Margaret said. "You're still angry at me for what I said to Liam, and this is your way of punishing me."

"I'm not punishing you. This isn't about you." But she wasn't sure. *Was* she moving out to punish Margaret for lying to Liam? And, in doing so, was she also punishing Faith? Maybe even herself?

Margaret picked up her empty wineglass from the table and carried it into the kitchen. The phone rang once. Heart thundering, Hannah glanced around for the receiver that was always getting lost under sofa cushions. By the time she'd found it, the line was dead. She went into the kitchen. Margaret was refilling her wineglass.

"Who was on the phone?" she asked her mother.

"Some guy for Rose," Margaret said.

"I thought it might be Liam."

"Some guy for Rose," Margaret repeated, her back to Hannah. "Next thing I know, she'll be moving out, too. Then Deb, although at least Deb's always likely to come back the next day. So *is* Liam moving in?"

"Damn it." Hannah glared at her mother. Anger, like a bucket of red paint, obliterated all other emotions. "Do you want to know a big reason I'm moving out?"

"All I know is you never mentioned moving out before you-know-who showed up on the scene."

Hannah gritted her teeth. Margaret *was* going to drive her crazy. Any minute now she'd start gibbering. She paced the room, trying to calm down. "I want you to listen to me, okay? Just listen. This has nothing to do with Liam. Nothing to do with Allan. Nothing to do with Prince Charles, nothing—''

''Prince Charles? What does he have to do with—''

''Listen to me, Mom. Just listen. I'm trying to tell you this has nothing to do with a guy. I'm not pregnant. I'm not getting married. No one's moving in with me. I just want a life of my own.''

''Well, you have a life of your own now.''

''No, I don't. I have a life under a microscope. Everything I do is endlessly discussed—''

''Discussed?'' Her mother's expression turned indignant. ''If you think we sit around discussing you, you're wrong. Like I said to Rose, Hannah's life is her business.''

''Mom, that's exactly what I'm talking about...'' What was the point? She peered into her mother's face. ''Be happy for me, okay? Think of all the extra time you'll have not cooking and picking up after me and Faith.''

Margaret managed a brave little smile. ''You're my life, honey, you and Deb and Faith. Whatever I do, I do willingly because I love you.''

THE NEXT DAY WAS a school holiday, and Hannah came home from her run to find Faith in the kitchen crouched next to a wicker basket.

''A late birthday present from me and Max,'' Rose told Hannah. ''My new sweetie. His dog had eight puppies. This little guy was the last one left.''

''My whole life, I've always wanted a puppy exactly like this.'' Faith held the tiny caramel color puppy up to her face, squealing as it licked her nose.

Rose laughed. ''Your whole life, huh? Wow, *my*

whole life, I've been looking for Prince Charming.'' She looked at Hannah. ''Cute, isn't he? The puppy, I mean.''

Hannah cupped her hand behind her neck where a massive knot of tension had not been relieved by the run. The rental agreement she'd signed clearly stated no pets. She looked at Faith, stretched out on the floor, flat on her stomach in deep eye-to-eye communion with the puppy, and walked over to check the cork bulletin board on the wall where telephone messages were pinned.

Allan had called. Liam hadn't. Not that she'd expected him to. Except she had. And he hadn't. No apology for disappointing his daughter. Nothing. She glanced at Allan's message. ''Just wanted to tell you I miss you,'' it read. Rose was watching her, so she opened the refrigerator and hid her face among the cartons of yogurt and cottage cheese.

''What did you have for breakfast?'' she called to her daughter.

''Ice cream,'' Faith said.

''Ice cream?'' Hannah glanced over her shoulder at Faith. ''For breakfast?''

''My specialty,'' Rose said. ''That and boiling water, but water's iffy. I tried to talk her into a jelly doughnut, but she wanted Ben and Jerry's.''

''Liam bought me doughnut holes,'' Faith said. ''And I ate three.''

''No kidding,'' Rose said. ''I bet you really like Liam, huh?''

''Uh-huh. He's nice. He put me on his shoulders.''

''Wow, that sounds like *fun,*'' Rose said. ''So are you guys going to do some more fun things with him?''

''Maybe if Mommy calls him. I did a picture for him.''

''Faith.'' Hannah emerged from the refrigerator and

glared at Rose. Then she addressed her daughter. ''Go upstairs and get all your clothes out of the hamper and bring them down so I can start a wash.'' She waited until Faith was out of earshot. ''Don't pump her for information,'' she said. ''If you want to know something, ask me.''

''Oh, lighten up,'' Rose said. ''What's the big deal? Liam's some sacred topic no one can discuss? Your mother's the same way. I mention Liam's name and she screams at me that it's none of my business. *Excuse me?* Aren't we all family here?''

Hannah put the kettle on for tea. One thing had just become a whole lot easier. If Liam still had any ideas about being part of Faith's life and taking her off to Ireland, he could damn well forget them.

''Hey, Mommy.'' Faith ran into the room, a pile of laundry in her arms. ''Guess what I'm going to call my puppy?''

Hannah stared at the dog, her mind blank.

''Spot?'' Rose asked.

Faith frowned. ''But he hasn't got any spots.''

''I'm going to call him Raisin. You know why, Mommy?''

''You okay, hon?'' Rose interrupted. ''You're not upset about…'' She nodded in the direction of Faith, now on her back, the puppy extended above her at full arm's length. ''I just thought since we all felt so bad when Turpin passed on, it was time for a replacement. And Faith's been wanting a puppy forever.''

''Forever,'' Faith echoed. ''And now I've got one. And his name is Raisin because he's got eyes like little raisins. Hey, Grandma,'' she called as Hannah's mother appeared in the doorway. ''I've got a puppy.''

''A puppy.'' Margaret shook her head slightly as

though she couldn't quite comprehend the situation. She looked from Hannah to Rose. "Where did he come from?"

"Me," Rose said, then she laughed. "Well, not me literally."

"No, Rose, I didn't think you meant literally," Margaret said. "Well, I just hope this apartment Hannah rented allows animals."

"Apartment?" Rose looked at Hannah. "You're moving out."

"Mom." Hannah gave her mother a warning look. Faith had been asleep when she'd gone on her run, so she'd decided to tell her later. That was before she'd learned about the puppy. The phone rang. Hannah watched her mother answer it. She could feel Rose staring at her, obviously dying to ask about the apartment. Margaret hung up and came to sit at the table.

"Well, how about this for a piece of news?" She looked at Hannah. "That was Helen. She's watching the local news." She lowered her voice and leaned across the table. "Liam was in some kind of brawl last night. The cops had to break it up."

CHAPTER TEN

LIAM SAT in a marina coffee shop eating a concoction of scrambled eggs, chilli peppers and avocado. He'd walked over to the marina from Miranda's house and brought a notebook with him, thinking about a song he wanted to write. He'd half finished it, then run out of inspiration. Another half-finished song to add to the pile. His life was full of half-finished things.

A waitress in white shorts and a blue shirt smiled at him and held a coffeepot above his cup. He glanced up at her, nodded and waited for the inevitable remark.

"Walked into a door, huh?"

"Right," Liam said. Since the fight the night before, he'd heard a dozen variations of the comment. "It was in my way," he said. The waitress smiled and he watched her move on to the next table.

The incident last night had turned out to be more of an embarrassment than anything else. He'd blacked out briefly but was fully conscious by the time the cops arrived. If the cop hadn't recognized him and Brid from a publicity photo, the whole thing would have been just another bar scuffle. As it was, he'd been treated to a lecture from the cop and warned to stay out of trouble. The bar owner hadn't pressed charges, but he'd obviously tipped off the media because the following morning, Miranda had woken him to say there was a reporter on the phone. He hadn't taken the call.

He ate a forkful of eggs, and speared a piece of avocado. He'd eaten more avocado since he'd been in California than he had his whole life. He pushed his plate aside and watched a gull make a dive for a bit of orange peel garnish.

At the zoo, Faith had charmed him out of some change to buy birdseed. She'd held out her palm for the birds to feed, then retracted it, squealing whenever a bird swooped down. He'd watched Hannah watching their daughter and told himself he wanted a life like that. Sunshine and family outings. And then he'd returned to Miranda's to hear that Brid hadn't come home and it was as though he'd stepped out of one world and back into another. Now, thinking of Faith and Hannah again, it seemed he had a foot in each world.

You have to make a choice, Brid had said.

He finished his food, glanced at the check the waitress had dropped off and put some bills on the table under his plate. His thoughts still on his daughter and her mother, he made his way back to Miranda's. Past a waterside bar, past a bagel shop and past a Realtor where the pictures pasted in the window showed million dollar properties with red-tiled roofs and ocean views.

At a pay phone, he dug in his jeans for Hannah's phone number. He listened to a phone ring three times, and then her mother answered.

"Don't hang up again, Mrs. Riley," he said, expecting to hear the click of a disconnection. "It's Liam. May I talk to Hannah, please."

"She doesn't want to talk to you," Margaret Riley said.

"She can tell me that to my face," Liam said.

"She's not in," Margaret said.

He leaned his back against the wall. From where he

stood, he could see the boats rocking in the slips. A middle-aged man in white shorts and a blue shirt wheeled a wooden cart down one of the gangways. "When do you expect her back?" he asked.

"I've no idea."

"Look, I don't want to cause a scene, Mrs. Riley," he said, "but this is the third time you've given me the runaround. I intend to speak to Hannah one way or another, if I have to camp out on your front doorstep."

"Why are you doing this?" Margaret Riley asked. "Why are you trying to push your way back into Hannah's life? She doesn't need it, neither does Faith. If you had any feelings for either of them, you'd leave them both alone."

"If you'll excuse my saying so, Mrs. Riley, that's my business. And Hannah's."

"Hannah's my daughter," she said.

"And Faith's my daughter."

She laughed, a humorless bark. "You can throw the term around, Liam, but you're not her father in the real sense of the word—"

"Because I was robbed of the chance to be."

"Robbed." She gave another laugh. "Look, if you're expecting an apology, you're going to be disappointed. If you were honest with yourself, you'd admit you weren't prepared for the responsibilities of taking care of a wife or child. And you're still not. My daughter sat at home waiting for you last night, while you were out getting arrested for a bar brawl."

Liam thought of the day Margaret Riley had told him about Hannah's abortion. She hadn't asked him in—they'd stood at the front door talking. Her teeth had been chattering and she had worn a gray cardigan that had a bulge in the sleeve just above her wrist. A tissue, it turned out, with which she dabbed at her nose continuously. He'd been reminded of his Auntie Maude; always a hanky up her sleeve ready to swipe snotty little noses. And always candy in her apron pocket. One of the few good memories of his childhood. Margaret had been so distraught on the porch that day that he'd had an irrational urge to assure her everything would be all right.

"You were a bad influence on her," she was saying now. "Do you have any idea at all what a fragile emotional state she was in? If her family hadn't stepped in, I hate to think what might have happened."

Liam shifted the phone to his other ear. Now, as he had back then, he wanted to hate her, but felt mostly sympathy. What did he know about the whole loving family bit? After his ma walked out, he'd been like an odd bit of luggage, carted around from place to place, no one quite sure where he belonged, or in any hurry to claim him. No big loss either if he went missing and never turned up again. For Hannah, things couldn't have been more different.

"Look…" he started. "That's in the past, there's nothing to be gained in going over and over—"

"It was all over the news about your bar brawl." Margaret went on as if he hadn't spoken. "Hannah was shocked, of course, although why it would surprise her I don't know. It goes with your lifestyle, as far as I can see."

"*Is* Hannah there?"

"Ever since you came back into the picture, nothing we do is right for her. She fights with me, she criticizes my sisters. We've bent over backward to make her happy and what does she do? Last night, she announces that she's moving out."

Liam said nothing, but the news surprised him. He'd

had the impression that Hannah and Faith were quite happy living in the family home. He tried to remember whether Hannah had said anything about moving during their trip to the zoo. He remembered her red eyes that morning.

''It's her life, of course, which is what I'm always telling her,'' Margaret said. ''Far be it from me to interfere. It's just her reason for moving out that upsets me. She denies it, but I know it's because she's got this idea that you were wronged and now she doesn't trust any of us, so she's uprooting herself and my granddaughter...'' Her voice cracked. ''Look, I'm begging you, please leave her alone.''

''I WANT TO MAKE Rocky something really incredible for dinner,'' Jen told Hannah as they walked down the aisles of the Trader Joe's on Pacific Coast Highway, checking out the bags of gourmet pasta and imported mustard. She held up a plastic bag for Hannah's inspection. ''Look. Squid pasta. See, it's shaped like little squiddy things.''

''But it's black.'' Hannah pointed out. ''You think he'd go for black food?''

''Yeah, good point.'' Jen set the pasta back on the shelf. ''They had this really cute heart-shaped pasta for Valentine's Day and I knocked myself out making a great alfredo sauce to go with it. He wouldn't touch it.'' She shifted her basket to the other arm. ''So what's the word on Liam?''

''Nothing... Well, I called the place he was staying in Huntington Beach and the woman who answered said he was out somewhere, so I guess they don't have him locked up in jail.''

''But he hasn't tried to call?''

''Nope.''

''Maybe he did and your mom didn't give you the message.''

''No, I don't think she'd do that. She'd figure I would find out somehow.''

''So how does Faith feel about moving?'' Jen asked.

''She isn't happy. She doesn't understand why we have to move if we can't take the dog, and now my sister and aunts are giving me these lectures about being selfish.'' Earlier that morning, as she'd left the house to drop Faith off at her friend Tiffany's, Deb had asked Faith for a few minutes to ''talk to Mommy about private stuff,'' then angrily accused Hannah of putting her obsession with Liam in front of Faith's happiness. And then Rose, who was thinking of moving in with her boyfriend, had begged Hannah to reconsider moving because it would leave Margaret alone. ''I'm suddenly the monster,'' Hannah told Jen.

''Screw them,'' Jen said. ''It's your life. Faith can go visit the dog at your mom's house. Don't let it get to you. What time do you have to pick up Faith?''

''Not till six.''

''Want to have lunch?''

''Actually, I think I'm going to track down Liam.'' She dug in her purse for her billfold, fished out a five-dollar bill for the parmesan cheese and pasta she'd picked up. ''Not because I give a damn if I ever see him again, but we need to have a little chat about his intentions regarding Faith.''

Ten minutes later, as she drove slowly along the street of expensive waterfront homes where Miranda Payton lived, Hannah tried to talk herself into actually parking the car, getting out, knocking on the door and asking Miranda if she could talk to Liam.

The problem was, she didn't want to do it. Didn't

want to see the beauteous Miranda, with her cleavage and hundred-watt smile. Didn't want to look like some desperate groupie stalking Liam. Didn't want to hear his justification for choosing Brid over Faith. Didn't want to be so damned obsessed with Liam Tully that she'd allowed him to invade her every waking thought and pretty much take over her dreams, too.

Faith. I'm doing this for Faith.

Outside Miranda's house, she peered through the tangle of bougainvillea to the front door. She lost her nerve and drove around the block again, past the house and back onto Pacific Coast Highway. At the next light, she pulled into the left-hand lane, made a U-turn and returned to Huntington Harbor. Miranda lived on a cul-de-sac. She drove past the house, parked two doors away outside a mansion with green-and-white awnings and a bubbling fountain in the front yard.

The engine idling, she tried to talk herself out of confronting Liam. Since he hadn't called, or come to see her, his talk about wanting to be part of Faith's life was apparently just that—talk. One option was to simply accept it. Deal with it by not dealing with it. As she'd pointed out to Liam, Faith would quickly forget him. Why stir things up?

A Mercedes convertible drew up behind her and parked at the curb. Through the rearview mirror, Hannah watched a tall blonde in white jeans and a black bikini top get out, then disappear into the tropical foliage.

Hannah pulled down the mirror, and stared at her reflection. God, why did she have to look so damn *wholesome?* If they were casting her in a movie, she would be the girlfriend from Iowa. She dug into her purse for lipstick. She couldn't let him just leave. Nothing had been resolved. If Liam walked out of her life again, it wouldn't be until they'd cleared up a few things.

As she pulled up outside Miranda's, the front door opened and Liam walked out. He wore baggy khaki shorts and a black T-shirt. *Liam.* Blue eyes, wind-tussled hair.

Once he'd been her life. Now he wasn't. Her life would go on without him in it. But God, no one had ever made her heart beat as hard as it was doing right now. Her face felt hot as she stretched across the passenger seat to look at him through the open window.

"We need to talk," she said.

ONE HAND ON THE ROOF of Hannah's little red Toyota, Liam leaned into the car. Her yellow shorts and sleeveless white shirt were all summery sunshine, but her face was tense; her fingers were locked in a death grip around the steering wheel. He met her eyes for a moment and then, on an impulse, climbed in and slammed the door.

"Drive somewhere," he said.

She didn't move. "You have a black eye."

"I hadn't noticed, but thanks for pointing it out. How's Faith?"

Her jaw tightened. "Faith's fine."

"I'm sorry I didn't make it over to see her last night."

"Really." She flashed a tight smile. "Well, that was easy, huh? You're sorry and now everything's fine."

"Hannah, look…I couldn't help—"

"Of course you could. You had a choice. You could spend the night hanging around bars tracking down your singer, or you could be with Faith. Faith lost out."

He looked at her. "I'm sorry, Hannah. I mean that. I'm sorry if my apology isn't enough. I'm sorry that I disappointed Faith. I'm sorry. What do you want me to do?''

''What do I want you to do?'' She stared at him. ''What do *I* want you to do? Well, let's see. For starters I want you to think about what you really mean when you say you want to be part of your daughter's life.''

''Hannah, look—''

''No, you look. Being a father isn't something you just do when it suits *you,* Liam. It's a full-time commitment, one you're obviously not ready to make. You might be her biological father, but you know nothing about what it really means to be a father. So, to answer your questions, what I want you to do is stay the hell out of Faith's life.''

Liam felt her anger like a blow to the chest. Her eyes blazing, body tensed, clearly ready to pounce on the next word from his mouth. It struck him that he'd never actually been the recipient of Hannah's anger. She'd been upset with him before, but she'd tended to withdraw rather than fight back. In the past, he'd never been quite sure where he stood with her. This time he had no doubt.

''Can we continue this somewhere else?'' he asked.

''I have nothing else to say.''

''Well, I do and I'd like a chance to say it. But not here.''

''Where?''

''I don't know.'' He saw the massive oak front door to Miranda's house swing open. Miranda's blond head emerged briefly, then disappeared. ''Anywhere. Someplace where there aren't multimillion-dollar houses and other testimonials to conspicuous consumption.''

She put the car in drive and pulled slowly away from the curb.

''I'm a hypocrite,'' he said. ''If it weren't for Miranda's multimillion-dollar place, we'd all be kipping in some fleabag.''

''One of your many character flaws,'' she said, but there was less heat in her voice.

''A veritable walking flaw,'' he said. ''That's me.''

''Does your eye hurt?''

''The pain is excruciating.'' He buckled the seat belt. ''What about the beach?''

Without a word, she drove out of the complex and north onto Pacific Coast Highway. He watched the jumble of signs and billboards, Hannah's anger beating a steady tattoo in his brain. A medical office advertised flu shots, the tanning parlor next door had an introductory offer. Doughnut shops and taco stands, yacht brokers and surfing shacks. The breeze through the rolled-down windows tossed Hannah's hair around, filled the car with the flowery scent he used to dream about. Her thighs and knees beneath her yellow shorts were completely smooth and lightly tanned. *You know nothing about what it means to be a father.*

''Seal Beach is the closest,'' she said.

''Fine.'' They drove down a street lined with small shops. Main Street the sign read. There had been a Main Street in one of the towns he'd lived in as a kid. Some place in Armagh, the sort of abandoned-looking crossroads with its strip of narrow, paint-peeled houses that only looked picturesque if you didn't wake up every morning in one of them. Two bars where his stepdad had spent most of his waking hours, a church in which no one he knew had ever set foot and a newsagent's where his ma bought packs of Players before she took a notion that she wanted to start her life over in Liverpool free of small boys and other encumbrances.

''Now for the difficult part,'' Hannah said as she

pulled onto the ocean front. ‘‘Finding somewhere to park.’’

‘‘Over there.’’ He pointed to a white van that was pulling out and watched Hannah’s arms as she maneuvered the car into the empty space. Tanned like her legs.

‘‘There,’’ she said after she’d got the car squeezed in between a dune buggy and a Mercedes convertible. ‘‘Pretty good parallel-parking job if I do say so myself.’’ She turned off the ignition, removed the keys and moved around to face him. ‘‘So?’’

‘‘Let’s go for a walk.’’ He got out of the car, came around to her side and pulled open the door. Hannah swung her legs around and sat there for a moment, looking up at him. He could hear gulls screeching behind him, the loud roar of the waves. Wind blew his hair, billowed the back of his shirt. A car passed and he instinctively stepped closer to Hannah. He’d worn an old pair of tan shorts that belonged to Pearse and he felt the warm air on his legs and then the brush of Hannah’s skin against his own. He saw the contact register in her eyes and everything seemed to stop for a moment. And then he leaned into the car and kissed her. When she didn’t immediately pull away, he kissed her again and his brain all but ceased to function.

‘‘Damn you,’’ she said a moment later. ‘‘I’m still furious at you.’’

‘‘Go ahead with it then.’’ She looked as dazed as he felt. ‘‘Hit me if it makes you feel any better.’’

She caught his face in her hands. ‘‘Shut up.’’

They kissed again, so hard that he felt her teeth against his lips. Another car zoomed past, inches from where he stood halfway into the car, Hannah almost reclining across the seats. He drew back to look at her.

"I changed my mind about the walk," he said. "I have a better idea."

HANNAH SAT UP, ran her fingers through her hair. Liam walked back around the car, opened the passenger door and got in. Dazed, she turned in the seat to look at him. No point now in telling herself this was all about Faith. It wasn't. She knew it and he knew it. Everything had suddenly changed. Later, her mind would kick in—the analysis, the second-guessing, the regrets. Right now, bodies ruled.

"I've got a guitar I want you to give Faith." He touched her knee, cut his eyes up to her face. "I left it in the tour bus. If I remember rightly, it's only a minute or so from here, on a lot behind Fiddler's Green. We can talk there."

She started the car. As good an excuse as any to find a place where they could rip off each other's clothes in private. With Liam giving directions, she drove. Her brain was a haze of jumbled thoughts and flashing warnings; her body felt liquid, every nerve loudly proclaiming that without immediate satisfaction, they would all gang up on her and drive her insane with lust.

Five minutes later, she stood behind Liam on the steps of the tour bus, waiting while he unlocked the door. Inside, it was dark and cool and smelled faintly of stale beer and cigarette smoke. A strip of sunlight glimmered from beneath the dark fabric covering the windows, faintly illuminated a small living area furnished with a couple of couches. The green digital numerals of a microwave glowed 4:13 p.m.

She heard the muffled roar of traffic on Pacific Coast Highway, the sound of her own breathing. Liam put his hands on her shoulders and kissed her again, and it was like drowning. No one had ever kissed her like Liam. No mouth had ever felt like Liam's. Everything about him seemed familiar—the wiry frame of his body, now hard against her own, the shape of his shoulders under her hands. Familiar and yet so dreamlike and insubstantial she wanted to preserve it somehow before it slipped away.

He took her hand, and led her to the couch, where they sat down and kissed again. She wanted him to keep on kissing her—if he kissed her until tomorrow, it wouldn't be enough. When they eventually parted, he reached past her to switch on a light and took a small guitar from a box beside the couch.

"This is for Faith," he said. "There's a note on the back to her."

Hannah took the guitar, and tried to emerge from the sexual fog. He'd printed Faith's name in big block letters, each letter outlined and shaded in a different color. With her finger, Hannah traced the *F*. Imagined him carefully lettering his daughter's name.

"Pearse walked in on me as I was doing that," Liam said. "Gave me a hard time about it, called me Daddy Liam. I threatened to knock his teeth out."

She set the guitar down. Why would that bother him? It wasn't something she wanted to dwell on right now.

"Brid got herself in a bit of trouble last night," Liam said after a moment. "That's what the scuffle was all about. I'd gone to find her and the idiot she was with didn't appreciate my showing up. She's finally admitted she needs help. We've got her back at Casa Pacifica until she's well enough to go on the road again."

Hannah said nothing. From the couch where she sat, she could see the pictures pinned to a bulletin board on the wall opposite. Brid in black lace, holding a guitar.

One of Liam, onstage. Newspaper clippings, a schedule of performances. She folded her hands in her lap. Liam sat close enough that she could feel the heat of his body. The strip of light from beneath the curtains fell in a bar across her thighs, disappeared, then reappeared just below the frayed edge of Liam's shorts.

Without a word, he drew her onto his lap, and they kissed until she was almost lying across him; her brain gone to mush, her body moving in rhythm to the thrust of his tongue in her mouth. They kept kissing. He pressed the flat of his palm against her crotch, held it there. She groaned and moved against it.

''What's this all about then, Hannah?''

She caught his hand, held it still. ''Well, I've got you figured out, Tully. The guitar was just a transparent attempt to get me into this den of iniquity.''

He nuzzled his face in her neck. ''You saw right through me.''

''Of course.'' Even stilled, the pressure of his palm was driving her crazy. She squeezed it between her thighs. ''You think I'm some little bimbo groupie?''

''Aren't you?'' He freed his hand, and made to push her off his lap. ''Off with you then. I'm only interested in ladies of easy virtue.''

''There's something contradictory about ladies and easy virtue,'' she said, ''but at the moment I'm not thinking too clearly.''

''Well, I can straighten one thing out.'' He grinned, his teeth white in the murky light. ''This should clear up any thoughts you might have that this is just about Faith.'' He kissed her neck, her throat. Stopped to look at her again. ''Despite your little lecture, I do want to be part of her life. I've never been as serious about anything before. But Faith isn't the whole picture. I can't think of her without you."

Hannah's arm was still around his neck, her legs across his lap. She thought about what he'd said. Weighed whether to say what was really on her mind, then decided that, if nothing else, they should be honest with each other.

"If we take Faith out of the picture, Liam, I think what we have together pretty much boils down to sex."

His grin broadened. "And that's a bad thing?"

"It depends. If it's the foundation of a relationship, we're off to a shaky start. We've been there. What did we know about each other when we got married? Nothing. And we had nothing in common…except sex."

"I bet if we'd taken up stamp collecting, we'd still be married today."

She punched his shoulder.

"Or lawn bowling. Except we'd have probably caused a scandal each time I threw you down on the green and had my way with you."

"Seriously though. We created Faith, and now here we are again…"

"And it's still all about sex?"

She squirmed around to look at him. "Tell me how it's anything else."

He undid the top button of her blouse, and watched her face as he undid the rest of the buttons. Kept watching as he pulled off her shirt and tossed it on the floor. Didn't take his eyes away as he snapped open the clasp of her bra.

"If you're trying to convince me otherwise," she said as he lowered his mouth to her breasts, "you're not doing a very good job."

He said nothing, just circled his tongue around her

nipples until she lost herself again in the feel of his hands, his mouth, his tongue. She didn't need his confirmation. It *was* all about sex. Always had been, always would be. Which was fine. Maybe every woman needed a guy like Liam. Purely for sex, because you couldn't count on him for much else. And then, he slid out from under her and stripped off her shorts and panties.

CHAPTER ELEVEN

THE SHORTS CAUGHT around her foot. He unsnagged them, lifted her legs and swept all her clothes to the floor. The couch was some sort of fake leather and it felt cool and a little damp under her bare skin. Liam stood above her for a moment, watching her. A little self-conscious and grateful for the dim light, she shifted slightly and clasped her hands behind her head. Still in his khaki shorts and T-shirt, Liam trailed his fingers down over her stomach, then kneeled between her legs.

"The last time I saw you naked, we had a fight." He kissed the inside of her thighs, and parted them with his hands. "Do you remember? We were living in that place in San José?"

"The place with the fire escape outside. There was a woman downstairs who…" She stopped, her breath uneven as she felt his tongue move inside her. A sound escaped from her throat, loud and surprised to her ears. Liam glanced up at her, caught her ankles and draped her legs around his shoulders. For an instant, she saw it all through the eyes of a detached observer. A couch in a dimly lit tour bus. Liam's dark head between her thighs. Her own pale body: breasts, stomach, bare feet on either side of his neck. An afternoon tryst. A little tawdry maybe, an experience she'd be unlikely to reveal to anyone, but more exciting somehow because of that.

Briefly she wondered about other women who may have lain on this couch with Liam.

And then she stopped thinking altogether. With his tongue inside her, she lost herself in heat and sensation. Her unchecked cries filled the air; her hips rose higher and higher. Building, building, her body arching spasmodically. A vibration had started somewhere inside her, a done of bees growing louder and louder. "Oh yes, *yes*..." Every nerve in her body was screaming now, the hum filling her brain.

"Liam, I'm...I think I'm going to... Oh yes, yes..." She collapsed against the couch. In an instant, Liam was out of his clothes and driving into her, his breathing harsh, his mouth against her neck.

When he came, moments later, he toppled off her, pulling her with him from the narrow couch to the floor. They both started laughing. Bodies, slick with sweat, legs still entwined, wedged between the couch and a low coffee table, they laughed and laughed and kissed some more.

"God, Hannah, I love you," he said. "I've never stopped loving you."

BUT EXACTLY WHAT they were going to do about it was another matter, Liam reflected as Hannah drove him back to Miranda's. Hannah had chosen to ignore his declaration. Had probably put it down to the sort of postcoital ardor that would cool almost as soon as the clothes went back on. She hadn't expressed similar feelings for him, and he hadn't asked. Now he felt let down and morose.

They'd had their fling—he could almost hear Hannah thinking—now he could make her life a whole lot simpler by getting back on the bus and riding off. Which was probably the best thing he could do for everyone in the long run, himself included.

But he wanted his daughter and he wanted his ex-wife. A few days ago, Brid had asked him whether he missed being close to someone. He'd responded with a joke. Either he hadn't really known the answer, or he hadn't recognized his own needs. Now he did.

Except that his daughter didn't know him, and her mother didn't love him.

"Beverly, that was the name of the woman downstairs," Hannah said suddenly. She turned to look at him. "That place in San José with the fire escape. Beverly lived in the apartment below ours. Beverly Mc-something or other."

Liam roused himself from his gloomy musings. "I don't remember a woman downstairs," he said.

"Really?" Hannah gave him a skeptical look. "You don't remember how we used to sleep outside on the fire escape because it was so hot in the apartment? One night, you had no clothes on and you said it didn't matter because no one could see you and then the next day Beverly said you had a cute butt. You don't remember that?"

He shook his head. Not only did he not remember, he didn't care. What the hell did any of that matter?

"That's what the fight was about." Hannah stopped for a light, turned again to look at him. "Beverly was always coming on to you. You have to remember her. Long blond hair, big boobs?"

Liam shook his head. "As I recall, we fought because I wanted you to sleep naked and you insisted on covering yourself up with this frilly little cotton nightie you had. Rosebuds around the neck."

"You remember that nightgown?"

"It's what you always wore."

"Oh God." She shook her head. "I guess I was kind of on the modest side. Prudish. Self-conscious. I don't know."

"I could never understand why."

She smiled.

"I'm serious."

"Oh come on, Liam. How could I not be? There were always women fawning all over you. Fantastic-looking women. They'd stare at me, and I knew they were thinking, 'God, what's he doing with her?' And then all the nights you didn't come home till three and I could smell cigarettes and perfume…"

"Proof, of course, that I was running around."

"Well, it didn't exactly take a huge stretch of imagination."

"Apparently not." He waited a moment. "If you thought I was running around, why didn't you say something?"

"Because…" She hesitated and shot him a glance as though to gauge his possible reaction. "It sounds crazy now, I know, but I was scared to have my suspicions confirmed. So I just kept them to myself."

"You thought I was running around, but you didn't say anything because you thought I'd leave you?"

"Pretty much."

"I'm sure the logic must be there somewhere, but I've got to say I don't see it."

"I told you it seems crazy now, but I loved you. It was easier not knowing for sure."

Loved you.

He'd hardly heard anything after that. A pulse throbbed in his temple. A grim need to get all the bad news over with made him push on. "Listen, Hannah," he said as she pulled up to the curb outside Miranda's house. "What would I need to do to make it work between us again?"

She parked at the curb and turned in her seat to look at him. Waited a moment before she answered. "I don't think it could ever work again, Liam," she said softly.

Her words seemed to hang there for a moment; the air in the car filled with them, echoing in his head. "And you've got all the reasons ready to trot out, I'm sure," he finally said. "You don't trust me. Our lives are too different. We have nothing in common. I'm always on the road."

"Are you arguing with that?" Hannah's tone was incredulous. "Can you really see yourself in a suburban tract home, going to PTA meetings and washing the car on Saturdays?"

"That's only one version of life," he said. "There are others."

"It's pretty much my version though. It's what I've always known. What I want for myself. What I think is best for raising my daughter."

"Our daughter."

"Sorry."

"What if I said I want to give that kind of life a try?"

"I'd say you'd need to give it a lot more thought."

"I could give up the touring," he said impulsively. "Get a job…I don't know, teaching music, or something."

She slowly shook her head. "It's not you, Liam. You'd never be happy. What about the band? What about Brid? The other musicians? You can't just walk away. You said yourself that everything comes second to your music. What about the commitments you've made?"

"Everything's on hold for the next week while Brid's in rehab."

"So fatherhood would be something to keep you occupied in the meantime?"

Her words hit him like shards, puncturing the balloon of optimism he'd been trying to get off the ground. "Give me a break, Hannah, will you? I know to you this is a bloody joke—"

"No, Liam, it's not a joke to me." Spots of color on her face now, Hannah's anger matched his own. "It's pretty damn serious. You're telling me you want to be a father to Faith, you want us to have a relationship again. I don't think it's a joke at all. I'm not about to have my life, or Faith's, turned upside down for something you decide on a whim."

"It's more than a whim," he said.

"How do I know that?"

He didn't answer immediately. And then he said, "Give me a week. Starting tomorrow, a week to be with you and Faith. We'll take her to school, do things together. Get to know each other. At the end of the week, we'll see what happens. If you're right and it turns out to be just a whim, I'll be on my way and you won't hear from me again. If it isn't, we tell Faith who I am and take it from there."

"If you're doing this to test whether there's any possibility for us, Liam, I can tell you right now, you're wasting your time. It'll never work."

"A week. It's not asking much."

She said nothing. They were sitting outside Miranda's, the car windows open. The air seemed glittery and golden, the way it did in California; he could smell flowers, orange blossom maybe, although in Miranda's neighborhood he hadn't spotted many orange trees. It wouldn't be a bad life. A house by the beach maybe—if he ignored all he'd heard about the price of homes in California. What he'd do for a living, what he'd do about the band and the commitments they had for the next year were matters he'd have to think about.

His arm was over the back of the seat and he touched his fingers lightly to Hannah's shoulder. Felt her skin, warm and smooth. They'd work something out. If she'd just believe in him, they'd work something out.

"Okay, a week," she finally said. "A week so that you can spend time with your daughter."

He grinned, almost light-headed with relief. "We'll pick Faith up from school."

"Okay," she said slowly. "But this *is* about Faith. A chance for you to get to know her. It's not about us. Forget what happened this afternoon. There is no us."

"Right, Hannah, if you say so."

"I do."

AND JUST TO ELIMINATE any doubts about the "us" thing, Hannah went to dinner at Delmonico's with Allan that night. Actually, Allan, along with Margaret, Rose, Deb, Helen, Faith and Douglas. Technically, it was Rose's Mystery Casserole Tuesday, but Allan had managed to convince everyone to join him and Hannah for dinner instead. Allan was clearly family.

They all sat around the window table eating bread sticks and drinking red wine while they waited for the food to arrive. In the middle of the adults, Douglas and Faith were coloring on paper placemats printed with outlines of Italy and pictures of pasta bowls to designate key cities.

Allan had his arm across the back of Hannah's seat. Every so often, his fingers brushed her shoulders. *Just as Liam's had.* Five minutes after they'd sat down, Hannah was wishing she'd stayed home. Maybe she had told Liam there was no "us," but she wanted to think about Liam making love to her. About Liam telling her he loved her. About Liam telling her he wanted to try again. She wanted to think about it, but more than that, she wanted to tell someone about it. To spill it all out, the excitement, the doubt and confusion, the fact that she absolutely couldn't go more than five minutes without thinking about Liam.

It'll never work. That's what she'd told him. So why did the need to see him again feel like a physical ache? She *hurt* to see him. Her chest, her stomach, her head. But it *wouldn't* work. Wouldn't, couldn't, and yet a stubborn little spark of hope refused to be doused. Maybe, just maybe. God, she had to talk to someone. But who?

"I think that would work, don't you, Hannah?" Margaret asked.

Hannah gave her mother a blank look.

Allan squeezed her shoulder. "Daydreaming, kiddo?"

Hannah gritted her teeth. *Kiddo.* Why was she here?

"Allan was saying it would be fun if we all went out on his boat tomorrow night," Margaret said. "If I pick up Faith from school, you can go straight to the boat when you get off work."

"Should we pack a picnic?" Helen asked Allan. "I have a wonderful chicken terrine recipe..."

"No, don't bother about it," he said. "Tomorrow's Wet Wednesday at the yacht club. They have a big barbecue after the race. The kids will love it."

"So, Allan?" Rose's voice was elaborately casual. "Do you actually belong to the yacht club?"

He smiled. "My family's belonged for as long as I

can remember. My father and grandfather, too. We've always enjoyed sailing.''

''Big boat?'' Rose wanted to know.

Allan shrugged. ''A fifty-foot Columbia.''

''Wow,'' Rose's mouth and eyes opened wide. ''That's *big,* huh? Listen, is it okay if I bring Max?'' She winked at Allan. ''He's my significant other.''

''Significant other du jour,'' Deb nudged her aunt.

''Does anyone have an Excedrin?'' Hannah asked.

''Excedrin or Advil?'' Helen dug a bottle of each from her bag and set them on the table.

Allan brought his mouth close to Hannah's ear. ''What you need is a back rub.''

Hannah smiled. And gulped down two Excedrin with a glass of water. God, life would be so much easier if she could feel something for Allan. She *wanted* to feel something for Allan. If only because the man had the patience to sit through a dinner with her family. By now, Liam would be restless; shooting her looks intended to convey that if he didn't leave in five minutes, the top of his head would explode. She entertained herself by imagining that she'd just announced her plans to bring Liam along on the little sailing trip.

Liam, who had made love to her on the couch of a darkened tour bus that afternoon. Liam, who had told her he loved her. ''I've always loved you,'' he'd said. *It'll never work.*

''So let's see how many people do we have coming?'' Allan asked. He started around the table with Hannah. ''You and Faith—''

''I can't make it,'' Hannah said. ''Neither can Faith.''

All eyes turned to her, and she knew she'd made a strategic mistake.

"Oh no." Helen made a little mewl of disappointment. "What a pity."

"How come?" Rose asked.

Margaret drank some wine and looked at her daughter. Hannah turned away.

"But I want to go on a boat," Faith said. "Why can't I go?"

"We'll talk about it later, sweetie," Hannah said. "I've already made other plans," she told the others. "But you guys go, it sounds like fun."

"Can Douglas come on our other plans?" Faith asked.

"So what other plans have you made?" Rose asked. "Sound mysterious."

Deb looked across the table at Hannah. "Liam?" she mouthed.

"*I* want to go on the boat," Faith wailed. "No fair, I don't want to have other plans. I want to go on the boat."

"Somebody is getting a little cranky," Margaret said. "Maybe Grandma needs to take you home."

"Faith." Hannah addressed her daughter who was decimating a bread stick. "Put the bread down and wipe your hands."

"Where were you this afternoon, Hannah?" Helen asked as the waiter arrived, plates of steaming food held aloft on a large silver tray. "I wanted you to see this darling little outfit I got for Faith at Nordstrom's. I brought it over to show you, but your mother said you were with Jen."

"The funny thing is I thought I saw Jen in Albertson's," Margaret said. "She was buying a pork roast. I remember thinking, that's weird, I thought Jen didn't eat meat. Anyway, it was just after four."

Hannah watched Rose sprinkle parmesan cheese on her linguini. Just after four. Around the same time she was making love to Liam. Maybe, she could tell Margaret. Maybe she could make her mother understand how confused and mixed-up she felt about Liam. Maybe she could describe to her mother how you just sort of go on with your life, not unhappy, but not really happy either, although you don't do anything to change it. And then you fall in love and it seems selfish and irresponsible, but it makes you happy and you just want to go on being happy.

Except that she wasn't in love. *She wasn't in love.*

"You remind me of someone." Rose eyed Allan through narrowed azure-blue lids that exactly matched the nylon jogging suit she wore. "That guy who used to play Marlo Thomas's boyfriend on *That Girl.* What was his name?"

"*That Girl.*" Debra hooted. "Jeez, Aunt Rose, how long ago was that?"

"I don't like this spaghetti, Mommy," Faith said.

"So why can't you go sailing tomorrow?" As she glanced over at Hannah, Margaret splashed red wine on the sleeve of her white blouse. "Damn." She dunked the corner of a napkin in her water glass and dabbed at the spot. "Can you change your plans, honey? I love it when both of my girls are together and we do things as a family. We don't do that so much anymore."

"Mommy. I *hate* this spaghetti," Faith said. "I want SpaghettiOs."

"What do you have that's so important tomorrow, anyway?" Margaret asked Hannah.

"Omigod," Deb said. "You'll never believe who just walked in."

"I HAVEN'T BEEN HERE for years," Miranda Payton told Liam as he held open the door of Delmonico's for her. "Frankly, I find the food a little old-fashioned, but it's kind of fun in a quaint, old-world way."

Liam breathed in the aromas of tomato and garlic and glanced around the small foyer. A bench along one wall and half a dozen folding chairs were all packed with people, indicating a wait was likely. Miranda was undaunted. All peach-colored silk and flowing blond hair, she swept past tables of diners, trailing cigarette smoke and calling loudly for the manager. Heads swiveled in the booths lining the walls. A large party over by the window all turned as one.

And then Liam saw Faith.

She seemed to appear from nowhere, her hair tied up with red ribbons, bread crumbs around her mouth. She beamed broadly, clearly pleased to have spotted him.

"I don't like my spaghetti," she told him. "If you want it, you can have it. Mommy's got lasagna and my grandma has…I forget what she has, but I don't like that, either. Can we go to the zoo again?"

Liam grinned at his daughter, surprised by the sudden and sharp upward turn his mood had taken. He had a mad urge to lift her onto his shoulders and gallop around the restaurant proclaiming to everyone that this was his daughter.

"Well, let's talk about this a bit." He caught her hand and led her to one side, out of the path of an oncoming waiter. He crouched so that they were eye-to-eye. Behind him, he heard Miranda complaining loudly about inferior service. And then her voice suddenly stopped and he sensed her putting two and two together. Faith was watching him, waiting for him to speak. "Tell me," he said, trying to rally his thoughts, ''what exactly is it you don't like about spaghetti?''

''I only like the kind that's in little circles,'' Faith said.

Liam peered past Faith's shoulder, trying to spot Hannah. ''What about little squares?''

''They don't make little squares,'' Faith said.

''She's talking about SpaghettiOs,'' Miranda said. ''God, revolting stuff. My mother's housekeeper used to try to feed it to me.''

Faith looked uncertain. ''I like SpaghettiOs.''

''So do I,'' Liam said, having no idea what they were. ''There's nothing like SpaghettiOs. In fact, you know what I think we should do? I think we should go and find your mum and buy three hundred tins of SpaghettiOs and eat them until SpaghettiOs come out of our ears.''

Faith giggled. ''You're funny,'' she said. ''They don't come out of your ears.''

''Well, they might if it was a really, really big bunch.'' Liam pulled himself to his feet, and glanced over at Miranda. ''I hate to leave you in the lurch, but I'm on a mission, all right?''

Miranda's face darkened. ''For God's sake, Liam.''

He shot a look at her over Faith's head, a look intended to convey that if she chose to make a scene about this, she'd be sorry. Then he addressed Faith.

''Let's go and talk to your mummy.''

He took his daughter's hand. It was soft, warm and sticky, just as it had been at the zoo on Sunday. Did all six-year-old girls have warm, sticky little hands? His own felt cold as Faith walked him over to the table where Hannah sat with her party of fifty. Or at least that's how many seemed to be gawking up at him over their dinner plates and brimming wineglasses. Fifty, maybe a hundred. Not one of them looking happy to see him. His feet were also cold and his heart was doing overtime; pounding in rhythm with the pulsing beat of his right eyelid. Miranda, still in tow, was asked by a waiter to extinguish her cigarette. Her response was a pithy and anatomically impossible suggestion, clearly audible over the Puccini on the sound system. Liam tightened his grip on Faith's hand and considered making a dash for it, yelling over his shoulder for Hannah to join them. A foot or so from the table, he made eye contact with Hannah, who looked nervous and tense, hardly surprising really—he felt pretty nervous and tense himself. God, who *were* all these people with her? He recognized her mother. Margaret's face was flushed, her expression strained. *Sorry, Margaret, I know you told me to stay away from her, but I ended up making love to her instead.* And there was the pirate's dad. And the pirate, not in costume tonight, though. The pirate's dad had his arm around Hannah's shoulder. Liam pictured himself taking the pirate's dad out. One quick blow to that chiseled jaw would do it.

''And here's Liam,'' Faith said, drawing his name out like a sidekick on a television show announcing the big star. ''He said we're going to buy a whole big bunch of SpaghettiOs and eat them until they come out of our ears. Okay, Mommy? We can give my spaghetti to Raisin.'' She looked up at Liam. ''Raisin can't come with me to our new apartment because you can't have dogs there.''

''Then we'll have to look for a place where you *can* have a dog,'' he said.

Hannah shot him a look, whispered something to the pirate's dad and eased her way out of the booth. Her face flushed, she nodded at the door, and he followed her, Faith's hand still in his. A moment later, they were outside the restaurant. Tall, skinny palm trees in the center median waved their frondy top knots at the dark blue sky and the night air felt cool and damp. That was one thing that had always surprised him about California. Even the hottest days cooled off rapidly when the sun went down. Hannah was looking at him as though she expected an explanation.

"The week isn't supposed to start until tomorrow," she finally said.

CHAPTER TWELVE

LIAM SHRUGGED. ''I didn't know you were going to be here.''

''Can we get SpaghettiOs?'' Faith asked.

''Faith doesn't like the spaghetti at that place,'' Liam said. ''I told her we'd get the stuff she likes.''

''Faith has a plate of untouched spaghetti inside the restaurant,'' Hannah said. ''Until she takes a bite, she really doesn't know whether she likes it or not.''

''But I don't,'' Faith wailed. ''I only like SpaghettiOs.''

''She only likes SpaghettiOs,'' Liam said.

Hannah gave him a long look. An eyes-narrowed, hands-on-hips long look.

''I'm just telling you what she likes,'' he said. ''And it's not the stuff in there.''

''I like SpaghettiOs.'' Faith released his hand, hopscotched along the sidewalk. ''SpaghettiOs, SpaghettiOs,'' she sang. ''I only like SpaghettiOs.''

''You heard her,'' Liam said. ''She only likes SpaghettiOs.''

''If you say that one more time, I'm going to hit you,'' Hannah said.

He watched her face. She was trying hard not to smile. So was he. Both of them, standing there with the waving palm trees and Faith singing about SpaghettiOs. He broke first and grinned at Hannah.

"You are impossible, Tully."

"SpaghettiOs?"

She raised a hand as though to swipe at his face.

Ten minutes later they were pushing a cart down the aisle of a supermarket. He watched Faith briefly disappear around the corner of Aisle 15—pasta, tomato sauce, olives—reappear, then take off again. "Shouldn't she sit in the cart?" he asked Hannah.

She gave him a scornful look. "Faith would be very insulted if she heard you say that. She hasn't sat in a cart since she was three."

He shrugged. "What do I know?"

"We have very strict rules about how far she can stray. No more than one aisle over from where I am, and she has to come back as soon as she hears me. Or else."

"Or else what?"

"Just *or else*. It's something parents say to kids."

"I'll remember that," Liam said.

Hannah gave him a look he couldn't read. She considered his interest in Faith a whim—he had little doubt about that—and was surprised by anything he said that suggested otherwise. Suddenly the week he'd asked for seemed so ridiculously inadequate that he felt himself sinking into the state Brid called his Misery Mode. "Snap out of it," she'd tell him when he'd succumb to the moody gloom, or as Pearse put it, the Celtic Crud. "You're a misery to look at and a bloody misery to be around."

"So where are we going to cook this gourmet feast?" Hannah reached for a can of SpaghettiOs. "I'm pretty sure you don't want to do it at my mother's house."

"I don't care," he said, although the idea of sitting in the family kitchen with the aunts and Margaret shooting him dagger looks wasn't loaded with appeal. ''Sooner or later Margaret's going to have to get used to me being around.''

''Let's make it later rather than sooner, okay? She's in this emotionally fragile state right now. My sister's pregnant and—''

''And I'm just one more problem she doesn't need, is that it?''

''Liam...''

''I'm sorry.'' He'd regretted the words as soon as he'd said them. ''This is about us, not your mother. And the last thing I want is a fight.'' He thought for a moment. ''The tour bus has a hot plate,'' he said. ''We could cook there.''

Hannah smiled, a doubtful smile that spoke volumes.

''Nix the tour bus?''

''After this afternoon, it has...certain associations that don't exactly go with cooking SpaghettiOs for Faith.''

He smiled, too—the gloom sent packing by the certainty that Hannah, despite her cool demeanor, had been as bowled over by their afternoon together as he had. ''You don't think I'd try to ravage you over a plate of SpaghettiOs.''

''The thought crossed my mind.''

He tried to look injured. ''I do have *some* moral principles.''

She raised a brow. ''No kidding?''

''Absolutely. They're good on toast with grated cheese.''

''Did I mention you were impossible?''

He kissed her neck. ''Did I mention you were fantastic today?''

''Did I mention that you're wasting your time if you think there's going to be a repeat performance?''

He put his arm around her shoulder, and brought his face around to kiss the side of her mouth. ''I don't believe you.''

''Wait and see.''

''Want to bet?''

''No, thank you,'' she said primly. ''I don't gamble.'' She glanced at him. ''Not that it matters to me at all, but...''

''No, I'm not sleeping with her.''

She steered the trolley into his leg. ''You didn't *know* that's what I was going to ask.''

''Weren't you?''

She grinned. ''Maybe.''

Faith reappeared, peeked into the basket. ''I don't see any SpaghettiOs.''

Liam took the can Hannah had been holding and dropped it in the cart. He looked at Faith. ''What d'you think? Five more? Ten? Six hundred?''

''Six hundred,'' Faith said.

''What if we split the difference and make it two?''

''Two's good, too.'' She grinned. ''Hey, I made a joke. Two's good, too,'' she chanted as she ran down the aisle.

''So did we establish a place?'' Hannah asked

''What about your new home?''

''There's no furniture there yet,'' she said.

''Electricity? Gas?''

''The utilities haven't been turned on.''

''Have you got the key?''

''Yes.''

''Good. I've got an idea.''

FAITH SAT CROSS-LEGGED on a blanket, a paper napkin tucked under her chin, shoveling SpaghettiOs, heated on a Sterno burner, into her mouth. Half a dozen candles set on paper plates around the room made flickering shadows on the walls.

"I like this place, Mommy," Faith said. "It's like camping, only better." She looked at Hannah. "But you don't get to pee in the woods."

"Faith." Hannah protested.

"When we go camping with Allan and Douglas, Mommy says we get to pee in the woods."

"Faith, I really don't think Liam cares about that," Hannah said.

"Yes, I do." Liam, studiously ignoring Hannah, smiled at Faith. "I want to hear all about it."

"She said we have to take flashlights so we don't trip over something," Faith went on, clearly encouraged by Liam's interest. "And Allan's going to cook marshmallows."

Hannah caught Liam's eye, held his glance for a moment. "Allan invited us to Yosemite this summer," she said. "Faith and I will have our own little tent, Allan and Douglas will have theirs." She saw a smile flicker across Liam's face; she knew he knew she was telling him that she wouldn't be sleeping with Allan.

"More SpaghettiOs?" she asked Liam, who was making a valiant effort to finish the food already piled on his plate.

"That's all right," Liam said politely. "I've had plenty. Help yourself."

"You have them, Liam," Faith said. "I want to see them come out of your ears."

"Yeah, Liam." Hannah said as she emptied the pan onto his plate. "Let's see them come out of your ears."

She tried unsuccessfully to keep a straight face. This was fun. Doing things with Faith was always fun; Liam gave it a new dimension. There is no us, she'd told him. But didn't they kind of feel like a cozy little threesome right now? Sitting here in an empty apartment eating canned spaghetti they'd bought because it was their daughter's favorite?

But a relationship was more than a picnic in an empty apartment. It took dedication, commitment, mutual respect. And as she watched Liam and Faith clown around together—Faith urging Liam to "eat, eat, eat"—she marched out all the reasons their marriage hadn't worked the first time and wouldn't work if they tried it again. Marched them out, paraded them for inspection, then tried to shoot them down. And just when she was just on the verge of deciding their relationship might actually work, a parade of nameless, beautiful women trooped through her brain, reminding her of the all-consuming jealousy and insecurity she'd felt before.

"Mummy's not paying attention," Liam told Faith. "Which is a pity, because she missed one of the best tricks of the evening." He winked at his daughter. "Right?"

"Right," Faith said. "You missed it, Mommy."

"What did I miss?" Hannah asked.

Faith gave Liam an uncertain look. "What did she miss?"

"Ah, come on, Faith. You know." He crooked his finger and she came over to him. With one hand, he brushed her hair aside, and whispered something in her ear. "Now tell your mum what she missed."

"You missed seeing SpaghettiOs coming out of Liam's ears," Faith said. "It was a really good trick, too."

She smiled at Liam. "You have talents I never even suspected."

He met her eyes. ''All I need is a chance to demonstrate them.''

Hannah looked away, then busied herself with picking up paper plates. Faith started telling Liam about the time that Douglas laughed so much that milk came out of his nose. Liam sat with his chin in his hand, his expression thoughtful as he interrupted Faith's description with questions. ''Just a minute now, Faith,'' he'd ask solemnly. ''Was this *skim* milk? Did it come out of *both* nostrils, or just one?''

For all Liam's concerns about not knowing how to behave around small children, Hannah reflected, he was succeeding incredibly well with his daughter—who was clearly enchanted by him.

''Douglas and Grandma and Auntie Rose and everyone get to go for a ride on Allan's boat tomorrow.'' Faith had moved on from the milk incident. ''But Mommy said we can't go because we have other plans.''

''But I think you're going to like those other plans.'' Hannah looked from Liam to Faith. ''Guess who's going to pick you up from school?''

''Grandma?''

''Guess again.'' Hannah felt a vague sense of trepidation. As she'd left the restaurant with Faith, she'd caught a glimpse of her mother's apprehensive expression. Now she was going to have break the news to Margaret that Liam would be picking up her granddaughter from school.

''If it's not Grandma...'' Faith looked from Hannah to Liam. ''Then it's...'' She pointed her finger at Hannah. ''Mommy.''

''And me,'' Liam said.

Faith grinned. ''*Liam.* Cool. Then we can all go out on Allan's boat.''

"Actually, I've got a better idea," Liam said. "I know a great big boat we can go on."

"As big as Allan's?"

"Bigger."

"Is it your boat?"

"No, but I have a special arrangement with the captain."

"Cool," Faith said again. And then she got up from the cushion she'd been sitting on and moved next to Liam. "Hey, Liam." She looked up at him. "You know something?"

"What?"

"I like you."

Hannah watched Liam's face. He was sitting cross-legged on the floor, his back against the wall. For a moment, he didn't speak and then he put his arm around his daughter and kissed the top of her head.

"That's good," he said. "Because I like you, too. A lot."

"And I love Raisin," she said. "He's the best dog in the whole world."

"But can he play a guitar?" Liam asked.

Faith eyed him for a moment. "He's a dog, silly."

Hannah remembered the guitar Liam had given her that afternoon. She'd left it in the car, thinking that she'd wait until Liam was there before she gave it to Faith. While Liam was telling Faith that he'd like to teach her to play, Hannah slipped outside. Liam smiled as she came back in, holding the guitar. "Liam has a present for you," she said.

He crooked his finger at Faith. "C'mon over here. I'll teach you to play it, then you can teach Raisin."

This struck Faith as so funny she dissolved in giggles and ended up spilling her glass of ginger ale down the front of her shirt. The lesson was postponed while Hannah stripped off the wet top. Belatedly she realized that she didn't have a replacement.

"Here. Wrap this around her." Liam pulled off his shirt, and handed it to Hannah. "Clean this morning."

Faith giggled even harder, rolling around on the floor now, hyped-up and overtired. Laughing and flinging her arms as she leaped around the room. A sprite, completely unselfconscious, clad only in a pair of red shorts.

"*I* don't have a shirt and *you* don't have a shirt," she told Liam between peals of laughter. "*You* don't have a shirt and *I* don't have a shirt. *Mommy* has a shirt, but *you* don't have a shirt. *I* don't have a shirt..."

Hannah met Liam's eyes. "She'll wind down in a minute."

"Hey, Hannah." He touched her foot with his own. "I love you."

"IT'S A SHAME she can't have her dog with her here," Liam said after Faith had finally fallen asleep on the living room floor on an improvised bed of blankets and cushions brought in from the car. "Have you spoken to the landlord? Maybe he'd reconsider."

"The lease was pretty clear about no animals," Hannah said.

"Let's find a different place," he said. "She should have a dog."

Hannah heard the word *let's.* She allowed herself a moment to consider what it implied. Togetherness, shared responsibility. She picked up a circle of spaghetti that had escaped her earlier cleanup. "This apartment is what *I* can afford, Liam. There aren't many places in my price range that allow pets."

"I'll contribute, I told you that." He glanced around

the empty, shadow-filled room. ''Look, give me the landlord's number, I'll have a talk with him tomorrow. If I can't get him to change his mind, we'll find something else.''

We. She felt her heart beat a little faster. It had appeal, this shared responsibility thing. Sharing, instead of assuming it all herself. Hannah couldn't remember a time when she hadn't felt weighted down by responsibility. ''Let me talk to her,'' she'd tell Margaret. ''I'll handle it,'' she'd say to Rose or Helen. ''Don't worry about it,'' she'd assure Deb. ''I'll sort it out.''

And now Liam was saying, *Hey, take a break. I can handle it.* And it would be so easy to allow that to happen. Easy and comforting…and dangerous.

She studied him as he lay stretched out on his back now, his hands pillowed behind his head. She averted her eyes from his bare chest and his flat stomach. Averted her eyes, but found herself mentally stripping off his faded jeans. Sex is sex is sex, she reminded herself. Don't confuse it with real commitment.

''When I was about Faith's age, maybe a bit older, this dog followed me home from school.'' Liam smiled, as though remembering. ''Black-and-white, he was. A little bit of everything. Bloody great feet and a tail that never stopped. My stepdad caught me opening a tin of beef and gravy for it to eat. Thrashed me and sent the dog packing.''

''God, that's awful. What a jerk.'' Hannah pictured him as the small boy he'd been—dark hair maybe overdue for a trim and their daughter's blue eyes—and felt as retroactively protective as if it had been Faith he was telling her about. ''What did you do?''

He grinned. ''I went looking for the dog and found it

waiting outside a bar in town. Knew its place apparently—the owner came out a few minutes later.''

''I think that's the first thing you've ever told me about your childhood,'' she said. ''I remember when I used to ask you, you'd just change the subject.''

''Not much to tell,'' he said, still on his back, hands locked behind his head. ''My ma couldn't take care of me and none of the aunties and uncles were clamoring for the job either. I got shipped around a bit, which is no doubt why I'm the sterling character I am today.''

''But your mother…'' She found herself struggling with the concept of a mother just abandoning a child. ''Do you ever hear from her?''

''Two or three years ago, she rang. Out of the blue. I didn't even recognize her voice. She'd been living in England and had hardly any trace of an Irish accent. Just wondering about me, she said.''

''That was it?''

''That was it. I might have been an acquaintance whose number she'd just rediscovered.''

''I wonder what she'd think about being a grandmother.''

''I've no idea.''

Faith shifted in her sleep, and Hannah glanced over at her. One of the candles flickered wildly, then went out. She watched as Liam got up to relight it then stretched back on the floor again. ''Do you think you'll tell her about Faith?''

''I hadn't thought about it until now,'' he said. ''But I might. It would be good for Faith to know she has family besides yours. Give her a look at the two extremes.''

''It's funny to think Faith has another grandmother somewhere.'' Hannah sat cross-legged, shoulders pressed against the wall. ''Margaret's so involved in Faith's life, I don't know how she'd deal with a competing grandmother.''

''In the long run it doesn't matter,'' Liam said. ''She's our daughter. The grandparents are just supporting players.''

''Tell that to Margaret,'' Hannah said.

''She'll find out for herself soon enough.'' He sat up, looked at Faith and rolled over to smooth the blanket covering her back. ''If I were the vengeful type, I'd take a lot of pleasure in the fact that your mother's lies are about to come back to haunt her.''

Hannah felt uneasy suddenly. His face gave nothing away, but she had a gnawing sense that if she dug a little deeper, she would discover something she'd rather not know. Unspoken resentment? Had he, just now, inadvertently shown his cards? Was it truly Faith and Hannah he wanted? Or the opportunity to turn the tables on Margaret? As the silence lengthened, she tried to mentally formulate a question, but it sounded paranoid, even to her ears, Still she couldn't shake the thought.

''*Stop it.*'' Liam shifted across the floor to sit beside her. He took her hand, brought it to his mouth, then set it down again. ''Stop telling yourself this won't work.''

She turned her head to look at him. The room was dark except for the flickering candles. From the makeshift bed, Faith made soft whimpering noises in her sleep. Hannah started to speak and Liam shook his head.

''I need you to believe in me, Hannah.'' Again he took her hand, held it on his knee. ''Once upon a time,'' he said softly, ''there was this wee little boy who wanted to make his ma happy because she was having a pretty rotten time of it, crying a lot and always sad. So he decided he'd have a bang-up dinner ready for her when she came home from work. Chops and roast potatoes and an apple tart for afters.''

Hannah smiled and he put his arm around her shoulders and drew her close. Swept by a wave of tenderness, she felt a sudden insatiable need to know more of these vignettes about his life, all the things that he'd never shared with her when they were married.

''Do you have any pictures from when you were a little boy?'' she asked.

''A few, not many.'' He squeezed her shoulder. ''But you're interrupting my story.''

''Sorry.''

''Right, well where was I?''

''Cooking dinner.''

''Ah yes, well that was a bit of a problem since the lad couldn't cook at all.''

She grinned. ''Still can't.''

''I'll ignore that. Anyway, not only couldn't he cook, he was also a bit short of cash. Hadn't a penny, actually. But he was a resourceful sort, so he went down to the grocer's on the corner and asked would they let him pay for the food by helping out around the shop, doing a few errands. Well, they laughed in his face.'' He paused. ''And that night his ma stuck her head in the gas cooker.''

''Oh, Liam...'' She'd been half smiling, anticipating the happy ending and what he'd said was so awful, she was stunned into silence. ''I don't know what to say.''

He ruffled her hair. ''Don't go getting maudlin. They got her in time. But wouldn't it have been a far happier story if the shopkeeper had trusted the kid?''

''Yeah, but trust isn't always so easy.''

''So I'm discovering.''

''Liam—''

"You've got reason enough to be skeptical, Hannah, but I swear to God I never ran around on you while we were married and I know without a doubt that if we try again, we can make it work. But you have to believe."

He kissed her then and she could taste the sweet tomato of the SpaghettiOs. Her back slid down the wall as they kept kissing. When he let her go, her mouth felt warm and numb.

A moment passed and he pulled himself to his feet. "Well, enough of that. It's late." He glanced down at his sleeping daughter. "I'll carry her out to the car."

Hannah watched him bend and gently scoop Faith up in his arms. She blew out the candles, locked the front door and followed them to the car.

"So, we're on for tomorrow?" he asked after he'd strapped Faith into the back seat of the car. "What time does she get out of school?

"Two-thirty. We can walk down there from the house."

"The house on Termino? Your mother's house?"

She nodded. "I'll let her know."

"Break the bad news, huh?"

"Come on…"

"After the boat, we could all have dinner somewhere." He grinned. "To counteract the SpaghettiOs."

"So who is it you know with a big boat?"

"Actually, I was stretching it a bit." His smile widened. "Isn't the *Queen Mary* docked in Long Beach? Pearse was telling me they've got these little water taxis that you can ride over on and I've heard there are all sorts of things to do on board. Don't tell Faith though. It'll be fun to see her face when she sees it. And," he added, "it *is* a wee bit bigger than Allan's boat."

She shook her head at him, then reached up to kiss him on the mouth. ''I don't know about you, Tully.''

And then they were both grinning, arms wrapped around each other. He leaned back against the car, drawing her to him. Beyond his shoulder, the small white wooden bungalows up and down the street glowed in the night sky and in that moment, it seemed absolutely possible that they'd be together forever. It was all she could do not to tell him that.

''How did it go?'' he asked a moment later. ''Our first day?''

''It went great, Liam.'' She wanted to say, *I love you Liam. I love you and I believe in you and I know it can work.* Instead she said, ''Really great.''

HE'D KISSED HER AGAIN after she dropped him at Miranda's; a soft tender kiss that left her feeling dreamy, floating on a fragile bubble of optimism. The feeling was still there ten minutes later as she turned onto Termino and pulled up outside her house. Her mother's house, Hannah thought.

She leaned her head back against the seat. This time next week, her home would be the apartment on Tenth where she and Liam and their daughter had just spent the evening. Images ran through her brain. Faith laughing openmouthed at one of Liam's jokes, paper plate of SpaghettiOs on the floor beside her. Faith, shirtless, dancing across the floor. Liam's face as he said, ''I love you.''

She did want it to work.

I want you to believe in me.

It would work.

CHAPTER THIRTEEN

THE OPTIMISM WAS STILL there the next morning. Bright and buoyant as a child's balloon, it bobbed gaily as Hannah got Faith off to school and was still afloat by noon when she called Margaret from school to suggest they meet for coffee at Babette's Feast.

Hannah was already sitting at one of the green wrought-iron tables on the outdoor patio when Margaret arrived.

"This is nice." Margaret smiled appreciatively, her eyes hidden by the knockoff Armani sunglasses she'd bought last week at the Long Beach Farmer's Market. "I'm very lucky, you know that? We both are."

Hannah grinned. "You lost five pounds this morning, too?"

Margaret leaned forward. "*Did* you?"

"No." She spotted the black-aproned waiter bringing their cappuccinos in white cups the size of soup bowls. "But I ordered a chocolate Napoleon for us anyway. So why are we lucky?"

"Having daughters." Margaret sat back in her chair as the waiter set down the food. "Daughters are nice to have," she said after he left. "My friends with sons are always complaining how they never remember birthdays, but you and Deb…well Deb's forgotten a few of my birthdays—but you never have and that means a lot to me, sweetie. Not to get syrupy on you, but I really treasure our relationship.''

''So do I, Mom.'' Given the strain of past few days, she felt a stab of hypocrisy. Was *treasure* overstating it? ''I mean we've always gotten along,'' she amended, almost thinking aloud, ''and I feel sad about the way things have been with us lately. That's one of the things I wanted to talk to you about.''

Margaret stuck a fork under the Napoleon's flaky crust. ''How many Weight Watchers points, do you think?''

''Screw Weight Watchers,'' Hannah said. ''This is a celebration.''

Margaret looked at Hannah over the rim of her sunglasses.

''That's the other thing I wanted to talk to you about.'' She smiled. ''I'm in love, Mom.'' *There, she'd said it.* Suddenly she couldn't stop smiling. The balloon bobbed brightly, liquid sunshine flowed through her, filling her with this incredible incandescent happiness. ''God, I'm so in love I could stand on the table and yell it out.''

Margaret's expression had congealed slightly. ''Do I need to ask?''

''Liam, of course.'' Even saying his name aloud felt terrific. ''Be happy for us, okay?'' The balloon had dipped ever so slightly. ''I want you to get to know him.'' She watched a sparrow hop across the patio's flagstone tiles. ''He's going to be a part of our lives. Mine, Faith's and yours. You need to understand that and accept it.''

Margaret put her elbows on the table, and studied her daughter's face. ''Would you be happy if you saw Faith running out into the traffic?''

"Oh, for God's sake...I am not a six-year-old child running into the traffic." The balloon had taken a precipitous drop, but she could send it aloft again. She broke off a piece of the Napoleon and ate it, choosing her words carefully. "Look, I have a great idea. In this morning's *Press Telegram* there was an article about this program at Western Memorial. It's in the neonatal intensive care unit," she went on, warming to the subject. "Premature babies respond well to the human touch—being cuddled and hugged—but the nursing staff don't have the time to sit and rock them so that's where this program comes in. It's called Cuddlers and every volunteer is assigned to a baby. I think it would be perfect for you."

Margaret said nothing. Arms folded across her chest, she stared at Hannah through her dark glasses while the sparrows chirped and twittered around them and the sun threw shadows across the table.

"What, Mom?"

"Don't patronize me, Hannah."

"How am I patronizing you?" Hannah heard her voice rise. "This is a wonderful thing. The babies get what they need, and the volunteers know they're providing a much-needed service."

"Kind of like giving an orphaned lamb to a sheep, knowing that the sheep will nurse anything put in front of it."

Deflated, Hannah just shook her head. "I thought—"

"You thought that if you found something else to keep me busy, you'd be free to run off with Liam."

"No, that's not it at all." She mashed a crumb with her finger. "I mean I do think it would be a good thing if you had some other interests, but—"

"You just don't get it, do you? You really think that

I'm only having sleepless nights because I have nothing better to do with my life.'' She pushed aside her coffee, clearly angry. ''Give poor old Mom something meaningful to do. I can just hear you and Deb—''

''Mom…'' Hannah frowned at her. Margaret's raised voice had drawn curious glances from the occupants of nearby tables. ''Keep it down, huh?''

''I don't care. I'm furious that you can be so blind and stupid about this man. Who was that woman with him in Delmonico's last night?''

''Miranda. He's staying at her place.'' Hannah felt her face go hot. ''I mean the band's staying at her place. She's married, Mom.''

Margaret lowered her sunglasses and eyed Hannah over the rims.

''What?''

''I've seen Liam twice since he got back, and each time he's been with a different woman.''

''Brid is his singer and I just explained who Miranda is.''

''Why does he need them traipsing around with him? Why does he need to bring his singer to his daughter's birthday party? Why does he go out to dinner with this Miranda? How come no one else in the band went along?''

Hannah felt her mood take a steep plunge. Margaret's voice had risen a notch with each question. She'd obviously been stewing over Liam's questionable fidelity for some time. Then she remembered Liam's words. *I need you to believe in me.* ''I don't care what it looks like to you, Mom, he's not sleeping with Miranda or Brid. He loves me, he wants us to be a family.''

''How do you *know* he's not sleeping with these other women?''

"He told me."

Light glinted off the lenses of Margaret's glasses. "Oh of course, why didn't I think of that. So what happens next? He goes off on his tours and you stay home and play house? Or are you going with him? And where does Faith fit into the picture?"

"We haven't talked about it. I'm just trying to tell you how I feel." A sparrow had hopped onto the table and was regarding her with bright black eyes. "Can you at least *try* to understand?"

"I'm sorry, but I don't think I can." Margaret folded her arms across her chest. "I just don't trust what's happening, period. I don't believe Liam's serious about this daddy thing. I don't believe he's thinking about what's best for you or Faith. He's a womanizer, Hannie, just like your father."

"Mom, you don't even know him. You've never even tried to get to know him."

"I don't need to. I lived with your father for enough years. I know the type. They love to have women around them. Oh sure, they've always got some excuse, but bottom line, they like women."

Hannah thought of Beryl, her father's longtime secretary who'd accompanied him on business trips. Of the young widow down the road who was always calling on him to fix something or other; of Margaret's various woman friends who seemed to inevitably end up on the couch talking to her father whenever they dropped by. All innocent on the surface, just like Miranda and Brid.

"Hannah, your father cheated on me until the day he dropped dead. I'd catch him in some lie, and he'd confess and swear it would never happen again. But it always did. That's the way some men are. And I'm telling you, a good-looking guy like Liam is not about to trot home faithfully every night, especially when there are kids running around and dishes in the sink."

"Liam's going with me to pick Faith up from school today." Hannah decided to ignore Margaret's gloomy forecast. She forced a smile. "He's pretty excited about it. So is Faith. We're going to take her to the *Queen Mary*."

"He's playing at being a parent, Hannah. And you want to buy into it. You're believing what you want to believe. We all do it at times. Unfortunately, it tends to blind us to the true situation."

"Well…" Hannah fished in her purse for her billfold. "I'm ready…"

Margaret shook her head, then reached across the table to touch Hannah's hand. "Look at me, sweetie. You've got to put Faith first in this situation, and I don't think that's what you're doing. What kind of a life is Liam going to provide for her? Forget all this starry-eyed nonsense about being in love with him. It's your daughter you need to think about."

"WELL, IS SHE A GIRLIE GIRL?" Miranda asked Liam as they walked the aisles of Ikea looking for children's furniture. "Or a tomboy?"

Liam smiled as he thought about the question. It was the day after the SpaghettiOs evening. He thought of the small but growing collection of things he knew about his daughter. "She loves animals, especially koalas, but also monkeys and giraffes. She doesn't like brussels sprouts or the spaghetti at Delmonico's, but she's very partial to—"

"SpaghettiOs," Miranda interrupted. "I think you owe it to her to break her of that little quirk. I can't believe you and Anna—"

"Hannah." Miranda had apparently developed a mental block about Hannah's name. Just an hour earlier, she'd referred to her as Hillary.

"Hannah then," Miranda said. "I still can't believe the two of you actually ate that revolting stuff just because a six-year-old child happens to like it."

"This isn't just any six-year-old child, Miranda. This is a six-year-old child with very discerning taste. I personally believe she's just ahead of the gustatory curve. A year from now, all those fancy restaurants you go to will be serving SpaghettiOs."

"You're impossible." Miranda drew up at a white bedroom dresser, pulled open a drawer, closed it. "Cheaply made." She moved to a vanity table, and ducked to glance at her reflection in the child's eye-level mirror. "God, do I need a facial. I think I overindulged last night. Unlike some people," she said, "who drank ginger ale."

"Nothing wrong with ginger ale," Liam said. He would have preferred a Guinness last night, but had no problem at all sharing a ginger ale with his daughter. "Tasted quite good, in fact."

"That's because you're besotted." Miranda sat down on the lower mattress of a bunk bed, and looked up at Liam. "If your daughter wanted chocolate-covered grasshoppers washed down with cherry Kool-Aid, you'd go along with it."

"Faith would never waste a good grasshopper with chocolate," Liam said. "They're much better with strawberry jam. I'd go along with the cherry Kool-Aid, though."

"Pearse told me this morning he's worried." Miranda picked up a lamp with a frilled shade, examined the underside. "He thinks you have no idea of what you're getting yourself into. He said between Brid's problems and this thing with the kid, he's concerned about the band.'' She set the lamp down, and looked at Liam. ''Just relaying his thoughts.''

Liam rubbed his hand across the back of his neck. The children's furnishing department of an Ikea store in suburban Orange County didn't seem like the place to tell Miranda what she could do with her relayed thoughts, but she'd said one thing he couldn't let pass.

''The *kid* happens to be my daughter. Her name is Faith.'' He walked over to a grouping of furniture made of some sort of fabricated material. Probably laminated plywood, he thought. But the pieces were painted in bright primary colors. A red bed; dresser drawers in yellow, green and blue. A small yellow chair set in front of a blue desk. He could see Faith sitting there. He just wasn't sure what Hannah would think of it. She should be here with him, but he'd wanted to surprise her and Faith. He'd pictured them this evening, walking into Faith's room all set up with the new furniture.

''Liam.'' Miranda touched his arm. ''Don't be mad at me.''

Liam ignored her and looked around for a salesclerk. Faith would also need sheets and blankets. No doubt Hannah had plenty of her own, but he wanted to do this for Faith.

''You've put so much into the band, all of you,'' Miranda said. ''Brid, Pearse, Mick. You can't blame them for not wanting it to fall apart.''

''It's not going to fall apart.'' Liam took a credit card from his wallet, and checked his watch. ''Pearse knows I'd never let that happen.''

''He said he's never seen you like this. I'll be honest with you, Liam, Pearse and I had a long talk last night.

Maybe we'd had one too many piña coladas, but Pearse said he thinks this girl—''

''Girl?''

''Amy is it? No, Hannah, that's right. Why can't I seem to remember her name? Pearse thinks she's a bad influence. All she wants to do is come between you and the band and she won't be satisfied until she's got you trapped in Irvine or somewhere with two more kids and a mortgage.''

''Right then,'' Liam said after he'd signed the credit card receipt. ''I'm ready.''

''Liam.'' Miranda caught his arm. ''I care about you, I really do. You are making such a huge mistake. At least take a little time to cool off before you make a decision.'' She smiled at him, all perfect teeth and glossy hair. ''Puerto Vallarta is lovely. I could make reservations for us.''

AS HE HEADED ACROSS the manicured grounds of Casa Pacifica looking for Brid, it occurred to Liam that anyone who hadn't seen the discreet sign noting a physician was on twenty-four-hour call could be forgiven for thinking that he or she had wandered into an exclusive hotel instead of a rehab center.

He found Brid lying on a lawn chair; eyes closed, her bare shoulders turning almost the same shade of pink as her bikini top. Liam tweaked her toe and she opened her eyes and smiled.

''Well, there's a sight for sore eyes.'' She sat up, and held out her arms to him. ''Howya, Liam.''

''Not so bad.'' He sat down on the grass. ''And yourself?''

''Getting fat as a cow,'' she said.

''You've still a long way to go.''

"Not with the way they're feeding me here."

"Just keep doing as you're told," he said. "I need you back on the stage beside me."

She studied him for a long moment. "What's wrong, Liam?"

"Pearse thinks the band's about to break up. He blames me."

Brid shook her head. "Blames you for what?"

"Breaking up the band. He told Miranda that Hannah won't be satisfied until I'm wearing a ring."

"*Miranda.*" Brid rolled her eyes. "A head case if ever I saw one. Pearse was probably trying to get into her knickers. No doubt he was feeling his drink and just letting off a bit of steam."

"You don't think it then? That I'd let the band be broken up?"

"Daft cod," Brid said. "You'd give up breathing first."

Liam grinned.

She gave him another long look. "But I think it says something that you had to hear me confirm it. Six weeks ago, you'd have laughed your head off if Pearse had said something like that."

"Six weeks ago Pearse wouldn't have said something like that."

"How are things with your daughter?"

"Grand." He smiled. "Fantastic."

"And it's killing you to think of how it'll be when we're back on the road again."

"It is."

"But you wouldn't be happy with any other kind of life."

"I know."

"Remember when I asked if you ever feel like putting down roots?"

He shook his head. "No, but I can imagine what I said."

"Something about taking aspirin and lying down until the feeling went away." She pulled a towel off the back of the chaise longue, wrapped it around her shoulders. "Maybe you should do that now, Liam."

HANNAH WAS CUTTING PAPER flowers from colored construction paper and trying not to let Margaret's parting advice completely ruin her mood when Allan stopped in her classroom just before two to pick up Douglas for a doctor's appointment. In a Zen-like trance—anything to block Margaret's voice in her head—she'd already cut out a pile of pink paper roses. Bouquets of yellow daffodils and purple tulips blossomed in colorful profusion across her desktop.

Allan picked up a paper rose, and studied it. "I really enjoyed meeting your family last night. Your mother's quite a character. They all are."

"Yeah, well…" Her face felt warm. "They like you, too, Allan."

"Unfortunately, you don't feel the same way."

"That's not true," she protested. "You're a terrific guy. I'm just—"

"You're just not in love with me." He folded his arms across his chest. "How were the SpaghettiOs?"

"Faith liked them."

Allan grimaced. "God."

"I know." She traced the edge of a rose with her finger. "I'm sorry about walking out on you. It was rude, I know."

He waved away her apology. "It bothered your

mother more than it bothered me. Not that I wanted to see you go, but I looked at you looking at that guy and I recognized I was fighting a losing battle.'' He perched on the edge of her desk, picked up a framed picture of Faith, studied it, and set it down again. ''Listen, if I'm out of line, just tell me. I'm talking to you as an attorney who's done some family practice law, Hannah, not as a guy who would like to marry you.''

''Allan…''

''Sorry, strike that last part.'' He paused. ''Liam is Faith's biological father, right? There's no doubt about that?''

She blinked. ''Of course.''

''Okay, I just needed to know. And when the two of you were divorced, there were custody arrangements?''

''No. My mother told Liam I'd had an abortion.'' She saw Jen poke her head around the door and mouth the word *later* when she saw Allan. Hannah peered up at the clock on the wall. Nearly time to pick up Faith. ''What's this all about?''

He looked at her as though debating how to answer. ''I'm concerned for you.''

Hannah sighed, exasperated. ''Join the club. God, I wish to hell everyone would stop being concerned about me and get on with their own lives.''

Allan looked offended. ''This is just a case of a friend helping a friend,'' he said. ''You've given me some great advice on Douglas. I'm just returning the favor.''

''I'm sorry.'' She touched his arm. ''I'm a little weary of discussing Liam. I went through it this morning with my mom.''

''How serious is Liam about having a role in Faith's life?''

''Very.''

"Do you realize he has a good case for a lawsuit?" He waited a moment. "I'm not an expert on this, but I'm sure he could probably bring civil litigation against your mother. He could also sue for joint custody of Faith. I'm assuming he intends to go back to Ireland?"

She nodded. "Look, you're making it sound a lot more adversarial than it is. Liam's already told me he'd like to have Faith visit him in Ireland. I'm hoping it doesn't come to that, but if it does we'll deal with it."

"You'd allow him to take her to Ireland?"

"He's her father, Allan."

"So you're sure that whatever happens, that the two of you can work it all out?"

"I think we can."

He gave her a skeptical look.

"What?"

"What if you're wrong? What if he meets someone else when he goes back to Ireland? Marries her even. He'd still be Faith's father. Still have all the same rights to have her with him. Do you want another woman bringing up your child?"

"Of course not."

"Then I'd suggest you protect yourself. And Faith. If you want my advice, you'll launch a prepreemptive strike and file suit to stop him from trying to take Faith to Ireland."

"That's your advice, is it?"

"Absolutely."

"And it has nothing at all to do with anything my mom said to you at dinner last night, right?"

Before he could answer, the secretary stuck her head around the door to say that the nurse from Faith's school was on the phone. Faith had a stomachache and a fever of 101 and could someone come and pick her up?

LIAM WAS JUST LEAVING Miranda's when Hannah called to say the trip to the *Queen Mary* was off and that she'd already picked Faith up from school. "I don't think it's anything serious," Hannah said. "Too many SpaghettiOs last night, maybe."

Liam, staring through the plate-glass windows of Miranda's sunroom and out at the shimmering blue water, felt suddenly bereft, as though the whole reason for the day had just vanished. The feeling frightened him. Maybe Brid was right. Maybe he should lie down until these images of himself in an apron barbecuing on the back patio with Faith and Hannah looking on went away. He realized Hannah had said something.

"Sorry?"

"I asked if you'd like to come by for dinner tonight," she said.

"Your house?"

"My mother's. I want you to get to know each other a little better. She's convinced that you're a scheming womanizer and that I don't know what the hell I'm doing."

He laughed, but without much humor. "Are you as confused about all this as I am?" he asked.

"Yeah," she said. "I probably am."

"Everyone giving you advice? Making predictions?"

"Yep. You?"

"Advice and gloomy prophecies. The consensus being that I've no idea what I'm getting into."

"Hey, Liam," she said. "Have faith."

SO WHILE THE BAND—without him and Brid—was doing a scaled-down gig at an Irish bar up in Pasadena, here he was sitting at the dinner table with Hannah's mother, her aunts and her sister, who were all clearly on their best behavior but not exactly welcoming him into the fold.

In an agony of indecision, he'd arrived with a box of chocolates for Margaret and flowers for Hannah. When Margaret took the chocolates, she'd said something about being on a diet and he realized he should have bought flowers for her, too, and maybe he should have picked up something for the aunts and the sister. Five minutes into the meal he was almost wishing he'd never come.

But truthfully he was glad to be here. Hannah sat next to him, her hand on his knee, and Faith, all better now, kept jabbing him with her small pointed elbow as she wielded her knife and fork. Every so often, she'd turn to grin at him and phrases like ''worthwhile sacrifice'' would drift through his brain as he imagined giving up music to have her in his life.

And although you could bounce a penny off Margaret's stiff expression, Hannah's sister Debra seemed friendly enough, as did Aunt Rose, who kept winking at him across the table and finding ways to bring him into the conversation, which, at the moment, was all about the price of houses in California—a topic Californians seemed to spend a great deal of time discussing.

''So anyway, Liam,'' Rose was saying. ''This guy I used to go with was also from Ireland and he said it's the same thing there. Germans buying up the west. Tearing down the thatched cottages and building these great big mansions on the water.'' She frowned, and scratched the back of her elaborately piled-up red hair. ''Or was it the south. Where's Clare?''

''West,'' he said.

''Cute guy,'' Rose said. ''Declan. Well, not cute exactly—he had a face like a potato—but I loved his accent.'' She winked. ''Tore all my defenses down, if you know what I mean.''

Hannah shot him a sideways glance and squeezed his knee.

Debra grinned. ''We don't know what you mean by defenses, Aunt Rose. Actually, we didn't know you had any.''

Helen cleared her throat. ''Do you own property, Liam?'' she asked.

''I do,'' he said. Hannah's hand was still on his knee. ''In Galway.''

''Gahlweh,'' Faith mimicked, and shifted around in her chair to look at him. ''You talk funny, Liam.''

''Faith.'' Hannah and Margaret said in unison.

''I didn't know you had a house,'' Hannah said.

''I bought it a couple of years ago.''

''A big house?'' Rose wanted to know.

''Big enough,'' he said. ''Too big for me, really. A family of five could fit comfortably in it.'' After that, everyone went silent. He looked down at the lasagna on his plate. Hannah had made it herself—apologizing in advance because she wasn't much of a cook. He felt Faith's elbow again, heard the chink of cutlery against plates.

Tried to imagine his life this way, sitting down to supper every night with all this family. He and Hannah would get their own place of course, but where? Even with last year's success, he wasn't making the kind of money to afford California real estate.

Margaret drank some wine. She set her glass down and looked at him from across the table. ''I remember Hannah telling me once that you never wanted to be tied down to one place. She said you were going to buy a gypsy caravan and roam around the country, just the two of you.''

''I don't remember saying that,'' Hannah protested.

''What's a gypsy caravan?'' Faith asked.

''Kind of like a Winnebago, honey,'' Rose said. ''Except that horses pull it instead of an engine.''

''Cool,'' Faith said. ''I like horses.''

''I used to ask Hannah what she would do if you had children.'' Margaret addressed Liam. ''And she just laughed and said exposure was good for kids.''

Rose laughed. ''Exposure to what?''

Helen cleared her throat again.

''I really don't remember that.'' Hannah turned to look at him. ''Do you remember that, Liam? The gypsy thing?''

''Actually, I do,'' he said. ''I'd always wanted a caravan. I still wouldn't mind one, come to that.'' He drank some wine, angry at his response. How bloody brilliant was that? If he was trying to make an impression, that was just the thing to say. No wonder Hannah's family wasn't pushing for him and Hannah to make another trip to the altar.

Margaret directed a frosty smile at him. ''Have you ever considered what you'll be doing…twenty or so years from now?'' She bent her head slightly to spear a slice of tomato on her fork, and eyed him from across the table. ''When you're getting older, looking toward retirement?''

''Liam's thirty-five, Mom,'' Hannah protested. ''Who thinks about retirement at that age? I certainly don't. Neither does Deb.'' She looked at her sister. ''Right?''

''Only that I damn sure don't want to be still waiting tables at Claim Jumper when I'm fifty,'' Deb said.

''Find a rich husband,'' Rose said. ''That's my philosophy. 'Course, *you'd* have to find a rich wife, Liam." She laughed. "Unless…oh shut up, Rose."

Helen gave her sister an arch glance. "Good idea, Rose."

"To answer your question, Margaret," Liam said. "No, I haven't thought that far ahead."

Margaret's gaze was fixed on Faith. "Well, Liam, if you're…contemplating a family, I would suggest that the future is something to which you *should* give some thought."

CHAPTER FOURTEEN

"SOMETHING TELLS ME I didn't exactly win over your mother tonight," Liam told Hannah as they stood in the kitchen washing dishes. "I should have lied and said, 'Yes, I've given it a lot of thought and I've decided brain surgery is the life for me with maybe a bit of investment banking as a sideline.' Would that have made her happy, do you think?"

Hannah drained the Chianti left in her glass. Faith was in bed, the others were in the living room watching *Survivor.* It seemed an appropriate choice, she thought wryly.

"Your goal in life isn't to make my mom happy."

"That's a good thing," he said, "or I'd be failing miserably."

Hannah draped the damp tea towel over the bar on the front of the stove. During lunch break at school, she'd skimmed through the *Los Angeles Times.* Actually, she'd been idly browsing the classifieds for herself, wondering about more fulfilling occupations than coaching the Taylor Beckers of the world to ace kindergarten exams.

A private academy in Studio City wanted a music teacher. She'd read the ad, reread it, then turned to the next page and gone on reading. But she couldn't stop thinking about it. Before she'd left to pick up Faith, she clipped the ad and stuck it in her purse. Now, her heart kicking up, she looked at Liam.

"I have something to show you." Her purse was upstairs in her room. She motioned for him to follow her. Inside her room, she closed the door and fished around in her purse.

Liam sat down on the edge of the bed. "Won't this raise a few eyebrows downstairs?"

She looked at him. "I'll keep both feet on the floor."

As he read the clipping she handed him, she watched his face and realized that she was holding her breath. The exchange with Allan had played in her head all afternoon. He'd raised a question she hadn't allowed herself to contemplate. The thought of Liam taking Faith to Ireland was only bearable if she pictured herself as part of the trio. But Faith in Ireland with Liam and…God, Brid—or an Irish version of Miranda Payton—helping raise Faith was more than she could bear.

He looked up at her. "This would do the trick, would it?"

She waited a moment, thinking about how to answer him. "It would be a stable and secure job," she finally said. "The money's not bad. You'd still be working in the music industry and you'd be here in California."

He held out his hand to her, and she sat down on the bed beside him. The room was warm and a little stuffy. The light through the pink floral lampshade by the bed glowed a rosy gold. Liam's eyes looked very blue. He put his arm around her shoulder, turned his head to kiss her. She could hear the TV downstairs. She knew Margaret had probably heard their feet on the stairs, in fact, had probably *listened* for the sound of their feet on the stairs. The kiss lasted as they fell against the bed, Liam on top of her, his erection hard against her groin. And then he sat up suddenly, as though a thought had just occurred to him. He leaned against the headboard.

"What about all the other stuff?" he asked.

"What other stuff?"

"My insatiable need to chase skirts for instance."

She picked at her fingernail. "I've thought a lot about that. Not you chasing skirts, I mean. Just the whole scene when we were married. I was so damn insecure that I managed to work myself into this constant frenzy of suspicion. I'm a lot more secure these days."

"Which isn't exactly a ringing endorsement of my fidelity."

"Maybe I had no real reason not to trust you when we were married. My mom said something today about believing what we want to believe. Maybe I almost wanted to believe you were running around because I was so damn sure you'd leave me eventually, I was just kind of preparing myself for the inevitable." She put her arm around his shoulder, and kissed the side of his mouth. "Plus, I could just tell myself you were a no-good jerk."

Smiling now, he studied the ad again. "We could live in Los Angeles. Buy his and her convertibles. A house with a swimming pool."

"On a music teacher's salary." She grinned. "Dream on."

"Something I've always been good at."

"Dreaming?" She got up from the bed, and locked her fingers behind her neck. "This is a huge decision for you. An incredible sacrifice—"

"It *is* a big decision, I'll grant you that. I don't see it as a sacrifice though. Not if I had you and Faith."

Hannah sat down on the bed beside him again. Something was stopping her from abandoning all resistance and saying, *Yes let's do it. Let's be a family again.* It was as though Liam were on the other side of a river and she couldn't quite bring herself to swim across the water that separated them. He was smiling, his hand extended. She wanted to be with him, but she couldn't quite do it.

"At least I can look into it." Liam glanced at the ad again. "I'll ring them tomorrow." He took her hand. "We're still on for the *Queen Mary,* right?"

"Yep." *The zoo, the* Queen Mary, *pretend camping in an unfurnished apartment. If they could just go on doing fun things, deferring reality, instead of dealing with dull stuff like jobs and security, life would be a whole lot easier.*

"IS LIAM YOUR BOYFRIEND, Mommy?" Faith asked the next morning as Hannah was pouring cereal into a bowl.

"Well, not exactly," Hannah hedged. "How come you're asking that?"

"Auntie Rose said he was your boyfriend."

Hannah poured milk into a bowl of Cheerios, and set it in front of Faith. "Don't forget to feed your hamster before you leave." Evasion by distraction, she thought. Not exactly the preferred La Petite Ecole method, but Faith was her daughter, not her student.

"I thought Allan was your boyfriend." Faith dug into the Cheerios. "Can people have two boyfriends?"

"Two boyfriends?" Rose shuffled into the kitchen. "Sure, honey, if you can manage it, more power to you."

Hannah frowned at Rose. She'd gone to bed after Liam left, then stayed awake half the night wondering whether it had been a mistake to tell him about the job. What if he took it and wasn't happy? What if he ended up hating her for forcing him into something he'd never really wanted? What if Faith wasn't happy having him around? She felt surly and distracted; her head ached with indecision.

"I like Allan, Mommy," Faith said. "Want to know why?"

"Huh?" She looked at her daughter who had left the table and was sitting cross-legged on the floor, the puppy in her lap lapping milk from Faith's cereal bowl. *"Faith."* Hannah grabbed the bowl, and set it in the sink. "The puppy has his own bowl to eat from."

"I like Allan because he has a little boy for me to play with," Faith said.

"And a big house on Riva Alto Canal," Rose said.

"Rose." Hannah glared at her aunt. "Shut the hell up."

"Oooh, Mommy said a bad word," Faith said.

"Mommy's not in a good mood this morning," Rose observed.

No, she wasn't, Hannah thought as she went upstairs to get ready for school. And her mood wasn't improved when she stopped to get a notebook she'd left in the study and found a downloaded page entitled: Getting Custody of Your Grandchildren.

Her face burning, Hannah read through the material.

According to the U.S. Census Bureau, in 1997, 3.9 million children lived in homes maintained by their grandparents, up 76 percent from 2.2 million in 1970. In a majority of the cases, grandparents were the primary caregivers. Despite this fact, it is not always easy for grandparents to get custody of their grandchildren. Courts are reluctant to award custody to anyone other than the parents.

> The law varies from state to state, but in general, grandparents cannot petition the court for custody if the family is intact—i.e. both parents are at home with the children. Grandparents may, however, intervene in a custody dispute. In some states, grandparents may also ask for custody if the child has been living with them for an extended period of time (e.g., six months, one year).

Margaret had underlined the last two lines.

Hannah barged into her mother's room. Empty, the bed made up. She ran downstairs to the kitchen. Rose was pouring chocolate syrup onto a slice of toast. Faith was grinning, her mouth rimmed with chocolate.

"Hey, Mommy," she said as Hannah stormed in. "Look what me and Auntie Rose invented." She held out the bread. "Want to try some?"

"No, I don't, thank you." Ignoring Faith's wail of dismay, she grabbed the toast and stuffed it down the garbage disposal. "You know better than to eat chocolate on toast for breakfast," she told her daughter. "Even if the adults around here don't."

"Uh-oh," Rose said in mock terror. "I'd better get out of here."

"Rose." Hands on her hips, Hannah addressed her aunt. "Where's Mom?"

"She left early. Something about an appointment downtown."

THE *QUEEN MARY* WAS NOT turning out to be one of his better ideas, Liam thought as he watched Hannah run down the promenade deck after a sulky Faith, who had told her mother that she wanted to ride a real boat that went somewhere, not a stupid boat that just stayed in one place. She wanted to ride in a boat like Allan's boat. She liked Allan. She was bored. She wanted someone to play with. She wanted to call Douglas.

Liam looked out at the blue water. White boats glided back and forth. Sailboats, power boats churning up a wake, darting red water taxis, a streamlined white vessel that went over to Catalina. He'd suggested earlier, in light of Faith's unhappiness with the *Queen Mary,* that they take the boat over to Avalon, stay the night and return the next day. Faith had brightened at this, but Hannah frowned and reminded him that she had a job to go to.

She'd been tense from the moment he'd arrived at the house on Termino. He didn't know what was wrong. She hadn't offered an explanation, and he hadn't asked.

He turned from the water, and watched Hannah walk toward him, holding Faith's hand. Hannah was saying something to Faith that he couldn't catch, looking down at her as she spoke. Faith nodded a couple of times, her expression still petulant.

"What do you have to say to Liam?" Hannah asked as they reached the window where he stood.

Liam felt a surge of anger. Hannah could force Faith to apologize to Allan, or to any of her other boyfriends; he didn't want his daughter apologizing to him because she'd behaved like a six-year-old. He ruffled Faith's hair. "That's all right, listen, I've got an idea—"

"No, it's not all right, Liam." Hannah looked at her daughter. "Faith?"

Faith kicked at the wooden deck with the toe of her red sandal. "Sorry."

"Sorry, who?" Hannah asked.

"Sorry, Liam."

Liam flinched. Sorry, *Liam.* His daughter had called him Liam. He looked around, almost blindly, wanting to strike out at something. She'd called him by his name before, but this time it felt like a wound reopened. Hannah realized her mistake and touched his arm. He pulled away. ''Let's get out of here,'' he said.

In silence they made their way to the elevator and off the boat. With no direction in mind, he started down a footpath that cut through a grassy verge along the edge of the water. He felt the wind in his face, saw the sunlight off the water. Something had gone wrong and he didn't know what to say to fix it. More to the point, he didn't know what had caused it to go wrong in the first place.

''Can we go in there?'' Faith pointed across the water to a circular blue building painted with sea creatures. ''I want to go in there and see the porpoise.''

''That's not the aquarium,'' Hannah said. She glanced at Liam. ''I don't know why Long Beach painted the convention center to look like an aquarium. The aquarium's down there.'' She nodded in the direction of a structure further across the bay. ''People are always getting it confused.''

''I want to go to the aquarium,'' Faith said.

''Not today,'' Hannah said.

''When?'' Faith tugged at Hannah's hand. ''When can we go to the aquarium?''

Anxious to turn the day around, Liam opened his mouth to suggest they go right now, then thought better of it. They all kept walking, past large rocks and boulders set along the water's edge. He stopped to look at a couple of boys with fishing poles sitting on the rocks. On some lower rocks, a couple of girls, maybe a little older than Faith, were jumping from one boulder to the next. Hannah and Faith had stopped, too, and stood beside him. He watched Faith watching the girls and edging a little closer. One of the girls jumped to a rock at the water level. The other one clambered down, arms waving to steady herself. Their laughter carried in the breeze.

"I need to go to the restroom." Hannah glanced over her shoulder in the direction of a low stucco building, then she caught Faith's hand. "Let's go."

"I don't need to go." Faith was still watching the girls.

"I'll watch her," Liam said.

Hannah took off across the grass. The girls on the rocks were both down at the water's edge, bending to look at a small tide pool in the hollowed surface of a rock. Faith looked at Liam.

"I want to go down there."

"Go ahead," he said. "I'll go with you." He took her hand and they climbed down three boulders. One of the girls waved to Faith.

"I know that girl," Faith said. "Her name's Yolanda. Can I go down where she is?"

Both girls were smiling up at Faith, calling for her to see the shells they'd found. Faith was clearly impatient to be with them. Liam checked his shoulder to see if Hannah had started back, but couldn't spot her. When he turned back in the direction of the rocks and water, Faith was on the boulder immediately below the one where he stood and had started to maneuver her way down, arms outstretched, to the next one.

"Hold on, Faith," he called as he scrambled down after her. "I'll give you a hand."

''Faith,'' one of the girls called out. ''You have to see this shell, it is so cool.''

''Faith,'' Hannah shouted from the top of the bluff. ''Come on, let's go.''

''She's fine, Hannah,'' Liam called over his shoulder. ''I'm watching her.''

Down at the water's edge, the rocks were green and shiny with seaweed. The girls held out dripping hands to show Faith what they'd found. Liam lowered himself onto one of the rocks. Faith was smiling now, a different child from the sullen one on the deck of the *Queen Mary*. He felt his mood lift as he watched her, wind blowing her hair about her face, billowing the back of her denim shirt. The trio had moved a few yards along the lower tier of rocks when he heard Hannah's voice behind him. He turned to see her climbing down the rocks to where he sat. Faith had also looked up to see her mother.

''Mommy. I have to show you this really neat thing.'' Her hands cupped, Faith made her way across the seaweed-covered rocks, her brow furrowed in concentration. ''It is *so* cool, you'll be amazed.''

Liam grinned and saw that Hannah was smiling, too. He put his arm around her shoulder, and pulled her to him. Infused with a sudden burst of happiness, he couldn't keep the smile off his face. He kissed the side of her mouth.

''Faith asked me this morning if you were my boyfriend,'' she said.

He felt himself tense slightly. ''And what did you tell her?''

Whatever answer she might have given was frozen by the splash of noise and confusion at the water's edge. In an instant Liam was down there, lifting his shaking, shivering daughter from the bay.

AT TEN THAT SAME NIGHT, Hannah sat in her bedroom talking on the phone to Liam. "Look, quit blaming yourself, okay? It wasn't your fault. We were both there with her, watching her. It was just an accident."

"I keep telling myself I should never have let her go down there in the first place."

"Kids play there all the time, Liam. Deb and I used to spend hours on those same rocks and I was younger than Faith. I even fell into the water a couple of times. It's no big deal. I mean you could see that for yourself. She'd almost forgotten about it by the time we got her home. She's fine. In bed and sound asleep."

"Right...well. You know her best."

She switched the receiver to her other ear. Liam wasn't convinced. She could hear it in his voice. Faith's tumble into the water had been the low point in an afternoon that never really got off the ground.

Mostly it was her fault. All day, she'd been unable to shake the stunned disbelief that her mother had, at the very least, considered the possibility of getting custody of Faith. She'd tried, unsuccessfully, to reach Margaret later in the afternoon when Hannah got home from school. Margaret was out. She hadn't returned by the time Liam stopped by to pick up Hannah and Faith.

In a masterpiece of bad timing, Margaret *had* been home when they'd carried Faith, wet and shivering, into the house. Without a word of explanation, Hannah had taken Faith upstairs. After Liam left and Faith was in bed, she'd felt too exhausted to confront Margaret. Liam's call came just as she'd drifted off to sleep.

"I called about the job," he said, after the silence between them had become uncomfortable. "They asked me to send a résumé." He laughed. "I've never written a bloody résumé in my life."

"I can help you with that," she said, sounding in her own ears exactly as her Aunt Helen had years ago when Hannah protested that she really didn't have the background to apply for a position at La Petite Ecole.

"Help me with what?" Liam asked. "I've played in bands. Other people's and now my own. How do you turn that into a résumé?"

"Well, the position *is* for a music teacher," Hannah pointed out without much enthusiasm. Maybe they were trying to do the impossible. Square pegs in round holes, that sort of thing. She felt tired and discouraged. "Listen, we can talk about it tomorrow." She yawned. "Right now I'm so bushed, I can't even think."

"Yeah..." Liam said. "Right."

She waited a moment. "You're not happy, are you?"

He sighed. "I'm so bloody confused about everything, Hannah. I don't know if I'm pushing you into something you don't really want. I don't know if I'm pushing myself into something I don't really want. I don't know if what we're doing is right for Faith. I just don't know."

"Liam..." A deep wave of tenderness for him made her throat close. If all of this was hard for her, how much harder must it be for him? Regardless of what happened, she would always have Faith in her life. Liam didn't have that certainty. "I love you," she said, surprising herself.

"That helps," he said after a moment. "A lot."

"Well, I do." Despite her own doubts and fears, it suddenly seemed vital that she reassure him. "I love that you care enough about Faith that you're willing to make this huge sacrifice to be with her. I love the way you are with her and I love you, Liam..." She stopped, self-consciousness halting the stream of words.

"Go on," he said. "I'm feeling better by the second."

"I feel as though I'm seeing a side to you I never

knew when we were married. It's as though I didn't know you then. I mean, I still don't really…''

''And when you find out that I have this thing for women in black corsets, leather boots and whips…''

''Humor is a distancing mechanism,'' she said. ''I learned the term from my Aunt Rose. She got a B+ in Intro to Psychology. Humor stops you from dealing with things you don't want to deal with.''

''Read any good books lately?''

''*Avoidance* is another term Aunt Rose told me about.''

''Is that right?''

''Yep. That's one thing that hasn't changed about you, Liam. It still kills you to talk about feelings, doesn't it?''

''Yeah,'' he said softly. ''I've never been good at that. Never had much of a chance to be good at it, come to that. But don't let that stop you from saying things like you just did. In fact, do me a big favor, would you, and say it again.''

Hannah rolled over on her stomach, phone melded to her ear, smile spreading across her face. ''I love you,'' she said.

''Ditto,'' he said. ''We'll work it all out, won't we?''

''Yeah.'' Still smiling. Believing, at least for now.

''And tomorrow? What's on the agenda?''

''Want to pick Faith up from school?''

''What time?''

''Come by about two. We'll walk down there.''

''How about if I make it earlier? Half-past twelve or so?''

''I'll still be in school. Why?''

''Oh, I don't know. An hour or so up in your bedroom has a lot of appeal.''

''Did I ever tell you you were bad news?''

"You might have mentioned it a few hundred times."

"Well you are," she said. "But I love you anyway."

She was still smiling as she walked downstairs, suddenly ravenous, to get something to eat. Halfway down, she caught the aroma of baking from the kitchen, heard her mother's voice and then Faith's saying something she couldn't quite catch. *What was Faith doing up at this hour?* Faith spoke again and then Hannah heard Rose's voice.

"...your mommy and Liam were *kissing* when you fell into the water?"

"They were sitting on the rocks and Liam had his arm around Mommy and I saw him kiss her," Faith said. "And then my foot slipped and I fell into the water."

Anger like a red haze in her brain, Hannah stood transfixed. Her mother was talking now, asking Faith whether she had ever seen Mommy and Liam kiss before. And then Faith was saying that Allan was her mommy's boyfriend, that she liked Allan because she could play with Douglas. Her heart beating so hard she thought it might actually burst in her chest, Hannah sat down on the stairs.

"So what about your mommy's new apartment?" Margaret asked. "Did you like going there with Mommy and Liam?"

"It doesn't have any furniture," Faith said. "So we had to sit on the floor and have candles. And then I spilled ginger ale on my shirt and Liam took his shirt off and then Mommy took mine off—"

"Mommy or Liam?" Margaret asked.

Something seemed to detonate in Hannah's head. She burst into the kitchen, plucked Faith and the blanket covering her up from the chair she'd been sitting on and left the room in a blur of movement; aware—as if in a dream—of Margaret's startled expression, of Rose darting aside to avoid being plowed down, of Faith's warm, wriggling body under the blanket as she was carried up the stairs, protesting that the chocolate chip cookies weren't ready and Grandma had promised she could have two.

In blind fury, Hannah set Faith down on the bed. She looked at her daughter and tried to bring her voice under control. "Listen, sweetie..." Her voice and body were shaking. "We're going on a kind of adventure, okay?" She went to Faith's dresser drawer, pulled out socks and underwear, dumped them on the rocker, opened another draw and gathered pants and shirts.

"But I want a cookie." Faith's voice turned tearful. "I don't like you, Mommy. You're being mean."

"Hannah," Margaret said from the doorway. "I think you need to calm down a little, okay? You're frightening your daughter."

Faith started crying, little whimpering sounds.

Her back to Margaret, Hannah clutched a pile of Faith's clothes. Her teeth were chattering, her body trembled. Behind her, Margaret was telling Faith not to cry. Mommy was just upset about something, Margaret was saying. Mommy would be fine. They'd all be fine. Still shaking, Hannah went to the closet and started to pull down Faith's overnight bag. A little red suitcase Helen had bought last Christmas. She tugged it out from under a couple of boxes, a jerky movement that sent it tumbling to the floor. One of the clasps had rusted and the case burst open, spilling assorted drawings and schoolwork Faith had brought home. In the few moments it took to stack them into an empty shoe box, reason trickled back in. Maybe this wasn't the way to handle the situation. Faith, already upset, would be confused.

Frightened. She had no idea why her mother and grandmother were fighting. Hannah took a deep breath, and tried to compose her face as she looked at her daughter.

"Hey, you know what?" She studied her watch, noting in her peripheral vision that Margaret was no longer in the doorway. "It is *late*. Really late. After midnight, in fact." Faith regarded her wide-eyed, not entirely convinced things were back to normal. "How about a bedtime story?" Hannah asked her daughter.

"What about our adventure?"

"Let's put the adventure off until tomorrow," she said. "What d'you say? It's kind of late for an adventure tonight."

"Can I have a cookie?" Faith asked.

Hannah pretended to consider. "It's very late, but if you brush your teeth really well afterward, I guess you can have one."

She tucked her daughter into bed, kissed her forehead and went down to the kitchen to get a cookie. From the living room, she could hear the TV, but no voices. She got the cookie, poured milk into a glass and carried it upstairs. Faith was already asleep. Carefully she closed Faith's door, set the milk and cookies on the hall table and walked across the hallway to Margaret's bedroom.

CHAPTER FIFTEEN

MARGARET, IN HER PURPLE ROBE, was sitting up in bed, a *New Yorker* spread across her knees, her bifocals down low on her nose. One side of her face lit by the bedside lamp, she listened without a word as Hannah demanded an explanation for the downloaded information. Demanded an explanation *and* an apology for grilling Faith.

"You have seriously overstepped your boundaries, Mom. You have absolutely no right—"

"No, as far you're concerned, I have no rights, do I? It's all about Liam's rights. To hell with the fact that I'm her grandmother. To hell with the fact that Faith has been a part of my life from the moment she first came into the world. I *watched* her come into the world. And now suddenly, it's all Liam this and Liam that." The *New Yorker* slid to the floor and she leaned over to pick it up. "I'm sick to death of it. If this was a responsible guy with a normal job and the means to provide my granddaughter with a decent home, it would be one thing. Maybe I wouldn't be happy about it, but I could accept it. But no, it's some damn foreign musician who has decided he wants to be a daddy and suddenly you've abandoned any shred of common sense. Well, I'm sorry, but if you're expecting an apology from me, you're not going to get it. And I'll tell you one thing. Faith would never have fallen into the water if I'd been watching her."

After that, Margaret burst into tears. By then it was after one and since there seemed to be no way to resolve things, Hannah left and went into her room. She dropped fully dressed across the bed, but she didn't fall asleep. She thought about the things she'd said to Liam, the things Margaret had said to her. Thought about how to make everything all right again. Around four in the morning, she went down to the kitchen and poured herself a glass of wine from Margaret's jug. But still she couldn't derail her brain. It kept running down the same track, colliding inevitably with Liam's rights as a father and her mother's rights as a grandmother who'd helped raise her granddaughter. Liam's happiness if he gave up his music, her own happiness and, overshadowing everything else, Faith's happiness.

When the room began to fill with hazy morning light, she gave up on sleep altogether, pulled on her robe and began to make coffee. Some time later, Margaret came down, dressed in a burgundy blazer and gray slacks. When Hannah told her mother that she and Liam would be picking up Faith from school, Margaret gave a brittle smile, picked up her purse and walked out.

For the first time in the four years she'd worked at La Petite Ecole, Hannah called in sick that morning. After taking Faith to school, she spent the morning packing clothes from her room and Faith's into cardboard boxes. Debra dropped by about ten. She'd just returned from a visit to the obstetrician.

"When you had Faith, did you feel like a grown-up right away, or did you still feel like a kid?" she asked Hannah.

Hannah, on her knees trying to decide what to throw in a sack for Goodwill and what to pack, sat back on her heels to look at her sister. Her head felt like cotton from not sleeping, and she suspected Debra was more interested in spilling out her own feelings than listening to hers, so she took the easy way out. ‘‘Is that how you feel? Like a kid still?’’

‘‘Kind of. I mean, here I am back home again with Mom fussing over me, nagging me about eating right, and I’m thinking, God, I’m going to have this kid who is actually going to need *me.*’’

Hannah looked at her sister. Debra’s face was flushed. She wore a baggy black T-shirt and gray leggings that ended just below her knees. Flopped on Hannah’s bed, a black baseball cap pulled low on her head, she looked less like a mother-to-be than someone who had just wandered out of a college class.

‘‘I mean, don’t you ever kind of resent Faith?’’ Debra asked. ‘‘Like, if you didn’t have her you’d be free to do all these other things, travel, bum around…I don’t know, it just seems like this huge responsibility.’’

‘‘It *is* a huge responsibility.’’

‘‘But did you think about that before you had Faith? Or did you just kind of…get pregnant?’’

‘‘I don’t know, Deb.’’ Hannah shook her head. She wasn’t up to philosophical discussion on motherhood. ‘‘I guess I didn’t give it a whole lot of thought.’’

‘‘Yeah…’’ Debra turned onto her side, face propped on her elbow. ‘‘Mom said the only thing you really cared about was Liam—’’

‘‘Mom said that, huh?’’ Hannah felt a return of last night’s red rage. ‘‘Well, Mom can damn well go to hell.’’

‘‘Hannah.’’ Deb regarded her with a faint smile. ‘‘What are you getting so mad about? I mean, sure you love Faith now and you’re a good mother and everything, but you were kind of like the way I feel right now.

It's like you weren't really a grown-up. You were just a kid who was obsessed with this guy and then you had a kid yourself. You were lucky Mom and everyone could help you out."

Hannah managed to finish packing the box she was filling with Faith's underwear and nightclothes. She excused herself to Deb, went into the bathroom and stood under the shower for thirty minutes. Afterward, as she dried her hair, she stared at her face through a clear spot in the fogged-up mirror. Her mouth looked strained, her eyes puffy. If only she could have flat-out denied Deb's assertion…

SHE WAS DOWN at the mailbox, picking up the day's assortment of catalogs and grocery store fliers when Liam pulled up thirty minutes early. The mail in hand, she watched him reach for something on the seat, then open the passenger door of the Mercedes. He walked to where she stood, a smile on his face and a bunch of pink roses in his hand. Despite everything, her heart sped up with no regard to the turmoil churning in her brain.

"Any million-dollar checks for me there?" Liam asked, with a nod at the mail she was holding. "Checks, fan mail?"

"Hi." She smiled. "No mail for you." His white T-shirt read: What's The Craic! Find Out In The *Irish Post.*

"All things considered—" she flicked his chest "—not the best thing to wear to your daughter's school."

He frowned, peered down at his shirt. "What?"

"Craic?"

He grinned. "It doesn't mean crack, it means fun. It's Gaelic. The *Post* publishes a calendar of what clubs are playing where.'' He shrugged. ''I see your point though. Kids could read it wrong.''

''Yep.''

''God.'' He sighed. ''I've a lot to learn, haven't I?''

''Hey...'' She glanced at the roses in his hand, up at his face, the smile gone now. ''You're doing fine, don't worry about it.''

He handed her the roses. ''Do you know what pink means?''

She shook her head. ''Do you?''

He grinned. ''No idea.''

''You're early. We still have about ten minutes before we pick her up.''

''Alert the media,'' he said. ''The first time in my life I've ever been early.''

''I'll take these into the house.'' Roses in hand, she started up the path, aware of Liam following her. She walked through the back door into the kitchen, felt him watching her as she bent to get a vase from one of the lower shelves. She carried the container over to the sink, ran water into it and began to arrange the roses. Liam came up behind her and put his arms around her waist. Dug his chin into her shoulder.

''Talk to me,'' he said. ''What's wrong?''

She stayed very still, suddenly on the verge of tears. ''Oh...stuff.''

''Stuff.'' His chin was still on her shoulder, his hands locked over her stomach. ''Bloody awful that stuff, isn't it?''

''Yeah.''

''What variety of stuff?''

''Everything.'' She exhaled. ''My mom's talking about wanting custody of Faith.''

He said nothing for a moment. Then he took her hand,

led her over to the table and they both sat down. Hannah looked at him in his Craic T-shirt, at the planes of his face, his mouth, and something just seemed to dissolve inside her. He leaned forward in his chair, put his arms around her again, stroked her hair as she cried against his chest. When the sobs subsided, she got up and mopped at her face with a paper towel. Then she sat down again.

"I don't think it will really come to that, but it's obviously crossed her mind." She sat facing Liam, her knees touching his. "Everything's such a mess. I feel as though my mother's become my enemy."

He got up, and walked over to the window. The roses, visible from the kitchen, bloomed in bouquets of red, yellow and pink. He turned around to face Hannah. "I wrote up the résumé last night. I brought it for you to have a look at. Maybe it would reassure Margaret if she thought…" He shrugged. "That I wasn't about to move the two of you to Ireland."

She sighed. "I'm not sure if your getting a job is really the answer, Liam. If you'd made the decision independently of me and Faith, it would be different, but—"

"I wouldn't be thinking about it if it weren't for you and Faith," he said.

"That's my point. What if you regret it a year from now?"

"There are no guarantees, Hannah. Life's a calculated risk."

"But how well have you calculated this one?"

"Okay then, here's the deal." He came to kneel by her chair. "It's never going to work if we're both pessimistic at the same time. Last night was my turn to sing the blues. You were the one who said we'd pull through, remember?''

She smiled slightly.

''Well, now it's your turn to wail and gnash your teeth. Go on. Do it while you can. Then it'll be my turn.''

Her smile broadened. ''You're nuts. You know that?''

''I love you. You know that?''

She nodded. Liam leaned forward to kiss her. He got up a few moments later, sat on a chair, pulled her up on his lap and kissed her again.

''Optimism alone isn't enough, though,'' he said. ''We need a plan. Tonight, after Faith goes to bed, let's have a talk with Margaret. Maybe we can get her to see our side.''

Hannah nodded. ''I guess it couldn't hurt.''

''Come on.'' He caught her hands. ''Cheer up. One of these days when we've got six kids and grandchildren running around all over the place, we'll look back on this and laugh.''

''You think so?''

''Absolutely. First, though, we need to do something about my shirt.''

''Take it off.''

He did. The shirt in one hand, he grinned at her. ''Now what?''

She laughed. Liam was wiry rather than muscular and his bare chest showed little evidence that he'd spent time basking under the California sun. But damn, he turned her on. Standing there in her mother's kitchen, blue-eyed and sexy in his black jeans that sat low enough on his belly that… ''I'll get you another shirt,'' she said. ''After you kiss me again.''

AND THEN THEY WERE OUT on the street, Liam in a yellow polo shirt Deb's ex-boyfriend had left at the house. Walking hand in hand down Termino to Faith's school with the sun warm on her back and the scent of orange blossoms in the air. As they crossed Ocean Boulevard, Hannah looked out at the strip of shimmering, postcard-blue Pacific visible behind Albertson's market and felt a surge of pure happiness that, like blinding sunshine, overpowered everything but the moment. Impulsively she brought Liam's hand to her mouth and kissed it.

"I love you," she said.

He stopped walking. "Say that again."

"I love you."

Liam smiled and looked so much like Faith that Hannah almost told him once more. They started walking again, swinging hands, Liam humming something she didn't recognize.

"You know something?" she said to him. "I wish we could just take Faith and somehow…encapsulate ourselves in our own little world. It's all the outside influences that screw things up."

"There's a spaceship parked outside Miranda's," he said.

"I'll get packed."

"I know what you mean, though," he said after a moment. "When I'm with you and Faith, I have no doubt we could make things work. And then…" He sighed. "Actually, there's some concern about the future of the band. What with Brid out of things for a while. Pearse thinks I've lost interest…"

"Lost interest?" Hannah looked at him. "Is he kidding?"

"Well, I've been distracted. Brid's having treatment, so there's some excuse for her missing practice sessions, but I've skipped a couple of sessions myself. The other night, for instance. I'd planned to go out for a quick meal, when I ran into you and Faith."

Hannah said nothing, but a cloud drifted across the horizon. For one evening, Liam had chosen Faith over his music. How many times could he make that kind of choice and not begin to resent the sacrifice?

"Ah, to hell with it all anyway." He squeezed her hand. "To hell with everything but the three of us. If we hadn't agreed to give it a week, I'd say let's pick up Faith and drive to Las Vegas and get married."

Hannah felt her breath catch. She recalled Margaret's words. ...*you've abandoned any shred of common sense.*

"ANY MINUTE NOW," Hannah said, "those doors will burst open and a bunch of little monsters will come tearing out. If you don't stand back they'll run you down."

Liam sat on the edge of a low brick wall, his eye on the green painted double door. His assurances to Hannah aside, tension gnawed at his gut, held his neck and shoulders in a viselike grip. Hannah's mother didn't just dislike him, she was actually ready to wage war against him. And the thing was, he couldn't blame her.

He thought of his mother, blowzy and peroxided when he'd last seen her. He'd been about ten and they'd gone to Dublin on the train. A job? A man? He couldn't remember why she'd taken him there.

For hours, they'd walked about the city looking for a flat she could afford. No one would take a chance on her. She hadn't enough to pay the rent, they'd tell her over and over. It was nearly dark when they'd left the last place and he knew—and she knew he knew—they'd spend that night sleeping in the train station. He could see now that it must have been the last straw for her. She'd stood on the street screaming at him to go away.

"I can't take care of you," she'd sobbed.

And here he was, years later, sitting in the sunshine waiting for his daughter, who went off to school every day in a neighborhood of pastel-colored houses with lawns manicured to smooth green velvet and windows that glinted in the sun. Glibly telling his daughter's mother that there were no guarantees in life, but they would work things out. He looked at the knot of parents waiting for their kids and wondered who exactly was fooling whom? A blond woman in blue cotton pants and a white shirt waved at Hannah.

"Tiffany's mother," Hannah told him. "Tiffany is Faith's best friend. They argue about once a week and Faith decides Beth's her best friend and she's never going to speak to Tiffany again. The next day they're inseparable."

Liam opened his mouth to speak, but just then the doors opened. He shoved aside his gloomy musings and tried to spot Faith in the tumble of kids whooping and yelling their way out of the building. "What is she wearing?" he asked Hannah.

"Red pants and a yellow shirt. She picked them out herself."

He smiled, kept his eye out for red and yellow garments.

"Tiffany has red curly hair," Hannah added. "Bright red. If you see her, Faith will be right behind."

"What does Beth look like?" he asked.

"Beth looks a little like Hannah, actually. "Light brown hair that she usually has in a ponytail."

"Is that Tiffany?" He pointed to a girl with a mass of long curls the approximate color of tomato soup.

''Yep.'' Hannah peered into the crowd. ''I don't see Faith, though. And there's Beth. I wonder what's keeping Faith?''

''Come on.'' He caught Hannah's hand, impatient to see his daughter. ''Let's go and get her.''

Hannah followed him, then called out to Tiffany, who was twisting her shoulders out of a dark green backpack. ''Do you know where Faith is?''

Tiffany dangled the backpack from her fingers. ''Her grandma picked her up.''

Liam glanced at Hannah. ''I don't understand,'' he said. ''She knew we were coming to get her, didn't she?''

''Of course she did. I'm going to check in the office.''

The secretary in the office had blue curls and wire-rimmed glasses. The name tag on the collar of her pale blue blouse read, Mrs. Smith. She addressed Hannah. ''Your mother came by at about ten and said she and Faith were taking a little trip.''

Liam stared at her. ''Did Faith know this?''

Mrs. Smith, who'd ignored Liam until now, gave him an uncertain look, then raised her eyebrows at Hannah as though asking for permission to answer his question.

''This is Liam Tully,'' Hannah said. ''Faith's father.''

''Oh…'' The woman's eyes widened slightly behind her glasses. ''I didn't realize… No, that's the funny thing. Faith's such a little chatterbox. I heard all about her visit to the zoo, so I thought it was a bit funny when Mrs. Riley mentioned the trip and Faith hadn't said a word.''

''How is it your mother's allowed to pick her up?'' Liam asked Hannah.

''I gave her written permission. She picks her up most

days because I'm at work.'' She looked at the secretary. ''You said they left about ten?''

''About that. I remember because I was taking a break. I'd just put a bran muffin in the microwave to heat when she came in.''

''A trip.'' Hannah shook her head. ''What kind of trip? Did she mention where? How long they'd be gone?''

''Sorry. I didn't even think to ask.'' Light from the windows glinted on her glasses. ''You didn't know about this?'' she asked Hannah.

''No,'' Hannah said. ''We didn't know about it.''

THEY RAN BACK to the house, neither of them speaking. Liam followed her into the kitchen, and stood in the doorway as she confronted Debra, who was sitting at the table.

''For God's sake, Hannah, calm down, will you?'' Debra lifted a glass to her mouth. ''Faith's with Mom. It's not like she was kidnapped by a stranger or something. Maybe they went shopping.''

''Mom knew we were picking her up.'' Hannah stood in the middle of the kitchen. ''Why would she take her out of school at ten without calling me first? God, why am I even asking that?''

She ran upstairs to Faith's room. The red suitcase she'd pulled down last night was gone. Someone, Margaret obviously, had gone through the boxes she'd started to pack. The box with the underwear had been emptied out. Hannah went into her mother's room. Margaret's overnight bag was gone. She came down to the kitchen again.

''You've no idea at all where they are?'' Liam was asking Debra. ''Your mother said nothing to you?''

"Nope. I'm sure she'll call in a while. You know how she likes to surprise Faith."

"Where are Rose and Helen?" Hannah asked her sister. "I thought you guys were all going sailing."

"That was Wednesday. Anyway, it kind of fell apart when you said you weren't going. I don't think Allan was too jazzed about schlepping the family along if you weren't part of the group."

Hannah closed the drawer she'd been searching. "Where's Rose?" she asked again.

"Over at Max's house and Helen's gone to some crafts thing," Debra said. "She's big on crafts things," she told Liam. "If you stand still for too long, she'll decoupage your head."

Hannah caught her face in her hands. "God, I can't deal with this. What the hell was Mom thinking? *A little trip.*" She peered at Liam through her fingers. "I'm sorry. This is obviously her way of keeping you from seeing Faith."

"You don't know that," Deb said. "Why don't you wait till she calls before you jump to conclusions?"

"Wait?" Hannah stared at her sister. "How long? An hour? A day? Two days? This is my daughter she's just taken off with, for God's sake." Her hands back around her face again, she paced the kitchen—over to the window, back to the fridge. She looked at Liam, who stood with his back to the sink, arms folded across his chest. "I'm calling the police," she said.

CHAPTER SIXTEEN

"DON'T BE CRAZY," Debra said. "You can't call the police on your own mother."

"I'll tell them Mom has a drinking problem. I'll tell them I'm worried about Faith's safety."

"Is that true?" Liam asked. "Are you?"

Hannah hesitated. The honest answer was no. Margaret was scrupulous about not driving even after just one glass of wine. Hannah's suggestion that Margaret cut down on her drinking had been motivated by her concern for her mother's health. Never for a moment had she believed that Margaret would ever do anything to endanger her granddaughter.

"What is wrong with you, Hannah?" Debra glared at her sister, then addressed Liam. "Mom's been picking up Faith from school from the day she first started and Hannah's never once said a word about a drinking problem. Now suddenly it's a big deal because Mom has a glass of wine in the evening."

"No, Deb, maybe it's a big deal now because Mom overstepped her bounds," Hannah said. "Maybe it's a big deal now because Mom seems to have forgotten that Faith has a mother *and* a father. Maybe it's a big deal now because Mom has my daughter, and I have no idea where she's taken her. Maybe—"

"Hannah." Liam caught her arm.

"No." She pulled away. "This is our daughter

she's...kidnapped. You want to just let her get away with it?''

''I need some fresh air.'' He turned to leave the room. ''Let's go outside.''

She nodded and followed him out of the kitchen.

''Hannah,'' Deb called, ''can I talk to you for a minute.'' She inclined her head to the hallway, where Liam was still visible. ''In private.''

''If this is about Faith, Liam needs to hear it, too,'' Hannah said.

He shook his head. ''I'll wait for you outside.''

''I hope you know you've driven her to this,'' Deb hissed a moment later. ''She's so damn worried about Faith, she can't see straight. You stand there asking what Mom's thinking and you see nothing wrong with letting Faith sleep on the floor of an empty apartment or hanging around with some guy who was too busy brawling in a bar to see his daughter. God, you've lost it, Hannah, you really have. While you were making out with Liam, your daughter nearly drowned, for God's sake. And you ask what *Mom's* thinking. What the hell are *you* thinking?''

Speechless for a moment, Hannah just stared at her sister. ''*Do* you know where Mom is?''

''No, I don't, but if I did, I wouldn't tell you. You're so damned obsessed with Liam, you'll put him before your own daughter. Mom said she tried to talk some sense into you when you guys went for coffee, but you wouldn't listen. *Someone* has to put Faith's interests first, Hannah.''

Hannah slowly exhaled. If she didn't get out of the kitchen, she was going to blow up. She walked away, found Liam sitting on the front step and sat down next to him. By now it was nearly five and the sun was low in the sky, filling the yard with long shadows.

"We need to find an attorney," she said. "I don't know where we stand legally, but that's the first thing we need to find out."

Liam said nothing and they sat in silence for a few minutes, her hand on his knee. She waited for him to say something; to put his arm around her, to indicate somehow that they were in this together, but he seemed suddenly inaccessible. *What are you thinking?* she wanted to ask him. *Talk to me.*

From where they sat, she could see halfway down the street. Margaret sometimes walked Faith from the house to the beach, two blocks away. Last summer she'd taken her to swimming lessons at the Belmont Pool. She watched the street now, willing her mother and Faith to appear. A new surge of anger at Margaret made her heart pound.

"Look, the main thing is we know Faith's in no physical danger. I mean, as awful as this is, we at least know she's with her grandmother. It's probably too late to find anyone still in their office," she said. Allan's name came to mind; he was the only attorney she actually knew. Not a good choice, she decided. Maybe Allan was in on this. "I'll call someone in the morning," she said.

Unable to sit still, she started pacing the lawn. "It's my fault." She stopped at the grouping of rosebushes at the far end of the lawn. Then she walked back down to where Liam sat. "The thing is, Mom does so much for Faith she thinks she has equal rights over her. It's my fault—I take responsibility for allowing it to happen." Back to the roses again. Her head throbbing, brain racing. "I truly don't think she recognizes that you have a claim to her."

Again she sat down on the steps. Liam sat on the top step, his feet on the concrete of the third step. His back was slightly bent, his head bowed as though he were reading something written on the ground at his feet.

"Liam."

He raised his head.

"Talk to me. Listen, I just thought of something. Jen should be home. Let me give her a call. Her sister went through this custody thing with her ex-husband last year. I could get the name of her attorney."

He scratched the back of his neck but said nothing.

"Hey, come on." She put her arm around him, and pulled him close for a moment. "Don't freeze up on me, Liam," she said softly. "I know this has got to be a nightmare for you. But we'll get through it."

"No..." He shook his head. "I don't think so."

"Sure we will. Her arm still around him, she tried to ignore the rigidity in his shoulders. "You were right with what you said last night about talking to my mom, trying to reassure her. I can see now, I didn't pay enough attention to how upset she's been. She's blown things out of proportion." She relayed Debra's comments about letting Faith sleep in the empty apartment, about falling into the water. "I don't know whether she really believes we've put Faith at risk somehow, or she's just using it as an excuse—"

"Either way, it doesn't matter," Liam said.

"Exactly. We just need to make her understand—"

He cut her off with a wave of his hand. "No, I mean it doesn't matter. I don't want to go through with this."

She sat very still for a moment. The hollowness in her stomach told her what her head refused to understand. "Don't want to go through with what, Liam?"

"This. The battle with your mother. Your family's

disapproval as though I'm this monster out to harm you and Faith. I don't need it.''

Hannah had taken her arm from around his shoulder. She sat with her hands folded in her lap. Words whirled around in her head like a blizzard of snow—settling, melting, forming patterns then immediately dissolving. ''But that's what I'm talking about, Liam—they don't really know you. If they did—''

''Neither do you, Hannah. And I don't know you. I got carried away with...'' He shrugged. ''Sex, chemistry.''

''Okay,'' she said slowly, willing reason into her voice. ''Let's put us aside. What about Faith? What about wanting to be part of her life? You said—''

''I know what I said, Hannah.''

''But this is a very small setback. How can you just let—''

''Tells you something about my level of commitment, doesn't it?''

''So you never meant any of the things you said?'' She didn't believe that. Still, she needed to hear him deny it. ''Talk to me, Liam.'' She put her hand on his arm. ''Please.''

She felt his arm relax slightly under her palm. He'd just had a temporary case of cold feet, she told herself. They'd work everything out. Maybe she'd overreacted. Her gaze drifted out to the street again. What *exactly* had the school secretary said?

Maybe Margaret had just forgotten that this wasn't one of her days to get Faith from school. Even as Hannah tried to grasp this thread, she knew there had been no mistake. Margaret had taken Faith in a deliberate attempt to keep her from Liam.

''It's a relief, actually.'' Liam's voice broke into her

thoughts. ‘‘You said all along that we could never make it work and you were right. The whole thing’s been tearing me apart anyway, not knowing the best thing to do. It’s a load off my mind to come to a decision.’’

‘‘I don’t believe you, Liam.’’ She twisted around on the step to look at him. Their eyes met for a brief moment and then he looked away. ‘‘I don’t believe you’ve suddenly changed your mind like this.’’

‘‘I think it’s best for Faith,’’ he said. ‘‘She was doing well enough before I arrived on the scene, she’ll do well when I’m gone. The pirate’s dad would probably be a better father to her anyway.’’

‘‘And what about you? What about what you want?’’

‘‘I’ll still have my music,’’ he said. ‘‘That’s enough.’’ After a moment, he stood, looking at her as though not sure how to bring the conversation to a close. ‘‘Well then…’’

Hannah stood, too. Anger pulsed in her temple, her chest. Fists clenched at her side, it was all she could do not to strike him. ‘‘Well then, what, Liam? Well then, I’ll never see you again? Well then, I only thought I wanted to be a father? Well then, I never meant any of the things I said anyway? Well then, it was a whim after all?’’

‘‘All of the above,’’ he said. And took off down the garden path.

She sat down again, immobilized by rage. Her face felt hot as if he’d slapped it. By her left foot was a terra-cotta pot Margaret had brought up to the house to plant petunias in. Her hand shaking, she curled her fingers around the rim and hurled it at the gate just in front of Liam.

‘‘Just a goddamned whim, Liam,’’ she shouted.

By ten that night, she'd moved everything she and Faith owned out of her mother's house and into the new place. Clothes, books, a few pieces of furniture, some boxes that had been stored in Margaret's garage. Rocky and Jen had helped her load all of it into his pickup truck.

Activity helped. Dry-eyed and resolute, she moved about the apartment, unpacking boxes, hanging clothes in closets, folding bed linens. In the kitchen, she drank from a can of flat, lukewarm Diet Coke. The utilities would be turned on tomorrow. For now, she was working by the glow of the candles they'd used the other night; carrying her cell phone from room to room in case it rang.

She carried a box of toys into Faith's room. Earlier, she'd frozen in the doorway, gawking at the brand-new furniture that filled the small space. A bright red bed, a blue wooden chest with yellow drawers. Only one person would be unaware that Faith didn't really need a new bedroom suite. The one time Liam had seen his daughter's bedroom, it had been late and he probably hadn't noticed the furnishings.

Wondering how he'd got the furniture in, she remembered that she'd given him an extra key. Now that simple act of trust, the togetherness and shared responsibilities it implied, seemed a mockery. She took a deep breath and all the emotions, pent up since walking into the school office that afternoon, broke loose and she sat on the floor with her back to the wall and wept. When she'd cried herself out, she started to call the police on her cell phone, then decided she didn't want to be on the phone in case Margaret called. Fifteen minutes later, she was shivering in the air-conditioned chill of the Long Beach Police Department.

“I’m not sure if this is technically a police matter,” she told the desk sergeant, “but my mother picked up my six-year-old daughter from school today, and I haven’t seen or heard from either of them since.”

“This is the child’s grandmother.” He was an older guy, maybe a grandfather himself, with a craggy, lined face and a bored expression. “She has your permission to pick up the child?”

“Well, yes. She picks her up most days, but this wasn’t her day and she knew I was supposed to…and we had this big disagreement last night.”

Her face burning, she thanked him and left the station. Five minutes later, her cell phone rang.

“Faith’s okay,” Margaret said. “I’m okay. We’re in an emergency room in Ventura… No, no, let me explain. Someone rear-ended the car, Faith got a bump on the chin, and the CHP insisted we get her checked out. She’s fine, really. Hannah, I’m so sorry. Everything just kept building, I could see Liam getting more and more involved with you and Faith and I’m sure I was putting my own spin on things, but when she fell in the water, I just couldn’t…I had to do something.”

HANNAH DROVE UP to Ventura early the following morning. Faith had a Band-Aid on her chin and slept all the way home. Margaret continued to apologize.

“Maybe the accident jolted my brain, too,” she told Hannah. “Remember how angry I got when you told me about that Cuddlers program at Western? I think it was because I knew, deep down, that you were right.” She smiled ruefully. “What *did* I have in my life without you and Faith?”

In Long Beach, Hannah pulled up in front of the house on Termino to let Margaret out.

''We're not coming in,'' she told her mother. ''Everything's in the new place.''

''Hannah, don't punish me.''

''I'm not.'' The engine was still idling. She couldn't look at her mother. ''We need to get home.''

''Look, what I did was wrong, I know that. But I've learned my lesson. I have all kinds of plans, sweetheart. I'm going to sign up for classes at Cal State, check out the Cuddlers program. I'll stop expecting you and Deb and Faith to fill all my needs.''

''Well, good. I'm glad you've got all this insight now that Liam's safely out of the picture. Bottom line though, you prevailed. Congratulations, Mom, you managed to drive him away again.''

AFTER THE SHOW, in the hot, noisy pub, amidst the happily rowdy crowd, Liam tried to shake the gloom that had descended upon him in the last week. It felt like wet, heavy concrete slowly oozing through his vital organs. Gray and viscous; smothering his brain, filling his lungs so that sometimes he had trouble taking a deep breath. Hardening around his heart.

It had been a week now since he'd walked away from Hannah. A week of telling himself he'd done the right thing, that it was better for everyone, especially Faith, if he just bowed out. Better that she go on believing her daddy was in heaven than to have him let her down, disappoint her—as he almost surely would.

A week in which he'd managed to convince himself that what Margaret had done had probably been a blessing in disguise. Without it, he'd have kept traveling along the path to a life with Hannah and Faith. The kind of life, he kept telling himself now, in which he would never have been really happy. And, in the process, he would have made Hannah and Faith unhappy. *So, thank you, Margaret.* He drank some beer. *You did us all a favor.*

And things were not all bad. Brid was better. That was something to be thankful for. Or at least she'd assured him she was better. She'd worked out some sort of telephone counseling arrangement with her shrink at Casa Pacifica and claimed she was ready to go back on the road again. He'd taken her at her word and rescheduled the canceled performances.

Tonight they'd played at a college campus in Santa Barbara. The show had gone well, despite teething problems with hired equipment and no sound check. A hardcore crowd of faithfuls had filled the front of the place and sung along with the music. Afterward, they'd all trooped down to an Irish bar at the end of the street. Brid was singing now, Pearse accompanying her on the tin whistle.

Liam sat there, nursing his Guinness, telling himself this was the life. And wasn't it? Hadn't he always been happy with it? The music went from jig to reel while feet stomped on the wooden floor. The fiddle, the whistle, the drum like a heartbeat. Someone played pipes for a bit and then Brid grabbed the microphone again and the noise subsided as she began to sing. Something melancholy about desire and remorse; of being left behind, abandoned.

He listened, transfixed until she was nearly through. And then he put down his glass and pushed his way through the crowd to the door.

Outside, the night was cool and the streets were full of college kids in blue jeans. They spilled out of the taco shop across the road, congregated in groups on the sidewalk, laughing and talking and shouting out to one another. His face felt hot and flushed, and he stood with his back to the wall, trying to explain away the feeling that had come over him in the pub.

"Are you all right, Liam?" Brid stood in the doorway, the pale, flimsy fabric of her dress blowing in the wind.

"I'm fine."

"That song went well, can you hear them in there calling for more?"

He nodded.

"There's a girl in there asking about you."

"I'll be in, give me a minute."

"You sure you're all right?"

"Leave off, Brid." He pushed past her into the pub, but she caught his arm, pulled him against the wall and fixed him with a look. "What?"

"What." She clucked her tongue at him. "How long have we known each other? You're a wreck."

"I'm fine. The show went fine."

"You're not fine."

"I am," he said. "Leave me alone."

"We're going to talk."

THEY WENT TO A DENNY'S a block or so away. He gawked at the plate of scrambled eggs and ham the waitress had set down in front of Brid and shook his head. "You go from one extreme to the other. You're actually going to eat that?"

"No, Liam, I'm going to fashion this—" she poked with her fork at the ham "—into a little hat and maybe I'll use the eggs for a facial. Of course I'm going to eat it. And stop watching me, or I'll dump it all on the floor."

Liam lifted the top of his bacon and avocado burger

to verify the presence of avocado. Two slices. He couldn't get enough of it. A few weeks from now, he'd be drooling at the memory of avocado. He glanced at Brid, who was busy segregating the pile of eggs from the ham. As a kid, he'd done the same thing with peas. God forbid that a small, shriveled, olive-green pea should come anywhere near his mashed potatoes.

Did Faith do that? Did Faith ever ask about him? Did she ever pick up the guitar he'd given her? Did Hannah think of him? Across from him, Brid cut a tiny corner off a piece of ham. So far he'd seen nothing go in her mouth. She looked up and caught him watching her.

''Pack it up, Liam. I mean it.''

''So this therapist really said to call him anytime?''

''He did.'' Brid stared at Liam across the table. ''His daughter died of anorexia, and he doesn't want to see it happen to anyone else, if he can do anything about it.'' She kept watching him. ''Either that, or he wants my body.''

''Skeletal as it is,'' Liam said, and Brid reached over and slapped his hand. ''Sorry,'' he amended. ''Fashionably slim.''

''Not if I keep shoveling this stuff down.'' Brid had now impaled ham on the tines of her fork and was studying it as though psyching herself up to actually put it in her mouth. She put the fork down and looked at Liam. ''So?''

He met her gaze. ''So what?''

''So what's wrong with you?''

''Me? Nothing.'' She kept watching him. ''Oh right,'' he said, pretending to understand. ''The chronic moodiness and flare for melodrama, you mean?''

''No, that wasn't what I meant, Liam. Although God

knows, we're all quite familiar with those qualities, thank you very much.''

''Then I've no idea what you're getting at.''

''Haven't you?'' She carefully set her knife and fork on top of her uneaten food. ''Right, then, I'm through.''

''You hardly touched it.''

''And I won't. Until you tell me what's making you behave like a lovesick cow.''

''A cow?'' He laughed around a mouthful of hamburger.

''Talk.''

''I don't feel like talking about it, Brid.''

''And I don't feel like eating.''

''I ended things with Hannah.'' He set the hamburger back down. ''I thought it was the right thing to do, but it's killing me.''

''You love her?''

''I never stopped.''

''Does she know that?''

''I told her. And then…'' He couldn't bring himself to discuss the whole episode. ''I changed my mind.'' He pushed at her plate. ''Still lots of food there.''

Brid fixed him with a look. ''You changed your mind? And is that what you told her?''

''Yeah.''

''God.'' She shook her head. ''Men. The whole lot of you are scared to death to let anyone get close, so you tax your little brains trying to work out ways to stop it happening and then when it does, you wonder, all big-eyed and innocent, what went wrong and how you can make it better again.''

''The male psyche according to Brid Kelly.''

''So that's really what you told her?'' she asked. ''Just that you changed your mind?''

He shrugged. "Words to that effect. I kept trying to see myself in her world, a little suburban house, mowing the lawns on Saturday. What it came down to in the end was I couldn't do it." He frowned at his plate, at the lurid green pickle slices, the congealing grease. "And then her family was putting up a lot of resistance," he admitted, still thinking about Margaret. Wondering as he had countless times since he'd left Hannah's how it had all ended up. Wondering what reason Margaret had given for taking Faith, although that one wasn't hard to guess. Wondering, too, how Hannah was coping. Thinking, as he had over and over, of picking up the phone to call Hannah. To find out, to explain. Deciding, as he had over and over, that he needed to put it all behind him and move on. "It's for the best," he told Brid.

"Right," she said. "It's written all over your face how happy you are about it all."

"I didn't say I was happy about it. I said it was for the best. Hannah's world isn't mine. By the same token, I can hardly expect her and Faith to give up everything and live like gypsies, following the band around." A waitress stopped at their table, looked at his plate, then up at him.

"You all done with that, hon?"

"I am." He glanced at Brid's plate, still some left but she'd made a dent in it. "I don't know about her."

"Not quite." Brid smiled at the waitress. "I'll have some more coffee when you have a moment." After the waitress left, Brid stuck her elbows on the table and propped her face between her hands. "We've had this discussion before," she said. "Remember?"

He frowned, sorting through all the advice he'd received since learning of Faith's existence. Advice from Brid, from Miranda, from the guys in the band.

"After your daughter's birthday party?" Brid prompted. "I told you then, you need to make a choice. It's one thing or the other. The kind of life you have now, or a different kind of life with a wife and daughter. There's no way you can have both, Liam."

"I know." The waitress brought coffee for Brid, smiled and set the check down on the table. Liam picked it up and studied it. "And I've made the choice. The next step is to convince myself I'm happy about it."

"BUT I HATE THIS PLACE, Mommy." Faith lay in bed, tears streaming down her face. "It's ugly and it smells funny and I miss Raisin. I want to go back to our old house. I want my bedroom and I want the tree-house bed."

Hannah sat down on the edge of the bed Liam had bought for his daughter, and tried to keep her voice and expression upbeat. In the week that they'd been in the new apartment, Faith's bedtime had become a nightly ritual of tears. Several times, unable to console her daughter, Hannah had brought the little girl into her own bed, where Faith would finally fall asleep, snuggled up so close that Hannah hardly slept for fear of moving and waking her up again.

"When can we go back to our house?"

"Sweetie, this is *our* home now. The old house is Grandma's."

"But I like that one better. I want that to be our house again."

"I know you do, but that's because we haven't lived here long enough for it to feel like our house." She smoothed Faith's hair. "Let's think about some things we could do here to make it feel like our house."

Faith brightened. "We could bring Raisin here."

Hannah took a breath. "Besides bringing Raisin here. What are some other things we could do? Tell you what..." Her brain scrambled wildly to think of something that would fulfill the objective, not cost too much, not involve pets or painting the walls, which was also prohibited. Faith was waiting, her expression hopeful. "How about we make some new curtains," Hannah said. "Red and blue to match your furniture."

Faith's expression darkened. "Why *can't* Raisin live here?"

"Because he lives at Grandma's house," Hannah said. "But you can see him whenever we visit Grandma."

"Tomorrow?"

"Well, maybe not tomorrow."

"When?"

"Soon, sweetie, I promise."

"But when, Mommy? I miss Grandma and Auntie Rose and Auntie Helen. I want to go home."

This time, Hannah didn't have the heart to correct her daughter. She leaned over to kiss Faith's forehead. "Listen, you need to get some sleep. Mommy needs to get some sleep. Tomorrow, we'll get the material for the curtains, okay?"

"I miss Grandma a whole lot," Faith said. "But I miss Raisin the most."

CHAPTER SEVENTEEN

AFTER SHE FINALLY GOT Faith to sleep, Hannah was too tensed up to sleep herself. She paced the tiny apartment, zeroing in on anything that would divert her thoughts from the endless playing and replaying of everything that had happened with Liam. In her bedroom, she hauled out all the clothes she'd initially jammed into the closets just to get them out of the way, and dumped them on the bed.

Order. If she couldn't impose a sense of order on her life, she was damn well going to whip her closet into shape. But as she segregated shirts and tops in color groups, further segregating them into casual and dress, she found herself thinking about Liam. As hard as she tried, she couldn't see anything good that had come from his brief involvement in their lives.

She hadn't seen or spoken to Margaret all week. She'd let the machine pick up all calls, and then ignored the red blinking message light. Each day after school, she took Faith to the park or beach, then stopped for a long, leisurely meal that didn't end until she figured it was too late for Margaret to drop by. By that time, Faith was irritable and sleepy, which added guilt to everything else Hannah was feeling.

But she'd been resolute: determined not to grant quick forgiveness, nor to slip back into the easy warmth of the family life. In the process, she'd also felt so lonely and bereft that she thought she would lose her mind.

But things *would* improve. Liam hadn't derailed her life. Not this time. He'd simply been an obstacle along the track. But she could circumvent it and move on. One small problem—she was no longer sure of her destination.

Where *had* she been headed before Liam's brief reappearance in her life? Continued employment at La Petite Ecole, coaching the Taylor Beckers of the world? Marriage, somewhere down the line, if not to Allan, to someone like Allan? A guy with comfortable, middle-class values, a guy who would feel entirely at home sitting around the family dinner table?

Even now, she still saw her mother's house when she thought about the family dinner table. Would there ever come a time when she'd think of herself and Faith as a family instead of a satellite in Margaret's orbit?

With the Goodwill bag full, she started sorting blue and green shirts, trying to decide whether each should have its own section, while also debating whether Liam had inadvertently done her a favor by making her question her destination. Deep in thought, she jumped, startled by a knock on the front door.

It seemed late for visitors, but the clock by the bed showed that it was only a little after nine. In the living room, she stood on tiptoe to peer through the glass pane at the top of the door. Rose, Helen, Deb and Margaret stood huddled together outside shooting each other uncertain looks as they waited for her to respond to the knock.

She opened the door.

"Ta-da!" Rose held out her arms. "You might think

you can shut us out of your life, but we're here to tell you you're wrong.''

Hannah stood with one hand on the edge of the door, struggling to keep her face composed. Rose, Helen and Debra all held bulging plastic grocery sacks and shivered a little in the cool night air. And on the lower step, her face a mask of anxiety, stood Margaret. Hannah bit her lip hard, pulled back the door and they all trooped in.

''Come on, Hanny.'' Rose enveloped her in a hug. ''Tell your old auntie you still love her.''

''*You're* going to be an auntie, remember?'' Debra patted her still flat stomach. ''Who do I talk to about morning sickness and stuff? Plus, it's not fair that I have to be the focus of all Mom's obsessive worrying.''

''Now, Deb…'' Margaret's wavering smile flickered and she looked from one daughter to the other. ''I'm trying, I really am.''

Debra rolled her eyes.

''*Girls,*'' Helen said reprovingly. ''Be nice to your mother.'' She surveyed the tiny living room. ''This is…a sweet little place. I think when you get it all fixed up, it's going to be adorable. You know, you can actually staple sheets to the walls. I've seen some wonderful patterns and the beauty of it is you can take them all down when you move out.''

''Grandma.'' Faith, sleepy-eyed but smiling, burst into the room and flung herself into Margaret's arms. ''I miss you, Grandma.''

And suddenly the apartment, which minutes earlier had been so silent, was full of voices and laughter. Helen called from the kitchen to announce that the freezer wasn't working properly. Rose was saying that she'd finally persuaded Margaret to go to a singles dance, and

Faith, still in her grandmother's arms, was demanding to hear news about Raisin.

"Omigod," Rose, who was in the kitchen now, said loudly. "This fridge must be older than I am. It looks *exactly* like the one we had growing up. Hey, Margaret, come and look at this. Remember how we used to defrost it with the hair dryer?"

"How big is Raisin now?" Faith asked Margaret. "When can we come home again?"

Hannah exchanged a look with her mother. Margaret had her arms around Faith's waist. Faith's legs, pale under her scrunched-up red nightgown, were wrapped around Margaret's hips. Faith would soon be too big for Margaret to pick up, Hannah thought. Tears stung her eyes and she turned away, busying herself straightening the miniblinds.

In the kitchen, Helen was still talking about the antiquated freezer and how the artichoke, feta and chicken casserole would thaw and get spoiled. Deb made some joke about pickles and ice cream and Rose was inquiring about the possibility of a cold beer. Hannah turned from the window to catch Margaret dabbing at her eyes.

"I'm sorry." Margaret looked at Hannah over the top of Faith's head. "I'm really, really sorry. God, I've missed you guys so much…"

"I know, Mom." Hannah swallowed. "We've missed you, too."

And she had.

They drove her crazy, she thought a little later as they all sat around the kitchen table—her kitchen table—demolishing the pan of brownies Helen had brought, but her mother and aunts were so much a part of who she was that she could never really sever the ties completely. They might stretch and fray—even to the point of almost breaking—but, ultimately, the ties were strong enough to endure. The thought made her feel happy and sad at the same time. Happy for herself; sad for Liam whose ties to her and Faith were so fragile, he could relinquish them in an instant. His loss, she decided.

"Grandma." Faith tugged at Margaret's hand to get her attention. "When *can* we come home?"

Hannah opened her mouth to speak, then decided to let Margaret handle the question.

"What do you mean, you want to come home?" Margaret scooped Faith up on her lap, tucked an errant strand of hair behind her granddaughter's ear. "You are home, my love. *This* is your home. And you know what? I think it's a pretty nifty home."

AND, GRADUALLY, the little apartment did begin to feel like home. Faith made friends with a girl two houses down who, she told Hannah, she liked even better than Tiffany. Hannah, with Helen's assistance, made curtains for Faith's bedroom windows, filled the window boxes with geranium cuttings from her mother's backyard and even planted a few of the hated nasturtium seeds that Margaret was only too glad to be rid off. Three or four afternoons a week, Hannah and Faith dropped by the house to take Raisin for walks along the beach.

One evening, mostly at Faith's insistence, Hannah invited Allan and Douglas over to dinner; another time, feeling lonely and a little blue, she went to dinner with Allan. At the end of the evening, she told him that she valued his friendship but wanted nothing more than that. He'd been sweet and understanding as he hugged her goodbye. "Have a happy life, kiddo."

At La Petite Ecole, Taylor Becker aced his kindergarten screening test and Deanna Becker was so thrilled she tried to give Hannah a gift certificate for a weekend at the luxurious Ventana Inn in Big Sur.

"Take your sweetie," Mrs. Becker urged. "The place oozes romance."

Hannah thanked her, but explained that La Petite Ecole's policy prohibited the staff accepting gifts from parents. Besides, she didn't have a sweetie. Which was just as well, because she'd signed up for landscape design classes at Cal State Long Beach. She wouldn't have time for sweeties.

THE WILD ROVERS PLAYED their final performance at a club in Hollywood where the audience seemed surly and bored from the first chord of the opening song. "Ah well," Pearse muttered to Liam as they trouped off stage, "you can't please them all." His sentiments exactly, Liam decided as he half listened to Pearse and Brid and some of the others talk about where to go for a few pints and something to eat. Like the audience, Liam felt surly and bored. As far as he was concerned, the moment they stepped off the plane at Shannon couldn't come soon enough.

"A lady here to see you, Liam," someone shouted from the front of the theater.

Liam stopped dead. He'd imagined this so many times since he'd walked away from Hannah. Right down to the night she'd finally appear, the last one of the tour. And now it was happening. He stood, immobilized. His shirt was sweat drenched from the show and he pulled it off, realized he didn't have another one and, grabbed a new Wild Rover T-shirts from the stack on the concession stand. Pearse's sister, who worked the table where the shirts were sold, gave him a questioning look.

He shrugged and headed back into the theater where a few diehards were still straggling out.

''Liam.''

Margaret. In a red blazer, white blouse and dark trousers, smiling but twisting her hands and glancing around her and looking about as out of place in a Hollywood club as any suburban granny would. Speechless, Liam stared at her. Disappointment hit him like a blow to the stomach—replaced immediately by fear that something had happened to Hannah or Faith.

''Is Faith all right?'' he asked. ''Hannah? Is something wrong?''

''No.'' She shook her head. ''Yes, well no, I mean they're both fine but...is there somewhere we could talk?''

They went to a nearby Subway, where Margaret said she wasn't hungry but she'd have some coffee. He *was* hungry but couldn't focus enough to decide what sandwich combination he wanted. Two cups of coffee in hand, he sat down at the table opposite Margaret.

''However much you want to do what's best for your children,'' Margaret said, ''there comes a time when you have to realize they're not children any longer and they must be allowed to make their own decisions. You might not agree with them, but...'' She shrugged and a smile flickered briefly. ''They might not agree with *your* decisions, either. Usually don't, in fact.''

Liam drank some coffee. A sense that Margaret had carefully rehearsed what she wanted to say stopped him from interrupting her.

''I should never have let you think Hannah had had an abortion. And I should have backed off when you returned. I should have had enough confidence to trust Hannah to make the right decision. But as I told her, we sometimes believe what we want to believe. I didn't want you to take her and Faith back to Ireland, so one way to prevent that was to cast you in the role of the philandering no-good. I made myself believe it and hoped that she would, too.''

''How do you know I'm not a philandering no-good, Mrs. Riley?''

She looked at him for a moment. ''I don't. But Hannah seems convinced you're not, and I need to trust her judgment.''

''How is Hannah?''

''Okay.'' Margaret stared into her coffee. ''But I think she'd be happier with you in her life again.''

''You *think?*''

''I know.'' She drank some coffee, then set the cup down again. ''I'm going to be honest with you. I would be far happier to see my daughter fall in love with an attorney who owns a house on Riva Alto Canal—''

''The pirate's dad.''

Margaret gave him a puzzled look.

''Nothing. Go on.''

''Anyway, my new resolution is to try to be supportive of whatever Hannah decides to do.''

''But you think—''

''I think she loves you, Liam.'' She shook her head in mock exasperation. ''So do something about it, for heaven's sake.''

HE ACCEPTED Margaret's offer of a ride back to Long Beach and, with forty-eight hours left on his visitor's visa, knocked on Hannah's front door step.

''Can I come in?'' he finally asked after she'd stared at him for several seconds. Without a word, she motioned him inside—where he made the mistake of telling her about Margaret's visit.

Big mistake. For the next fifteen minutes—he'd checked his watch—he sat on the couch saying nothing as Hannah paced around the room; railing on about her mother and her aunts, about how she *just* could not believe that they hadn't learned their lesson and were they ever, *ever,* going to stop interfering in her life and she could fight her own battles thank you very much and she certainly didn't need Margaret tracking him down on her behalf as if she were some desperate, pathetic woman who couldn't keep a man and if he imagined for a moment, an *instant,* that she had nothing better to do with her life than sit around waiting for him to make up his mind, he'd better damn well think again. And then she seemed to run out of steam.

"The place looks different," he said into the silence that followed her outburst. "With the furniture and everything. It looks nice."

"Liam. I want you to go, okay?"

He looked at her. Her hair was clipped up with this black-and-white plastic dog thing, and she had on a pair of baggy gray sweatpants. Beneath the faded blue shirt that read, Got My Dog, Got My Horse, Don't Need No Damn Man, he could see the outline of her breasts. No bra. He remained seated.

"I mean it."

"What if I said that I was here because I wanted to be here?"

She shrugged, walked to the door and pulled it open. "Life is full of the things that we *want.* For example, I *want,* really, really *want,* just for once in my life to be left alone. No family interference, no one breathing down my neck. But, God, what are the chances of that ever happening?''

''Come back to Ireland with me. That should help.'' It wasn't what he'd intended to say, it had just come out. But it didn't seem like a bad idea and when he saw something flicker in her eyes, it was all the encouragement he needed. ''I'm serious, Hannah. Come on, close the door and let's talk.''

Her hand was still on the door. ''There's nothing to talk about, Liam.''

''At least close the door then.''

She did, and sat down on the arm of the couch. ''I'm not going to Ireland with you. We might as well establish that right now.''

''I just hit you with it, I know, but think about it.'' He could hear his voice speed up; enthusiasm like a whip, driving his words to move faster. ''It would be great, terrific. We'll live in my house in Galway. Near the recording studio. It'll be just like a regular job, at least for six months or so. We can get Faith into a good school.''

''Liam, she's six. I can't uproot her from her family and take her off to a foreign country.''

''We're her family,'' he said, but Hannah was clearly unimpressed. ''Look, it's wonderful for her to have your mother and aunts, but it wouldn't hurt her at all to know there was a life outside of Long Beach, California.''

She shook her head. ''It won't work, Liam.''

''It could, if you wanted it to.''

''Well, maybe that's it. Maybe I don't want it enough to make that kind of change.''

''Or maybe you're scared to leave the nest.'' He could see he was losing, so he decided he might as well fire all his weapons. ''It's comfortable for you here, isn't it?

Your mother and aunts twittering around, fussing over you. Maybe they get on your nerves at times, but on the whole it's safe and nonthreatening and you never really have to challenge yourself, do you?''

Hannah stood up. ''You're incredible, you know that? You're asking *me* to uproot my life to follow you across the world. You're talking to *me* about not challenging myself? Where the hell is the challenge for you, Liam? Huh?''

''Hannah, come on—''

''No.'' She pulled open the door. ''Go. Leave.''

''Your mother gave me a ride down here.''

''Oh really? So you just thought, 'Oh, I'll hop into bed with Hannah.'''

''Well…''

''Well, tough. *Walk* over to my mom's house. I'm sure she'll be happy to drive you back.''

OF COURSE sleep was out of the question. If the mental picture of Liam walking through the darkened streets of Long Beach looking for somewhere to spend the night didn't make her feel guilty enough, the anger at Margaret kept her brain working at a furious pitch rehearsing all the scathing things she would say to her mother once she'd calmed down enough not to actually kill her.

At one in the morning, she was wandering around the apartment, looking for something to organize. At two, she was sitting at the kitchen table trying to work out a filing system for the recipes she'd clipped from newspaper food sections. When she suddenly realized she'd been staring blankly at the same recipe for a while, she forced herself to concentrate on the title. *Irish soda bread.*

Maybe it was a sign.

Follow Liam to Ireland, bake Irish soda bread, have babies and live happily ever after. She got up from the table, and wandered into the bathroom. She looked at her face in the mirror, and pulled the stupid dog barrette out of her hair. Faith's *101 Dalmations* barrette. God, what a dork she must have looked.

Why hadn't she even considered his suggestion? She didn't love him enough? She *was* scared to leave the nest? Last spring, a little bird—a baby bird—kept flying against the kitchen window, bumping its head against the glass before it flew away, looking stunned.

She had flown the nest once, gotten a little bruised, then returned to be soothed and consoled. And Liam was right, it was pretty comfortable with everyone chirping and twittering all around. Now she had her own baby bird and it was scary to think of flying away again. Sure, she'd moved out of Margaret's house, but nothing else had really changed. Margaret, Rose and Helen—even Deb—were all there for her when she needed them. All there for her even when she *didn't* need them, which was probably more to the point. Maybe it was time to stop fooling herself. Maybe it was time to leave for real.

THE DAY AFTER Hannah told him never to darken her door again, Liam found himself driving south on the Golden State Freeway in a compact rented from Budget, and having serious misgivings about what he'd just done. By the time he turned onto the 710 heading back to Long Beach, he'd started rehearsing the reasons he would give to the Celtic Arts Collective for changing his mind about taking the position they'd just offered him.

He'd called the collective on a whim—there was that word again—after reading an article in the *Hollywood Reporter*. As luck would have it, there was a position he might be interested in. If he'd like to come up and talk to the director, he'd been told, maybe they could work something out.

So he'd made the trip to Burbank today and had accepted the job.

He'd be doing a bit of everything—developing new talent, helping to promote Irish music and culture and teaching guitar classes a couple of days a week.

"We can't pay you much," the director told him, "But you'll have the freedom to work on some of your own music and if your wife is working, too, you'll do okay."

His wife. Liam hadn't corrected the administrator's assumption and now the thought of Hannah as his wife filled him with equal parts exaltation and dread. Dread, because if she were still of the same mind as last night, he'd created a bit of a mess for himself.

And everybody else, come to that. Before he left for the interview, he'd told Brid and the fellows in the band that he was probably going to quit. And, determined to show Hannah he was serious, he'd told his manager to put an indefinite hold on plans for the European tour.

But now he felt less certain that he'd done the right thing.

In fact, by the time he pulled up outside Faith's school, he'd all but convinced himself that the best thing he could do now was let everyone know that he'd experienced a temporary bout of insanity and nothing he'd said or done in the past twenty-four hours should be taken seriously.

And then he got out of the car and walked across the road to wait for his daughter.

AT THREE, Hannah sat on the grass across the road from Faith's school, slightly apart from the knot of parents on the other side of the road. Her head lowered slightly, the visor of her baseball cap and dark glasses shielding her eyes, and—she was pretty sure—her face from Liam, she watched him take in the parents waiting by the entrance. He looked good. Terrific. Stylish in dark sage-green pants and a long-sleeved cotton jersey a shade or two lighter.

He hadn't seen her, hadn't looked across the street in her direction. Which was good, because she had no idea what she would say to him if he did. She drew her knees up to her chest, wrapped her arms around them and propped up her chin. Still eight minutes to go.

She imagined various scenarios of what would happen when Faith walked out. In one, Liam spotted his daughter before she did and he and Faith came over to where she was sitting. In another, she was the first to see Faith, she grabbed her daughter's hand and they made a quick getaway before Liam noticed them. In the third, they both spotted Faith at the same time, Liam smiled at her, birds twittered in the trees and they all walked off into the sunset, hand in hand.

Or none of the above.

She watched Liam say something to a woman in a red dress. The woman smiled up at him. She probably thought he was cute, which he was. Hannah chewed the edge of her thumbnail. God, her heart was going crazy. *I love you.* She could just walk up to him and whisper it in his ear. Cut through all the other stuff. *I love you.*

If she could get her brain past the thought that he was back because Margaret had intervened. He'd left because of Margaret. He was back because of Margaret. It was almost comical. Like a soap opera. What will Margaret do next? Tune in tomorrow for the next episode of *As*

Margaret's World Turns. Or maybe, *As Margaret Turns The World.* Better yet, *As Margaret Turns Hannah's World.*

A thought struck her. Was saying no to him last night actually an act of rebellion against Margaret? When Margaret had seen him as evil incarnate, she herself had rushed to his defense. But now that he had Margaret's blessing, could it just be that…nah. She pulled herself to her feet, brushed grass off the back of her shorts and sauntered over to where he stood. Came up behind him and tapped him on the shoulder.

"Hey."

He turned and smiled at her. "Hannah."

"You know that old saying about cutting off your nose to spite your face? Don't ask me to explain because I get a headache even thinking about it." *On the other hand maybe Margaret had been just using reverse psychology…God, no, she couldn't think about that, either.* "Anyway, I just wanted to tell you…that you look very nice. And…" She kicked at the grass with the toe of her sneaker. "I love you."

Liam made a melodramatic swipe at his brow. "Phew."

"What?"

"I've just taken a job in Burbank which I'd have absolutely no interest at all in doing if you didn't love me."

"A job?" She stared at him. "What kind of job?"

"This nonprofit group that's trying to promote Irish arts. Music, theater. That's why I'm all dressed up. I drove straight here from the interview."

"Wow." She smiled at him. "That's fantastic…isn't it? You're pleased about it?"

''Yeah...'' He shrugged. ''Sure. I'll still have time to write some of my own stuff. It'll work out.''

She watched his face as he told her about what he'd be doing. He sounded okay about it, but something was missing from his voice. The spark she always heard when he talked about his music. ''Are you sure you'll be happy? What about the rest of the band? Brid? The European tour?''

''Listen.'' He caught both her hands in his and looked into her eyes. ''Stop worrying about whether I'm happy. Just tell me this makes you happy.''

She swallowed. His expression was solemn now, his eyes dark. How could she not be happy? What more proof did she need that he loved her? ''Liam, I just want to be sure...it's such a huge sacrifice for you.''

''Happy? Or not happy?''

''Just—''

''Happy? Or not happy?''

''Okay, happy. Of course I'm happy. Who wouldn't be?''

''Well, maybe you won't be when I tell you what I've found out about the price of houses.''

''Houses? You've already looked at houses?''

''Not in any great depth, but enough to depress me.''

''We could stay in my place...'' She caught herself and grinned. ''Our place? The place I'm renting.''

''I want Faith to have her dog,'' he said.

Hannah smiled then. Couldn't stop smiling. A few kids had started to trickle out of the school. If she lived to ninety, she thought, she could never repay him for the sacrifice he'd made today.

''I think I see our daughter on the schools steps.'' Liam put his arm around Hannah's shoulder and they started walking across the grass. ''The girl with the frizzy ginger hair must be Tiffany, right?''

''Yep.'' Hannah squeezed him to her side and reached up to kiss the side of his neck. ''Thank you, Liam. I mean it. I don't even know what else to say. I'll make you happy, I promise.''

He stopped walking. ''I can see I'm going to have to give you a stern talking to. And you're obviously a bit thick, so I'm going to say this very slowly. *My happiness is not your responsibility.*'' He took her face in his hands and kissed her mouth. ''Got it?''

She started laughing. ''God, I'm getting just like my mom.''

''Remember that no one forced me to do this. It was my choice. I did it because I want a life with you and Faith and…this is the way it worked out.''

And since I turned down your first suggestion, Hannah thought, *what alternative did you have?* But she kept the thought to herself because Faith, in a pink polka-dot dress and white sneakers was tearing across the grass, hair and knees flying, face ablaze.

''Mommy. Liam.'' She beamed at both of them but saved her biggest smile for Liam. ''I've been thinking about you,'' she told him.

''Have you?'' His smile matched hers. ''I've been thinking about you a bit, too.''

Faith turned to Hannah. ''Can we all do something fun, Mommy?''

Hannah glanced at Liam. ''My plans for the rest of the day were grocery shopping and organizing my sock drawer.''

He grinned.

''I've become very big on organizing lately. When

your closets and cabinets are in order, other parts of life don't seem so chaotic."

"She's organizing *everything*." Faith rolled her eyes dramatically. "You wouldn't believe it."

"Will your socks stage a revolt if you don't marshal them into order this afternoon?" Liam asked.

Hannah bit back a smile. "I'll risk it." She looked from Liam to Faith. "So what fun thing do you want to do?"

"*Queen Mary,*" Faith said.

"I thought you didn't like the *Queen Mary*," Hannah said.

"No, I did." Faith's smile faded for a moment. "I was just in a bad mood."

"Were you?" Liam frowned. "Hmm. I don't remember that."

"Well, I was. But today I'm in a good mood. Want to know why?" She smiled up at him. "Because you're here."

FOR THE REST OF THE AFTERNOON, Liam carried his daughter's words in his head. A little gift he'd take out every so often, examine and smile to himself. He smiled while they ate ice cream on the dock and he reached over to taste Faith's bubble-gum sundae. And in the red water taxi that carried them over to the *Queen Mary*, bobbing across the bay, the wind and sea spray in their faces. And during the Ghost Ship tour of the old liner, listening to spooky accounts of ill-fated passengers reputed to still haunt the decks and cabins. Faith had gripped his hand and shivered dramatically. Hannah had smiled at him and he'd told himself he'd done the right thing. They *would* all be happy. He could live without the band and the touring. He'd sell the house in Galway, make California his home, wear the bloody barbecue apron if he had to. They'd all live happily ever. They would.

Around five, Faith had announced that she was hungry and they'd ended up in a downtown café called Super-Mex, where, Hannah insisted, they made the best carnitas tacos she'd ever tasted.

''You were right.'' He pushed his empty plate away. ''Best carnitas tacos I've ever tasted.''

Hannah gave him a skeptical look. ''Have you ever had carnitas tacos?''

''No.''

She pushed his arm. ''Tully. I don't know about you.''

He caught her hand and felt it go very still. Faith sat next to Hannah. Faith, all pink-cheeked and sleepy-eyed from the boat ride and the tortillas and beans she'd just demolished. He kept holding Hannah's hand as he addressed his daughter. ''Here's the thing, Faith. I love your mum. A lot. And you're not so bad yourself.''

Faith grinned. ''And you're not so bad yourself, Liam,'' she said.

''Thanks. So anyway, I'd like to marry your mother and I was wondering what you might think about that.''

''Marry her?'' Faith's eyes turned saucer like. She twisted around to look at Hannah. ''Hey, Mommy. Liam wants to marry you.''

''My goodness.'' Hannah fanned her face with her hand. ''A proposal.''

''So what do you think about that, Faith?'' Liam asked. ''Your mother and me?''

''I think it's cool,'' Faith said. ''Huh, Mommy?''

Hannah smiled as she looked into his eyes. ''Way cool.''

''But I want to be sure I'm doing the right thing,'' he

told Faith. ‘‘You don’t think she’d rather that I just cleared off? Left her alone to organize her cupboards?’’

‘‘She already organizes way too much,’’ Faith said.

‘‘You think it’s a good idea then? Marrying your mother, I mean?’’

‘‘*Yessss,*’’ Faith said loudly. ‘‘Now can I have another Pepsi?’’

‘‘Listen, Faith.’’ His voice confidential, Liam leaned across the table. ‘‘I’m no expert on elocution, but I believe the preferred usage is, ‘May I have another Pepsi?’’’

‘‘*May* I have another Pepsi?’’

‘‘No.’’

Faith grinned. ‘‘You’re funny, Liam.’’ Up on her knees, she looked at him for a moment. ‘‘So if you and Mommy get married, you’ll be my stepdad. Just like when Tiffany’s mom got married.’’

Liam exchanged a quick glance with Hannah, decided to let her respond.

‘‘Well, this is a little different, sweetie,’’ Hannah said. ‘‘It’s a long story, but Liam really *is* your daddy.’’

Liam watched Faith’s face as she considered this. Such a short and simple explanation of a long and convoluted journey. He wondered whether the answer would satisfy her.

‘‘But I thought my daddy was in heaven,’’ Faith said, after a few moments. ‘‘What happened? Did you come back?’’

‘‘Well, it’s a long story,’’ Liam said. ‘‘But you have the gist of it. I’m back and I’m here to stay.’’

‘‘Cool,’’ Faith said.

HANNAH STOOD in the doorway of Faith’s room, watching Liam tell his daughter a bedtime story. Actually, he'd already told her a couple, in an outrageously broad accent that she herself could hardly understand. Most of it, she was pretty sure, had been lost on Faith, but it didn't seem to matter. Faith lay on her back, covers tucked up to her chin, smiling at Liam, clearly enchanted.

"And a knock came at the door," Liam was saying. "And Lady Wilde opened it to see a witch with two horns on her forehead and in her hand, a wheel for spinning wool."

"How come she had two horns?" Faith asked.

Liam scratched his head. "D'you think it would better if she had just one then?"

Faith grinned, sleepy now but willing to be entertained. "No, two horns are good."

"Well, the witches began to sing an ancient rhyme. Strange to hear and frightful to look at they were, those witches with their horns and their wheels. 'Rise, woman and make us a cake,' they said." He turned to look at Hannah. "I think she's out."

"That's what happens when guys tell women what to do," Hannah said.

"Is that so?" Liam followed her into the kitchen and they stood in the middle of the room, his hands on her shoulders. "You mean if I told you to take off all your clothes, you'd fall asleep?"

"Well, it depends. What would you do after I'd taken off my clothes?"

He kissed her on the mouth, guided her to the wall and pressed hard against her. "God, Hannah, I have no idea what I'd do. Have you any suggestions?"

"Yeah, a few." Still watching his face, she undid his belt buckle, unfastened his pants and slid her palm down over his stomach, beneath the elastic waist of his shorts.

"Would it have anything to do with where your left hand is right now?"

"It might." She smiled into his eyes. "Can you rise to the occasion?"

"I think I already have."

His body shuddered in a quick spasm and he buried his mouth in her neck, nipped at the skin on her collarbone. They kissed, mouths soft and open, bodies dissolving together. She felt languid, sensual, catlike. Jazz should be playing, she thought as she arched her neck to reach his mouth. Fear of Faith waking up and walking in on them stopped her from dropping to her knees and taking him in her mouth.

"We'd have to be very...circumspect. Faith isn't used to waking in the morning to find a man in my bed."

"I'm glad to hear that."

And then she took his hand and led him into the bedroom.

CHAPTER EIGHTEEN

THE NEXT DAY she drove over to Huntington Harbor to see Brid Kelly. Liam had gone up to L.A. to iron out visa details and wouldn't be back until early evening. As she pulled up to the curb, she thought of the last time she'd stopped by Miranda Payton's house. She'd been geared up to do battle with Liam for disappointing Faith. This time her mission was quite different.

Miranda Payton answered the door. She wore a short white terry-cloth robe and her hair was piled into a disheveled top-knot. Her eyes widened when she saw Hannah. "Liam's not here."

"I know. I'm here to see Brid."

Without a word, Miranda turned and called into the house. Moments later, Brid emerged at the top of the stairs. Unsmiling, she stared at Hannah but made no move to come down. Hannah looked from Miranda to Brid, but neither women spoke and she felt a definite tension.

"We've never met." She addressed Brid. "But I'm Hannah Riley, Liam's—"

"I know all about you," Brid said.

"I'd like to talk to you, if you have a few minutes."

Brid shrugged.

Hannah shifted her weight from one foot to the other and licked her lips. She wished Brid would come down the stairs and Miranda would go away. From somewhere in the house, she could hear canned laughter coming from a television set. ''Can I buy you coffee or something?'' she asked Brid. ''Breakfast? I haven't eaten yet, there's a place on the Coast Highway.''

''I don't eat breakfast,'' Brid said.

''There's coffee here if you want some,'' Miranda said.

''I wanted to talk to you about Liam.'' Hannah peered through the expanse of hallway and up at Brid's shadowy figure on the stairs. ''About the band and everything…''

''The band?'' Brid gave a mirthless laugh. ''What's there to talk about? You've managed to make short work of the band. It's no big loss, as far as I'm concerned since I intended to quit after this tour anyway, but Liam might as well be cutting off his left arm.''

''He's had a brain lapse,'' Miranda said. ''Six months from now, he'll wake up and regret what he's done.''

Hannah pushed at her hair. This was none of Miranda's business. Unfortunately, she was at Miranda's front door; Brid was on Miranda's stairs, making no move to come down, and Hannah had the feeling that alienating Miranda wouldn't help endear her to the singer.

''Liam's told you about his job with the Celtic Arts Collective?'' she asked Brid.

''He has.''

''He swears it's what he wants to do.''

''It's not,'' Brid said.

''That's what I wanted to talk to you about.''

''Celtic Arts Collective.'' The derision in Brid's voice was clear. ''Putting Liam into something like that, sitting him behind a desk to do…whatever…would be like tak-

ing one of your palm trees back to Ireland and expecting it to flourish.''

''He's got this thing about the kid,'' Miranda said, ''and it's blinding him to what he really wants.''

Hannah looked at Miranda and decided she didn't care whether she alienated her or not. ''The kid is my daughter. Liam's daughter. And her name is Faith.''

''Do you love Liam?'' Brid asked. ''Really love him?''

''Yes, I do,'' Hannah said, softly.

''Then please don't let him kill his soul.''

''TELL ME ABOUT YOUR HOUSE in Galway,'' Hannah said that evening. She and Liam were in the kitchen of her apartment, trying to whip the stew Liam had sworn he knew how to make into something edible enough to serve the family, who were all coming over for dinner. ''Is it in town?''

''Just outside.'' Liam shook pepper onto the browned meat. ''What if we added tomatoes?''

''In Irish stew?'' Hannah shrugged. ''It's worth a try, I guess. So what about the schools? Are they pretty good?''

''My manager's daughter is doing well enough. Joel's always talking about all the prizes Carolyn's taking for this and that and she's a terrific reader. Last time I was at his house, she read me some bits from *Black Beauty*. Why?''

''Just wondering...'' She tasted the stew. ''God, Liam.''

He grinned. ''Bad?''

''At least one of us had better learn how to cook.''

He opened the fridge. ''Worcestershire sauce.''

''Couldn't hurt.'' From the bedroom, she could hear

Faith and Tiffany laughing together. ''So about your recording contract—''

''Nixed.''

She glanced at him. ''But it doesn't have to be that way. You could—''

''I've made the decision, Hannah. Let's leave it at that.'' He poured a stream of Worcestershire sauce into the pan. ''Maybe we should wait for your mother and aunts to get here and work their magic on the stew. Why didn't they ever teach you how to cook?''

''I *can* make cakes and lemon chicken,'' she said. ''Actually, we should bring Faith in here to help us. My mom's turned her into quite the little cook.'' She threw some frozen chopped onion into the pan on the stove. ''So anyway, after you're through with recording, you'd begin the European tour?''

''Right.'' Wooden spoon in hand, he glanced over his shoulder at her. ''What's all this about, Hannah?''

''I've been thinking.''

''Lie down.''

''I'm serious. I'm thinking that it would be good for Faith to have a broader experience. See what it's like to live in another country.''

''For a holiday, you mean?'' He shrugged. ''I'd have to check with the new boss. It might be a while before I could get the time off.''

''I was thinking of something more long-term.'' She came up to stand behind him, put her arms around his waist. ''Like actually moving there.''

He went very still. ''You're telling me you want to come back to Ireland? You and Faith?''

''Yep.'' She kissed the back of his neck. ''In fact, the more I think about it, the better it sounds.''

He turned to look at her, his expression unreadable.

''What brought about this change, Hannah? I thought we had it all settled.''

''We did. Now I've unsettled it.''

''I don't know what to say. You've taken me completely by surprise. What...'' He shook his head. ''Why?''

''Because...'' She was about to tell him about her conversation with Brid, then decided against it. Besides, it wasn't the main reason. ''I really want us to be a family, you and me and Faith. I want us to create new experiences together, to grow together. I'm not saying we couldn't do that here, but I like the idea of starting our new life together somewhere completely different.''

Liam took a couple of beers from the refrigerator and held one out to her. ''You don't have to do this for me, Hannah. I'm fine with the plan we had.''

''I'm not doing it *just* for you.'' She took the beer. ''I'm doing it for us. It's...I don't know, time to leave the nest.''

He laughed. ''A bit of a long flight, isn't it?''

''Maybe.'' *But I love you enough to risk it.* ''We'll make it. Trust me.''

''God.'' A smile stretched across his face. ''You're sure you want to do this?''

''Yeah...I do. We need to sit down and talk to Faith about it, of course. But she's young, so she'd adjust pretty quickly. You wouldn't have to give up the band. If the European tour is in the summer, we could even go with you. Anyway, I have this new appreciation for tour buses.''

''We'll fly,'' he said. ''Tour buses are for the young and crazy.''

She grinned.

''But what about you. Are you going to be happy?''

"Yeah." She nodded, even more sure of her decision now she'd told him about it. "I really do want to try something different. I've been in a rut for a while now. I just didn't recognize it. Faith provided me with an excuse to never leave my comfort zone."

"I doubt that you'll find much call for Mediterranean plants in Galway."

"Maybe not, but I bet roses do really well there. I'm excited, Liam, I really am. It's an opportunity for a whole new start. There are all kinds of ideas I want to explore."

"I could build you a greenhouse," he said.

"See? Next thing you know, I'll have a thriving roadside stand. Maybe a converted gypsy caravan. Who knows?"

"What about your mother?"

"Hey, she was the one who brought you back." She smiled. "Actually, I think she'll be happy for me. For us. She'll miss Faith, of course, but deep down she recognizes that we're our own family now. You and me and Faith."

"We'll invite her over for the wedding," Liam said.

EXACTLY TWO MONTHS LATER they stood in the back garden of Liam's stone cottage outside Galway. Hannah, shivering in a cream linen dress that skirted her knees, carried a bouquet of pink roses, just a shade darker than Faith's bridesmaid's dress. Margaret wore yellow silk, Helen and Deb were in blue and Rose made her own statement in a red velvet pantsuit with leopard trim. Brid, accompanied by Pearse on the tin whistle, sang as Hannah walked down the pathway to meet Liam, who stood waiting under a vine-covered arbor.

After the ceremony, they all crowded into the tiny

kitchen to drink champagne as they stood around the stove watching Helen, a navy apron tied around her waist, whisk a hollandaise sauce for the eggs Benedict keeping warm in the oven.

"Happy?" Liam had his arm around Hannah's shoulder.

"Very." She squeezed his waist. "Faith looks pretty happy, too." Through the kitchen window, she could see their daughter tearing across a stretch of brilliant emerald-green grass after Raisin and a large black dog she had named George. "I think she's going to do just fine."

"So, Liam," Margaret said. "Let's talk nuts and bolts. As soon as you get back from your honeymoon, you're going to start building the mother-in-law cottage?"

"Actually, I thought I'd get the hammer and pop outside as soon as I've finished this glass of champagne," he said.

"Now, Margaret..." Helen gave her sister a look. "Don't pressure him. He and Hannah need some time alone together."

"Speaking of being alone together," Rose said. "I just checked out the bedroom. Looks pretty cozy."

Liam winked at Hannah.

Hannah shook her head, trying hard not to smile. "What do I have to do to get away from them? I move to another continent and they're still poking their noses into my business."

"Ah well," Liam said. "That's the way it is with families, isn't it? The thing is they mean well."

"We do," Margaret, Rose and Helen said in unison.

Liam laughed aloud, and Hannah's heart swelled at the genuine happiness she heard in the sound. *I loved you when we were first married,* she thought. *But that didn't come close to how much I love you now.*